O F
L O V E
A N D
L I F E

Three novels selected and condensed
by Reader's Digest

O F
LOVE
AND
LIFE

The Reader's Digest Association Limited
LONDON

The Reader's Digest Association Limited
11 Westferry Circus, Canary Wharf, London E14 4HE

www.readersdigest.co.uk

Printed in France

CONTENTS

Judith Krantz

The Jewels of Tessa Kent

On the night Tessa Kent wins the
Oscar for Best Supporting Actress, she
promises herself a present—a string of
pearls from Tiffany's. These pearls prove
to be just the beginning, for when she
marries one of the world's richest men he
adorns her with a collection of fabulous
jewels. But tragedy strikes and Tessa is
forced to take stock of her life. She realises
that she must win back the heart of
somebody who was once close to her, and
to do this she may have to sacrifice her
beloved collection . . .

Prologue

QUICKLY, TESSA KENT stepped out of the bank and crossed the New York pavement. The door of her parked limo was held open by the driver. She slid inside, grateful that she'd left a coat on the seat when she'd entered the bank. It had been a morning of indecisive early fall weather, but now the afternoon sun had disappeared behind rain clouds on this mid-September day in 1993.

'Where to, Miss Kent?' Ralph, the driver, asked.

'Wait right here for a while, Ralph. There's something I want to see,' she answered impulsively, surprising herself, and pulled the coat over her shoulders.

All through the endless afternoon at the bank, she'd kept herself going by promising herself that the instant she was able to leave, she'd return as quickly as possible to her apartment at the Carlyle Hotel, take a long, lavishly perfumed bath, put on her oldest, softest *peignoir*, have a fire lit in the generous fireplace of her bedroom, and stretch out on the pile of pillows flung down on the carpet. She intended to put the past three days firmly behind her, sipping a distinctly alcoholic drink and looking straight into the flames until she was so dazzled by them that her mind would unclench and a pleasant emptiness would take over.

Yet, as soon as she entered the limo, Tessa Kent abruptly understood that it was still too soon to escape into that peaceful moment. Something was missing, a sight that would put an absolute punctuation to the process she had just completed, the witnessing of a three-day inventory of every last one of her jewels except the few she was wearing.

She needed to see her jewels actually leave the protection of the bank. She needed to watch them being brought out into the street and whisked away in three taxis and three ordinary cars by six couriers and a twelve-man armed security team that would carry tens of millions of dollars worth of jewels in the scruffy briefcases and sturdy shopping bags that had been selected to attract no attention.

If she didn't see that final scene of the drama, she'd still be able to imagine that her jewels slept in the darkness of their velvet cases, piled high in their vaults, ready for her to come and pick out those she would wear to an opening night at the theatre or a black-tie party or dinner in a favourite restaurant. Something deep in Tessa's psyche demanded that she recognise, with her own eyes, the fact that her jewels no longer belonged to her, that now they were gone for good.

Since her marriage, eighteen years earlier, Tessa Kent, the most internationally adored of American movie stars, had never been seen in public unadorned by magnificent jewels. They had become a signature as utterly specific to her as the sound of her voice, the shape of her mouth, the colour of her eyes.

Suddenly Tessa saw the first of the couriers, carrying three shopping bags, appear at the entrance to the bank. On either side of him, seemingly busy in conversation, were two of the armed guards, clad in banker's grey. One of the taxis that had been circling the block for hours pulled up beside Tessa's limo, paused briefly as the three men got in, and then continued up Madison Avenue.

As she watched more couriers and guards walk out of the bank and disappear into their carefully choreographed transportation, she felt a complex mixture of feelings: loss, excitement, relief, anticipation and nostalgia, all jumbled together. Dominating every emotion was hope.

'You can take me back to the hotel, please, Ralph,' Tessa told the driver as soon as the couriers had left the bank. The limo had barely covered two blocks when a heavy rain began to fall.

'Oh, perfect!' Tessa exclaimed. 'Stop wherever you can, Ralph, I'll walk.' As her driver knew, rain was her friend. With a big black umbrella skilfully deployed, she could roam the streets of New York without being recognised.

Blessing the foul weather, she pulled a beret down until it reached her eyebrows, kicked off her shoes and put on the boots that lay waiting in the back of the limo. She shrugged into the light raincoat and picked up an umbrella.

'Let me out at the corner, Ralph. I'll walk all the way back.'

As soon as the limo came to a stop, Tessa hopped out, opened her umbrella and strode rapidly across the street in the direction of 5th Avenue. She struck out uptown at a fast pace, breathing deeply. Enjoying herself in a way so frequently denied her, Tessa continued up 5th Avenue past St Patrick's Cathedral and was three good blocks beyond it when she stopped and changed direction. At thirty-eight, she hadn't been inside a church for years. But something about today drew her back to the great bulk of the cathedral, drew her up the steps to the doors, drew her inside. She closed her umbrella. Old habit took over as she dipped her fingertips in the font of holy water, crossed herself, and genuflected before slipping into one of the pews at the back.

She would just sit here for a few seconds and then flee, back out to the delicious freedom of the busy, dripping streets, Tessa thought. Sit and bask in the vast singing hum of busy silence that had a colour and a texture and a scent uniquely its own.

Without willing it, Tessa found herself on her knees, her head bent. She was praying—she who no longer believed in prayer—as ardently as when she'd been a girl, but praying without words, praying purely for the sake of prayer.

The hope she had felt earlier in the afternoon returned, stronger than ever, illuminating her heart. She was safe here, Tessa thought dreamily, and the tears she had held back for many, many days splashed comfortingly down the backs of her hands.

One

AGNES PATRICIA RILEY Horvath, whose daughter, Teresa, would become Tessa Kent, lay in bed at three in the morning. She had been woken, as usual, by obsessive, angry thoughts about her husband, Sandor, and the way in which he dominated the upbringing of their only child, who now, in August 1967, had reached the age of twelve.

Her parents had opposed her marriage to Sandor Horvath in 1954 and they had been right, Agnes told herself. She was humiliated to the marrow of her bones as she relived her folly, lying next to Sandor in those private hours.

If it weren't for Sandor's stern prohibitions, Agnes reflected furiously,

Teresa would be well launched on her career, a career about which there wasn't the smallest question.

Her daughter had been born a star—yes, a star!—by virtue of her extraordinary beauty and the unmistakable dramatic talent she'd exhibited even as a small child. That wasn't a mere mother's pride talking; that was the opinion of everyone who'd ever seen her, Agnes told herself, trembling with frustration. Teresa should be making movies, or at the very least commercials. But no, her husband, unable to move away from his rigid, old-fashioned, European ideas of what was correct and proper for a young girl, had steadfastly refused to let her take the girl to New York, where she could meet the influential people who would recognise how exceptional her daughter was.

Night after night, Agnes Horvath asked herself what had possessed her, when she was a mere eighteen, to insist on marrying a man who was foreign to the devout, Irish Catholic world in which she had her enviable place as the youngest of five sparkling, black-haired, blue-eyed Riley daughters. Why had she set her heart on a refugee from communist Hungary, a music professor of thirty-five?

Sandor had been an amazingly handsome man, who spoke English with more elegance and precision than any American boy. This charming and romantic stranger had swept the unsophisticated provincial fool she had been off her feet. Savagely Agnes reminded herself she'd been too immature to realise how quickly his fine-boned, intellectual, sensitive beauty would become infuriating when she weighed them against the rules and regulations he imposed on her.

Now she was thirty-one, her marriage was thirteen years old, and Agnes Horvath had known for at least half of it that she'd made the biggest mistake a deeply religious Catholic woman could make. No matter how great her rage against her husband, there could be no thought of divorce. But even if the mere idea of divorce had not been a sin, what training did she have to make a living for herself and Teresa on their own? Agnes Riley had been brought up to be a protected wife and a devoted mother, like every other woman of her generation.

Sandor earned a good salary as the head of the music department at an exclusive girls' school in Stamford, Connecticut, not far from their home on the oldest edge of the rich community of Greenwich, where they lived in order to be near their daughter's school. Teresa was a student at the aristocratic Convent of the Sacred Heart, where many daughters of millionaires were her classmates.

In all fairness, Agnes reminded herself, turning over in bed, she had to admit that Sandor worked hard, and the whole family respected her elegant, learned husband. Her sisters had married local boys in nearby Bridgeport, where she'd grown up. Each of her sisters had produced a sprawling brood of ordinary, unremarkable kids. When she took Teresa to their frequent family gatherings there was no doubt about whose child was the centre of attention. Teresa's singularity was a subject of family pride rather than any sniping or competition. From the time she was a tiny baby she had so fine and rare a quality that a party would have been incomplete without Teresa to marvel at. Her own sisters, Agnes knew, were in awe of the child she'd brought into their limited world. Her cousins vied for her attention.

'Teresa's becoming spoilt,' Sandor had grumbled angrily after the last Riley get-together. 'She used to be a satisfactory child, docile and obedient, but lately, I warn you, Agnes, I sense that there's something going on inside her that I worry about . . . some sort of rebellion under the surface, something I can't put my finger on. And I definitely don't approve of that "best friend" of hers, that Mimi Peterson. She's not even a Catholic.'

'You're imagining things,' Agnes had snapped. 'Every little girl has a best friend, and the Petersons may be Protestants but they have the good sense to realise the quality of education at the Sacred Heart Convent. And they truly appreciate Teresa, which is more than her own father seems to do.'

'How can you say something so unfair?' he demanded, stung. 'I love her too much for my own good, but, Agnes, the world's a difficult place and Teresa's not a princess, whatever you may think. The way you dote on her is shameless . . . it comes close to the sin of pride, if you ask me.'

'Sandor!'

'Pride, Agnes, is too high an opinion of oneself.'

'Do you imagine I don't know that?' she asked, outraged.

'Too high an opinion of one's offspring, can, like pride, lead to the sin of presumption.'

'When I need a priest's interpretation of sin, Sandor, I know where to go for it. How dare you preach to me!'

'Agnes, in less than a year Teresa will be a teenager. I've seen your sisters go through enough trouble with their own teenaged children. Why should we be different? If only . . .'

'If only we'd had more children? Don't you dare, Sandor! I wanted them as much as you did. Are you saying it was my fault that I had those miscarriages . . . ?'

'Agnes, you can't possibly be starting this nonsense again. Please stop talking about fault. The Blessed Virgin didn't mean it to be, and we must accept that.'

He did blame her, Agnes Horvath brooded angrily, but never as much as she blamed herself, no matter how futile and morally wrong she knew it was to use the word 'blame' about a situation that was in the hands of God alone. But at least she had Teresa, and wasn't one Teresa worth a houseful of ordinary children?

She wished her parents wouldn't fight about her, Teresa thought in misery as she tried to go to sleep. She couldn't hear them from her room, but she knew that another of their quarrels was hatching.

For a long time she had believed she could change her mother's disappointment, make her father less severe. But nothing had worked. Her mother was utterly concentrated on her; her father was suspicious and disapproving. Teresa's home life was so tense that it made her want to scream. There was never a time in which she could take a deep breath, feel a sense of contentment, and, most important of all, *feel safe*. Oh, how she yearned for a safe day, a safe hour, even a safe minute, in which all pressure would dissipate and be replaced by easy, loving, unqualified approval.

If it weren't for Mimi she didn't know what she'd do, Teresa thought. She didn't know how she'd manage to keep on pretending to be the good little girl her father expected her to be as well as enduring the burden of being her mother's 'pride and joy'. If her parents knew everything about her, they'd *die*, Teresa told herself, caught up in a combination of defiance, shame and guilt.

But at least she could escape the atmosphere of her home, when she went over to Mimi's big, luxurious house to do their homework together. She and Mimi, another only child, were sworn blood sisters, and Mrs Peterson—lively, easy-going, and expensively dressed—was too busy playing bridge or golf every afternoon to give a thought about what the two little convent girls were up to.

'Teresa, sweetie, you're a good influence on Mimi,' she'd say if she came in before Teresa had left for home. 'She never got her homework done before you started studying together.'

But Mrs Peterson had no idea how easy the homework was when Teresa and Mimi put their heads together and attacked it. Both bright, they could polish it all off in an hour. And then, at least twice a week, they'd 'engage in an adult experience', as Mimi called it.

The Petersons' bar was crammed with bottles of everything any liquor store could supply. Teresa and Mimi, sharing Mimi's bathroom glass, would pour three jiggers full of whatever drink took their fancy, replacing what they took with water, and carry the glass up to Mimi's room.

They'd lock the door and sip slowly, taking turns, giggling like maniacs as each reported the fascinating alterations they felt in themselves.

They hadn't yet used the same bottle more than once and they'd never dared make a second trip downstairs for more. They were always careful to brush their teeth and use mouthwash before Mimi's mother was expected home.

The Petersons were a couple in their mid-thirties who, Mimi reported proudly, still loved a good time. On their exploration of her parents' bedroom they found a large collection of *Penthouse* and a smaller-sized publication called *Variations*, which contained erotic short stories. Two drawers of Mrs Peterson's dresser were filled with sexy underwear. Mimi and Teresa would select several pieces at a time—tiny, lacy panties, garter belts that attached to slinky black stockings, dainty push-up bras or transparent chiffon teddies—and carry their loot swiftly back to Mimi's room, where they'd try on everything, using pairs of her mother's high-heeled shoes to see themselves at best advantage.

As for *Penthouse* and *Variations*, they pored over one issue at a time, discovering that some of the subject matter was heart-pounding and passionately fascinating. Teresa couldn't keep from thinking about all the forbidden, unutterably exciting things a man and a woman could do together—except when she was brooding on the certainty that she was going to go to hell after she died.

It was amazing, Teresa thought grimly, that she was able to lie with such calm to the priest at confession, producing a normal series of venial sins in the red velvet, padded phone booth of the confessional. But she knew the truth. She was guilty of lust, the sin of impurity, and of gluttony, the sin of drinking too much. When she and Mimi dressed up and admired themselves she was guilty of the sin of pride . . . their sessions certainly didn't conform to the 'normal pride in a neat appearance' the nuns talked of.

Every single week of her life, she was committing yet *another* mortal sin by not confessing, so her sins were not forgiven, but lay on her heavily and painfully, almost too much to endure.

Yes, the certainty of hell for a sinner who hadn't confessed and wasn't absolved had been seared into her at weekly catechism classes for seven years. It wasn't knowledge she could question any more than she could question the fact that she was a girl or an American.

In their freshman year at Sacred Heart's high school, soon after they both turned fourteen, Mimi and Teresa grew closer than ever.

In the course of the past year they had worked intensively on their looks. Both girls had falls of fake hair that reached halfway to their waists, styled in a long flip. Both of them were adept at applying mascara, eyeliner and eye shadow in shades from dead black to turquoise, and they owned a dozen lipsticks in colours ranging from deep red to frosted pale pink. They had practised walking in the fashionable shoes they bought and kept in the back of Mimi's closet, until they felt totally at ease in them. They had fishnet stockings and tights in every colour and they had made themselves dark, micro-skirts which they wore with clinging little sweaters.

'We look like absolute whores,' Teresa said one Saturday night in mid-September when she had been allowed to sleep over at Mimi's. Her voice was filled with admiration. The two girls had groomed themselves to perfection and now they were alone in the house, for Mimi's parents had gone out to what promised to be a long night at the country club.

'You're absolutely wrong. We're divine, and I have an idea,' Mimi said, inspired. 'We're going to Mark O'Malley's party! It's tonight, we're dressed, and my parents will never know if we're back in time. Oh, Teresa, I triple dare you!'

'Absolutely not. I'm not allowed to go out on dates, not till I'm sixteen, my father says,' Teresa said gloomily, flinging herself down on Mimi's bed.

'Come on, it's only going to a party, not another of your dreary mortal sins.'

'Correction: it's *crashing* a party, and not even you, silver-tongued one, can convince me that's the same thing as "going" to a party.'

'What's the worst thing that can happen?' Mimi demanded. 'We'd be asked to leave? Oh, I don't think so, my lovely one. There's no question in my mind that when Mark O'Malley lays eyes on us he's going to be very glad that we've favoured him with our presence. He'd have asked us himself if he knew we existed.'

'Maybe,' Teresa said with a shrug. 'Sure, maybe the captain of the football team at Greenwich High would be so overwhelmed by our charm and beauty that he'd have begged two convent girls to be his guests, that's not impossible, but somehow we've escaped his eye, even though we've never missed a game he's played in. So forget about it, and stop bugging me.'

'Teresa, pay attention. I'm *going* to that party and *so are you*. You've got a crush on Mark O'Malley. You've had it for years and I'm sick of listening to you carry on about him. You're just playing hard to convince so this is going to seem like my fault when I'm actually doing you a huge favour.'

An hour and a quarter after the party had started, Teresa and Mimi slipped casually into the large crowd at Mark O'Malley's house. They were quickly absorbed, blending perfectly with all the other older girls.

'Let's have a drink for courage,' Mimi murmured.

'Darn it, Mimi, we decided we wouldn't drink so we'd keep our wits about us.'

'Oh, for Pete's sake, all they have is this kind of fruit punch. At least carry a glass so you'll have something to do with your hands.' Mimi sipped in a ladylike way. 'It's mostly pineapple juice, Teresa, try it.'

'All right, but we can't just stand here; we have to mingle . . . but don't go so far away that I don't know where you are.'

'I'll keep my eye on you—oh, Mark, hi! This is a great party! You invited the world.'

'I guess I must have.' Their host smiled down at both the girls, fully aware that he didn't know them, but who cared with girls this cute? Wrong: the blonde one was cute; the dark-haired girl was flat-out gorgeous. No way he could ever have seen a girl so beautiful and let it slip his mind.

'Anyone for a dance?'

'Thanks,' Mimi said quickly, 'but I'm waiting for my date to get out of the john. Teresa, why don't you dance with Mark?'

'Teresa,' he said. 'Nice name. Come on.' He took Teresa's glass of punch and put it down, grasped her firmly by her upper arm and led her away.

'Do you talk, mystery guest? Or do we need your little friend to interpret for us?'

'I can speak for myself,' Teresa said hardily, summoning all her reserves of dramatic power to get the words out. Mark O'Malley up close was far more devastating than he was from a distance at a game. He was as tall and muscular as any fully grown man, his curly dark hair as long as the school regulations would permit, his eyes bright and blue and smiling, with a man's confidence. She could feel nothing but the warmth of his hand on her arm.

'How old are you?' he asked suddenly, stopping in midstride.

'Eighteen, why?'

'I thought you might be older. You make the other girls look like kids.'

'No, just a simple eighteen.'

'But experienced?'

'What's that supposed to mean?'

'There's something about your eyes.'

'Maybe I'm what they call an old soul,' Teresa said, smiling slightly. This wasn't so hard, after all.

'In a young body. I've never met a sexy old soul before . . . good combination.'

'Aren't we going to dance?' Teresa asked.

'Oh, I don't think we really want to, do we? You can't talk when you dance, and somebody might try to grab you away from me. I think what we want to do is get some more punch and find a place to get to know each other . . . I know just the place.'

'But Mimi . . .'

'Your friend can take care of herself, can't she?'

'If anybody can.' Teresa laughed and relaxed.

'She's the one who talked you into crashing my party, isn't she?'

'Oh!'

'Don't be embarrassed, I'm glad you did. Where do you two go to school?'

'Oh, just a little private school in Stamford.'

'Where'd you see me?'

'At a football game.'

'Well, I'm flattered my party lured you here. Or have you broken the hearts of all the boys in Stamford already? What's your last name, lovely mystery girl?'

'Carpenter.'

'Well, Teresa Carpenter, come on upstairs with me so we can chat without interruptions from this horde of bandits. I want to find out more about you . . . I'd like to see you again, take you out on a real date.'

'I don't think so,' Teresa said slowly as they mounted the stairs.

'Don't think you want to see me again?'

'I don't think I want to go into a room alone with you.'

'Don't "want to" or don't think you should?'

'I don't think I should.'

'I'll be good, I promise.' Teresa looked up at Mark's face and saw nothing there but lively interest and a touch of amusement at what he thought were her flirtatious wiles. He didn't realise that she'd never been alone with a boy in her life who wasn't a first cousin.

'I thought you wanted to get more punch,' she temporised, as he opened a door.

'I have my own private stash. I'm the host, remember?'

'Oh—it's your bedroom!' Teresa said as she walked in. She stopped dead and looked around at the football trophies and banners on the wall.

'What did you expect?'

'I wasn't thinking. I'd better go down.'

'Teresa! Sit down on that window seat and stop being silly. You act as if I'm going to attack you.'

'How do I know you're not?' she asked lightly, repressing the tremor in her voice.

'I've never attacked a girl in my life. To be frank, I've never had to, never wanted to. Yeah, that's better, sit down and get comfortable. Now, did you break up with your boyfriend? Is that why you're here, to make someone jealous? Because you could, you know, you could so easily, just by looking at me the way you're looking now.'

'Looking? There's nothing special about my look.'

'You look . . . let's see . . . sort of as if you might take to me if you knew me better.'

'You seem . . . likable enough,' Teresa said, gulping her drink as she tried to make herself realise that she was alone with Mark O'Malley, the boy she'd been in love with for years, an agonised, passionate first love, a hopeless love for this boy who was the hero of the entire high school, the boy who had always been the focus of her fantasies. She felt the wild beating of her pulse in her forehead and the thumping of her heart, and she couldn't make herself stop looking at his mouth.

'Could I have some more of that?' she asked, holding out her glass. It tasted harmless, and her mouth was dry with excitement.

'Sure thing. My dad made it and then he and my mom took off for the country club. They said they'd be back by the stroke of midnight to make sure that every last rotten kid was out of the house. I'll be glad when college starts and I get out from under their eagle eyes.'

'My parents are the same way. I can't wait to be on my own.'

'Where did you apply?'

'Oh, the usual places.'

'With a fallback, right? Somewhere you're sure you can get in?'

'Naturally,' Teresa said with nonchalance. What college would be a good fallback, whatever that was?

'Which one?'

'Uh . . . Smith.'

'Very funny. Come over and sit closer. For an incredibly beautiful girl you're an awful liar. Did you know that? Or else you've got a great sense of humour. Or a genius IQ. Which is it?' He leaned towards her and kissed her lightly on the lips. 'Oh, nice. Nice. Here, give me another kiss . . . wasn't that nice?'

'Oh my God . . . oh, Mark, *yes*!'

'You've got to stop crying, Teresa,' Mimi hissed as soon as they reached the privacy of her bedroom, after a taxi ride during which Teresa shook with silent sobs.

'I can't. I can't. Oh God, Mimi, I can't stop.'

'Teresa, damn it, you terrified me! One minute you were there and then you disappeared with Mark. I looked everywhere for you, I didn't do anything else all evening. I don't know what I would have done if you hadn't shown up eventually. Where the hell were you?'

'Oh, Mimi, I can't . . . it couldn't have happened, tell me it couldn't,' Teresa pleaded through her unstoppable tears.

'*What* couldn't?' Mimi whispered, cold with fright.

'I can't tell you, I can't talk about it, I can't.'

'You damn well better or I'm going to tell my mother that Mark O'Malley did something awful to you. Your hair's a mess, you've lost your bra, you're in shock . . . Mom knows his mother and they'll get to the bottom of this!'

'No! You'd never—'

'The hell I wouldn't.'

'No, no, please, Mimi, stop!'

Mimi pulled Teresa's chin up with all her strength and inspected her devastated face.

'That bastard! He won't get away with this. Shit, it's all my fault, I was the one who triple dared you. I could kill myself.'

'He didn't rape me!'

'Then you'd better tell me exactly why you're carrying on like this.'

'We . . . made love, I think . . .'

'Teresa! You *never* made love, that's crazy. You've got it all mixed up. Tell me exactly what happened, don't leave out anything.'

'We started out just kissing, nicely, just kissing. Sitting on the window seat of his room. We had a couple of glasses of punch . . . two, maybe three, it must have been stronger than I thought. And then, little by little it got more . . . hot and heavy and we ended up lying on top of his bed and we were necking, you know, and then, I guess we were petting . . . heavy petting . . . he took off my sweater and my bra and kissed my breasts and sucked on my nipples and then—'

'I knew it, he raped you!'

'No, Mimi, I *wanted* him to, I helped him do it. I took off my panties myself, I couldn't stop myself. I can't tell you the crazy way I felt, I just wanted to finally find out, and then I *had* to see . . . I had to see what it looked like in real life, not just in photos, so I let him take it out and put it on my stomach.' She fell silent.

'So that's the reason you're crying like crazy? He put his cock on your stomach? What next?' Mimi demanded.

'I touched it . . . a lot . . . I couldn't stop touching it . . . he was so hard and he got even harder . . . and the harder he got, the more I wanted to touch it . . . and then . . . and then . . . he put the tip of it in.'

'*He put it in!* Jesus Christ, Teresa! Didn't you put up a fight?'

'No . . . I mean I didn't tell him not to when he asked me if he could. . . I wanted to feel it . . . you know . . . *inside*. Just the tip of it. I had to know how it felt, more than anything. It was so big and I wanted it so much. I was so . . . it was like being out of my mind, nothing else existed . . .' Teresa whispered. '. . . And then, oh God help me, then, after just a few seconds, *with only the tip in*, oh, Mimi, he came. *Inside me*. He just gave this shudder and made this sighing noise and he came. He didn't pull out, he didn't wait!'

'Shit! That's not rape, that's pure stupidity. What an asshole! But you're a virgin, so there's nothing to worry about. What did he say?'

'He said he was sorry and if I'd wait a little while he'd do it again, only much slower, so I'd enjoy it.'

'He didn't know you were a virgin?'

'He never got in far enough to find out. He thought I was eighteen, he thought I'd been around. Oh, Mimi, what am I going to do?' Teresa cried out in anguish.

'Stop that crying, take a hot bath. I'll give you two of my mother's tranquillisers and a sleeping pill, and you'll go to bed and never think about it again. Does he know where to find you?'

'I lied about my name and said we were from Stamford.'

'With any luck he'll never see you again and he'll never recognise you anyway without make-up. The whole thing is over. *Over*. And I don't want to hear anything about sin. You didn't know what you were doing, he got you drunk, it wasn't your fault. Do you understand that, Teresa?'

'I understand what you think, Mimi. But I know what I did. I didn't have to do it, but I did. I sinned, and there's nothing you can say that will ever change that.'

'Mimi, I think I'm pregnant.' Teresa was so pale with panic that Mimi's heart skipped a beat. Hastily she rose and locked the door to her room.

'You're a virgin; how could you be? You're late, that's all,' she said, taking Teresa's cold and shaking hands and rubbing them to bring some blood into her fingers.

'I've never been late since I got the curse a year ago, and now it's been four whole weeks since that party. I finally made myself look up sperm in the encyclopedia at school. They swim incredibly fast and they can live for a few days inside the vagina.'

'But you're a virgin! It's simply impossible. It can't happen.'

'Mimi, it can. A hymen isn't a solid barrier. Face it, it *has* happened,' Teresa said through trembling lips that belied stoic words.

'You'll have a miscarriage or whatever it's called. Tonight, tomorrow, you're only just fourteen, you can't have a baby,' Mimi babbled in fear.

'That's what I've been telling myself,' Teresa said wearily. 'I've been praying on my knees for hours and hours every night, praying for God to take the baby. It's His decision. He can stop a pregnancy.'

'Oh, damn it, Teresa, if only you weren't such a Catholic! My mom knows a doctor, he's a perfectly good one—'

'Don't even say it, Mimi. Never, absolutely never. As bad as I am, that's the one thing I can not do. Never. *Ever.*'

Agnes Horvath had never experienced morning sickness when she was pregnant with Teresa, but when she heard, three days in a row, the smothered sounds of vomiting coming from Teresa's bathroom before her daughter finally appeared, pale and red-eyed, late for breakfast, unable to eat, and mumbling something about stomach flu going round the school, she began to suspect. When Teresa arrived home from school each day, the stomach flu miraculously cured until the next morning, her heart was speared by the truth.

But Teresa was a virgin, to her knowledge. Teresa had never been alone with a boy, to her knowledge. Teresa, to her knowledge, had never yet been kissed.

But Teresa must be pregnant. Teresa her daughter, perfect and adored, for whose future she had lived, was a stranger to her; immoral, unclean, evil, cunning, lying, and damned to hellfire for eternity.

On Friday morning Agnes lay in wait outside Teresa's bathroom. As the girl emerged, deathly pale, her mother gripped her by one arm and slapped her with all her strength across her cheek.

'*How could you do this to me!*' she spat, and slapped her again, on the other cheek. 'How? How? You filthy slut!'

Teresa burst into tears and would have fallen to the carpet if Agnes's clutching hand hadn't been keeping her upright.

'Shut up! If you don't, I'll hit you until you do! Do you think you have a right to those tears? I'm the one who should be crying,' Agnes panted in rage. 'I'm the one you put aside because your lust was stronger than your love for your mother.'

'No . . . no . . . it had nothing to do with you,' Teresa wailed.

'It has *everything* to do with me. You know that lust is a mortal, deadly sin and yet you chose it, just as you chose the influence of Mimi Peterson rather than mine—she must have had a hand in this. How else could you have met a man? But who has watched over you all your life? Who has given you everything she could? Who managed to find the money to send you to Sacred Heart? Who has nourished your talent? Look at how you've repaid my love. You are beneath contempt. I have no words to use for the kind of girl you are. All my pride and love was folly.'

'Mother!' Teresa cried in anguish.

'Don't call me mother. No daughter of mine could do what you've done. Who is he? No, don't tell me! I don't want to know any of the vile details. You disgust me! We're going to see Father Brennan this minute. After you confess, we'll talk to him. He'll know where to send you.'

'What?'

'You don't think this is the first time this has happened, do you? There are places for evil, godless, shameful sinners like you, places to stay until the baby is born and adopted.'

'But it'll be months, months! I can't just disappear.'

'Teresa, you've ruined my life. I've lived for you, the person I thought you were, a person who doesn't exist. Are you too stupid to imagine how the stain, the gossip will spread? Pregnant at fourteen! Don't you see that no decent man will ever have anything to do with you? I'm giving you a second chance, don't you understand? Not because you deserve it. You deserve nothing but punishment, and you will be punished, Teresa, trust in that.'

'But how can I vanish and then come back without people guessing?'

'It means all of us moving, as far away as possible, some place where no one knows us. Your father will have to sacrifice his job and find work in another school. I'll tell him tonight.'

'He doesn't know? Only you?'

'It's not a man's business to know until he has to,' Agnes said grimly. 'Go get dressed for church now. And don't forget your rosary.'

'**H**elp me to understand you clearly,' Sandor Horvath said to his wife that night, after she'd told him everything. 'You expect me to give up my position and find another job?'

'You have to. There's no other way. I've thought of everything and it's the only way we can hide what's happened.'

'And Father Brennan will arrange to send Teresa to this place in Texas to wait for the birth and the child will be adopted by strangers? And then she'll come home and forget all about it?'

'Adopted by a good Catholic family. We can be sure of that.'

'And you can be sure I refuse!'

'Sandor! You can't refuse! You can't let her go away for six or seven months and then come back here. Everybody would be counting on their fingers. Everybody would know. We might as well take out an announcement.'

'Agnes this child is our grandchild. I will never consent to give up this child. This is my flesh and blood.'

'We can't afford to be sentimental. Teresa's future—'

'I don't give a damn about her future! What you ask goes against everything I believe in and I simply will not do it. And you can't do it without my consent.'

Agnes looked at him and realised immediately that nothing she could say would move him now, unless, unless . . . he'd agree to the plan of last resort that she'd made during the four days she'd spent thinking.

'Sandor, if we moved, if you got another job, somewhere where nobody knows us, I could . . . bring up the child as . . . my own. I'm only thirty-three. It would seem perfectly natural.'

'The baby would become our child, Teresa's brother?' he asked slowly.

'Or sister, but yes, our child, yours and mine.'

'And how would Teresa feel about that?'

'How she feels doesn't matter. She's given up any right to be considered. Do you think that the penance Father Brennan gave her wiped away her sin?'

'Did he give her absolution? Did she receive the Sacrament of Penance?'

'Yes.'

'Then God has forgiven her. Can we do less? I'll start enquiries about another position tomorrow.'

'Thank you, Sandor.'

Secretly thrilled by the prospect of a grandson, a grandson to continue his name and his blood, Sandor quickly discovered a teaching position in the music department of the Harvard School, a well-known private boys' school in Los Angeles. It didn't pay as much as his present job, but it answered the problem of putting distance between his family and everyone they knew, and it was available immediately.

Within weeks the Horvaths moved to a small rented house in rustic Reseda, a ranchlike section of the San Fernando Valley. Agnes had made her family believe that the move was prompted by an offer so magnificent that she couldn't ask Sandor to turn it down. Only Mimi Peterson knew the truth. She and Teresa parted in tears, knowing that they'd never be allowed to be together again.

'Can't you at least send me a message when the baby's born, so I'll know you're OK?' Mimi asked.

'I'll try, but don't write back, whatever you do. I'll know how you feel, I'll know you're thinking of me. Oh, Mimi. I'll never forget you.'

The months in Reseda passed more slowly than Teresa would have believed possible. She couldn't go to school, nor could she walk around window-shopping on any of the main streets of the nearby small towns, where a decidedly pregnant teenager would turn heads.

Throughout the long winter months of her pregnancy she was a prisoner at home, with only the few uplifting paperbacks her mother grudgingly bought her, the local newspaper, and daytime television to keep her company.

Teresa's loneliest moment of each week came on Sunday morning when her parents got into her father's car and left her alone while they went to mass in the Reseda Catholic Church. She longed to be allowed to go with them, parched for the human contact and warmth of the service, aching for the consolation of communion, but of course it was impossible to show herself and arouse curiosity.

Teresa tried to attract as little of Agnes's attention as possible, since her mother's rage had only deepened with the isolation and the strangeness of California. Once Teresa's morning sickness had passed, she felt her robust health return. Neither mother nor daughter mentioned the need to see a doctor until Teresa felt the child move within her.

'Oh! It just kicked me,' Teresa exclaimed, with excitement.

'Isn't that nice for you.' Agnes turned away, shaking her head in disgust.

'Shouldn't I go to a doctor, just to see if everything's all right?'

'Of course it's all right. A baby is always all right when it isn't wanted, every woman knows that, the only ones you lose are the ones you're dying to have,' Agnes said with a bitter laugh. 'Don't you realise that there's a good reason why you can't have medical records? A doctor would only ask questions you must never answer, starting with your age. Any doctor will remember your face and your youth. This baby is going to be born in the county hospital under my name and the less trace there is of it in connection with you, the better.'

'You still have hopes for my future, or you wouldn't bother being so secretive,' Teresa said, suddenly illuminated with knowledge.

'Of course I do. Look at all I've done to give you an intact future, to provide you with a blank slate so you can make something of yourself. Do you realise how much you have to thank me for? Do you?'

'Yes, Mother. I do. I always will.'

The baby born on June 15, 1970, to Agnes Patricia Riley Horvath and Sandor Horvath, was a girl. One busy intern remarked to a busier nurse that the mothers were getting younger every year, but otherwise it was an unremarkable birth of a healthy baby on an unremarkable morning after an unremarkable labour.

The patient known as Agnes Horvath was discharged from the hospital two days later and returned to Reseda with her parents. No one at the hospital gave a thought to the whereabouts of the father. The baby's birth certificate gave her name as Mary Margaret Horvath, daughter of Agnes Patricia Riley Horvath and Sandor Horvath.

A week later the baby was baptised. Sandor Horvath had made no intimates at Harvard School, but he had struck up a casual friendship with one of the history teachers, Brian Kelly, who Sandor discovered was both a good Catholic and a married man. Brian and his wife, Helen, were surprised but flattered to be asked to become the child's godparents.

'How could I not have realised you were expecting this happy event, Sandy,' he said. 'You're a dark horse, never telling me.'

'My wife is superstitious; she asked me not to talk about it until it happened,' Sandor answered. 'She's had two miscarriages since Teresa.'

'Mary Margaret is a splendid baby,' he said, carefully touching her head.

'Isn't she beautiful?' Agnes snatched the wailing baby away from Helen Kelly as quickly as she decently could. 'No, darling, don't cry,' she crooned. 'Don't cry. Your mommy won't let anything bad ever happen to you. No never, my own, sweet little Maggie will never, ever have anything to cry about.'

'Maggie? Is that what you're going to call her?' Teresa asked her mother in amazement. Throughout the ceremony she had stood to one side, watching quietly. The worst pain of the milk that had made her breasts rock-hard and hot for three days was mercifully gone, though her breasts still ached dully.

'It's my grandmother's name, you know that, Teresa,' Agnes said impatiently, too engrossed in the baby to look up.

'I guess I missed that part of the discussion,' Teresa said, feeling even more out of touch with anything to do with the baby than she had before. From the moment they had arrived home from the hospital, her mother had attended to every need, every cry, every sign of discomfort the baby had made, ordering Teresa to leave the baby alone, stay out of her way, and stop bothering her.

'Teenagers,' Sandor said indulgently. 'We know about their attention span, don't we, Brian?'

'All too well.'

November 15, 1971

Dearest Mimi,

I hope you still live at your old address. Even though I always write "Please forward if necessary" on the envelope, it's like putting a message into a bottle and throwing it in the ocean, since you can't answer me and it's been just over two years since we came here.

Everything's changed for the better since my last letter. We've moved to Santa Monica because my mother decided that Maggie should be brought up on this side of Los Angeles. It's so pretty here and cooler than the Valley. We've rented a cute little house and my father got a promotion, so now he's head of the department again.

I'm on a full scholarship at Marymount. It's a *really* good school with a terrific drama department. Sister Elizabeth, who's in charge, is a ball of fire, and I think she likes me.

The other girls, most of them anyway, are pretty snooty. They all seem to have known each other all of their lives, lots of them are very rich, and the big deal here is all about which girls, two years from now, will make their debut at a ball! There have been a lot of sweet-sixteen parties lately, but when I turned sixteen I didn't say anything about it to anyone, since my mother would never have given me a party and anyway, I didn't know who to ask. Did you have a party? I like to imagine that you did and that it was absolutely wonderful. And that you missed me a little.

I'll bet you're wondering about Maggie. Well, you shouldn't worry. She's got my mother hanging over her every waking minute and lots of her sleeping minutes. My father too, when he's home. They absolutely *adore* her. They've truly convinced themselves that she's their very own little girl. She has a mop of jet-black curls and very pink cheeks and my mother's bright blue eyes. Maybe I've been brainwashed because of circumstances, but the whole maternal thing—I just don't feel it, Mimi. Nothing.

I feel that Maggie truly is my sister. She calls me 'Tessa' because she can't pronounce Teresa. It used to break my heart when I came home and she was still taking her nap and I had to go straight to my room and do my homework, when I knew she was going to be waking up any minute, all smiling and smelling heavenly and warm and squashy. But that was my mother's favourite time to be alone with her, and anyway, I really needed the time to concentrate on my school work. After all, I have my scholarship to keep up, which pretty much means getting all As.

This is all for now. If anything amazing happens, I'll write again before next year, but I have a feeling that life is just going to go on like this until I'm eighteen and go to college.

With all my love, a million happy, slightly belated returns on your birthday, have a wonderful year, and have a lot of fun for me, but not *too* much.

I'll never forget you,
Teresa

'Teresa, I'll be picking you up at school tomorrow afternoon,' Agnes said, opening the door and looking in on her daughter.

'Don't tell me it's time to get my teeth cleaned again,' Teresa protested peering up from her homework.

'No, as a matter of fact I'm driving you into Hollywood to an audition for teenaged girls. Paramount is doing a remake of *Little Women* and they're looking for young actresses. You're as ready as you've ever been, and your father's agreed at last. Be sure to wash your hair after dinner.'

'No! Really? You're not kidding?' Teresa jumped up in excitement.

'Certainly not. Why would I be kidding?' Her mother said coldly.

'But it's been years . . . you never said anything more about . . . I imagined you'd given up on that idea.'

'Give up? After all I've done for you?' Agnes's eyes flashed in anger and a clear edge of unmistakable contempt.

'Why did you wait till the last minute to tell me?' Teresa asked, ignoring her mother's familiar look, a deeply wounding look she tried not to let herself dwell on. 'I could have reread that book.'

'I have no idea what part they're reading for,' Agnes replied. 'This isn't something you can study. In any case, I found out about it only two days ago in the *Los Angeles Times*—they're holding auditions all week at a casting director's office. I have a sitter for Maggie.'

'Oh, Mother, Mother, thank you!'

'There's only one way you can thank me, Teresa, and that's by doing well. I have no illusions that you'll get a part in the first movie you audition for, but there's no reason why you shouldn't eventually justify the sacrifices we've had to make for your sake.'

'What should I wear?' Teresa asked, trying to head off the well-worn subject of sacrifice as quickly as possible.

'There won't be time to change, and in any case you're better off wearing your uniform. It doesn't hurt to let people know you're a Marymount girl, and something classic looks better than trying too hard. Anyway, they won't care about your clothes. Just sit down and finish your homework, Teresa.'

'Yes, Mother.'

As soon as Agnes closed the door, Teresa studied her face in the bathroom mirror. Clear, very white skin with a faint rosy blush over her cheeks, as if she'd just come in from cold, crisp air, a blush she'd always had no matter what the weather. Her nose was straight and long enough, it seemed to her, to be in proportion with her other features; she had her father's high cheekbones and his extra width of jawbone at that special point under the ear where the jaw meets the neck; her eyes had always been a colour she could never quite figure out, an odd shade of green with a hint of grey; her mouth was generous, her neck long. Teresa flashed herself an experimental smile. No question but her teeth were her best feature, she thought. Thank God you couldn't see her gums—that would have been a misfortune, considering the width of her smile.

People had always thought she was beautiful, Teresa reflected; she'd often heard them say so, either to her face or when she wasn't supposed to be listening. She honestly couldn't see what they meant, dearly as she'd like to. Her face was just the face she'd grown up with. She wished she could manage to convince herself that she was beautiful. It would make the audition so much less frightening.

Peggy Brian Westbrook, the veteran casting director, and her young assistant, Fiona Bridges, opened fresh Cokes.

'How many does this make today?' Peggy enquired wearily.

'Cokes or girls?' Fiona asked. At the age of twenty-six, she was ambitious in a way that belied her blonde, placid, classically Anglo-Saxon features. She had been in Hollywood three years, having apprenticed herself to Peggy to learn the art of casting.

'Either. They all taste the same and produce the same results. Too sweet, and they make me burp.'

'About five Cokes, rough estimate, and fifty-six girls.' Part of Fiona's job was to keep detailed notes for Peggy.

'This is day three and we don't have anyone who's even vaguely possible. Not a Beth, not an Amy, not a Meg and obviously not a Jo.' Peggy said plaintively.

Children, followed by teenaged girls, were her least favourite casting assignments, but this one was for her favourite director, Roddy Fensterwald. Roddy was adored by women, for all the good it would do them. How did such an openly gay man manage to be so seductive, she wondered, not for the first time.

'Ready for the next hopeful unknown?' Fiona said cheerfully. She buzzed the receptionist. 'Right, please send in the next girl, Ginger.'

Outside in the reception room, Teresa sat stiffly, torn between studying the pages the receptionist had passed out to all the girls in the room, and observing the other hopefuls. There wasn't another girl who wore a school uniform, Teresa thought miserably. Almost all the others were dressed in a version of the latest look: slim trousers with a bell-bottom flare, and ribbed clinging sweaters in colours that matched their trousers. At least half of them sported the shag, Jane Fonda's hairdo that had swept America, and all of them wore make-up that enhanced their natural prettiness.

'Teresa Horvath, please,' the receptionist announced, opening the door into the inner office. Agnes rose with formidable composure. 'Come along, Teresa,' she said.

Teresa followed her, standing as straight as possible, her shoulders back, her head high.

'I'm sorry, Mrs Horvath, but Mrs Westbrook prefers mothers to wait outside during an audition,' Ginger said with a pleasant smile.

'What!' Agnes said in the beginning of outrage.

'She doesn't make exceptions.' Ginger's smile never wavered. 'Go on in, Teresa.' In a rush of sudden gratitude, Teresa walked past her mother and closed the door to the office behind her.

'Hello, there,' Peggy said, from behind a table littered with cans of Coke and sheets of photos. 'Thanks for coming. This is Fiona Bridges, my assistant. Teresa, that's right, isn't it, or do you have a nickname?'

'Yes,' Teresa heard herself say. 'Yes, I do. It's Tessa.'

'Lovely.' Peggy's jaded attention was immediately jerked into life by the clear, distinct melody of Tessa's voice. 'Now, Tessa, why don't you tell us something about yourself, come on over here where we can see you.'

Tessa moved forward and stood in front of the table, her hands firmly clasped behind her to hide their trembling. They had such friendly smiles, these two women. What was the worst thing they could do, after all, except send her away?

'I'm sixteen,' she said, 'and I live in Santa Monica with my parents and Maggie, my baby sister. We moved to California more than two years ago from Greenwich, Connecticut. My mother's from a big Irish family and my father came here from Hungary back in the 1950s. Now he's head of the music department at the Harvard School. There's nothing particularly exciting about me, except that I've always wanted to act. No, that's wrong. I *have* always acted.'

'Do you have any professional experience?' the casting director asked. As Tessa recounted the simple outline of her life, Peggy had felt unexpected chills racing up her arms.

'I've never been in anything but a school play,' Tessa answered. 'This is my first real audition, unless you count the ones at school.'

'I see,' Peggy said slowly. 'So you wouldn't have any head shots, any eight-by-ten glossies?' Good God, a schoolgirl without an agent or experience or even pictures . . . But those chills . . . how long had it been since she'd felt chills when an unknown spoke?

'I have snapshots in the family album, but my mother didn't bring them,' Tessa answered. 'I didn't know I needed glossies.'

'Actually, you don't. It's just that some of the girls leave them behind so we'll remember what they look like.'

'Just think of the girl in the dumb uniform,' Tessa laughed with an utterly spontaneous sense of the ridiculous, a wonderfully affirmative sound that rang through the little room.

Peggy and Fiona looked at each other swiftly. Normally, at a first audition of an inexperienced unknown, they'd just chat, make notes, and send her on her way. But neither of them would have dreamed of letting Tessa go without a reading.

'Take off your blazer and sit down, Tessa. Let your hair out of the ponytail so we can see it, and undo the top buttons of that very well-ironed blouse, so you can breathe a bit,' Peggy continued, writing a note to Fiona. *That laugh! Trained voice???*

'Have you had voice lessons, Tessa?' Fiona asked.

'No, I haven't, but I sing in a choir. And my father's very insistent on proper speech.'

'Choir?'

'At the Convent of the Sacred Heart in Greenwich and now, at Marymount.'

'And all your acting has been done in Catholic schools?' Peggy probed gently.

'I haven't been to any other kind of school, or to summer camp either. But the Madams at Sacred Heart put on a wide range of plays, and so do the Sisters at Marymount.'

'You've been given the four pages—sides—we'd like you to read. The context of the scene is that Jo March, the part you're reading, is having an argument with her older sister, Meg, who's dignified and proud and proper. Jo is independent and tumultuous and rebellious. Fiona will give you your cues. You read the lines that are underlined. I think you should read the scene over again first, to feel familiar with Jo.'

As Tessa bent her head over the pages, Peggy and Fiona turned their swivel chairs away from her and conferred quietly.

'Isn't she much *much* too beautiful for Jo?' Fiona whispered. 'Jo isn't supposed to be a raving, tearing beauty, she's a tomboy whose "hair is her one beauty", remember? Tessa's not at all the character, except for her height and her hair.'

'Miss Bridges, this is Hollywood. Kate Hepburn played Jo in 1933 and she was never an ugly duckling. Casting to type bores me, anyway. All the other girls have to be pretty but Jo has to knock you right off your chair because she's the heroine.'

'I'm as ready as I'll ever be,' Tessa said.

Fiona started to recite the cues she'd memorised in the course of the past three long days. Tessa read without gulping the words, giving herself an instant to look up from the pages whenever she could, look straight at Fiona and say the next line as if she'd learned it, as if she were living it, before having to consult the script again.

In spite of this being a first reading, Tessa's luminous intensity was immediately switched on. Tessa *became* Jo March as if she'd been inhabited by an uncompromising spirit. To Fiona, the words she'd spoken so often became fresh with meaning as she awaited Tessa's response. Then, so suddenly that Peggy shivered in surprise, the four sides were over and the reading ended.

But I want to hear what she says next, I need to hear her, Peggy thought. This hasn't happened in ten years. Fifteen! 'Thank you, Tessa,' she managed to say, calmly. 'That was excellent.'

'Is that it?' Tessa asked in evident disappointment, withdrawing from the character slowly and dreamily. She struggled to put on her blazer, the young, arched fullness of her breasts evident for the first time against her starched white shirt.

'Oh, no, I doubt that'll be it,' Peggy said, blowing her nose violently. She had tears in her eyes, another thing that hadn't happened for fifteen years. That's not it, not if I know anything about this damn business, and I do. This girl is *unconditional*; it's all or nothing with her. She knows all those essential things you can't teach.

'Ginger,' she said, buzzing the secretary. 'Would you please ask Mrs Horvath to come in?'

Agnes entered, wearing a resolute smile.

'Mrs Horvath, can you bring your daughter back tomorrow?' Peggy asked without ceremony. 'There are some more pages I'd like her to study overnight. Oh, and be sure she wears her uniform again, if you don't mind.'

'Tomorrow? Of course,' Agnes said, coming forward quickly.

'But, Mother, tomorrow afternoon there's that field hockey match with Westlake—' Tessa reminded her, unwillingly.

'Sister Elizabeth told me not to bother about it if these ladies wanted you back.'

'Sister Elizabeth? Don't tell me she's still at Marymount!' Peggy Westbrook exclaimed.

'Do you know Sister Elizabeth?' Tessa asked in amazement.

'She was head of the English department and also coached the plays when I was there, a long time ago,' Peggy confessed.

'We just did *Saint Joan*,' Tessa offered eagerly.

'What part did you have?'

'Joan.'

'And you satisfied Sister Elizabeth?'

'She said I was right for the Maid of France, that's all. She doesn't give an opinion if she can help it.'

'So I remember. Thank you, Tessa. We'll see you tomorrow. And, Mrs Horvath, please leave your phone number with the receptionist.'

After the door closed behind Agnes and Tessa, Peggy and Fiona sat in silence for stunned seconds, both of them struck by the sudden flat dullness of the room.

'What was that business about *Saint Joan* and Sister Elizabeth?' Fiona ventured.

'Sister Elizabeth never, ever put on a production of *Saint Joan* unless she'd discovered someone she considered worthy of the part. To my knowledge she hasn't put on *Saint Joan* in twenty years.'

Two

TESSA WOKE UP one summer morning in 1974 feeling defiant before her feet hit the floor. Today was Saturday, a day on which, by rights, she should have at least a few free hours to herself. But every single minute was scheduled. Right after breakfast she had a riding lesson, a new skill her agent insisted she needed to develop; then home to shower and change for a talk with her business manager over lunch. After lunch she had to change for an interview set up by the producers of her new film, *Gemini Summer*. The interviewer, a French journalist from *Paris Match*, would be accompanied by a photographer who wanted to 'follow her around' all afternoon. As soon as that major ordeal was over, her mother expected her home for dinner, here in Santa Monica. She was going to be nineteen in six weeks' time, but there was no space for *her* in her day, Tessa realised, as she brushed the hair that fell in a drifting cascade of natural waves.

Yet this past March, on Oscar night, when she'd won the Best Supporting Actress award for Jo in *Little Women*, Tessa had promised herself a present. She'd had to postpone buying it because of the demands on her time, and the longer she waited, the more alluring it became. She craved it, this gift from herself to herself, the Oscar present and the major nineteenth-birthday present she wouldn't be anywhere near Tiffany's to buy on her actual birthday. Tessa came to a decision. She was going to play hooky. She was going to Tiffany's this morning and that was that.

She picked up the phone that had been recently installed in her bedroom and called Fiona Bridges, her just-as-recent personal assistant, and told her that she thought she might be coming down with a cold and that her riding lesson had better be cancelled. She hated to lie, but she didn't want even Fiona to go with her when she bought her present. It should be a private moment, a secret delight, with nobody looking on and giving advice.

Tessa carefully considered what to wear. She wanted to look like someone who had every right to expect service at Tiffany's and at the same time she didn't want to risk being recognised. Finally, Tessa decided on her best green linen suit, with a white silk shirt. She poked and pulled at her hair until it fell untidily around her face, concealing her features. She decided not to put on any make-up.

Then she phoned the local taxi company. As soon as she saw the cab stop at the front door, she was out in a flash, calling 'Bye, Mother, have to meet Fiona,' before her mother could stop her.

'Tiffany's in Beverly Hills,' Tessa told the driver, feeling a sudden surge of freedom as the cab pulled away quickly. She hadn't been this excited since the audition that had won her the part of Jo. She had talked Steve Miller, her business manager, into letting her open a little current account of her own. What if every last penny of the money she'd made were tied up in those safe investments that Steve told her would give her financial security when she was too old to work?

'I'm young, Steve,' she'd told him, amazed. 'I can play *ingénues* and leading ladies for another twenty years and I'll still only be thirty-eight. That's practically middle-aged! Then, when it's time, I'll move into character parts. You'll see, Steve, I plan to get older in some wonderful way, maybe a dignified, distinguished way, like an English actress, or in a sexy, fascinating way like a French actress. I'll play anything—mothers, maiden aunts, teachers, taxi drivers, nuns, you name it—because I intend to keep on working until I drop dead from real old age one day.'

He'd laughed at her, but eventually she'd managed to get him to fork out $3,000, more money than she'd ever believed she would have in her possession. Tessa's never-used chequebook lay snug in her handbag.

The taxi stopped in front of Tiffany's at the corner of the Beverly Wilshire Hotel. She'd never been in the store—she'd hardly ever been to Beverly Hills, for that matter—yet she didn't linger to gape at the windows but marched through the door as if she'd done it dozens of times before. She moved with her characteristic walk, coltish yet swinging, both youthful and immodestly alluring, slightly boyish but enduringly graceful, a walk she was never to lose.

Swiftly Tessa cruised around the store, her proud head on her proud neck set at a critical, appraising angle. The salespeople all seemed to be occupied with customers, and for a minute Tessa stood still and looked around. At five feet seven inches, she was so perfectly made that she looked taller, and her disciplined posture was commanding without her realising it. She made a vivid sight in her green suit, this tall, slim girl with a treasure of almost black hair tumbling around her face.

'May I be of assistance?' asked a man's voice. Tessa turned to see a pleasantly smiling, reassuringly middle-aged man.

'Yes, thank you. I'm looking for . . . a pearl necklace.'

'You've certainly come to the right place,' he nodded. 'Let's go over to the back of the store. That's where we keep our pearls.'

Tessa followed him to a long counter where, under glass, lay dozens of pearl necklaces and earrings.

'Are these for a gift or for yourself?' the salesman asked.

'For myself,' Tessa answered, her voice tentative as she realised that pearl necklaces came in more varieties than she had ever imagined.

'Well then, if you can give me some idea of what you have in mind . . .?' He gestured at the abundance of choice.

Tessa heard herself say, 'I really won't be able to tell you much until I try one on, will I?'

'That's absolutely right,' the salesman agreed. 'Even two necklaces that seem identical to the naked eye will look different on your skin.' On this girl's very white, extraordinarily perfect skin, he thought, any necklace was going to look exquisite.

'Of course,' Tessa said, looking down at rows of pearls that all seemed to be the same colour.

'I assume you're looking for a sixteen-inch necklace?'

'Probably,' Tessa said guardedly.

'It's the most useful length. You can wear a sixteen-inch strand with anything from a ball gown to a sweater,' he said, trying to decide whether her amazing eyes were more green than grey. Tessa looked up at him. Far more green, he decided, a green like early spring in the forest. 'When you get to eighteen inches there's always the problem of the necklace dipping under your collar.'

'Then let's go for sixteen,' Tessa said, relieved to have one element isolated from the other possibilities.

'As for the millimetre . . .?' The salesman paused tactfully. The size of the pearl determined the price.

'The millimetre,' Tessa mused, not betraying the fact that she was entirely at sea. Was the millimetre the diameter of the pearl? 'The millimetre, yes, naturally. Now what would you buy, if you were me?'

'For a young woman, I usually recommend eight and a half to nine millimetres, not too big a pearl, not too small, and it's always appropriate. This strand, for instance,' he said, reaching into the case and pulling out a necklace.

'Is that eight and a half or nine?' she asked.

'Both,' he answered. 'A discrepancy of one half millimetre is standard in a necklace of uniform size.'

'Oh, of course, because they're natural,' Tessa said hastily, realising that pearl divers couldn't be expected to pop up out of the ocean with a bunch of pearls that were exactly the same size.

'Not natural, no.' The salesman repressed even the hint of a smile. 'These are all cultured pearls. You can only tell the difference if you X-ray them. There haven't been any natural pearls available since the 1930s, unless you buy them at auction, and then they're fabulously expensive.'

'At auction?' Tessa said shocked. '*Secondhand pearls?* I'd never do that. How would you know what you were getting?'

'Precisely.' Her mouth was utterly fascinating, the salesman thought. It was sharply incised at the corners yet rising to an unusual plumpness. 'I think the only way for you to decide,' he continued, 'is to sit down in our private room and try on a number of necklaces.'

'Fine,' Tessa agreed quickly. Out of the corner of her eye she'd noticed several people looking at her with the kind of interest that she'd learned meant that she'd been recognised.

The salesman unlocked the case, extracted three identically sized necklaces, and escorted Tessa to a small room lined in grey velvet, where there were a desk, a chair, and a large round mirror on a stand. He laid the necklaces out carefully on a square of velvet.

'Which one would you like to start with?' he asked Tessa.

'That one,' she said, pointing at random. He undid the clasp and, standing behind her, fastened the necklace round her neck.

Tessa fell silent in wonder. There was something softly mysterious about the necklace, as if a light were gleaming from deep within each pearl. But the lapels of her suit held her shirt too close to her neck for her to get the full effect, so she shrugged her jacket off and flung the silk collar of her white blouse back, so that she could see as much as possible. Still her hair obscured many of the pearls, so Tessa fumbled in her handbag for the wide elastic band she kept there and quickly made a ponytail.

'Ah, that's better,' the salesman approved, with what little breath remained in his lungs after watching Tessa take off her jacket.

Still Tessa said nothing, absorbed in the effect of the pearls.

'Not exactly what you have in mind? Here, try these,' the salesman said, whisking the necklace away and replacing it with another. 'They have a slightly more creamy tone.'

'Mmm,' was all Tessa could manage.

'Not these either? Now here's a strand with a definite silvery quality,' he said, replacing the second necklace with the third.

'They all look pretty much the same,' Tessa commented, finding a crisp tone from somewhere, unwilling to commit herself to anything until she found out what they cost.

'I'll go and get a few more strands. You've just begun to look,' the salesman offered immediately. As soon as she was alone Tessa examined the tiny white price tags that hung by a thin string from each necklace. Each one was the same price, $3,400. Shocked and dismayed, she sat back, trying to decide what to say to make a graceful exit. But before she had time to find the right words, the salesman was back with three more necklaces.

'These are between twelve and twelve and a half millimetres each. With your height, the length of your neck, and the width of your shoulders, I suspected that you'd probably be happier with something larger. Now,' he asked, as he closed the clasp of one of the new necklaces, 'tell me if I'm right or not.'

'Oh,' Tessa said, fighting down a hysterical laugh, 'you're right. These do more for me, there's no question about that.' And they did, oh, they did! These were exactly the pearls she'd had in mind. These were her dream pearls, gleaming with a pink-white magnificence, precisely the right size.

'How much are they?' she asked simply.

'Fourteen thousand five hundred.'

Tessa looked at herself for long minutes, expressionless.

'There's one problem.'

'I know. You want earrings to go with them. That won't be a problem at all.'

'It's not that. I have only three thousand dollars in my current account and I don't have a credit card. So I'm afraid I'll have to leave these here,' Tessa sighed. She should have known better than to let him put them round her neck.

'But, Miss Kent, we wouldn't dream of expecting immediate payment! The manager is opening a house charge for you as we speak.'

'He is?' Tessa said blankly.

'Yes, he told me who you were when I went out to get these neck-laces. I have to admit I didn't know . . . I rarely get to the movies. I didn't even watch the Oscars, but please accept my congratulations.'

'A house charge? *A charge account at Tiffany's?*' Tessa breathed, unable to believe his words.

'You can keep them on and wear them right out to lunch. I'll just remove the price tag for you,' he said, as he quickly snipped the thread. 'Now, they're yours! You've made the perfect choice, if I may say so. Perfect! Now, shall I bring you some earrings?'

'I think I'd better come back later for the earrings,' Tessa said, smiling freely for the first time since she'd entered Tiffany's. 'I'm having lunch with my business manager and I don't want him to have a heart attack.' She got up, put her jacket back on, and took the band out of her hair.

Tessa Kent walked out of the private room, wearing her first real pearls, straight into a burst of applause. Dozens of people had gathered round the door and were waiting to see her emerge.

Startled, she stopped, but almost immediately she threw her head back and began to laugh. 'Thank you,' Tessa said, as she walked easily and happily through the crowd, stopping now and then to sign an auto-graph. 'Thank you so much.'

Agnes Horvath stood by the stove in her kitchen while the water came to a boil for tea, listening to the laughter that came from Teresa's room, where her daughter and Fiona Bridges were packing for Teresa's flight to London the next day. There she would rendezvous for costume fittings and make-up tests with David Lean and the cast of his new film, an epic set in sixteenth-century England, in which Teresa would star as the young Mary, Queen of Scots. Peter O'Toole and Albert Finney would be playing her second and third husbands, and Vanessa Redgrave would play Queen Elizabeth, Mary's first cousin and nemesis.

Or rather, Agnes thought with the ever deepening affront she had learned to mask, *Tessa Kent* was packing for London. Tessa Kent the phenomenal young star, Tessa Kent, Agnes told herself with a burst of bitterness, for whom her own name was not good enough. Teresa Horvath, that ingrate, had allowed herself to be re-baptised by her agent, Aaron Zucker. An agent handpicked by Roddy Fensterwald who had directed *Little Women*.

Agnes added sugar to her tea and held the cup so that it warmed her cold hands. Still, the laughter came from above, shutting her out, just as she'd been shut out of everything else. When Teresa had started working on *Little Women* she'd become so busy that she might just as well have left home. She'd left school against her wishes, but there was nothing they could do since she was over sixteen. Whatever little time she wasn't needed on the set was devoted, under Zucker's decree, to lessons in fancy new activities: ballroom dancing, driving a car, horse riding and tennis.

Her own role, Agnes reflected as her tea grew cold, had long ago been reduced to running a bed and breakfast, nothing more than a convenience for a daughter who grew more independent, more self-assured and more sophisticated every day. It seemed as if a glittering scarf of Teresa's triumphs, a wide mantle of sparkling stars and silvery moons, flashed perpetually about her shoulders. This image burned into Agnes as she watched the happy girl dashing here and there.

A car and driver were at her beck and call. Fiona Bridges worked with the fashion designers whose clothes Teresa wore for her frequent appearances at premieres and award shows, chose her escorts, directed the girls who answered her mail, arranged time for journalists and photographers from all over the world, all with the advice of a publicity firm.

And now Teresa would be off, flying away to England with more brilliant success in sight—Mary, Queen of Scots and Queen of the Isles, that most tenacious of Catholic queens, that passionately devout Queen— just the sound of the words was deeply romantic. Agnes sighed heavily, unable to bear her own dreary life.

'We're starving, Mother,' Teresa said, bounding into the kitchen. 'Is there anything to eat? Packing is hungry work.'

'Finished already? But you'll be gone for months and months.'

'All done! Fiona decided that almost all of my clothes just won't do, and anyway, I'll be in costume much of the time and she can always shop for anything I need. For big nights, designers will send me stuff.'

'How convenient,' Agnes said, glaring at Fiona. It was Fiona who'd

JUDITH KRANTZ

taken the place that rightfully belonged to Agnes. She was the lucky one who had all the fun and excitement of being intimately associated with a star. She, Teresa's mother, could have done anything Fiona did and done it better, Agnes thought in cold hurt.

'Mother? Food? I don't see anything interesting in the fridge.'

'Call room service,' Agnes snapped, and left the kitchen abruptly.

'**Agnes**,' Sandor said that night, after Maggie had been put to bed, 'What happened with you and Teresa this afternoon?'

'Nothing "happened". I barely saw her. You spent more time with her than I did before she and that Fiona creature went off together.'

'She told me that you'd been upset with her because she and Fiona invaded your domain demanding something to eat. She asked me to tell you that she was sorry to have been so thoughtless. She also said that when this next picture's over and she gets back to Hollywood, she's going to move out and become responsible for herself.'

'High time,' Agnes said, refusing to betray her feelings of rejection.

'I didn't agree. I believe that it's proper for a young woman to live under her parents' roof until she gets married. But she made a case for herself and she made sense. We simply don't live in the style to accommodate the traffic and service a movie star has reason to expect.'

'Damn you, Sandor! For a lifetime you insist that everything in our lives be as strictly Catholic as if you were the Pope's brother, and then, when you see Teresa becoming rich and famous, you suddenly change. She's a sinner, Sandor, a sinner, have you forgotten?'

'I've forgiven the sin, Agnes. I've told you that before. But you've never forgiven, never forgotten, have you?' he said, his voice trembling with anger. 'Have you ever prayed to stop being angry at our daughter? Of course you haven't, because it's still with you and you can't let yourself give it up. You're consumed by the sin of envy. You envy our daughter's success.'

'You know nothing about me and you never have,' she retorted, drawing herself up in rage and scorn. 'But you, Sandor, have you looked at yourself? Where are your precious spiritual values now? Drowned in the sin of covetousness, that's where. Not for yourself but for your daughter.'

'"Covetousness,"' he said slowly, shock on his fine features, 'I hadn't thought, but perhaps you're right. I hadn't seen that in myself, but yes, it's not impossible. I'll discuss it with Father Vincent tomorrow.'

'**Brian**,' Sandor Horvath said to his friend, Brian Kelly, Maggie's godfather. 'We've come to know each other pretty well in the past few years, wouldn't you say?'

'Sure thing, Sandy. I'm only sorry that our wives haven't managed to hit it off better.'

'But at least you and I don't have that problem. I look forward to our lunches more than you realise.'

'Same here, Sandy. Is there something wrong? You don't sound happy at the moment.'

'Nothing wrong, just a favour I'd like to ask you, in your capacity as a godfather.'

'Ask away.'

'I've written a letter I'd like to have delivered thirteen years from now, if I'm not around to deliver it myself.'

'Come on, quit kidding.'

'I'm perfectly serious.'

'Delivered to whom?'

'Maggie.'

'You're not talking about a will?'

'You don't need a godfather for that, Brian.'

'All right, assuming that you're not around, which isn't going to happen, what about Agnes?'

'It doesn't concern her. It's between me and Maggie. That's why you're the one person I can count on to make sure this letter gets to her, wherever she might be, when she's eighteen.'

'Give it to me and forget abut it, unless you change your mind. I'll keep it in my safe-deposit box until she's eighteen. And if, God forbid, I'm not around myself, I'll have arranged for it to be delivered.'

'You're not curious about what's in the letter?'

'Of course I am, but I know you wouldn't go to this trouble if it were something you could tell me.'

'Thank you, Brian. You relieve my mind more than I can tell you.'

Yesterday, David Lean told her that Mary Queen of Scots was the first woman to have played golf. Was the young queen also the first woman to have almost frozen to death in the royal apartments of Edinburgh Castle while waiting for the sun to come from behind a cloud, or would Tessa Kent enjoy that distinction, Tessa wondered? Clad in an elaborate dressing gown, fit for a nine months' pregnant queen, with the great necklace of black pearls Mary had always worn, and a mound of padding on her belly, Tessa stood motionless, framed by an imposing medieval window. The castle's dramatic height above the city exposed it to the chill wind whistling in from the sea.

Tessa, riveted to her mark by the window, from which there was a

270-foot sheer drop down basalt cliffs, told herself firmly that it was a warm afternoon in mid-June of 1566 when no woman of the period could possibly have felt the cold. Behind her she felt the tension of a unified crew praying for the precious rays of light to return, all conversation stilled in anticipation, every technician at the ready, the camera operator ready to roll film as soon as David Lean, the director, spoke. There were barely ten seconds left to be shot in this scene as the queen looks through the window into the distance of the Firth of Forth and speculates aloud about the importance of the sex of her anticipated child, but they needed those ten seconds to set the scene for the birth of the baby boy, James VI, who eventually became James I of England, heir to Queen Elizabeth I.

Tessa began to shiver, slightly but uncontrollably. Then suddenly she heard the sound of quick footsteps moving towards her and, almost before she could wonder that anyone would dare to move on the set, she was engulfed in a heavy garment, deliciously warm from body heat, held round her tightly and protectively by a man's strong arms.

'What the hell do you expect from this girl, David? Death in the line of duty?' a voice shouted as the sun appeared.

'You bloody, bloody fool!' the director screamed. 'Take that thing off her and get the hell out of my set!'

'Can't,' the strange voice said calmly. 'There seems to be a button tangled in her wig.'

'Wardrobe!' someone shouted, and Tessa felt quick fingers attempting to separate her wig from whatever was enveloping her so comfortingly.

'Now look at her,' the wardrobe woman cried in despair. 'The wig's all crooked and her necklace is broken! Hair, props, quickly!'

'Never mind, we've lost the light,' David Lean said with frustration.

'Shit, I didn't realise . . .' the strange voice said.

'If I thought you had, I'd kill you with my bare hands, you crazy son of a bitch. Oh, Tessa, sorry. You can move now. Eddie, tell everyone it's a wrap for today.'

Tessa turned, expecting to see the intruder being manhandled off the set. Instead, he and Lean were wrapped in a laughing bear hug.

'Next time you do that, Luke, I'm throwing you headfirst through the nearest window.'

'Just keeping an eye on my investment, David,' her would-be rescuer replied. 'I didn't know you were shooting; there wasn't the slightest sound in here.'

'You might have asked yourself why we were all standing around holding our breath but all you saw was a lady in distress. I expect nothing less of you. Tessa, this is Luke Blake, unfortunately one of my most cherished friends. Luke, this is Tessa Kent.'

'I appreciated feeling warm, even if it was only for a second,' Tessa said, taking the hand he held out to her. With her hand in this man's hand she felt more than warm, she felt *safe*, she thought in confusion— safe in a way she'd never felt before in her entire life.

A feeling of amazing discovery was rising in her chest, so powerful she was afraid that she was going to burst into tears. Such a thorough conviction . . . how was it possible? Her eyes sought Luke Blake's. Warmth was in them, too, human warmth as powerful as any force of nature, telling her that he approved totally of everything about her. His gaze had intelligence and humour, but it was the warmth that was all-important.

'Here, have my coat back,' Luke Blake said. He was big and burly in his heavy ribbed wool sweater, with dark red, curly hair, cut very short; open, weathered features; a dominant nose; and a most authoritative flash in his blue eyes. He was obviously an urbane man, yet he had the look of someone who spent his life outdoors, Tessa thought, to say nothing of the commanding set to his shoulders and his interestingly firm, imperious mouth with amused corners.

'Tessa's going right down to wardrobe,' the director replied.

'Have it anyway, you don't need to freeze on the way there,' Blake insisted, helping Tessa carefully into his duffle coat, giving her padded stomach a friendly pat. 'Hello, James, you little rotter,' he said. 'Never even protested when Auntie Elizabeth cut off your mother's head, did you? Kids—always looking out for themselves.'

Australian . . . why did it take me so long to realise? Tessa wondered as his slight but perceptible accent registered.

'Why, Luke, can you possibly have been reading history?' Lean asked in amusement.

'Certainly. Enough so that I know what happens to Mary after the film's over. I don't have tunnel vision, unlike you, David. I get interested in these characters. When you're finished with Mary you'll be roaring off with another script and another bunch of actors, forgetting that poor girl imprisoned by her cousin for the next twenty years, you can't deny that.'

'You make me feel like a savage.' He laughed.

'All directors are savages. You're a disgrace, letting Miss Kent stand there covered in goose bumps. I'm almost ashamed to know you. However, in view of the past, dinner tonight?'

'Of course.'

'Goodbye, Mr Blake,' Tessa said. Maybe he'll invite me too, she thought. 'How should I get your coat back to you?'

'Don't give it a thought; I have others. Anyway, aren't you and I planning on dinner tomorrow night? We can discuss it then.'

'You're staying around?' Lean asked, in surprise.

'Indefinitely. If I'm welcome.'

'I warn you, one false step and I'll glue you to the floor.'

'A small price to pay.'

'Tell me about her, David,' Luke Blake asked as they sat down to dinner, without formality or preliminary.

'You might at least ask how I am, and how the film's going. It's your twenty-five million pounds that's paying for it, as I remember.'

'Bloody details. Tell me about Tessa Kent and stop playing games, cobber,' Luke said, grinning fondly at the great director.

'She's out of your class, boy.'

'Who decided that?'

'Everyone. I've known you too long. You have a bad record. Forty-five years old and never married, the man who's kept half the available great ladies of the last quarter century. You're asking about a barely twenty-year-old kid who's more innocent than any actress I've ever worked with, a girl who still lives at home. Not your kind of material, old friend, not in your wildest dreams. Not bedable, not keepable, not obtainable at any price.'

'So it would seem.'

'Don't even think about it,' he said warningly. 'There are some things in the life of Luke Blake that shouldn't happen. Tessa Kent is one of them.'

'"Shouldn't"? I don't see where you get the authority—or the bloody nerve—to make that judgment.'

'The age difference.'

'Besides that?' Luke said, waving it away.

'She's a virgin.'

'I have to admit that you're never wrong on that score.'

'And a Catholic.'

'Well, so am I as a matter of fact, lapsed thirty years ago, but still a cradle Catholic, to say nothing of having been an efficient altar boy.'

'You'd never seduce a virgin, Luke, that's just not your style.'

'You're right. I'm basically a good sort of chap.'

Lean laughed. 'Shall we look at the menu?'

'I'm going to be late,' Tessa moaned in agitation to Fiona, who was helping her get dressed.

'You look gorgeous now, for goodness sake,' Fiona said. 'You've been fussing for an hour. What's the matter with you, anyway? Luke Blake's got to be more than twice your age, and let me tell you, the man's been round the block a time or two or ten.'

'Fiona, why can't you let me enjoy myself? I've never dressed for a real date before and you know it. All I'm doing is having dinner with a man who was nice enough to try to keep me warm.'

'I'm trying to warn you, in my own subtle way.'

'You think he's going to try to add me to his list of conquests?'

'"Think?" I haven't the slightest doubt of his motives. I bet he's never bought a woman dinner without the intention of getting her into bed in the back of his mind—no, make that the front of his mind. And succeeding nine point nine times out of ten.'

'Fiona, have you ever gone out with a man without the possibility of sex, not necessarily that night, but maybe, just maybe, sex *sometime*, entering into the disgusting swamp of your brain?'

'You're right. I'm as bad as any man ever born. That is, if we're not considering obvious noncandidates, like, oh, let's see, the local minister, or college professors, or my best friends' fathers, men like that.'

'I wouldn't trust you with any of the categories you just mentioned, except my own father,' Tessa laughed, doing up her black velvet trousers and standing so that Fiona could zip her into her black velvet Regency-cut jacket, trimmed with heavy white-lace stand-up collar, and cuffs that fell to her fingers.

'Go, meet that man, Tessa, you fool.' Fiona shooed her out of their suite. 'He's waiting in the lobby. Shall I stay up for you so you can tell me all about it?'

'Good night, Fiona. See you tomorrow.'

'Thank you for the thermal long johns and the electrically heated socks,' Tessa said as she sat down to dinner in the small, perfectly appointed French restaurant with tables set at a pleasant distance from each other. 'They came this morning first thing.'

'Did they help?' Luke asked, barely able to speak as he looked at her face framed in white lace. She was like a portrait of a young Renaissance princess, so radiantly, luminously beautiful that you could study the painting for hours, yearning to have been alive when she existed in real time.

'Actually, I had to take them off after the first half-hour. Mr Lean's childbirth scene was messy, sweaty stuff, but the baby's going to be born tomorrow, thank goodness, and after that they'll be more useful than you can imagine.'

'How does a virgin know how to play a woman having a baby?'

'Exactly how do you know I'm a virgin?'

'Oh.' He fell silent and dropped his eyes in embarrassment.

'Is it common knowledge, does it show somewhere, or did you just assume it?' Tessa demanded, her eyes flashing mischief.

'David told me,' he admitted.

'Out of the blue? As if virgins are as rare as unicorns and you had to be alerted when there's one in the neighbourhood, like a special tourist attraction?'

'Actually he was warning me not to pursue you.'

'I hope you told him to mind his own damn business.'

'Something more or less like that.'

'Does he also think I'm not old enough to be let out alone with such a hardened sinner as you?'

'Definitely. Who told you I was a hardened sinner?'

'Everybody. It's common knowledge.'

'Well, that makes us even, doesn't it? Two of a kind? Two of an opposite kind, that is.' I'm babbling, he thought. I'm not making sense, except, I don't feel foolish.

'That makes us people who shouldn't even be having dinner together,' Tessa said serenely.

'Is that why I feel so blazingly happy with you?'

'I don't know.' She shrugged her shoulders in an eloquent gesture of ignorance. 'I don't know you at all, certainly not what makes you happy. I just know you're kind and good and I feel something with you I don't feel with anybody else.'

'What is it you feel with me?'

'Safe,' she said quietly. It took all her courage, but she was determined to tell him. 'Totally and completely safe. As if nothing bad can possibly happen to me, as if you'll protect me from all the frightening, hard, awful things in the world. It's crazy, it makes no sense at all. I've just met you, but I've never felt this way before. It's like discovering that I can be a completely new person. It happened to me yesterday when we shook hands. I decided I should tell you because it's too important to keep secret. I don't mean to make you feel any sense of obligation. I don't realistically expect you to take care of me for a single second, but I wanted you to know.'

'You have to know that what you just said would scare the living daylights out of most men.'

'I felt you were tough enough to take it. And if I'm wrong, it's better for me to know now. I thought about it all night.'

'I thought about you all night long, too.'

'What sort of things?' she asked without coyness.

'About the facts that you're very young and a virgin. I discovered how amazingly important that virginity is to me, and I never knew that about myself. Your age isn't of consequence, but the fact that you've never made love with a man . . . that's different. I've been with a lot of women, but there wasn't one of them who didn't have some experience. It's got to be the old altar boy in me. I have no right at all, considering the life I've led, to prize virginity so much. I'm not absolutely clear on why virginity is deeply mysteriously meaningful, and, for me, wonderful beyond words, but it is. Enormously.'

Tell him now, Tessa thought. Tell him now, before this conversation goes further. But tell him what? She *was* a virgin, and giving birth hadn't changed that fact. The three-second episode with what's-his-name didn't count; she'd been drunk and not responsible. The only kisses she'd experienced since had been before a camera. She'd never even been allowed to go out on an unsupervised date. There was nothing to tell except the part she'd confessed and been absolved of, and that was between her God and herself. She took a deep breath and sat back in her chair, glad to forget the ridiculous idea of telling him the truth.

'Is that what makes you feel happy with me?' Tessa asked with wry curiosity.

'I felt that way before I knew damn-all about you expect that you were freezing. It started right after I put my coat around you. It's something about your eyes and your smile and your voice.'

'All those women you've had, did they make you happy?'

'Not one, not truly, or I'd have married her.'

'You don't frighten me, either,' Tessa said as lightly as she could, suppressing a tremor with her actress's skill. She had to change the subject or the surprising, inexplicable tears of joy that menaced her might rise to the surface. She felt atoms of happiness swirling and churning and slowly turning into a solid pillar somewhere in her chest. 'What sort of things do you like to do?'

'Sail a small boat and fly a small plane,' he said, thinking of priorities, 'and marinate a rack of home-grown lamb in my home-made sauce, and dance a samba in Brazil and eat a Peking duck at Mr Chow's in London and read until three in the morning and go to auctions and ski the fall line and, oh, I almost forgot, kiss pretty girls. And take care of my business. What about you?'

'Me? Not fair!' Tessa said indignantly, instantly jealous of his easily produced list of delights that included so much enviable experience that had nothing to do with her. 'I haven't had time to choose what I'd like to do because I've been so busy taking the lessons my agent decided I should take. I can dance, but not a samba, whatever that is. I love to read, but I don't even know what a Peking duck looks like. You're over-privileged, Luke Blake. Where do you live?'

'Here and there, more or less. I have a place in Melbourne and another in Eze-Village, Provence, but I rarely spend more than a few weeks in Australia and a few weeks in the South of France every year. That's where I go to unwind. I have business all over the world, so I roam about, living in hotel suites most of the time.'

'What sort of business?'

'Mining, milling, brewing, finding new ways to dig things out of the earth.'

'Why can't you just leave the earth alone?' she said, provokingly.

'I often wonder. My great-grandfather started it and I'm trapped in the family business. Now too many people depend on me to even think of stopping.'

'Under the circumstances, with all this rape of the planet you're hopelessly involved in, in spite of certain philosophic reservations for which I give you very little credit, don't you think we might have something to eat?'

'Did I forget to order?' he asked in wonder.

'Not even a drink.'

'Lord, I'm sorry. What will you have?'

'I'll try a Blake's, see what all the fuss is about.'

'You've never had a Blake's?'

'Never had a beer, actually.'

'Waiter, two Blake's, please.'

'I'll try, sir,' answered the waiter in the most authentically French restaurant in the aristocratic, sophisticated old city. 'But I'm not sure we have that particular brand of beer.'

'Shocking. Well then, bring us a bottle of champagne. I'm sure you have Dom Perignon. What shall we drink to, Tessa?'

'My first real grown-up date,' she said with decision.

'You don't mean—you can't mean—me?'

'You. And about time, I think.'

The next morning Tessa was pulling on her jeans and sweaters for her early-morning wardrobe call when Fiona came in with a note and a bunch of pallid daffodils. Tessa tore open the note, read it twice, turned quickly, and hurled the daffodils into a wastepaper basket.

'He's gone!'

'What? Let me see that.' Fiona grabbed the slip of paper and muttered, 'Have to leave for London suddenly, hotel florist not open, hope you like daffodils, keep warm, et cetera, et cetera.'

'Do you *believe* that?' Tessa raved.

'I still don't know how last night ended,' Fiona said, reaching for a pragmatic tone.

'He brought me back to the hotel, escorted me up to the door of our suite, looked into my eyes for a very long time, as if he were memorising them, kissed me gently on the top of my head, and abruptly left, leaving me standing there stupidly waiting—I don't know what I expected but it was definitely not that after we'd both said things . . . things that I thought meant . . . obviously I was wrong . . . meant that we liked each other very much. More than very much. Oh, Fiona, we *weren't* flirting, I was so sure of that. We were speaking from our hearts.'

Tessa's eyes were full of incredulous disappointment and disbelief. She felt utterly abandoned that she could barely comprehend what had happened. How could she ever reconcile last night's long dinner, and the intimate, serious, revealing conversation that had lasted until late in the evening, with the note she'd just received? Until she'd read it, she'd been plunged into a pool of tremulous emotion, so new in her experience of life that she'd been up all night long, alternately examining everything she had said to Luke and Luke had said to her, reliving every detail, abandoned to her happiness, her heart so full that she'd wept for joy.

'But, Tessa, he doesn't say he isn't coming back,' Fiona said, as briskly as she could, but still sounding only a hollow note of hope.

'When? The very next time he has business in Scotland? Between trains in five years?' Tessa abandoned her attempt at brittle scorn and cried out, 'What kind of man could do a thing like this, Fiona? Can you explain it? You know men. Is it typical? Is it something I should have expected? He *had* to leave for London? Why didn't he even mention that detail last night when he was so busy telling me how blazingly happy— yes, those were the words he used—I made him? Can you think of a single reason, even one, that makes any sense?'

'Damn, I was afraid of this,' Fiona said viciously. 'A bloody hit-and-run driver.'

'You were so right. And you can say "I told you so" as much as you want to—I deserve it. Oh, what a fool I was!'

'Tessa darling, I'm sick that you've been so badly hurt, but Luke Blake wasn't for you and you knew it all along. Come on, admit it. The guy's middle-aged and more than lived-in. You're ten thousand times too

good for him, too young, too fresh, too talented, with too many wonderful things that are going to happen to you. Your life's just beginning.
Don't waste your energy on him. You're going to be late as it is and you
have a long day's work. Come on, let's go. They'll feed us in wardrobe
and that's what we need, both of us.'

Three days later, on a Saturday afternoon, Tessa found herself alone in
her suite. Fiona had just left for a cashmere shopping trip in the heart of
cashmere country, but Tessa was too deeply plunged into depression to
feel any temptation to go with her. She'd slept only fitfully and eaten
almost nothing, unable to stop going over the fatal dinner in her mind.
Only sheer discipline had enabled her to get out of bed each morning
and go to the set. All her energy had bled away, except what she had to
summon for the camera.

She didn't want a single sweater or scarf that reminded her of
Edinburgh, Tessa thought apathetically. She couldn't wait to leave
Scotland next week after the film wrapped and she was free to return to
gloriously warm Los Angeles.

'You should learn to play solitaire,' she said out loud to her reflection
in the mirror. Her eyes, in the clear northern light, seemed more distinctly green than ever, although they never lost their faint overlay of
grey, like the most illusive wisp of smoke through a tropical rain forest.

The phone rang. 'Mr Blake would like to know if he might come up,
Miss Kent,' the concierge said.

'No!' Tessa slammed down the phone, her depression turned into a
lightning strike of pure rage. What was he doing here? Come back to
feast his eyes on a virgin, like some sort of vampire? Come up to say
goodbye for ever, I'm off to fly my plane around the world? Come up to
tell her about the delights of the latest Peking duck he'd gorged himself
on in London? Or the dozen pretty girls he'd kissed? She wouldn't
bother to spit on his shadow.

The phone rang again. 'What is it this time?' Tessa asked furiously.

'Mr Blake would like to know when it would be convenient for you to
see him.'

'Never! Never, tell him that, tell him I said never, and I mean never!
And don't call me again. I've been working all week, I'm trying to rest
and you keep interrupting me, don't you understand that?'

'I'm most dreadfully sorry, Miss Kent, it won't happen again.'

She was so angry she found herself pacing the floor, unable to sit still.
They say that murderers can't keep away from the scene of the crime.
Come to gloat, had he, she thought bitterly?

There was a knock on the door.

'Yes?' Tessa said neutrally. It was probably the maid.

'Let me in, Tessa,' Luke Blake demanded.

'*I will not.*'

'What's wrong with you? Didn't you get my note?'

'It came.'

'Then why won't you let me in?'

'I don't want to see you.'

'That's impossible. Of course you do.'

'Get away from my door or I'll have you thrown out of the hotel.'

'I own this hotel.'

'Is that supposed to be some sort of threat? I don't care if you own this whole miserable city!'

'Tessa!' he shouted, his voice severe in its demand.

She didn't answer, waiting for him to leave. Several minutes passed before she heard his footsteps retreating. In less time than seemed possible, Tessa heard the tramp of heavy footsteps and a shout of warning to stand back, then saw the door to her suite splinter under an assault from two burly firemen armed with axes.

'It's in the bedroom,' Luke directed them. As they rushed to the bedroom he looked at Tessa, open-mouthed and immobile in shock, standing in her quilted pink bathrobe. 'I should have guessed it,' he said finally. 'You detest daffodils.'

'Are you insane?'

'Probably. But what does that have to do with it?'

'I have nothing to say to you. Get out of here, you and those firemen.'

'Chaps?'

'Yes, Mr Blake.'

'It's OK, Miss Kent managed to put it out herself. I'll have the door put right tomorrow.' He tipped them and sent them off.

'Tessa, I'm utterly hopeless at writing to people, I should have called . . .'

'There was nothing to say.' She tightened the sash of the bathrobe round her waist and grew taller in freezing dignity as she looked at him with biting scorn, her eyes dismissing him as the smallest and least worthy of any pitifully abject creature that has ever crawled on the face of the earth.

'But, at dinner—'

'Forget that dinner. Wipe it out of your mind. I was feeling exceptionally vulnerable. I said things I didn't mean . . . I was being actressy . . . over the top. I didn't realise how far over I'd gone or how ridiculous I'd been until it was too late. Obviously you're accustomed to saying things you don't mean, you've been doing it for a long time, haven't you? I didn't understand that since I haven't met your kind of man before, fortunately for me. Once is more than enough.'

'Tessa, I meant every word.'

'Oh, please, Luke, that's not necessary,' she said, producing a marvellously indifferent ghost of a smile. 'I don't need your empty reassurance, although why you feel the need to repeat your performance is beyond me. Does this amuse you in some twisted manner? I'm tired, and I'd like you to leave at once.'

'God, I'm a fool! You couldn't have known. No wonder you're acting like an avenging angel.'

'Known what?'

'I went to London to get something for you, something important I'd known existed for years, but the man I thought had it said he'd just sold it, so I had to go to New York and it turned out I had the wrong information, so I had to go to Geneva. I got there in the nick of time; Sotheby's was selling it at auction the next day, so I had to stay overnight . . . Anyway . . . here it is.'

He took a small blue leather box from his pocket and tried to give it to her.

'I don't want anything from you,' Tessa said, recoiling, and the box slipped from his hand.

'I keep getting it wrong.' Luke hit himself on the forehead in frustration. 'I've never done this before. Could I start over?'

'I asked you to leave,' Tessa repeated, with no hint of thaw in the glacial hardness of her voice.

'Tessa, hear me out,' Luke demanded, standing foursquare in the middle of the room. 'Before we even had dinner I knew that you and I were going to get married. I'd given up hoping that I'd ever find a woman I could love, and then, you—you, Tessa, you happened to me. One word from you and from that second on there was never the slightest doubt about it in my mind. I knew. My God, that sounds as if I think this is all about me and what I want, but it isn't. It's about you, too. So I decided it had to be something special, your engagement ring, I mean. That's what's in the box.'

'You've spent three days chasing after an engagement ring for somebody you've never even asked to marry you? Is this some kind of playboy's bad joke?' Tessa asked, so armoured against him that she was unable to recognise the sound of truth in his words.

'Don't you want to marry me?' Luke asked, surprise in his voice for the first time.

'Marry you? How would I know something as important as that after one dinner?' Tessa responded, with the first possibility of belief.

'It was much more than dinner,' Luke said relentlessly. 'You said you loved me and I said I loved you.'

'Never!' she shouted, outraged again. 'The word love never passed my lips, or yours.'

'Tessa, it was the subtext of our entire conversation, of every word we said to each other,' he insisted.

'No, it was not!'

'Then listen to the simple text, Tessa. I love you. You're the only woman I've ever loved, and I insist that you marry me,' Luke informed her, more commanding than ever, his eyes dominating her eyes, refusing to let her get away from him, continuing to defy her attempts to build a safe emotional barrier between them.

'So, you "insist" do you? That's irresistibly romantic,' she said as scornfully as she could. She must not hope.

'Answer me,' he demanded.

'I don't have to,' Tessa answered, holding on to her grievance as if it were a bastion that would keep her safe from the future.

'Ah, I knew it, damn it, I *knew* I should have called, but I was running from one airport to another and I'm sorry you don't like daffodils—'

'I *adore* daffodils!'

'Don't you love me?' Luke asked. 'Can you look at me honestly and say that you don't?'

'I don't know how I feel,' Tessa answered, maintaining her dignity. She could refuse to hope, but she couldn't look at him and say she didn't love him.

'Will you marry me, Tessa?' he asked, unsmiling.

She looked thoughtful, considering the situation. Did a proposal of marriage constitute a basis for hope, or would she make a fool of herself again?

'Tessa, Tessa, please say you will.' He was finally reduced to pleading, something he didn't know how to do. 'You're driving me mad and I know you're enjoying yourself, damn it. Don't say you're not, because I won't believe you. All I want is a yes. I don't deserve it, but love has nothing to do with merit.'

Tessa turned away, to hide the fact that her eyes had filled with tears of joy. Pushed to the wall, she acknowledged that she'd never been able to truly get over the hope that he'd return, not even in her lowest minutes. She finally admitted to herself that her life had been spent looking, although she hadn't known it, for this one particular man, this one particular destiny, and no other. It took her seconds of intense concentration to be able to speak clearly, but she wanted her words to be uncompromising.

'I love you totally, and I wanted to marry you the minute you took my hand.'

'Thank God,' he said with great relief, stepping forward, gathering her in his arms and kissing her lips over and over until she couldn't bear the burden of such confusing, unfamiliar rapture for another second. She pushed him away long enough to whisper, 'Where's that ring that's so special that you made me suicidal over it for three days?'

'It must be here somewhere.' Luke groped around on the floor until he found the box he'd dropped. He turned on a lamp against the twilight that was creeping into the room, and opened the lid.

It was a perfect heart-shaped stone, cut in facets, as big, Tessa thought, as a huge chunk of hard candy—and it was green, a marvellously soft green, the most mysterious, elusive colour she'd ever seen.

'It's the colour of your eyes in a certain light,' Luke told her as she stared at it, speechless. 'It's a green diamond, the rarest of natural colours after red, and red was wrong. Except for the "Dresden Green", this is the biggest green diamond in the world. What's more, it's a chameleon.'

'"Chameleon"?'

'It changes colour. It's the only diamond that does so. It turns yellow in the dark. I knew I had to have it for you, instead of some obvious blue-white rock.'

'It's shockingly beautiful,' Tessa said, daring to lean a little closer.

'Will you put it on, Tessa, darling?'

'It will change my life,' Tessa said, with a faint, odd feeling of reluctance. The ring, in spite of the soft fire of its colour, was as triumphant, as regal as a queen's tiara. Was she ready to wear it, to carry it off? It had implications she couldn't begin to understand, but she knew they were buried in the extraordinary stone.

'Any engagement ring I give you will change your life, even if it's just a cigar band.'

'True,' she replied, gathering the courage to extend her hand. The ring fitted her finger perfectly. It sat there like a tame butterfly from a magic planet far away. Suddenly Tessa exploded in giggles.

'What's so funny?'

'Fiona! Fiona . . . she said I was ten thousand times too good for you, and I agreed . . . now how am I going to explain this?'

'Tell her she's absolutely spot on, but I bribed you.'

'Holy shit, Tessa, you can't do it!' Aaron Zucker screamed, holding the phone as close to his mouth as possible—as if Tessa would be convinced by the sheer volume of his conviction.

'Give me one good reason,' Tessa laughed. 'By the way, you're invited too, so get your plane tickets; it's only ten days away.'

'One good reason? I'll give you twenty. This is madness! You've had offers for the leads in the three best scripts I've seen in years, you're the hottest new star in decades, you'd be throwing away opportunities right and left that I'd give my left nut for, you're too young, you've never left home before, you don't know this man, in fact you don't know diddly about men in general or, even worse, in particular. You're making a life decision without my guidance—'

'Aha, I thought that was it,' Tessa chortled, delighted with herself. 'I'm getting married without my agent's approval, that's your real problem, Aaron. Your feelings are hurt.'

'I'll bet your parents don't approve either,' Aaron shouted.

'I haven't told them yet. Isn't it any satisfaction to you to know that I called you with my news first?'

'Why haven't you called them?' he asked suspiciously. 'I bet it's because you're sure they won't approve either. And what's the big rush? Why do you have to get married ten days from now? It's obviously not a shotgun wedding. I just don't get it.'

'We won't have time for a honeymoon if we don't—Luke has to be back in Australia in three weeks. But most of all we don't want it to turn into a circus, we want to keep it as private as possible. No publicity, Aaron, that's the most important thing, and you must help me on that. I'm counting on you.'

'What did you say this guy Luke's last name was again?' Aaron asked in a more normal volume, hearing in Tessa's voice her determination to do this insane thing no matter what he thought about it.

'Blake.'

'Like the beer?'

'He is the beer.'

'You're marrying a brewer?' he asked incredulously.

'His great-grandfather was the brewer. Luke's basically in mining and other stuff too complicated to explain.'

'He's *that* Luke Blake?'

'So now you're impressed? So now it's all right with you, now you're excited for me? Aaron, I'm ashamed of you.'

'Isn't Luke Blake, Tessa, come on, *Luke Blake*, a little . . . mature . . . for you?'

'Nope. We're perfect for each other. Our ages don't matter one little bit.'

'OK, whatever you say, but, Tessa, what about your career?'

'I'll still make movies, but only one a year.'

'*What?* Tessa, you can't mean it! One a year . . . why not just retire, turn into a little housewife and get it over with?'

'Now, now, Aaron, don't exaggerate. Luke and I have discussed the whole thing thoroughly. Outside of one film a year, I'll be with him. When I'm working, he'll stay wherever I am.'

'Where will you be based?' Aaron moaned.

'I have no idea. Luke's a rover, he goes where the problems are. We'll be gypsies together, with a place in Provence and one in Melbourne, for whenever we both have some time off.'

'One picture a year,' Aaron said, regaining a little composure. 'Well,' he sighed deeply, 'it might not be everything that it could have been, considering how fast you've become a star, but one film a year, if it's the right one, will be enough to keep your career on a steady track.'

'You're feeling better already, aren't you, Aaron? But no scripts, no matter how good, that need a day more than three months shooting time. You'll have to be very picky or I won't consider it. Now, when are you getting your plane tickets?'

'Today, today! But why are you getting married in Monaco?'

'It seems that . . . Luke dropped in on these good friends who live there so he could tell them he was engaged, and they want to give the wedding, absolutely insisted on it as a matter of fact, and since Monaco is central enough for everybody to get to—'

'Are they anybody I'd know?'

'Princess Grace and Prince Rainier.'

'Holy . . . cow.'

Agnes put down the vacuum cleaner and picked up the phone.

'Mother, oh, Mother, I'm so glad I got you. I didn't know if you'd be home.' Tessa's voice didn't reveal her fluttering heart. She knew that there would never be a good way or a good time to break the news to her mother, and hearing her 'hello' had been enough to make her feel like a mistrusted child again.

'And just where did you think I'd be, Teresa?' Agnes was as dry as if Tessa were calling from around the corner. Long distance worked no wonders on her.

'Shopping, out with Maggie . . . it's not important. I'm delighted that I reached you right away because . . . well, you'll probably never believe it, I can hardly believe it myself, but I'm engaged . . . engaged to be married.' The telephone air was empty. 'Did you hear me, Mother? I said I was going to get married.'

'The last time you called home, not long ago at all, you said you and Fiona had been each other's dates for the whole picture, that you hadn't had any other social life. How could you possibly be getting married?'

'Look, Mother, I simply hadn't met him the last time I called. I admit it *is* sudden, but he . . . Luke . . . is so incredibly wonderful, and I'm so happy. I'm so certain about this, there's not the slightest doubt in my mind . . . oh, you'll love him when you meet him.'

'Teresa, for heaven's sake, stop carrying on. You realise, don't you, that you haven't made any sense up till now? Can you tell me exactly who this miraculous stranger is, this man you've decided to marry after knowing him for no time at all?'

'His name's Luke Blake, he's an Australian, a close friend of Mr Lean's. David says he's an absolutely wonderful guy and—'

'I wasn't asking for David Lean's testimony or opinion,' Agnes cut in. 'I assume this Luke person isn't Catholic, Teresa?'

Finally, Tessa thought, finally the one question I can answer in a way that will please her without qualification.

'Luke was born and bred a Catholic. He was even an altar boy. We're going to have a religious ceremony in a cathedral. That should satisfy you, Mother, after all the worry I've been to you.'

'It's a relief, I'll say that much.' Agnes paused. It was some relief to know that there would be—presumably—one less occasion for sin in Teresa's life, but there were major drawbacks that the girl naturally hadn't thought about, bad Catholic that she was.

'You realise that rushing into an impulsive marriage with another Catholic is much worse than if he weren't Catholic?' Agnes said severely. 'You don't know this man, you're merely infatuated with him. If it's a mistake, and at your age it must be, you'll be in a terrible situation. A Catholic marriage can only be ended by the death of one of the spouses.'

'Mother! How can you think that way, why do you say these things? You'd turn the best wine into the sourest vinegar if you could. I can't imagine ever wanting a divorce from Luke.'

She'd known it would be bad, Tessa thought, but this was worse than she'd expected.

'Of course you haven't thought about divorce. No girl ever can be realistic when she imagines she's in love.' She was an expert on that particular error, Agnes thought bitterly. But it wasn't something she would ever tell her daughter. 'How old is your young man, Teresa?'

'Older than I am, but he's never been married. In fact, he's never even been truly in love before—'

'I asked you how old he was, Teresa.'

'Forty-five.'

'Have you gone stark raving mad?' Agnes shrieked.

'His age doesn't matter. I'm in love,' Tessa said, barely managing to keep her voice under control, 'and I'm going to get married. You don't have to accept it or like it or approve of it because there's not a damn thing you or anyone else can do about it.' Tessa was finally angry. 'The ceremony is in ten days. I hope you and Father and Maggie will come. I'm planning on having Maggie as my flower girl. I'll get a bunch of dresses ready so there will be something perfect for her to wear,' Tessa announced with the composure that came of knowing that whatever she said would make no difference to her mother now.

'Teresa, I warn you, this is the mistake of your life, and you won't be able to count on me to get you out of it this time. Of course, I assume he doesn't know about your past; you're not that big a fool. He'll never learn it from me, if you're worried on that score.'

I wondered if she was going to bring it up, Tessa thought. I shouldn't have wondered; I should have known. Her voice grew lilting and easy as she changed the subject without a pause.

'We're getting married in Monaco, Mother. Luke has a place near there. We've decided on a Low Mass in St Nicolas's Cathedral. Luke is sending planes for you and Father and Maggie and the whole Riley family. You'll all be staying as his guests at the Hotel de Paris. The other guests are Luke's top executives and their wives plus his stepbrother, Tyler, and Tyler's wife and kids. Luke doesn't have much family.'

'I see.' Agnes paused and allowed a silence to develop. 'Yes, I understand it now, Teresa. You're marrying a man with money.'

'Luke is an enormously rich man, Mother, although he doesn't talk about it. But if you think I'm marrying him for his money, you don't know me at all. When you meet Luke, you'll understand everything,' Tessa said, as patiently as she could. 'You'll know immediately that it's not about money. You'll see the difference in our ages doesn't mean anything. You can't make judgments now.'

'Why do you care about my judgment? You're going to do this no matter what I think.'

'I suppose I must have been hoping that you could be happy that I'm happy, even if you don't approve. Is that really too much to ask?'

'I can't lie to you, Teresa. I think this is utter folly.'

'So be it. I'll send you all the details as soon as I can. Oh, by the way,

Princess Grace is giving the wedding reception, lunch at the palace after the ceremony.'

'Goodbye, Teresa.'

Agnes put down the phone and stalked around the living room, unable to sit down and consider the news. All she could see in her mind was a kaleidoscope of jagged fragments of imagined scenes: Teresa in the arms of someone who looked like Cary Grant; Teresa covered in a coat of white mink with a train that dragged on the ground; Teresa covered with pounds of diamonds, with a private jet and her own Rolls-Royce and the most beautiful clothes ever designed; Teresa with houses all over the world and in each one of them, among the large staff, some unknown, pathetic, dried-up little woman, whose job it was to vacuum the floors. Teresa laughing as she moved further and further away into the otherworldly stratosphere of people who were all famous and rich and beautiful.

Finally, exhausted, Agnes flopped down into a chair. She'd lived for people to appreciate her daughter, she told herself. She'd fought with Sandor so that Teresa could be exposed to the opportunities for fame and fortune. Why did she hate it now, so much that it was almost unbearable? She fell into a reverie from which she was aroused by one name. Grace Kelly. *Princess Grace* was giving her daughter's wedding reception! As she composed herself, more of the details Teresa had given her in the last minutes of their phone conversation returned to Agnes. Private planes; the Hotel de Paris; a wedding luncheon in the palace—she'd be at the bride's table with Princess Grace and Prince Rainier. The mother of the bride was always the most important person at a wedding besides the bride and groom themselves. And her sisters knew nothing yet!

Oh, this would cap everything; they'd never recover, she thought, suddenly full of energy. Her sisters had been thrilled when Teresa won the Oscar for *Little Women*, but that was nothing compared to this! It would be the high point in the lives of the entire Riley family.

Agnes was poised to pick up the phone to call her eldest sister when she suddenly remembered Teresa saying she wanted Maggie to be her flower girl. Oh, no, Teresa, she thought, you're never getting married in church before a priest with your illegitimate daughter walking before you, strewing flower petals, with no one in the world to suspect. No, my girl, sinner that you are, that's not going to happen while I'm alive to prevent it. Yet, what could she do to stop it?

Hastily Agnes ran over various scenarios. She knew Sandor would agree with her about this; he'd think Teresa's brazen plan even more a defiance of the sacredness of the Sacrament of Marriage than she did.

She'd tell Maggie that it was a grown-up party and children weren't invited. She'd get somebody to take care of Maggie for the few days that they'd be away. Perhaps Helen Kelly. After all, she was Maggie's godmother. And she'd tell Teresa that Maggie had developed a high fever and something that the doctor suspected might be German measles the day before the flight.

There was nothing she could do to prevent Teresa from marrying a man she barely knew but she wasn't going to be allowed to have absolutely everything she wanted. Maggie wasn't going to be part of this . . . this . . . sacrilege.

# Three

'PROMISE ME IT'S OVER,' Tessa demanded faintly out of her haze of exhaustion, as she and Luke drove up the Moyenne Corniche on their way to Luke's farmhouse just below the high-perched town of Èze-Village, where they were going to spend their honeymoon. 'Promise me we never have to do *that* again.'

Luke glanced at her profile. Tessa's splendid head was thrown back on the leather seat. Her eyes were closed, and the faint mauve shadows that he could glimpse on the tender skin under her lower lashes were infinitely touching. Her lips, so ardently, alluringly prominent, were parted slightly in fatigue. Only Tessa's flashing waves of hair, liberated from their elaborate wedding coiffure and taken by the wind, still seemed to possess any spirit. In the light of the approaching sunset, he thought he could see an occasional red glint in the darkness of its strands.

'Not unless you insist on repeating our vows on our tenth anniversary,' he answered her tenderly. 'In which case I'd have to agree. Of course I'd try to talk you out of it. I'll say "paparazzi" over and over again until you'd changed your mind.'

'You'd have to say it just once,' Tessa sighed, thinking of the outrageous mobs of photographers and journalists who had only been held in check by Monaco's formidable police force. 'We should have eloped, Princess Grace or no Princess Grace. I've learned my lesson. Never let anyone give you a wedding no matter how generous she is. No, make that, especially if she's generous. I couldn't have taken one more minute of being a bride. Is a person supposed to enjoy her own wedding?'

'Oh, I shouldn't think so, darling, I've never heard of anyone who did.'

'Then why did we do it?'

'It's a rite of passage or something.'

Or something, Tessa silently agreed. Something she should have had the good sense to have avoided. And most of it was her fault. The wedding itself, this morning, had been a dreamlike blaze of white: clustered garlands of white flowers spilling down from large baskets suspended under dozens of splendid crystal chandeliers, high banks of white flowers and tall white candles at the altar. Her progress down the centre aisle of the vast stone cathedral had seemed like a promenade in a garden, a slow, proud promenade towards her beloved. Oh, the wedding was a dream and the only details she could remember about it were the times she'd peeped at Luke's face as he knelt on his prie-dieu during the ceremony and the joyful strength of his voice when he answered that he took Teresa for his lawful wife.

If she hadn't had the idea of inviting all her family, every last aunt, uncle and cousin, maybe the three days preceding the wedding might have been delightful. But she'd been greedy, she'd wanted them all to witness her happiness, and that's where she'd gone so very wrong. Her memories of family gatherings were of a relaxed clan of giggling, gossipy, warm-hearted women and beer-drinking, joking men, all good-natured and feeling at home in their skins. But during the entire time in Monaco they'd been on their best behaviour, as stiff as if they'd been stuffed, afraid to make any kind of gaffe, and solemn and careful of speech in a manner more suitable to a funeral than to a wedding. They'd danced so sedately at the wedding luncheon in the palace itself that it was hard to remember them pulling up the rugs at home and showing off their prowess. They hadn't even dared to have one glass too many of the champagne.

And the wedding lunch wasn't the worst of it, Tessa reflected, too frazzled to open her eyes and look at one of the world's most thrilling views of the Mediterranean as Luke drove skilfully up the steep, twisting mountain road to Èze. The single worst thing of all was the way her aunts had treated her mother. It had started when her parents had arrived without Maggie, who was sick at home, on a different plane than the one that had brought the rest of the family.

Much of Tessa's time had been spent at the Hotel de Paris with her mother and her aunts, and it had grown more and more painful to watch the . . . reverence, there was no other word . . . with which Agnes's sisters surrounded her. Her mother had been elevated beyond any sisterly relationship. She wouldn't have begrudged her mother a second of her glory, Tessa thought, if she hadn't known how she really felt.

As for her cousins, the very same cousins she used to have so much fun with, they hadn't managed to feel comfortable with her, Tessa realised. It was as if she had become so different that there was absolutely no common ground. And all their children! The ones she'd so grandly insisted on including—was that the way kids acted now? Constant squabbles, whining, teasing and talking back to their parents.

Yet, on the other hand, Tessa reflected, Tyler and Madison Webster had taken her in with ease and pleasure, delighted to see Luke so happy. Luke's stepbrother and his wife, a handsome young couple from Essex County in the New Jersey hunt country, had been the only guests at the wedding who'd been perfectly natural with everybody, from her father to Prince Rainier, from a shy wife of one of Luke's executives to the youngest of her badly behaved second cousins.

Of all the guests who'd known her before she'd started making films, Mimi alone had remained herself, as devilish and free-spirited as ever. She had waltzed around in Tessa's suite wearing nothing but lace bikini underpants and high heels. She was as irrepressible as ever, detailing the pros and cons of her long train of boyfriends at college, demanding that Luke provide her with an Aussie exactly like him. Only Mimi, and Tessa's small group of Hollywood guests, had the fun that she'd wanted them all to have.

Oh well, her intentions had been good, Tessa told herself. She felt the solid wedge of tension between her shoulders begin to disappear as the wedding memories stopped occupying her mind. She could feel the light of the late-afternoon sun grow dimmer on her eyelids. Maybe . . . maybe, she'd just take a little nap until Luke stopped the car . . . they should be there soon . . .

Tessa woke up slowly, with the feeling she normally associated with a particularly good night's sleep. Oh, she thought, without opening her eyes, why weren't naps more appreciated? She must ask Luke . . . Luke!

She sat up abruptly. She was still wearing the dress she'd put on after the reception, and there was a warm quilt covering her, but she seemed to have been napping right in the middle of a large bed in a room she'd never seen before. Luke must have carried her in from the car. There were heavy beams overhead and arched windows were cut into the thick stone walls. Tessa hurried over to the nearest window and looked

out. A long field of still unharvested lavender, its spiky, concentric clus-
ters planted in strict rows; olive trees; cypress trees; vines that crept
round the outside of the window—nothing unexpected for a farmhouse
in Provence. Not if you ignored the colour of the light . . . light the clear
colour of dawn, not of sunset.

I must have slept at least thirteen hours, maybe more, Tessa thought,
wrapping the quilt round her shoulders.

The first door she opened was that of a perfectly appointed bathroom, where Tessa discovered that her cosmetics bag had been placed,
unopened, by the side of the basin. She hastily splashed her face with
water, brushed her teeth, took off her crushed dress, and decided to
take a quick shower.

Next she searched the closets for her suitcases without success.
Wrapped in a large bath towel big enough to fasten into a sarong, Tessa
opened the other door in the room and almost fell over Luke. He lay
there, fully clothed, like a faithful bodyguard, sleeping on a runner in
the corridor, huddled in a nest of pillows and covered by another quilt.

She knelt by his side and scratched the back of his hand gently. He
slept on. She kissed his earlobe lingeringly. Nothing. She pulled gently
and then less gently on various short tufts of his hair. His breathing
didn't even change. With determination Tessa removed her towel and
crept under the quilt stark naked. Surely he'd feel that she was there and
wake up . . . wouldn't a person know when someone had joined him
under his quilt?

Tessa unbuttoned Luke's shirt. She put her head next to his chest and
puffed all over it, thinking to wake him with her breath. Luke slept on.
Tessa reflected. She could unbuckle his belt. Yes, that would be the next
logical thing to do. She unbuckled it easily and unzipped his fly easily,
considering that she'd never done either of those things before except
on a pair of her own jeans. Luke rolled his head away from her, but otherwise there was no change in his sleep. Tessa followed the line of hair
on his chest down past his waistline, pulling firmly on it at every step.
Wouldn't you think that if somebody pulled your stomach hair, you'd
wake up? Squirming until she could reach lower, Tessa took Luke's
penis in her hand and cuddled it, without moving. It felt . . . friendly,
she thought, not at all frightening and more responsive than its owner,
since he continued to sleep while his penis showed signs of acknowledging her touch. Fascinated, she continued to hold it as it grew larger
and longer and harder. Soon it was so big that the only way she could
take its measure was to move her hand up and down its length.

'Hey! What the hell!'

So that was the secret of waking him up.

'You were sleeping,' she said accusingly, not letting go.

'Stop that!'

'Aren't you supposed to like it?'

'I do, but let go!'

Reluctantly, Tessa abandoned her discovery and raised her head to a level with Luke's. 'Good morning,' she said demurely.

He snorted with laughter at her tone. 'What convent did they teach you that in?'

'I was merely following my natural instincts.'

'Oh, darling,' he said, covering her face with kisses, 'I hate to repress your instincts, but not on this floor.'

'What are you doing out here, anyway?'

'I brought you in from the car and put you in the middle of the bed. Then, when you didn't wake up for hours, I didn't want to move you, so this seemed like the best place to wait, where you'd find me when you woke. My God, you're naked!'

'I wondered when you'd notice.'

Luke scooped her up, quilt and all, and carried her back into the bedroom and deposited her gently on the bed.

'Will you wait here, without going anywhere else, just stay put, while I brush my teeth and take a quick shower?' he demanded.

Tessa waited for him, overcome with curiosity, anticipation, and anxiety. Her mind refused to function as she looked at the beams of the bedroom ceiling without seeing them. When Luke returned he peeled off his towel, and rolled under the quilt next to her. He drew closer to her and traced her eyebrow with his lips, then he kissed her with tiny, soft kisses along the curve of her bone from her eyebrow to her nose. Gently he turned her head so that he could kiss her lips. Mutely, Tessa returned his kisses, but Luke could tell, from the tension he sensed in the trembling pressure of her mouth, that she was filled with apprehension. Of course she is, he thought, what could be more natural? He modulated his passion to her timidity, keeping his kisses utterly undemanding, reining in any sign of his desire. For long minutes they lost themselves in a chain of soft, almost tentative kisses, while his fingers were plunged into her hair, caressing her skull with calm, reassuring movements. Some time after he felt her lips grow more confident, Luke allowed his mouth to stray from her mouth to her ear, leaving no fraction of its lobe untouched, and then he kissed her down the long, firm curve of her neck; and when he reached her shoulder he kissed her along the fragile skin at the base of her neck. Each time he reached her collarbone, his mouth retraced its journey down from her ear, never venturing lower and never breaking its rhythm.

Tessa's breathing grew faster with each voyage of his lips from her ear to her collarbone, until, suddenly, she flung back the blanket and revealed her high breasts, their small pink nipples as erect as if he'd been sucking on them without mercy. 'Put your mouth on them,' she panted 'and leave my ear alone, you're driving me crazy!'

'That's more or less the idea,' Luke mumbled, as he bent his head toward the points of flesh whose delicacy had grown so bold. Tessa reached her arms out blindly for him, but Luke drew the lower part of his body out of her reach so that she couldn't again tantalise his rearing penis. She needed so much more to make her ready, he thought, so much long and careful preparation, yet she could have no idea of what her touch did to him. They lay facing each other while he cupped each of her breasts in his hands so that he could move quickly from one nipple to another, using his tongue, his teeth, his lips, firmly holding back the full force of his passion, entirely focused on giving her delight throughout every cell of her exquisite nipples that grew more engorged by the second. Tessa squirmed under the quilt that covered her from her waist down, trying to push it off, but Luke's superior strength prevented her. Oh no, he thought, you won't make me rush you, you can't make me take you before you're so excited that it won't hurt.

Suddenly, with a lightning change of pace for which he was unprepared, Tessa gathered up all her strength, freed herself of the quilt, and in one swift movement raised herself up off the bed, pushed Luke over on his back, threw one leg over him, and straddled him. Stunned, he felt her grasp his penis and pull it back from his belly so that it stood at a right angle to his body.

'No!' he cried, but Tessa was already arched above him, her expression rapt and isolated in an absolute purposefulness. Her eyes were tightly closed as she guided his penis directly between her parted thighs. She circled the head of his penis in her fingers and lowered herself until he was just inside her flesh. 'Oh,' she said to herself, 'oh . . . yes . . .'

'Darling . . .'

'No, don't move, don't say anything; I have to do it myself,' she commanded. He lay absolutely still, disciplining himself with all the authority of his maturity, fascinated by her intent caprice, as a fraction of an inch at a time she pressed down onto him with her taut, quivering body. Both of them barely breathed, her lips were pressed firmly together, there was no sound in the room as moment by moment, at a pace determined by Tessa, she resolutely impaled herself on him. It seemed to

Luke that she was as ruthless with the pain she must be feeling as she was ruthless in her insistence on his passivity. She looked like a stranger, with the fierceness of an Amazon branding her brow, her teeth pressed into her lower lip. Time stopped until finally Tessa gave a deep breath and Luke became aware that he was enclosed, up to his hilt, in her warmth. He looked up at her face, close to him now, her lips finally parted, her eyelids fluttering, an expression of relief re-creating her face, familiar again.

Only then did he dare to fold her in his arms and, making certain that he didn't move too quickly, gather her closely to him and turn her over, so that he was above her. He stayed motionless, watching her face as a smile came to her lips, a complex inward smile of accomplishment, pride, and astonishment.

'Look at me,' he whispered, but she kept her eyes closed, her smile suddenly teasing. 'Look at me, my darling,' he insisted, and she opened her eyes and saw his, bright with tears. 'Did I hurt you?' he asked.

'Only a little, because I could control it—it's all right now—why are you crying?'

'Because you're my virgin bride and it's more beautiful than anything I could ever have imagined.'

'But I'm not a virgin any more.'

He drew back slowly, until his penis left the cave of her body, and then, with infinite care, he pushed it in again as far as it would go, filling her completely. 'No,' he said, '*now* you're not a virgin any more.'

'I never knew people could be domestic for four whole days in a row,' Luke said, as he and Tessa cleaned up the kitchen after the lunch they'd walked into the village to buy: a newly baked baguette, sweet butter, fresh ham sliced from the bone, and five kinds of cheese. 'Would you like to go out for dinner tonight? We're invited to a party on board a yacht.'

'So love in a farmhouse has already made you itch for social life,' she sighed mockingly.

'It's not social life; it's the sheer brutish macho satisfaction of showing you off to a roomful of people, knowing that every man there feels desperate envy of me. I'm going to be profoundly jealous and utterly possessive and I'm going to flaunt you all over this little planet. Thank God you're much too young to want children. By the time you're—oh, maybe thirty—I suppose I'll be able to face sharing you with them.'

'Why didn't you mention any of this sooner?'

'I truly didn't know it until we got married.'

Tessa had reached a point at which it was emotionally and physically painful to be further away from Luke than the next room, and then it was only possible to endure this separation for a few minutes at a time. She couldn't fall asleep, no matter how he'd satisfied her, until he'd drifted off and she could lie in his arms, remembering each honey-and-fire-filled hour of the safe, safe day. Even as she felt their breathing merge, she could barely allow herself to drift into dreams and waste these exquisite minutes.

'Yes,' Tessa agreed, forcing the light words, 'by all means, let's go to the party. What should I wear?'

'A little black dress.'

'But I don't have one with me. How about a little white dress?'

'Is it plain?'

'It's as plain as plain can be,' she assured him. 'Is this some new fetish of yours? A plain white wardrobe?'

'You'll understand it all at the proper time,' he said, coming to stand behind her, his arms crossed in front of her so that each of her breasts was lightly enclosed in his warm hands. He buried his face in her hair as Tessa bent her head in swift, docile delight. They stood without the slightest movement, barely breathing, as Luke's penis rose, under his trousers, and grew, jerking slightly and swelling upward against the small of her back.

'In the kitchen?' she gasped her heart beating so heavily that she thought he must be able to hear it.

'Bedroom,' he groaned. 'Understand now why I didn't want to make the bed?'

'I knew why. I didn't think you'd make me wait this long.'

All afternoon they lay in bed, making love, dozing, and making love again, sometimes as playful as animals in a zoo, sometimes deeply earnest, caught by the voluptuous gravity of a whirlwind of passion that Luke, for all his experience, had never known before.

As the sun began to set, sated for the moment, they prepared themselves for their evening out. Although it had a matching chiffon stole with a wide, hemstitched border, her strapless white dress looked like nothing on the hanger. Yet when she put it on, its finely pleated, Grecian shape, cleverly draped, outlined her body to below her hips, eloquently justifying its Dior label. When she whirled in front of the mirror the short skirt, unpleated, swished around her thighs and kissed her knees. When she leaned forward, she could see that the bodice of the dress began no more than a hairline above the top of her nipples.

With a final twirl in front of the mirror, flourishing her engagement ring at an imaginary audience, Tessa picked up her wrap and presented herself to Luke, who stood in the living room of the farmhouse, clad in the unaccustomed formality of a white linen suit, a blue shirt, and a yellow tie.

'That's your plain white dress?' he inquired, '"as plain as plain can be?"'

'You said a yacht,' she reproached him, 'and anyway, show me where it's not plain, just show me one bit of decoration.'

'It's perfect,' he assured her, 'but close your eyes.'

'Why?'

'Because I said so.'

Tessa stood with her eyes tightly closed. What now, she wondered, shivering, as she felt him fumble at the back of her neck and heard a slight click as a heavy necklace was settled round her neck. Suddenly the lobes of each ear were embraced by a weight of cool metal. Luke took her shoulders and guided her steps until she stood in front of her bathroom mirror. 'You can look now.'

'Good God!' From a necklace of five huge, pear-shaped emeralds, brilliantly graduated in size and mounted in thick crusts of diamonds, hung a pendant fashioned from a single giant pear-shaped emerald, an emerald almost the length of her little finger. It lay on her breastbone, rimmed in its own diamond setting, a fathomless drop of the very essence of green. The earrings were great round emeralds, of a colour perfectly matched to the necklace, set in large diamond domes.

'They're your wedding present, but I didn't want to give them to you until you were ready for them. They're inappropriate for a girl.'

'But I am a girl.'

'No, you're a woman now, Tessa.'

'But I'd never . . .' Tessa turned this way and that, falling into a reverie as the fabulous emeralds exerted their spell. 'They're so alive—I always thought emeralds were a hard green with a sort of blue flash.'

'Most of them are now. But these are very, very old ones, the aristocrat of emeralds. They were mined in the 1500s, in Colombia. The pendant once belonged to Alphonso XIII when he was King of Spain.'

'"Old" emeralds, what a strange word to use,' Tessa said dreamily, moving her shoulders so that they caught the light in an explosion of sparks. 'Oh, Luke, should I be such an easy mark? I didn't know I loved jewels until you gave me the ring. And now these . . . is there something wrong about feeling so . . . thrilled? So absolutely saturated with excitement and delight?'

'Are you asking me as your spiritual advisor?'

'There's no one else around to consult.'

'You're not kidding, are you darling? Underneath you really mean it, you really feel that there has to be something wrong with enjoying them, don't you?'

'Maybe,' she said sheepishly. 'Jewels must be the most purely materialistic enjoyment there is.'

'Feeling guilty about something that isn't wrong is a waste of time. For more than four hundred years these stones have made women happy. Today it's your turn. Now listen to me. I want to feel free to give you jewels and I don't want to be deprived of that pleasure. But, if you're really disturbed by it, I'll stop. It's your decision, but couldn't you try, at least, to get used to it? For my sake?'

'I guess so,' Tessa said after a pause for reflection.

They were still sleeping the next morning when Luke woke to a repeated knock on the front door. Cursing under his breath, he recognised the voice of Len Jones, his second-in-command, whom he'd left in charge of the business. Len had been instructed not to disturb him.

Sliding quickly out of bed, he left Tessa tucked under the quilt as he pulled on his robe and went to answer the door.

'Luke, I'm sorry, but I had to let you know—'

'Bloody hell, Len. Whatever it is, couldn't it have waited?'

'I'm terribly sorry, but no, it couldn't have. It's Tessa's parents. It's bad news, Luke, the worst. They were in a taxi on their way home from the airport . . . it was sideswiped by a tanker truck. The driver and Tessa's father were killed instantly, her mother's still alive but she can't last long . . . the people who are taking care of Tessa's sister called me at the number you sent them . . .'

'Damn, damn, damn! Look, go back to the office in Monte and arrange for my plane to be ready to leave from Nice in three hours. No, two and a half. I'll get Tessa ready.'

Slowly Luke walked back to the bedroom of the farmhouse. He sat on the side of the bed for a few minutes, unable to wake Tessa to the news. Everyone's parents die, he thought, but not with such brutal suddenness, not at the end of their daughter's wedding festivities. He lifted a strand of her heavy hair and rubbed it lightly between his fingers. He worshipped her, he admitted helplessly. He would give almost anything to spare her this.

With the tip of a cautious finger, he caressed the back of her hand, hoping, at least, to wake her into a moment of brief happiness before he had to tell her the news. 'Tessa,' he whispered, 'Tessa, Tessa darling, wake up. Wake up, my little sweetheart . . .'

'Can she speak?' Tessa asked the nurse as she approached the door of her mother's room in the intensive-care unit of St John's Hospital.

'She's said your name, from time to time, but that's all.'

'Can you leave me alone with her?'

'Of course. Ring when you need me.'

Tessa pushed the door open and forced herself to approach the bed. Only a few strands of her mother's hair, dark, curly, and still incongruously alive, identified her as the handsome woman she had been. Tessa was too deeply shocked to cry. She sat in the chair by the hospital bed.

'Mother, it's Teresa. I'm here, Mother.'

Agnes's eyelids remained closed, but her lips moved slightly.

'Mother, can you hear me? It's Teresa.'

'Teresa,' Agnes said in a dry whisper. 'I'm dying.'

'No, Mother, no you're not, you'll get better . . .' Tessa's voice trailed off at the expression of faint scorn with which her mother received her false attempt at comfort.

'Listen, Teresa . . . important, don't tell husband about Maggie . . . never . . . never . . . never . . . promise me . . . important . . . my pride . . . my life work . . . don't ruin . . . worked so hard . . .'

'Mother, don't worry. I won't tell anyone anything, but don't worry about Maggie. Luke will take care of everything, everyone. Maggie's safe, I'm safe. Mother, I love you.'

'Proud of you . . . good girl . . . don't spoil your life . . . I always loved you best . . . always . . .'

'Mother. Mother!' Tessa searched her mother's face. The spark of life had suddenly but unquestionably blown out. She knelt and prayed at length for her mother's soul.

'Always loved you best', her mother's last words . . . why did they surprise her, Tessa asked herself in desolation. Hadn't her mother put her first as long as she could remember? Believed in her, fought for her, planned for her? Used all her power to keep her from the consequences of her mistake? And how had Tessa repaid her mother? She'd deceived and mocked her with Mimi; she'd replaced her with Fiona; she'd taken her devotion for granted or scorned it as meddling—this woman who'd had such a tiny measure of love in her life.

Painful tears, tears of shame, filled Tessa's eyes. Agnes had been a hard mother to love, and she'd never forgiven her for getting into trouble when she was a teenager, yet nothing could change the fact that for years she'd been the chief joy of her mother's life. Her mother had been as good a mother as she'd known how to be, as she'd been able to be, Tessa realised, sobbing for the young, hopeful Agnes Riley, who'd believed she was making a romantic marriage, sobbing for herself and the understanding she'd reached too late.

Behind her she heard the steps of the nurse returning. Tessa rose to her feet.

'Oh, Miss Kent, she's gone. I'm so very sorry. Was she able to recognise you before . . . ?'

'Yes. She was . . . herself . . . until the end. More than ever herself.'

'Is she?' Luke asked as Tessa walked slowly into the waiting room.

'She's gone. She recognised my voice, she said a few words, but then she . . . I watched her die . . . one second she was alive and the next she just . . . wasn't . . . she was only thirty-eight . . . oh, Luke, I wish I'd been a better daughter, but it's too late.'

'Oh, my darling, my Tessa, don't say things like that,' Luke urged, pressing her tightly against his shoulder. 'Nothing can make this accident worse than it is except thinking like that.' He patted Tessa's back as if she were a child who had fallen and hurt herself, but she made herself draw away from him, knowing that if she broke down again she'd never gather up the courage to leave the circle of his comfort. In time she'd have to absorb the loss of her parents, but now she had an immediate duty, a responsibility that couldn't wait.

'Luke, I have to tell Maggie. The Kellys promised not to say a word until they heard from me. We should go there right now. Oh, Lord in heaven, how—no, *what*—am I going to tell her?'

'The truth, what else is there?'

'A five-year-old child? This was the first time they'd ever left her. They were her whole life . . .'

'There's no way to get around it, darling. You have to tell her about the accident.'

'I know.'

'I'd tell her for you, but she's never laid eyes on me.'

'Oh, Luke, Luke, there are some things even you can't protect me from,' Tessa said. 'What you can do is deal with the hospital administrator and call Father Vincent at their church—it's St Charles of the Holy Saviour in Santa Monica—and start making the . . . arrangements, while I go and talk to Maggie. I think it would confuse her to meet you for the first time at this moment. I won't be alone—Mimi's waiting downstairs in the car. You were an angel to know that I'd need her and to get her here so quickly. Then we'll all come back to the hotel with Maggie. Fiona should be there by then.'

'Your aunts are waiting to hear. I can take care of that too.'

'Oh, would you, darling? They know you and I'm not sure when I can get to a phone.'

'Right. Just tell me something before you leave. Is Maggie . . . just how emotional and sensitive is she?'

I'm not sure, Tessa thought. I don't truly know her that well.

'I refuse to believe this,' Mimi said as they sat side by side in the limo, the window raised between them and the driver. 'A bride and an orphan in six days. No wonder you look so . . . I can't find any word but "blank".'

'I'm not letting myself feel any more emotion than I can help, not until I've told Maggie. At least my mother and I managed to say we loved each other before she died. We did, you know, in a strange and difficult way. I realise that now, Mimi, when it's too late.'

'Was she able to say anything else?' Mimi asked hesitantly.

'Oh yes, she managed to make herself very plain. With her last words. She told me never to tell Luke about Maggie, never to tell *anyone* about Maggie, never to, I guess she meant "destroy", or something like that, her pride, her life's work. She kept herself alive to tell me that, I'm sure of it.'

'But—'

'What?'

'Well, I mean, you weren't *planning* to tell, were you?'

'I don't know what to do, Mimi. After all, Maggie . . . is my daughter.'

Tessa began to weep again not merely tears over the loss of her parents, but tears of utter confusion. Her mother's dying words resonated in her ears no less strongly than Luke's when he'd told her, over and over, how deeply important it was to him that she was a virgin. And she'd tacitly confirmed that lie each time he'd said it. Over and over. There had been exactly one perfect chance, one ideal moment to tell him about Maggie, on their first evening together, and she'd rejected the opportunity with every bit of intuition and instinct and reason she possessed. If she made herself tell him the truth now, he'd never believe in her again, never trust her again.

'Tessa! Stop it right now!' Mimi handed her a wad of Kleenex. 'You don't have time to cry! Now listen to me. Maggie has only known one mother in her life, not two. You're her big sister, the one she's damn lucky to have, the sister who can make sure that she spends the rest of her life being happy and taken care of. If you're thinking of some damn stupid moment of truth, some need to bring up the past, stamp on it!'

Tessa blew her nose and listened to Mimi.

'Remember your mother's last words, Tessa. You simply can't go against them! The truth Maggie knows is that her parents and your parents are the same people and they're dead. What on earth would you have to gain by stepping forward and claiming Maggie now? What a media orgy that would be if it ever got out, and how wouldn't it? Give me a break! "The Secret of Tessa Kent's Bastard Child!" Please! She's yours anyway. No one can take her away from you; you're her next of kin.'

'I know.'

'Then where's the problem? You must have a major self-destructive streak if you ever *dream* of telling him. Shape up, girl! You're thinking crazy. Luke doesn't ever need to know.'

The wake had been in full swing for several hours when Mimi took Tessa aside. 'Do you think you could split for a few minutes?' Mimi whispered in her ear. 'I've got to get some fresh air.'

They walked down the stone pathways of the Hotel Bel-Air, inhaling the rich scents of the flowering bushes and fragrant annuals that were planted in thick borders everywhere, until they came to a quiet courtyard with a central fountain and a wooden bench.

'Maggie was so composed at the funeral it scared me,' Mimi said.

'I know, I noticed the same thing. Oh, Mimi, would you believe that I can't even think straight about my parents? All I can think about is what to do with Maggie.'

'I can't tell you what the answer to that is, but I do know the one thing you can't do, not ever, and that's raise her, you and Luke.'

'But that's the natural—'

'It would be, if she were your sister, no matter how complicated it got, but in the circumstances, no, Tessa, just plain no. Find another way.'

'Why, Mimi, why? I could carry it off, I'm an actress, he'd never guess.'

'Maybe not, but I'm thinking of you, living each day fooling him and fooling her and trying to fool yourself, what is quaintly known as "living a lie". You wouldn't make it, Tessa, not for long.'

'You can't know that!'

'I've been your friend for ever, remember? You and your crazy sense of guilt and sin. Teresa Horvath, the last of the big-time sinners—do you think I've forgotten, or that you've basically changed? Sooner or later, as Maggie grows up and gives you the usual problems kids give, the big sister façade would disappear and the maternal instinct to tell her what to do would take over. You'd crack, Tessa! You couldn't avoid making a slip, or you'd give up and just confess the truth, but before that happened, you'd be a wreck. Always nervous, always watching yourself trying not to act too motherly, always keeping an eye on Luke's reaction to the two of you together, always afraid of doing too much for Maggie, or worse, not enough.'

'You've always loved to tell me what to do!' Tessa protested.

'You wouldn't be the woman Luke married any more,' Mimi continued, paying no attention, 'and he wouldn't understand why, and of course he'd blame Maggie. My God, Tessa, you had exactly four days together before this happened. You're a couple of barely newlyweds with a lot of adjustments to make like everybody else—you hardly know each other when it gets down to that, to say nothing of the major age difference, which I've been too polite to mention till now. Luke's a guy who can have anything he wants, and children haven't been high on his list. Don't tell me *that's* an accident.'

'He's never wanted children,' Tessa admitted miserably. 'He said, maybe in ten years . . . I'll only be thirty!'

'Well then! You simply *cannot* take on the burden and responsibility of a five-year-old child on top of everything else, not when there are four aunts, each one of whom made a point of telling you that she wanted Maggie to come and live with her, each one of whom has plenty of child-rearing experience. You're her sister, who visits her whenever you can and brings her wonderful presents and ends up being the person who understands her best, the person she can really talk to and confide in, the person whose advice she follows. You're her fairy godmother, instead of the person who tells her to finish her homework and eat her peas.'

'Oh, Mimi, hasn't it occurred to you that I *know* I'm not Maggie's sister, that I *know* I'm her mother, that I *know* I have a duty towards her? I was never allowed to mother her the way I yearned to, but there was never a minute when I didn't love her. No matter what I do, I'm going to be wrong, there's no honourable way out of this.'

Tessa pressed herself tightly into the shelter formed by Luke's lap and chest and arms and let herself go completely, weeping as loudly and unselfconsciously as a child. Luke did nothing to stop her, gripping her as tightly as he could without hurting her. High time, he thought, high time.

After a long while, with a final descent into a diminishing series of whimpers, Tessa started to dab at her eyes with the hem of her nightgown.

'Tessa, darling, I know I told you that I didn't want to share you with kids for ten years, but that was before and this is entirely different, and what I said shouldn't count any more.' Luke set his lips sternly. 'We'll bring up Maggie. We'll hire the best nanny in the world to travel with us. Then when she's old enough for school, we'll get her a tutor too, several tutors if necessary, and by the time she's, oh, eight or nine, whenever little girls usually go away to boarding school, we'll send her off, so she could make friends of her own age. There are some marvellous schools in Switzerland or England, even in Australia, wherever she'd be happiest, and she could be with us on vacations.'

'But Luke, Maggie's in kindergarten now, she's already had two years of preschool, and next year she starts first grade. Children need to be "socialised" from day one.'

'They do?' Luke looked blank. 'Socialised?'

'I honestly didn't remember either, until you started making those sweet, impossible, mixed-up plans. Look, I think that the most important thing is for her to be brought up in a family with kids roughly her age, so she has a normal family life. I can't say I liked my cousins at the wedding, but at least some of them are the right age, with young families. I think that while you're in Australia I should take a trip back East, take Maggie with me and spend time with each of their families. There's got to be one family Maggie could fit into happily.'

'Hmm,' Luke murmured. 'Let's talk this over in the morning. I promise you we'll find a solution. It's too complicated to settle tonight and, anyway, you look so exhausted. I bet if you went to bed and I held your hand, you'd be asleep in minutes.'

'I'll try,' Tessa agreed, yawning.

As Luke watched Tessa fall into a profound sleep, he thought about her cousins, a bunch of impolite, classless oafs, in his opinion, with a mob of ill-mannered, unappealing kids. He had no intention of letting his wife's sister be brought up with them. There was another solution.

Very early the next morning, Luke got up quietly, leaving Tessa still deeply asleep. He called his stepbrother, Tyler Webster, who had attended the funeral and was due to fly home in a few hours. He asked him to meet him in half an hour in the dining room.

'Good of you to have dressed so quickly, Tyler.'

'Least I could do, Luke.'

'Tyler, there's something very, very important you can do for me.'

'Just ask,' Tyler replied.

'It's something that won't go unrecognised—in fact, something that will be most highly rewarded, even by your standards.'

'Luke, come on guy, you already do more than enough.'

'I'm aware of that,' Luke said, concentrating on spreading marmalade carefully on a piece of toast.

The Webster family lived entirely on Luke's largesse. Charming Tyler combined fatal bad judgment with a talent for laziness. He had never been able to keep a job for more than two months. Luke's father had thrown him out of the family business in less time than that, but because Dan Blake loved his American second wife, Tyler's mother, he had made Tyler a generous allowance, so generous that Tyler was able to concentrate on his one serious passion. Riding horses beautifully was the only occupation for which Tyler was fit.

After his father's death, Luke had continued the allowance, and when an unresisting Tyler had been married by Madison Grant, a plain Jane from a good family, a clever girl who knew that Tyler was her best chance at a good life, Luke had increased the allowance and bought them a stud farm near Madison's family's home, in the New Jersey hunt country. Luke paid for everything, from the children's schools to Madison's beautiful clothes and the parties she gave so well. The stud itself, even under a qualified manager, just about broke even, but in years when it lost money, Luke made up the difference without flinching.

'Luke, what's up? You look so serious.'

'I want you and Madison to bring up Maggie, Tessa's sister.'

'What?'

'There's no one else who'll do. Maggie's aunts are too old and her cousins aren't suitable. She's a dear little girl and she needs to be in a good, stable, loving family environment. Tessa and I aren't going to be leading that kind of life—there's a worldwide business to run and there's Tessa's career. How old are your children now?'

'Uh . . . wait a minute . . . right, Allison's eight, Candice's ten, and Barney's, gosh, four and a half.'

'Spot on. Barney can share his nanny with Maggie. As I remember you have a guest suite, right? Good. Plenty of room for Maggie. What I'd appreciate your doing, right now, is calling Madison and telling her to pack herself and the kids up and fly out here today. They can take the company's New York plane; they'll gain three hours, so they can be here before dinner.'

'Today?'

'The sooner Tessa knows that Maggie's going to be happy in her new home, the better for everybody.'

'Oh, sure, I can understand that. Gosh, I wonder what Madison's going to say.'

'She'll understand, Tyler. You won't even have to explain when she knows how important it is to me. Essential, as a matter of fact. Waiter, could you bring a phone to the table please?'

Madison Webster and her three children walked over the bridge in front of the entrance to the Hotel Bel-Air, as unrumpled as if they'd just driven over from Beverly Hills. Maggie stood shyly, but holding her ground, as the introductions were made.

'Well, well, so this is Maggie! What a dear little girl you are,' Madison said, bending down to kiss her cheek. 'I'm so glad to meet you.'

'Thank you,' Maggie mumbled.

'Barney, why don't you shake hands with Maggie,' Tyler suggested.

'How old are you,' Barney demanded, looking Maggie in the eye.

'Five.'

'You're older than I am but I'm taller than you. Much taller,' he announced with satisfaction, a big, warm, friendly grin splitting his freckled face. He took her hand in his and squeezed it tightly, pumping it up and down. 'Wanna play?'

'Play what?'

'Just play, Maggie. Come on, I'll show you. I know lots of good games, fun games. Maybe we'll build a tree house, you'll like that.' Barney didn't bother to say hello to his uncle Luke or his new aunt. Without letting go of Maggie's hand, Barney tugged the little girl away into the gardens, both of them soon breaking into a run. Maggie's laugh rang out as they rounded a corner and vanished from sight.

'Me Tarzan, you Jane,' Tessa said, smiling for the first time in days.

Four

LUKE DIDN'T KNOW, and Tyler didn't notice, that Madison Webster steadily saved healthy amounts each year, investing them in a deeply conservative mutual fund with a steady performance record. Her personal dreaded rainy day would only come if Luke died. Without him, the Webster family would have no income at all.

Maggie's arrival four years earlier had been a guarantee that, as long as the little girl lived with the Websters, they could count on receiving far more money from Luke than they had before—a guarantee made in writing by the law firm Luke employed in Manhattan.

Why *couldn't* she like Maggie? Madison asked herself in irritation.

Why couldn't she feel even a flicker of genuine warmth for the nine-year-old? Maggie's presence in their house had, from the day she arrived, ensured a minimum of thirteen years of respite from any rainy day, since she would certainly live with them until she was eighteen. Even when she went off to college, Madison told herself, Luke would unquestionably agree that she'd need a home to come back to for school vacations.

But every time she laid eyes on Maggie, she was reminded of how much she owed Luke, or was it how much she owed Maggie? There was no getting away from it: when Maggie called her 'Aunt Madison' she rejected the term in her mind. They had decided it was the least confusing form of address for a child of five who was—too ridiculously for words—Tyler's stepbrother's wife's sister. But she wasn't Maggie's aunt, damn it, and Tyler wasn't her uncle. Maggie didn't come from their kind of background. She was an unfeminine thing, always dashing around with Barney as if she were another little boy, her unruly hair looking as if it had never been brushed, her face as if it had never been washed. None of the exquisite, and totally inappropriate, party dresses or fine sweater sets that she brought back from her visits to her sister had ever survived more than a few weeks of Maggie's treatment.

You could always tell when Maggie was in the house: the sound of her bold laugh, entirely too loud and too frequent, the sound of her feet—couldn't that child ever walk instead of running up and down stairs? Maggie acted as if she owned the place, Madison thought bitterly, and although the child couldn't possibly realise it, in an indirect way she did, for every acre of their handsome property belonged to Luke, and Luke and Tessa had no heirs other than Maggie.

Madison sighed, thinking of her own daughters: Candice, the exceptionally pretty one, who was now fourteen, and Allison, who might or might not become the extraordinarily beautiful one, but was now, at twelve, merely promising. If only some of their breeding had rubbed off on Maggie!

Well, all she could say was that whatever momentarily fortunate mix of Irish and Hungarian genes had produced the ravishing Tessa hadn't been in operation when Maggie was conceived. Everything about her high colouring, with skin so white, and cheeks so red, with her thick thatch of black curls and the fierce blueness of her eyes, screamed 'Black Irish'.

Not that she had anything against the Irish. Goodness knows, she wasn't a snob, Madison assured herself, but there simply didn't happen to be any living in the neighbourhood. Nor enrolled at Elm Country Day, where Maggie was the only child who had to be driven to confession every Thursday and catechism every Saturday. Thank the good, reasonable Episcopalian Lord that she had the excuse of going to her own church on Sunday, so that she could send Maggie off to Mass with Elizabeth the cook.

'Maggie, do you really have to get up on that pony?' Barney begged, as he watched from the rail of the riding ring. 'You know you're not supposed to ride her without a grown-up around.'

'I've got to keep practising,' she said, stubbornly, 'or she'll never get used to me.' Maggie gave her new pony lump after lump of sugar in the forlorn hope that they might ensure good behaviour.

Her mount, Fairy, was a Welsh pony, a recent ninth-birthday present from Luke, the equivalent of a valuable thoroughbred horse. Unfortunately, Fairy was smarter, Barney knew, than she should be: an overbred, neurotic animal with a well-developed mean streak.

'Maggie, you stink on a horse, why won't you admit it? There's nothing to be ashamed about.'

'Yeah, well tell that to everybody around here. If you can't ride, you might just as well be dead.'

Muttering prayers to the Holy Mother and the Infant Jesus under her breath, Maggie led the pony over to the rail, stopped her, and scrambled into the saddle. She settled herself, adjusting the reins perfectly, and gave Fairy a gentle nudge to get her started.

Maggie's real problem was that she was petrified of horses. Every horse looked menacing to her. She hated their rolling eyes, their slobbering lips, their nightmarish nostrils. This fear was something that was impossible to confess, when everyone in the Webster house and every girl at school lived to ride.

'Lookin' good,' Barney called encouragingly. Once he'd seen that Maggie's pony was trotting, he'd mounted his own horse, a sturdy, trustworthy little mare, and was following her round the ring. He watched carefully as Maggie somehow urged the pony into a canter. This was where she usually got into trouble. He watched closely as she tensed up, pinching the pony with her knees in an effort at control. Her legs flopped around, her upper body became rigid as she became conscious of her legs, and soon she was jerking the pony in the mouth, trying to get it to stop. Annoyed, Fairy broke into a gallop. White-faced but silent, Maggie hung on, pulling harder and harder on the reins.

Barney easily kicked his mare into a gallop and pulled up alongside, grabbing the reins and gradually slowing the pony down.

'Thanks,' Maggie said, biting her lip.

'It's nothing. Fairy has a mean temper. Come on, let's stop now.'

'No,' she insisted, setting her face in a ferocious grimace. 'I'm going to get Fairy to canter properly if I have to stay here all night.'

Oh, no, Barney thought, there went his baseball practice.

Four years earlier, when Tessa had agreed with Luke that Maggie would be happier living with the Websters than with any of her Riley cousins, she had accompanied Maggie to New Jersey while Luke had gone off to a board meeting in Melbourne.

For a week Tessa had lived at the Websters' house, sharing the guest suite with Maggie. The instant devotion of Barney, a pint-size, gallant cavalier who was fascinated by Maggie and never let her feel alone, had touched Tessa's heart. Candice and Allison were pleasant, kind children and Madison and Tyler had both been so welcoming, so full of assurances that one more child round the dinner table would be a joy to them, that Tessa had finally managed to incorporate into her heart as well as her brain all the reasons why this separation was not just the best but the only possible good solution.

During Maggie's first year with the Websters, Tessa made as many flying visits as she could manage, but soon she realised that these visits were fundamentally unsatisfactory. They disrupted Maggie's adaptation to her new life, they obliged the Webster family to surround an unexpected guest with gracious attention and she wasn't able to be alone with Maggie in the way she had hoped. Having Maggie visit her had none of these disadvantages, and so from 1976 the little girl went to visit her sister when it could be arranged during school vacations or on holidays.

Although Luke tried hard to take a real interest in Maggie, Tessa soon realised that the visits were more joyful for her and Maggie when they could be alone together. During these private, precious days together, days that depended on Luke's being away in some far part of the globe where he'd be too busy to need his wife's company, on Tessa's not being in the middle of making a movie, and on Maggie's being able to get out of school—days that were possible to arrange only several times a year—Maggie was able to bask in her sister's full attention.

Tessa had a collection of dolls and toys she kept for Maggie to play with, but the little girl lost interest in them as soon as she discovered the joys of 'dressing up'. Maggie would rig herself out in bits and pieces she found in a trunk crammed full of fabulous odds and ends that Tessa accumulated by becoming friendly with the wardrobe head on every picture she made. Tessa would create a story to go with the costume Maggie had created, a story in which Maggie was always the heroine.

The other sort of 'dressing up' was a far more solemn affair, for it involved Tessa's jewellery. Luke liked to see her wearing jewels at all times, no matter how casual the occasion. Tessa had huge, unfaceted cabochon sapphires, almost as simple as deep blue glass pebbles, in invisible platinum settings, to wear with jeans and denim shirts; and ropes and ropes of real seashells inset with precious stones, a mermaid's dowry, to wear with bathing suits. She slept in a fabled string of Imperial jade, of an intense green, because Luke superstitiously believed it warded off sickness. But for all her serious clothes, the clothes she wore when she entertained Luke's business associates or met Hollywood people, she had a vast choice of extraordinary jewels.

When Maggie visited her, often the two of them would spend an entire afternoon in her dressing room, as Tessa told Maggie the history and stories behind some of her jewels, modelling them first and then decking Maggie out in them and letting her observe herself in the mirrors to her heart's content.

What a bloody bore, this Yank institution, these Oscars, this lumbering, pretentious, blatantly commercial sideshow that had managed to make itself a source of mindless, gaping worldwide attention, Luke Blake thought, as he roamed angrily around the living room of his suite at the Hotel Bel-Air in Los Angeles. The television set was tuned in to the 1982 Oscars, although the sound was off and had been off since the beginning of the broadcast.

Hours earlier, in the middle of the afternoon, Tessa, dressed and ready to present the Best Picture award, had stepped into her limo, escorted by Roddy Fensterwald.

Luke had accompanied her himself the previous year, because then she'd been up for her second Best Actress award. He wouldn't have considered letting her sit in the audience, waiting for the results throughout the endless evening, without him, but tonight Tessa wasn't nominated for anything and her function was purely ceremonial. She'd be planted backstage for hours, she'd told him, in her most persuasive tones, and there was simply no reason for him to endure hours of tedium.

She'd been a vision when she'd left the hotel in the brilliant spring sunshine, wearing a strapless lilac satin ball gown, with a wide sash bound tightly round her waist above a multitude of petticoats that caused the enormous skirt to move as lightly as a swaying bell. It was the first time she'd worn the latest present he'd given her: the entire Fabergé *parure* he'd assembled of imperial Russian jewels; the great web of a necklace that had belonged to a grand duchess, the splendid pendant earrings, the eight bracelets, and the hair ornaments like giant snowflakes. The jewels, inspired by eighteenth-century design, were made with infinite delicacy. Their deep garlands, elaborate swags, and extravagantly complicated bows made Tessa sparkle with every movement of her head, as if she'd been sprinkled with frost and ice.

She'd turned to him, her face bright, untroubled. 'Don't even bother to turn the television on until after nine, darling,' she'd reminded him as she kissed him goodbye. 'There's no possibility that the show will run less than four hours, and I'll be on last.'

Did she guess, he asked himself, did she have the faintest idea of the shameful, grotesque torments of jealousy that afflicted him when he had to share her with her work? Was that why she'd spared herself his presence tonight, so that she'd be free to enjoy herself with her peers?

As he trod a restless path from the window to the television set and back again, he examined his behaviour with Tessa for the ten thousandth time and came to the invariable conclusion that during their marriage he had managed to keep the toxic fumes of his jealousy from escaping into the air of real life. But what if Tessa was even more sensitive than he believed she was? Could she know what he was feeling?

Luke sat down in front of the television, glancing at his watch and back to the screen. There was that quick audience shot, there was Roddy, sitting far up front with Maggie beside him in the seat that Tessa had wangled for her. Maggie, he mused. How could a girl almost thirteen years old so thoroughly embody absolutely everything that was meant by the 'awkward age', and still come out of the same gene pool that had produced Tessa? Maggie wore braces, both upper and lower, and suffered from a constant plague of pimples. Her ridiculously abundant hair was either frizzy, curly or limp, depending on the day; and, worst of all, she hadn't stopped growing. She was taller every time he saw her, with breasts that already looked like those of a grown woman.

Impatiently—it was not yet near the time he could expect to see Tessa—Luke flung himself back in his chair and closed his eyes and drifted into a reverie. Strange, how Tessa never truly stopped protesting at the jewels he gave her so often, never understood how entirely necessary it was for him. She still thought in terms of generosity and extravagance, not guessing at the deep, secret pleasure that compelled him to *mark* her as his property. Yes, he thought with voluptuous pleasure, every new jewel *branded her* once again as belonging exclusively to him.

Often there were nights when he'd whisper to her to take off all her clothes and lie down on their bed. She knew exactly what he wanted, lying there with her eyes tightly closed, while he slowly covered her from her neck to her feet with the contents of her jewel cases—a goddess bound by chains of gems, a goddess who allowed him to make whatever use of her pleased him. Which way would he take her tonight, Luke asked himself, when she came home from the Oscars? Which way would make her forget most thoroughly that any other world existed except the one they inhabited together?

The day after her birthday in August 1985, Tessa stopped taking the Pill. Luke had said he'd be ready for fatherhood, or at least ready to contemplate it, by the time she was thirty, and thirty she was.

She decided not to tell him of her decision. Normally Tessa told Luke everything important, but she didn't want making love to become a self-conscious act, with conception in the back of their minds. And, she admitted to herself, what if he were to suggest postponing having a baby for one more year, and then another?

Tessa understood Luke Blake's nature far better than he realised. Yes, he was as intensely, jealously possessive of her as any man could be, and she gloried in his possessiveness. Yes, he was thoroughly, hopelessly selfish about how she spent every second of her time when she wasn't actually working on a movie, and she gloried in his selfishness. Yes, he wanted all of her attention when he wasn't working, and she gave herself to him gladly in an undivided way.

Tessa knew that in the deepest sense she conspired to join Luke in their tight, exclusive relationship, one that some, perhaps most, women might find stifling. But to her it was essential, for with Luke she continued to live in the heart of that sense of safety she was still consciously aware of needing every day of her life, an emotional safety that no amount of her own success could ever guarantee. She'd never forgotten the years before he'd come into her life and transformed it with just the touch of his hand.

But now she wanted a baby. She'd waited without showing her impatience, she'd kept her part of the bargain—well, perhaps it hadn't been a bargain but just a statement Luke had made—but now was her time to get what she wanted. No, what she *needed*.

In April 1986, Tessa missed her period. She said nothing to Luke, waiting to be sure. Every day she expected to experience the morning sickness she remembered, the horrible bouts of vomiting that had alerted her mother to her pregnancy. Had they started in the first month or the second? She couldn't recall.

To Tessa's relief, Luke's business travel had slackened somewhat in recent years, as he found more good men to work for him in different parts of the world. That spring they were able to spend a long, quiet time at Èze, a time she contrived to make as inactive as possible, pleading fatigue after the completion of her latest film. For the next three weeks she cocooned herself, ambling up the road to the village from time to time but otherwise sitting contentedly on the terrace outside the farmhouse. She spent hours reading or merely daydreaming, as she gazed at the new leaves on the grapevines, watched the circles of lavender grow taller by the day, listened to the gentle wind in the cypress and olive trees, and basked like a cat in the sun of the Midi.

How would they live when they had a baby? Tessa wondered. She found it impossible to decide, with all the world open to them. All she was certain of was that their existence would be very different from the life they had led up till now. She would give up work for years, if not for ever. Luke would simply have to travel much, much less. They would stop their nomadic existence and finally establish a true home somewhere. They might even buy a house in California, where they'd always stayed at a hotel during her bouts of film-making. Why not Santa Barbara, one of the most beautiful places on earth? All she really knew was that they would settle down, she promised herself, or it wouldn't be fair to the baby.

'Now, about this matter of your breasts,' Luke said several nights later, as he pushed the straps of her nightgown down and weighed them in his hands.

'What about them?'

'They're fuller than they've ever been, and warmer, like two just-baked loaves of bread. Heavenly bread. And your nipples are getting slightly bigger and just a touch darker.'

'Goodness! The things you notice . . .' she protested feebly.

'Darling, when did you plan to tell me?'

'When I was . . . sure.'

'What would it take to make you sure?'

'Another few days, maybe a week . . .'

'And if I said I was sure, would that do it?'

'If you said you were happy, that would make me positively sure,' she said in a small voice.

'Happy? That isn't a big enough word for how I feel. Tessa, I love you so much . . . how long do I have to wait for our baby?'

'Seven months, or a little less.' She laughed for joy.

'Aren't you a little behind schedule?'

'Huh?'

'I thought we'd agreed at thirty. I've been waiting for nearly a year, and doing my bit to help, as you might have noticed.'

'You remembered!'

'I never forget a promise.'

'So you won't mind sharing me?'

'I'm only human—from time to time, I probably will. But I've had you to myself for more than ten years, the best years of your life some people might say, certainly the best of mine.'

'What if the best years are ahead?'

'But they are, darling,' Luke assured her, trying not to remember that he'd just had his fifty-sixth birthday and she was still only thirty. Thirty, my God, he'd been a kid at thirty. Nothing but a kid. 'You know I almost never agree with what people say.'

Tessa stood outside the cheese shop in Èze-Village. Normally she loved to go in and pick out each of the five cheeses they always bought, but today the thought of the pungent interior of the shop was suddenly repulsive and she'd told Luke to go in by himself.

'We don't need cheese that much,' he assured her. 'It can wait.'

'No, don't be silly, darling. I'd rather stay outside, but that doesn't mean you have to deprive yourself. I'm fine, honestly,' she'd responded, all but pushing him into the always-crowded store.

But was she fine, Tessa asked herself? She still hadn't had a minute of morning sickness, but the feeling of well-being she'd enjoyed only a week earlier had departed, leaving her nervous and jumpy, instead of deliciously languid. It was impossible to know whether she had been pregnant for two months or several weeks longer, but now, as she waited, she resolved to drive down to Monte Carlo this very afternoon and see a gynaecologist.

What was taking Luke so long, she wondered? Suddenly the gentle sun seemed far too hot, the light breeze far too strong, the quiet street much too noisy. Was it the first sign of a mistral? Most likely. And that would account for her nerves. She took a step forward to rap impatiently on the window of the cheese shop and almost stumbled, grasping the trunk of a chestnut tree. As Tessa stood holding onto the tree, she felt a severe cramp beginning in her abdomen. She pressed herself tightly against the tree, trying to stop the pain, to crush it before it could grow, but it mounted rapidly upwards, gaining in intensity. Unable to remain upright, she bent over, doubled up, still grasping the tree, and saw in horror that blood was dripping from the bottom of her slacks, pooling darkly between her sneakers and dripping onto the cobblestones of the street. Jesus, she prayed, Jesus, no, *no*, but by the time Luke had gathered her up and carried her to the car, driving down to Monte Carlo as quickly as possible on the dangerously twisting road, she understood that she was having a miscarriage. She didn't need a doctor's opinion to tell her why the bleeding, the terrible bleeding, hadn't stopped.

During the next year, Tessa had another miscarriage in the middle of her third month. Her doctors, the best in Los Angeles, insisted that they could find no reason for this inability to maintain a pregnancy. Two miscarriages in a row were absolutely not a sign that she would never have a child, they assured the Blakes. Tessa was only thirty-one and although, strictly speaking, she was not at the peak of fertility, she was well within her prime. Luke was as vigorous as a man half his age. After six months had passed, they advised them to try again.

Luke was fifty-seven now. On his birthday Tessa saw a man who had barely changed since the day she'd first laid eyes on him. Yes, there was grey in his thick, dark red hair, but only at the temples. His features, those powerful, weathered features she had loved at first sight, were certainly more deeply lined around his mouth and eyes, but otherwise he was indestructible.

Before Tessa's second miscarriage, they'd bought the family home she'd daydreamed about, choosing Los Angeles because there Tessa could be closer to her work. Luke no longer asked that she make only one film a year, since he understood that work was her best therapy now.

They settled in Beverly Hills, high up in the winding roads north of Sunset in a house of old whitewashed brick, timbered in the style of a *manoir* in Normandy, and covered with flowering purple trumpet vines. Four acres of land descended from terraced gardens down to a swimming pool and finally to a tennis court. It was as peaceful here as at Èze, Luke said, and even the vegetation was uncannily similar.

Now Tessa and Luke found themselves part of the Hollywood scene. It suited them both, at this particular time, to welcome distraction, to accept a number of invitations, and, to Luke's quiet pleasure, it gave Tessa many more chances to wear her most important jewels. Even now, at the peak of the lavish 1980s, when great jewellery was being worn by many women, Tessa's vast collection was indisputably of the highest quality, the most extravagant and the most original owned by any woman in one of the richest communities on earth.

'What shall I wear with this tonight, darling?' Tessa asked, turning round to show him the white silk linen dinner suit she'd chosen for an intimate dinner party in a private room at Le Dôme, where Fiona was celebrating the completion of her first production. 'Don't you think, maybe rubies?'

'Yes, absolutely,' Luke said, smiling at her from the armless slipper chair in her dressing room, where he liked to sit and watch her finish dressing.

'But which rubies?' she responded, vanishing into her closet where her built-in wall safe was open. 'Luke, come on in here and help me choose . . . no, never mind, I'll bring out the trays and let you see everything,' Tessa said, as she emerged from the closet laden with six black velvet trays of jewels.

Tessa screamed and dropped the trays. Luke was slumped sideways in the chair, his left arm hanging to the floor, his head and shoulders following the line of his dangling arm.

Tessa ran to him, using all her strength to push his upper body back into the chair. His head flopped forward, his chin rested on his breastbone.

'Luke! Luke! What's the matter?' she begged. 'Open your eyes, for God's sake. Is it your heart?' He didn't move, didn't open his eyes, didn't speak.

In a panic that gave her superhuman strength, Tessa managed to pull the phone table towards her and dial 9-1-1 while still propping Luke up in the chair with one hand on his shoulder. He had fainted, she thought, she mustn't let him fall. Tessa managed to give the emergency operator the address of the house and the fact that Luke had passed out, before dropping the phone and attempting to take Luke's pulse. When she reached for his wrist he started to fall forward towards her. She abandoned the attempt, wrestling with his weight to keep him in the chair.

Tessa was still holding Luke steady and imploring him to speak to her, when two paramedics burst into the room. She stood back only when they laid him down on the floor. One of the paramedics checked Luke's pupils and took his blood pressure while the other checked his pulse and quickly reached for the defibrillator paddles. 'We're going to shock his chest,' he explained to Tessa.

'He's never had a heart problem,' she cried, incredulously watching the bizarre activity that had suddenly erupted in the fortress of her home. 'His heart is perfect. What's wrong, what's wrong with him?'

'I don't know, ma'am,' one of them answered. He had no intention of telling her that the paddles showed only a flat, straight line that indicated no electrical heart activity. That duty was for the doctors.

'How could you not know?' she shouted. 'Do something, for the love of God, do *something*!'

'Yes, ma'am, we're doing everything possible,' he told her, reassuringly.

The paramedics exchanged a look. The man's pupils were fixed and dilated, there was no pulse, no blood pressure, he was asystolic, but they were trained to go on the basis that there was always hope. They shocked his chest, put an airway down his throat, and put an IV into his arm to try to push medication into him.

'Call the hospital,' one of the paramedics told the other. Suddenly three firemen entered the room, responding to the initial call Tessa had made. One of them carried an oxygen tank, the others helped to strap Luke onto a stretcher. The paramedic on the phone said quietly, making sure that Tessa didn't hear him, 'We're coming in, yes, asystole, fast as we can.'

The paramedics, the firemen carrying the stretcher, and Tessa, grabbing her bag, all ran down the stairs to the ambulance that waited by the front door. Tessa climbed into the ambulance and tried to gather Luke in her arms even though he was strapped to the stretcher. Neither of the paramedics tried to stop her.

'We'll get him to the hospital as quickly as possible,' one of them said. He would not tell this poor woman that her husband was dead. He'd known it the minute he'd looked in his eyes. It had been pointless to try the techniques they used for heart-attack victims. It must have been an aneurysm, he thought. Nothing else could kill as quickly.

Maggie and all the Websters flew out to Los Angeles as soon as possible after Fiona had called to tell them that Luke was dead.

Madison, Tyler and Maggie dropped the others at the Beverly Hills Hotel and went directly to Tessa's. There they found Fiona, Aaron Zucker and Roddy Fensterwald already gathered.

'Where's Tessa?' Maggie asked as soon as she saw the little group huddled round a coffee table in the living room.

'In her bedroom. She won't come out,' Fiona said, 'and she won't let anybody in.'

'Do you mean nobody's seen her since it happened?'

'Just me,' Fiona answered. 'She gave the hospital my name last night and I went to pick her up and bring her home right away—there was nothing she could do at the hospital—but when we got here, she ran upstairs to the bedroom and locked the door. She won't answer the house intercom and she hasn't rung for anything to eat. I listened at her door but I couldn't hear a thing, not a sound, and no matter what I said, she wouldn't answer.'

'I think we should break the door down,' Roddy said.

'Fiona,' Maggie asked, 'what was she like at the hospital?'

'In shock. Total. She wouldn't talk to me, she wasn't crying, she was barely breathing. I don't know if she even realised who was driving the car home. I must have been the only person she could think of to call because she knew I was at Le Dôme.'

'What did the doctors tell you, exactly?' Maggie said, still trying to comprehend what had happened.

'He had something called a cerebral aneurysm,' Fiona answered wearily. She'd already had to explain this to Roddy and Aaron. 'Some people are born with the possibility of it happening. You can die from it at any time, or live to a ripe old age, it just depends. The pathologists at the hospital did the autopsy and called me this morning.'

'Oh,' Maggie said in a small voice. 'So Tessa still doesn't know why Luke died.'

'I agree with Roddy,' Aaron said. 'We've got to do something, we just can't sit around here while she's going through this all by herself. Can't we take the door off its hinges?'

'Let me try to get her to open it first,' Maggie said. 'I'm the only one here who's family.'

'You're right,' Fiona agreed. 'Do you want me to come with you?'

'Oh, yes, please, Fiona. I need someone to show me the way, this is the first time I've been here.'

As they walked up the staircase, Fiona, who hadn't seen Maggie for several years, was amazed by the steadiness of her step. She's not a kid any more, Fiona thought, but how old can she be? Surely no more than seventeen?

At Tessa's door, Maggie knocked. When she received no answer she spoke through the door, raising her voice so that it was impossible that it wouldn't be heard.

'Tessa, it's Maggie. I'm here, Tessa, I'm here for you. Please let me in. You can't stay in there all by yourself, you need to be with somebody. I'm your sister, Tessa. Luke wouldn't want you to be alone now. You know he'd want you to be with your sister. Please let me in.'

'Maggie? Are you alone?'

'Fiona's here with me, but she'll go away if you want.'

The door opened and Tessa stood there, still wearing the white suit she'd had on the night before.

'Maggie,' she said, without any inflection, without any sign of surprise at Maggie's presence. 'Maggie, have you heard about Luke?'

'Yes, Tessa, that's why I'm here. May we come in?'

'Something happened to Luke, Maggie, something I don't understand.'

'I know, Tessa. Please let me come in.' Maggie and Fiona both entered the room, stepping carefully over the dozens of ruby necklaces and bracelets and earrings that lay scattered all over the floor where Tessa had dropped the trays.

'Where did you come from, Maggie,' Tessa said in a mechanical voice from which all emotion, even curiosity, had bled away.

'From home, Tessa. Tyler and Madison are downstairs, and Aaron and Roddy.'

'So many people,' Tessa remarked, slowly. 'And Fiona, you too. Do they all know that something's happened to Luke?'

'Yes, Tessa, they know. They came to be with you. We love you, Tessa,' Fiona said.

Only after the Requiem Mass was Tessa finally able to begin to accept the fact of Luke's death. For five days, despite Maggie's and Fiona's entreaties, she shut herself up in her room once more and mourned for Luke, unable to stop weeping, sleeping only an hour or so at a time, waking hideously to a nightmare that never ceased, eating only when her body insisted. Luke, her one and only love, was gone, her safety was gone. There was nothing left to live for, but no way to die.

Eventually Tessa's mind began to work again. She must learn to live without Luke, she understood, since she was still alive. If she could only *act* as if she had strength, perhaps she would eventually find some measure of true strength, Tessa told herself, with all the courage she could fake. Searching in the only direction she knew, Tessa took the first step to stitch up the tattered rags into which her heart had been ripped. She phoned her agent and asked him to come to the house.

'I need a job, Aaron. Within a week.'

'Tessa, Tessa, what kind of crazy idea is that?'

'I have to have it, Aaron—a location shoot, as far away as possible, as difficult as possible, something that will keep me from thinking or feeling for as many hours of the day as possible.'

'Wouldn't it be better to—'

'What?' she interrupted him, 'sit here and mourn? I could spend the rest of my life doing that, Aaron, and never have the slightest reason to stop. The alternative is to go back to work. I know that's what Luke would have wanted me to do. And if I don't, how can I keep on living? Work is the only thing I know how to do now.'

'But what about Maggie? She wants to come and live with you. She hopes so much that you'll let her. She'll be such a comfort to you.'

'Oh, Aaron, Aaron, Maggie is such a darling, but she has no idea how bad an idea that would be for her. She may be ready to sacrifice an all-important year of school, but I'm not ready to let her do that. All I can hope to be, Aaron, for a long, long time, is a woman who is using her work to survive. No one can "be a comfort" to me.'

Now that the first numbness had worn off, she saw clearly what was right for Maggie. She was free now to tell Maggie the truth, to claim her daughter, to claim the only child she'd ever have, but that revelation would bind Maggie more strongly to what she imagined, so wrongly, so sweetly, was her mission of comfort. She must wait to tell Maggie, until she felt less needy, less vulnerable. She must wait until she had done the long work of mourning that remained to her.

Five

SHE WOULDN'T HAVE TO STAND it much longer, Madison Webster told herself, sitting at the desk in her bedroom, as she listened to Maggie clatter down the stairs, off to one of the countless events that marked the end of her last year in high school. That—that *peasant*—would be out of the house soon. She didn't need to provide a home for Maggie any longer, not for another second, yet for the sake of appearances she obviously couldn't throw her out until her graduation, Madison thought, as she bent over her accounts.

Her own impressive funds, built up through thousands of domestic economies, seemed minor compared to the $20 million Luke had left Tyler in his will. Although the settlement of Luke's complicated estate was not yet final, they were far richer than she had ever dreamed they'd be.

Aside from what Luke had left them, he'd arranged the affairs of his company in exceptionally good order, leaving $10 million each to his six top men, dependent on their pledging to remain in the employ of the company for the next ten years, and he'd passed on his position as chief to Len Jones, who had been his second-in-command for so long. He'd left $70 million to various charities, and everything else, the bulk of his estate, had been left to Tessa, except for another $20 million he'd left Maggie, to be kept in a trust until she was thirty-five, with Tessa named as one trustee and his tax attorney the other.

If Luke had enough money to leave $170 million to others, Madison wondered, biting the inside of her lips, what must Tessa be worth? She couldn't begin to imagine.

As for Maggie, clearly it was Luke's intention that she now be in Tessa's charge. Let Tessa cope with her sister for a change!

Anyway, chances were Maggie would spend most of her holidays with classmates, just as she'd encouraged Barney to do. That boy hadn't been home for almost a year, what with a summer at a friend's ranch in Nevada and Christmas and Thanksgiving in Boston and Philadelphia. He was such a popular boy that his disappointing marks didn't matter. The main thing was that he was making exactly the kind of friends she'd hoped he'd make when they'd decided to send him to Andover, when he was twelve, more than five years earlier.

Even though it was soon going to be too dark to ride, Maggie wandered down to the stables and perched on the fence surrounding the empty practice ring. It was almost twilight on this soft spring Friday evening, a week before graduation. All the horses had been turned out to the fields, the six stable hands had gone home to their own lives, and she had the place to herself. She was surprised to feel a piercing nostalgia as she gazed at the scene of so many childhood hours of fear and humiliation. Yet she didn't feel anything but anticipation at the prospect of going away to college, leaving the cold care of Madison, who had never once greeted her with a trace of warmth.

No, her nostalgia was not for her years in this house where she was, at best, tolerated. Her sense of loss was centred entirely on the time she'd spent with Barney, her faithful protector, who had forgotten her, disappearing into a world of grand new buddies and social vacations.

Damn Barney to hell, anyway! He was only seventeen and a half and she was about to be eighteen in a week, a grown woman feeling sorry for herself because she'd been ignored by a boy, a mere adolescent, who wouldn't mature for years.

She was at the top of her class academically, Maggie told herself fiercely, she was popular with all the other girls, she was editor of the school paper and president of the debating team, she was highly computer literate, she'd been accepted by the University of Michigan, where there were guaranteed to be men, genuine grown-up men, thick on the ground.

She knew she'd meet the right guy during freshman year. It was impossible for anyone as ripe, as eager for experience as she was, not to find a guy. She wanted to fall in and out of love as many times as was possible. Four years of serial love affairs, Maggie promised herself with a wide smile—wasn't that the underlying purpose of higher education?

She'd have to keep her grades up enough to stay in college, but fundamentally she was going to major in passion. And when she graduated she was going to go to New York City and get some kind of wonderful job and have another five years of love affairs before she even thought of getting married.

She'd been stuck in boring, limited horse country for most of her life. If ever a woman needed to be liberated it was she. There was a vast, marvellous world out there that she was going to bite into and chew up, piece by delicious piece, Maggie promised herself. She was going to be a raving success, she knew it in her bones. She took a deep breath, revelling in her sense of all the exciting, unknown adventures that were going to happen to her.

'Hey,' said a quiet voice behind her.

Maggie almost fell off the fence in surprise, prevented by a pair of muscular arms grasped round her waist.

'Don't say anything. It's me, Barney,' he whispered urgently in her ear, and lifted her easily off the fence so that she stood in front of him.

'What are you doing here? You're not supposed to get out of school till next week. What's going on? Why are you whispering?'

'I've been expelled.'

'Shit! Why?'

'Pot party, I made the buy and they caught me on the way to my room where the other guys were waiting.'

'Oh, Barney, you asshole! What happened to the others?'

'They said they didn't know what I was up to, a surprise to them.'

'Nice guys.'

'Why should they risk admitting anything when they didn't have any weed on them? I'd have done the same. So I'm out, one year short of graduating.'

'How'd you get here?'

'On my bike. I have a second-hand Harley I fixed up so it's better than new, kept it in a garage in town. Bikes are my thing, my real thing. I'm so good with bikes you wouldn't believe it.'

'Wow, *Easy Rider* all over again,' she drawled.

'You got it, I'm reinventing the genre,' he grinned.

'And what are Ma and Pa Webster going to say?'

'That's the part where it could get nasty. Let's go in the tack room and figure out a lie.'

'Barney, you're delusional. The school'll notify them. You'd have it easier escaping to Alcatraz.'

'I've already escaped from Alcatraz. I took off as soon as I was kicked out. Didn't pack, just got my bike and headed home.'

'Alcatraz? I thought you liked school.'

'Nope, not really. I'm academically deeply lacking, but mechanically brilliant. I tried to be a real preppy but my heart wasn't in it. I made a lot of friends, but they're busy planning to turn into their fathers, and that isn't for me. I want to work with my hands, run a bike shop. Only problem is I don't dare tell my folks, they'll never allow it. A blue-collar son! They'll make me get a college degree from any tenth-rate place that would have me, even if they have to bribe one.'

He opened the door to the tack room, turned on the light, and closed the door behind them.

'Whew! Safe at last. I figured I might find you still trying to learn how to stay on a horse, so I came down here first, left my bike behind the barn.'

'I can damn well stay on any horse in the Essex Hunt.'

'Bet you can't,' he said. 'Bet I still have to save your ass.'

'What'll you bet?' Maggie challenged him.

'A kiss.'

'What kind of bet is that? If I can't ride I kiss you, if I can ride you kiss me? Heads you win, tails I lose? No thanks.'

'OK, no bet. I believe you.'

They faced off opposite each other, unable to stop smiling in sheer joy at the sight of each other. She'd never been so glad to see anyone in her life, Maggie thought. Barney had shot up, he was well over six feet tall. His streaky blond hair, tangled by his long ride, flopped over his forehead; his face was tanned; his pleasant, lively boy's face had turned into that of an almost-man, strong but still changing into what it would eventually become. His impudent grin and his freckles were the only fleeting reminder of the boy she'd known since she was five.

'Do you know what a sexy, lovely girl you've turned into?'

'Of course.'

'Well, I didn't.' He put his hands on either side of her face and bent down and kissed her full on the lips, a long, lusty kiss that detonated like a depth bomb in her belly. Her eyes opened wide in astonishment as she kissed him back voraciously. The tack room whirled around her; bridles and saddles, hunt caps, rows of polished boots, dozens of photos of horses—everything blurred and she staggered with dizziness. Only Barney's arms kept her upright.

'You liked that,' he said, stunned by her response.

'I did. I'd like more. Over here, on the sofa.'

'Maggie, we're not related or anything, are we?'

'Not even kissing cousins. We're just old friends.'

'Oh, God,' he groaned, 'you're so gorgeous, so grown-up. Where have I been?'

'Too busy to notice me.'

'I must have been stupid.'

'You are. Shut up.' She reached up for him with her open, impetuous, curious, innocent lips, groaning with hungry haste and need, adoring the touch of his searching tongue. She quivered with delight as he explored her mouth, lacing her fingers in his hair to bring him closer, kissing him all over his face, smelling his unfamiliar, delicious, rough skin. She rapidly pushed and pulled him round so that she could kiss his neck and his ears and his forehead, returning always to his open mouth and his hot, eager, shamelessly seeking tongue.

'I've got to feel your breasts,' he muttered into her lips. Maggie ripped the buttons of her blouse open and exposed her breasts to his hands and his mouth, catching her breath in bliss as she felt his touch, so warm, so firm, so focused. She lay under him, pushing upwards, as he greedily sucked her nipples and madly rubbed her mound, under her jeans, with a penis that felt like a club. In a minute they both came, fully dressed, Maggie gasping, Barney with a muffled scream.

Too shaken to say anything, too surprised to move, they lay one on top of the other, holding each other tightly. After a minute Maggie, crushed, eased herself out from under Barney's body and lay next to him, hugging him close. He was limp from the unexpected power of his orgasm; she was weak with a pleasure greater than she'd ever known.

'And we didn't even *do* anything,' Barney finally said in wonder.

'We didn't?'

'Not really.'

'I never have,' she admitted. 'Have you?'

'Yeah, not much though. You're so . . . fast.'

'Is that good?'

'Damn right. Oh, Maggie, I've got to do it again.'

'I do too.'

'Touch me this time, touch me, please. I've always loved you, Maggie.'

'I know.'

'Can you take off your jeans? I want to touch you too.'

'OK, but that's all, just touching.'

'I promise.'

In seconds both of them were naked, kissing and nipping at each other, looking at all their secret places, exploring each other's bodies almost roughly, trying to hold back from the only thing they really wanted, until, as mad with curiosity as with need, they both had to give in and explore each other frantically between their legs, fingers wet and ruthless. Soon, much too soon, they were both racked by profound, piercing, slowly widening and exploding orgasms that neither of them would forget for the rest of their lives.

Maggie returned to her room by a back staircase while Barney settled down to sleep in the tack room. No one saw her as she shakily made her way home and closed her door behind her. She sniffed herself. She'd never smelt the aftermath of sex on herself before, but she knew instantly that the first thing to do was to take a shower. The pungent odour was all over her, on her hands, on her jeans, even her hair reeked wonderfully of Barney.

After her shower Maggie put on clean pyjamas and got into bed so that she could say to a curious maid that she didn't feel well enough to eat. She turned off her lights, lay back on her pillow, and finally let herself think about what had just happened to her.

Barney, Barney, was all she could think at first, still dazzled by a trembling buzz that made her nerves zing. Barney was seventeen and a half years old, Maggie told herself. A man-boy, half-grown, who had the terrifying power to make her do crazy things. She was scared witless by the thought of how helpless she would become if she lay in his arms again, kissed him, smelt him. She'd never be able to stop with just petting and the kind of touching they'd done tonight. Barney, darling, beautiful Barney, no! She knew ten times more about sex now than she had a few hours ago *and she wasn't going to do it.*

She was on her way to college; he'd been thrown out of school and didn't want to go back. She was on her way to many years of adventure; he had no ambitions beyond his dream of a bike shop. Both of them had their lives ahead of them but they didn't want the same things. Sex and their still-childish love wouldn't be enough. The real world would crush them. They were simply too young. Kids, both of them.

What had happened to all her sense of adventure and her eagerness to get out and stir the world up around her? She asked herself. The answer came clearly. Nothing had happened. She still intended to have it all. Barney's appearance here tonight had changed nothing fundamental. The timing was wrong. She couldn't change her own dreams for Barney, sweet, loving, heavenly, glorious Barney, even if she would never forget him. It was over. It had to be over. There was no choice.

It was, Maggie thought as the tears streamed down her cheeks, her first one-night stand.

The next day, at lunch, Maggie found herself alone at the table.

'Where are my aunt and uncle?' she asked Elizabeth, the cook, as soon as she could find her alone.

'They left to fly up to Barney's school, that's what I heard them say at breakfast. There's some sort of big trouble.'

Maggie wandered down to the stables, dawdling along the path. Barney couldn't be in the barn or the tack room or the stable hands would have seen him.

'I thought you'd never show up,' he said, stepping out from behind a grove of trees. 'Come here, come here, darling Maggie. I've been up all night thinking about you.'

'No, Barney,' she said, standing in the middle of the path. 'It was the most wonderful, exciting thing that's ever happened to me. It was bliss, Barney, but I can't, not again. I can't even kiss you.'

The amazed hurt on his face went through her heart, but she faced him firmly. 'I love you too much to dare to love you more.'

'Come here and explain what you mean.'

'No. I'm going back to the house. I just came to tell you. And there's something else. I know that they've gone to make a fuss and get Andover to take you back, and maybe they'll manage it, but I think you should do what you're good at, what you want to do. Go to New York and work with bikes, and get what you really want. Make your own life, don't let them force you into anything. You're different from them.'

'You came down here to give me career advice?' he asked incredulously.

'Yep, I did. Do you need any money?'

'Christ!'

'Well, do you?'

'No, I have enough.'

'Will you let me know where you are in New York?'

'Will you come to visit me?'

'I don't know, maybe some day, but first I have to go to college, Barney. I have to grow up and so do you.'

'Oh, God, I hate it when you're right.'

'So you know too.'

'Yeah. We're too bloody young. Now. We won't always be, Maggie. Don't forget that. Don't forget me. I loved you from day one. I love you now. I'm going to love you *always*. You're *my* girl Maggie. I'd better split. I'll let you know where I am. Give me just one kiss.'

'I'll owe it to you. One kiss and we'll be back where we started yesterday. Good luck, darling, darling Barney. Goodbye.'

'Maggie, come on in the kitchen as soon as you get a chance, I have something to ask you,' Elizabeth whispered with an air of secrecy, the day before Maggie's Saturday-night birthday party. Madison had realised reluctantly that it was her duty to celebrate the occasion, considering the size of the legacy Luke had left Tyler, although why he'd felt it necessary to leave Maggie an equal amount she'd never understand.

During the past week, since Barney's expulsion from school, Maggie had barely seen the Websters, both of whom were beside themselves with anger at their son and the need to find him and somehow place him, willy-nilly, in another school so that he could get into college next year. If they hadn't turned the plans for Maggie's birthday party entirely over to Elizabeth, they would probably have forgotten about it, Maggie thought, but the cook was perfectly capable of managing a dinner party for Maggie's graduating class of twenty-three girls without any instructions from Madison. What special treat had Elizabeth dreamed up? Maggie wondered, as she made her way into the large kitchen.

'You're not going to show me my birthday cake in advance, are you?' she said, grabbing Elizabeth round the waist and planting a kiss on each of her cheeks. 'Isn't that supposed to be bad luck?'

'Maggie, come in the pantry,' Elizabeth said with unaccustomed seriousness. 'I don't know what to do about this.' She handed Maggie a letter addressed to her. 'Here, read it.'

Maggie opened the envelope and scanned the single page. It was a short note from Barney, asking Elizabeth to give Maggie, and only Maggie, his address in New York. He was fine, he said, but he didn't want his parents to know where he was until he had a job and could support himself, because nothing would make him go back to school.

'What should I do?' Elizabeth asked. 'Should I show this to Mrs Webster?'

'Give it to me,' Maggie said. 'They're worried sick about him. They have to know he's OK.'

Relieved, Elizabeth turned over the paper to Maggie and went back to her preparations. Maggie memorised the address, tore the letter into bits, and put it in the trash. She promised herself to go into town that afternoon and empty her bank account so she could send Barney money to live on until he could pay her back.

Maggie waited impatiently until Madison and Tyler returned for lunch.

'Barney called while you were out,' Maggie said, as soon as they arrived. 'He wanted you to know that he was fine but he said he wasn't going back to school and you shouldn't worry; he's looking for a job.'

'Shouldn't worry?' Madison screamed furiously. 'Shouldn't worry, after what he's put us through!' She sounded relieved but doubly furious. 'Where was he?'

'I asked but he wouldn't tell me, I'm sorry.'

'God, what I would give to get my hands on that rotten kid,' Tyler raved. 'Who the hell does he think he is? How could he treat us this way? What kind of future does he think he has? A job? Who would employ him? He must be lying around smoking marijuana with a bunch of dropouts just as bad as he is.'

'He sounded together,' Maggie ventured, 'not drugged at all.'

'As if you could tell over the phone,' Madison scoffed. 'Why on earth didn't you get more out of him? I'll bet you didn't try. How can we find him? How dare he hide from us!'

'I did try,' Maggie protested, 'but he's doing his thing.'

'Oh, that phrase! It makes me sick. Well, obviously there's nothing to do till he runs out of money and turns up on the doorstep. Oh, and Maggie, speaking of turning up, Tessa is coming to the party tomorrow. It's supposed to be a surprise.' Damn Maggie, she thought, for not having prised Barney's whereabouts out of him; they'd always been thick as thieves.

'Tessa's coming?' Maggie cried, stunned with joy.

'She's taking the Concorde over from London, arriving at the Carlyle tomorrow morning, driving out here for the party, spending the night at the hotel, and returning Sunday.'

'Oh, I don't believe it!' Maggie rejoiced, flooded with happiness. Months ago she'd given up all hope of seeing Tessa on her birthday.

As she had planned, as soon as possible after Luke's death almost a year ago Tessa had replaced Michelle Pfeiffer, a flu victim, at the last minute on a major movie set in a small Greek village. The role had kept her working for four months. Then, with only a week for hurried costume fittings, she'd made a Merchant–Ivory film in the English countryside, and she was now in a Jaffe/Lansing production due to be made in and around Paris and London.

Tessa had sold the houses in Beverly Hills and in Melbourne. HEART-BROKEN STAR WILL NEVER REVISIT SCENES OF PAST HAPPINESS, the story in *People* had said, and, Maggie reflected, they had it right. Tessa seemed to have jettisoned all her baggage except for her jewels. In rare photographs of her in the past year, she had been covered in gems. She must need, Maggie realised sadly, to wrap herself at all times in the protective armour Luke had given her.

'Tessa's going to a lot of trouble for just one party,' Madison said sourly, annoyed at Maggie's expression of radiant expectation.

99

How like Tessa, she thought, to show up once a year and get all the credit for having made an enormous effort.

'Oh, Madison, she *is*, she is!' Maggie gulped and ran out of the room in a hurry because she was about to burst into happy tears.

Two days earlier, Tessa found herself with a free day stretching in front of her. London was at its best, spreading its humming vastness out beneath a sky of a singular transparency.

She stretched out in a canvas chair in St James's Park and contemplated the passage of three tiny white clouds that punctuated the exquisite pastel of the sky, framed in a circle of treetops. She could live here, she thought idly, if every day were like this one. She could buy a house in London if she hadn't spent last winter here, grimly accepting what any Californian would think of as a twilight zone, with lamps lit well before four in the afternoon. But it might be amusing to have a small place, just a mews house, with a little garden, only for the spring and fall, so that she wouldn't always have to live in hotels . . . With a start of surprise Tessa realised that she was making a plan. It was the first time since Luke had died that she'd thought of the future. Galvanised, she jumped up from her chair and started walking rapidly through the park.

If she could make any plan, even a tentative one based on the weather, she must be well along in the mourning process, Tessa told herself. Mourning Luke had been like having an invisible wound that left no outward trace. She could only judge its healing by the way her mind worked. She had reached this point by living one day after the other, hanging on, enduring. Every morning she willed herself to get out of bed and go to work, never thinking of her future. So . . . time had passed, enough time, apparently, although she would never have known it if she hadn't imagined owning a mews house. If she were well enough to consider that, Tessa thought with a leap of joy, she could allow herself to be with Maggie without clinging to her and dragging her down into her grief.

Maggie would be eighteen on Saturday, Tessa reflected, hurrying back to the hotel. The concierge could, *had* to get her tickets on Concorde so that she could tell Maggie the truth without any further delay. Maggie could spend the summer with her in London before going back to start college. They'd have months in which to begin to learn how to be mother and daughter . . . if . . . Maggie would accept her after she'd told her everything that had happened.

Tessa broke into a run. There was so much to do, so much to plan. So much to hope for.

On the morning of her birthday Maggie woke early, feeling very important. She'd had dreams of strange rapture, like dancing on clouds of gilded meringue, that vanished as soon as she'd woken, but they'd left her feeling light, graced and poised.

After her shower she posed naked in front of her full-length bathroom mirror, admiring her rosy, abundant, sexy adult self from all possible angles. Then, for a mad minute, she capered about in honour of the kid she was leaving behind. As she dressed, Maggie realised to the full how major an occasion today was going to be in her life.

Tessa would be arriving in New York well before noon, Maggie thought. What if she took the bus into the city and met her at the hotel? Elizabeth could drive her to Essex to catch the bus, and she'd have time alone with her sister before the party. Turning the idea over in her mind, with mounting excitement, she rushed down to the kitchen for breakfast.

'Well, here's your annual birthday card,' Elizabeth said with a smile. 'Your godparents in California never forget, do they?'

Maggie ripped the envelope open and found that it wasn't a card, but a letter from Brian Kelly enclosing a sealed letter addressed to her. To escape Elizabeth's kindly but prying eyes, she took the two letters into the deserted dining room to read.

My very dear Maggie,

As you know, your father was one of my closest friends and I treasure the honour he did me in making me your godfather. When you were five years old, your father gave me this letter to deliver to you on your eighteenth birthday in case he was no longer on earth to do it himself. I've often wondered if he felt a premonition, poor dear man. I've kept it in my safe-deposit box for thirteen years.

Dear Maggie, have a wonderful day. Both of us send you all our very best wishes and many happy returns. You must be a very grown-up lady by now.

With our fondest love,
Brian and Helen

Wonderingly, reverently, Maggie turned over the enclosed letter. The envelope, yellowing at the edges, was heavily sealed and addressed to Miss Mary Margaret Horvath.

Mary Margaret, she thought. My father thought of me by my full name. How strange that I never knew that.

She held the letter, turning it over and over, postponing the moment of opening it. A letter from her father, written thirteen years ago, was too important to open here, she thought. She hastily took both letters to her room, where there was no chance of Madison or Tyler walking in.

Maggie put Sandor Horvath's letter carefully on her desk and slowly slit the envelope and removed the letter. The paper was stiff and so heavily creased that it was hard to smooth out, but the elegant handwriting was as easy to read as calligraphy.

Beloved Mary Margaret,

I pray that you will never receive this letter. I am fifty-four years old and, given a merciful God, should be alive to be with you thirteen years from now, on your birthday. But there is no way of knowing the future and I am determined that you should be told the truth about your birth when you have reached the age of reason and, I hope, compassion. If it is within my power, I will tell you the following facts myself when you turn eighteen, but if I am no longer of this world, someone must tell you, and there is no one I trust but myself.

Mary Margaret, your sister Teresa is your mother. She gave birth to you when she was still but fourteen years old. We do not know who your father was. Your grandmother, Agnes, and I decided to bring you up as our own child. This was done for several, all-too-human reasons. First of all, we wanted to spare Teresa the great disgrace of bearing an illegitimate child. In the second place, your grandmother wished to keep all knowledge of this disgrace from her family, and I, for my part, wanted another child. For that reason we came to California to live, where everybody we know believes you to be our child, not our grandchild.

Your mother, now twenty years old and known to the public as Tessa Kent, is about to leave our home and go to Scotland to make a motion picture. At the age of sixteen, when you were only two, she became a film star. I do not know when she intends to tell you the truth about your birth, but I pray every night that it will soon become possible for her. On that day I will destroy this letter. Until that day, all three of us, your mother, Teresa, and the two of us, Agnes and Sandor Horvath, your loving grandparents, are mired in this lie, which deprives you of knowledge of your true mother.

You are a good, sweet child, Mary Margaret, and you have given me great joy, but I have never felt that I had a right to that joy with the knowledge I possess. I have always blessed you, and will always bless you, every day of my life. Forgive me if you can.

Your grandfather,
Sandor Horvath

As she read the letter, Maggie had instinctively risen from her desk chair and retreated to the bathroom, where she could lock herself in. She reread it twice more and then once again, seeking time to absorb the shock.

Long before the final reading, Maggie's emotions had galloped ahead of her mental process and assumed a vile, jagged, threatening shape that filled her chest and abdomen and pushed inwards on all her vital organs, making it almost impossible to breathe.

She was overcome by an intense desire to hide, to disappear from a world that contained this story of betrayal and secrets and lies, all directed at her since she had been born. She was without rights, without a place of her own, a fraud, a mistake everyone could lie to, manipulate, put down or take up at will, a sin to be confessed, a disgrace, a thing to be hidden but never acknowledged. A thing, a thing, not a person.

For a long time Maggie knelt on the carpet, the letter scattered by her side, bowed over so that she could rest her head on the floor and protect it with her hands, gathered into the smallest space she could take up, too beaten down for the relief of tears, a solid wad of pain.

Slowly, gradually, thoughts gathered, strength returned. She was Maggie Horvath, and Maggie Horvath *was* a person. No matter how unwanted she'd been, no one could take that away from her. The web of the letter dropped away and Maggie was left with one piece of certainty: *She existed and Tessa was her mother.*

Maggie got up off the floor and looked at herself in the mirror. She looked like the same person who had woken to such happiness that morning, yet now she was reeling with pure rage. The pain inside her had condensed into an anger she could barely contain. Her eyes were bright with it, her cheeks flaming with it, her heart beat with the power of it.

She dressed for Manhattan in minutes. She packed a small suitcase, grabbed her handbag and walked downstairs, pausing only to pick up the keys to Madison's car from the hall table. She hadn't taken the test for her driving licence yet, but she'd known how to drive expertly for years, and within an hour and a half she'd parked in an uptown garage near the Carlyle. She left her suitcase in the car, walked briskly to the hotel, and had herself announced at the reception desk.

'Please go up, Miss Horvath,' the clerk said, after he'd called upstairs. 'Miss Kent is in suite nine hundred.'

'Thank you.'

As she got out of the elevator Maggie saw Tessa standing in the hallway at the door to her suite, arms open in welcome, her words tumbling out, her smile filled with excitement.

'Maggie! Darling Maggie! Madison must have told you . . . I . . . I wanted it to be a surprise. I have so much to tell you . . . but I hardly recognise you, you've changed, you're so very much more grown-up than a year ago. Oh, give me a kiss, my Maggie.'

'I don't think so,' Maggie said, walking past Tessa into the sitting room.

'You're not too old to give me a kiss, are you?' she said, bewildered.

'You're much too old, Tessa.'

'*What?*' The smile was still on Tessa's face.

'You're thirty-two. Isn't that too old to lie to your daughter?'

They faced each other mutely. Maggie's expression a fierce, frozen challenge as she searched Tessa's face, watching the smile fade and the eyes fill with the beginning of comprehension.

'I came on purpose to tell you . . . I couldn't before because—'

'*Liar.*'

'No, truly—'

'*Lie!* I'll never believe anything you tell me, ever, ever, ever!'

'Oh, God! I can't blame you, but Maggie, please, *please* lis—'

'Don't you wonder how I know?'

Tessa was shocked into silence, unable to keep from turning her face away from Maggie's look of flaming accusation.

'I had a letter from a dead man this morning. Sandor Horvath. Not my father, *your father*, Tessa. He didn't trust anyone to tell me the truth—he knew you pretty well, didn't he?—so he wrote me thirteen years ago and left the letter with my godfather to send.'

'You can't understand,' Tessa said, sinking down onto a sofa. 'I don't expect you to understand yet, but I was only fourteen. Fourteen. You should try, at least, to understand that, you've been fourteen, you know what it would have meant. How could I have taken care of you? I did what they told me. I had to obey them to survive.'

'I don't blame you for any of that,' Maggie said in a level tone.

'Oh, Maggie . . .' Tessa turned to her with a look of hope beginning to flare in her lovely eyes.

'I blame you for everything else. I blame you for what you did to a little five-year-old child who believed everything you did was wonderful. I blame you for sending me to live with those terrible people when you married Luke. I wasn't even invited to the wedding. I was only five; it wasn't too late to become my mother once you were married. You could have kept me with you, you could have claimed me. But you abandoned me for ever when you married Luke. How could you have been cruel enough to do that to your *own* child? I blame you for sending me away for thirteen years to the Websters, people who never had any liking for me, much less a drop of love, people who weren't my family, who treated me like an intruder. Except for Barney, the cook is my only friend in that house.'

'Maggie—'

'How much did you pay them to keep me? It must have been a fortune to keep Madison halfway civil. But you would have paid anything, wouldn't you, to keep from having to take care of me yourself? You were too busy being a star, too busy being married to a rich man, too busy jaunting around the world, too busy living for Luke, too busy being the famous Tessa Kent. There was simply no room in your wonderful, brilliant life for a child, was there? I grew up without love, except the little bit you spared me when Luke was away and you allowed me to visit, allowed me to play with your jewels. Your jewels around my neck instead of your arms.'

'You should have said something!'

'*I* should have said something?'

'I thought you were happy with the Websters.'

'Even if I had been, they're nothing to me. You're my mother. *My mother!* How could you leave me with them? How could you pretend to be my sister? How could you spend so little time with me?'

'Luke didn't know,' Tessa whispered. 'He never knew.'

'What's that supposed to mean? What does that have to do with anything? Luke's been dead for a year. Even if I believed you never told him, and I don't believe it for a second, once he died you could have told me.'

'I couldn't then,' Tessa cried. 'It wouldn't have been fair to you.'

'This is where I came in, Tessa,' Maggie said. 'I don't want to see you again, ever. I don't want anything from you, ever. I don't want the money Luke left me; nothing will make me take it. Tell Madison I took her car and I'll send her the claim ticket for it. And tell her to cancel the party, I won't be going back there.'

She turned and walked towards the door as quickly as possible. It swung shut behind her as Tessa, immobile, was unable to follow her.

'I came here to tell her,' she told herself in small voice, hugging herself and rocking back and forth. 'I came here to tell her, but I couldn't before, could I? *Could I?*'

A few minutes later Maggie found herself sitting on a bench in Central Park, so drained by the revelations and emotions of the morning that she couldn't imagine how she'd ever get up again.

The past was entirely past: over, finished, dead. College was out, because that would mean having her bills paid by Tessa, and any future relationship with Tessa was unthinkable. Even as she thought of Tessa, she felt absolutely nothing—no sense of loss, not even a flicker of anger, just an empty blankness devoid of pain.

The future was hers to invent. Her assets? The money, the $800 she had planned to lend Barney, was still safe in her bag. She had a suitcase back in the car filled with whatever she'd packed this morning, she was dressed in her best light spring suit, and her shoes were beautifully polished. She had Barney's address. All in all she was in a relatively rich position to begin a new life. She needed a job and a place to live.

Resolutely Maggie returned to the garage to get her suitcase, gratefully used their rest room, and took a taxi to Barney's address, a brownstone converted into single rooms in a shabby street on the Upper West Side.

Barney's name was scrawled next to one of the buttons on the downstairs panel, but when he didn't answer she sat on the second step of the short flight of outside stairs and waited for him. She welcomed this opportunity to decide what to tell him.

Not a word about Tessa, she concluded instantly. Madison and Tyler. They were reason enough, Maggie thought, watching, in an increasingly dreamlike state, the lively action of the crowded, noisy, dirty and almost certainly dangerous street. Eventually, as she clasped her handbag tightly in one arm and threw the other round her suitcase, her lids closed over her weary eyes.

'Maggie!' Barney scooped her up and held her tight. 'Oh, my Maggie, I thought I'd never see you again! Oh, sweetheart—'

'Barney! Wait, please *wait*. Shut up and listen to me and try to understand. You've got the wrong idea, I know how it looks, but I haven't come to be with you. I've run away. I'm *never* going back. If Elizabeth hadn't given me your address I'd have gone to a hotel.'

'Run away? It's your birthday. You can't run away on your birthday,' he blurted, totally confused.

'It's as good a day as any other.'

'Maggie, for Pete's sake, what's going on?'

'I've had it up to here with your folks. I know you probably love them, but I had to get out. Your mother and I have always had problems with each other and when I realised I was eighteen and legally free, I got out. I gave them your message, by the way. Your mother said you'd be back when you ran out of money.'

'The hell I will!'

'I didn't argue with her.' Maggie grinned. 'For a change.'

'Come upstairs, birthday girl. We can't talk here,' Barney said, taking her suitcase and leading the way up two flights of stairs to the room he'd rented.

'It's not a palace, but it's home sweet home,' he said proudly, opening the door on a back room with one curtainless window looking out on a dusty tree. The walls were already all but concealed with bike posters, he had a futon on the floor partly covered by a threadbare rug, and a table held the essentials for living: a tape deck, a hot plate and a can of insect spray. An ancient refrigerator hummed in the corner, and the sink on the wall had room for a soap dish and a toothbrush. A mirror hung above it. The room, even the window, looked clean if nothing else.

'There's a closet, and a john down the hall. I can cook and do my dishes, and my neighbour has a shower he'll rent out for a quarter for five minutes,' Barney said proudly.

'It's perfect. It's you, Barney. The real you. Where's your bike?'

'Safe in the shop. I got a job at a big Harley repair place, entry level but plenty of room to rise to the top. I already know more than most of the guys there but I'm playing it cool, not letting them know yet.'

'Wise,' Maggie said, reclining as sedately as possible on the improvised couch. 'Are you liking it?'

'I love every second. And I'm a reformed character.'

'You? In one week?'

'Yeah, me. Lifting weights, no beer, no pot, early to bed, saving half my salary. And I figured out how to cook hamburger and scramble eggs. Want something to eat, my beautiful birthday girl?'

'I'm starving.'

'Listen, you take a nap, you're half asleep already, and I'll go get something for an early dinner. We'll celebrate being free.'

'No, Barney, I have to get a place to live first,' Maggie said regretfully, gazing at him. If only she could kiss him . . . she sat up quickly.

'Hell, you could stay here for just one night,' he said indignantly. 'I wouldn't jump you.'

'You wouldn't?'

'Not "jump" . . . exactly. Maybe . . . more like a suggestion . . . a birthday commemoration? You're only eighteen once.'

'Nope, no can do,' she said briskly, making herself stand up. 'Do you think there are any rooms to rent in this building?'

'It's full up. This was the last room, a lucky break. But at the drugstore there's a bulletin board for the whole neighbourhood, people selling stuff, looking for soul mates, lost cats, room-mates. We could go look.'

'Forward, comrade. Do they make sodas in this drugstore?'

'Maybe they did, forty years ago.'

'Find anything yet?' Barney asked. He'd bought Maggie an ice cream cone and a Coke while she investigated the bulletin board in the store.

'Lots of local colour and one possible room-mate. Listen to this. "Wanted, to share part of rent: female, open-minded, unshockable, immaculate, quiet, NONSMOKER, no pets, no tattoos, no body piercing, no post-Beatles music. Private room and bath. P. Guildenstern." And it gives a phone number.'

'Sounds like a weirdo. "Immaculate *and* unshockable"—and what does "no tattoos" mean?'

'It sort of sounds like me. I'm going to call her. What have I got to lose?'

'How do you know it's a woman?'

'I don't yet,' Maggie laughed, dialling the number on the wall phone.

'Hello?' said a deep, gruff voice.

'P. Guildenstern?'

'Herself,' the voice said, in its normal feminine tone.

'I saw your notice. My name is Maggie Horvath. No tattoos, unshockable, nonsmoker. Is the room still available?'

'That depends.'

'On what?'

'On whether I think you seem like a suitable person.'

'I'm immaculate, too.'

'That's always a subjective judgment. Come on over and let me see for myself. It's three blocks up from the drugstore, top floor. I have a German shepherd, trained to attack if you make a false move.'

'I'm harmless. All right if I bring my cousin to check you out?'

'Man or woman?'

'Man.'

'No, leave him one flight down. I'll leave the door open so you can scream if you think it's necessary.' P. Guildenstern's voice trembled slightly.

'I'll be right over.' Maggie put down the phone. 'She's ten times more scared of me than I am of her, Barney. I bet she doesn't even have a tabby cat.' She finished her cone, looked at herself in the mirror of her compact, wiped a speck of chocolate ice cream off her lip, applied a little powder, and smoothed her hair. 'Do I look nice and clean?'

'Distinctly nice, definitely clean,' Barney agreed, using all the verbal restraint at his command.

Breathless from the climb to the top of the six-storey building, Maggie knocked at the bright blue door on which was tacked a tiny card engraved with the word '*Miniatures*'.

The door opened on a stout chain and P. Guildenstern looked up at her with wide grey eyes attempting a fierce stare. Maggie looked down at a dainty woman of perhaps five foot one inch, whose mass of curly red-blonde hair was tied back from her neck with a black velvet ribbon. She had a charmingly delicate face with a small, piquant, pointed nose and Victorian rosebud lips. A German shepherd almost as tall as she was stood at attention by her side, on a short leash.

'Good afternoon, Miss Guildenstern,' Maggie said gravely.

'Good afternoon,' she answered tentatively.

'I'm Maggie Horvath. I just called.'

'Oh, good. I couldn't be sure. Sometimes strangers ring . . .' she said vaguely, while she inspected Maggie rapidly and keenly from head to toe. 'Is your cousin downstairs?'

'Barney, give a yell,' Maggie called.

'I'm down here,' Barney called up from the fifth-floor landing.

'Tell him to stay there.'

'It's OK, Barney. Just stay put.'

'My name is Polly,' P. Guildenstern said, unlocking the door but keeping the dog on the leash. 'Please come in.'

'Oh, how wonderful.' Maggie stood stock-still, astonished by the large skylight that let a flood of late-afternoon sunshine into what was clearly a studio. 'You're an artist.'

'I paint miniature portraits.'

'What do you paint on?'

'I use vellum, or what passes for vellum laid on card—what does this have to do with the room?'

'Nothing, I was just interested,' Maggie explained, peering across the studio at a work table.

'You may take a look at the room now.'

'Does that mean you think I look like a suitable person?'

'Fairly suitable,' Polly Guildenstern said with a considering sniff, walking down the hallway and unlocking a door. 'It's stuffy,' she apologised, throwing open both of two barred windows, 'but of course I keep these locked when there's no one here. You can't be too careful.'

Maggie looked around. A canopied four-poster bed, hung with rather tattered pale blue and white damask, dominated the room. The walls were covered with an old floral paper in dim but still-gay yellows on white. Elegant floral fabrics, some satin, others taffeta and silk, were draped over two French armchairs, made three skirts of different lengths on a round table, and were used freely as draperies at the windows. A patched floral rug covered the floor. Nothing matched, everything had mellowed into shades of faded pastel, and everything went together. It was like stepping into an illustration from an old book of fairy tales.

'Oh, it's heaven!' she gasped.

'There's a closet and a small but complete bathroom. Would you like to look at it?'

'Oh, yes, but there's no place to cook.'

'So it would seem. But nothing is quite what it seems, don't you find?' Polly asked, drawing back a four-panel screen painted with vines and revealing a compact little kitchen.

Picking up a nest of plastic measuring spoons, Maggie burst into tears. She couldn't stop sobbing once she'd started, and she sat on the floor and cried her heart out.

'Not the spoons?' Polly asked, giving her a box of Kleenex.

'No,' Maggie gulped, and dissolved into fresh tears.

Polly sat on the bed and let Maggie recover herself slowly.

'I'm sorry,' Maggie finally was able to say. 'I've had a tough day and it all hit me at once. And it's my birthday, on top of everything. I'm eighteen.'

'I'm twenty-six, and you need a cup of tea.'

'Oh, yes, please.'

'Is two hundred dollars a month all right?'

'Am I suitable?'

'Absolutely. But first we have to talk. Come back to the studio and I'll make tea.'

Maggie sat quietly, after repairing her make-up, while Polly boiled water and measured tea leaves into a pot.

Polly, she observed, was wearing a white cotton dress she must have bought in a vintage clothing store, covered with a pinafore made of a sprigged material that she was certain must be called dimity, although she wasn't sure what dimity was. White ballet slippers and a locket round her neck completed the outfit. Passing strange, Maggie thought, but strangely suitable.

'You see,' Polly said, passing the sugar in a silver bowl, 'I'm a lesbian. It's only fair to let you know.'

'I don't care, one way or another,' Maggie told her truthfully, trying not to look too surprised.

'Still, you might reasonably wonder if I am attracted to you. That's why I put "no tattoos or body piercing" on the notice. I only like my own gender when they are tattooed and pierced. Not that it has to be evident at first glance. I have a weakness for black leather and boots . . . on others. As I said, nothing is quite what it seems. You're a very pleasant-looking girl but simply not my type—I'd never rent to my type.'

'That sounds . . . sensible.'

'I learned that the hard way. She broke my heart.'

'Did it mend?'

'Oh, yes, many times,' Polly giggled deliciously. 'I have all the virtues except fidelity.'

'Oh, my God. Barney! He's still waiting! I'd forgotten him.'

'I take that to mean your cousin is the faithful type?'

'Madly faithful.'

'Well, let's offer him a cup of tea, in that case. Go tell him to come up.' Polly called her dog. 'Stay, Toto,' she ordered him.

'Toto!' Maggie whirled round.

'Don't dare laugh.'

'Barney,' Maggie called, 'you can come up now.'

'About time,' he growled, mounting the stairs two at a time.

'Polly, this is Barney Webster. Barney, this is Polly Guildenstern and this . . . this is Toto.'

Barney looked around the studio, shaking his head in wonder. 'This place is great! Have you been here long?'

'About five years. Would you like a cup of tea?'

'Yes, ma'am,' said Barney. 'So, have you two worked things out?'

'We've covered the necessary ground,' Polly said with her lilting giggle. She handed Barney a cup. 'I believe you wanted to check me out.'

'It's not important,' Barney said hastily. 'You look very . . . ladylike . . . I mean, proper and nice, very nice.'

'Thank you,' Polly replied. 'Now, in what way are you two cousins?'

'Well . . .' Barney hesitated. 'It's sort of complicated. My dad's step-brother was married to Maggie's sister, before he died.'

'Hmm . . . then you're not really cousins?'

'But we were brought up together,' Maggie said hastily, as she felt the blood rise to her cheeks. 'When we were little, that is.'

Polly's keen glance travelled from Barney to Maggie and immediately comprehended the essentials of their relationship. She smiled gently to herself. Very sweet, she thought, and harmless. Straight people were so simple to figure out.

'Barney, Polly's an artist,' Maggie said hastily, following the speed and import of Polly's sweeping appraisal. 'She paints miniature portraits on vellum.'

'No kidding?'

'Some day I'll show you some of my favourites,' she promised.

'Great! Maggie, I'll go and get your suitcase.' Barney put down his cup. 'Then we can go out for dinner.'

Six

'MAGGIE, XEROX ALL THESE papers, file them, give the originals to Miss Hendricks, bring me two boxes of large paper clips and three packages of little Post-its, get rid of that stale bagel, empty the coffee machine and refill it, then report on the double to Mr Rexford in Coins. He has some work for you that has to be done immediately.'

'Yes, sir.' Maggie hastened to the Xerox machine, anxious to get these tasks for Mr Jamison of Animation Art out of the way so that she could go downstairs to Coins, whose immediate neighbours were the departments of Tribal Art, Arms and Armour, and Collectibles. Collectibles was her personal favourite of the fifty-nine different departments at the venerable auction house of Scott and Scott, and one into which she never failed to cast an eye, no matter how rushed she was.

In her three months working as a temp, Maggie had never had a job she found as interesting, confusing and overwhelming as this one. Collectibles charmed her because it was sometimes possible to see, through a half-closed door, the resident expert inspecting the great varieties of objects people brought in to Scott and Scott to find out if they could be sold at auction, objects that had included dolls, stuffed animals, corkscrews, croquet sets, farmers' tools, sports equipment and antique toys.

The Monday after she'd moved into her room in Polly Guildenstern's apartment, Maggie had looked in the Yellow Pages under employment agencies and made an appointment with the largest one that listed temporary help. With her computer skills and her absolute willingness to do anything, no matter how lowly, she'd hoped she'd find no trouble getting jobs, and she'd been right. Now, at Scott and Scott, she felt a sense of opportunity, a possibility that she might have fallen into a job that could last for a while, because the auction house operated with as small a permanent staff as possible.

Scott and Scott, although considerably smaller than Sotheby's or Christie's, was a global auction house with thirty-nine offices in twelve countries. It held several hundred auctions a year, and only a larger and more computer-savvy staff could have managed to keep up with the workload, Maggie noticed as she raced around, hailed by dozens of harried people who needed her help *immediately*. The constant calls of 'Maggie, I need you over here' gave her a feeling of identity that helped to combat the adjustment she was slowly making to living on her own and being completely responsible for herself.

It helped enormously that Polly so often invited her to share the savoury stews she cooked so well. It helped to know that Barney was nearby if she needed him, but she couldn't seek his company in the familiar framework of their former friendship, because the discovery of their mutual passion had blocked them from being alone together.

Maggie took comfort where she could find it, however. It helped that she had acquired the outward persona of a New Yorker. She soon realised that if she dressed in black from head to toe she could blend into the local look at any level. Afternoons patiently chasing bargains in the bazaars of the Lower East Side had yielded two black miniskirts, one wool, the other leather; black sweaters; an ankle-length black wool coat; a wide black belt; tall, black, low-heeled boots; and opaque black panty hose, all for less than $100. For another ten dollars Maggie had bought herself long, vivid mufflers in bitter orange, sulphur yellow and screaming green, and she parted reluctantly with twenty dollars for a pair of small, sterling silver hoop earrings that went with everything.

Too much hair, she'd decided, looking at herself in the mirror, and she'd taken herself off to a cheap drop-in barber shop and had had it cut defiantly short. Maggie's only make-up was black mascara and bright red lipstick, her only beauty aid Pond's Cold Cream. When she had finished putting herself together, the aggressive flag of a knotted muffler flying behind her as she dodged traffic, Maggie became a very primer of a New York career girl, the crackling blue of her eyes and the vivid pink and white of her complexion so enhanced by their crisp black frame that she looked like a piece of walking pop art.

Still and all, she was lonely. She could not allow herself even to think about Tessa. That was a closed subject. In any case, what had Tessa ever been to her but a few postcards and an occasional visit to an unreal world? She was better off without her. No, Maggie decided, the reason for her loneliness must be that she regretted, more than she wanted to realise, the plans she had made for college.

Being a temp, even at a world-famous auction house, was a far cry from being a freshman at a great university, she thought as she went to wash out the coffee machine. To her irritation she saw that there was a very tall man blocking the sink. He wore an ancient tweed jacket and baggy grey flannel trousers.

Maggie planted herself behind him, tapping her nails on her empty coffee maker, hoping that the noise would alert him to the fact that the sink was not a place of meditation. He had, she saw, dismantled another coffee maker and spread its pieces over all the available surface.

'Missing something?' she finally asked, as he showed no sign of doing anything but stare helplessly.

'Yes, as a matter of fact, I'm missing any notion of what to do with this damn thing.'

'I'll do it,' she said impatiently. 'Couldn't you have asked a temp?'

'I'm a floater, I'm not supposed to bother a temp,' he answered, turning gratefully and peering down at her through his glasses. She was as appetising, as fresh, as tasty looking as a nectarine at its moment of perfect ripeness.

'A "floater"?' Maggie asked, bending over the sink. 'You mean there's something lower than a temp?'

'A temp, they told me, has to have real skills; a floater . . . floats, drifts, levitates . . . to wherever there's assistance needed, selling catalogues, moving stuff, cleaning stuff, making coffee, but silently, without creating undesirable noise.'

He nattered on deliberately, his object to engage her attention for as long as possible. 'My brief, as I understand it, is to act swiftly, silently, helpfully, unquestioningly, above all, *floatingly* . . . I'd be more, a great deal more specific, but this is my first day here.'

'So you didn't go to college?'

'I have a master's in Fine Arts from Harvard, a degree from Business School, also Harvard, and a year studying at the V&A in London,' he admitted ruefully.

Stunned, Maggie looked up at this overeducated moron.

'The V&A?' she asked curiously, as she took inventory of the tall young man with a lot of fine red-brown hair that badly needed cutting, big hazel eyes that were really interested in her for some reason, a two-day growth of reddish beard that needed shaving, a long but handsome nose, horn-rimmed glasses and a large, well-shaped mouth.

'The Victoria and Albert Museum. They have a programme that's almost a necessity for people like me . . .'

'People like you?'

'Ceramic and porcelain people.'

'You sound fragile,' she laughed, giving him the reassembled, refilled coffee maker. 'My name's Maggie Horvath.'

'I'm Andy McCloud,' he said, offering her a large, warm hand.

'Andy!' A secretary scurried up behind them. 'For Pete's sake, will you bring that damn coffee! A whole meeting on Musical Instruments just walked into my boss's office.'

'Got to go. If I take you to dinner will you show me how to make coffee?'

'Dinner?' Maggie asked, surprised at this abrupt invitation from a stranger.

'Tonight, meet you after work.' He dashed off, almost dropping the full coffee maker in his hurry.

She had a date, Maggie thought excitedly. Her first real date! Andy McCloud, wordy, messy, incompetent, and surprisingly attractive floater, had asked her for dinner. It would be wonderful to make a new friend.

'Well, here's the choice. We can go back to my place and you can show me how to make coffee over drinks, or we can have drinks and dinner first, and then have the coffee lesson,' Andy McCloud said, after he and Maggie met at the employees' entrance to Scott and Scott.

'If I didn't know that you really can't make coffee, I'd say that was the best way of getting a girl up to your place that I've ever heard of.'

'I suppose a girl like you has good reason to be suspicious of every man she meets.'

'And what kind of a girl is that?'

'A sophisticated New Yorker who gets hit on—I believe that's the correct phrase, is it not, or is it dated?—by every man who sees her.'

'How perceptive of you. You've described me perfectly.' Maggie beamed at him.

'Which shall it be?'

'Drinks and dinner first. You see, I never actually promised to teach you how to make coffee. I only sounded surprised that you wanted to have dinner.'

'So you did,' he said, remembering their exchange. 'I've been presuming on your good nature.'

'Without knowing a thing about me except that I had to get you away from that sink so I could use it.'

'But you see, you don't look like a person who would refuse to impart vital, job-related knowledge. You look essentially good and kind, as well as frighteningly luscious,' he said, tucking her arm under his and rapidly walking in the direction of 3rd Avenue.

'Here we are,' Andy said, whisking her inside a dim cave of a small bar. 'This is an old-time place, no innovations, no happy hour, no television, just a jukebox that doesn't work. Now, what are you drinking?'

'Dry sherry, please.' Madison always drank that, Maggie thought. It must be proper. She pulled her arms out of her coat and placed it beside her in the booth. The lack of bright lights in the bar didn't prevent every man within sight from observing her with close attention. Maggie in her unadorned black sweater, Andy thought, was almost unbearably juicy: a girl with big breasts who didn't flaunt them, and wasn't coy about them, just let them stand at attention and speak eloquently for themselves.

'Joe, the lady will have Tío Pepe and I'll have Absolut on the rocks. Maggie,' he said invitingly, 'this is the kind of place in which people tell each other the high points of their lives, so I'll let you go first.'

'I have no intention of telling an almost perfect stranger my life story. I'd have to know you much better,' Maggie said, trying for a tone of composed, worldly aloofness.

'Quite right. Reveal nothing until you know to whom you're speaking. So, about me. You already know my education and what I do. Born and bred right here on the East Side of Manhattan, the usual two parents, one older sibling, female, several cousins, all female, usual youthful traumas, two engagements, five unhappy romances, currently completely unattached.'

Maggie giggled. 'You used more words describing your job as a floater than you did in telling me your life story.'

'I was stalling for time, trying to figure out how to ask you for dinner without seeming too abrupt, but I couldn't quite figure out how to do it.'

'You managed quite well. Now, what about those engagements?'

'Broken by mutual consent.'

'Why?'

'General immaturity.'

'Ah, I see.' She sipped her sherry carefully. Her fingers itched to take off his glasses and get a better look at his golden-brown eyes. Did he have long lashes? . . . Impossible to tell.

'Well, I'm still young,' Andy said. 'There's time to find the right girl. I'm just twenty-seven.'

'Twenty-seven and only a floater!'

'You have to start somewhere.'

'What do you want to be when you finally grow up?'

'An expert, of course.'

'In ceramics and porcelain?'

'That would be the basic idea,' Andy McCloud replied, repressing a smile, thinking of his many intense years of specialised education. Maggie had great natural dignity but he'd bet she wasn't much more than twenty-one. 'Now, may I hear a little about you, Miss Horvath, or do you have more questions?'

'Parents dead,' Maggie answered promptly. 'No siblings, brought up by distant connections, no money for higher education, no engagements, currently unattached.' She copied his telegraphic style; it was ideal for leaving out things she didn't intend to talk about.

'Elementary school?' he probed, finding her unnecessarily mysterious. From her account she could be an alien. Yet everything about her—her body language, her accent, her gestures, her attitudes revealed a girl of a class he recognised, the class he belonged to.

'Just a little country school.'

'And how long have you been a temp?'

'Oh, quite a while.' Maggie's tone indicated a long, interesting and varied career.

'What did you do before that?' he asked, determined to get some concrete detail out of this girl who was growing more maddening and more alluring by the minute.

'I was a journalist, but I didn't think I had a future in it.' Considering that it was a high-school paper, that was certainly true.

'What about love affairs?'

'None of your business,' she answered. Barney didn't count as a romance; he was her oldest friend, an impossible partner in lust and confusion. 'Is the inquisition over?' she asked.

'My God, I have been giving you the third degree, haven't I? It was rude of me. I apologise. How about another sherry? Or are you starving?'

'Oddly enough, no,' Maggie said, coming to a decision. 'What I'd really enjoy is . . . is . . . a cup of coffee.'

'Joe, check please, right away.'

They took a taxi to a building off Madison Avenue. Could Andy possibly still live at home with his parents? Maggie wondered as they strode quickly through the handsomely appointed lobby to the elevator.

'It's rent-stabilised,' he told her, reading her thoughts as he unlocked the door. Inside she just had time to gain an impression of wood panelling and walls of bookcases before he turned her round and took her in his arms.

'May I?' Andy McCloud asked, bending his head to try to look into her eyes.

'Only if you take off those glasses,' Maggie answered, doing it for him as she spoke, trembling with eagerness.

'Oh, Maggie, are you real?'

'Try me,' she whispered, reaching up and twining her arms round his neck so that she could easily reach his lips. Yes, she thought, as he kissed her over and over again, as firm on his feet as a tree, oh, yes. She half-closed her eyes as she let him lead her into another room and sit her down on the edge of a bed. She pulled off her boots and her panty hose, and lay back of her own accord, squeezing her eyes tightly shut. Who would have guessed that he had such demanding lips? she wondered. Who would have expected him to be lying naked next to her so quickly? Who would have imagined that he could strip off her clothes so adroitly, a man who couldn't even assemble a coffee maker?

'Maggie, aren't you ever going to look at me?'

'No, not yet.'

'Why not?'

'Because I want to be surprised,' she whispered, pulling his head down to her breasts. The contrast between the silky hair she twisted between her fingers and the rogue scrape of his beard as he concentrated all his attention on her breasts with a controlled but unmistakably violent hunger, a hunger that announced that he was in no hurry to satisfy it, told her that she had to do with a man, not a boy.

His mouth was deliberate and crafty, brushing her nipples only long enough to promise further attention, while he knelt on either side of her body and raptly marvelled at the whiteness of her breasts and the perfection of their form. Each time he imprinted his hard mouth on them he left a mark that receded slowly, so that soon both her breasts wore a rare and rosy flush, while her nipples, all but untouched, filled and stood erect in circles of deepest pink, their tender surfaces stretched upwards in a way that begged for the easement of his tongue.

Too soon, he thought, too soon. She had run the show so far, but now the power was in his hands and he chose to grasp her hips even more tightly between his knees and let his mouth drift, slow kiss by slow kiss, away from her breasts and down the fragrant skin of her torso, almost at random, ignoring her attempts to stretch upwards towards his mouth. She wanted to be surprised and he vowed to himself to do his best.

Now that Andy's head was too far away for her to grasp his hair, Maggie stretched out her arms and caressed his shoulders, revelling in the solid forms of his tense muscles and the vigorous tufts of hair under his arms. Her mouth was dry with desire, her lips open with an unuttered plea, when suddenly she felt him elude her touch as he moved downwards on the bed, holding her thighs apart with his elbows, his hands stern and commanding as he opened her wide, parting her dark pubic curls far enough to bury his tongue between her legs.

She held back a scream, panting, almost holding her breath. She'd read about this, dreamed of this, but the reality and the dream had nothing in common. The warm roughness of his artfully pointed tongue meeting the delicate concavities of her body was far wilder and more arousing than anything her imagination could have created. She listened with all of her senses as his lips and teeth joined his tongue, fastening themselves on the distended, hard, secret arrow only Barney had ever touched. Maggie was utterly silent. Only the muffled sound of his sucking existed until, soon, with a shriek, she came with a series of acute, frenzied spasms that arched her body high off the bed.

Not until she lay almost quietly, but still shivering, did he push himself into her with exquisite carnal precision, seeking his own sure pleasure without hurry. Abruptly he stopped, startled at the resistance he met. 'Maggie? Maggie?' He pulled away.

'Yes,' she sighed, smiling to herself.

'Jesus, Maggie! You're a virgin!'

'I told you . . . none of your business . . .' she breathed languidly.

'But . . .'

'Please,' she murmured, sliding down on the bed, tilting her pelvis upwards, urging him back towards her, and rubbing one finger shamelessly on the base of his spine, 'don't stop now, I couldn't bear it.'

'**W**here's a temp? I have to have one desperately! Somebody, find me a temp!'

Maggie looked up from the Xerox machine to see Lee Maine, the head of the press office, standing in front of the elevator doors.

'I'm a temp,' she said, leaving the machine. 'What can I do for you?'

'Man the battle stations! This is ridiculous! I have to go to Philadelphia in ten minutes to work on the American Primitives sale and there's nobody in my blasted department! My second-in-command had a premature baby over the weekend, I still haven't replaced the little traitor who defected to Sotheby's last week, and my last remaining assistant just called in sick with flu! Damn all three of them! Now listen closely. I want you to sit in my office and answer phones, take messages, tell one and all I'll be back tomorrow. If anybody in this place tries to get you to do something else, anything at all, tell them Lee Maine said she'd strangle you with her bare hands if you so much as left the desk. And while you're at it, take a look at the piles of work on the other desks. Maybe you'll find some little thing you can to do between calls, but don't leave the office, on pain of death. That phone must be answered! We live by the phone!'

'Got it, don't worry. Do you want me to call you with messages?'

'Good God, no, don't tie up the phone lines. I'll be back tomorrow. And you'd damn well better be there,' she warned. Lee Maine belted herself into a long red coat, jammed a black astrakhan hat on her head, and, pulling on her long gloves, took off without another word, leaving Maggie to find the press office.

Within five minutes she'd settled herself at one of the three assistants' desks and started eagerly going through the various auction catalogues she found lying there. She soon realised that many of the sales coming up, according to the dates on the catalogues, were unaccompanied by any sort of press release. Memos, all begging for releases, were tucked into many of the catalogues.

Did Lee Maine have any idea what an unholy mess her department was? Maggie wondered, as she bent over a computer. If some of these releases weren't written at once, they risked appearing only a week or so before the sales involved.

In her days running the school paper at Elm Country Day, Maggie had been accustomed to putting out the paper almost single-handedly, writing everything from humourous columns to thoughtful editorials. She found a file of old press releases and quickly realised that there was no mystery to them. She could write as well as or better than the sample releases, she thought, grinning to herself.

In spite of frequent phone interruptions, by lunchtime she'd finished the work on one desk and started on the second, finding a floater to bring her a sandwich and a secretary to sit by the phone while she made a hurried visit to the ladies' room. By nine at night, Maggie had finished every press release that had been left undone on all three assistants' desks, printed them out on the laser printer, and stacked them in a pile on Lee Maine's desk, each attached to the relevant catalogue. Next to them she put the dozens of phone messages that had arrived during the day.

The next morning she was sitting primly at one of the desks outside Lee Maine's office when the press office head arrived, in a flurry of questions. 'Who called? Any emergencies? Did you find anything you could manage to do?'

'Everything's on your desk,' Maggie said, biting her lip in nervousness. Had she presumed? Lee Maine disappeared into her office, closed the door behind, and stayed there for half an hour without buzzing. Suddenly she rushed out.

'What's your name?'

'Maggie Horvath.'

'Do you insist on being a temp?'

'Good God, no! My ambition is to be a galley slave.'

'Perfect. You're hired. Only don't work this hard or they'll cut my staff down to just you and you'll burn out at this pace.'

'What—what do I call myself if anybody asks?' Maggie ventured, electrified with excitement.

'Press officer for Scott and Scott.'

'*Press officer?* Oh, Miss Maine, thank you.'

'Thank me? I'm the lucky one. And call me Lee, everyone else does. When did you get here? At Scott and Scott I mean, not this morning, because you must have slept in the office last night.'

'I started last fall, in September.'

'Good grief! It's almost March—you've been a temp for more than five months. What's wrong with the people here?'

'Nobody ever asked to see what else I could do. Xeroxing has been my chief mode of self-expression. Sending a fax made my day.'

'Madness, sheer madness,' Lee Maine said in wonder. 'All right, Maggie, take these round to where they're needed and report back here. I've got to rush down to the sales rooms. Wait a sec, that still leaves nobody to answer the phones . . . well, find a temp somewhere, grab her, and make sure she stays here till one of us gets back.'

'Will do. What should I tell the personnel department?'

'That you've been promoted—no, make that hijacked, full time—that you're working for me now, exclusively, and they'd better find another temp to take your place.'

'Miss Maine . . . salary?'

'Whatever you've been making, plus twenty-five dollars a week and lots of free lunches. PR is about free lunches, among other things, including keeping this auction house going almost single-handedly.' Lee Maine disappeared with a wave.

Press officer, Maggie said to herself, *press officer*! Oh, yes! Polly would be thrilled for her. And Andy . . . Maggie, in her daze of delight, suddenly remembered Andy, still a floater. How would he feel?

She probably wasn't going to have a problem with Andy's reaction to her new eminence, she decided. He seemed quite content with his humble position. Yet she had to admit that his job was ten times more interesting than that of a temp. Since she'd known him he'd floated to Toronto, Mexico City and Los Angeles. 'They always need somebody to go out for pizza,' was Andy's standard comment when Maggie enviously asked him the details of his travels.

During the past few months, he'd been floating in the loftiest of departments, doing his vague, many-faceted, unimportant thing, what-ever it was, in the executive offices, which she'd never yet entered. She'd seen Hamilton Scott and Mrs Elizabeth Sinclair, the owners of Scott and Scott, from a distance and plagued Andy with questions about them, to which he only replied that they were "just plain pizza lovers only with more money".

Perhaps the reason he gave the impression of aimlessness, the reason he didn't take floating more seriously, Maggie thought, was that his true destiny was to work as an expert, and floating was only a matter of being able to call himself employed until he moved into a position in Porcelain and Ceramics. But how long would he have to wait? Now that she came to think about it, she didn't know Andy's timetable for success any better than when she'd first met him.

Tonight, since they hadn't seen each other for several days, Andy had been so ravenously intent on making love that she hadn't had a minute to tell him about her new job, Maggie realised, as she sat up in bed and watched him nap. If he didn't wake up soon she'd have to get up and scramble eggs or perish of hunger.

The depth of Andy's sleep began to irritate her seriously. Why were men so exhausted by sex that they had to restore themselves with a trip of unconsciousness? She'd never felt more alive! But how could she generalise about men when Andy was the only man she'd ever known intimately?

Andy had never actually said he was in love with her, but then she'd never told him she was in love either, Maggie brooded. The truth was that she didn't know if she was or not, her only yardstick for love was still Barney, and that was such a complicated, tormented, tangled web of emotion, that she couldn't compare it to anything but itself. Andy was charming, funny, whimsical, wonderful to look at, but . . .

Maggie lay back on the pillow, wondering if her black clothes were the right gear for a press officer. Twenty-five dollars extra wasn't enough to branch out into anything but one more piece of black, she decided, poking Andy gently. He turned over seeming to fall more deeply asleep. She buried herself under the covers and pulled his ears and blew on his eyes until she was satisfied that he was rising up out of the depth of sleep. She wasn't going to wait another minute to tell him her news.

'Andy, Andy, darling?'

'Yeah, yeah,' he mumbled, aggrieved. 'What time is it?'

'Dinner time. Listen, Andy, do you know who Lee Maine is?'

'Lee . . . great gal . . . think Uncle Hamilton . . . always . . . had sorta letch for her,' he yawned, still three-quarters asleep.

Maggie pushed him away, recoiling. '*Uncle Hamilton!*'

Shocked fully awake, Andy blinked at her. 'Did I say that?'

'You said that. Uncle Hamilton *who*, Andy?'

'Well, obviously . . . oh, shit!'

'If Hamilton Scott's your uncle, Elizabeth Sinclair's your aunt! You're some sort of Scott! How could you not have told me?'

'I didn't want it to influence you,' he replied, looking badly caught out.

'In what way?' Maggie demanded, hopping out of bed, pulling a robe around her and standing wrathfully against a wall as far as she could get from him.

'It was damn stupid but I thought it could have made you like me more, or less, depending . . .'

'I could have played up to you because of your connections? Don't you know me better than that?'

'Of course I do! Shit, Maggie, that's the last thing you'd do. You're the most emotionally honest person I know, but by the time I got to know you, I'd let it go so long I didn't know how to tell you. There never seemed to be an exactly right time.' He struggled out of bed with as much dignity as he could muster, wrapping a blanket around his waist. 'You can see the problem, can't you?'

'I'm very good at seeing exactly that sort of problem.'

'There are only a few people at Scott and Scott who know who I am: Lee and some of the department heads, and the head of the international office . . . people I've known practically all my life. My floater job has been a way of training me.'

'By going out for pizza?'

'Well, pizza was just a euphemism. I've actually been working my ass off learning the ropes. I need the practical experience of seeing how everything runs, from top to bottom, from the day a consignment arrives until it's sold and paid for. Eventually, unless I screw up big-time, I'll become head of Scott and Scott. It won't happen for many years, of course, but none of the other kids in the family wants to go into the business. Aunt Liz has two married daughters in California, with their own busy lives; both of Uncle Hamilton's sons are doctors; so that leaves me.'

'The porcelain and ceramic expert,' Maggie said flatly.

'That's perfectly true. There's no reason why an executive can't be an expert too. That's why I went to business school, so I'd have both kinds of training. Oh, come back over here, sweet, beautiful Maggie. Don't look at me as if I were a monster.'

'Is this apartment really rent-stabilised?' she asked, not moving.

'Yes, thank God. But I don't live on a floater's salary, I have what is known as a small but adequate private income.'

'Is there anything else I should know?'

'Well . . . yes.'

'Don't you think you'd better tell me?'

'Hellfire and damnation! Next month I'm going to Geneva.'

'For a sale?'

'No . . . for a year. Oh, Maggie, I can't help it, Uncle Hamilton made the decision. I'm going to be working directly under the head of the Geneva office, for upper-level training, and then I'm going to the London office for more of the same, another year or so, maybe more.'

'That's two things,' Maggie said. 'Maybe even three.'

'You can see that I intended to tell you everything. How could I leave for all that time without explaining why?'

'No, that would have been too much to lie about, even for you,' Maggie said, from behind the closet door where she was quickly getting dressed.

'I wasn't lying, Maggie! I just wasn't being straight with you!'

'You're playing with words.' She emerged, ready to leave, her sulphur-yellow muffler wrapped tightly round her neck, her eyes narrowed in disgust. 'You've lied every night we've spent together since you knew me enough to trust me. You would have kept on lying tonight if you'd been even half awake. Lies of omission, steady omission of the truth, is as much a lie as any other kind, Andy. Didn't you ever learn that at Harvard?'

'But Maggie, you can't leave, I'm crazy about you!'

'Were you planning on taking me to Geneva?'

'How could I? But I thought—'

'That it would be much easier to wait till the last minute and then just drop the bomb.'

Andy fell into a silence of admission while Maggie studied his face. No, she'd never been in love with him; how could she have ever wondered if she was? There was a strong physical attraction between them, nothing more. The hurt was in being lied to, but that particular hurt would always be the most painful, the most unforgivable one for her because of her past. Andy had behaved the way many men would when they want to keep a girl without making a commitment to her, and, in all fairness, she'd never asked for more, not so much as hinted.

'Andy, don't do this again to another girl. It stinks, it's beneath you, it isn't fair,' she said gently. 'But I owe you, so I forgive you.'

'Owe me? What are you talking about?'

'I owe you for a glorious, five-star, incredibly thorough and imaginative erotic education. It's going to be marvellously useful in the future. After all, Andy, remember: you were my first. I certainly never planned for you to be my one and only.'

'Oh, Maggie! Don't go!'

'Goodbye, Andy. I have to go out for pizza.'

Seven

W HEN SHE REACHED thirty-six, in August 1991, Tessa formed her own production company. There had been no lessening in the number of scripts offered to Aaron for her attention, but too many actresses were discovering that there were fewer roles for them as they approached forty for her to assume that the same thing wouldn't happen to her.

Although Tessa, in the most thorough inspection of her looks, still couldn't find any damage to her skin, her features, her hair, or her body, she knew that through some change behind her eyes, through some difference in her expression, she had changed vastly from the girl who'd started by playing Jo March in *Little Women*. She'd been in front of the cameras for twenty years and it showed in a million ways that no moviegoer could pin down but each one would recognise.

Fiona Bridges had been willing to join Tessa in the new production company in exchange for Tessa's commitment to do one film a year for the entity, leaving her free to make pictures elsewhere. To have this call on the services of a star as internationally adored as Tessa was vitally important to Fiona. As partner in Kent–Bridges Productions, she had taken two or three giant steps. Aaron Zucker had been retained to be business manager for the company, as well as continuing to serve as Tessa's agent.

'No full-frontal nudity,' Tessa stipulated, as they celebrated the formation of the new company.

'That the only no-no?' Aaron asked. 'How about hookers, addicts, abused women, serial murderers—that sort of thing?'

'That's Oscar nomination material for any actress of my age.' Tessa giggled. 'If you can find a script in which, at some point or another, I'm committed to an institution, preferably maximum-security, where I don't wear make-up, have no costume changes, and never get my hair washed, it's almost a sure thing. However, there's got to be a white phone in my cell.'

'And Fred Astaire takes you out dancing once a week,' Fiona murmured, 'and they let you wear your jewellery.'

'Fiona, darling, you've always understood me,' Tessa remarked lightly, wondering what Fiona would say if she knew that since Luke's death she'd continued to buy herself extraordinary jewels on many of the special occasions he had observed, spending princely amounts of her enormous wealth on what had become a necessary part of her life. She owned so many treasures that there wasn't an important jeweller who didn't notify her when a truly exceptional gem came into his hands. She had progressed from a woman who merely wore the jewellery a man gave her to a woman who was considered a serious private collector.

Kent–Bridges's first success had been a film in which Tessa played a lawyer defending a character played by Bruce Willis on murder charges. The picture owed fully as much credit to Willis's splendid performance and the chemistry between them as it did to her own performance, but his salary had chewed deeply into their profits.

Now, a year later, in the fall of 1992, not long after Tessa turned thirty-seven, she had set her heart on making a film in which the meatiest part belonged to her.

'Aaron, have you finished the biography of Lady Cassandra Lennox?' she asked impatiently.

'Considering that it's nine hundred and ninety-seven pages long, I'm proud to say I finished it last night. That's over three hundred pages a day and my wife's ready to leave me. Again. I've been reading till two in the morning.'

'Well?'

'Hey, I didn't think women could get away with that sort of stuff back in Queen Victoria's time. No wonder she was considered the most scandalous woman of her era. All those lovers, all those little bastards she popped out so easily, all that travel from one court of Europe to another, all that stealing other women's husbands—who wouldn't admire a dame like that?'

'But did you find out about the rights?' Tessa asked impatiently.

'I sent you a memo on it this morning. The guy who wrote it, Dr Elliott S. Conway, flatly refuses to sell. To anybody. He's had a heap of offers. Dr Conway maintains that Hollywood would only sensationalise Lady Cassandra, turn her into something she wasn't, leave out the important things she stood for. He spent seven years researching her life and he says there's no way he'll allow anyone to turn it into a two-hour movie. He wants people to read every page of the entire book.'

'That's ridiculous. How could Cassandra be shown as more sensational than she really was? And nobody refuses a movie deal,' Tessa said, more amazed than irritated.

'He doesn't appear to be aware of that. The guy's a history professor at

Columbia, with a major ivory-tower attitude.'

'I've got to meet him,' Tessa said resolutely. 'I *have* to play Cassandra. It's *my* part, and that's all there is to it. Aaron, can you arrange it through his agent? I'll fly to New York any time and meet this absurd professor.'

'What if he won't take a meeting?' Aaron asked.

'Tell his agent I'm a devout fan and all I want to do is buy him a drink, tell him how brilliant and wonderful his book is, and get my very own copy autographed.'

'What if he doesn't fall for that line of sickening bullshit?'

'Oh, Aaron, you've been around me so long you take me for granted,' Tessa sighed. 'If he's any kind of man he'll want to meet me.'

'I'll give it my best shot,' Aaron said, repressing a groan.

Two weeks later Tessa waited in a bar far uptown on the West Side near Columbia for Dr Elliott S. Conway, who was, at this point, half an hour late. He'd declined to come downtown to have a drink at the Carlyle Bar, or in her suite, because, as he put it, he had severe limitations on his time. He could at least have the courtesy to be prompt, Tessa fumed, tired of pretending to be engrossed in a copy of *The Life of Lady Cassandra Lennox* while avoiding making any eye contact in a bar jammed with men who were staring openly at her. She couldn't remember the last time she'd been in a bar by herself, Tessa thought. Had she ever done so?

She'd prepared herself for this meeting as carefully as possible. She'd had a burgundy suit designed which, without being in any way a costume, possessed a subliminal Victorian influence in its silhouette: a tightly laced waist, a full skirt, a wide-lapelled jacket that outlined her breasts and opened, at her throat, on a blouse of precious white lace. Round her neck she wore a dog collar of small pearls that clasped at the front with a cameo, delicate cameo earrings hung from her ears, and her dark hair was brushed into a highly modified version of a Victorian hairstyle, up off her neck and into a careful array of curls. Tessa was certain, as she left her hotel, that she'd stopped well short of looking over-the-top, but she hadn't reckoned on the uniform of blue jeans and baseball jackets that the local barflies wore.

Calm down, Tessa told herself. A man who habitually drank in a sinister gin mill like this wouldn't even notice clothes, wouldn't have the subtlety to realise that her eagerness to buy the rights to his book was emblazoned on her back.

'Let me see the book,' a man said, sitting down next to her, wearing a bulky leather jacket and corduroy trousers. As Tessa yelped in surprise, he took it away from her and laid it flat on the bar table, open to the halfway point. Then he flipped through the following chapters, quickly opening the book to certain pages, until he came to the end.

'Either you've really read it or somebody else has,' he said, extending his hand. 'I'm Sam Conway. Which was it? You or somebody else?'

'Me, of course,' Tessa answered, bewildered. 'What were you doing?'

'Checking. You can tell if a book really has been read. You open it in the middle and if it falls flat, the back's been cracked. Then you look for the signatures, folds of printed paper stacked on top of each other and glued to the backing, each one the same length, and you can see if they've been skipped or not.'

He was young and burly, a huge man, and he didn't fit her expectations of a dour, arrogant, ancient Herr Doktor Professor. With his long, tough, battered nose, the quirky, humourous light in his eyes, his capable big hands and his badly cut, untidy thatch of curly blond hair, shades lighter than his heavy eyebrows, he looked as if he needed to be on a horse, or on a small boat in a stiff breeze, Tessa thought, as she studied him.

'Why would I be here if I hadn't read the book?' Tessa asked.

'Someone could have read it for you and given you coverage—that's what they call a reader's report.'

Tessa laughed. She'd known what coverage was since she was sixteen. 'Aren't you going to give me a pop quiz? Cassie has no secrets from me that she didn't keep from you, Professor. And how come it's Sam and not Elliott?'

'Elliott's not my style. Samuel's my middle name. How come you call her Cassie?'

'That's my own private name for her,' Tessa answered. 'Lady Cassandra Lennox seemed too long after the first three hundred pages. I hope you don't mind.'

'I think of her as Cassie, too. A pisser, wasn't she?'

'A first-class pisser.'

'What are you drinking? Oh, by the way, sorry I'm late. A student tried to talk me into a passing grade and it took a long time to say no, and explain exactly why.'

'Why didn't you say yes and get here on time?'

'Can't do that,' he said, shocked. 'Where are your morals? So what'll it be?'

'Vodka straight up,' Tessa ordered, hoping that the alcohol might sterilise the bar glass, that notorious conveyor of germs.

'Jim, two Stolis straight up, very cold. Bring the lady a straw.'

'How—?'

'I read minds.' He grinned at her, with a flash of whimsical complicity Tessa was not accustomed to inspire in strangers. 'You don't exactly look at ease. This place may be humble but they do use a dishwasher. Still, you'll be happier with a straw.'

'Well, I admit, I didn't feel comfortable before you showed up,' Tessa said, opting for the charmingly frank approach. 'I've just realised that I've never been in a bar alone in my life, much less one where a mob of guys are staring straight at me.'

'Well, by showing up here, you just made me at least four hundred bucks.'

'What?'

'I said I'd bring Tessa Kent in for a drink and everybody bet me five bucks apiece I couldn't do it. That's why they're all checking you out, making absolutely sure I'm not pulling a fast one, as if a Tessa Kent lookalike could possibly exist. I guess they want their money's worth.'

'My God, how *old* are you!' Tessa exclaimed.

'Thirty-eight.'

'And still playing fraternity house tricks?'

'Why not?'

'But you're a full professor, you have a doctorate in some deeply meaningful subspecies of Victorian history, you've written a great, great book. Aren't you too old to—?'

'Soul of a teenager. That's what my wife said.' He shook his head rue-fully at the memory.

'Wife?'

'Ex-wife. I couldn't get rid of the soul.'

'How many wives?'

'Only one, long gone. I was much worse in my twenties.'

'Children?'

'Nope. You?'

'No one.' Her fingers fluttered all complications away. 'Fancy-free.'

'Soul of a teenager?'

'I grew up fast, at fourteen. I never had time for one.'

'That's too bad,' Sam Conway said seriously. 'You missed something wonderful. But it's never too late. Hang around me, you'll see: it's catching.'

'I'd like to hang around you,' Tessa said, taking the plunge resolutely. 'I'd like to play Cassie.'

'Well, of course you would. That's why you're doing a most wonder-fully subtle impression of that ravishing creature in her prime. But I don't want to sell the rights to the book.'

'Sam, look, you may be immune to money but don't you realise how many people will be exposed to the story of Lady Cassandra Lennox if a film's made? You're not being fair to her. A movie would make Cassie a household word, all over the world, with millions of people seeing the film when it's released two years from now at a time when they've practically stopped buying the book. That means a major return trip to the paperback best-seller lists. Then, every time the movie is run on television, more multiples of millions of people will watch it. And a percentage of them will go right out and buy the book and read it for the first time. Why do you think *Gone with the Wind* is still in print?'

'*Gone with the Wind* is the perfect illustration of what I don't like,' Sam said, turning so that he could look at her closely. Intensity darkened his dark blue eyes. The man filled the room, Tessa thought. He was off the wall, yes, but what presence he possessed! She could imagine him lecturing to a mesmerised classroom.

'Now *Gone with the Wind*, there was a book full of history, slanted towards the Southern point of view, I grant you, but still history, crammed with vivid research. The script included five per cent or less of the book. The Civil War was treated as a plot device, just enough to hold the romantic narrative together.'

'But there's no war in your book,' Tessa retorted passionately. 'It's not a true historical tome; it's the story of one real woman's amazing life, she's front and centre the whole time. She *is* the narrative, the spine of the story. Every page lives and breathes Cassandra Lennox. You wrote biography like a novel and now you're thinking like a historian.'

'And you're talking like an agent.'

'*I am not!*' Tessa glared at him in fury.

'Just kidding, take it back, wanted to see what you'd say,' he said, stumbling over his words at her rage. 'You're talking like an actress who's fallen in love with a part, aren't you?'

She sat in sullen silence.

'Well, aren't you?' he persisted. 'Yes or no?'

'True,' she snapped. 'Did any of the others talk to you like me?'

'No, it's all been agent-to-agent talk. I haven't gotten into it at all. I just keep saying no.'

'Shouldn't you be less rigidly academic, more flexible and, most of all, more thoughtful about the future of your work?' she prodded him.

'I played football to get through college, never had much of an academic attitude till I discovered history. Shouldn't you be more show biz, more snotty, more Hollywood?' His grin told her that he wasn't to be influenced easily.

'I hope you're having fun,' she said coldly.

'I am,' he said, looking pleased with himself.

'It must be ego-gratifying to have every major star in Hollywood wanting to play Cassie,' Tessa said.

'Not particularly,' Sam Conway replied slowly, suddenly sounding uncharacteristically bashful. 'What is ego-gratifying is that *you*, Tessa Kent, want to play Cassie. I kept seeing you as I researched and wrote the book. I know this sounds totally corny, but you've always been my favourite movie star. I wouldn't sell my book because I was saving it for you. But I wanted to see if you'd read it. *I wanted you to come to me.* My adolescent soul again, and my adolescent crush on you.'

'Oh.' She could only look at him, her lips parted in astonishment. He was blushing violently, but he held her gaze until she dropped her eyes.

'You know what?' he mumbled. 'Let's go ice-skating at Rockefeller Center, this minute. You're dressed just right. And we can tell our agents to make a deal tomorrow. Sound good to you?'

'I haven't ice-skated since I was sixteen,' Tessa stammered.

'Don't worry, I'm a whiz. I'll hold you up, won't let you go. Can't have Tessa Kent flat on her ass in front of her public.'

'Sam, I'll be a great Cassie, I promise you.'

'I knew that years before you did. Jim, put this on my tab and collect my winnings. So long, guys. Well worth losing five bucks, wasn't it?'

As they left the bar in a storm of applause, whistles and catcalls, Tessa thought that she knew what it felt like to have the soul of a teenager after all.

Maggie settled herself as comfortably as she ever could in a plane, and reflected thankfully that there was no one on the flight to present her with a birthday cake and wait for her to blow out twenty-three candles, no one who knew, as she returned to New York from Hong Kong, that this June day in 1993 was her twenty-third birthday.

She'd been gone two weeks, working the publicity mill for all it was worth. For a month preceding the trip she'd worked in New York with the Chinese wire services and the two English-language Hong Kong newspapers, as well as with journalists from the most important of the dozens of magazines that crowded the Hong Kong newsstands. Once there, she'd held a press conference attended by more than a hundred journalists. She'd organised every detail of the catering and flowers for the week-long exhibition and the actual sale, held in the Regent's largest ballroom. During the sale she'd dashed between journalists and the bank of phone bidders, finding out which purchasers were willing to let their names be used. She'd kept herself going on room-service scrambled eggs, tuna fish sandwiches, and long dawn and late-night swims with which she religiously released her tension in the Regent pool.

In addition to the commissions on the hammer price on the many millions achieved by porcelain, Chinese furniture, Chinese paintings, and the results of the jewellery sale—largely jade, watches, and the fancy coloured diamond so admired by the Chinese—she was returning with the 10 per cent commission on $1.7 million that had been paid for a rare and extraordinary fine jade necklace. A world record for Scott and Scott or any other auction house. The price of that necklace, in addition to the great success of the entire sale, had finally established Scott and Scott as a major player in Hong Kong.

Maggie sipped another glass of the champagne the flight attendant kept bringing her. Five years in the auction business, she was convinced, counted for more than fifteen years in any other job. Any press officer had to be prepared to be pushed, not just to the edge, but *over* the edge, totally and utterly consumed by the business at hand, and auction followed auction relentlessly.

As she'd advanced in the press department, she'd earned more money. It still wasn't much—public relations never paid well—but she managed to make her salary cover her brutal haircuts that were essential to her look, expensive panty hose that wore like iron and were a true economy, shoes she tended so carefully that they lasted for ever, and a very occasional replacement to her all-black wardrobe. By being fanatically careful about expenses, Maggie had managed to rent a cheap two-room apartment one flight down from Polly. It gave her the advantage of the increased privacy she now wanted and the reason to start buying at auction for herself.

Her apartment was, Maggie thought dotingly, as eclectic as you could get. It was still fairly empty, but everything in it mattered to her. She didn't entertain there and probably never would. Lunch almost always took place at a fashionable restaurant as, sometimes with Lee and sometimes alone, Maggie became friends with the many journalists a press officer needed to know: the ladies and gents of the art and antiques magazines, the fashion magazines, the general interest magazines, and the specialised magazines for collectors.

'May I offer you a little more champagne?' the flight attendant asked.

'Please,' Maggie said, holding out her glass. This stuff wasn't getting to her; she was still too high on the last two weeks to be touched by wine. She was the luckiest girl in the world, Maggie decided, as she drifted off to sleep.

On the first Saturday night in September 1993, just as business hours were ending, Maggie met Barney at Chopper Dude's, the custom motorcycle shop he'd opened with a well-financed partner several years earlier.

Maggie and Barney had reached an agreement never to talk shop. Even the brand names of the bikes competing in the Daytona 500 remained as foreign to her as the very existence of a Philadelphia Chippendale tea table remained to him.

'Take me out of this testosterone-as-a-lifestyle pit,' she demanded. 'I have something to talk over with you.'

'Where the hell have you been? I haven't seen you for months,' Barney complained as they walked down 9th Avenue.

'Working,' Maggie said briefly, mindful of their agreement.

'Working too hard to give me a quick call?' he asked, hurt.

'In Hong Kong,' she said tersely.

They turned off the noisy street into a little bar with pretensions to Barcelona chic and sat silently, waiting for their drinks, happy just to be together. Barney looked so much older than he was, Maggie thought, scanning his beautifully muscled body. A man now, a man to be reckoned with.

But it didn't matter how safe he said his beloved bikes were; she distrusted them all, not for anyone else, but only for him. How many women felt the same way? she wondered. She'd never understand the relationship of men and speed.

'So what's your problem?' Barney asked, finally. 'It can't be about your job so it's got to be about a guy.'

'It's not about a guy,' Maggie said slowly.

Relief washed over him. He'd dreaded the day she'd meet the right guy, dreaded it for years. No matter how good it might be for her and how inevitable he knew it was, how bound it was to happen in the course of her life, he honestly didn't know how he'd live through it.

He'd tried fruitlessly not to worry about it, but he'd never managed to forget the possibility every time he thought about Maggie, and that was often. How did she *dare* to get more luscious? It infuriated him! She'd slimmed way down—not that he thought she needed to—without losing her fabulous tits, and she'd accomplished some evolving and mysterious alteration of her black uniform, so that she resembled every other chic, unmistakably New York woman from the neck down. But Maggie's skin looked as if she spent her days in a rose garden near Connemara, wearing a sun bonnet. No woman in Ireland had eyes as blue, he was convinced, and certainly no one had ever managed to make hair so short into hair so sexy. Or have a laugh that gave every man in earshot a hard-on.

'If it's not about your job and it's not about a guy, you must want to buy a bike,' he said.

'Great guess, but just off the mark. No, Barney, believe it or not, it's about my future. I've had a job offer from another auction house, a much bigger house, at more money, with more opportunity.'

'Which one, Sotheby's or Christie's?'

'How'd you know their names?' Maggie was startled.

'Classic car and bike auctions.'

'And that's dumb of me, because of course we have them too, so I should have realised.'

'Well, which?'

'Sotheby's.'

'Why don't you want to take it?'

'I've thought and thought about it, and it keeps coming back to loyalty. Lee and Hamilton and Liz have just been so damn good to me. They've trained me, they've moulded me, patiently and with kindness. I love all of them.'

'I don't think you should consider moving,' he said with complete conviction.

'Why not?'

'Because you said you loved all of them. That's the best reason I've ever heard for staying put.'

'Hmm . . . I thought it was loyalty . . . but no, it is love . . . everyday love, basic love, just about the most important thing in the world. I knew I should ask you—Barney, what's that on your arm?'

'Nothing,' he said, hastily rolling down his sleeve.

'Show me,' Maggie demanded.

Sheepishly, he rolled his sleeve back, revealing the edge of a tattoo.

'Oh, for Pete's sake, not you too! Let me see that awful thing.'

'No.'

'Yes,' Maggie insisted, using both hands to yank the fabric almost up to his shoulder. A good-sized heart, pierced by an arrow appeared on his bicep, adorned with M on one side and B on the other.

'Oh,' she said and lapsed into silence. After a minute she asked, 'How many others do you have?'

'That's the only one. You can search my body if you don't believe me.'

'I believe you.'

'Happy Valentine's Day, retroactively.'

'Thank you, Barney,' Maggie said gravely, more touched than she was willing to admit.

'I'll never have another, you know that, don't you? And I wasn't drunk when I had it done . . . I'd wanted one for years.'

'I do know, I do, sweet Barney. You're such a romantic, aren't you? You'd ride off to war for me, you'd fight dragons for me, you'd jump into a pit of snakes and cut their heads off for me, wouldn't you?'

'Damn it, Maggie, you know I would,' he said passionately, fussing with frustration. 'I'd do anything in the whole wide world for you. I'd go into outer space for you, with or without a spacesuit, but unfortunately, that doesn't seem necessary right now. You're riding high.'

'So are you,' she replied absently, thinking hard. She had to deal with this . . . thing . . . about Barney sooner or later. It had been going on for five years; it stood in the way of her ever caring about another man, or even, if it came to that, wanting to care. And it wasn't sensible or healthy for Barney, either. That new tattoo proved that he hadn't forgotten, that he still cherished what he mistakenly thought were romantic feelings for her. Without them he'd have found other girls, and many of them, long ago. They'd both be happy if they weren't stuck in their shared past. As long as they remained inaccessible to each other, they'd remain slaves to their old fantasies. But a fantasy realised, a fantasy acted on, would be a fantasy no longer, just mundane reality that could be easily judged for its true value, and discarded, leaving them free.

'Maggie, you're a million miles away. Not still thinking about that job offer?'

'No, just . . . relaxing. It's Saturday night, remember? Date night.'

'Except that this isn't a real date; it's just the two of us,' Barney drawled wryly. 'Two old buddies, comrades in arms, pals for life, like a couple of leathery cowboys sharing a bottle for old times' sake, just as if you didn't know that I'm in love with you, more than ever. Fuck! I shouldn't have said that.'

'Barney . . . ?'

'What?'

'Oh, Barney, I don't know . . .' she sighed.

'Maggie, you? You always know. You're the one with all the answers about us. Right from the beginning. Not that I'm bitter; I just sound bitter. Oh, hell, so maybe I am a little bitter, who cares? I can live with it.'

'What if you didn't have to?'

'I'd be a happy man, but don't kid yourself; it's not gonna happen just because it makes you feel more comfortable to think it might. It's not your problem, Maggie,' he said brusquely. 'It's mine, don't worry about it.'

'But what if? . . . Barney, what if you could stop feeling bitter?' Maggie persisted. She sat up straight and looked him directly in the eye. She knew she was blushing, but she didn't care. This had to be said and said clearly. 'I'm talking about making love, you and me, the way we never did, and getting it out of our systems.'

'Is that . . . is that,' he asked carefully, 'what you really think would happen?'

'I'm sure of it,' Maggie answered, overcome by the rightness of her thought process. 'It's logical and it makes perfect sense.'

'Hmm. What if you got me out of your system but I didn't get you out of my system? What then?'

'Barney, remember how right I was before, that day when you left home? Even you had to admit that we couldn't make love then. Well, I'm right again. Now we can, now we're old enough,' Maggie insisted, made more stubborn and impetuous by his unexpected resistance. 'We both have fantasies about each other that have to be exposed to daylight, or they'll persist, or even get worse.'

'Let me get this absolutely straight, so I don't take advantage of your theory. You propose that we make love, in cold blood, so we won't moon around about each other any more?'

'Exactly,' she answered, her eyes shining with conviction. 'No more mooning, it's childish.'

'When and where?' he asked quickly.

'Tonight. The sooner the better. We could go to my place or your place, it won't matter.'

'You know you're nuts, don't you? Completely, absolutely nuts.'

'I've never been saner in my life,' she said urgently.

'Let's go to your place. Then I'll be the one who has to get up and go home afterwards, not you.'

'Fine.'

'Now?'

'Now,' Maggie said, with resolution, even though her mouth was dry and her feet were cold and she longed for him with her palms and her fingertips and she ached for him in the pit of her stomach and the back of her neck, it must be now because once it was over, once it was real, she wouldn't feel this unendurable need again.

Maggie woke up in the middle of the night, woke up completely, as if it were broad daylight, and knew, without a single doubt, that she had never had a happier minute since she'd been born. Everything in her life had led to the harbour of this bed in which Barney lay quietly sleeping on his back, an arm flung across one of her breasts. She felt as open and fertile as a newly planted field in spring, ravished, teeming with possibility, lying, rich and receptive, under the light of noon. She eased herself away cautiously so that she could turn round, lean on her elbow, and gaze at him in the dim beam of the streetlamp that filtered through her curtains.

He was the stuff of dreams, this man of hers, he was the pink-silver of a spring dawn, the honey of a summer afternoon, the moth-dreaming indigo of twilight. And if she hadn't been brilliant enough to prove that to herself, once and for ever, she might have missed understanding that he was the love of her life, and always had been, Maggie thought, suddenly terrified at her close call.

How many women had Barney conquered to make him into such a magnificent lover? she wondered. She suppressed a pang of jealousy. Neither of them should ever ask each other any questions about what they'd done while they were waiting for each other. The past no longer existed.

'Have we reached the part where we stop mooning about each other yet?' Barney asked sleepily, his eyes still closed.

'Oh, no, no, no, not yet.'

'Not ever? Promise?'

'Never, my love, *never*.'

It had been a year, Tessa realised, one whole year since she'd met Sam Conway. Her thirty-eighth birthday had come and gone with the end of the summer of 1993, but in her happiness she hadn't given a thought to something as unimportant as a birthday. Sam and she had been inseparable since that night they'd gone ice-skating.

She'd fallen in love twice in her life, both times at first sight. How many women had ever been that fortunate? The girl who'd known instantly that Luke Blake was the man for her had become a woman of thirty-seven, a woman who lived alone, a woman who'd learned to get through each day, forcing herself to *act* courageous until she became truly courageous. She had spent five years without Luke, years in which no other man had entered her consciousness.

And then Sam. Such a different man from Luke, this new love of hers. Sam was not a restless rover over the face of the earth. Sam, Tessa had discovered, was a contemplative man who found his deepest satisfaction in teaching and writing. His antic sense of humour, his essential boyishness, and his love of mischief masked the fact that he measured success by his own sure standards: delivering a good lecture, inspiring his students to ask thoughtful questions, finishing a chapter of his new book. Even one good page was enough to bring him deep pleasure.

They lived life at a slower, quieter pace than she'd been used to. Sam's work at Columbia had kept them in New York during the academic year. Over the summer they'd gone to seminars at Aspen and Berkeley, where he'd been a guest speaker, and she'd managed to get him to Los Angeles for a few weeks, long enough for Sam to get to know Fiona and Aaron as well as the brilliant script writer, Eli Bernstein, who was working ten hours a day turning *The Life of Lady Cassandra Lennox* into a film.

When the two men had met they'd liked each other immediately and plunged into a conversation about the psychology of Cassie that continued for days. Afterwards, Sam felt that he and Eli agreed entirely on what made Cassie tick. Even if he was going to have to use only the highlights of the book to make the script short enough to work for a movie, it would still be an epic film.

That script should be finished soon, Tessa realised, as she returned to her apartment in the Carlyle after a day of lazy shopping while Sam worked in his office at Columbia. She bought only casual clothes now for her new understated world.

Tessa's jewels, except for a few basic pieces, like her triple strand of pearls and the engagement ring she always wore, were put away in their bank vaults. She'd bought no new jewels. She'd gone to no auctions, looked at no catalogues. She'd utterly lost interest in the world of gemstones.

Nevertheless, Tessa clung to the existence of her jewels in memory of Luke's love and that major portion of her own existence that was embodied in them. Her jewels were the twelve years of her life with Luke; they were the personal collection she'd amassed to try to comfort herself after his death. In ways too complicated and symbolic for her to put into words, her jewels were an absolute extension of herself, Tessa recognised.

Occasionally, when Sam was teaching a late class and she found herself alone, she thought about them, visualising each piece safe in the shelter of its velvet box, and wondered how it would feel to wear them again in public. Had there really been a day when, wearing lilac satin and illuminated by a web of Fabergé diamonds, she'd presented an Oscar in front of the world?

Since she'd met Sam, Tessa had automatically refused all film offers, even those that would be shot in Manhattan, because she hadn't wanted to alter the rhythm of her new life with him. However, once Eli completed the script, and that shouldn't be more than a few more months, she'd have to go to the Coast for the casting process—Lady Cassandra's lovers demanded a full roster of strong leading men—and inevitably, a start date would be set. The locations of the film were all English and European. How many of them would require her to travel and how many interiors could be reproduced in Hollywood? she wondered. She was torn already between the prospects of a role she'd been born to play and a man she didn't want to leave, not for a day.

'Do you know anything better than Midol for cramps?' Tessa asked Fiona, towards the end of one of their frequent, coast-to-coast phone conversations about the progress of the script.

'Midol and gin,' Fiona answered. 'Why?'

'I've got them bad, really worse than ever,' Tessa said miserably, her brow wrinkled in pain.

'Haven't you seen your doctor?' Fiona questioned.

'Almost a year ago to get another prescription for the Pill, right after I met Sam. I figured I didn't want to get pregnant and have another miscarriage. I had my annual checkup then, but my cramps weren't bothering me all that much at the time.'

'This is what my mother did,' Fiona advised. 'She'd take three Midol, fix a glass of room-temperature gin and put it on her bedside table, wrap herself round a hot-water bottle, and tell the family to leave her alone. She was usually all right the next day. It's a well-known home remedy.'

'I can order some in a minute, from room service.'

'Well, take a good slug. Just remember to hold your nose when you swallow,' Fiona advised, 'and you should feel better soon. What about a hot-water bottle? As I remember, you don't have one.'

'I'll have them send to the nearest drugstore. Sam would go, but he's at Yale for a week, giving a seminar. I knew I'd get my period now so I didn't go with him.'

The next day Tessa, haggard and weak, answered Fiona's phone call.

'Well?' Fiona asked, anxiously.

'Now I have a truly hideous hangover on top of the cramps,' Tessa said. 'And I refuse to drink gin again, ever. It's poison. Your mother should be ashamed of herself.'

'Tessa, you've simply *got* to see your gynaecologist.'

'If she says warm gin, I'll be surprised. Home remedy, indeed!'

Dr Helen Lawrence, whom Tessa saw the next day, was a small, middle-aged woman with a pleasant manner, and she had the reputation for doing the most gentle pelvic exams in town. After Tessa dressed, Dr Lawrence invited her into her office.

'I'd like you to have an abdominal and pelvic ultrasound, Tessa. It's possible that you might have endometriosis. In any case, that's the first thing to rule out.'

'Endometriosis? What's that?'

'One of the most common causes of painful periods. Some of the uterine lining gets outside the uterus and develops implants, which bleed into the abdominal cavity.'

'Does the test hurt?'

'Ultrasound? Not in the slightest,' Dr Lawrence said, handing Tessa a card for an outpatient radiology facility.

'Does it take long?'

'No. I'll go ahead and make an appointment for you. There's a very good radiologist there, Dr Henry Wing.'

'Please, Helen, just let me know when. I want to get this over with before my guy comes back.'

'Miss Kent? It's Dr Wing.'

'Yes,' Tessa said anxiously. 'I've been waiting for your call. Do I have endometriosis?'

'No, there's no sign of it.'

'But there's got to be something!' Tessa exploded, as much in anger at not getting a quick answer as in fear at what no answer might mean.

'I do see some evidence of an enlarged pancreas, Miss Kent.'

'Is that the problem? Cramps from the pancreas?'

'No, there's no connection. I'd like you to go for a test called Computerised Tomography, a CT for short. While the doctor is at it, he'll do a CT-guided needle biopsy.'

'A . . . biopsy . . . ?' Tessa asked. 'A biopsy of what?' she asked, keeping her voice as level as she could make it. A flutter of confused apprehension began to rise in her stomach.

'Of your pancreas.'

'Why?' she demanded, fear of her fear making her sound bold.

'The pancreas is, as I said, enlarged. We have to find out why.'

'Oh, this is so typical! You go to a doctor for a pimple and the next thing you know he sends you to a leper colony! What if I don't choose to go, Dr Wing?'

'I think you should talk it over with Dr Lawrence, before you make any decision. I can only tell you what the ultrasound showed.'

'I certainly will! Goodbye, Dr Wing,' Tessa said, narrowly preventing herself from slamming down the receiver. It was natural and normal to feel apprehension about another of their damn tests, Tessa told herself, who wouldn't? One test always led to another, nothing ever had a simple answer. But mostly, she told herself, she was furious at the medical profession, every last one of them.

'Tessa, I want you to see one more doctor,' Helen Lawrence said calmly, after she'd learned the results of the CT and the biopsy. 'Her name is Susan Hill.'

'What kind of doctor is she?'

'A medical oncologist,' Helen Lawrence said quietly.

'An oncologist?' Tessa said, so stunned that she could feel her heart turn over in her chest. 'But . . . but Helen, an oncologist's a cancer doctor! Is that what you're suggesting? You know perfectly well I couldn't possibly have cancer. That's out of the question. How could I possibly need to go to a cancer doctor for cramps?'

'Your cramps are complicated. You need a doctor who knows more than I do,' Helen Lawrence replied, her voice firm.

'But a cancer doctor! That's insane! Why can't *you* handle my problem, Helen, why do you think I came to you? I don't want to see anyone else. Why are you handing me over to every damn doctor in this damn city?'

'Tessa, I know how you feel, but like it or not, you really need to see someone who knows more than I do,' Helen Lawrence insisted. 'I've made an appointment for you. Dr Hill will see you this afternoon. Fortunately she had an opening in her schedule. You'll like her, Tessa.'

'Oh, no doubt about that. I'll be crazy about her. I've always wanted to meet a medical oncologist.'

How could a cancer doctor be so wholesomely pretty, have such flaming red curls and look no more than thirty-eight? Tessa wondered, trying to distract herself as she sat in front of Dr Susan Hill's desk.

'Dr Hill, how long have you been an oncologist?' Tessa asked nervously, feeling as if she should be seeing a wise old man instead of this young woman.

'I've been in practice for twelve years, Miss Kent,' she said, smiling.

'May I call you Susan?' Tessa asked impulsively. She'd feel more comfortable if she didn't have to say 'doctor' every five seconds.

'Of course, in fact I'd prefer it. And I'll try to call you Tessa, even though that seems a bit like name-dropping.'

'Good. Why did you pick this particular specialty, Susan? How come you didn't want to be in something more agreeable—dermatology, for instance, or plastic surgery?'

'Because there's such immense progress being made in the field of cancer,' the doctor answered, an enthusiastic smile flashing across her face. 'It's the single most fascinating area of medicine today. This is where I can do the most interesting work and see real results.'

'So, tell me, what's wrong with me?' Tessa asked abruptly.

'I've studied the radiology and biopsy reports carefully.' The doctor's smile faded. 'They indicate a tumour of the pancreas.'

'A tumour—you mean a cancer?'

'Yes.'

Tessa felt death inhabit her body. Death, unmistakable. She closed her eyes and dropped her head, raking her hair back from her face with all the strength of her hands. She was going to faint, she thought dimly, through an icy mist.

'Put your head between your knees . . . Yes, that's it, way down. Stay like that and breath deeply, long, deep breaths. Take your time. Don't lift your head until you feel ready.'

Eventually Tessa fought through the mist and faintness. She fought the word 'death'. Cancer *wasn't* death; cancer was cancer and she could be cured of it. She felt the doctor's hands on her shoulders, steadying her.

'Where exactly is the pancreas?' Tessa asked lifting her head. Chemotherapy, she thought. Ten to one that's what she'd have to have, but her hair grew amazingly fast. If it all actually fell out, she could always wear wigs while her hair was growing back in. She was accustomed to wigs.

'Look at this chart, Tessa. Here's the pancreas, that transverse organ, that looks like a longish, horizontal piece of liver, thick at one end, thin at the other. It's surrounded by the duodenum here, the liver here, the spleen and the stomach. Your particular tumour is right here, at the thin end, where I'm pointing.'

'It's a nasty-looking organ,' Tessa said with as much bravado as she could. 'What's the purpose of it?'

'It's a gland that secretes pancreatic juice, a fluid made of different enzymes that help in digestion, and it also secretes insulin.'

'How important is it? Is it indispensable, Susan, like a heart or a liver?'

She was asking the right questions, Susan Hill thought, and going straight to the point. Tessa Kent was a smart, direct woman, making that serious effort certain patients were capable of to be thoroughly informed about something they've never before, under any circumstances, wanted to understand or even think about.

'No, it's not actually indispensable. There are some patients in whom the pancreas can be removed surgically. Then they can be maintained on artificial pancreatic fluid and insulin injections for the rest of their lives.'

'"Some patients"—do I need that operation, Susan?'

'No, Tessa, you don't. The only time to operate is when the tumour is confined to the pancreas. Yours is not. You see, one of the problems with this particular tumour is that it doesn't cause any symptoms, such as pain, in its early stages, so it's rarely discovered at a time when an operation is possible. You wouldn't have known you had it at this point if you hadn't gone to a doctor for other reasons.'

'So if Helen Lawrence hadn't sent me to Dr Wing . . .'

'Exactly: you couldn't have known yet.'

She only answered the questions a patient wanted to ask, Susan Hill thought. It was vital to let them set the pace of their tolerance for knowledge. No two patients were alike. They all had different comfort levels at which they could accept or permit themselves to learn things. Tessa Kent looked, from the brilliant determination in her extraordinary green eyes, as if she were going to keep on going right to the end. If that was her choice, she had every right to know as much as it was possible to tell her.

'You said the tumour isn't confined to the pancreas?'

'No.'

'Where did it spread to?' Tessa persisted.

'Certain lymph nodes close to the pancreas, the celiac nodes. Yours are enlarged, a sign that an operation isn't possible.'

'Well, you can't get rid of my pancreas. So that's one option I don't have,' Tessa said, squaring her shoulders. 'What *will* you want to do next? What treatments are available? Is it going to be chemo or radiation or a combination of both? What exactly are you planning to do to me?'

'I can't be "exactly" sure, until we talk it over. We have treatments for pancreatic cancer that will prolong life,' Susan Hill said carefully.

'Prolong . . . what the hell kind of word is that? It could mean anything! Look, Susan,' Tessa demanded, suddenly ferocious, 'say I take every single treatment you can throw at me, how long can I expect to be OK, after that?'

'That—that differs in each case.'

'*Damn it! Give me an average.*'

'Even if the treatments are successful, the tumour will eventually return—'

'How soon?' Tessa interrupted savagely.

'In a year and a half, perhaps two, perhaps a little bit longer.'

This was where they'd been heading, but most people would never come this far; most people would not ask such precise questions. Susan Hill felt sick. Nothing, no amount of experience, had ever hardened her to this moment.

'*So soon? So soon?*' Tessa whispered. Her features were stone, her eyes almost black with shock.

'Tessa, in medicine there aren't any hundred per cent guarantees, I can only give you my best opinion, but I could be wrong, nothing is an absolute . . .'

'Susan,' Tessa said desperately, 'wait a minute. Susan, you said, perhaps longer than two years. Tell me what's the longest I can expect to be OK if everything goes well, the treatments work out perfectly and I get very lucky.'

'It's an inexact projection. A little longer, a few months, perhaps even a little more . . .'

'And then? *What then?*'

'Tessa, there isn't a permanent cure for pancreatic cancer.'

'You mean that I have an *incurable* cancer? You're telling me that even all the treatment in the world won't make it go away?'

'Yes. Yes. Tessa, I wish I could say you were wrong but you're not. There are no miracles in this kind of cancer. I'm as sorry as it's possible to be. The most important thing I can offer you, Tessa, is a minimum of pain. The tail of the pancreas is where a tumour gives the least possible pain and most of that can be handled with narcotics. I believe in the most aggressive pain management possible.'

Tessa was silent, trying to think through the iron casque of shock that enveloped her and invaded her brain with numbness. Wasn't there something else she could ask, something that would give her some hope?

'Does everybody have treatment?' she asked, finally, barely able to offer the question.

'No, they don't. They decide they don't want treatment, they don't want the side effects, since, well, since it's not going to fix the problem permanently.'

'I see. If there's no "fix", Susan, the people who do choose to have treatment—why do they pick it?'

'Usually to be as certain as possible to be around for some special event, a child's graduation from college, for instance, or a grandchild's wedding or a golden wedding anniversary.'

'So . . . so. That means I must be . . . very young . . . for this.'

'You are. Extremely young.'

'Is there anything I don't know? I don't want to go home and remember some question I forgot to ask.'

'Tessa, I've almost never had a patient walk out of this office who asked every possible question, but you have. You know all the options.'

'You mean the lack of options, don't you?'

'This isn't one of the days I'm glad I went into oncology. I'm here for you, Tessa, for everything. Any questions, no matter how small, any fears, any medication, anything at all, at any time of day or night. That's my job. That's what I do. Will you let me know as soon as you've decided how you intend to handle matters?'

'Besides die, you mean.'

'I mean I'm here for you . . .'

'Thank you for being so honest with me.' Tessa got up carefully and forced a small smile.

'See you around, Susan.'

'Yes, Tessa. Whenever you want, remember that.'

Three hours after she had left Susan Hill's office, Tessa snapped out of a time period she would never rediscover in detail again, and found herself sitting in the Madison Avenue office of an unknown travel agent, about to sign an agreement to take a ninety-six-day world cruise that started in January in Los Angeles and crossed the Pacific going towards Hawaii and points west, following the sun.

'I'm sorry,' she babbled to the travel agent, trying to hide her confusion. 'I've just realised that I really can't take off ninety-six days. I'm so terribly, terribly sorry to have wasted your time. Please forgive me, I'm so very sorry.'

'But Miss Kent, you insisted . . . I pulled every string to get the accommodation . . .'

'I'm so sorry. I'd really love to go, but it just isn't possible. Do forgive me, I'm sorry,' she blurted, and fled, carrying with her a full burden of shopping bags. She'd raided Bergdorf's, Tessa noticed as she dumped the contents of the bags on her bed back at the Carlyle. She'd bought cruise clothes of every sort. But everything could be sent back to the store tomorrow, Tessa knew, and with that, she began to weep, slowly at first and then more and more violently. She was shaken by hugely mounting sobs, wrenching, painful sobs, wave upon wave of them, until she slowly stopped only because she had wept as much as her raw, aching eyes and throat would endure.

When she was able to look at her watch, Tessa realised that she must have been lying on her bed, her pillow over her head, pounding the mattress, for hours. She had a murderous headache and a hungry pain at the pit of her stomach.

How could she possibly be hungry? Tessa thought as she phoned room service for a double order of scrambled eggs and toast. She stood under a hot shower for a long time, and then, wrapped in her towelling bathrobe, took off the metal covers that had kept the eggs and toast warm, spread the toast with the entire contents of a pot of jam, and wolfed down everything, just to fill her stomach. She went to the bar and made a compress of ice wrapped in a napkin. She locked the door to the apartment, lay down on her sofa, put a big tumbler filled with iced vodka within reach, and adjusted a heap of pillows under her, intending to move the compress from place to place to try to make her eyes feel better.

In a few seconds Tessa was shaken by a rage so destructive that it made it impossible for her to remain motionless on the sofa. Gulping the vodka, and pouring more, she paced back and forth, muttering to herself in an incoherent monologue. She'd like to kill somebody, yes, more than anything; she'd like to hit and hit and hurt and hurt until somebody died. If she had the power she'd order a hundred executions, she'd hurl thunderbolts, she'd wipe out cities. She would, she meant it, she yearned to do it, she thought in a concentrated passion of fury that lasted for hours until, weak and drunk, she fell on her bed and slept dreamlessly, without moving.

She woke up at three in the morning, disorientated at finding herself in her robe, lying on top of her quilt, her feet freezing. For a minute she remembered nothing of the previous day, and then it all came rushing back in a blast of realisation so horrifying that she didn't think she could survive.

Tessa stared in utter confusion at her image in her mirror. She didn't look like a woman with no more than two years to live. If she was lucky, two years and a few months. If she wasn't, a year and a half. She'd only just turned thirty-eight. In two years she'd just reach forty. Forty was nothing!

But she'd never reach forty. She'd never celebrate the birthday that foolish, lucky women complained about in make-believe misery, even lied about. Why wasn't every birthday a brilliant triumph to be toasted and celebrated, another year you could boast about because you'd survived? Were people utterly crazy, not to realise that survival was a gift of the gods, to take it for granted, to actually feel bad about getting older? *About having lived more life?* What were wrinkles, what were forty extra pounds or weakened muscles or grey hair, except signs of the best of good luck?

It was too much to bear. It was too unfair. It was the most unfair thing she'd ever heard of happening to anybody. Nothing that had ever happened was unfair compared to this, not even Luke's death. It was the ultimate unfairness and no one to blame but some cells gone mad. Yet Tessa felt as if she'd been targeted, as if some malevolent force loathed her, specifically her, with a direct, evil calculation that had already measured out the dose of poison that would kill her twice over.

She only knew one thing with any certainty. She wasn't going to have any treatment. No chemo, no radiation. She wasn't interested in spending one second in a hospital or a doctor's office. She felt a blanket of the blackest depression, bleak, dismal and hopeless, start to sneak over her, smothering and all-but-irresistible, and Tessa knew that if she didn't think of something else quickly the two years she still had left could be spent, would be spent, in a hell of self-pity. She had used up years of her life mourning Luke. After he'd died, she'd actually believed she had no reason to live. How stupid she'd been! How wasteful! All those priceless days thrown away on grief. There was no time left, not a day, not a minute, to mourn for herself. It was a luxury she couldn't afford.

What did she have left? she asked herself, trying to focus. Sam? But how long could she keep this from him? Her work? She couldn't play Cassie, she couldn't count on having the time to finish the film; they'd never get insurance on her now anyway. So, at best, she could assist Fiona in some way. All her friends in California and New York? Friends, Sam, work. Wasn't that more than a lot of people ever had? It was, she tried to tell herself, it really was. She had decades of stardom to look back on . . . Luke, she'd had her life with Luke. She'd had her year with Sam. How many women could say as much? Wasn't that enough? No, it wasn't. It was *not* enough.

She was going to be denied most of the experiences of a mature woman, there was no getting away from that. She would have no forties, no fifties, no sixties, no three score and ten. She would never accept it, she could never forgive it, but she knew it was a fact she had to bite into with all the power left to her.

But . . . but . . . there existed one experience no one could refuse her, one way to still create, to leave something behind that would show that she had lived a life outside her films, some bit of her that would survive and make a difference.

She could make her peace with Maggie. She could know her daughter again. She could try to heal the rift between them.

Maggie. She had a daughter and her daughter would have a daughter or a son some day. No cancer could take that chance away from her. A daughter who had inherited half of whatever she was would eventually, inevitably, have children of her own, descendants . . . her descendants, who would know that Tessa Kent had lived . . .

Her excited thoughts slowed down. It had been roughly five years since Maggie had refused to accept the millions Luke had left her. She had been too young to understand the financial consequences, but the gesture had said clearly that she was not too young to have made up her mind, once and for all, that her mother was cast out of her life.

But that could not be allowed to stand.

In five years, Tessa calculated, on fire with her idea, Maggie *must* have changed, must have mellowed. Five years were for ever, she knew that now. Maggie was an adult; she'd passed her twenty-third birthday months ago. Tomorrow, yes tomorrow, she'd go to see her, go straight up to that apartment she was living in, that apartment Tessa had quietly had checked out by a private investigator every six months, and confront Maggie, yes, have that confrontation she'd never dared to risk before because she believed that Maggie would shut the door in her face and that had seemed to much to endure. What a vile coward she'd been, to let so much time go by. She'd tell Maggie that she only had a short time to live, *force her*, force her, to listen, just to *listen*. That's all she asked.

No one could turn down a dying woman.

Eight

WHEN TESSA WOKE UP later that morning, after a few hours of fitful sleep, she knew, even before she opened her eyes, that the confrontation with Maggie she had been so convinced about in the middle of the night was a lousy idea.

If she presented herself as a dying woman, as a case for pity, no real relationship could be established between them, much less any honesty. There must be another way to reach Maggie, a way that didn't involve anything to do with her health.

Maggie's work at Scott and Scott—that was the only path left to her, Tessa realised as she ate breakfast. She'd known Liz Sinclair socially and casually for years. They had many of the same acquaintances from the days when Luke was alive, and there wasn't anyone important in the auction business she didn't know.

Why? How? What reason could she give Liz Sinclair to explain that she had to talk to Maggie Horvath, had to see Maggie Horvath?

Suddenly Tessa knew what to do. She had Liz Sinclair on the phone in minutes.

'Tessa Kent, what a lovely surprise! I couldn't imagine how you'd managed to disappear from sight in the last year, although I did hear something about a devastating professor, hmm? How are you, Tessa? It's been so long, Hamilton was just saying–'

'Liz, I haven't time to be polite. Just assume we've had ten minutes of charming small talk. I intend to auction my jewels, everything but my green diamond and a few strings of pearls.'

'Tessa!'

'For charity, of course. That goes without saying. Scott and Scott has the auction . . . no Liz, don't interrupt, there's no need to compete with another auction house, no need to give me a guarantee, it's yours on one single condition. I don't want to work with Lee Maine on the publicity. She's tremendously good, I know, but I want to work exclusively with Maggie Horvath. Liz, I know that Maggie's made it a point of pride never to trade on it, but she's my younger sister. I was born Teresa Horvath.'

'What? Good grief, Tessa, I had no idea . . .'

'I know you didn't. Maggie and I have actually been, well, I suppose one could call it, at arm's length, for the past few years. Actually an estrangement. We haven't spoken, can you imagine? Silly family stuff. I want to end that. Now. Quickly.'

'But, but . . . sell *all* your jewels! Tessa, are you sure? You could never duplicate . . .'

'Liz, what a tender-hearted woman you turned out to be,' Tessa said, impatiently. 'Hamilton would be shocked if he heard you. Of course I'm sure. They're only . . . things. Very lovely things, but they don't have hearts.'

'Well, no, of course not, Tessa—' Liz said, still almost dumbstruck by this turn of fortune.

'I expect you to make it the biggest single-owner auction since the Duchess of Windsor's,' Tessa continued. 'My jewels are easily equal in quality to anything she had, and there are a great many more of them. *And I'm alive, Liz.* Not a dead duchess. I can publicise the sale from here to Saudi Arabia and I will. But it all depends on your delivering Maggie to work on the publicity with me. She won't want to do it, I'm pretty sure of that. And if she refuses, I won't sell the jewels, not anywhere. And it has to be quick, within six months, no more. I know that's short notice, less than you need for your usual preparation, but that's the way it has to be,' Tessa said firmly. If she allowed more time, how much would she have left in which to be with Maggie, be with her as a proper mother?

'I understand. I'll call you as soon as I've talked to Maggie.'

'Maggie, Mrs Sinclair wants you to go up and see her right away,' one of the assistants said, after she'd answered the interoffice phone.

'She say why?'

'No, just get moving.'

'Miz Liz,' Maggie said cheerfully upon entering Liz's office. 'You wanted to see me?'

'Yes, sit down, Maggie, and have some tea.'

'No tea, thanks. What's going on?'

'It's complicated, Maggie. It concerns the future of the house. I'm offering you a chance to help me with a great opportunity, one I never dreamed we'd have.'

'An opportunity? What kind?' Maggie asked eagerly.

'We've been offered a historic sale of one of the finest, most famous private collections in the world.'

'Oh Liz, great news! What's the sale?'

'It's a sale, Maggie, that will make Scott and Scott a worldwide household name for the first time since it was founded. It will open the door to dozens, hundreds of other great sales in the future. People will think of us who've never even considered consigning their property to Scott and Scott. It will change our future for ever.'

'But you still haven't told me what it is. Are you trying to make me beg? And what about Lee? Why are you telling me first?'

'Because you have it in your power to make sure that this sale takes place. You also have it in your power to prevent the sale, to keep it from ever happening.'

'Oh, Liz! For heaven's sake! How could that ever be?'

'Maggie, the sale . . . it's . . . the jewels of Tessa Kent.'

'You . . . you . . .' Maggie stopped and looked away, shaking her head in total negation.

'Maggie, I know she's your sister. She called this morning and told me. I know the two of you have problems, but Maggie, dear Maggie, you see the only reason she's willing to auction her jewels is to get a chance to be reconciled with you. She wants you, not Lee, to handle the press. How terrible can that be, Maggie? It's a job you're thoroughly capable of doing. Tessa said she'd never sell her jewels unless you were in charge of the publicity.'

'No, Liz, no, she can't get at me through you.'

'Maggie, whatever the problem is with you and Tessa, believe me, as the two of you get older, you'll *need* each other. The ancient hurts and hostilities will come to seem unimportant, even absurd. In time you'll forget the details. But the two of you sisters will have something priceless together in the years to come, someone to talk to who remembers the same family things you do, who came from the same parents and grandparents, who understands you from the earliest days, who speaks your language the way no friend ever can . . .'

'Liz, I do realise what family sentiment means,' Maggie said, forcing herself to sound patient and reasonable. 'But what went wrong between us isn't something any auction can change.'

'You don't know, you can't be sure of that! Tessa's willing to help with the publicity on this in every way, travel with the jewels to previews and exhibitions, pose for any pictures, do any television. Oh, Maggie, just think what that would mean to us! Her only stipulation is that the auction has to take place no later than six months from now. She intends to give the proceeds to charity, maybe that has something to do with it. It will mean a mountain of immediate work. I'll get you all the extra help you need—'

'She said six months? Exactly that and no more?'

'Yes.'

'Then you can't expect me to give you an answer in six minutes,' Maggie said, red-faced with suppressed words as she took her leave.

'Polly, I have to talk to you,' Maggie yelled through the door. She'd left the office right after she'd talked to Liz and hurried home to take counsel with Polly, the only person she had ever told about Tessa.

'Keep your hair on. I'm coming.' Polly unlatched her door and watched calmly as Maggie dashed in like a furious ball of dark tumbleweed, turning round and round for a place to light.

'What's the matter? Had a fight with your very own Barney? Already?'

'Of course not. It's Tessa, can you believe it, after all these years? She's blackmailing me the strongest way she knows how. She's offered Scott and Scott an auction of her jewels—but only on condition that I run the press on it, meaning we'd be in daily contact for six months. Liz has just been at me, telling me that the future of the house depends on me, and me alone. Pure blackmail. That, Miss Polly, is why I'm in a state.'

'Mercy.'

'How well expressed, how finely spoken. Mercy, indeed. Tessa's probably got the greatest collection in the world except for a few Saudi ladies who can't wear them in public, the several wives of the Sultan of Brunei, and Queen Elizabeth.'

'She must really be desperate to make up with you, Maggie,' Polly said, in her most serious, thoughtful voice.

'Guilt, pure guilt. Although why it struck her now I can't imagine.'

'I can't either. But something's better than nothing. At least she feels bad enough to sacrifice her jewels.'

'And I'm supposed to make her feel better about all those years of rejection by helping her make a terrific success of the auction? Hah—at least it's for charity.'

'Something tells me that she wants to feel better by getting closer to you. I'm sure she can't be eager to part with her jewels. She could just give the money to charity if that were all it was. Why are you still so opposed to trying for some sort of, oh, I don't know, I hate to say "relationship" but I can't think of another word to replace it.'

'Oh, not now, Polly, not when I'm so happy,' Maggie cried fervently. 'I've put her out of my mind, forgotten about her. Why reopen old wounds?'

'So you still want to punish her? The way you do when you regularly send her letters back without reading them? Now you won't work on a big exciting auction—wouldn't that be good for your career?'

'Damn right it would. Of course what motivates Liz is the world-beating, slam-bang auction that's going to make such a difference for Scott and Scott.'

'So now you're punishing Liz and Hamilton and the entire house of Scott and Scott too, not just Tessa Kent? Can't you let it go? Can't you stop being so desperately proud, stiff-necked, hard, stubborn, impossible? That's certainly not the Maggie Horvath I know and love.'

'When were you elected to become the voice of my conscience?'

'The day you moved in, a sad, lonely case, really needing a place to live, and I fed you for months, or rather years to be exact, and became your best friend and still am.'

'*Low blow.*'

'Well?'

'I'll think about it.'

'**W**ant to eat here tonight, sweetheart, or go out for Chinese food?' Sam asked Tessa soon after he arrived back at the apartment, three days after she'd spoken to Liz Sinclair.

'How hungry are you?' Tessa asked, holding him as tightly as she could.

'I'm not really. I had a big lunch with the head of my department.'

'Could we just sit here for a while? I have something I have to tell you.'

'That sounds ominous. You haven't stopped loving me? You don't want me to pack my bag and go?'

'Nothing like that. This is all about me.'

'Now that'll be a treat—you talk about yourself less than any female I've ever known. If you weren't so absurdly famous, you'd be my wonderful little secret, my very own private woman of mystery.'

'Sam, sit down, drink your drink, and listen to me. Don't interrupt. I have to get this out all at once.'

'Tessa, what the hell—'

'Just listen. *Please*. When I was fourteen I had a baby. Maggie. Mary Margaret Horvath. My parents brought her up as my sister, to hide the disgrace. By the time Maggie was three I'd already made *Little Women*. I'd become Tessa Kent. I neglected her shamefully, I was too wrapped up in my own future, too full of ambition, too high on my own totally wonderful self, to even *think* of getting to know her. I had plenty of opportunities because I lived at home for the next three years, but I allowed my mother to take over Maggie completely. I never even put up a fight. I was . . . grateful; it meant one less distraction in my exciting, brilliant, self-important life.'

'Oh, come on Tessa, that's not you at all, that's—'

'Then I met Luke and married him,' Tessa continued without giving Sam a chance to say more. 'I was twenty, Maggie was five. I never told Luke about her, although now there's no question in my mind that if I had, right at the start, he would have accepted the fact that Maggie existed. Hell, he was forty-five, a grown-up, a kind man, and I knew he was crazy about me. There was a window of opportunity, and I blew it. He wanted to think I was a virgin, right from our first date, and I let him believe I was. That was the worst of my lies. Afterwards, I couldn't admit I wasn't. I lied and lied, even on our wedding night.'

'Tessa, you're so hard on yourself, you were a kid—'

'The week Luke and I were married, my parents died in an accident and Maggie was left all alone. I let her go, Sam. I let her go to Luke's stepbrother's family, the Websters, and grow up there. My daughter could have grown up with Luke and me, with a mother and stepfather, but I never had the courage to admit she wasn't my sister. I was an utter coward, a shameful coward.'

'Tessa—'

'Don't, Sam, let me finish. I visited Maggie from time to time, and she visited me, not nearly as often as it should have been. I never truly knew if she was happy or not. I could have found out, but I kept our relationship bright and easy and utterly superficial. That was easier for me. My life with Luke came first. All the real family Maggie ever had was this remote movie-star creature who threw glamour dust at her every once in a while. Barney, the Websters' son, adored her. That's all the real love she got, Sam, from the time she was five until she was eighteen. She's twenty-three now. Even after Luke died I didn't tell her.'

'Then why now?'

'Wait! Maggie found out I was her mother when she was eighteen. I'd finally decided the time had come to tell her, but she found out first. She's never spoken to me since, or opened a single letter I've sent her. There's one chance left. Maggie works in publicity for Scott and Scott, the auction house. I called a friend there, one of the owners, and told her I'd sell all my jewels at auction, but only on the condition that Maggie would work on the sale. That way we'll be thrown together and she'll have to talk to me, and maybe . . . but I don't know yet if she will or won't.'

'Do you have a lot of jewels?' he asked, in surprise. 'All I've ever noticed is this unbelievable green rock and some pearls. Oh, and those cameos you were wearing the day we met.'

'Oh, Sam, darling Sam, yes, I have jewels. I just don't wear them with you or your friends. They're a . . . distraction.'

'You mean something like a million bucks' worth of jewellery?' he asked incredulously.

'Tens of millions.'

'That just might have made the wrong impression at faculty parties.' Sam gave a snort of laughter. 'When will you know?'

'When Liz Sinclair calls me. I have very little hope.'

'If there is an auction, when will it be?'

'I told them it had to be held in no less than six months; I don't want this situation to drag on and on.'

'Will it take up a lot of your time?'

'Almost all, and I'll have to travel a lot to publicise it.'

'Tessa, we've been together for a year and you've never said a thing about Maggie. Is it because of the auction that you told me the whole story tonight?'

'No, Sam, no! I couldn't stand lying to you any more, lying by not saying anything, even though chances are you would never have known.' She couldn't tell him everything at once, Tessa thought with a twinge of guilt.

'And even though you thought I might stop loving you. Admit it, you did think that. I know you so well now, I could tell.'

'But how *can* you keep loving me, Sam?'

'You made one hell of a lot of mistakes, rotten judgment calls, you were a lousy mother and not even a decent sister. But that was then and this is now, and there's hope for you, Tessa Kent. So you thought I would change, you actually believed that was possible?'

'Yes.'

'I guess you don't really know me yet,' Sam said, grabbing her and pulling her close. Tessa sobbed into his shirt for long, relieved minutes while he kissed her hair and patted her back as if she were a baby. Finally, she looked up at him and said, 'You haven't even asked what this will do to the movie schedule, how long we'll have to postpone starting production.'

'What movie?'

The next day Maggie, grim-faced but bowing to her own intensely rooted loyalty to Scott and Scott, agreed to handle the publicity for the auction of the jewels of Tessa Kent.

A preliminary meeting was immediately scheduled for the following morning, a meeting that would include only Liz and Hamilton, Tessa, Maggie, Monty Foy, the director of Scott and Scott's jewellery department, and Juliet Tree, the director of marketing. As within every auction house, the big sale, or the prospect of one, was a tightly held secret known only to the few top people who would work on it from the very beginning.

Everyone but Maggie had arrived and taken their places round a table by the appointed time. Earlier that morning Liz had gathered Monty Foy and Juliet Tree together and told them that the only reason Scott and Scott had the prospect of Tessa Kent's auction was that Maggie Horvath was Tessa's younger sister. Unless Maggie ran the press, there would be no sale, but they must not make any reference to that fact during the meeting. They had to be informed, she realised, so that they wouldn't make a gaffe about the absence of Lee Maine, who normally would have been there.

Tessa had refused to sign the Master Consignment Agreement even after she'd telephoned her with the news that Maggie would participate, Liz thought, tapping her foot. Tessa was waiting to see if Maggie was actually going to show up, in spite of Liz's assurances, and by now Maggie, who was usually so punctual, was ten minutes late.

The presence of Tessa Kent certainly did nothing to lower the level of tension in the room, Liz noted, trying not to look at her watch. To all of them, even to her, Liz realised, Tessa Kent was the sum of many things, the unforgettable roles she'd played, the Oscars she'd won, the sheer mythology of her Hollywood glamour, the cloak of inaccessibility she'd drawn around herself for twenty years, her position as Luke Blake's widow, and, of course, her jewels, that incredible collection of jewels that was not, until the contract had been signed, theirs to sell.

'Sorry! Sorry everybody, the bus broken down, we all had to get out, the next three buses were so full that they didn't even stop, so I had to walk the rest of the way,' Maggie said breathlessly as she slid into the vacant chair between Juliet Tree and Monty Foy. She busied herself with opening her handbag and taking out a notebook and pencils, not looking at anyone in the room, a neutral expression fixed firmly on her face.

Tessa's heart was cleft by a burst of thanksgiving at the sound of Maggie's voice. She could find no armour to protect herself from her emotions. She felt as bare, as stripped, as she'd ever felt in her life.

'I believe we can get started now,' said Liz Sinclair, managing to remain majestic as she slid the Master Consignment Agreement across to Tessa, who was seated next to her, and indicating the place for Tessa's signature. As soon as Tessa scrawled her name, Liz continued. 'From now on, Maggie, you're to travel with a car and driver. Your time's too valuable to be wasted.'

'Great,' Maggie responded, opening her notebook and arranging her pencils according to some unknown order.

She won't look at me, Tessa thought, but oh, she's here, she's here. Tears started into her eyes as she stared hungrily at Maggie, a self-assured New Yorker, transformed into one of the bright-eyed, swift, strong, stunningly self-possessed young women who strode the streets of the city as if they owned them. Maggie, her flamboyant, downright voluptuous daughter, who owed her nothing, whose difficult path through childhood and adolescence had been traversed without her. Maggie who'd created herself triumphantly, with the only cards she'd been dealt. Maggie, almost unbelievably, was here today, ready to go to work. Maggie, her daughter.

'Maggie,' Tessa managed to say, 'you look wonderful.'

'Feelin' fine,' Maggie replied, with a nod at the room in general.

She won't say my name, Tessa thought. She won't look at me. But she's here. We've made a start.

'How'd the meeting go?' Sam asked eagerly even before he'd kissed Tessa.

All yesterday evening, he thought, she'd been negotiating her way across a tightrope of nerves in a way that was foreign to his experience of her. She had been so wound up that she could talk of little other than the fact that today, this very afternoon, since all the jewels were now in the possession of Scott and Scott, she'd find herself in the same room with Maggie for the first time since the day she'd signed the auction contract.

'I'm not sure,' Tessa answered in a white, muted voice, her vitality and conviction lost. 'I may have blown it.'

'What are you talking about?' he asked, tipping her lips up for a kiss. 'You said this was just a preliminary strategy meeting. How could you even, with all your amazing ability to screw up your life, possibly blow a six-month effort right at the beginning, darling?'

Tessa gave him a smile that was no more than a faint gesture.

'Tell me everything that happened,' Sam ordered, 'from the beginning, so I can explain it to you, because you don't make sense.'

'There were seven of us, sitting around a conference table—Lee Maine has lent the room to Maggie for the duration, and—'

'Who were they? Pretend you're a historian, baby. I want details.'

'Besides Maggie and Juliet Tree and me, there was Janet Kovitz, Maggie's assistant, and another girl I hadn't met before, Dune Maddox by name, a rakish, very social blonde with more brains than you'd think to look at her. Also there were two floaters Maggie recruited—kids, Sam, probably no more than twenty.'

'Were you the only grown-up there?'

'No, Juliet Tree's in her forties, a true professional who's been at Scott and Scott for years, an elegant woman, the tailored suit type, who seems a bit square. Obviously Maggie's a cult figure; the others are all Maggie clones, like Janet, even down to the haircut, and except for Juliet they treat her word as writ.'

'So you're sitting there with a bunch of females. Then what happened?'

'I pushed my chair just far enough away from the table so I wouldn't seem to be intruding on Maggie's turf, since she was running the meeting, and I sat back and listened. She explained how they announce an important auction, keeping it totally secret until the actual morning of the press conference, so it makes headlines all over the world. She said Hamilton Scott would make the announcement of the sale and then I'd speak, explaining why I'd decided to auction my jewels and telling the press that the proceeds would go to cancer research and answering questions.'

'So far, so good.'

'Juliet wanted to know if I had any scrapbooks and I told her that Fiona had made them of every picture ever published of me since my first film and I'd let her know to send them here right away. They need the pictures for the catalogue and to distribute to magazines.'

'But there must be thousands upon thousands of photographs.'

'There are. The idea is that every magazine that does a story on me will get entirely different photos from different movies and different occasions when I was photographed in real life wearing my jewels. Maggie's going after the big television interview shows, too. I didn't question it, just said I'd be available for anything except lying in my tub with bubbles up to my armpits.'

'Will you mind if anyone gets wise to us? You've kept it so quiet all year.'

'Mind? I'd take out an ad in *Publishers Weekly* if you'd let me. Will *you* mind is more the question.'

'I wish everybody knew,' Sam answered. If only she'd marry him! She'd been on the verge, before the auction came up, but now all her emotional focus was turned towards Maggie.

'Your study'll be off-limits anyway,' Tessa continued. 'Photographers won't want me in front of a desk.'

'You can do this stuff in your sleep, can't you?'

'Just about. I publicised every picture I made, but I never did an interview just for the sake of keeping my name in front of the public. That's probably why I'm supposed to be something of a recluse. Anyway, I gave all the press department an open invitation to come and take a good look at this place so they'll have an idea of how it could photograph. Janet and Dune jumped at it.'

'What about Maggie? Doesn't she want to see it too?'

'Clearly no. She told them she was delegating all questions photographic to Dune and Janet.'

'So far, strictly as a historian, I don't see where you blew it.'

'Maggie made absolutely no eye contact with me, *none*, Sam, even though we had been in that meeting for at least two hours. She looked at all the others whenever she talked to them, but I could have been completely invisible. She never once, *not once*, used my name, Sam; she referred to me as "the consignor" as if I weren't right there in the room, and managed to make it sound as if she were just being terribly correct and polite. She was actually *ceremonial*, as if I were the hundred-year-old hereditary ruler of some feudal country.'

'So then you blew up?'

'No, nothing that sensible. Then I suggested that since we were all going to be working together for a long time, we should be like people on film sets, at least my sets, and use first names. I asked everybody to call me Tessa, because that way Maggie would have to go along with the rest of them.'

'Well, what's wrong with that?'

'They all looked at Maggie, as if for permission, and she raised her eyebrows slightly as if I'd said something embarrassingly over-friendly, and that's when—oh, shit, Sam, I was so frustrated by the icy, determined way she was giving me the invisible treatment—I explained that Maggie had been leaning over backwards to be proper because she didn't want to trade on or presume on the fact that we were sisters.'

'Hmm.'

'What's that supposed to mean?'

'Not much, I wasn't there. How did Maggie react?'

'She didn't. They did. They were rocked by the news. You could literally feel their astonishment hit as they took in the word "sisters". They were incredulous and shocked, but, to their credit, they held it down pretty well. A couple of them blurted out "sisters?" and Juliet looked as if she'd just solved some large puzzle, and Maggie didn't say anything at all, just kept on consulting her notes, so I blundered on, doing a Miss Innocence number, and I said that I'd assumed they must all have heard by now, that Liz Sinclair and Hamilton Scott and Lee Maine knew and I simply imagined that everyone in the publicity department would know . . . I really blathered all over the place, fool that I am.'

'How can you be so sure if she didn't react?'

'Because the entire rest of the meeting Maggie *still* didn't look at me or use my name, and I could tell that she'd become ten times colder than before, and now she was deeply resentful, because I'd pushed too hard and confronted her.'

'OK, so you've had a setback, I won't try to tell you otherwise, but you haven't "blown it", darling,' Sam said after a moment's thought. 'You've put a modified version of the truth out in the open, so at least you don't have to go around acting as if you two had never met before, which would be pretty hard to keep up for six months, especially since other people at Scott and Scott already know.'

'Do you really think that or are you just saying it?'

'I really think it. You know I don't soft-pedal things to you. When you get right down to it, it's not the sister stuff that's the big deal. It's the mother–daughter connection that's making her act the way she does, and that's been going on for so long that it won't go away until . . . it goes away. Somehow. Or other.'

'Oh, Sam, I was so awful!'

'You were natural, you weren't on guard, you were too happy to see her, you wanted to shout from the rooftops. You weren't very smart. Even you, darling, have moments like that. But, remember, you've still got six months. Anything can happen. Six months is a long time.'

'Oh, Sam. Six months? Six months! They'll go by so quickly!'

'You can accomplish miracles in six months. We've only been together a little more than a year and I can't even imagine how time passed before I knew you.'

'I guess . . . time . . . is always relative,' Tessa said in a small voice, drifting to the window and looking out blindly. Six months, not even two full seasons of one year. One day Sam would be a fine old man, a famous old man, still teaching, still writing, happily married, the father of a family, one day, thirty or forty unimaginable years from now. Oh, Sam, when you look back, will you still think six months was a long time? Will you have any idea how much I would have given to grow older, year by year, with you?

Nine

Tessa carefully checked the laden tables that room service had just brought up to her apartment. About six weeks earlier she'd started inviting the auction team of the press department to an early breakfast every Friday morning so that they could sit around in comfort and assess the work done in the past week.

It was the only way to keep herself firmly focused on the progress of the complications of the publicity schedule, Tessa had decided, after a number of meetings at Scott and Scott had been interrupted by unrelated phone calls or questions from the members of the press office who were handling the publicity on Scott and Scott's other auctions.

With Liz Sinclair, Juliet Tree and occasionally Monty Foy, who was composing the part of the text that related to the history and quality of the jewels themselves, Tessa had weekly meetings at Scott and Scott to work on the layout of the catalogue, which was almost ready to be printed and mailed. Never, everyone agreed, had jewels been photographed so imaginatively and alluringly, and never would there be better shots of an owner wearing the jewels in the company of famous people at glamorous parties.

When Tessa studied the photographs, culled from Fiona's scrapbooks, she found herself at a strange distance from them. Yes, there she indisputably *was*, not more than eight years ago, in a pale-blue satin strapless Givenchy gown, dancing with the king of Spain at a ball in Venice, wearing yards of cornflower-blue Kashmir sapphires as lightly as if they were bubbles; there she was laughing with Tom Hanks, Tom Cruise and Kevin Costner at an opening night party only three years ago, in a short, unadorned black satin shift and a throwaway pair of oval diamond earrings. They could easily look, to the untutored eye, as if they were costume jewellery, because the diamonds were that startlingly pure bright, flawless Fancy Vivid Yellow that only the Sultan of Brunei also possessed. They were set in a $9 million pair of earrings, unbuyable at less than $300,000 a carat . . . *but there she wasn't.* Not really. Another world, another life, another woman. Her emotional removal was a blessing, Tessa thought, or else she might well have felt regret at the way she had chosen to use these six priceless months of her life, as it became more and more certain that Maggie wasn't going to soften one whit towards her, no matter how much time they spent in the same room.

The concierge announced the first of the troops from Scott and Scott, and soon they were all gathered around the tables, helping themselves to platefuls of the enormous breakfast Tessa had provided—everything from croissants for the delicate eaters, to scrambled eggs and smoked salmon, or baked ham and sausages with pancakes, for those who jumped at the prospect of a hearty breakfast, instead of their usual fare.

The atmosphere at this morning's breakfast was especially exciting, Tessa realised, coming back to the present moment, because tomorrow, on Saturday morning, she, Maggie and Dune were leaving on a nonstop flight to São Paulo, where the first foreign exhibition of the highlights from the collection would take place the following Monday night. Scott and Scott was giving a gala reception in the ballroom of the luxurious Maksoud Plaza Hotel, where they were all staying, to which every potential bidder in South America had been invited. On Tuesday and Wednesday there would be wall-to-wall private appointments for those women who wanted to try on the jewels and inspect them carefully, since they couldn't be taken out of their cases during the exhibition. Dealers would have to travel to New York before the auction for the same privilege. São Paulo, the South American equivalent of New York, was not just a centre of vast wealth and big business but a hub of journalism, and a press conference had been called for Monday afternoon, which hundreds of reporters from all over South America were expected to attend.

Security was as important as publicity in any foreign exhibition and Tessa, Maggie and Dune would be travelling on one plane and the jewels in another. The jewels would be accompanied to the airport in New York by one large group of inconspicuous security men and would be met by another such group hired by Scott and Scott's São Paulo office. A heavy force of Brazilian police would keep the jewels under armed surveillance during their stay in Brazil.

While the others were in the middle of breakfast, Maggie, who was seated close to the door of the living room, put down her plate and slipped out, unnoticed by anyone but Tessa. After a few minutes of hesitation, Tessa followed her.

The door to the guest bathroom was open and the room was empty. Where had she disappeared to? Tessa wondered. Worried, she looked next in the empty bathroom off the library and finally went to her own bathroom, where a dressing room and closet were separated by an inside door from the toilet.

The door to the dressing room from the hallway wasn't entirely closed and, as Tessa stood outside, she heard the unmistakable noises of vomiting, violent and uncontrollable, relieved for seconds as Maggie gasped for breath. Finally, she heard Maggie flush the toilet and cross the marble floor towards the basin.

Holy Mary, Mother of God, Tessa thought. Morning sickness. She'd never forgotten that sound. Tessa found herself clasping her arms across her breasts with her hands at her throat, as she closed her eyes and automatically whispered a prayer.

Don't go in, she told herself, fiercely trembling with the desire to rush to Maggie; don't you dare to go in. Remember what happened the last time you intruded on her right to privacy. She's pregnant but you may not, *you must not*, discuss it with her. She is pregnant with your grandchild, but you must seem not to know. She's pregnant and you don't know who the father is. She's pregnant and you don't know when she'll have the baby, or if she'll have the baby, and you may not, dare not, must not ask!

Hastily, Tessa blotted tears of excitement and joy from her eyes and fled down the corridor to rejoin the others.

Maggie gazed wide-eyed at herself in the mirror. She spat out the mouthwash she was gargling because she was grinning so widely that she'd almost swallowed a mouthful. Good God Almighty, so *this* was why she hadn't had a period in so long! A baby, Barney's baby. Contraception didn't always work, she'd always known that, but she hadn't guessed how marvellous it would be when it didn't. What would Barney say, what would Polly say, what would Liz Sinclair say? What difference did it make what anyone said? Maggie thought, her heart jumping with wild happiness. What would Tessa say when she found out she was going to be a grandmother? She frowned at herself in the mirror. Tricky, all this, especially leaving for Brazil tomorrow. She'd just sit on the delicious knowledge, hug it to herself, until she'd had a chance to tell Barney. She gargled one more time, splashed her face with cold water, reapplied her lipstick and set off sedately for the living room. There had better still be some croissants left . . . she was starving!

Maggie frowned and consulted her watch once again as she and Tessa waited in the VIP lounge for their 8.00am flight to São Paulo. Dune should have joined them at least a half-hour ago. How could she, the most obsessively reliable of all her assistants, have failed to realise how vitally important it was for her to be on time this morning? The plane would be ready to load in twenty minutes.

'Miss Horvath? There's a phone call for you,' an attendant said. 'You can pick up right here.' Maggie grabbed the phone and listened grimly as Dune, sobbing with anger at herself, informed her in disbelieving outrage that she'd broken her ankle running for a taxi and was calling from a pay phone in a hospital emergency room, where she was waiting to have it set.

'Oh, Maggie!' Dune wailed. 'How could I have done this to you?'

'We should have sent a limo for you, too. Don't worry, no big deal. I can handle it alone. Feel better, take care.'

Maggie walked over to Tessa and told her the news.

'Oh, that poor girl! She must be miserable,' Tessa said, even as she reproached herself for being thrilled by Dune's accident, which left them inescapably alone for the first time.

'She is,' Maggie said, tightlipped.

Tessa and Maggie, lacking the hapless Dune, each took a window seat in the two first rows of first class, one behind the other. They spent the uneventful nine-hour trip with only the most perfunctory communication. In the São Paulo airport, at six in the evening local time, they were met by the capable and very elegant Señora Marta Pereira, the director of the local Scott and Scott office, accompanied by her two senior employees. They were driven through the immense metropolis of 16 million people in an air-conditioned Bentley that had been rented for the occasion, and soon they were settled in their magnificent suites on the top floor of the Maksoud Plaza Hotel. It was spring in Brazil, although, except for the temperature and the masses of spring flowers in their suites, there was no way to glimpse any countryside, even from their elevation, so sprawling was the city itself.

Before she unpacked, Tessa phoned Sam in New York and told him about Dune's accident.

'Until the press conference on Monday afternoon I'm totally at loose ends here, darling. I've finally got Maggie to myself and it's obvious that she's going to keep herself so busy that I'll never be alone with her,' she said sadly, almost with resignation. What else had she expected, anyway?

'Tomorrow she's planned a whole day around Marta Pereira, who she's already adopted in the place of Dune, so we'll never be alone, but there's nothing I can do about it; I can't tag along when I'm unnecessary.' Tessa paused while Sam spoke.

'What will I do? I'm going to order something light to eat and go to bed early. It's lucky that I brought three books with me; Sunday promises to be a long, lonely day. I'll call often. Oh, I do love you!'

In the middle of the night Tessa was woken by a faint but persistent knocking on her door, coming from the circular entrance that led to her bedroom.

'Who is it?' she called, startled.

'Maggie.'

Tessa switched on a light, jumped out of bed and ran to open the door. Maggie stood there in her bathrobe, her eyes huge.

'I didn't want to bother you . . .' she faltered, standing unsteadily in the doorway.

'Maggie, what's wrong?' Tessa cried, pulling her into the room.

'I—oh, hell—I'm bleeding.'

'Oh, no! The baby! Lie down on the bed right away, yes, flat, feet up on this pillow.'

'How did you know?'

'I heard you throwing up yesterday. How long have you been bleeding?'

'I can't be sure. Fifteen minutes ago I woke up and went to the bathroom and noticed . . . it was brownish, at first, and then there was some bright red blood . . .'

'Any cramps?'

'No, just the bleeding.'

'I think it's a false alarm, just spotting, but I'll get a doctor immediately.' Tessa sounded more reassuring and knowledgeable than she felt. If ever, this was the time to convey calm and self-possession.

'Why a false alarm?' Maggie gasped.

'I've lost two pregnancies. I could *never* have made it down a hotel corridor on my own. I had terrible cramps and I lost blood like mad. Now keep quiet, take deep breaths and try to relax.'

Tessa picked up the phone and spoke to the night operator.

'Operator, this is Tessa Kent. What's your name? Dolores, excellent. Now, Dolores, contact the general manager, at his home, immediately, and tell him to call me at once. This is an emergency. After you've reached the general manager, call the night manager and tell him to come up immediately to Tessa Kent's suite with an empty hot water bottle and two buckets of ice cubes. Thank you, Dolores. I'll hang up so the general manager can phone me directly, you understand?'

She turned to Maggie, whose face was twisted with apprehension. 'I'm going to get some towels, it won't take a second,' Tessa said. She hurried to the bathroom and returned with an armful of towels.

'Here, I'll pull your pyjama pants off over your feet, and you put one of these between your legs.'

She turned to answer the phone. 'This is Tessa Kent. Thank you *señor*. Yes, it's an emergency. I need a top gynaecologist in São Paulo here in my suite *immediately*. What's the best hospital in the city? Good. Now, please call the Albert Einstein and tell them it's for Tessa Kent. I'm in an emergency situation. Ask for the department of gynaecology and write down the names and home phone numbers of their top doctors. Explain that it's for me, Tessa Kent. Call them at home, ask the first one who answers to come here for me, Tessa Kent, at once. Tell him it's an emergency, *señor*.' Tessa turned back to Maggie.

'I never thought I'd hear those words so often in two phone calls,' Maggie said in a weak voice.

'Which words?'

'Tessa Kent.'

'They work best. Oh, that must be the ice,' Tessa said, relieved, scrambling to open the door to the night manager. She took a tray from him and told him to go downstairs to wait for the general manager. Quickly, she filled the hot-water bottle with ice cubes, wrapped it in a hand towel and placed it low on Maggie's abdomen.

Soon a knocking on the door announced the arrival of the night manager, the general manager, and a short, powerfully muscled, handsome middle-aged man who announced that he was Dr Roberto Goldenberg.

'Thank you, gentlemen, thank you so much,' Tessa said, shutting the door on the hotel men and admitting only the doctor.

'Miss Kent, what seems to be your problem?' Dr Goldenberg asked in a deep voice that resonated with self-assurance.

'It's not me, it's my daughter, Maggie. She may be having a miscarriage. I've got her flat in bed with an ice pack on her belly.'

'How long ago did it start?' he asked, as he hurried across the entrance to the bedroom.

'I'm not sure. She woke me up about half an hour ago.'

'You work quickly, Miss Kent. From the hotel manager I imagined you must be having triplets this very minute.'

'Where were you in medical school, Doctor?' Tessa demanded.

'Harvard, and later Johns Hopkins. Hello, Maggie. I'm Dr Goldenberg,' he said, smiling. 'Now, let's take a look at you. *Mamãe*, wait in the sitting room, please,' the doctor said, bending over Maggie.

Vanquished by a superior force, Tessa retreated, reassured by the doctor's manner, and huddled in a chair in the sitting room. After some time she was joined by the doctor, who sat down next to her.

'In my opinion, Maggie's not having a miscarriage,' he said, patting her hand kindly. 'The chances are very low, although you realise that they're never zero, that she will lose this pregnancy. This kind of spotting is frequent, and it has almost stopped. However, it's best to be on the super-cautious side for the next three days. The most important thing is rest and plenty of fluids.'

'Did you give her all those instructions?'

'I'm telling you, isn't that enough?'

'You're going to have to repeat the rest part to Maggie. She's down here to work and she won't listen to what I say.'

'She'll obey me,' Dr Goldenberg promised, with a chuckle.

The doctor looked at Maggie severely, as Tessa stood by his side. 'Listen, Maggie, I've told your *mamãe* and I'm telling you: the only way to be sure you don't lose this baby is to stay exactly where you are, with your feet up, and rest for three days. Drink lots of fluids, eat what you want, but *stay in bed*. You can get up carefully and slowly walk to the bathroom. But you absolutely cannot go downstairs and run around that exhibition you were fretting about. You may not! Under *any* circumstances.'

'Oh, Dr Goldenberg, I have so much responsibility,' Maggie protested weakly. 'This couldn't happen at a worse time.'

'Someone else will take care of everything, count on it. Your *mamãe* will manage that as well as she managed to get me here in the middle of the night. Now, Maggie, it's time for you to sleep. I'll come back and check on you later in the afternoon tomorrow.'

Tessa closed the door behind Dr Goldenberg and marched into the bedroom armed with a feeling of complete authority. Maggie was sitting up in bed, with the beginning of a potentially rebellious expression on her face.

'But, Tessa—'

'You heard what the doctor said, Maggie. You're not going anywhere.' Oh, the simple joy of saying those words, Tessa thought, words every mother must have said a million times.

'Why did Dr Goldenberg expect you to know all the details?'

'I guess in Brazil the *mamãe* is the first to find out.'

'Well, you *were*. I didn't know until a few seconds before you did. Yesterday was the first time I had morning sickness. I didn't have any today. Oh, God, do you think I'll have it again tomorrow?'

'Probably not,' Tessa said with more conviction that she felt.

'It could just have been a fluke,' Maggie said dismissively, looking concerned. 'The worst of it, besides being out of commission, is I can't reach Barney to tell him. He took that gorgeous Ducati he's in love with and went off with her for the weekend. Damn!'

Tessa waited a few well-timed seconds before she murmured, without any inflection at all, 'Ducati.' Oh, God, let Maggie not be involved with a man who didn't adore her.

'His new motorcycle. Very special, I gather. Barney owns a custom bike-building shop. Don't even ask, but he does well, very well.'

'Barney,' Tessa all but hummed in a way that kept any element of question out of her voice. Tensely she waited for Maggie to reply.

'You remember Barney! For heaven's sake, Tessa, you can't have forgotten Barney?'

'The only Barney I remember actually seeing with my own eyes wasn't quite five years old.' Barney, she thought, with a leap of her heart, remembering the little sunburnt boy who had taken care of Maggie from the moment he met her. Barney: protective Tarzan to Maggie's timid Jane.

'But we've talked and talked about him! Don't you remember how he'd never leave me alone? Always pestering me?'

'Barney Webster? . . . Your old faithful Sancho Panza?' She started to breathe again in relief.

'Tessa, really! There's *never* been another Barney in my life.'

'He certainly never gave up, did he? Getting you *gravida* seems an ultimate form of pestering, if you ask me.'

Maggie giggled, sleepily. 'Neither one of us ever gave up.'

'Will he be happy?'

'Beyond happy . . . way, way beyond happy,' Maggie said faintly, as she closed her eyes and fell silent.

Tessa watched her intently until she was satisfied from the changed sound of Maggie's breathing that she was fast asleep. Now that Maggie wouldn't be disturbed, Tessa began the slow, stealthy labour of tugging, inch by inch, two deep, heavy armchairs until they came together near the bed. She positioned them so that they faced each other and formed a short, downy couch on which she planned to curl up for the night. She found a pillow and an extra blanket in a closet and snuggled down, her knees bent, in what seemed to be a fairly comfortable position, and drifted into sleep.

Many hours later, Maggie woke to find Tessa sleeping alongside the bed. Soundlessly she slid out of bed on her way to the bathroom.

'Where do you think you're going?' Tessa asked, one eye flying open.

'The john. I thought you were sleeping.'

'I was.' Tessa sat up, threw off the blanket, and yawned. 'And then I dreamed you were trying to escape, so I woke up.'

'I'll be back one of these days,' Maggie said, putting one foot down in front of the other in slow motion, with a show of caution.

Tessa scampered to the second bathroom of the suite to splash icy water on her face and run her fingers through her wild hair to try to smooth it down. Every limb ached because of her awkward sleeping position, but she welcomed the evidence that they'd both managed to get some rest. She quickly rejoined Maggie, who'd dutifully returned to bed.

'Any bleeding?' she asked, trying to sound casual.

'Nope. Not a sign. And I feel terrific. In fact I'm starving.'

'Oh, Maggie, that's the best sign of all! What would you like to eat?'

'A gallon of orange juice, bacon and eggs, piles of toast, strawberry jam, tea. Oh, my God, what time is it?'

'Two in the afternoon. I'll open the drapes and order for both of us.'

'If I had morning sickness, I must have slept through it. You can't get it after lunch, can you?'

'All I'm certain of is that it's not something you can sleep through,' Tessa said, as the springtime sunlight flooded the room, 'although I have heard of rare women who have all-day sickness from day one through the delivery.'

'They must be passionate to have a baby, to put up with feeling hideously queasy and throwing up for nine whole months.'

'Umm.'

'That means you're wondering how passionate I am about it, aren't you? Oh, Tessa, I want a baby with Barney more than I want anything else in the world. I never expected to feel this way. It wasn't in my plans, at all. Of course, now we'll have to get married. Oh Lord, do you think we have to invite Tyler and Madison?'

'There's no way out of it,' Tessa said, her heart jumping in jubilation at this question. It was the first time Maggie had asked her advice in many years.

'Well, they probably won't stay long if they even show up. I'd give a lot to see Madison's face when she finds out I'm going to be her daughter-in-law. Mrs Barnaby Alcott Webster. I love it! Oh, here's breakfast, or is it lunch? Doesn't it look good?'

Maggie was half-finished with her eggs when her hand flew to her mouth.

'Sick?' Tessa jumped up, alarmed, immediately ready to help Maggie to the bathroom.

'I just remembered! Marta Pereira! I'm supposed to meet her at three.'

'She'll call up from the lobby. I'll explain that I'm taking your place. Trust me, I'm good at making up convincing excuses, as well as a demon at checking arrangements. I'll pretend I'm you and I won't be satisfied with anything but pure perfection.'

'That's all very well for today,' Maggie admitted, glad to be vanquished, 'but Tessa, tomorrow! The press conference and the gala reception at night. Every single potential important bidder from all over South America! What am I going to do?'

'Guess?' Tessa asked, repressing a smile.

'I'm going to stay here in bed, flat on my back,' Maggie muttered, 'and let you handle everything, which you're perfectly capable of doing, as I'm aware, without anyone's help. After all, you're Tessa Kent and, more than the jewels, Tessa Kent is what they're coming to see.'

Taking great care to make no noise, Tessa opened the door of her suite, late on Monday night, only to find Maggie lying in bed, still reading.

'I couldn't possibly sleep,' Maggie explained, putting down her book, 'until you came back and told me how it went.'

'It was a fantastic success, a brilliant, glorious gala!' Tessa exclaimed, excitedly flinging down the cape of silver lamé that swirled in pleated folds around a bare, slender column of silver satin. 'Oh, Maggie, I was riding so high I could have personally auctioned off every last piece in the exhibition for twelve times its high estimate, but Marta wouldn't let me. She's still down there making appointments for women to come to try on the jewels—they're keeping the pieces here two extra days because they can't handle the requests in less time than that.'

'But—'

'No, don't worry, she called New York and cleared it. We'll go back as we planned. Oh, I wish you could have been there! Such glorious people, such superb clothes. They really know how to dress up . . . it was the way I imagine Hollywood must have been in the fifties. I felt a bit of a country mouse.' Tessa pulled out the pins that kept her hair swept up high and let it tumble down around her flushed face.

'You must be exhausted. You've been on your feet for two days,' Maggie said.

'Oh, maybe just a little, but it doesn't matter . . . you only live once.' Tessa yawned and stretched, and unzipped her dress, letting it slither to the floor. Maggie lay back with her eyes half-closed until she heard Tessa return from the bathroom in her bathrobe and sit at the dressing table to take off her make-up. Maggie pulled herself up on on her pillows with quiet determination, while Tessa, her back turned, concentrated on silently turning the lid of a jar of cleansing cream.

'*Who was my father?*'

'Oh! Good God! You scared me! I thought you were sleeping.'

'Who was he?' Maggie demanded firmly. 'I want to know all about him, every detail. Don't leave out a thing. I would have asked sooner but I didn't want to upset you before the big night.'

'Your father's name was Mark O'Malley and you look very much like him. He was tall and beautiful and as Irish as they come, and he had your curly dark hair and your marvellous big blue eyes, and he was seductive and confident and had a charm no one could resist. Like you. He was a local hero, Maggie, the captain of the high-school football team. I was besotted with him for two years.'

'Two years? You had a two-year romance with him?'

'Hardly that,' Tessa answered soberly, remembering. 'He didn't know I existed . . . my love was a mad, completely one-sided passion. I adored him from a distance, I dreamed of him night and day. It was first love, and there's nothing like it. All-consuming. You ought to know, you and your Barney. Finally, when I had just turned fourteen, a friend and I crashed a party at his house and I met him. I told him I was eighteen and he believed me. I looked much older than I was and I dressed the part. He never knew my name, he never knew I'd got pregnant, he never saw me again.'

'That son of a bitch!'

'No, no, Maggie, don't say that! I had on a lot of make-up; he thought I knew what I was doing. I led him on, actually. He certainly didn't have to force me, so you can't blame him. Blame me, I'd had too much to drink and I wanted to.'

'So how in the name of God did you get knocked up?' Maggie asked.

'He was . . . overly . . . aroused . . . and when he . . . ah, when he . . . penetrated me, he only managed . . . about an inch . . . before he had an orgasm, and that was that.'

'An inch! That's how you had me? An inch! You were still a virgin, for Christ's sake?'

'I was, but who would believe me? Your grandparents didn't want to know. I was a sinner and that was enough.'

'So I owe my existence to a horny high-school hero with super sperm who suffered from premature ejaculation and a horny high-school girl who let him put it in. Great. Just great.' Maggie shook her head at the ways of yesteryear.

'Well, think of it this way: if it hadn't happened, you wouldn't be alive.'

'Oh, God,' said Maggie, 'an inch, an inch, one lucky inch . . .' and she began to giggle so hard that the mattress started shaking. 'An inch, an inch, I owe my life to just one inch . . .'

'Stop it, you're getting hysterical,' Tessa begged, beginning to laugh herself. 'Please, Maggie, honestly it wasn't funny at the time, but you made me tell you all the details . . . oh, oh, I admit it's really . . . too ridiculous . . . that's all it was, an inch . . .'

Maggie and Tessa gave full rein to their fill of mirth until they both fell silent with the realisation that this discussion wasn't over.

'When I got that letter from my grandfather,' Maggie said, solemnly, 'what just about killed me was not the whole teenage mom story, because anyone would understand that, but the fact that when you could have acknowledged me, you didn't. I totally get it that when you became famous at sixteen you couldn't be allowed to have a kid, but what about when you married Luke and my grandparents died? That's where the whole thing sucks! Since I was supposed to be your sister *anyway*, not some stranger, why didn't you and Luke just take me instead of sending me to the Websters?'

'There are a dozen answers to that, none of them any good.'

'Yeah? Well, tell me a few, just for my information.'

'Luke never knew you were my child, that was the beginning of it.'

'You never told him?'

'I . . . he wanted to marry a virgin. It was terribly important to him, a real obsession.'

'What right did he have to want a virgin!' Maggie sputtered with rage. 'Luke was a hundred years older than you; he'd had a million women. What gave him the right to want a virgin? Was he some kind of god who demanded a virgin sacrifice?'

'Oh, Maggie, if only I'd dared to ask him that! I was too stupid, too much in love, too young. I wanted him too much; I believed he could keep me safe. Oh, how I needed to feel safe! It was like suddenly being able to breathe fresh air after being underground for years. I was desperate. I'd never felt safe in my life, especially after I got pregnant . . . I don't expect you to understand or forgive me, I'm just telling you exactly the way it was. I was afraid to lose Luke, so I lied by letting him believe it, and then, afterwards, I couldn't even consider telling him the truth because it was such an enormous and fundamental lie. Maggie, I believed our life together was founded on his believing me. Depended on it. Even on our wedding night—I played up to it.'

'But you'd had a child, couldn't he tell?'

'The doctor who delivered you assured me that he'd done me a favour and stitched me up so that I was "as good as new". I found out what that meant the first time Luke and I made love.'

'OK, so you got away with passing as a virgin. But the man totally, absolutely *adored* you. I know that, so why couldn't you admit it sooner or later, once he couldn't live without you?'

'I was a criminal coward, Maggie. Luke had a terribly jealous temperament and he hated my career, but he let me have it anyway. I didn't want to disturb that delicate balance we'd created. Luke was demanding and controlling, but even though his world revolved completely around him, I had become the most important element in it. He was incredibly generous in so many way, to so many people.'

'He bought people,' Maggie said in a low voice.

'Yes, he did, one way or another, Maggie, but he didn't buy me. I allowed him to set the terms of our life because I *liked* it that way. I didn't have to do it, don't you understand? I wanted to! Deep down, I wanted to be dominated, to be all the things Luke wanted me to be. I told you, it made me feel *safe*, and I thought I couldn't live without that. I took the easy way. The lying way. The longer I did it, the more it became the *only* way.'

'But after Luke died, why couldn't you have told me then?'

'That's the one thing I got right, Maggie, the one action I'm proud of. I knew I had to just set my teeth, keep busy and do my mourning alone. If I'd let you sacrifice your last year in school to be with me, it would have been thoroughly wrong and horribly unfair to you. As soon as I discovered that I was able to make plans again, my first thought was to claim you. But you'd received that letter . . . and it was too late.'

'More than five years ago . . . I can't believe it,' Maggie murmured.

'Maggie,' Tessa said, 'you do believe, don't you, that I never understood how you felt about the Websters? I thought you were happy with them.'

'I never wanted you to know.'

'But I should have guessed!'

'You couldn't have, not possibly. I'm a pretty good liar myself, and I can keep it up for years, like you. Maybe it's a talent that runs in the family . . . your mother, then you . . . and me.'

'You don't have to let me off the hook.'

'Maybe I want to,' Maggie said impetuously. 'Maybe I'd rather have a mother I can love than a sister I won't look at and don't speak to.'

'Maggie, oh, Maggie, do you mean that?'

'Isn't it time?' Maggie said, opening her arms and pulling Tessa close, so that she could lay her head on Tessa's shoulder and feel the sweet, necessary, longed-for comfort of her mother's embrace.

'When?' Dr Helen Lawrence echoed Maggie's question. 'I'd guess in about five and a half months to six months, more or less, but I wish you had some clue as to when you got pregnant.'

'I always used my diaphragm,' Maggie laughed.

'Always?'

'Well . . . maybe,' Maggie said thoughtfully, remembering the frenzied, incredulous, magnificent haste of the first night with Barney. 'Maybe there's the possibility that I forgot, just once, in the spirit of the moment, as it were.'

'Even if you always used it, there's a failure rate. But since you're so thrilled to be pregnant, it doesn't matter. '

'Well,' Maggie defended herself, her eyes rolling with mischief, 'at least my diaphragm worked for five years. Do you remember when I first came to you to be fitted? I didn't know any doctor's name but Tessa's.'

'Of course. You were just eighteen. Now tell me, how's Tessa doing?'

'She's simply marvellous. She totally wowed them down in São Paulo. She did her job and my job and everything went better than it would have if I'd been on my feet.'

'What about her appetite?'

'Her appetite? I honestly didn't notice.'

'It's so vitally important for her to keep eating,' Helen Lawrence fretted, sitting forward and fixing Maggie with earnest eyes. 'I was very upset when Dr Hill told me Tessa had decided against any chemotherapy or radiation, but obviously,' she sighed, 'treatment would have made it impossible to make all these public appearances for the auction that you've been telling me about.'

Maggie, too stunned to seize the deeper meaning of the doctor's words, felt brute instinct tell her to maintain her calm at any price.

'Obviously,' she agreed in a voice that revealed nothing.

'Maggie, are you able to notice if she's feeling any pain yet? Susan Hill has all sorts of methods of keeping it under control, but of course, knowing Tessa, if she had a job to do, she wouldn't use anything as strong as Roxanol, which really does the trick.'

'Roxanol?' Maggie asked casually, her nails biting into her palms.

'Morphine in an elixir, a liquid form. It tends to slow you down and numb you, you're not as alert or sharp as usual and you won't be as willing to make the effort to eat. Food aversion is such a difficult thing to do anything about. Whatever you can do to get her to increase her fat intake is important, Maggie, since you're travelling with her and seeing her every day. Most people with her kind of cancer lose a shocking amount of weight.'

'Fat intake?' Maggie parroted, sitting straight in her chair by using all her will-power.

'She's never carried any extra weight, Maggie, you know that as well as I do.'

'True, but how about . . . about her kind of cancer?' Maggie said carefully, keeping her face as immobile as possible and her voice utterly level. 'I don't quite understand it.'

'That's not surprising. Most people don't. Pancreatic cancer is so rarely diagnosed before it's spread. There usually aren't any symptoms until it's too late. If Tessa hadn't come to me for something else she wouldn't have known for months. Quite possibly not even now.'

'Too late to cure it, you mean?'

'Too late to treat it. Maybe some day there will be a cure, but not yet, Maggie, that's the terrible pity of it. Thank goodness you're having a baby—that's going to be a great happiness and distraction for her. She'll have months and months to enjoy your baby, with any luck.'

'Only . . . months? Not . . . a year?'

'Oh, yes, maybe a year, even a little more. We just don't know.'

'Do you think . . . would it be a good idea . . . if I suggested that she stop making these trips?'

'No, absolutely not. Obviously South America agreed with her. She'll know when she feels too tired to travel. Anyway, it's her choice how she spends the time she has left,' Helen Lawrence said briskly as she got up to show Maggie to the door. 'Now be sure to take those vitamins I prescribed for you and make an appointment for a month from now with my nurse. I'll call you as soon as I have the results of your blood work, but from everything I've checked, you couldn't be healthier and you're perfectly all right to travel.'

Maggie walked up Lexington Avenue as purposefully and quickly as she always did, although she was absolutely aimless. Everything she passed, every store window, every traffic light, every man and woman on the street looked unnaturally bright and clearly outlined. She crossed the street when other people crossed the street, she avoided the taxis that made their turns too close to the kerbs, she kept from being jostled with her habitual agility, she put one foot quickly in front of the other to keep up with everyone else, but she wasn't conscious of anything except Helen Lawrence's words.

Maggie reached the Carlyle. Without bothering to have herself announced, she took an elevator directly up to Tessa's floor. She rang, and when the maid opened the door she pushed by her and walked into the living room, where Tessa was arranging flowers.

'I saw Helen Lawrence this afternoon. She told me. About you. About your cancer.' Her voice was hard and furious.

Tessa carefully adjusted a rose and straightened up, putting off the minute she'd have to look at Maggie's face.

'Helen must have thought you knew,' she said calmly. 'I was going to tell you in my own way, Maggie darling, but not yet, not until I had any real symptoms. I feel perfectly fine. I wouldn't believe there was anything wrong if I didn't know.'

'Don't "Maggie darling" me! *How could you, Tessa?* How could you be so cruel to me? Why didn't you just leave things the way they were? Everything was great before you came along and dangled an irresistible auction in front of Liz. God damn you, Tessa, I didn't need you. I had my own life and you weren't part of it. I never gave you a thought. But now! How could you arrange it so that I'd find out what it was like to have a mother? You knew before you started that I'm going to lose you, but no, you weren't satisfied to let me live my own life, you had to make me love you—'

'But that wasn't—'

'Don't tell me that! It was! You know you hoped I'd love you when I got to know you. Deny that!' Maggie challenged Tessa, her anger as unstoppable as breaking surf.

'I can't deny that I wanted us to mean something to each other,' Tessa said in a voice that was all but demolished by Maggie's rage. 'I didn't want to die without your forgiving me for the way I neglected you. I had to try to explain why it happened, no matter how ashamed I was of myself.'

'*Yourself!*' Maggie shouted. 'Always yourself! That's all you thought about, *your* needs and *your* reasons and *your* feelings and *your* lies and why you did this and why you did that for thirteen whole lousy years! Did you ever put yourself in my place? Even for a minute? Just look at the way you acted in São Paulo, knocking yourself out, taking care of me as if the world depended on it. Why didn't you take care of yourself? You *knew* and you slept on chairs. You *knew* and you spent your precious energy running around a hotel doing my job. How do you think that makes me feel? Guilty, that's how, guilty as sin . . .'

'There's not one single thing I did on that trip that will shorten my life and a rest cure wouldn't make me better. But seeing your baby . . . that's going to make a big difference to me. I was just being selfish again.'

'I understand that, damn it, but it doesn't help. I feel so terribly guilty. Why couldn't I have opened at least one of the letters you kept sending me? Why did I never try to find out your side of it? Oh, Tessa, I can't bear it . . . I don't know what to do.' Maggie faltered, as her storm of emotion swept her suddenly into the tumult of tears she hadn't been able to shed.

'Come and sit down here.' Tessa tugged Maggie down onto a sofa and pulled her close. She wiped away the tears that streamed unceasingly down Maggie's hot face, smoothing her curls and giving her little kisses all over the cheek she could reach. 'Don't blame yourself! You were right to resent me. If I hadn't found out how little time I had left, who knows what I would have done? Left you alone, in all probability. I never thought of it from your point of view, only from mine.'

'Oh, Tessa, what are we going to do now?' Maggie sobbed.

'Stop crying, I guess, and start living again.'

'I love you, Tessa. I've always loved you, even when I thought I didn't, but now I love you so much more. You know that, don't you?'

'Yes, my own darling, my daughter, my little girl, I do. That's what we're going to do now, love each other, very hard and very much. That's the only answer I can think of.'

'You're going to tell me something you think I don't want to hear,' Sam whispered to Tessa as she lay naked in his arms that evening. 'Eli's finished the script, hasn't he, and they want you out on the coast tomorrow.'

'Why do you say that?' Tessa asked, her voice muffled in his chest.

'Because I've never been seduced the way you seduced me tonight . . . I felt like an innocent, young, untutored broth of a lad in the arms of a magnificent female who had decided to make a real man out of me. Is this what actors mean by "getting into the part?"'

'You thought I was being Cassie? Passionate Cassie?' Tessa asked, lifting her head.

'Passionate Tessa with something . . . astonishingly new, something I'd never even dreamed of before.'

If only it were that, Tessa thought, burrowing again into his arms. If only her frenzy had been Method acting, instead of a driving need to make love one last time before she had to tell him about her sickness, a last celebration of pure sexual playfulness during which he wouldn't know about her cancer, in which such awareness couldn't cross his mind while they were together.

'But what you don't know, and couldn't guess,' Sam continued, 'is that I've made arrangements to begin my sabbatical year early so I'll be able to spend it with you, while the picture's being made. I'll do research during the day and be there when you get back at night, or whenever you have a free minute. How does that sound to you?'

'Like a dream of impossible bliss.'

'Nothing impossible about it—it's already arranged with the dean of my department.'

'But it can't be, Sam.' Tessa sat up in bed, leaned against the headboard, and pulled a robe over her naked body. She took a shuddering breath and reminded herself that if she didn't tell him now, she'd have to do it tomorrow because she couldn't let him find out the way Maggie had. 'It can't be because I can't make the film and I can't make the film because I have cancer,' she said, forcing her voice to be as ruthlessly direct as a well-thrust dagger.

Sam swung his feet to the floor, his body reacting against the blow before his mind.

'I don't believe it.'

'Yes, you do. You know I wouldn't say it if it weren't true.'

He looked at her sitting with her arms folded defensively over her breasts, her hands balled into fists, and moved quickly towards her, until he could hold her fiercely close. 'Tessa, we'll fight it together, darling. You're going to be all right, I promise you.'

'No, I'm not going to be all right, Sam.'

'*Don't say that.* Whatever it takes, you have to do it.'

'There's nothing to do.'

'For God's sake, Tessa, what kind of quack told you a thing like that? Tomorrow we'll find the best doctor in New York.'

'Sam, Sam darling, listen to me. I've been to one of the best doctors in New York. I have pancreatic—'

'*God! No!*' He let her go abruptly, stood up, and punched the wall so hard that she could hear a bone in his hand break.

'Sam?' Tessa asked in the sudden silence.

'My father died of it.'

'So you understand.'

'Yes.'

'How old was he?'

'Almost eighty. Tessa, did you get a second opinion? You're much too young, there's something wrong . . . it's simply not possible . . .'

'I'd get a second opinion, if it would make you feel better, but I've had ultrasound and computerised tomography and a biopsy and a consultation with a top oncologist and there's no doubt. It's inoperable and I refuse to have treatment that would eat up whatever time is left. It's very early, Sam. I have at least a year, maybe even two . . . Yes, just hold me, keep holding me, don't ever let me go.'

'I won't, my beautiful girl, I won't.'

Ten

SAM SAT NEXT TO TESSA in the comfortable chairs that were arranged in the upstairs owners' lounge of the main auction room, where they would be able to witness the auction without being stared at. Tonight they were alone with the panoramic view of the heads of everyone in the room, and binoculars were provided so that Hamilton Scott, at the podium, seemed only feet away. Although they couldn't see the numbers on the bidders' paddles, they could hear perfectly through the loudspeaker in the lounge.

People were still being seated as Sam restlessly readjusted his pair of binoculars. He and Tessa had been sitting here for almost an hour, with floaters popping in every now and then to ask if they wanted anything to eat or drink. They'd been smuggled in early through the employees' entrance so that Tessa wouldn't have to run the gamut of the huge crowd outside Scott and Scott, attracted by the arriving parade of the invited society figures and celebrities. The mob outside was further enlarged by the presence of mobile television trucks from all three networks and CNN, who would be reporting on the auction as soon as it was over, when they could finally interview executives from Scott and Scott as well as the departing bidders.

Would this hellish auction ever start? Christ, he couldn't wait for it to be over, couldn't wait until Tessa could finally put an end to the infernal round of travel interviews, photographs and more travel. He knew that if she had said, at any point in the past month, "enough", she could have returned to private life and let the auction take place under its own steam. But somehow, once she'd started on the publicity, Tessa hadn't been able to cut it short by one minute. It used up a merciless, profligate, reckless amount of time, time Tessa didn't have, although that wasn't his judgment to make.

Tessa had accomplished the one great single shining thing she had set out to do: become a mother to Maggie. It had meant spending more time than he had imagined possible when she first told him about her plans, but every minute that she worked and travelled with Maggie was a minute of motherhood reclaimed from all the years that had been lost.

Even if he had known about her cancer when she'd first told him about the auction, he wouldn't have said a word to influence her against the idea. He didn't have the right, nor did anyone else, Sam thought, watching Tessa scanning the room, exclaiming excitedly when she caught sight of someone she knew, her binoculars constantly returning to Maggie as she watched her daughter move deftly through the ranks of journalists, bending here and there to distribute chosen morsels of information.

'Darling,' Tessa said, turning to Sam. 'Immediately after the auction, Maggie's coming back to the Carlyle with us. There's something special I want to ask her. Would you mind if she and I had a drink at the bar and talked while you go on upstairs?'

'Of course not. I'll be knocked out. That's what watching people spend tons of money in public does to me. The only time I went to Las Vegas I fell asleep under the blackjack table.'

'Ah, but tonight it's in a good cause.' Tessa smiled at him, a strangely mysterious smile on her passionately formed lips, with such a loving look glowing in her eyes that he had to clench his fists not to cry out. Had she ever looked so vividly alive? Had her face ever been so deeply expressive? She'd never gone for that second opinion and he'd never mentioned it again. Mutely they'd reached an understanding that they had time, plenty of time, for whatever Tessa wanted to talk about, whenever she felt like it.

All Sam knew was that he was on board for the whole trip, he'd be there for her, unequivocally, every step of the way. He loved her more extravagantly each day. All he could do was to hide, as well as he could, the bleak, blank prospect of a future without her that drilled him through and through by day and by night.

The loud crack of Hamilton Scott's hammer brought the buzz below to an abrupt halt. 'Good evening, ladies and gentlemen,' he announced in his rich, extravagance-inspiring voice. 'Welcome to the Scott and Scott Building, and to our historic sale of magnificent jewellery from the collection of Miss Tessa Kent.'

As Tessa and Maggie entered the Café Carlyle, a burst of cheering and applause broke out as Tessa was recognised. The news of the results of the auction had travelled all over the world the instant it finished, and in Manhattan, radio, television and word of mouth had spread the story in less time than it had taken them to drive back to the hotel.

One hundred and sixty-two million dollars had been attained, more than three times as much as the largest single-owner sale of all time, that of the Duchess of Windsor in 1987. Not a single jewel had gone for less than five or six times its high estimate, and every record ever made for every category of gem had been broken.

Tessa waved and smiled to the startled, congratulatory crowd as the head waiter led them to the secluded table she'd reserved earlier in the day. The champagne she'd ordered was poured immediately and she relaxed against the banquette, sighing with relief.

'Why do I have the feeling that I'm here for a reason known only to you?' Maggie asked. 'Why am I suspicious because Sam insisted that he was too sleepy to join us? He looked wide awake.'

'He developed a bad case of auction fever,' Tessa laughed. 'I've never heard a man get so excited. What he needs is to take a tranquilliser and go to bed.'

'Was he surprised that you had so many jewels?'

'He'd flipped through the catalogue once or twice, but I don't think it sank in until tonight. When the auction began and he actually saw and heard an emerald necklace being sold in a few brisk minutes for seven million dollars . . . he was knocked for a loop. Even I was stunned.'

That was the only time during the auction that she'd had to fight back tears, Tessa thought. The memory of that magical night in Èze with Luke, the perfume of the lavender, the warm wind of Provence, that marvellous white Dior dress she'd worn for the first time . . . oh, had it really happened a million years ago and was it possible that there'd never be another night like that again for her?'

'So was I, and I'm used to auctions,' Maggie admitted. 'Those people went crazy! They just had to have a piece of you at any price. You or your legend; I guess they're indivisible. It's hard to wrap my mind around it.'

'I bet Liz and Hamilton aren't having any trouble getting their minds around their ten per cent commission.'

'It's an easier sum to swallow. Almost bite-size. Now, Tessa, tell me why I'm here and you're not upstairs with Sam.'

'Actually, darling, I'd like to offer you a job.'

'What?' Maggie exclaimed, almost choking on the Sprite she'd ordered instead of champagne. 'I've just finished the biggest piece of work in my life and you want to offer me a job? What exquisite timing. Ma, don't you think I deserve a vacation?'

'"Ma"?'

'Yes, I've decided that suits you. Only when we're alone, of course.'

'I love it. I feel like a Ma. Now, Maggie, pay attention. The new foundation will start out funded by the hammer price of everything sold tonight and the profits on half a million catalogues. That's a lot of money. I started to make my will today and I left most of Luke's money to the foundation as well.'

And more than enough to Maggie, Tessa thought, so that she and her children would never be dependent on any man, no matter how much she loved him. But she'd find that out later, when she couldn't protest. And her Tiffany pearls and earrings, which Maggie would actually wear, as well as a glorious three-strand necklace of perfectly matched natural pearls, which she'd probably only wear when she'd grown into them.

'Holy Mother!'

'Exactly. There will be, eventually, a great deal more than . . . several billion dollars for the foundation to work with, with additional funds coming in every year. This foundation needs someone I trust to run it. I don't want to have to count on strangers. I'd like you to consider becoming the head of the foundation.'

'A billion! My God, Tessa, I don't know *anything* about running a billion-dollar foundation!'

'Of course you don't. But you're smart, you're enormously well organised, Maggie mine, and accustomed to working with all sorts of people, and getting them to work with each other. That's the uniquely important thing. For the rest, you'd be able to hire professionals to teach you how a foundation works and pay consulting fees to the best oncologists in the world to guide you in the right directions. It boils down to the basic question of whether you'd rather be doing that or something else.'

'But what about the baby, Ma, your grandchild-to-be?'

'That's the chief thing on my mind. Were you planning to go back to Scott and Scott after the baby is born?'

'No, I want to stay home for two or three years and find something I can do part-time. Barney's doing amazingly well so we can easily afford a housekeeper and I can take care of the baby and do other work besides.'

'You could run the foundation from home,' Tessa said quietly.

'How could I possibly? A billion-dollar foundation?'

'It's not like running a billion-dollar business. Of course you'd have staff. And very good salaries, for you and for them. And an office, to put the staff in, to have a place to meet with the professionals you hire and consult with. But you don't actually have to go to an office to learn and think and ask questions and gradually arrive at the point of making decisions, these days, do you? As far as the money is concerned it would be administered by the same people who administer Luke's estate for me now, so you wouldn't have to worry about that. And it's not as if you'd have to snap right into it. That money wouldn't go anywhere until you felt sure of what you were doing. You'd take little steps and then bigger steps, you probably wouldn't be ready to take giant steps until the baby was in kindergarten—'

'Would I be pregnant again by then?'

'How would I know?' Tessa asked, astonished.

'You know I'm to run the foundation, I thought you might know that too.'

'Oh, Maggie! *Really? Truly?* You'll really do it? You can't have any idea how marvellously happy that makes me. Oh, darling!'

'How could I resist? The more you talked about it, the more I realised I'd resent having anybody else do it. It's your foundation, Ma, the Tessa Kent Foundation, and who else has a better right to make sure it's run on a shipshape basis than your daughter?'

'That's the other thing . . .'

'Tessa? What other thing! Do you have more plans for me?'

'Not plans exactly . . . a question. Now, when I go back to my lawyer to finish drawing my will, do you want me to say that the foundation is going to be run by my daughter—or my sister?'

'Oh, hell. That's a big one and I never thought of it.' Maggie sat absolutely still for minutes, chewing her lip. Finally, she started to speak.

'You can't set up such a huge foundation without making news. It's literally impossible to keep the details out of the press. If you say your "daughter", it becomes a major news story and it will never die. If you say your "sister", that's just a truth that's been around for a long time. It's not news, it's normal.'

'I want it to be your decision entirely,' Tessa said.

'Oh, God, I don't know what to say,' Maggie cried. 'I want people to know I'm your daughter! But I desperately don't want to spend the rest of my life having to explain—'

'—why I didn't say so sooner.'

'Yes.'

'Do you want time to think about it? Talk to Barney, mull it over . . .'

'Or talk to Polly . . .'

'Polly knows!' Tessa exclaimed.

'Oh, she knew first. Well, outside of Barney, Sam, Mimi, Polly, you and I, when you get right down to it, there's nobody else I care about so much that I feel a burning need to tell them. Since we all know, that's enough for me. Tell the lawyer to write "sister"—oh, my God, Doctor Goldenberg!' Maggie clapped her hand over her mouth.

'He was convinced that I was too young to be your mother,' Tessa said with a wicked laugh. 'If he ever reads about it, he'll think I pretended to be your mother to get his full attention. He thought that anyway.'

Eleven

THE FIRST WEEK in June 1994, not long before Maggie's twenty-fourth birthday, her baby was born, a daughter she and Barney named Teresa Marguerite. They called her Daisy from the minute she was placed in Maggie's arms.

Now, on a honeyed Sunday in September, glazed with topaz light that unmistakably trembled on the verge of autumn, Daisy was little more than three months old. All her short life had been spent in a restored farmhouse in Fairfield County, Connecticut, surrounded by her court of Maggie, Tessa and Sam. Only Barney went to the city each day, riding his bike back and forth.

After the auction, Tessa had kept herself busy house-hunting in the countryside for weeks, until she'd discovered this old farmhouse with its forty overgrown but flourishing acres, its wealth of noble trees surrounded by low stone walls. She'd known at once that it was destined to be hers, and then Maggie's and Barney's.

It had been a home for more than 200 years, and its last owner had been careful to restore the plumbing and add a new kitchen without disturbing its old-fashioned charm of nooks, corners and wide porches, and cool, low-ceilinged rooms with wide floorboards and huge fireplaces. It was both a rambling and an embracing house, casually done in an informal style that offered an abiding sense of repose.

It was, Tessa knew, more than a bit of a grand gesture, to give a young couple a newly done-up country house, but she had made a pact with herself to do absolutely everything she wanted most to do, and not ask permission of anyone.

Every morning and afternoon, for three-quarters of an hour, at what had been identified as Prime Daisy Time, after her need for sleep had been satisfied and before she grew hungry again, Tessa and Daisy were left alone together, communing with each other on a wide porch swing heaped with pillows. Daisy alternated between lying on a baby seat that supported her back and held up her head so she could recline at ease and look out regally at the world, and a place in the curve of Tessa's arm, where she snuggled, nuzzled, chuckled, slavered and cuddled contentedly.

'Don't you wish it wasn't September, Daisy?' Tessa enquired in the low, intimate voice she always used with the baby. 'Don't you have the feeling that the summer has come and gone in a flash, that swift, splendid July, that basking, brilliant August—over already? I can hardly believe it. I wish I could tell what's going on in your mind, Daisy. Perhaps a month is but an hour to you, perhaps a lifetime, but I'm convinced that you know more than anybody gives you credit for.'

Daisy, in her baby seat, held out her arms to Tessa with a little cry. Carefully Tessa undid her tiny seat belt, lifted her up and tucked her into the cradle of her arm. The baby immediately snatched Tessa's finger and put her green diamond ring in her mouth.

'I do believe you must be teething, Daisy,' Tessa told her in admiration. 'So young to start, or are you right on schedule? And just why do you look at me like that? I wish I understood why you have so many questions in your unblinking eyes. Is it because there's so much to learn, or could it be that I interest you?'

She'd see Daisy sit up, Tessa thought, as she let the baby play tug-of-war with her finger. She was a strong child. At the rate at which Daisy was growing, she'd certainly be sitting up on her own some time in the next few months.

She'd see Daisy crawl. But would she see her struggle to her feet holding on to a piece of furniture? Or take her first step? Or totter from one piece of furniture to another?

She'd recently graduated—if you could use such a word, Tessa mused— from a simple pain patch to a form of time-release morphine sulphate that lasted from eight to twelve hours. Between the two she kept herself pain-free and she'd adapted her schedule so that she felt most alert between Prime Daisy Time and that precise moment in the afternoon when the infant started to fret and it was time to let Maggie whisk her away.

If only she were one-tenth as hungry as this baby! Maggie was breast-feeding Daisy six times a day, and her appetite was a never-ending astonishment. Sometimes Tessa stretched out in an old wicker chair and watched companionably as Maggie nursed Daisy on the porch, but at other times, when it was more convenient for Maggie to nurse her in the big, cosy kitchen, she drifted away, unobtrusively. Kitchen smells, even those that had once been delicious, had grown intolerable.

Although she refused to climb on a scale, or look at herself naked in a mirror, Tessa knew by the way her clothes fitted that she'd lost an enormous amount of weight. Months ago she'd taken to wearing her full linen shirts outside of trousers, tightly belted so that they wouldn't fall off her hips. Her clothes floated around her, hiding her outline. Every day she made sure to get enough sun to maintain a glowing tan. She used the brightest red lipstick she could find, and she let her dark hair float in its deep, shining waves without restraint.

A girl of summer, she mocked herself, as she looked quickly in the mirror and then looked away. She had the same lack of interest in the still-undiminished beauty of her face as she had in the pile of scripts that lay, growing daily, on the porch near her swing. She hadn't told Fiona the truth, hadn't told Roddy, hadn't told Aaron, hadn't told Mimi, with whom she'd never lost touch. They all thought it was her refusal to be separated from Sam, by a year of location filming, that had made her decide not to play Cassie. Better that than their shock, their solicitude, their pity, and their inevitable phone calls, Tessa thought, jealously hoarding her energy for the people she loved the most.

As July and August had passed, a general agreement had been reached, almost without discussion, that they wouldn't move back to New York this year. Sam worked on his new book for hours every day. Maggie spent some of her time, while Daisy napped, communicating by fax with Dune Maddox, whom she had easily lured away from Scott and Scott to work as her primary assistant on the start-up of the foundation.

What bliss it was, Tessa realised, to look at the old trees that sur-rounded the house, already showering a lazy leaf from minute to minute, and know that she didn't have to leave this place just because the wheel of the year was about to turn. They'd settle into the seasons, Tessa thought dreamily as she delicately smoothed the wisps of dark hair on Daisy's head. Soon they'd be in the middle of the slowly explod-ing fireworks of a New England autumn . . . then the snug, snowy, ease-ful, firelit winter . . . the delights of spring lay ahead . . . too far ahead to bother to anticipate . . . today was enough; each second was enough.

Sam, who had grown up in the country, had already ordered a vast supply of firewood and snowblower for the driveway. Maggie had bought extra blankets and a wardrobe of larger, warm baby clothes, even a tiny snowsuit. Barney had become an instant captive to the big vegetable garden he'd created on a whim from well-grown seedlings a few months earlier. Now he'd sent for a dozen seed catalogues and com-mandeered Sam's services for the harvest.

Daisy's head moved restlessly and Tessa looked down to see the baby's vivid blue eyes with their long dark lashes fixed on her with extraordi-nary concentration.

'If you were a man, Daisy, I'd say you must be in love with me, but that seems unlikely, given your gender and your tender age.' Daisy reached for her finger and began to gnaw vigorously on the diamond.

'But when you're older, and you ask your mother about her mother—and you will—Maggie can show you the auction catalogue—instead of some faded photo album . . . it's all in there, Daisy, at least the part I wanted the public to know. Your mother can tell you the rest, the part I wanted her to know. Then there are the things a woman never tells, but if you're so smart, you'll figure that out for yourself. Will my life be something you can't imagine leading, Daisy? There are so many moments now when it seems like that to me. Strange . . . it didn't truly begin, you know, until one afternoon in 1971, when everything changed in an instant. It was twenty-three years ago . . .'

Daisy looked up suddenly, turning her head alertly, and Tessa wiped a little drool from her chin. 'What a sense of timing you have,' Tessa said admiringly, as she watched the small figures of Maggie, Sam and Barney hurry across the bright lawn, each of them carrying a basket of newly picked vegetables.

'Yes, Daisy, yes, they're all coming, just as fast as they can.'

JUDITH KRANTZ

IT WAS NOT UNTIL Judith Krantz was forty-eight that she started writing fiction. At the time she was the West Coast editor of *Cosmopolitan* magazine and took a leave of absence to write, telling only a few friends what she was doing. 'In fact,' says Judith Krantz, 'it was my husband who made me write my first novel. It took him fifteen years of nagging, fifteen years of telling me that I was a novelist, and after fifteen years I decided to give in and show him I couldn't write a novel. Halfway through writing the first chapter of *Scruples*, I was having the time of my life.' *Scruples* became an international best seller, a hit TV mini-series and launched Krantz's career.

In her novels, Judith Krantz writes mostly about women in business, all striving for success. 'I'm the mother of two sons. Recently I realised that for over twenty years I've unconsciously been creating my own missing daughters in the form of my heroines. In *The Jewels of Tessa Kent* I decided to confront my daughter complex head-on and see where it led.' Although her novels have been described as glamorous fantasies, Judith Krantz researches each book meticulously. 'My husband's been in the film business, both movies and television, since we've been married. In a sense it's my business too, so I didn't have to research any of the film-making detail at all in *The Jewels of Tessa Kent*. As to the workings of an auction house, I was given free rein to research the world of jewellery by a great friend, Andrea van de Kamp, who is the West Coast director of Sotheby's. She introduced me to all the New York Sotheby's people and I was able to see auctions being held from every vantage point. I also did a lot of library research and spent time at the Gemological Institute of America and spoke at length to John Block who's in charge of jewellery auctions at Sotheby's, to make sure that all Tessa's jewels were correctly described.'

Judith Krantz herself does not have great personal experience of buying jewellery at auction. 'I've only done so once and that was here in Beverly Hills. I get all the worldwide catalogues, but I'd never buy anything I hadn't actually tried on. I don't "collect" *per se*, but, over time, I have accumulated a very adequate jewellery wardrobe. My mother left me a lot of jewellery, but it was all stolen. After that there were years in which I wore only a watch, fake pearls, fake pearl earrings and a pin or two. However, after I wrote *Scruples* I bought myself diamond earrings . . . and never looked back. I much prefer to pick out my own jewellery, whenever I think it's an appropriate time to reward myself for finishing a book or for a birthday or anniversary. I then take my husband to see the jewellery to make sure he likes it too. He hates to shop so it's a good thing it isn't up to him!'

Judith Krantz has been married to her husband Steve for over forty-five years, has two grown-up sons, a beautiful Bel Air residence and a house at Newport Beach, California. Like her heroines, she has worked hard and achieved success.

Frankie McGowan

~

A KEPT WOMAN

*Beautiful Serena Carmichael
has it all: money, status and
a family she adores. Then,
suddenly, it all comes to an end.
Her banker husband disappears
and she realises that she has been
little more than a kept woman.
Abandoned by her wealthy
friends, she has to face reality
and find her own way.*

Chapter One

~

THE FAINT SOUNDS of the shower behind the closed door on the other side of her bedroom roused Serena from sleep. Stretching out a hand she fumbled for the lamp switch, forcing her eyes open to examine the bedside clock. The slim black hands swam into focus. A groan escaped her as she registered the unearthly hour. She snapped the light off and let her head fall heavily back onto the pillow.

Six o'clock. She knew before she opened her eyes that there would be an empty place beside her. It had been a long time since she had allowed herself to hope that her day might start in a more leisurely, more intimate way. The pleasure of waking to see Stephen's dark head still next to her had never been a certainty. These days it was a rare bonus.

Serena sat up on one elbow, pushing her blonde hair out of her eyes as the bathroom door opened and Stephen's shape filled the doorway.

'Hi,' she called drowsily. He paused and came over to her, one towel wrapped round his waist, rubbing his hair dry with another.

'I missed you,' she yawned, reaching for his hand. It was cool, still damp from the shower. 'We couldn't sell your ticket at such short notice. Melanie says I should divorce you. What happened?'

'Usual stuff. Malcolm let the meeting drag on, fretting about losing Bretil's interest—he's just not getting back to us. Afraid it's going to be like this for a while,' he warned her.

Serena closed her eyes. 'So what's new,' she grumbled. 'Nothing for it. I'll have to take a lover.'

'Then you'll have to get him past me,' he said, sinking down on the edge of the bed, slipping his hand under the sheet and between her thighs. She gave a sleepy growl.

'Forget it, Buster,' she said removing his hand. 'I can't be bought that easily.'

'No?' He sounded amused. 'Believe me, everyone's got their price.' He leaned over and dropped a kiss on her mouth. 'Even Melanie. Tell her I'll write an obscenely large cheque and a grovelling apology.'

Serena gave him a lazy smile. 'Excellent. Actually it was a bloody awful concert. I rather envied you having an excuse not to turn up.'

He walked towards his dressing room. 'Not if you'd been where I was, you wouldn't. Even a godawful concert has to be more interesting than waiting for Malcolm to make a decision.'

'How is the beautiful Rupert?' she asked, lifting her head to pummel the pillows into a more comfortable shape.

'Still beautiful, still useless.' She wondered how it was possible for him to stay so calm, so detached. Rupert Chawton Browne had been personally hired by Malcolm Brisley Jones, the chairman of Draycott Mendes Merchant Bank where Stephen was head of corporate development, for no better reason than Rupert's family name stretched back to Norman times and his future held an earldom. This blatant social mountaineering had resulted in ludicrously long hours for Stephen, unravelling the problems created by the harmless but inept Rupert.

'Honestly, darling, you should put a stop to it. First bloody Malcolm foists that idiot onto you. Then you have to find him something to do, which he screws up the minute he opens his mouth, and then you have to spend time you could be spending with me bailing him out.'

'Hey, hey,' he interrupted. 'If Malcolm gets off on greasing up to Rupert's family, at least he's not interfering anywhere else in my life.'

Serena slumped back on the pillows. Hopeless. Nothing distracted him from the main event in his life—his job. It wasn't that Serena and the children came lower down the list. They were just on a different one. 'Well, you're going to kill yourself at this rate,' she finished morosely. 'I hope Malcolm will be satisfied when I'm a widow.'

He laughed. 'But just think of what a wealthy one.'

'What good will that do me? There's only a limited number of clothes you can buy in black.'

'Nonsense. Turn yourself over to Paula. Or that idiot Miranda. That's all they think about.'

Serena wrinkled her nose. 'Not Miranda. Poor girl's in a bad way—that bloody husband of hers.'

She stopped. Partly because Stephen wasn't in the least interested in the woolly Miranda Hooper, but mostly because, after the concert the night before, Miranda had begged her to take her home. She was feeling too distressed to face the dinner that her friend Melanie had spent weeks arranging and had made Serena promise to stay silent about the cause—she had just discovered her husband's affair.

Stephen paused in the doorway. 'Oh? What's he done now? Screwed the nanny?'

'No. Forget it. It's just that I had to miss Melanie's dinner and she's furious with me, so you'd better add another nought to that cheque.'

He gave a grunt. 'You're too soft. Every time he plays away from home, Miranda comes sobbing to you. And every time you drop what you're doing and listen to her. And what difference does it make?'

He closed the door. He was right, she thought glumly. Stephen tackled problems head on. She could not imagine him bothering to repeat advice to someone who had turned it down the first time.

Five minutes later, dressed in a pinstripe suit, pale blue shirt and navy silk tie, Stephen emerged from his dressing room and paused to pick up a black leather wallet lying on the bedside table.

Serena, now wide awake, watched him as he briefly checked its contents. It was a pity, she thought, that Mrs Owen couldn't see him. Stephen's immaculate appearance was her handiwork. Olwen Owen had presided over Serena's household for the last seven years. Such was her regard for the proper order of things that she had never invited Serena to call her anything other than Mrs Owen.

But it was Stephen whom Mrs Owen really claimed as her employer. Stephen who featured frequently on the financial pages of the papers, who dined regularly with the Chancellor and members of the Cabinet. Even more satisfying to Mrs Owen's notions of grandeur was when the Chancellor came to Belvoir Square and she, Mrs Owen, was charged with overseeing the caterers.

The care of his Savile Row suits and the laundering of his handmade silk shirts had become a cause in her life. These days the sight of Mrs Owen carefully arranging Stephen's clothes in colour-graded lines raised nothing more than a resigned sigh from Serena, who thought her devotion to his needs excessive.

She did, however, draw the line at having Mrs Owen take control of her own wardrobe. Beyond the practicalities of organising laundry and dry-cleaning, Serena firmly excluded her from her dressing room and was amused, if a little surprised, when Mrs Owen made no objection.

Very occasionally Serena would gently remonstrate with Mrs Owen when her zeal for her job threatened to mobilise a mass walk-out of the rest of the staff. When the last cleaner the agency had sent to assist Mrs Owen had stalked out midway through hoovering the stairs, Serena assured her housekeeper that as long as the house was clean and tidy she didn't mind the odd mite of dust.

'Mrs Carmichael,' had been the indignant response. 'You don't understand these people. Demand more than you need and you'll get the standard you expect. Accept less and they will take advantage.'

Cranky and snobbish she might be, but Serena knew she was excellent at her job and that was, in the end, all that mattered. Especially to Stephen. It was her dedication to Stephen's welfare that had prompted Mrs Owen the day before to sever all links with the current shirt service they were using, when they did not, in her view, achieve the perfection Mr Carmichael's shirts deserved.

Serena sat up in bed with a guilty start, remembering she had promised to relay this change to Stephen. 'Oh God,' she muttered. 'Stephen?' she called, halting him as he began to close the door. 'Totally forgot. Mrs Owen's in a pelter about your shirts. She fired Personal Valet yesterday. Leave her a note will you? Say "quite right" or something.'

Stephen leaned his head against the door frame and sighed. 'Can't you just tell her for me?'

'It isn't the same. Oh, go on,' she cajoled him. 'One line, that's all.' He grunted his assent. 'Love you too, Grumpy,' she teased. 'Hey, come back I haven't finished.'

But he hadn't heard her. She scrambled out of bed onto the polished landing, calling down to him. 'I bet you've forgotten. Chrissie's weekend off. I'm leaving early so I'll be at the cottage by six.'

He nodded and went on down the stairs. 'And lunch at my mother's on Sunday,' she added. She blew him a kiss and returned to bed.

It was six thirty. Stephen's driver would be waiting outside to open the door of the car, hand Stephen the *Financial Times* as he eased his tall, lean frame into the back seat, before walking briskly round to take his seat behind the wheel. Less than twenty minutes later, Stephen would climb out of the car at the main entrance to Draycott Mendes.

To Serena, Stephen had always been the most extraordinary man. Supporting him, protecting him, was as much a part of that as loving him for himself. Stephen's success was their success and she found it incredible that anyone would think she found it arduous to be there for him. She knew how hard he worked, although Stephen saw nothing unusual in his hours. If you made an effort, he reminded her, you got noticed and got on. Making an extra effort had got him a first at Cambridge. Pushing that extra inch secured him a place on the corporate ladder the week after he graduated.

It was what Serena had noticed about him when, aged nineteen, she had first seen him. Making an effort. Exerting himself to talk to the very dull wife of a tedious but titled landowner at the equally tiresome drinks party to which Serena had been invited.

Well, perhaps it wasn't the first thing she noticed about Stephen. The first was purely physical: a force in her that led to sleepless nights and loss of appetite, especially when she surveyed the competition for Stephen Carmichael's attention.

Later, when Serena had moved in with Stephen to his minuscule flat, the panicky feeling of having a permanent temperature left her and was replaced by an obsessive need to make Stephen see it had not been a mistake. She blotted out the fact that it had been Stephen's urging that had brought her to this mews just off Sloane Square, to the united disbelief of her parents, university lecturers and friends.

Being in love with Stephen was a full-time job. Each morning for the first week she scrambled out of bed to cook him breakfast. She soon found it wasn't wanted. 'It's just me being a boring bugger,' he told her apologetically, as she stood in the tiny kitchen clutching a frying pan and an egg. 'I just don't eat breakfast.' She looked aghast. 'And the space between getting up and leaving is when I do all my thinking for the day. It's me. I'm just uncivilised first thing.'

So she trained herself to stay where she was until he had left the house and learned to immerse herself in his life in other ways, which was a daunting task since they had little money. She might, she told him, be the gently nurtured and only child of a baronet, but she was adept at stretching meagre resources to great effect.

Eventually her parents came to support her decision and even developed a cautious regard for Stephen on the grounds that he appeared to love their daughter and that his determination to succeed was confounding all the critics. Sir Stafford and Lady Margot Armitage maintained a brave and united front when Serena and Stephen married hastily but beautifully in the parish church near their home in Wiltshire.

The bride wore a dress of moiré silk and the groom looked impossibly handsome. *Harpers & Queen*, who covered the fairy-tale occasion for their diary pages, tactfully refrained from mentioning that the bride was also four months' pregnant.

The newly-weds were both astonished to see how good Serena became at being Stephen's wife. Though not of a domestic disposition, she learned to cook, and listened when his colleagues came for drinks or dinner. She worked out the right questions to ask, making them feel smart and powerful and eventually more than happy to include the young Carmichaels into their social lives and Stephen onto their list of those to consider when the right moment came along.

Their lives moved rapidly on, which in later years Serena would say was the reason she managed to hang on to her sanity after her first child died a day and a night after she was born. They named her Anna and Serena held her just once, staring into the tiny still face that was her daughter, not knowing how such terrible grief could be endured.

Less than a year later they brought Louise home to their new house in Holland Park. There, two years on, Harry was conceived. Then, without telling her, a surprise he said, when the children were five and two, Stephen had driven her to Belvoir Square, five floors in a pretty garden square just round the corner from Kensington High Street.

'Melanie?' Serena tucked the phone under her chin, pulling her robe on. 'I'm truly sorry. It was a kind of crisis that I wasn't expecting.'

'Huh,' Melanie muttered. 'Miranda's a walking crisis. Who is it this time? Oh, don't bother—I know you won't tell me. But what excuse did Stephen give? We could have got another ten grand if he'd been around to sweet-talk that German banker.'

As usual, Serena felt defensive at the lack of understanding about her husband's punishing hours. 'Locked in meetings and I won't hear a word against him. Anyway, he's left you a cheque.'

A *hrumph* sound came down the phone. 'You're too forgiving. If it had been the first time . . . oh, all right. I love him to bits. Better?'

'Not much. But as I do, it hardly matters. Hey, must dash. Sounds like a minor earthquake going on upstairs.'

An hour after Stephen had left the house, Serena's day began. She could hear Chrissie—Louise and Harry's nanny—making the first of the usual several attempts to rouse Louise, followed by a sharp thump as Harry dived from whatever piece of furniture was doubling as a launch pad onto the centre of his bed.

Serena pushed back the covers, took a quick shower and dressed in record time. Before she reached the floor above she was already calling out to Louise to get a move on. Chrissie called good morning and went back to her own room to dress.

It was a practised and familiar routine. When Chrissie, a good-natured, easy-going young girl from Yorkshire arrived, two years before, she had accepted that Serena had no intention of relinquishing her children to anyone else unless her husband, or her commitments to the charity Babyways—of which she was a founding member—demanded her time. The best of it for Chrissie was that she got chunks of spare time that others in her nanny circle did not.

'Buck up, LouLou,' Serena called to her daughter, who was leaning against Chrissie's open door, quizzing her about her new boyfriend, and waited to make sure that Louise had at least made an attempt to start the day before opening Harry's door. She ducked as he sprayed his space gun in her direction, firing at imaginary aliens.

'Where are you going?' demanded Harry, lowering the lethal-looking weapon, eyeing her black skirt and blue tailored jacket.

'Committee meeting,' Serena explained, swooping him into a hug, letting him go as he wriggled from her grasp. She moved around the room, opening drawers and assembling his uniform. With a final plea to get a move on, repeated to Louise, who was sitting on the edge of her bed gazing in disgust at her school skirt, she disappeared downstairs.

Stephen's note to Mrs Owen was lying on the table. Serena grinned as she took in the two scrawled lines. She moved it to where it would be seen as soon as Mrs Owen came in.

'Oh, LouLou, just *try* to eat something,' she pleaded fifteen minutes later, depositing boxes of cereal on the table for Harry to choose from. Louise yawned, rubbed her eyes and surfed idly through breakfast television, ignoring everything her mother put before her.

'Daddy doesn't have breakfast,' she argued, tossing her dark bob out of her eyes, 'so why should I?'

'Because Daddy has breakfast meetings,' Serena replied calmly, determined not to be drawn into an exasperated exchange by Louise's current passion for thinness. It was absurd. She was, at twelve, as lean as her father—tall too—a softer version of his dark good looks. Harry was as blond as Serena was. At nine he was small for his age, with a gentle nature, unlike Louise's more fiery one. Louise, just like Stephen, was impatient to get on with life. Harry, like Serena, was more content to observe.

'I am gross already,' Louise wailed to an unimpressed audience. 'No one seems to care that I am obese.'

Serena ignored her, telling Harry to eat in a civilised manner and stop spilling cereal everywhere. He licked his spoon before letting it clatter back into the bowl and scrambling away from the table. The usual last-minute frenzy of finding lost scarves and donning coats was more frantic than usual, since Serena was casting around for the minutes of the last Babyways committee meeting. Finally, she swooped the entire family before her through the hall and out of the house.

As they piled out, they passed Mrs Owen hauling her thin frame up the stone steps. All the way up to the door she grumbled about the traffic and Mr Owen's refusal to get a car with an odds-on chance of starting first time in the morning.

'Oh, poor you,' Serena sympathised, trying not to sound rushed. 'Why don't you have a cup of tea, relax. I'll be back later—I want to leave by four if I can—oh, and there's a note from Stephen. Says you should work for him at the bank.' She grinned.

At the bottom of the steps Serena turned to kiss Louise goodbye and with a sigh eyed a strange lump round Louise's waist. 'Open your coat, Lou,' she commanded.

A short eye-to-eye tussle ensued before Louise complied and revealed a skirt rolled thickly over at the waist to bring the hem a more fashionable four inches above her knees. 'If you listened and sent me to a decent school, I wouldn't have to look so *sad*,' Louise retorted bitterly as she unfurled the skirt to its regulation length. 'It's gross.'

'Oh, c'mon, sweetheart, it isn't anywhere near as bad as some,' Serena assured her, and waved her off with Chrissie at the wheel of the Peugeot.

Serena hurtled across London to Hampstead to decant Harry at his prep school. She called Paula Van Stuckley from the car to warn her she might be late. Then, as she slowed for the lights at the Marylebone flyover, she stabbed out her hairdresser's number and had her highlights put back half an hour in case the meeting ran over.

After that she called Christie's and told them she would stop by after lunch to pick up the package containing a first edition of Yeats, which she planned to give Stephen for an anniversary present.

Thirteen years of marriage had left Serena more calmly in love with Stephen than gripped in the grand passion that had made her abandon university and a career. That passion had been softened by familiarity and two children. He had not lost his physical attraction for her, nor his ability to interest her—and that, lately, was the problem.

It was just tiredness, she consoled herself. Stephen so badly needed a holiday, that had limited more passionate moments. She had organised a whole month in Cap Ferrat in the summer, but after four days installed in their villa, and endless phone calls going to and from London, she knew that it wasn't going to work.

'Never mind, darling,' she had soothed, as he flopped down onto a lounger on the villa terrace. 'They'll get used to making a few decisions without you.' She saw immediately she had said the wrong thing, and groaned. 'I mean, until you get back,' she amended.

Stephen had left the same night. Serena and the children came home three weeks later, as planned, having spent the rest of the holiday without him.

Serena turned the car into the side road alongside the hospital and began searching for a meter. Her hopes were now resting on a new-year holiday with Stephen once the children were back at school, but she would not hold her breath.

She gave a sigh, inched her way between parked cars and ran across the road to the glass and chrome entrance of St Biddulph's. The fourth floor—the Wendover Wing—was where the monthly committee meeting of Babyways was to be held, for the first time, in George Kincaid's office. It had been Serena's idea to switch committee meetings to the eminent consultant's rooms at the hospital. Of late, Serena had felt the committee was losing sight of why they were meeting, sliding more into an excuse for lunch at fashionable restaurants.

'Awareness,' she told George Kincaid when they had all met up at a fund-raising dinner about a month before, 'isn't just about raising money, is it? It's about making sure that every new mother knows what can be done to help premature babies. And we don't do that. Why? Because we're not organised properly. We should have meetings that are conducted on a professional, businesslike basis—no fancy lunches.'

George Kincaid was gynaecologist to a clientele drawn from *Debrett's*. He loved the Babyways fund-raising evenings to which his Angels, as he smilingly referred to them, brought their rich husbands, since he would be the sole beneficiary of the event, and his reputation as the leader in his field enhanced. His knighthood, in his view, became even closer.

There was only one blot on George's perfect horizon. Gracing their fund-raising efforts was one thing, but all these women traipsing across his empire, poking their noses into what he was doing with the money they had raised, was just bloody outrageous.

He began to arrange his features into an expression of pained regret, and might have succeeded in deflecting Serena, had it not been for Malcolm Brisley Jones, who was attending the party in the hope that his pretty but bored second wife might be invited onto the committee. He had taken the opportunity to slide his arm round Serena's waist while he listened to her proposal and broke in: 'Splendid idea. Businesslike. That's what I like. Oh, c'mon George, what's the problem with that?'

George swallowed hard and accepted defeat gracefully. 'Problem? Why, no problem at all. I was just surprised, because I've been thinking much the same thing myself. Splendid. Good. I'll just have a word with Paula to see if we can start next month.'

Serena waited until George had found his hostess before turning to

Malcolm and giving his arm a squeeze. 'You're a wonder,' she grinned. 'He would never have agreed if you hadn't said something.'

'Oh, stuff,' Malcolm disclaimed, but she could see he was pleased, and he was too busy feeling charmed by Serena to recall the point of his presence at this party.

Meanwhile, George Kincaid, ostensibly listening to Paula congratulating him on his brilliant idea of moving Babyways into the Wendover, watched Serena. He felt a pang of frustration at the ease with which she got things done. Paula might have grabbed the chair when Serena had gracefully declined, but it was Serena who quietly kept the charity buoyant. And she made him wary.

He'd known her for years. Since Anna in fact. Not that Anna was one of his babies. Too late for that. He'd just picked up as best he could the consequences of a negligent and elderly country GP, who had failed to spot the danger signs. No one in their right mind would have allowed Serena to travel up to London in that condition had they known. They met because he was on duty that night, and he had said, 'Go home, grieve and learn to want another child.' Within three months she was back, pregnant with Louise.

Now Serena passed the nursing station and nodded a pleasant good morning. Further along she slowed her step to glance into the room where Louise and Harry had been born. She hesitated. Same room, the room where George Kincaid had broken the news to her that her first daughter had not survived.

It was because of Anna, now buried next to Serena's father in a Wiltshire churchyard, that Serena had become a prime mover in raising money for a premature baby unit. She felt relieved that it was now a reality, just wishing—oh God, how she wished—that it had been there for Anna.

At the end of the corridor she pushed open the light oak door and joined the meeting that was just being called to order by Paula. An hour later, as the meeting broke up, Serena had agreed to chair a meeting on Monday morning at her house to discuss the cabaret for the Easter Ball at Hurlingham.

As she let herself into the house, Stephen's secretary phoned to tell her that Stephen would be taking her to dinner. She would need her passport and would not be home until Monday morning. Could she pack a weekend case for him? Serena let out a shriek.

'Isn't he amazing?' she demanded of Melanie Westfield twenty minutes later, having despatched Mrs Owen to pack Stephen's case.

Melanie's silence told her that 'amazing' was not the word she would have used.

'Didn't you tell him that it was Chrissie's weekend off?' Melanie demanded. 'How can you go just like that? God, it's you who's amazing. And OK, I'll chair the meeting if you're not back.'

At five, with Chrissie already en route for her weekend off, Serena had dispatched Louise and Harry to friends and her cases were waiting in the hall.

Serena was on the phone when she heard Stephen come in, and quickly brought her conversation with her mother to a close. 'Sorry. Stephen's here . . . must dash. I'm really sorry about lunch on Sunday. It's my fault I should have reminded him,' she lied. It was easier. 'He's so busy,' she rushed on. 'It's our anniversary tomorrow, he's actually being very thoughtful.'

Her mother's 'of course' came just as Stephen strode into the kitchen. Thirteen years had not softened Lady Armitage's view of her son-in-law who had, as she saw it, robbed Serena of many choices in her life by allowing her to give up her degree course to look after him.

'Darling,' Serena exclaimed as she rang off and turned to hug him, 'you're a perfect angel. Where is it? Rome? No, it can't be. Too far. Please tell me, it's Paris?'

He laughed at her eagerness and kissed her. 'Buck up, darling, car's waiting, plane's waiting and most of all I'm waiting.'

It was, of course, Paris. A thin mist had followed them from the airport, hovering in trees, presenting a mournful view of Serena's favourite city. 'Shame we didn't get married in April,' she commented, turning back into their room at the Ritz from where she had been peering down at the Place Vendôme. 'I mean instead of November.'

'Grateful little soul, aren't you?' Stephen called from the sitting room where he was using the phone. 'I seem to remember you were not keen to wait at the time . . . Barbara? What news? See if he's there. I'll wait.'

Serena strolled through to run a bath, pinning her hair up as she walked between bathroom and bedroom, preparing for the evening ahead. She had plenty of time. Stephen never made just one call and always received several back.

She was ready, except for her dress, and was wrapped in a silk dressing gown when Stephen finally appeared, loosening his tie.

'Everything all right?' she asked lightly, looking at him in the dressing-table mirror. She adjusted her hair, already perfectly in place.

'Sort of,' he said, disappearing into the bathroom, emerging seconds later, pulling his shirt over his head and dropping it to the floor. 'Small change of plan. Nothing spectacular. They've managed to set up a meeting with Jacques Bretil, the guy from Banque Commerciale. The old man told him I was in town and he's delaying leaving for the country just to have lunch with me tomorrow. It's an amazing stroke of luck.'

'*Steph-en,*' she wailed, turning to face him. 'How can you say that? It's our weekend. Can't someone else go?'

He crouched down beside her and took her hand, gazing intently at her. Serena glared at him. 'I love it when you sulk,' he teased. 'Hey,' he coaxed. 'It's not so bad. We've got two whole nights here and we don't have to get the plane back until Sunday evening.'

'*Sunday?* You said Monday. I've got Melanie to cover for me *and* the children could have come back Sunday night, which is much better for them, *and*—' She stopped as Stephen produced a small white box from behind his back and held it out to her. It was tied with thin gold ribbon. 'What's that?' she asked, hanging on to her position for just a little longer.

'Present. Well, go on, open it.'

Inside a pair of pearl-and-gold drop earrings glinted back at her from a box marked Van Cleef & Arpels. 'You idiot,' she said crossly, throwing the box at him. 'They're beautiful and you're infuriating and . . . oh, damn you. Go to your silly lunch.'

He kissed her on the mouth. 'I'll make it up to you,' he promised. Serena gazed steadily back at him, fixing her new earrings in place. 'You'd better,' she murmured, getting up and pushing him gently backwards towards the bed, sliding her robe off as she went, 'and it had better be good.'

It was a familiar but practised intimacy. Stephen was back to his normal self. It had been almost two weeks. Her beautiful earrings got tangled up in her hair and they were, of course, a little late arriving at the restaurant.

Over dinner she gave him the Yeats, which he adored, reaching for her hand to kiss it. Later they strolled back in contented silence, their fingers entwined, threading their way through brightly lit but nearly deserted streets.

At the Pont de la Concorde they crossed the river, pausing because it was Paris and for lovers. Stephen pulled the fur collar of Serena's coat up round her ears and wrapped his scarf round her. They gazed down into the murky depths of the Seine, swirling angrily below them.

'Scary,' Serena said, shivering. 'Not romantic at all. We need warm sunshine, accordions, artists and poets.'

Stephen began to laugh. 'Accordions I can't do, but I might be able to help you with poetry.' He delved into his coat pocket, retrieving the slim volume of Yeats. 'Now where is it? . . . Ah, here,' he said, finding the page he wanted. '"When you are old and grey and full of sleep, and nodding by the fire, take down this book . . ."'

'All right, all right,' she begged. 'I give in. Anything but your idea of romance. Name your price.'

'A kiss,' he said, and pulled her to him.

She shrieked, but complied as two passers-by glanced curiously at them. 'You drive a hard bargain,' she announced as they moved on.

He gave her an odd look. 'There!' he said, 'I've proved a point.'

'And that is?' she asked, taking his arm. Stephen carefully stored the book in his coat pocket and then reached down, lightly tugging one of the earrings he had just given her. She looked up as he chuckled.

'As I said, my precious, everyone's got a price.'

The next morning she went for a stroll along the Boulevard St Michel, stopped at a small café overlooking the Seine and settled herself outside. The damp mist from the day before had given way to a bright but still sharply cold day. She wound her wide cashmere shawl up to her ears.

Serena felt peaceful. For a long time now she had felt Stephen slipping away, caught up in his work, sliding further into his own world. Even if it was just for a day, Paris had been enough to restore something of the old Stephen to her. She ordered a second coffee and waited at the café until she guessed Stephen would have finished lunch and her weekend could resume. She avoided the word she knew was more accurate. Her life could resume.

Chapter Two

SERENA READILY ACKNOWLEDGED that she was in the fortunate position of being a wealthy woman because of Stephen. He was passionate about life, and filled theirs with indisputable evidence that he was clever as well as successful. A discerning eye and a talent for investing in new young artists brought him to the attention of serious dealers. A wine cellar was stocked with vintage champagnes and clarets bought at auction. His children were sent to expensive schools and his library was that of a man who was well read.

He had brought his family from a cramped little mews house to their present splendour through his genius for getting what he wanted, a regard for the discipline of hard work as the route to success, driven most of all by a contempt for his father's dissolute lifestyle.

Wilfred Carmichael had spent his life travelling, gambling and womanising, using money that had been left to him by his father, who had won it on the football pools. Stephen was still in his first year at Cambridge when Wilfred dropped dead in a nightclub in Nice. The debts he left were considerable. But these were nothing compared with the legacy of his reputation.

A year later, his mother, who was fifteen years younger than Wilfred, had departed to set up home in Tuscany, with only a vague suggestion that, if he was at a loose end, he would be welcome to join her in her mountain home. When Serena met Stephen, he had lived on his own for five years.

True, Stephen was not destitute. In a rare show of strength against her husband, when she saw what was happening, his mother had insisted that Wilfred set up a small trust for each of her sons that was enough to support them in reasonable comfort until they found jobs. But it was only a fraction of the money Wilfred had squandered.

Serena had expected Stephen to feel grateful that his mother had stepped between him and hardship. Instead he was angry.

'My mother was hopeless with him. If she'd divorced him years before, she would have got far more, rather than hanging on to a man who cared nothing for her. You have no idea what it was like trying to shake off his reputation. The only decent thing he did was to die abroad so that for the last few years no one knew just how bad he'd become.'

Serena said nothing. In spite of Stephen's indifference to his mother they remained in touch and continued to antagonise one another whenever they met. She admired him for such loyalty.

Jasmine Carmichael, known to everyone as Minnie, was something of an artist in her own right. A tall, lean woman with strong hands, her loosely assembled hair streaked with grey, she was indifferent to fashion and never wore make-up. Those who knew her could never understand what she had in common with Wilfred. Now established in a small villa in Lucca, Minnie was happier than she had been in years. She had been able to live economically enough to return to her first love of painting, earning enough modest sales to make abrupt and infrequent trips to London to see the younger of her two sons. The older, Toby, lived in Cape Town.

Minnie had attended their wedding, given them one of her paintings and told Serena—watching Stephen as he moved among the wedding guests—that Stephen was his father's double.

'His father's?' Serena repeated.

'Mmm,' Minnie nodded. 'A fondness for the good life.'

'Heavens,' Serena's eyes widened. How little she knows her own son, Serena thought, amazed at such a judgment. Couldn't she see, wondered Serena—too polite to say so and indeed not knowing her new mother-in-law well enough to point it out—that Stephen was nothing like his late and—shocking to Serena—unlamented father?

Slowly Serena had come to realise that Stephen's hunger for success was his driving force. Not for a moment did she doubt that she and the children were loved, but it was many years now since she had acknowledged that her marriage would survive only if she gave Stephen the room he needed to power his way to the top.

After their weekend in Paris, Serena's hope that Stephen would cut back on his hours was short-lived. Christmas was spent in the country, but the romantic holiday she had planned in the new year to Antigua, once the children were back at school, was cancelled at the last minute.

'Antigua?' Stephen looked blank. 'Oh God, sorry, Serena, I forgot. Hopeless. It's just not on at the moment.'

Serena fell silent. It was after midnight and they were in the drawing room. For the past week he had been locked in his study until the small hours. Last night he hadn't come home at all, spending what little was left of it in the hotel where he had been with business associates sorting out the havoc caused, once again, by the hapless Rupert Chawton Browne.

'If Rupert's so hopeless why's he in banking?'

'Not hopeless, just not very committed.'

He directed the remote control towards the television, snapping it between channels looking for a City update. 'The trouble with you,' he said, 'is that you spend too much time wondering what everyone else is doing, while some of us keep our eye on what matters. What does it matter about Rupert? He's simply cosmetic. A joke.'

Serena started to protest that he wasn't a joke to the outside world. Because of Stephen's discretion, Rupert was publicly regarded as an asset, because Malcolm treated him as such, and it was all so unfair. But Stephen just yawned.

'Look, Stephen,' she said, trying not to sound like a whinge, knowing instantly she had failed. 'I was only thinking of you. Ever since Paris you've been working your socks off. I worry, that's all. I'm entitled to worry, aren't I? Stephen, are you listening to me?'

'Yes, yes, yes.' He struggled to his feet, putting his glass down with a snap. 'I'm listening. It's just a particularly tricky time.' He cut across as she opened her mouth to ask why it was tricky.

'Can't talk about it, you know the rules. Look,' he said, rubbing his eyes and letting his fingers drag down his face, 'why don't you buzz over to Rome, do some shopping, eh?'

She glared at him. 'Is that all you think I do? For God's sake, give me some credit. How could I leave now? You're under pressure. It's no fun for me either. You snap my head off all the time. I hardly see you.'

'All right, all right.' He picked up his drink and tossed it back. 'I understand, only'—his voice dropped to a more gentle tone—'not now, eh?'

She knew that voice. 'No, of course not. Not now. Bed?' she invited.

'In a minute,' he said, as she stood up. 'You go on. I'll be up later.'

She had hoped to celebrate Stephen's fortieth birthday at the end of January on a sun-drenched beach, but, deprived of this, Serena planned a party instead. She phoned Barbara, his secretary, and asked if she would make sure that Stephen left the office on time.

Barbara's voice was chilly. 'I'll do my best of course, Serena. But Stephen doesn't always tell me about the meetings he arranges. I can only vouch for those I organise.'

Serena stopped. 'Of course,' she agreed. 'I only meant you could remind him.' She replaced the phone.

She toyed with the idea of ringing Malcolm's secretary, but then remembered that she could be much worse than Barbara where wives were concerned. Malcolm and his second, much younger wife were coming to this party. Last time they had all dined together at Malcolm's house, Serena had noticed that Malcolm's wife clearly fancied Stephen. Malcolm could see it, too, and was miserable.

'And Stephen,' Malcolm's wife cooed, indicating his place next to her, 'you here.' Her breasts strained against a too-tight dress.

Poor old Malcolm, thought Serena, taking her place much further down the table. 'Serena, next to Rupert, and Malcolm,' his wife wagged her finger at him, 'you're not to flirt with Paula.'

Weeks later, planning Stephen's party, Serena frowned at the list in front of her. If there had been any way of not inviting the Brisley Joneses she would have willingly used it, but Stephen wanted them included.

On the day of Stephen's party Malcolm Brisley Jones's secretary phoned to apologise and to say Malcolm couldn't make it after all. She didn't give a reason and Serena didn't ask for one. This did not cheer her as she might have expected it to. She knew Stephen would be irritated.

Meanwhile, the florists were already working downstairs. Caterers would be installed at midday. She ticked off the list in her hand. Charles Westfield was going to propose the toast after Richard Van Stuckley had made his speech. Paula phoned Serena just after breakfast to say that Richard was only too pleased to have been asked. As he had offered himself, ruling out more appropriate candidates like Charles, Serena assured Paula that Richard was the perfect choice.

She wondered if Paula knew about Richard's infidelities. The last one had been the subject of one of her rare rows with Stephen. Serena had not known that Richard Van Stuckley, senior member of the Cabinet, charming and urbane, upholder of family values, had taken his mistress to Serena and Stephen's country home. Serena's fury, when she discovered this, had alarmed Stephen.

'Paula can be an absolute pain at times, but she is loyal to him and considers herself a friend of mine,' she stormed. 'And it won't do you any good if that bloody girl runs to the *Sun* and our cottage is plastered across the tabloids as a "Minister's love nest", will it?'

Although Richard resented the fact that he was never allowed to use the cottage again, he was nervous that Serena might tell Paula, so he always remained outwardly pleasant and attentive.

At eleven, she was dismayed when another guest dropped out. A close colleague of Stephen's was needed urgently at the same meeting as the chairman, which meant that the chairman's deputy would undoubtedly be ringing to cancel as well.

Serena started to feel nervous. At this rate it was likely that Stephen would not show for his own party. She called Barbara again, but this time she got the junior secretary who said Barbara had gone to lunch and Mr Carmichael was expected any minute. Serena left a message for Stephen to call her at the hairdresser's. She might still be able to get him to wriggle out of the meeting if she got to him before Malcolm did.

There was a pleasant buzz of activity as she left the house for the salon. Simon, her hairdresser, whizzed her through in record time, for which she left a handsome tip. She picked up her dress from Bond Street and headed home. It was almost five. All Serena had to do was check everything was in place, and then be ready by seven forty-five for the first guests' arrival. Still no word from Stephen, and the junior secretary had said Barbara had been asked to help out in the chairman's office. And no, Mr Carmichael wasn't at the meeting. She was quite, quite sure.

Serena breathed a sigh of relief, switched off the car phone and swung the car into Belvoir Square. The chance of Stephen doing a no-show at his own birthday had now been safely deflected. Serena reached into the back of the car to collect her parcels and then set the alarm.

It occurred to her, as she approached the shallow steps leading up to her front door, that there were an unusual number of cars in the square. Dark saloons. As she put the key in the lock the door was pulled open from the inside. Serena stared at the woman in front of her.

'Natalie,' she exclaimed, leaning forward to embrace the dark-suited woman, 'what brings you here so early? Goodness, you gave me a fr . . .'

Her voice tailed off. Natalie Silverman, senior partner in Beresford, Wright, Stephen's lawyers, took her arm and pulled her gently into the house. A series of images flashed before Serena. Mrs Owen's pale, stern face by the door to the kitchen. Silence when the sound of her children's voices should have been filling the house. Stephen's study door open, papers everywhere. She could see the backs of two men who were dismantling the computer. The clock was pointing at five to five. Serena wheeled round, dropping her parcels.

'Natalie, what is it? Don't frighten me. Is it Stephen? Oh my God, he's had an accident—'

'Serena, you must be calm.' Natalie, still clutching her arm, ushered her into the drawing room. One of the men came forward.

'Mrs Carmichael?'

'Yes?' Her voice was cracking. It came from a great distance. She was holding on to Natalie. She didn't know why.

'Have you any idea where we might find your husband?'

Serena looked at Natalie and back at the man. 'Stephen?' she repeated. 'His office. Here—I mean later he'll be here. It's his birthday. Why? Please, for God's sake, *tell* me.'

The second man came forward and motioned Natalie to make Serena sit down. 'Mrs Carmichael,' he addressed her. 'I'm sorry to have to tell you, we have a warrant for your husband's arrest.'

Serena gazed at him. She tried to speak, but the words were caught in her chest. Her eyes flashed around the group.

'Don't be so absurd. Is this some kind of bad joke?' But even as she said the words, she knew it wasn't, and as the man slowly shook his head, Natalie's hand closed over hers and a noise like a gun being fired echoed in her head.

Her eyes flew open. It was still dark. She groped for the light beside her bed, her hair damp with sweat, straining to hear if Harry or Louise had woken. It was four in the morning. The house was silent.

No one stirred. She slumped back on the pillows. She hadn't meant to go to sleep and she felt guilty that she had given in to this brief moment of oblivion, a respite from the terrible feeling of shock. Not knowing where Stephen was, terrified that he might be dead. And the silence. The dreadful silence that roared in her ears. She began to shake, huge gulping sobs racked her body. Sheer fear. She swung her legs to the floor and moved stiffly towards the window.

Below her was a scene that was bizarre and frightening. They were still there. Still waiting. All waiting for Stephen: the press corps were encamped outside the door and the police inside it. By that time, the bank had admitted that a large but unspecified amount had gone missing from several accounts, along with their head of corporate development, and the Serious Fraud Office had put out an alert for Stephen Carmichael.

Mechanically she went into the shower and turned the taps full on. Immediately a gentle knock came on her bedroom door. Oh God, she'd forgotten. The policewoman monitoring her in case she tried to phone Stephen, or slip away to do herself in.

She crossed to the door and opened it a few inches.

'I'm sorry, Mrs Carmichael, I just wanted to check you were OK. Can't you sleep?'

Serena stared curiously at her. 'Sleep?' she repeated. 'No. Dozed. That's all.'

'Would you like a cup of tea?' the young woman asked anxiously.

If it meant she would go away and leave her to her shower and to think, then she could make all the tea in China. Serena gave a weak smile. 'Yes. Thank you.'

By morning every paper splashed the story that a well-known merchant banker was missing. Headlines on breakfast television were dominated by it. By six, the BBC weighed in with several interviews—bank staff who claimed to be variously 'shocked' or suffering from 'disbelief'. By nine, all interviews had been vetoed on the orders of the bank who, in their panic, had not had time to brief their employees. Andrew Beresford had also threatened to slam injunctions on the entire staff for prejudicing his client's right to a fair hearing when he came forward, as he confidently predicted he would.

Melanie Westfield was let in early next morning to be with Serena until her mother arrived from the country. Harry and Louise were kept upstairs by Chrissie, with orders not to let them see any news bulletins, answer the phone or catch sight of any newspaper. Serena had explained that Daddy had been delayed somewhere. As soon as he phoned, she would tell them. Louise gave her a level stare. Harry just nodded and slid his thumb into his mouth.

Mrs Owen, whose husband had arrived to sit it out with her in the kitchen, was told not to speak to reporters.

'There's been a mistake, a dreadful mistake,' Serena told the silent Owens and Chrissie. No one believed her.

Three o'clock. The house was silent. Serena pushed herself, still fully clothed, to a sitting position. Not as good as the night before when, dosed up with Seconal, she had slept for six hours. But better than the five days after she had been told, when she couldn't sleep at all.

Across the room, the door to Stephen's dressing room was slightly ajar. Through the gloom Serena fixed her gaze on it, seeing him in the doorway, the perfectly groomed merchant banker.

If it hadn't been so tragic, she reflected, she might have laughed at Mrs Owen's face when the fraud squad had trawled through his wardrobe, searching for disks that Draycott Mendes claimed were crucial to their pursuit of a successful prosecution.

Serena had stood, rigid with rage, as they went through her husband's most personal possessions. Each day the house was crowded with detectives mobilised by the Serious Fraud Office. She never saw the financial investigators brought in when Draycott Mendes had first suspected Stephen might be doing the unthinkable. They had been secretly called in by Malcolm, unwittingly alerted by the hapless Rupert, who as usual stumbled into a file that made no sense to him, and for once took his clumsiness to Malcolm's deputy to unravel, rather than to Stephen . . . All of them closing in on Stephen, silently waiting to trap him.

Malcolm. Malcolm with whom they had dined only a few weeks before knew, absolutely must have known, that the man he was entertaining so lavishly in his own home was under investigation on his instructions. How could he have been so devious? How could they have believed Stephen would not have seen the trap waiting for him? Of course he had fled. If Malcolm could be so treacherous not to ask him, after all those years of loyal and selfless devotion, to explain the discrepancies, Stephen would have seen he had little chance of his innocence being recognised. She repeated this not only to herself but to anyone who questioned her. It had to make sense, she urged herself. It had to.

Serena locked herself in the bathroom, leaned her head against the cool tiles and took several deep breaths. Even then, the ever-present policewoman tapped and asked if she was all right.

'Go away!' Serena shouted through the door.

'Mrs Carmichael,' the woman said, 'you know that until your husband comes forward, we have to know if he tries to contact you.'

Serena opened the door and stood back so that the woman standing outside had a clear view into the white-and-blue tiled room. 'You have searched me for phones, and clearly the bathroom does not have one. Please,' she asked wearily, 'just leave me alone, will you?'

But they didn't. A saner, more rational voice, which hovered just below the surface of her anger, knew they couldn't. But she was not ready for the saner voice. Not when her bank accounts were frozen, Stephen's picture flashed on every news bulletin. Not while the world had gone mad. Surely to God, it would end soon?

Natalie Silverman arrived each day to protect Serena's interests. Andrew Beresford had instructed Serena to say nothing unless he or Natalie were present. He wondered when she would crack. The icy calm that Serena had maintained since the first wave of shock had suffused her was unreal.

Her phone calls were monitored and a system to track any call, should it come from Stephen, hooked up to the telephones and the fax line. Phone records were checked for calls overseas. Mobile phone records were similarly screened. Until all of this had been put in place, Serena was asked not to leave the room unless accompanied by the police-woman. A fierce argument followed, because Serena refused to see her children in the presence of the police, and a compromise was reached.

'Let them stay with Melanie,' begged her mother. 'They can't stay here like this. Let them go to school.'

'I can't,' Serena said. 'How do I stop those vultures taking pictures? What will it look like? Just think. Two privileged children being dropped off at their expensive schools, while their father is wanted for lifting millions from his company?'

'But that police officer said the press aren't allowed to take pictures of children no matter what their father has done.'

Serena leapt to her feet and gripped the fireplace. 'I don't care. I don't trust anyone. They stay here until . . . the fuss dies down, or'—she took a deep defiant breath—'until I hear from Stephen.'

She turned and looked beseechingly at her mother. 'Sorry. Sorry, sorry.' She sank down beside her. Margot reached out to grip her daughter's hand. It was cold, unresponsive. Margot tried again, leaning forward, speaking quietly, but with urgency. 'Serena? Listen to me. The children need to get out of here. Watching you suffer is purgatory for them.'

'No, no, no. The children stay with me. They need me.'

Margot slumped into silence. The children could, should leave the house. Margot had been in Belvoir Square now for over a week and was desperate for the children to experience normality. But they weren't normal any more. Nor would they ever be. Not now. They would always be the children of 'disgraced banker, Stephen Carmichael'.

Only a fool would believe in Stephen's innocence. An innocent man would not allow his wife to suffer in this way. Watching Serena clinging so stubbornly to the belief that Stephen would phone or any minute walk through the door, Margot longed, more than anything she had ever longed for in her life, that he would, to ease her daughter's pain.

Her daughter needed her. She needed someone to lean on. She hadn't mentioned it, and Margot had refrained from drawing her attention to it, but the phone, which rang incessantly, was rarely for Serena. And was anyone surprised? Their friends had been questioned by the police, there were reputations on the line, careers to be considered. Who could blame a little reserve until the dust had settled?

It was an excuse. Margot wondered just how many real friends Serena could rely on. Apart from Melanie, not many were braving the press corps to see her. Two or three had called, had hugged her, agreed there must be a rational explanation and tried not to exchange uneasy glances while Serena was in the room. Nice women, bewildered at what had happened, but hopelessly incapable of offering comfort.

The door of the drawing room was pushed cautiously open. Margot looked round to see Harry framed in the doorway. His small anxious face mobilised Serena into action in a way that her mother's entreaties failed to do. She held out her arms and Harry ran to her. Margot rose quietly from her seat and went in search of Louise.

Louise's unquestioning acceptance of her lot concerned Margot. Louise was a rebel, but at twelve she had to have something to rebel against. Without her mother's attention, she did not know how to rebel.

Margot now found her staring silently down into the garden four floors below her bedroom window. She looked round as her grandmother came in. Margot slipped an arm round her shoulders and gave her a squeeze. 'I'm all right.' Louise responded to the gesture with a gruffness that did not fool her grandmother.

'I know you are,' Margot replied, mustering a cheerfulness that exhausted her. 'It was just me that needed a cuddle. I do wish all these people would go away, don't you?'

Louise continued her examination of the view from her window. 'They won't until Daddy gets back.' She paused and then said in a strangled voice, 'I've missed Alice's party as well.'

'Darling,' Margot cried, 'when was it? Oh, why didn't you say?'

Louise shrugged. 'Saturday. It doesn't matter,' she struggled on fiercely, 'can't stand her anyway. She's such a cow.'

'LouLou!' Margot checked back a rebuke. No one had called to ask if Louise was OK. Certainly no one called Alice. Louise was right, Margot sighed to herself. What a cow.

Melanie picked Louise and Harry up just after seven that night. They were smuggled out of the house with the help of the police and their neighbours, a quiet, retired colonel and his wife, who agreed instantly to allow them to lift the children over the garden wall that divided the two houses, and from there into the cobbled street beyond.

Serena watched her children's progress, hugging them both and promising to see them the very next day.

'Mum,' whispered Louise, as she was about to be lifted across the wall, 'come with us, don't stay here.'

Serena kissed her and gave her a fierce hug. 'Don't worry about me, darling,' she whispered back. 'I have to stay here in case Daddy calls.'

Louise hesitated. 'He will, won't he, Mum? Then it will be all right again, won't it?'

'Absolutely,' Serena whispered back. 'Take care. Yes, yes, she's coming.' She stepped back as the pleasant-faced young officer, perching on the dividing wall, reached down to lift Louise off the ladder to join Harry already being whisked away to Melanie's car.

Dear God, Serena covered her face with her hands as her children disappeared into the night. What is happening to us? Stephen. *Stephen.* Where are you? Why are you doing this?

Chapter Three

~

SERENA MOUTHED A SILENT thank you at the picture emblazoned across the newspapers of the Cabinet minister who had been discovered in a discreet hotel with an indiscreet young model. Overnight, the chaos enveloping the house in Belvoir Square was upstaged. News teams were rapidly redeployed to push the doorbell of the arrogant MP, who was trying to bluster his way out of a mess of his own making. With no progress in locating the missing banker, and Serena's continued refusal to grant interviews, the cold and bored press corps vanished.

The few visitors who called to offer comfort dwindled. It was beyond her even to discuss it, but Serena knew there was widespread anxiety among those who had been called on by the police to discover if anyone had had a clue as to Stephen Carmichael's activities.

The daily calls from the police and Melanie continued. Eventually the children came home, and, without a press corps to note their every move, their lives resumed a kind of routine that, curiously, helped.

Andrew Beresford's role was restricted to the battle with the banks to keep Serena afloat, once it had been established that she was not implicated in Stephen's fraud.

'Thank God for that,' Margot said, as Serena came back into the room from a routine meeting with Inspector Donald Trewless.

'For what?' Serena asked, lowering herself into a chair.

'All those dreadful people,' said Margot, peering out into the deserted square as the detective's car drove away. 'All rushed off to plague the life out of someone else. Maybe now we can get back to normal.'

'And what would that be, exactly?' Serena asked, drily.

Margot looked flustered. 'Darling, I didn't mean . . . I, oh you know what I mean,' she ended, crossly.

'I know. Don't get your hopes up just yet. Inspector Trewless says they'll be back. What they do is come back when the fuss has died down and they think that you'll be ready to talk to them—yes, I know, complete waste of time, but there's still the big picture to take.'

Margot looked blank. 'Big picture?'

Serena made a fuss of pouring herself more coffee. 'Of course,' she said lightly, 'when Stephen comes home.'

Her mother's mouth opened and then closed. Whatever she was going to say was left unsaid. Instead she nodded vigorously. 'Absolutely,' she said, stoutly, 'of course.'

Serena wasn't fooled. She gave Margot a small smile. She knew she should tell her mother she looked tired, that the exhaustion etched on her face was unfair, but she had nothing left for anyone.

During the day she longed for night so that she could stop making an effort. Then she could escape to her own room to be alone without someone following her, her mother anxiously trying to make her eat, the children watching her face, waiting for a smile.

Haunted by images of Stephen lying dead somewhere, or with amnesia wandering in some strange city, she was glad none of her family could see her wrap herself in his dressing gown, burying her face in the soft towelling robe with its faint smell of his aftershave. Certainly, no one was there to witness the moments when she crouched on the grey velvet carpet rocking herself, moaning like a wounded animal.

The sight of the betrayed wife of an MP might well distract the public gaze from the shifty behaviour of a missing banker and the misery of the banker's wife, but it didn't, Serena told herself, stop the litany of horrors waiting for her each morning.

All Stephen's assets were frozen. The bank, with enough documentary proof that irregularities on a vast scale had emanated from accounts controlled by Stephen, had found no difficulty in having an injunction granted in their favour. Everything was under threat. The house, the cottage, the ponies, the cars. All bought, claimed Draycott Mendes, with defrauded funds. The bank's revenge had been swift and savage. 'What do you mean?' Serena whispered, when Andrew Beresford took her through the debts. 'They can't take the house away . . . Can they?'

'You have no assets of your own—yes, I know, but a few pictures and some family silver and furniture is not going to pay off the amount missing. Whatever Stephen did—OK, or didn't do—had a knock-on effect right across the board. It will be months before they unravel the mess. It runs into millions.'

Serena gasped. 'Millions? Impossible. Andrew—there's been a terrible mistake. Show me? Where are the millions?'

'Probably in a Swiss bank account,' he told her bluntly. 'He's been planning this for some time.'

'You don't know that,' she said stubbornly. 'If that were the case Stephen would have made sure he protected me and the children—he would have put the house in my name.'

Andrew shook his head. 'Afraid it wouldn't have made any difference. The evidence for the funds going walkabout starts a good seven years ago. It would have been seen by the courts as intent.'

'But surely to God, the court can't blame me and the children?'

'Courts are not interested in you. They're on the side of the victim.'

'But I'm the victim,' cried Serena.

'No, you're not. The bank is.'

Serena's cash flow dried up at an alarmingly quick rate. Bills that would normally have been paid by banker's order from Stephen's account were starting to be returned to her for payment. Mrs Owen had finally broached the delicate subject of her salary, which had not turned up in her account. Nor had Chrissie's, who had said nothing.

Serena was mortified. She found Chrissie upstairs, folding Louise's scattered clothes. 'You should have said something,' she scolded her.

'Serena, honestly, I'm fine,' Chrissie protested. 'As long as you can feed me I can hang on for a bit.'

Serena gave her a hug and walked slowly downstairs. Hang on for a bit? She didn't have the heart to tell Chrissie just how bad things were.

Charles Westfield came over that night. He wrote out enough cheques on her behalf to ward off tradesmen who on another occasion would have been happy to wait for payment. Chrissie and Mrs Owen were paid up to date.

'I hate this,' Serena mumbled. 'I know I should be grateful and I am, but it's not what I want. I wouldn't have asked, only Melanie insisted.'

'Quite right, too,' Charles replied, not looking up from the kitchen table where he was busy writing. 'Just a little temporary help from a friend until you're back on your feet. No big deal, is it?'

Serena watched him. 'And . . . of course Stephen will put it all right when, well, when things settle down.'

Charles glanced up at her. 'Of course,' he said heartily. 'And a very large dinner will be extracted as well.'

She look bleakly at him. This was difficult for both of them. She, because she was humiliated, and he, because the furious exchange he'd had with Melanie earlier hung over him. Charles had to fight back a strong impulse to tell Serena to stop believing in Stephen. But Melanie had been appalled at the idea. 'Charles, don't say a word. Just make her take some money—oh, for God's sake, just pay whatever will keep her afloat. Anything. Charles, she'd do it for me.'

'But I wouldn't do what he's done,' Charles protested. 'He's a ghastly prat. God knows how she never suspected. She's not stupid.'

'No, not stupid. Just loyal.'

Charles paused in the act of pouring himself another drink. 'What about all her other friends.'

Melanie grimaced. 'Exactly. Tell me about it. What about Miranda? Remember all those evenings Serena spent with her when her first husband left her? Where is she now? Telling anyone who cares to listen that she wasn't a particularly close friend of Serena's. And Paula never misses a trick to badmouth her, either. At the moment we're all she's got.'

Faced with Serena, the burden of being her only friend struck Charles more forcefully than he cared for. His innate sense of decency roused anger in him that Serena was so easily abandoned, but it wasn't enough to chide his friends.

Watching him now, Serena knew that too. For a brief moment their eyes locked. Charles looked ill at ease. He could have murdered Stephen.

'Of course,' she said valiantly, as Charles repeated that Stephen was bound to surface soon. 'As a matter of fact, Andrew has fixed for me to see Stephen's bank manager. I'll pay back everything. Bless you, Charles.'

Serena could no longer avoid telling Mrs Owen and Chrissie that she would have to let them go.

'No more than I expected, of course,' Mrs Owen said tightly. 'I can't work for nothing. I'll be off then. No point in hanging around.'

'No, of course not,' Serena agreed, hurt by the older woman's eagerness to go, and not a little puzzled by it too. She reached out and picked up two parcels lying just behind her on a small console table. Both were gift-wrapped, the first with a label written in Louise's familiar rounded hand: *To Mrs Owen, we'll miss you, lots of love LouLou and Harry*. Inside, as Serena knew, was a red wool scarf patiently knitted by Louise and a clay dish made in Harry's crafts class.

'Oh, very kind, I'm sure,' Mrs Owen said, stuffing them into her bag.

'And this is from us . . . I mean, me.' Serena held out the second gift. 'No, open it when you get home. I think you'll like it.'

It went the way of the first one, rammed down the side of Mrs Owen's capacious bag. Serena wondered if the delicate porcelain figures, always admired by Mrs Owen in the past, would survive the journey home.

'Well, goodbye.' Mrs Owen stuck out her hand and grasped Serena's for a brief second and then walked rapidly out of the room.

Dear, loyal Chrissie offered to stay on without pay until the future for Serena looked a little more certain, but Serena refused to hear of it. 'You are the most special person to us,' Serena told her gently and gratefully, 'but you have a life to lead, and I have no idea any more when mine will return to normal. I can care for the children myself and my mother is more than willing to help out if I get stuck.'

They looked at each other and began to laugh.

'Give me a break,' Serena begged, 'I'm not that hopeless.' She put her arms round Chrissie and hugged her. 'Come and see us, whenever you want and write to the children. That, I really would appreciate.'

'As if I wouldn't,' sniffed Chrissie, wiping her eyes.

Minnie Carmichael had never enjoyed an easy relationship with her daughter-in-law. She did not dislike her she simply felt puzzled by her. Once, on a rare visit to Belvoir Square, she had watched while Serena, who was not in her view daft or submissive, shushed the children and coaxed her husband into a good mood, when she herself would have told him to stop sulking. There was also a suggestion that Serena deferred to him a little too easily. Once she had been tempted to say to Serena: love him less, help him more to laugh at himself, but it was easier to remain silent.

Neither of her sons pleased her overmuch, but at least Toby, racing through marriage after marriage, had not inherited Wilfred's weakness for wanting what he couldn't have. She winced. Stephen had simply taken it a stage further. She would not have admitted it to anyone, but Minnie knew, as Serena refused to believe, that her son was guilty. She felt a most terrible sense of failure.

Stephen, so clever but so furious with the world. For days after his disappearance she had switched from terror—not knowing where he was—to fury that he could have been so stupid. Such a hard son to live with and even harder to live up to. So what was the point in torturing herself now? There was work to be done.

Even while she was grappling with the knowledge that her missing son was now regarded as a criminal, she knew she must support Serena. She wasted no time in phoning her, and had immediately offered to come to London.

At the time Serena was too bewildered to register the novelty of Minnie seeking her out, and assured her she was surrounded by a lot of people. It was perfectly true. The police and the press had made sure she wasn't left alone for a minute.

Minnie's latest letter to Serena was, as ever, mercifully lacking in sympathy, restricting her observations to what she could do of a practical nature. It did not escape Serena that Minnie was not protesting Stephen's innocence. She wrote:

> At this distance it is difficult to offer a lot. I do, of course, feel for you and cannot imagine what Stephen must be thinking of, letting you go through all of this. I really had hoped by now some news would have emerged. If I thought I would be of use I would come to London, but I doubt it. Besides you have so many friends who must be driving you mad with their constant presence, but even so, are obviously more helpful, knowing your life on a day-to-day basis as they do.

Serena lifted her eyes from the page and gazed out onto the garden. It looked a little neglected. So was she. *So many friends.* She gave a mirthless laugh. Chrissie and Mrs Owen had gone. The children were at school. Andrew Beresford was due to call her later, and Melanie had been deflected from making her daily visit by Serena telling her she would be locked up with him for most of the day.

It had taken an effort. Melanie's staunch support was not a surprise to Serena, but she knew that the time had come to usher Melanie back to her own life. Letting Charles Westfield pay some bills had been agreed in the days when she was expecting to hear Stephen's voice at the end of the phone. But Melanie's own life was bound up with all the people who were now shunning Serena. Business, friends, children and weekends were all woven seamlessly into each other's lives. The strain on the Westfields, if it came to a 'Serena or us' impasse, was one she wasn't prepared to risk. Serena liked them too much to allow that.

Nor did she want Melanie to know about the sale of some of her own paintings and some jewellery left to her by her grandmother, which had taken place the previous week, discreetly through Andrew Beresford, to pay for the children's school fees.

Schools. Serena sighed. Louise was suffering. Girls can be such bitches. Old enough to know what had happened, they knew why their parents were discouraging them from including Louise. And who could blame them for protecting their families from scandal? The school wanted to enter her for a scholarship place, but Louise had already asked to be taken away. She was bright, sharp and proud. She was like Stephen. She didn't want her classmates' sympathy any more than she wanted their derision. Each afternoon, when Serena came to collect Louise, her heart was torn apart by the sight of her standing alone by the doorway, pretending to be absorbed in a book. She was learning, in such an agonising way, just how cruel the world can be.

Harry was faring slightly better. His friends were too young to understand the full scale of how his little life had been disrupted and were not interested. But Harry was slow. He was never going to be the academic Stephen dreamed he would be. Scholarships were not in order.

Unable to bring any new solutions to her children's immediate future, Serena resumed Minnie's letter:

I hope you will not be silly about this and refuse all offers of help. You have the children to think of. Perhaps instead of birthday presents, they would like me to send tickets for them to stay here during the summer—you too of course—but I was rather thinking about the small respite you might get if they were safe with me. I leave it to you to let me know.

She folded the letter and began to stack the breakfast dishes into the machine. The day ahead stretched before her with unanswered questions, self-doubt and recriminations to keep her company. Why couldn't

Stephen confide in her? Had she been so wrapped up in her own world that she hadn't noticed her own husband tottering on the brink of a breakdown? Why did it not occur to her that he was in trouble?

Why he did it was not a mystery to her, now that she had had time to think about it. Checking the dates given to her by the fraud squad she was not surprised that, while the start of his fraudulent activities was tracked back as far as the year they came to this house, it was the arrival of Rupert and the astonishing rise of Rupert's star that had generated the cracks, and prompted carelessness to set in.

As the days passed she fluctuated between hope and despair. Sometimes she plunged into total panic when images of their life together began to blur, like a faded photograph. She struggled to get a clear picture of Stephen, but he remained out of focus, out of reach.

The children had gone to bed. The kitchen was silent except for the sound of the dishwasher humming gently. On the table in front of her a mug of coffee had grown cold. Ten o'clock. The doorbell rang. Surprised, she pressed the intercom.

'Serena? It's me. Richard. Am I disturbing you?'

Richard Van Stuckley at this time of night? Richard Van Stuckley at all was a shock. Paula had made no attempt to get in touch with her and she herself was not his favourite person. Not after her ban on him using their cottage. Hurriedly she ran up the stairs from the kitchen, pausing only to throw open the door of the drawing room and turn on the lamps.

'Just an impulse.' Richard smiled as she led him into the now more welcoming room.

'How nice to see you,' she lied. 'Let me get you a drink.'

As she handed him a tumbler of whisky she could smell brandy on his breath and saw that his eyes were a little bloodshot. She moved towards the windows and drew the curtains, shutting out the night.

'How's Paula?' she enquired, but not remotely interested.

He waved his hand indifferently. 'Fine, I expect. Don't see a great deal of each other.'

She resisted an impulse to point out that if he spent less time with other women he would have more to devote to his wife. Instead she smiled and said, 'I expect you've been busy.'

He nodded and took a gulp from his drink. Serena moved to a sofa opposite the one on which Richard was sitting and hoped this visit would not last long. If he had come to offer help she would have been astonished. For a while Richard described his busy life, and Serena deftly dealt with any enquiries about Stephen.

'If I had any news, I would be delighted to tell you,' she said quietly, 'but there isn't. I'm sorry to be so boring.'

He looked at her and tossed the rest of the whisky down his throat. She moved to refill his glass, but he was there before her. 'No, no,' he waved her back to her seat, 'if you don't mind, of course?'

She shook her head and he lifted the decanter to replenish his glass. Instead of returning to his own seat, he sat down beside her, too close.

'Look, Serena, I know we haven't always got on. But it's rotten what's happened. To be frank,' he went on earnestly, 'I've only just discovered that the girls have not been seeing much of you.'

She opened her mouth to speak, but he interrupted.

'Oh, don't pretend with me, Serena, we've known each other for too long. Don't defend them.' Richard sailed on, ignoring her bewildered look. 'Anyway, I thought I'd drop round myself. I thought you might need someone to talk to, depend on.'

Serena was surprised but quite touched. 'It's kind of you, Richard'— she smiled more warmly at him—'but Andrew Beresford is handling everything for me. Thank you, anyway.'

He stretched round to put his glass on the table behind him and took her hand. She was too astonished to pull it away.

'Serena.' He moved even closer. 'I know what you're going through. It would be so easy for me to help you, and no hardship either. I've always thought you were a very beautiful woman.'

He was obviously drunk and harbouring several hideously erroneous illusions about her. She was acutely aware of being alone in the house except for the children. It was imperative that he went. 'Richard, I am not in need of the kind of . . . comfort you are suggesting.' She attempted to stand up to signal that the visit was now over, but he pulled her down beside him, pinning her against the sofa. 'Richard,' she pleaded, twisting away from him. 'Get off me. Please. Richard—' Her voice rose to a scream as she felt his hands grip and grind into her breasts.

'That's right,' he panted, trying to control her pounding fists. 'That's it. Fight me for it. I've always wanted you . . . My God,' he screamed, suddenly releasing her. 'You bitch!' With a last furious lunge she had grabbed the decanter of whisky and hit him with it on the centre of his back. The contents spilled down his expensive cashmere jacket and dribbled onto the white silk sofa.

It was the respite she needed. She wriggled off the sofa, raced into the hallway and made for the front door. Her hands shook as she released the catch and then, trying to steady her nerves, she walked back. From the doorway she said breathlessly, 'Get out. Directly opposite you will see a dark saloon. The driver and his passenger are detectives. They watch me the whole time. One word from me will have you arrested.'

'You stuck-up bitch,' he spat at her. 'I was doing you a favour. And any ideas you might have of telling anyone that I came on strong to you will be laughed at. Who's going to believe a fucking crook's wife?'

'Out.' She could hardly breathe and she was shaking uncontrollably. As he pushed past her out of the house, she shrank back against the wall. Swiftly she closed the door and slid slowly to the floor, her eyes tightly closed, fighting to control the frightened and angry gasps that were exploding in her chest.

Her only consolation as, minutes later, she swabbed the silk sofa, was that Richard had believed the dark saloon, owned by her neighbour, was that of a fraud squad detective.

She was not surprised to read some days later a reference to Richard's friendship with Stephen being dismissed as mere acquaintance.

It was because she felt humiliated by the scene that she had at first tried to deal with it herself. In her weakened emotional state, her judgment had been scrambled and she felt she was somehow to blame.

In the end, distress mingled with rage at such an assault, proved too much, and Melanie was given a stammering and largely incoherent account of what had taken place.

'Not surprised,' Melanie snorted when she had finished. 'He did it to Jane Marshall when she and Paul split up for a bit.'

'No!' Serena exclaimed. 'What happened?'

'Much the same. The old "You must be lonely" routine. She told me she started sobbing and screaming and then the au pair came downstairs and started hurling books at him, until Jane had to beg her to stop.'

Serena looked awed. 'Good God, he must be fed up with women all over London beating him up.' She and Melanie began to giggle.

Later, Serena said, 'It's just the idea that he thought I would give in to him. Christ, Mel,' she groaned, 'do I look like easy meat?'

'Rubbish,' Melanie retorted angrily. 'You know you don't. You're not to blame in any way. Any one of us on our own would be a target. Frankly I think we should take a stand over this.'

But Serena was adamant. 'No, listen to me,' she pleaded, 'if you blank him you'll have to cut Paula out as well and it isn't her fault. And if you blank her it means Miranda will be put on the spot and Charles will be dragged into it because he works with Bill Hooper. See?'

The mention of Charles's business life being affected worked on

Melanie. Serena was relieved when she saw the uncertainty on her friend's face. 'Honestly, Mel,' she said, 'it was just the need to tell someone and I feel so much better already. I just felt so grubby. Truly, much better now. Promise.'

Andrew's voice was quietly furious. 'Look, Serena, she hasn't said anything that is untrue. She's entitled to her opinion.'

'Opinion? God help me, Andrew. What did I ever do to her? Why? Oh my God, the children. Can't we sue her?'

'For what? Telling a filthy tabloid what it was like working for the man the world's police are looking for? Did you have any idea she'd go to the papers?'

'Idea? Are you serious? None. She was here for seven years and she was paid on the dot, holidays honoured, we gave her decent presents at Christmas and on her birthday. Why?'

Serena was shouting, pacing up and down. Louise stood in the doorway of the kitchen listening, her face pale and solemn. Serena could do nothing to protect her. Harry began to cry.

The *Daily Messenger* had paid Mrs Owen a fair sum of money to describe life with Serena Carmichael, whom they referred to in the centre spread as 'A Kept Woman'. The feature, ghosted by a staff writer, was a concoction of fantasy and cringing cliché.

She wanted only the best from those who worked for her. She would check everything and woe betide me if it wasn't up to her standards. She was a stickler for things like that . . . Never worked a day in her life, glorified hostess, that's all.

Serena chose not to retaliate. She knew that it would simply prolong the agony for them all if she did. Chrissie had fired off a letter to refute everything Mrs Owen had claimed, but it was put on the letters page and went unremarked.

Her only solace was Mrs Owen's claim that the Carmichaels' disagreements were often over friends.

Mr Carmichael came to me one day to tell me that his best friend, the MP Richard Van Stuckley, wanted somewhere to work with his secretary on a top-secret government paper and asked me to make sure the cottage would be well stocked with food and wine. He told me not to trouble Serena with his private arrangement with Mr Van Stuckley because even Mrs Van Stuckley—for security reasons—shouldn't know. But Mrs Carmichael flew into a rage when she found out and he wasn't allowed to stay there again.

Serena winced when she thought of the scene in the Van Stuckley house when that was revealed. Richard would be mortified. And Paula? Poor deluded Paula.

Melanie just sniffed. 'Paula had it coming,' she snarled.

Chapter Four

~

S ERENA WAITED in the drawing room, gazing unseeingly out over the garden square opposite. She stood well back from the window so that her presence went undetected. It was July and very hot. An occasional breeze drifted through the open sash windows, stirring the white voile curtains into a gentle floating wave.

Louise and Harry were safe in the country with Melanie and Charles Westfield, driven there late the night before by Serena.

The house was still, the room silent except for the steady tick of the clock. She had insisted on being alone when she heard.

She glanced round at the clock. It was nearly midday. Andrew had promised to phone the minute he had a decision.

Cautiously she leaned forward, risking discovery—and with more hope than conviction—to see if the waiting photographers in the square below were showing any sign of flagging. Even though they were standing around restlessly, they were clearly dug in.

Serena's attention was suddenly caught by a bustle of activity as a black Jag inched its way round the square. The waiting pack closed in, flashbulbs exploded. Serena recognised the figure emerging from the car. The last lingering absurd hope died in her. She didn't have to be told the news. Andrew would have phoned if it had been different. She straightened her shoulders just as he opened the door.

'How long?' she asked, handing him a tumbler of whisky. 'How long to find somewhere else?'

Andrew rolled his drink between his hands. 'No rush,' he said carefully. 'But it might be as well to have somewhere to go. At least start looking. Or at any rate have a contingency plan. Maybe your mother's?'

Serena shook her head.

'No. Not my mother's. Not anyone's. I'm going to manage on my own.

224

I'm fed up, Andrew. Tired of people shrinking away from me in case I ask for help. Embarrassed that friends like Melanie and Charles urge me to live off them. And,' she hesitated, 'I want to prove something. That I wasn't just a kept woman leeching off a rich husband.'

'Serena—' he began, but was stopped by the look on her face. It wasn't an expression he was used to seeing. Harder, less giving. He reached over and squeezed her hand.

'You know where to find me,' he told her. 'Any time. You know that.'

Later that day Andrew Beresford arrived home to find a parcel had just been delivered. Inside he gazed at an original L. S. Lowry that had once hung in Serena's hallway, an inheritance from her father.

On account, said the note, signed with a flourishing *S*.

Serena's T-shirt was sticking to her back. Her legs ached and her linen skirt was crumpled. The relief of collapsing into the chair in front of Mr Stanley's desk, out of the sweltering heat of south London in August, was such bliss that at first she let him talk to her.

'Hmm. Four beds,' he repeated, drumming his fingers on the table, clicking his way through lists scrolling up on the screen in front of him. He glanced at her. 'Got to be rented?'

'Yes.' Serena insisted. 'And not too big,' she reminded him. 'I'm sure it's not impossible.'

Darren Stanley gave a doubtful shake of blond spiky hair. He looked about fourteen. His tie was loosened, his jacket had been discarded and there were damp patches creeping down from his armpits. Serena thought fleetingly of the courteous young man from the Knightsbridge firm Stradbrooke Properties who had arrived to assess her house a month before. In a dark linen suit and discreet tie, he had murmured instructions to an assistant. They had not troubled her for anything. And why should they? The house, and everything in it, was owned by the bank.

'It's not easy, four beds,' Darren was saying. 'Popular area as well. Got MPs on the phone day and night, I have, begging me to find them something because it's within the division bell . . . Not an MP, are you?' He peered at her. 'You look familiar.'

Serena felt her heart beat double. She shook her head. 'No. I'm . . . no one. Just looking for a house.'

Darren looked disappointed. Relief flooded through his client.

Draycott Mendes had finally decided to allow Serena to keep enough from the sale of the house to rent somewhere in London. Malcolm Brisley Jones had personally urged the board to help Serena as much as they could. They were bitter and angry men, but few had disliked Serena. Most had appreciated her warmth and genuine good nature. Now they were all united in their pity for her.

A string of interested buyers viewed the house over three days. Stradbrooke Properties had found a buyer almost immediately. Serena's instinctive eye for turning a grand house into a stylish but warm family home had been the subject of much envy. The fact that the house was also the home of a wanted banker had encouraged rather than deflected interest. The buyer was an Indian diplomat who wanted to be installed by the end of the summer, in time for his children to be enrolled in English schools.

To her relief the fuss created by Mrs Owen had begun to fade. If only that deceitful and cunning woman could see me now, she thought, trudging from house to car, car to estate agent. 'Kept Woman' had rankled. But what else had she been? No income to call her own, relying totally on Stephen, it had never occurred to her to be independent. She could see now it had been a mistake. But who could blame her? She had lived no differently from her friends. In the end, none of it was hers. How could it have been when the courts had decided it could all be taken because it all belonged to Draycott Mendes?

Louise and Harry had been dispatched to stay with Minnie in Lucca for two weeks while Serena went house-hunting. At first Louise had refused to go, not relishing the prospect of two weeks with her grandmother, but promptly relented when she discovered that, for the first time in their lives, she and Harry would be flying alone, to be met by Minnie at Pisa.

Armed with the best that Darren Stanley could come up with, Serena now trod up the path to a mid-terraced Victorian house, which the photocopied sheet boasted had off-street parking. A brown van was parked in front of the living-room window, a child's bike was propped by a tin dustbin and two black bin-liners were shoved inside the porch.

The doorbell whirred as she waited on the cracked doorstep. At least inside it can't be any worse, she consoled herself. After a decent interval she rang again. No answer. Slowly she walked down the path and at the gate stopped to check the address. Today she had seen seven houses. Six had been hopeless. And this one she couldn't even get into.

The reasons why she had chosen this small pocket of London were hard to remember now that she was here. Dimly she recalled Melanie saying it was one of those areas that was easy to reach—but who would be coming to see her?

She would try one more house. Just one, and then go home. There must be something in this area that was a reasonable size for her and the children, where they could start to live again.

She turned her car into the main road and drove two blocks until she came to Foster Street. She parked her car and began to walk slowly up the narrow road with its tired trees, flanked on either side by uniformly dull houses in red brick. Number forty-two was towards the far end. The door was painted blue, the knocker was hanging off, and she could see the frames on the sash windows needed replacing. Silently she gazed up at the net-curtained windows, fighting a desire to turn and run.

Stephen. Oh, bloody Stephen. Her gaze drifted from the worn-out brickwork. She noticed the minuscule area between the road and the door. A willow tree occupied almost its entire space. She sighed. So much for the front garden. Utterly hopeless.

A small breeze rustled through the still air. Serena gazed despairingly at the fronds on the tree swaying unevenly, lifting the trailing leaves to reveal a circle of smooth brown stones in which some pansies were struggling to be seen through a tangle of weeds. Serena stood very still and for a long while just stared at the patch of garden. She had to live somewhere. If the flowers could do it, maybe she could. With a deep breath, she walked purposefully up the path and rang the bell.

'It is *not* smaller than Harry's, just a different shape. Look, I'll show you.'

Serena began to pace the length of her daughter's new bedroom, while Louise leaned against the wall, one foot tucked up behind her, scuffing the brown flowered wallpaper with the heel of her shoe. Her arms were folded tightly round her waist, and she was glaring sullenly out of the window to the garden below. She wouldn't look at Serena, who was struggling to control an impulse to shake her.

'There. Four feet longer than Harry's but just one foot narrower. Overall area exactly the same. Lou, are you listening? Darling, please. I'm exhausted. This is not for ever, just until Daddy comes home.'

She stopped, quailed by the furious flash in Louise's eyes. Stephen's eyes. The anger died in her. Such a tough little face, so angry with the world and who could blame her?

Serena wanted to hug Louise and tell her it was going to be all right, but they both knew that it wasn't. Her shoulders sagged. She gazed around Louise's new room. Until her daughter had stormed downstairs to ask why Harry was getting a better room, she had been doing rather well. No disabling panic, no lurching stomach at the sight of boxes, one after the other, containing all that was left of her old life disappearing through the front door. Not even a tear as she turned the car out of the square following the van.

It was not her car, of course. That had gone. This one she'd hired for a few days. There wasn't going to be a car by the end of the week. She'd decided that, too, was an unnecessary expense. What she found odd was that this new parsimony no longer caused her any pain. Just relief. Blessed, sweet relief that nothing more could be taken from her. If she didn't have it, they couldn't take it. It was so simple. And if she didn't ask, she didn't owe. If she could have only bits of what she once had, she would have none of it at all.

Both Margot and Minnie had offered to find the money somehow to keep the children at their present schools.

'And where does it end?' Serena asked her mother. 'I keep LouLou at Collingham House, but then what? Do I make her suffer even more by allowing her to accept generosity she's not able to return, not able to keep up with everything she once took for granted? The holidays, the ponies—oh, you know what I mean. It would be too cruel.'

To Minnie she said, 'You are kind beyond belief. I'm perfectly sure it's what Stephen would want, but,' she studied her reflection in the mirror over the phone and then turned away, not able to stop the bitterness, 'but I can't afford what he wants any more. As a matter of fact, we all know now, I never could.'

Ten months after she had lazily kissed Stephen goodbye as he disappeared down the stairs on what should have been a routine day, she was embarking on a new life. The children had started at their new schools two months before, Serena driving them each day there and back across the river.

Ten months since she had felt him, touched him, talked to him. Almost a year learning how to manage without him. She was worn out with missing him. She missed his smell, his presence, his strength. She also missed sex. No lean, warm body to curl against and to drift into sleep tangled up in someone's arms. No one to laugh softly into the dark at a shared joke. God, she missed him so much.

She could not believe that he didn't miss her too, or that he could not find some way of contacting her. Sometimes the need for him was overwhelming, but there were times—for which in calmer moments she felt ashamed and treacherous—when she hated him so much she couldn't breathe.

About a month after Harry had started at Dunton Road Juniors, the head, Jack Billington, a comfortable man in his thirties, had called her in. He spoke to her of a child she barely recognised. His lack of social skills, commitment, cultural orientation were discussed until Serena was convinced he had muddled up her son with another child.

It was perfectly possible. His office was open house to a stream of children. How could he tell which was Harry—a bereft ten-year-old plucked from the gentle nurturing of an expensive school and plunged into one that asked for nothing more than survival of those who seemed willing to learn?

Jack Billington had done his best to reassure her that they understood, but that Harry could not command all his attention and needed Serena to soothe his fears, be a bit more robust. Serena felt faint. More? She had nothing left to give.

She had politely listened to everything he had to say, but he wondered how much she had absorbed. Encourage him to invite other lads home, he had suggested. But who? She had already brought the subject up with Harry, but he just resolutely shook his head. She had hoped so much that after his visit to Minnie a new confidence might make it easier for Harry not to be so afraid of the world.

Lucca had been a surprising success; even Louise had come back with no greater complaint than Harry was sad, positively *sad*, the way he wanted to keep painting. But with no one to witness her doing anything more glamorous than eating out on her grandmother's terrace in the evening, or walking a mile to a tiny restaurant in the little hamlet of Carleagia for pasta and *panna cotta* and—she reported with a sly look at Serena—accompanied by a glass of red wine, she had been more entertained than she thought it cool to admit.

Serena wondered what miracle had prompted Minnie to gauge her granddaughter's urge for a grown-up life so correctly. She smiled as Louise disappeared to unpack and she settled down to study Harry's efforts at watercolours, carefully rolled into a cardboard tube supplied by Minnie.

Why she thought such lifted spirits would survive the move, she now couldn't say. It was November. Two months since Louise had started at St Saviour's, a girls' school now a short bus ride away, and Harry at Dunton Road Juniors, which was a five-minute walk from the house.

Serena began to gather up discarded bin-liners littering the room that had contained Louise's CDs, videos and magazines, and started to fold them carefully to give her an excuse to stay, while she tried to think of something to say that would comfort both of them. Through the open window soared the raking voice of their new neighbour, beseeching her children to take the dog out before he crapped all over the garden again.

Impatiently Serena banged the window shut, making Mrs Plaxton with her frizzy blonde hair, too-short skirt for her plump legs, and shapeless T-shirt glance up and wave. Serena turned away. Mrs Plaxton had already introduced herself, hot on the heels of Cheryl Tosney who lived opposite. Cheryl had very quickly worked out exactly who Serena was, and was delighted to see someone so infamous reduced to Foster Street, and excited that property prices might now soar.

Betty Plaxton, with her three terrifying children and her ferocious dog Sovereign, was unimpressed with Serena's association with a man on the run. Since both her brothers had done time and a distant cousin was in Wandsworth for receiving, she horrified Serena by her suggestion that they were sisters under the skin.

'Bloody blokes,' she announced cheerfully, catching Serena as she staggered up the path, loaded down with the contents of her car. 'All the bloody same. Not Les.' She jerked a thumb towards the house. 'His back stops him from getting into trouble—and me as well,' she shrieked. 'Tell you what, though,' she paused and glanced surreptitiously across the street. 'Watch her,' she mouthed indicating Cheryl Tosney's house. 'She tried to pull my Les. Believe that?'

'Bet,' a voice bellowed from within. 'It's nearly twelve.'

Betty stopped and gave a squeal. 'Oh my God, is that the time? Work calls. Nice meeting you. Pop in if you need anything. Take us as you find us,' she called, disappearing into her house.

Serena turned back into the room where Louise was still in a massive sulk. I am not ready for this, Serena told herself. None of us is. She impulsively and fiercely folded her arms round Louise's stiff little body. There was no response.

Serena pretended not to notice that her attempts at making up were being resisted. Instead she kissed Louise's hair and released her. 'What about switching to the spare room?'

Louise shook her hair. 'No, thanks,' she yawned. 'I suppose this will do. They're all crap.'

'*Louise*,' Serena said wrathfully. 'Don't speak like that.'

'Sorr-ee,' Louise replied airily. 'Anyway, where's the phone?'

Serena watched as she clumped down the stairs. After a while she heard her ask for someone called Daphy. Louise stopped talking as Serena squeezed past her in the hallway.

'My mother,' she heard her explain. 'Yeah, cool. Come round, it's a right doss house.'

Serena wheeled round, a protest already springing to her lips, but Louise had turned her back to avoid her. She briefly closed her eyes and counted to ten before pushing open the door to the living room.

For someone who had lost everything, she had an extraordinarily vast amount of stuff to unpack. Tea chests and cardboard cases were piled on the floor. The Georgian rent table, the chiffonier and the grandfather clock that had once belonged to her grandmother sat in this narrow room, which ran the length of the house, like disapproving old retainers forced to consort with the kitchen staff. At least the house is warm, she consoled herself, crossing the narrow passageway and down two steps into the kitchen, where Harry was sitting munching biscuits and watching a portable television perched on top of the fridge.

'OK, darling?' Serena asked, hoping he would be too absorbed in his television programme to notice that it had been several hours since a proper meal had been put before him.

He nodded without taking his eyes from the screen. The lead for the electric kettle was hanging out of a box of food that had come with them. She plugged it in, found a mug and unearthed a box of tea bags. It had been a long day with only a few small reprieves.

The noise from the television finally drove her to seek the sanctuary of the living room. She moved some boxes from a small velvet chair and sat down. Just five minutes to herself. That's all she asked.

Through the walls she could hear a low rumble and a distant voice could be heard raised in fury. 'Bradlee Plaxton. Get back in here, or I'll break your bloody neck.'

'Can Harry come out to play?' Serena choked on her coffee and wheeled round at the sound of a voice in her empty kitchen.

Two small children stood gazing blankly at her, one as plump as the other was thin. The girl was about ten, her small snub-nosed companion a couple of years younger. Behind them a large Alsatian, straining and panting on a short plaited lead held by the girl, was digging his hefty haunches in the doorway, refusing to budge.

'Harry's ill,' Serena snapped. 'God, Alana,' she went on crossly, 'you nearly gave me a heart attack. How did you get in?'

'Door's open, innit?' Alana Plaxton said. The middle child and only daughter of Betty and Les shot Serena a look full of scorn and hauled the panting animal into the kitchen.

Serena had to admit, to her shame, that she was a little afraid of the rough and disorderly Plaxtons. She knew Harry was scared stiff of Ellis, a wiry eight-year-old, but rather awed by the masterful Alana.

'Oi, El,' Alana called to the small boy who had darted ahead of her into the room and was calmly flicking through the channels on the television. 'Leave that, I like Ricci Lake. She gets real pervs on.'

Serena watched helplessly as the two of them contributed to the chaos already at work in her kitchen. A pile of washing-up as well as a stack of ironing stared accusingly at her. The swing lid of the waste bin strained to contain the evidence of last night's fast-food supper.

Stuffed among the litter was another letter sent by Harry's headmaster, asking her to make an appointment to see him. By half term, Harry appeared to be getting worse rather than better.

Finding the will to tackle it all had failed her. A black scrunch ribbon held her hair back off her face, stray strands tucked carelessly behind her ears. She wore no make-up and although it was a fine spring day outside and the kitchen was warm she had been sitting hunched over the table in a thick black sweater, her legs encased in the bottom half of a pale grey track suit. Each day she wore something belonging to Stephen. A scarf, a sweater, pyjamas. Today it was a pair of skiing socks.

Margot had rung just after breakfast to say she was on her way, refusing to be put off any more. Harry was upstairs in bed waiting to see if the stomach ache he had complained of as they were leaving for school that morning was leading anywhere. It was already twenty past two and in an hour's time she would have to leave to meet Louise from the bus.

The arrival of these two forceful children in the middle of the afternoon finally felled her patience, along with the wit to ask why they were in her house when they should have been in school. Serena reached over and snapped off the television. Ellis promptly snapped it on again. 'Oi,' he said unabashed. 'I woz watchin' that.'

Serena had spent the morning negotiating the crowded aisles of the local supermarket. She had then had to deal with an officious woman from the DSS, who had been sent to check Serena's request for financial assistance. The visit, like all those from people concerned only that she did not get or take anything beyond that which the State provided for penniless women, was unannounced.

For ten minutes Mrs Cottenham roamed the house. Then, satisfied, she sat heavily on a chair in the kitchen and lectured Serena on what she was and was not entitled to. Finally she rose to leave, busily tucking notebooks and pens into her bag, splaying leaflets on the table that would guide Serena through the regulations governing her entitlement to assistance.

Serena too rose, perfectly polite, and moved to hold open the door. 'Thank you for coming.' She held out her hand. 'Most kind,' she added as Mrs Cottenham inched past her.

'Yes, well. Good. You know where to find me,' she muttered as she walked down the path.

A KEPT WOMAN

Harry had remained in bed while she had been at the supermarket, ordered to stay there where he would be safe. She hated leaving him but the alternatives were not attractive. Cheryl Tosney across the road would have been over like a shot. Bored and idle, Cheryl had developed an uncomfortable fascination with Serena, but as she was also a fund of local knowledge she had become useful.

In the few months Serena had lived in Foster Street, she had grown to tolerate Cheryl, even allowing herself to be amused by her. Today, however, was one of the days when the prospect of Cheryl's incessant chatter and gossip did not amuse. It simply wasn't to be borne. Nothing was. Today was just for getting through.

And now there was this unceremonious arrival of these two ghastly children, who seemed to regard her kitchen as their own. 'Ellis was bored,' Alana told Serena firmly. 'We want to play with Harry.'

'Well, I'm sorry, Alana'—it took enormous effort to be pleasant—'it's very sweet of you, but that's not possible. Harry had a wretched night—'

She stopped as Alana nudged Ellis, and they began to giggle.

'And I'm extremely busy,' Serena continued, warily eyeing Sovereign, whose lead Alana was no longer holding. 'I'm expecting Harry's grandmother this evening, so why don't you run along and when Harry's better—' Serena let out a terrified shriek as Sovereign flattened her against the draining board. She lashed out wildly to grab the leash, but her flailing arm caught several half-full mugs and a couple of glasses. Crockery and glass shattered in a shower of cold coffee and Ribena as they hit the floor. Diverted, Sovereign dropped on all fours and began pushing his long nose into the debris. Serena gripped the edge of the sink for support. 'Alana,' she breathed furiously, 'get that dog away. He'll cut himself.'

To her relief, but more to her surprise, they didn't argue. 'And now,' she said as Alana pulled Sovereign away from the mess on the floor, 'please go home. *Go. Get out, get the fuck out of here.*'

'OK,' said Alana cheerfully. 'I'll come back later, shall I?'

Serena closed her eyes in disbelief as the door crashed behind her uninvited guests. Swearing at two children? She hadn't, had she? 'Oh so what,' she muttered. She gave a weary sigh, turning to the sink.

Automatically she ran water into a bowl, squeezed in some floor cleaner and bent down to deal with the mess. Gingerly she picked out the largest shards of china and glass and mopped up the pool of liquid snaking across the floor. If he is alive, she thought, as she wiped the brown stains from the front of the green and cream cabinets, he must be thinking of me, he must be as scared as I am, missing us, lonely and lost. He's just waiting for the right moment to let me know. But what if he can't? Now we've moved. Who would tell him where we've gone?

But she knew that was a nonsense, her letters were being forwarded, the telephone company were diverting her calls; but everything was screened by the Serious Fraud Office, and that's why he couldn't.

These days she was more or less left to get on with her life. Inspector Don Trewless had dropped by shortly after she had moved in. He had stayed for an hour, drinking coffee, in this very kitchen. If anyone had seen them, he might have been an old friend. And in a way that was almost what he had become. Two people forced to stay in each other's life, neither crossing the boundary of acquaintance into friendship, since neither trusted what the other would do should they discover Stephen's whereabouts. And how could it be any other way? She leaned back on her heels and absently re-wiped the surface she had just cleaned.

'Mum?'

She looked round. Harry stood in the doorway, a sweatshirt pulled over his pyjamas, his hair ruffled, his feet bare.

'Don't come in,' she ordered. 'I broke some cups.'

Harry gazed at the bowl and the cloth. 'Have they gone?' he asked.

'You mean those nightmares from next door? Yes, darling, they've gone. Ghastly, aren't they?'

'Ellis is horrible,' he muttered. 'Not Alana, though,' Harry said, staring anxiously at her. 'She's OK. Actually I think she's my friend, only I'm not sure. Can she come and play later? Mum? Is that OK?'

Chapter Five

~

MELANIE HAD WARNED Margot that she was in for a shock: the children were in a mess, she had said. Louise had grown sullen and shockingly rude. She had gone native, she said, and who could blame her? How else was she to survive? And Harry was absolutely cowed by it all. All that imaginary illness.

'But is it?' Margot asked Melanie. They were talking on the phone before Margot had set off for London. They talked a lot, but Serena was not aware of it.

'Harry ill? Never,' Melanie said firmly. 'He just finds it easier to stay in bed than face the playground bullies. And who can blame him, poor little chap. And while you're there, see if you can get her to see that headmaster chappie. She ignores all his letters.'

Margot had set off for London half hoping that Melanie had exaggerated, but she could see for herself that she hadn't. Louise so full of rage, and no one to listen to her. And Harry looked perfectly well, but he just wouldn't get out of bed. And those clothes Serena was wearing. Where in the name of heaven had she found them?

'What's wrong with them?' Serena asked glancing down at the tracksuit bottoms and the black sweater now carrying the fallout from her tussle with Sovereign. 'What should I wear?' she asked. 'Chanel?'

Margot fought back a desire to scream at her daughter to stop hoping. She now hated Stephen with an intensity that shocked her. She had stopped reassuring Serena that he would never have deliberately landed her in this dreadful mess. She thought the words would choke her.

'Don't be silly, Serena,' Margot sighed. 'Of course not. It's just that I thought you might feel better if you wore something more . . . well, you.'

Serena gazed steadily at her mother. 'Of course they're not me. Me is packed away upstairs in boxes. I'm not me,' Serena said in an off-hand way, as if she was discussing the weather. 'Not any more. I don't know who that other person could have been. Not noticing her husband was cracking under the pressure, letting all those people touch him for favours for their charities—no one now to speak up for him. Oh God,' she glanced at the kitchen clock. 'Where's that bloody plumber?'

'It's like trying to get her to see that she should think of herself first— like on aeroplanes,' Margot whispered down the phone to Melanie next morning, while Serena was closeted with someone from Social Services. 'Where they tell you to put on your life jacket; you must put your own on first otherwise you're useless to everyone around you.'

At the other end of the phone at her house in St John's Wood, Melanie rolled her eyes. 'Well, who's going to get that through to her? You know, Margot, don't you think it's almost as if she is doing penance for something? She blames herself for his lordship's "breakdown" and this is her way of atoning. Can't you make her see he was just an overbearing, self-absorbed crook? There was nothing she could have done.'

'I know, I know,' Margot agreed, no longer prepared to defend Stephen. 'We've got to do something, we really have.'

In the event neither of them was called upon to do anything. Jack Billington was not a man to be trifled with. When Serena did not answer his letters, he contacted the children's department. And now this woman with her cream shirt, red jacket and neat black pumps was sitting here telling her that Harry was a problem.

Harry was home again for the third day running and Serena had been forced to admit, after this woman's gentle probing, that she had not thought it worth while to take him to a doctor.

Barbara Hill winced as the front door to Serena's house slammed. She looked up as Louise came noisily into the room, slinging her school bag across a chair, claiming that there were no lessons that afternoon. She had brought Daphy with her, who wore her Afro hair in tight little plaits, livid green eye shadow smeared across her lids. Like Louise she was wearing a short black skirt, thick black tights and heavy shoes. Louise stopped when she realised her mother had a visitor. 'Louise, isn't it?' Barbara asked.

Louise nodded as Barbara Hill consulted her notebook. 'St Saviour's? Your school, I mean. Is that right?'

Louise nodded again but more warily, shooting a glance at Serena who smiled faintly. 'Hello, darling. I'll get you some soup or something in a minute. Miss Hill won't be much longer.'

Barbara Hill frowned, and continued to address Louise. 'And the reason you're home at this time is—what?'

Daphy edged out of the room, but Louise stood her ground. 'Felt like it,' she answered defiantly.

'Lou, sweetheart,' Serena protested.

Both ignored her. 'Well, suppose you discuss it with your mother,' Miss Hill persisted. 'And try and feel like going back after you've had some lunch. And who's that with you?'

Louise blocked the doorway. 'No one, I mean a friend. She's come to borrow my history notes.'

'Well, that's a relief because for a moment I thought she might be bunking off. So she'll be going straight back to school as well, will she?'

A sullen look was all she got in return, as Louise backed out of the room. Seconds later the front door slammed and through the window Barbara Hill saw the girls glancing towards the house before they disappeared. She wrote something in the margin of her notebook, then turned to Serena. 'How often does she do that? St Saviour's doesn't have free afternoons or lessons, especially not at Louise's level. Have you never asked what she's doing?'

What Louise was doing? She was racing like a hoyden around Foster Street, crazy about every boy who passed the door, and incapable now of expressing herself in any other way except to say she was pissed off or couldn't be 'arsed'. Serena witnessed the brutalisation of her daughter like a woman watching a piano roll down a hill, not knowing how to stop it. She nodded. 'Of course. I think she was just feeling a bit cornered. She would have gone back. I know Louise.'

'Even so,' Miss Hill refused to be sidetracked or fooled, 'I think she needs a tighter hand.'

Serena stared politely back. Of course she did. But whose?

Barbara Hill sighed and studied the notes she had made. Finally she looked up and said, 'Don't you think, Mrs Carmichael, that you should at least go and see Mr Billington? You clearly need help and so does Harry. And Louise. I'm having trouble finding anything to say that would help your case . . .'

'Case? What case?' Serena spoke sharply. 'What are you talking about? I'm not a case.'

'Oh, but you are,' Barbara Hill contradicted her. 'You most certainly are. You tell me you see none of your old friends, you have no close relatives apart from your mother. You have no work colleagues, no outside interests. I agree'—she held up a hand to stop Serena interrupting—'all of this is difficult for you. But it's a bleak picture and I want to prevent you becoming a family in which our intervention will be necessary.'

A sudden flash of Louise and Harry being taken from her rose up before Serena's eyes. She half rose from her seat and then sank back with a small gesture of defeat.

'Look, Mrs Carmichael.' Barbara Hill closed her notebook and put it on the table beside her. 'I know what's happened to you, and I know what it must be like—'

Serena's eyes widened in disbelief. 'You know?' she asked, her voice dangerously calm. 'You know, do you, the effort it takes to open my eyes each day? You know,' she continued, staring into Miss Hill's eyes, 'do you, what it's like to imagine your husband dead or ill, and not know for sure? You know, do you, that every night when I go to sleep, I dream he will be back, and I have to deal with waking up and knowing he isn't . . . Tell me, Miss Hill. You know what that's like, do you?'

'No,' she said gently, 'I don't know that. But I know that you're depressed. Depression leads to exhaustion and exhaustion leads to neglect and then it's easier to take refuge in the past. I see someone who won't or'—she held up a hand as Serena opened her mouth to protest—'can't help herself. For whatever reason. Look, I can't tell you what to do, but I can tell you what will happen if you let these kids slide out of your sight. And that's what's happening.

'You're not a daft woman, you're bright,' she went on with what

Serena thought was a touch of frustration in her voice. 'You're right, I don't know how you feel, but I can see how it's affecting you. I have no idea if you can do anything about it, because frankly I don't know what you were like before all this. But I do know that everyone has a choice in your situation.' She paused. 'You can do something. It's as simple as that.'

'What do you mean?' Serena turned on her. 'Do you mean a job?'

'Maybe.'

'And who looks after my children? I have no money, no one to turn to. The police tap my phone, my mail is checked and my children are bereft of a father.'

'But they do have a mother. Don't you count for anything in their life? Don't you think they need you more than ever?'

For a few seconds they stared at each other. Neither spoke. Eventually Barbara picked up her raincoat. 'It's up to you. Now, shall I tell Mr Billington you'll be coming to see him?'

'I don't know. Let me think . . .' Her voice trailed off.

Barbara Hill moved towards the door. 'Look, call me.' She placed a card on the table and a leaflet outlining the help available and another pile of forms. Then she left.

For a long while Serena just sat and stared into space. This had to stop. These strangers just turning up, prying. Forms, forms, forms. She lifted the latest batch and glanced resentfully at them. Her life reduced to an entry in all those boxes. Without thinking, she began to tear the forms in half, then into quarters, and then halved those again. When the paper was no more than confetti, she carried it through into the kitchen and pressed the pieces down on top of the rubbish in the swing bin. Heaving on both sides she wriggled the black bin-liner loose, tied the top and took it outside and dumped it in the corner where the refuse collectors would remove it later in the week. Harry and Margot would be playing upstairs on Harry's computer. She walked slowly to the gate and gazed up and down the road.

It was just how you looked at these things, she decided, sitting on the edge of the low wall. Foster Street had signalled the end. But what if it was just the beginning? What would Stephen want her to do? She tried to recall his voice, his smile, the impatient lift of a hand to push his hair back off his face, but it all melted into a blur.

Large drops of rain began to plop on the pavement. She studied them until her shoulders were damp and Margot's voice brought her back to the present. Then she turned and walked back into the house. She went upstairs to see Harry and persuaded a reluctant Margot to return to Wiltshire.

'You'll like Alex. At least, Harry will. My brother's great with kids. Not like me. He got the real thing. I got Dunton Road Juniors.'

Serena smiled politely as the man in front of her chuckled at what was clearly a well-honed family joke. 'See him. You don't have to go back if you don't want to, but'—he looked at her, his head on one side—'I think you will.'

'Who knows?' she agreed, lightly glancing at the card he had handed her and placing it in the pocket at the back of her handbag. 'But there's the small matter of money. Actually'—she gave him a faintly embarrassed look—'I don't have any at all, so this might all be pointless. I have no idea what child psychologists cost.'

'Family,' he corrected. 'He treats the whole family. And it won't cost you anything. He does have a private practice, but he does NHS work as well. You'll have to be referred to him, but there shouldn't be a problem—Barbara Hill will send a note to your GP saying she recommends some sessions for Harry. She'll suggest Alex. He knows his stuff.'

Jack Billington leaned back in his chair, swivelling gently around as he spoke. Harry had returned to school the day before and arrived home with a note for Serena to say the head would see her the following morning. It occurred to her that she hadn't actually agreed to see anyone, but Barbara Hill had guessed, correctly, that Serena would not ignore Harry's headmaster yet again.

So here she was, swept along by a man who saw Harry as a problem. 'I think we both agree that there is a loss in Harry's life that needs addressing.' He paused. 'We both know,' he said gently, 'that Harry's depressed. That's tough for a child. But he is.'

She could feel the tears welling up in her eyes. She swallowed hard and nodded. 'Forgive me,' she began, 'for being so, well, so reluctant to talk to you. It's just that I needed to get so much sorted out. I just didn't want—well, don't want actually—for Harry to be regarded as a problem. If I hadn't been in such shock myself then it wouldn't have come to this, but then it wouldn't have happened, would it?'

He appeared not to notice her incoherent efforts to explain. 'Harry comes from a different background from most of these children, but,' he said gently, 'he wasn't fitting in terribly well at his other school, was he?' He dropped forward in his chair, frowning over a piece of paper in a file lying open on his desk. Serena recognised the logo on the paper and the familiar scrawl of Harry's former headmaster.

Jack Billington gave her a level look. Her shoulders dropped. 'Have you ever thought that Harry might have needed help in the long run? Don't you think that—well, OK, it isn't the ideal way to identify a problem, but now that we have, something can be done?'

An honest voice told her he was right. Money had subdued rather than confronted and solved a problem within Harry. She knew Harry's problems had been exacerbated, not created, by his new life.

'Don't you think we all have problems that we don't have to worry about, unless life takes a sudden twist?' she demanded. 'No one knows how they'll behave until they're tested. Harry had his safety net taken away, that's all. It's not his fault, it's other people's fault. It's my fault.' Her voice broke in a sob. She stopped, aghast, raising one hand to briefly cover her eyes. 'I'm sorry,' she whispered. 'Ignore me. This is not like me. I'm not—I mean, this isn't your problem.'

'But it is,' he said and, quietly reaching into a drawer to his left, he pulled out a box of tissues and held them out to her. 'And I don't want to ignore you. If I did I wouldn't have asked to see you. Harry is not your exclusive problem, while he's here he's mine as well.'

Serena blew her nose. 'You've been very kind.'

'Nonsense,' he said. 'I'm being practical. I want an easy life—which is a bit elusive these days.' He began to rise to his feet. Serena followed suit. 'Let's agree, then, that you'll see Alex and I'll do my best to get Harry to join in more. Yes?'

She nodded and he held open the door.

Faced with a bored clerk, it did not take Serena many minutes to establish that, while she was adept at organising a charity lunch for dozens of rich women, with the influence to pull a celebrity to grace it at a moment's notice, none of these virtues seemed to be regarded as advantageous for any of the jobs on offer at the Jobcentre.

'You're not making it easy for me, Mrs Carmichael,' the young woman said. 'You don't want to work full-time or at nights. You want to be home during the holidays. What about this? Ward orderly at St Wilhemina's?'

'But I know nothing about nursing.'

The girl laughed. 'That isn't what's required. They need someone to help give the patients lunch, tidy up a bit, generally help. No nursing involved. And your form says you've worked for a hospital. They generally want someone from either eight till two or two till eight. Couldn't you get someone to meet your kids from school—or take them?'

A week later Serena presented herself at St Wilhemina's. She took the bus as far as Camberwell Green and then walked. Cheryl Tosney was not who she would ever have envisaged employing to care for her children.

In fact it was Cheryl who had suggested it when Serena had mentioned she ·was looking for someone who wouldn't want a fortune, someone who could be at her house in time for her to leave.

'You know it makes sense,' Cheryl insisted. 'Besides, I could do with the extra,' she added, surveying herself in the mirror in Serena's kitchen. 'My highlights need doing something rotten.'

'What about Kevin?' Serena asked. 'Won't he mind you abandoning him every morning so early?'

Cheryl screamed with laughter. 'Mind? He wouldn't notice if the Russians invaded before midday. No, do him good.'

Promptly at seven fifteen, fully made-up and wearing one of her extensive wardrobe of shell suits and high heels, Cheryl left her house and minced across to Serena's, where Louise, half dressed, yawning and absorbed in breakfast television, barely acknowledged her.

Serena smiled apologetically. 'She's not at her best at this time. And Harry. Darling? Cheryl will walk you right to school and I'll be waiting outside when you come out. Now, have you got everything? Your lunch box is on the fridge, oh and . . .'

'Now, now, Serena,' Cheryl interposed, ushering her towards the door. 'You just get off. Me and Harry will be just fine. Go on, off you go.'

Serena looked uncertainly at the children. Louise was indifferent, Harry apprehensive. She hugged them both and then, grabbing her coat, absurdly near to tears, she fled out of the house and walked in the crisp early-morning air to the bus-stop in the main road.

St Wilhemina's was located in the centre of an erratic collection of Victorian buildings. A wide, curving, black asphalt drive led past boiler rooms and the hospital laundry and opened up into a bleak square from which a series of paths dissected the grounds. Ahead lay the main entrance with a reserved space for ambulances outside. A glass-and-brick extension to the left added to the grey Victorian building, with a greater regard for economy than design. A galaxy of signs pointing to X-ray, Outpatients, Maternity, Accident and Emergency and a long list of wards with depressing names were listed on an adjoining board.

Serena had to quell an overwhelming desire to turn and run. Only a sharp rebuke kept her facing in the same direction. This way, she lectured herself, you stay outside the system, even though the money's a pittance. This way you don't have to answer any more questions.

She adjusted the strap of her bag and walked up a narrow ramp and into the hospital, following the signs that led her to the Maud Frierley ward for geriatric patients. It was ten to eight. Just time to phone home and see if everything was OK.

Serena leaned against the tiled wall of the sluice room and eased her shoes off. An Australian girl called Becky was pushing soiled bed linen into huge cotton bags and then handing them to Serena, who secured the necks with yellow tape before hurling them into a wooden trolley, ready to be trundled away by a porter to the laundry.

'You'll never get them on again,' Becky warned, indicating Serena's discarded shoes.

'Not sure that I want to,' Serena replied, massaging one bare foot against the other. Under her overall, she could feel a thin trickle of sweat running down between her breasts. Her neck and forehead were damp. Every available window on the floor had been flung open to contend with the heat of a warm June day.

Very little of what Serena had been asked to do was what she had expected. She had been told she would be helping on the ward, but no one had prepared her for the sheer drudgery or the risk involved in a great deal of it. On the second day on the ward, one of the harassed nurses, joining in the rush to aid an elderly man, who appeared to have gone into cardiac arrest, had pushed the medication trolley at her and told her to get on with it.

'Just the paracetamol, you dummy,' the nurse hissed at her as Serena started to protest. 'Even you can do that, surely to God?'

Uneasily she started to work her way through the list, glancing furtively at the thin, severe figure of Sister Mary Burton, who was berating a junior nurse for allowing a visitor to enter the ward out of hours.

'What a cow,' the nurse muttered, rejoining Serena halfway through the round. 'You think she'd welcome a visitor, wouldn't you? No one ever comes to see the poor sods. Oh God, there goes Mr Haworth. Grab him will you?'

No one had mentioned, either, that Maud Frierley was a mixed ward where dignity was a disposable commodity, and where two or three elderly male patients were inclined to remove their pyjamas at a whim and go for a walk.

'Just as well most of the women haven't a clue what day it is,' Becky muttered, helping Serena to get Mr Haworth back into his pyjamas. 'I'm going to ask for a pillow to be put over my face if I end up in a place like this.'

Serena just nodded, too shocked to say anything. That had been two months ago. She had had two months of washing incontinent or feeble-minded patients, emptying bedpans or soothing wandering wits had been easy compared with dealing with the heartless Sister Burton. Any sign of compassion towards her patients was taken as a poor reflection on her management skills and, as Serena knew to her cost, any sugges-tion about how they might improve the lot of the abandoned generation was seen as a threat to her authority.

'Sit them at the table to eat their meals? *At the table?*' Sister Burton could not have sounded more incredulous if Serena had suggested taking the entire ward to lunch at the Ritz. 'If I thought getting these patients up and over to a table to eat lunch would contribute to the smooth running of my ward,' she stormed at Serena, 'I would do it. But it won't. Understand? To do that I need another pair of hands and I haven't the money to do it. Got that?'

'But it's only a question of two or three patients at the most,' Serena tried to point out. 'It would only take me a few minutes . . .'

'A *few minutes?*' breathed Sister Burton. 'If you've got a few minutes to spare, my dear, you clearly haven't nearly enough to do.'

'I'm so sorry,' Serena said quietly. 'I just thought . . .'

'Then don't,' Sister Burton snapped. 'For heaven's sake get a move on. Mr Merrow will be doing his round in an hour and I want this ward looking like the Hilton. Got that? And take these down to Records,' she added, thrusting a pile of buff folders into her arms, 'if you've got so much time on your hands.'

'Yes, Sister, of course,' Serena replied, ignoring the sarcasm. She walked down three flights of stairs, through Outpatients, until she reached an open hatch next to a door marked RECORDS.

'Hi,' she said through the hatch to a girl in a white coat and horn-rimmed glasses sitting at a nearby desk.

'Serena.' The girl got up and came over to relieve her of the stack of buff folders. 'So you haven't put Sister Burton in traction yet?'

Serena laughed. 'Give me time. She's not quite up to speed today. She's too busy preparing for the great man's visit. How's life?'

Stacey Barclay shrugged. She was, Serena decided, a remarkable-looking girl, tall enough to make her carefully chosen tailored jackets and skirts look a great deal more expensive than they were. She'd been at the hospital for a year, moving south to be with her boyfriend, leaving behind a well-paid job in the local council, not to mention a close-knit family. It was a friendship that Serena had come to enjoy.

'Wait for me when you get off and I'll walk down to the bus with you,' Stacey whispered, seeing her boss approaching.

Serena gave her a wave and turned to make her way back to the ward, where a lone nurse, who looked almost dead on her feet, was consulting a list of patients. Sister Burton was in her office. Becky and a stout black woman called Nonie were swishing wet mops down the ward.

'Shall I start with Edith?' Serena asked the nurse.

'Oh, Serena,' the nurse looked up with relief. 'Thanks. I'm glad it's you, I just couldn't take another morning with bloody Nonie, she's so rough with them, they get upset and then we have to sedate them.'

Serena walked round to the other side of Edith's bed. 'Hi, Edith.' She smiled down into the vacant eyes, pressing the thin hand lying across the blanket. 'How does a luxury bath sound to you?'

As she began to turn Edith on her side, she glanced around the ward. Frierley had made Serena realise, as nothing else had done quite so forcibly in the last eighteen months, that unless she helped herself no one would. In spite of her sheltered life and pampered marriage, there was a strength of character that had always been there but never allowed to flourish until now. A stoicism that had never been tested was making itself felt. The pay was poor, and after tax and fares and paying Cheryl there was little left over. But what was in her pay packet was hers, not a handout from the state. And with it came the return of a modicum of control. This wouldn't be for ever, she knew that.

She looked down and smiled. 'Here we go, Edith,' she said cheerfully to the skeletal figure in the bed. 'And then I'll help you into a clean nightie. Let me know if you feel uncomfortable, won't you?'

Edith Ambleton, nearly ninety and so stricken with bronchitis she had been removed by a health visitor from the home where she had lived for nearly fifty years, lifted a feeble hand and returned Serena's clasp. The nurse glanced across at Serena in surprise. She had never seen Edith smile before.

At noon, Robert Merrow marched onto the ward followed by a young registrar. Serena was successfully spooning cereal into a patient's slack mouth when she saw Sister Burton's signal to her to stop while the great man consulted his notes.

'Would you mind if I continued?' Serena asked quietly. 'This is the first time she's eaten for two days.'

Sister Burton's refusal was drowned by Robert Merrow's agreement. 'Certainly, certainly. Good sign,' he nodded. 'Nothing much more to be done, really. Carry on, nurse.'

'Oh, but I'm not a nurse,' she began, but stopped, partly because Sister Burton glared at her but mostly because Robert Merrow was staring intently at her, puzzled. He opened his mouth to say something and then changed his mind. Serena hastily turned her head away. She would not deny who she was, but nor did she want anyone to identify her. When she turned back, Robert Merrow had already moved on and the old lady was waiting for the next mouthful of food.

'**W**hy do you do it?' Melanie asked, noting approvingly that Serena had rearranged her living room since her last visit. The lamps that had once adorned her drawing room in Belvoir Square now cast a warm, welcoming glow across the room. The curtains looped back with taffeta ribbon softened the squareness of the windows and a glass vase stuffed with sunflowers provided a burst of colour against the plain walls.

Serena stretched her legs out and crossed her ankles. 'Because it suits me, I'm here for the kids in the evening, and it won't be for ever.'

She was looking better, Melanie noted with relief. Her hair, now piled loosely into a knot on top of her head, was no longer highlighted, and her make-up was confined to a splash of lipstick, but the improvement was noticeable.

About time too, Melanie thought grimly. It was a year and a half since it all happened and she talked about this Alex quite a lot.

'So what's he doing for Harry?' Melanie sipped her coffee.

'A lot. Harry sees him once a week and they talk about all kinds of things. He's terrific with him.'

'Don't you sit in on the sessions?'

'Well, at first I did. But then Alex thought Harry might respond more if I wasn't there. I expect he tells him I'm an ogre.'

'Nonsense,' Melanie snorted. 'Harry adores you. What does he say about Stephen?'

'I don't know. I'm not sure they've even got to that yet.'

'Heavens!' Melanie exclaimed. 'I suppose he knows what he's doing.'

'Yes. Absolutely. I have complete faith in him,' Serena replied. 'He's kind and—well, not gentle precisely, more understanding, if you see what I mean. You don't have to spell it out for him. Anyway, enough of us. How's life? Charles?'

'Well,' Melanie began, seeing that she was unlikely to get any more out of Serena—she was so secretive these days. 'The dreadful Paula has fallen out with Miranda over who was to choose the celebrity for the next ball. The rest of us are staying out of it. But George is angling for his knighthood and wants someone political.

'Incidentally, Malcolm asked about you. So did Meryl Holt. She, um,' Melanie glanced uncertainly at Serena, 'she asked if you'd like to have lunch some time?'

'Maybe.' Serena smiled faintly. 'I'll take a rain check on it.' Meryl Holt was an American, the wife of a Wall Street financier, Ryland Holt, whose company had moved him to London. Serena and Stephen had met them when they were staying with friends in the States, and they had got on well together.

Melanie left an hour later, pleased to have seen Serena, with plenty to report to Charles that would soothe both their minds. But she knew that lunch with Meryl was unlikely to take place. She turned her car over Westminster Bridge and drove thoughtfully home.

Chapter Six

~

ALEX BILLINGTON knew what it was like to see his own family break up and be separated from his children most of the week. This was, Serena decided, in his favour rather than something that could create doubt about his ability to mend broken lives.

For a while, apart from shaking hands with Harry and ruffling his hair, Alex Billington said very little to him, instead engaging Serena in quite ordinary small talk until—she wasn't sure how it happened—she found herself flicking absently through the pages of a magazine in a small anteroom, occasionally glancing at her watch while Harry explained the complexities of his computer game to Alex.

He was, she guessed, somewhere in his late thirties, although it was hard to be absolutely sure. Successful, well-regarded. Older than his brother and built on more slender lines. His fair hair was receding but he wore quite youthful clothes: baggy cotton trousers, a denim shirt under a cotton jacket, which she recognised as the designer item it was. His manner was gentle and he seemed to be familiar with nearly all schools of behaviour therapy. Jungian was, however, his favourite.

'Not mother's fault,' he explained cheerfully. 'Unlike Freud who can't point the finger fast enough.'

'Well, by all means, let's go with Jung,' Serena said. 'I've always thought he had a better handle on our dreams than Freud.'

He groaned. 'Don't tell me you're an expert.'

'Dream on.' She laughed, then became serious, choosing her words carefully. 'I wouldn't want to duck out of the blame, you know.' She fiddled with the strap of her bag. He gestured for her to go on. 'I mean, what if I am? To blame, I mean. If we're going to be realistic, it probably is me that's Harry's problem. But all I ask is that you must be honest with me. And that's OK too.' She knew she was sounding melodramatic. 'You mustn't worry because I've tried to prepare myself for it.'

'You mustn't beat yourself up like this,' he said quietly.

It was then that she horrified herself by bursting into tears. Swollen, convulsive sobs shook her, which she made worse by trying to suppress them. The tears were for Harry.

She tried telling him, but he just spoke soothingly over her, urging her to cry all she needed to, when all she wanted was to stop. Poor, broken little Harry, who had done nothing to deserve the demons invading his life and *she* was getting the sympathy.

'And are you also prepared for being blameless?' Alex asked gently, as she pulled a handful of tissues from the box he extended. Serena blew her nose. 'You may only be guilty of being a caring mother.'

The letter signed S. Maxfield, posted the day before, was curt and asked if Serena would come to the school on a matter of urgency.

'What's this about, Lou?' she asked.

Louise shrugged. 'What?'

'This letter.' Serena battled not to shout at her. 'Darling, let me have it. Why have they posted this? Why didn't they give it to you to bring home? What is it? Homework? No? Oh, Lou, not bunking off?'

'What would you know about bunking off?' Louise retorted rudely.

'*Lou*, that is no way to speak to me . . .'

'No? *No?* Then how do you want me to speak to you?' Louise suddenly flared up, wrenching open the door as she spoke. 'You don't speak to me at all. You talk to Harry. Lovely goodie-two-shoes Harry.'

'Louise, stop it.' Serena tried to calm her. 'Of course I care about you.'

'No, you don't. I've got the curse and have you asked how I feel? No.'

'How can I know unless you tell me . . .'

'I don't *want* to tell you. Go and see the bloody woman. See if I care.'

'*Louise.*' Serena ran after her. But Louise was too quick and was out of the front door and down the path before Serena could reach her.

Her age, Alex had said reassuringly when she phoned to cancel Harry's appointment. She hadn't meant to pour it out to him, but he seemed to draw it out of her, getting past her defences.

'You're right. You read about it all the time. I'll let you know how it goes. Thanks, Alex. It isn't your problem—Louise, I mean.'

'Nonsense,' he said cheerfully. 'Any time I can help, Serena, you know I will. Now, I normally see my other patients at my home,' he told her, by which she knew he meant his private patients. 'Why don't you bring Harry to the house on Saturday morning. Ten o'clock?'

At ten past four that afternoon, Serena was shown into the interview room at St Saviour's and confronted by Louise's year teacher.

'She's a bright, sharp-witted girl who has a good future, but she is wasting it by using this school to beat up the world,' said the brisk woman who sat behind a cluttered desk. She spoke brusquely with no preamble, checking a report in front of her.

'No homework submitted for over a month, bunking off lessons, insolence to her teachers, and yesterday, which is why I've asked to see you,' she said clasping her hands together, 'she was part of a gang of girls who pushed a teacher flat on her face.'

Serena gasped. 'Oh my God. Why? Is she all right?'

'Shaken and a bit bruised. And you had no idea about this?'

'No. None.' Serena gripped her hands into a fist in her jacket pockets.

'We don't tolerate violence on any level, Mrs Carmichael.'

'Of course not, but surely it was an accident?' Serena interrupted, rallying her wits just enough to defend Louise.

Mrs Maxfield shook her head impatiently. She was clearly in no mood to be sympathetic to a mother who didn't even know why she had been summoned to see her.

'It was not an accident. It was deliberate. I don't believe Louise instigated it, but she didn't stop it or step back from it.'

'I can't believe this.' Serena shook her head. 'Louise is headstrong and unhappy. But for heaven's sake, the child is only thirteen and she's come through so much. Surely you can understand that?'

'I can understand. But I don't condone. And she is nearer fourteen than thirteen. Mrs Carmichael, I am very aware of Louise's background and I am not attempting to underplay the shock of it, but I can tell you there are children in this school who have suffered much more serious deprivation than Louise and they don't resort to this. This is an official warning, Mrs Carmichael. One more step out of line and we will suspend her from school.'

In all of this, it wasn't until she had left the interview room with Mrs Maxfield's advice that she should get Louise in order, stop her from thinking she could break life's rules and get away with it, that she realised she had not once felt sorry for Louise. Just frightened for her.

Alex was inclined to take a more serious view of Louise's unrepentant stance, as described to him by Serena, than the actual crime.

'I know Susie Maxfield,' he said, pouring a mug of coffee for Serena and leading the way into the conservatory that led off his kitchen. 'Her manner is a little abrupt, but then she's not running Roedean is she?' He smiled down at her. Serena was tall, but he still towered over her.

'Here,' he said indicating with his coffee mug a couple of wicker chairs. 'Sit over here. It's such a stunning day, isn't it?'

Serena relaxed against a pile of cushions in one chair while he settled himself into its twin on the other side of an open door that led on to a small oasis of a garden. Beyond was a perfectly manicured lawn stretching down to an apple tree. The scent of jasmine drifted in on the summer breeze. Harry was engrossed in unravelling a computer game on Alex's son's computer which, Alex had assured Harry, Spencer wouldn't mind in the least. She had to remind herself this was a professional visit.

'No, Susie is a good egg,' Alex explained, cradling his mug in both hands, one leg flung over the arm of his chair. 'She's just seen it all.'

'So what does she mean: Louise is using school to beat up the world?'

'I think'—he coughed, throwing a self-conscious grin at Serena— 'Susie's quoting me, to be honest. Louise won't face the real problem probably because in the middle of all that anger and frustration she needs you and wants you to tell her what to do next. And when you don't, she takes it out on the nearest whipping boy. School.'

Serena stiffened. 'You're saying that I am Louise's problem?'

He groaned, reaching out his hand to briefly grip hers. 'No, of course not. I'm saying the reverse. You're most likely to be Louise's solution. Only it might not seem like it at the moment.'

She stared doubtfully at him. She the solution to a child who slammed doors in her face and screamed her hatred of her? 'I wish I could get Louise to talk to you,' she said, leaning back on the cushions. 'But she won't. Won't talk to anyone, I mean. Except a friend of hers called Daphy and some boy called Damon who has three earrings in one ear and calls LouLou "Babe".'

Alex chuckled. 'Give her time. Meanwhile, Harry, I'm pleased to say, is much more relaxed. Who is Stacey, by the way? He likes her.'

'Stacey? She's a dear. Works at the hospital. Mid-twenties, pretty. She's got a ghastly boyfriend who treats her badly, but she takes all the blame for everything he does. She comes over for supper when he's away— which is often.'

He looked thoughtfully out across the garden. 'Talking of which, I was going to ask if you would like to come to supper one evening?'

For some reason her stomach fluttered uncomfortably. Her eyes widened in astonishment. 'How kind,' she began, a little flustered. 'But I don't think I could, not yet, I don't think I'm ready for . . .'

'For what? Supper with someone who enjoys talking to you?'

Serena felt her throat constrict. Panic gripped her. She no longer felt safe. Alice. She suddenly recalled Alex mentioning his relationship with an artist called Alice. The yet-to-be-met Alice had shared Alex's weekends for the last three years.

'Alex, it's most kind of you, but I couldn't.' She swallowed hard. 'I mean Alice . . .'

'Alice?' There was a slight pause before he said, 'Of course, I meant Alice and I would like you to come to supper.'

'Yes, of course you did.' Serena thought she would keel over with embarrassment. 'I just meant,' she began, 'I just meant Alice might not want a stranger foisted on her, that's all.'

'Nonsense,' he said easily. 'I'll get her to call you.'

On the bus going home, two things had to be considered. The first and most obvious being that she had made a first-class fool of herself, the second was what would she have done if Alice had not existed and there was only Alex to consider.

For a wild moment she had been going to say yes. The vision of looking pretty and feminine and being flirted with and—oh God, who was she kidding?—to have sex that would exhaust her with its passion and ferocity had, for a brief moment, made her feel dizzy.

She looked down at the Saturday-morning shoppers pushing slowly along the crowded pavement, running into congested knots as pedestrians converging from different directions, trying to ease their way round pavement stalls. Outside McDonald's the bus slowed to manoeuvre its way past a parked car. Idly she watched as the glass doors swung in and out, disgorging groups of teenagers and small children. It took her a few seconds to register the couple pushing through the crowd gathering around the door. She strained across Harry to follow their progress as they disappeared into the crowd.

There was no mistake. It was Louise, draped around the boy with the three earrings, who called her 'Babe'. Louise was giggling up into his face, wearing a tight pink jumper that ended inches above the waistband of a pair of black jeans that imprisoned her legs, and thick clumpy shoes. None of these things, Serena thought frantically, were Louise's. Or at least not that she recalled.

She half rose out of her seat and then slumped back. By the time she reached the pavement, Louise would have disappeared and, anyway, the bus was already gathering speed. All she could do was hope that Louise would be careful and come home soon. Sex suddenly lost its allure. It was a fiend waiting to spoil her daughter and wreck her life.

Alex's house had mobilised familiar pangs of longing. Alex himself had stirred feelings best left where they were. Harry nudged her to start getting off the bus as the stop nearest to Foster Street approached. And then, she thought as she went down the stairs, there was Stephen. Stephen who was still her husband, Stephen who she still yearned for. How could Alex, until he had disrupted that private and protected world known only to Serena, have known what a powerful effect a simple, if misleading, invitation would have on her?

He was a good, kind—and yes, attractive man. But it was the treacherous seduction of sex, not Alex, that had distorted her feelings. Having arrived at that conclusion, she felt almost light-headed with relief. The bus creaked to a halt at the corner of the High Street. Anxiously she looked back down the road, knowing there was no hope of seeing Louise but trying not to imagine what she might be up to.

They crossed the road to the supermarket where Harry pushed the trolley, occasionally scooting it along with one foot. They passed through the crowded check-outs and, although Harry volunteered to carry one of the bags home, the other three pulled Serena's arms heavily downwards.

Slowly they walked up Foster Street. Cheryl was leaning on her gate gossiping to one of the neighbours. She waved a hand at Serena, who smiled and nodded back as she turned into her gate. Alana and Ellis were weaving about the pavement on their skateboards.

''Lo, Harry,' Alana called. 'Wanna go?'

Harry hesitated, looking quickly at Serena. The last thing she wanted was Harry playing in the street. But she was no proof against the eager look on his face. 'Can I, Mum?' he whispered. 'Just here, no further?'

'Of course!' She grinned back at him. 'I might even watch once I've dumped all this shopping.'

He dashed off and she turned into the house. Who would have thought it, she pondered, putting the shopping away. This time last year Harry would have been in the country riding his pony, or . . . she stopped and gazed into the distance. It wasn't last year, was it? It was the year before. Nearly two years.

She frowned, trying to remember what it had all been like. But she couldn't. The vision of her driving down the M4 was easy to conjure up, but the feeling of being protected, cosseted, eluded her. She switched the kettle on. The seamless way her life had drifted from that one to this troubled her. So much so that she couldn't now recall when one had stopped haunting her and the other had taken over. She took her coffee and wandered into the living room and glanced out at Harry speeding past, held up by Alana. No sign of Louise.

At times like this she felt Stephen's absence more acutely. Not there to turn to, to take the burden from her. But then, a more honest voice reminded her, there were times when she had trouble recalling what it was like being with Stephen.

Just after four, Louise came home. Fury that she had caused her so much anguish soared, but in the end relief and Alex's admonition to try and keep calm, to see Louise's resentment and rebellion as a way of getting her attention, won.

'So, there you are,' Serena exclaimed. 'I saw you coming out of McDonald's, but that was hours ago.'

A wary look crept into Louise's face as she stood in the doorway, hands dug into the pockets of her jeans. 'Taken to spying now, have you?'

Relief dissolved. The pact shattered. 'Louise,' she breathed furiously, slapping down the tea cloth on the draining board, 'if you are rude to me once more, I will really let you see just how tough life can be. Why didn't you tell me you were going out?'

'I didn't know I was, until after you'd gone. Why?' Louise retorted sulkily. 'What's wrong with that? Why should you mind? You were out.'

Serena rested her hands on the kitchen table and leaned towards Louise. 'Mind that you went out? No. Mind that you didn't have the courtesy to tell me? Yes. Don't do it again. Clear?'

'What if I do? You didn't ask me if it was OK for you to disappear with Harry for the whole morning. I haven't made a fuss.'

Serena took a deep breath. 'I am making a "fuss" as you put it because I was worried about you. You know perfectly well that I didn't have much of a choice about this morning's appointment—and I asked you to come, remember?'

'No, thanks.' Louise gave an exaggerated shudder. 'I'm not into being treated like a nutcase . . .'

'Nutcase?' Serena exclaimed. 'That's a charming way to describe someone as normal as Harry not having your confidence, your ability to make friends. Nutcase indeed. And don't slam the door, do you hear?'

Serena was exhausted when she left the hospital. Sister Burton had piled up the chores today, and tonight she was going to Alex's house for dinner. Eight o'clock, Alice had said. Informal, they would dine out of doors if the weather held.

She was going to go by bus and order a taxi to bring her back. That was the easy part. Harder to decide was what to wear. Black, she thought finally. There was the linen, sleeveless dress she had bought from Harvey Nichols three years ago. And maybe just a pair of earrings.

The amber and jet ones her mother had given her on her twenty-first.

There was also Minnie to call with some dates for Harry and Louise to go to Lucca in the holidays. God bless Minnie, she thought fervently. Nearly three weeks this time—although Louise had kicked up a terrible fuss at the prospect. But at least she could keep the money coming in. Then two weeks staying with Margot—or maybe Margot would come up? She must suggest it. At least that would placate Lou. And she would take a couple of weeks herself. It would just work.

'Can I give you a lift?' Robert Merrow was leaning out of the car window, dark glasses shielding his eyes. She hesitated.

'It's kind of you, but I live . . .'

'I know where you live,' he said. 'Otherwise I wouldn't have offered you a lift. Besides I want to talk to you.'

'Me?'

'Yes, you. Be a good girl, will you?' he added plaintively. 'I don't want to set tongues wagging, so just hop in.'

Serena looked around. Curious eyes were already taking in the scene of a senior consultant in a Jag fraternising with a ward orderly. In the end she swung herself into the passenger seat and he drove off.

'You're Serena Carmichael, aren't you?' he said almost immediately. 'Stephen Carmichael's wife.' Unperturbed by her silence, he carried on. 'What are you doing in a dump like this?'

'Mr Merrow,' she began, 'it's kind of you to give me a lift but my reasons for working here, like my life, are my own private affair. I appreciate it might look odd, but believe me, it is one of the saner things that I have had to deal with in the last year or so.'

'OK. But tell me something. Why did you take this job? Why not something more, well, upmarket?'

Serena sighed. 'So easy for you to say that. Who would give me a job where the gossip wouldn't have been dreadful? Besides, I have no real qualifications and I can't work full-time because of the children. Anyway, I don't think the job is a bad one, just hopelessly paid.'

'And how long do you plan to do it?'

'Well, funny you should say that,' she said. 'I really will have to get something else—it's finding something that isn't full-time.'

'What about four mornings and one full day? Thing is,' he said, 'I run a private practice just off Harley Street, specialising in nutrition and digestive problems, and I need a good receptionist. Someone who's discreet, looks good, and isn't fazed by difficult patients. Good money too,' he added, mentioning a sum that was three times her salary at St Wilhemina's. 'Thought you might consider it.'

Alice didn't so much move around the table as drift. She looked what she was, an artist. Serena knew from conversations with Alex that Alice was thirty-six, had no children of her own but adored his two. A halo of frizzy russet curls framed a face that reminded Serena of a silent-movie queen, with its pencilled-in eyebrows over startlingly blue eyes.

Alice was stunning to look at, but after less than an hour in her company Serena decided she was also tiresome. Then she felt terrible because she wasn't at all sure if this impatience with a woman she had barely met was rooted in the fact that Alex was tied to her. After a moment or two reflecting on this, she decided it was an unbiased view. After all, she didn't want Alex for herself.

Three other couples, the director of an art gallery whose wife, a designer, was abroad, and Serena made up the party. If they knew her history they were too polite to mention it.

Alex introduced her as someone he had met through his work, which was perfectly true, if a little misleading. As she listened to the art-gallery director bemoan the lack of subsidies, she noticed Alex keeping a protective eye on her and felt touched by his concern. When the opportunity presented itself, she smiled across at him to let him see she was fine.

The weather had held, so the meal was served in the garden. 'Not exactly ambrosial, but you will forgive—long day, more thrown together than prepared, I'm afraid,' Alice cried gaily.

Alex sat at one end of the glass-topped cane table, Alice—when she sat at all—at the other. 'Serena, do sit here, next to Gordon, and Tricia, here next to Alex.' Alice went on in this way until everyone was seated. Serena sat between two male guests, who seemed to be as amused by their hostess as Serena was unsettled. She found it hard to equate this frivolous woman with the paintings of hers that she had seen in Alex's study. Elaborate swathes of fearless colour had nothing to do with this dippy display of helpless femininity.

Throughout the meal, they were constantly being called on to reassure Alice that dinner was delicious. First she invited them, with a small frown, to consider if they didn't think she had not put *quite* enough teriyaki sauce in the vegetables which accompanied the roast salmon, and later, would the pecan struedel cheesecake have benefited from less cream? All this drew a chorus of protest from everyone, Serena dutifully joining in, since the meal was perfect.

Later, when the conversation, mostly of people and times of which she had no knowledge, left her feeling stifled, Serena was ashamed to realise that what she missed was being amused, made to laugh, by the very people whom Alex's friends could only discuss.

The evening was winding down, the conversation at the other end of the table slightly drunk. The man next to her, who had spent the last hour describing his entire career to Serena, said, 'Alex says you're a volunteer at St Wilhemina's.'

Serena took a sip of coffee, glancing in surprise at Alex who knew she was not. 'Actually I work there. I help on the geriatric ward, but I've just accepted another job, so I'm looking forward to that.'

'A job, Serena?' Alex's voice came down the table. 'What's all this?'

Alice glanced quickly from one to the other. 'How exciting,' she said. 'Do tell all, Serena.'

'Oh, please,' Serena said quickly. 'It's nothing special.'

'Nonsense.' Alex rose to his feet, holding his wine glass, and came to perch on a low stone wall just behind her chair so that she had to swivel round to face him, her knees just inches from his. 'It's wonderful news. I know you disliked the job you were doing.'

Serena paused. Disliked? No, she had never disliked it. She felt frustrated and angry at a system that could push frail and dependent women like Edith back to a home where they would have even less support, but not dislike. Robert had told her about Edith in the car going home. 'She won't be back,' he revealed. 'They need the bed. She's improved more than they thought, which means she can't stay.'

'That's dreadful,' Serena protested. 'Poor Edith. She has no one, just some ghastly daughter-in-law who never comes to see her.'

'Well, now she'll have to, won't she?' he said brusquely. 'Now, what about this job?'

The money was good, too good to ignore. 'Just give me enough time to sort out how I'm going to organise my children,' she had said.

'So? Tell me?' Alex said encouragingly, squeezing her hand.

It was a warm, friendly gesture, but at that precise moment with Alice gazing intently at them, a fraction disturbing. 'Nothing much to tell,' she assured him, sliding her hand from under his. 'One of the consultants wants me to work for him at his practice just off Harley Street. Running the office, overseeing patients, that kind of thing.'

'But that's wonderful,' he enthused. 'Why didn't you tell me?'

All eyes were on them. Alice's were watchful.

'Well, I only heard this afternoon and I was seeing you—I mean both of you,' she glanced at Alice, 'this evening.'

Serena felt a stab of annoyance that she had been forced to justify herself. 'I still have to work out the details; I mean the children have to be catered for. It isn't absolutely settled.'

He was still sitting near to her even though she had clearly come to the end of the explanation. 'I'll keep you posted,' she promised. To her relief there was a ring at the doorbell. 'That'll be my cab,' she said, rising quickly. 'Alice, that was a wonderful evening. Thank you both so much.'

Alex rose to his feet. 'I'll see you out.'

'Me too,' said Alice.

It was only when she was halfway home that Serena realised that Alice had not so much drifted but run after them.

Cheryl said she rather liked the idea of working a few more hours. 'Just the one full day, is it?'

'All the other days he has hospital rounds, surgery, that kind of thing. The point is, Cheryl, I won't need to ask you to do it right through the holidays because they'll be going to my mother-in-law in Italy for a bit and my mother is going to stay for a couple of weeks and he's said I can take the two weeks before they go back to school as holiday.'

Cheryl waved all this aside. 'No sweat.' She shook her head. 'Soon as the holidays finish, we'll give it a whirl.'

Stacey came round that evening with a bottle of wine to celebrate. 'Wish it was me,' she sighed. 'But Barry wouldn't hear of me working in the West End. He likes me to be there when he gets in.'

Serena said nothing. At first she'd tried to encourage her to stand up to the overbearing Barry, but knew it was useless. Stacey was in awe of him and, Serena suspected, frightened of him.

'Well, let's see how I get on,' Serena said, topping up their glasses. 'Tell you what, on my first pay day we'll go out to celebrate.'

'You're on.' Stacey laughed. 'Here.' She reached into her bag and pulled out a book on computer games. 'I found this for Harry. It was in that shop on the corner of the High Street. How's the lovely Louise?'

Serena just grimaced. 'Sulking. She's not too thrilled about going to Lucca next month, but Minnie says at this age they're easily diverted. At least, she says Stephen—' She stopped, glancing quickly at Stacey.

'Take it easy,' Stacey said. 'Hey, Minnie's right. Fourteen isn't for ever.'

'I know, it just seems like it,' Serena replied. She leaned back in her chair. 'By the way,' she said, her eyes closed, 'if you find out where Edith is, let me know, will you?'

The Carlyle Clinic, where Robert Merrow had his practice, was just off Harley Street in a tall redbrick house. The clinic occupied the whole of the ground floor, a calm oasis of pastel colours, plush carpets and fresh flowers. At the front, in a room overlooking the street, pink and blue armchairs with plump cushions and deep seats were arranged in small groups round low tables. Here patients waited for their turn to see Robert Merrow in his luxurious consulting room.

The staff, including Serena, numbered four people. Two nurses, one who worked in the dispensary and the other whose prime function seemed to be to shuttle patients from the waiting room to Robert Merrow's office. A part-time secretary, who dealt with his correspondence, announced herself as Jill. She eyed Serena critically and just rolled her eyes when she heard that she had never come into contact with a computer, let alone felt equipped to operate one.

'Never mind.' She sounded resigned. 'You'll learn. It's hardly NASA.' Serena's job was to keep the patients happy, make and confirm appointments and keep track of their notes.

'And play agony aunt to the ones who don't think their treatment is working and keep them from nagging Robert. He hates it.'

It took Serena less than a day to realise two things. The first she could deal with, which was that she would be bored witless with so little to do and with such patients to deal with. Her second concern, and the one that disturbed her, were the patients themselves. Stick-thin women with no evidence of any kind that their problem was any greater than a desire to remain that way. Rotund businessmen who took their medication to the next expensive restaurant. Sad, middle-aged women fighting the effects of gravity, and others who were so obese it was not Robert Merrow they needed, with his pills and injections, but a halfway decent doctor who would provide a very different kind of help.

Her first sight of Cindy Moreton scared the life out of her. Cindy was a model and exquisitely beautiful, with a sweep of blonde hair falling over one shoulder. 'I need to see Robert again this week,' she told Serena when she emerged from his consulting room. 'I've got to go away on Friday. I'd like to see him Wednesday.'

'Of course,' Serena said, turning to tap into the computer. The girl seemed nervous. 'I'm afraid Wednesday is rather full,' she told her. 'Would Thursday be all right, he seems to have a free—'

'I said Wednesday. If I'd wanted Thursday I'd have said so.'

Serena kept her eyes on the screen, gritting her teeth. 'If you'd like to wait a moment, I'll ask Mr Merrow if he can fit you in. Would you mind taking a seat in the waiting room and I'll find out.'

It was then that Serena saw Cindy's wrists. As she reached for her bag, the sleeves of her jacket fell back, revealing a skeletal arm. Her hand, with its bony fingers, appeared too large to be part of such a limb.

'What's the matter? Why are you staring?' she demanded.

'I'm sorry. I wasn't staring. I'll be with you in a minute.'

Instead of phoning through to Robert, Serena waited until he was free. 'It's a girl called Cindy Moreton. She's rather agitated, wants to see you on Wednesday, but you're full.'

'Oh, just be firm with her,' he said easily. 'She's a spoilt brat.' When he saw Serena hesitate, he asked, 'Anything else?'

'Well, only that she seems incredibly thin and . . . and as I said agitated. I just wonder if there might be something else wrong with her.'

Robert surveyed her. 'If there is, I'll soon find out. Now, be a good girl and just get the next patient sent in.'

She nodded. Cindy was waiting for her.

'Mr Merrow said he can only see you on Thursday, I'm afraid. Either that or perhaps you could wait until you come back from your trip?'

Cindy bit her lip, glaring at Serena. 'Oh, fuck him. Fuck the lot of you,' she muttered, and stormed out.

It wasn't until she was due to go to lunch that Serena saw the dispensary open for the first time. A woman called Bridget, with over-permed grey hair, presided over the white-tiled room where patients duly reported after a session with Robert. Serena was left with no doubt about the nature of Robert's real business. Stacked on a table at the back of the room, just out of sight of the patients, were rows of plastic containers filled with brightly coloured tablets, like Smarties without the chocolate.

On the third morning, Serena waited until Jill walked into her small office just off the reception area and followed her in. 'I just wondered if any of the patients had genuine problems,' she explained.

Jill just laughed. 'Oh, don't worry, he knows what he's doing.'

'It's not that,' Serena said quietly. 'It can't be right.'

'Course it is,' Jill said cheerfully, as she sorted through a pile of post. 'Perfectly legal.'

'But look at this,' Serena interrupted. 'File after file marked "GP not to be informed". How can that be right?'

Jill sighed. 'Well, they're all over twenty-one and he doesn't just dole out pills. I mean he takes blood and urine tests and checks their blood pressure. They're quite safe.'

'Dear God. Doesn't he understand this is just exacerbating the problem?' Serena whispered urgently.

Jill walked past her and closed the door to her small office and leaned against it. 'Now, listen to me,' she said firmly. 'There is nothing illegal about what's going on.'

'No, I know that, but it's just that he's encouraging some damaged people who need help, not pills.'

'You don't know what they need. You're not a doctor. Serena, I know what you're thinking, but believe me you're wasting your sympathy. Look at these people. Do you really think if Robert said, "Go on a diet, exercise", they would? Course not. Forget it. If it wasn't Robert it would be someone else. They know what they're doing, believe me.'

'I wish I knew what I was doing,' Serena muttered, walking back to reception, 'let alone them. Oh God, what a mess.'

Chapter Seven

THE AFTERNOON WORE ON with the steady procession of those Serena had come to refer to as the usual suspects.

Brian Conway rolled in with a lascivious wink at Serena. According to Jill he had enjoyed expense-account lunches for so long he was beginning to believe that his sales figures were diminishing in direct proportion to his expanding girth. All of which he thought could be reversed if he lost weight.

'Here,' he said to Serena, brandishing a brochure in her face. 'You should try this. Solo agency. Great place, but those babes like their guys to be a bit lean, know what I mean? You'd do well there. Come with me if you like.'

'How kind,' she murmured, hearing Jill choking behind her. 'However, I have a partner,' she lied. 'He'd be a bit cross if I suddenly went er . . . solo.'

Brian Conway chortled and waddled away to the dispensary. 'He tried to pull Cindy Moreton once,' Jill giggled.

'He couldn't pull a hair from his head, revolting little man,' Serena snapped.

At five a middle-aged woman called Madeleine Selway appeared, shyly presenting herself at reception. On this hot summer afternoon she looked ill and tired. 'The "change", you see,' she confessed, her cheeks going pink, moisture standing out on her upper lip. She dabbed at her forehead with a tissue. Serena glanced at her in alarm.

'Let me get you some iced water.' She led Madeleine to a quiet, cool corner, and pressed her into a comfortable wicker chair before going to fetch the water, which Madeleine sipped gratefully.

'Much better,' she smiled, handing the glass back to Serena. Serena glanced quickly round to make sure no one was waiting to book in.

'Mrs Selway,' she began. 'This is nothing to do with me. But why are you doing this? You look fine to me—better than fine. Do you honestly think this is doing you any good?'

'No. Probably not. But you see it's not as easy as you think.'

To Serena's horror, large tears welled up in the older woman's eyes. 'Mrs Selway, please, what is it? You mustn't cry.' Serena took her hand.

'Sorry, dear, it's just that I blame myself. I let myself go, so easy—bringing up the children, so busy, we forget to look after ourselves. Well, you've obviously been a great deal more sensible, haven't you?'

'That's not true,' Serena contradicted her. 'I'm like this because . . . because all the women in my family have been built on lean lines.'

'Lucky you.' Madeleine sighed. 'It's difficult for Colin when appearances count so much. And to be honest, I'm doing it for myself as well. Anyway, the good news is I've only got another pound or two to go and then I'll have reached my target. Now,' she patted Serena's hand, 'let me just toddle off to the little girls' room and I'll be fine. Oh look, there's Robert waiting for me. I'll just be a moment.' She smiled past Serena and gave a little flicker of her fingers to Dr Merrow who was looking curiously at the scene in front of him.

Serena rose hastily to her feet. 'She was feeling a little faint,' she explained, hoping the truth wasn't too evident.

'You should have fetched Jessie,' he said, referring to his nurse. 'That's her job. Send Mrs Selway in when she emerges, will you?'

All the way home, she wrestled with giving in her notice. The Carlyle Clinic was not for her. Unfortunately the money was. The sight of the bills plopping through the door no longer sent panic waves through her, and the children had both had birthday presents that had even made Louise forget she was a cool dude and show signs of pleasure. Just until the end of the summer, she decided as she joined the crowd pushing towards the escalator. Then she would get something else to do.

It was odd coming home to an empty house. The children had left the day before to stay with Minnie in Lucca, while Margot had hung on to her wits and humour just long enough to wave them off with a hug and a silent cheer before hastening to stay with an elderly cousin in a remote village north of Inverary to recover.

Serena threw her bag on the kitchen table and flicked the switch on the kettle. Yawning, she reached over to the answering machine. There were two messages. Her mother to say she had arrived safely at her cousin's and the second from Alex saying he would call later.

The sun was still hard up against the back wall of the house. Serena unlocked the kitchen door and took her coffee outside, safe in the knowledge that the Plaxtons had gone to Benidorm.

She settled herself in a canvas chair, swinging her bare legs onto the low table. She lifted her face to the sun. The heat, the journey on a packed tube and a crowded bus all had their inevitable effect, and she drifted off to sleep while the sun crept over the roof.

The distant rap of the door knocker roused her from a muddled dream. She stumbled from her chair at the insistent knocking and ran barefoot to the front door.

'Stacey,' she exclaimed, pushing her hair out of her eyes. 'I dozed off in the garden. Lovely to see—' She halted. 'Stacey? What's wrong? Stacey, tell me, what is it?'

Reaching out she pulled the weeping girl into the hall and closed the door. Serena grabbed hold of her, half lifting, half carrying her into the sitting room. A livid bruise was beginning to make its presence known just under Stacey's chin and her shirt was torn. Serena didn't have to be told. That bloody man she was living with.

'Don't move,' she ordered and ran back to the kitchen. Armed with a basin of water and pulling a bottle of witch hazel and some cotton wool from the cupboard, she rejoined Stacey.

'What did he do?' Serena asked, pulling a bottle of brandy from the cupboard and pouring some into a glass. 'Here, drink this. Go on.'

'Oh Christ, Serena.' Stacey choked as the brandy hit the back of her throat. 'I said I wanted to go back to my parents for a bit. Just to think, you know. He went berserk. It was my fault. I shouldn't have sprung it on him . . .'

'Oh, for God's sake,' Serena muttered, soaking some cotton wool with witch hazel. 'You don't thump someone because they've taken you by surprise unless they're burgling your home. Sit still, this will help.'

Stacey just wept, clutching the damp pad to her sore face, reproaching herself until Serena could bear it no longer.

'Stacey,' she gently admonished her. 'I'm not doing you any favours if I agree with you. He's a pig. No man should hit a woman. You can't go back there. He'll do it again. You know he will. Stacey'—she dropped to her knees in front of her—'stay here,' she urged. 'Just for a few days, the children are away. It won't be any trouble.'

Stacey closed her eyes, still weeping softly, and shook her head. Serena knew she was wasting her breath.

An hour later she watched Stacey, calmer, but still visibly distressed, turn her car in a three-point turn in the narrow road and roar away. Back to the man who needed her more than she needed him, but had tampered so successfully with the scales of responsibility that an innocent woman would be begging him to forgive her.

Afterwards she knew that if Stacey had not left her feeling so frustrated and angry she would probably not have agreed to supper with Alex when he rang later that evening. But she did.

'You need someone to talk to,' he sympathised. 'A bit of one-to-one for yourself. I'll pick you up in half an hour. Don't argue.' And then he added after a short pause, 'Please?'

They went to an Italian restaurant in Fulham, where Alex was obviously a favoured customer. At first she thought the owners might jump to conclusions, and she asked Alex quite clearly how Alice was so that they would know that she knew about her and it was all above-board.

Alex studied the menu. 'I think,' he said, not lifting his eyes from the task, 'you'll find the oysters particularly good. And Alice is fine. On a course at the moment. Sent her love.'

'How kind.' She smiled back and began to study the menu. 'Yes, the oysters sound wonderful.'

'Good.' He handed the menu back to a hovering waiter and ordered for both of them, including an excellent wine.

It had all been so long since she had been entertained in a halfway decent restaurant and this was more, much more than halfway. She felt almost euphoric and something of the woman she had once been began to surface. She made him laugh, and teased him. By the time they left to go home, Serena felt so relaxed she had forgotten her initial qualms, delighted that they shared so many views on so many things.

Outside Foster Street he got out and came round to open the door. 'Do come in for a coffee after that wonderful meal,' she suggested warmly.

Alex glanced at his watch. 'Why not?' he smiled. 'As a matter of fact I wanted to ask you something about Harry.'

'Harry?' She paused with her key in the lock. 'Is he all right?'

'Fine,' he soothed. 'I was thinking about suggesting someone else he might see instead of me.'

Her heart sank. More change. 'Of course,' she said. 'Let me get the coffee and you can tell me why.'

When she returned he was sitting on the sofa, legs crossed, one arm stretched along the back.

'So why do you want to refer Harry to someone else?' she asked, handing him the cup.

'Two reasons. One, I think he has moved on sufficiently to join a colleague of mine. Harry's a great kid and I think he has made real progress. What I'd like him to do now is to join a group of children who paint. He loves it; I think he must take after his grandmother.'

Serena remembered Minnie saying that Harry had a good, unusually good, eye for colour. 'Well, fine,' she smiled. 'You frightened me for a moment. I thought you meant he had real problems. No, that's good. I'm delighted. But he will still see you, won't he?'

He leaned forward, his elbows on his knees, his hands clasped. 'Not in that way. No. I think,' he spoke slowly, carefully, 'I'm not the best person for him any more.'

'Oh, rubbish,' she cried. 'You've been wonderful. Harry goes to school now so much more easily. He couldn't have done that without you.'

'Thank you, but I don't think you understand.'

'Understand what?'

He looked sideways at her. The room felt very still. 'Understand that I cannot treat a child when I'm interested . . . more interested than is good for me, in his mother. I'm sorry, Serena, this is hell for you.'

'No. No.' She closed her eyes briefly. 'Not hell. How could it be hell to be told by someone like you that they're attracted to you. The hell is what it alters, not the feelings.'

He laughed. 'Goodness, I feel very threatened. You're a psychologist at heart. And need it be hell?' He couldn't keep the hope from his voice.

'Possibly not,' she sighed.

He hadn't asked her how she felt. Somewhere in the flattering shield he had thrown around her, she felt locked in rather than protected. But she also knew that it was a long time since she had felt emotionally aroused. And she loved the feeling. She felt suspended from judgment and conscience, removed from making a decision she knew was right but didn't want to make.

When he moved to sit beside her, she didn't stop him. Nor when he leaned forward and looked at her for a long moment before kissing her very gently. She felt a small explosion of shock at an intimacy she had not known for so long and, without thinking, she clung to it.

He pushed her carefully backwards, his hand sliding her skirt towards her hips, and she shut her eyes and let him, feeling his body ease over her to cover her own, propelling her gently down into a swirling dark well that almost disabled her senses, but not her mind.

'Alice.' She began to push him away. 'Alice,' she reminded him breathlessly. 'Alice has to be considered. And,' she added slightly more urgently, 'and Stephen. You've forgotten. I'm married.'

'I haven't forgotten,' he whispered, lifting his head, trying not to see the panic that now filled her eyes. 'I just want you to.'

'I can't,' she whispered back. 'Not yet. No, please, I mean it. Forgive me.' She struggled to sit up, not looking at him. 'My fault entirely.'

He said nothing, just leaned back, one hand covering his eyes, the other stretched along the back of the sofa.

'No,' he said wearily. 'My fault. I was dishonest with everyone. Alice, you, myself. The trouble is, falling in love at my age hurts twice as much because it's twice as hopeless. We don't come uncluttered, do we? And you're right,' he reached out and caught her hand, 'it's what it alters that's the real damage.'

As a grey early-morning light began to signal the end of a very long night, Serena rose and made herself a cup of tea. It was just after five. What had she started? What a fool. Why, when she was beginning to make sense of life, did she have to plunge it back into chaos? Later, as she hung on to a strap on the tube taking her to work, hollow-eyed from lack of sleep, Serena winced at her own behaviour.

Alex had left shortly afterwards, calmly insisting that his was the blame for rushing her. She had been vulnerable, while he had been—was—too besotted to think clearly. He seemed determined to shield her from her own behaviour.

And what behaviour, she grimaced. She had not charmed him, she had flirted. Convincing herself she was simply being the perfect guest, she had instead confused a man who she knew, *absolutely* knew, wanted little encouragement to see if his feelings were returned. A declaration, an acknowledgment that she was desirable had been her subconscious goal. It was a test of her power, she thought glumly, and Alex had been the experiment to prove she could still arouse such strong passions.

In this miserable mood she arrived at the door of the Carlyle Clinic. Jill was already there bustling between Robert's office and her own cubbyhole off the reception area. 'Oh dear, bad night?' She paused, registering Serena's unmade-up face and hollow eyes.

'Mmm.' Serena pulled a face. 'Something I ate, I think. Much better now.' Armed with a strong black coffee, she activated the answering machine for overnight cancellations and messages. Among those was one from Madeleine Selway, who asked if Serena could ring her back.

There was just time to slap on some mascara, slick a lip gloss over her mouth and call Stacey.

'It's fine,' Stacey said brightly. Too brightly. She raced on. 'Barry's really sorry and I am too for dragging you into it. I can see what it looked like. But he really is going to make an effort. Hey, listen, must go. Your friend Edith, by the way, is now in a home in Sussex. There's a letter here for you. I think it's from her.'

'Edith? Heavens. She must have got someone to write it. Drop it in the post, would you? I'll get it in the morning. Talk soon.'

Then she checked Madeleine's number and called her.

'Thank you, my dear,' Madeleine's voice sounded tired. 'I'm just calling to cancel my appointment. Actually all of them . . .' Her voice broke. Serena strained to hear her.

'Mrs Selway . . . Madeleine . . . what's wrong? Are you all right?'

'I will be. It's just that Colin told me he wants a divorce. Last night.' She gave a brittle laugh. 'Just when I'd reached my target weight as well.'

'Oh, Madeleine. I'm so sorry. Is there anything I can do? Have you got someone with you?'

'Yes, yes. My daughter. She's on her way.'

Robert Merrow simply shrugged when Serena told him what had happened. 'Now she'll lose weight anyway,' he remarked casually.

A small ripple of disgust went through her. Quietly she picked up the files from his desk from the first patient and left him.

'Serena,' he called after her. 'It's not a wonderful idea to get personally involved with any of the patients.'

She stopped and turned back. Dear God, had Madeleine said something? 'I'm afraid I don't know what you mean,' she said.

He raised an eyebrow. 'No? I thought you might have guessed. Brian Conway. Says you're . . .' he glanced down at his notes. 'A right "go-er". None of my business, but it's sensible, however unintentionally, not to give out the wrong signals, especially to male clients.'

Serena walked back and leaned across his desk. 'Robert,' she spoke icily. 'I would rather go out with a man wearing a frock and clutching an axe than walk to the end of the street with Brian Conway. In fact almost any man who comes here. Have I made myself clear?'

Robert Merrow narrowed his eyes and looked at her, his head on one side. 'Perfectly, my dear. And have I?'

'As crystal,' she said with studied courtesy. 'Is there anything else?'

He shook his head, already immersed in a report.

By the time she had allowed Cindy Moreton to browbeat her into asking Robert to see her without an appointment, Serena's head was in the grip of a pounding headache. Cindy had been prepared to wait, even though there were three clients for Robert to see before he got to her.

When she next looked up she was surprised to see the emaciated girl had gone. Probably gone to feed her meter. The last patient had just gone in. 'Jill,' Serena called, 'I'm just going to get something for my head. Won't be more than a minute.'

Jill waved her hand in acknowledgment as Serena headed for the cloakroom. As she opened the door, she heard a gasp and saw Cindy Moreton standing by one of the two sinks. Both women gazed in horror at each other. Cindy because she had clearly not expected to be interrupted. And Serena at the sight of Cindy's ribs painfully stretching through blue veined skin, the ball and socket that kept her arms in place barely concealed. She was also inhaling deeply on what looked like an asthma inhaler.

'Dear God,' Serena whispered. Closing the door and leaning with her back against it. 'Cindy, for Christ's sake, you need help.'

Cindy grabbed her cotton sweater from the armchair where she had flung it and stuffed the asthma inhaler into her open bag. 'I don't,' she breathed. 'Get out of my way.'

Serena ignored her. 'Stop this,' she begged.

'Get out,' Cindy cried, hugging the sweater to her. 'Get out. And I do get asthma.'

Instead Serena slipped the bolt across the door to prevent anyone else coming in. 'This could be the biggest favour anyone's ever done for you,' she spoke rapidly. 'I'll give you a chance to do it yourself but, believe me, I'm going to check. I don't want to see you here again. If you do I'll make sure you never work as a model for anyone. Understand?'

'It's my metabolism, you interfering cow,' Cindy panted, trying to struggle back into her sweater. 'I'm like this—'

'Oh pleeese,' Serena stormed back. 'Do I look stupid? You have a hyped-up metabolism and you need pills to make it faster? I'm going to go back to reception and tell Robert you cancelled. Then tomorrow I'm going to call your agency—'

'Do that. Do what you fucking like. There's nothing wrong with me. Nothing. Do you understand?'

Serena just shook her head. 'Yes. I understand you have a problem—'

It was as far as she got. Cindy threw herself against Serena, pulling her away from the door screaming, 'Let me out. Let me out of here.'

From outside Serena heard a rustle and then a banging on the door. 'What's going on in there?' Bridget called out in alarm. Then came Robert Merrow's furious voice joining in, 'What the hell's going on?'

Serena sagged against the door frame. Slowly she slid the bolt back and opened it.

'I'm out of here,' Cindy muttered, and pushed through. They looked after her and then back at Serena who stood waiting for Robert to erupt.

'My office, Serena. Now,' he said curtly. 'Jill, look after reception.'

Inside Robert's office, Serena gazed calmly at Robert Merrow. 'Before you say anything, Robert,' she began, 'let me just say this. Cindy Moreton is anorexic and using a prescribed drug to encourage her condition. Her presence here cannot be helpful.'

'I will be the judge of that,' he breathed furiously. 'What do you think you're doing, telling me—a doctor—how to treat my patients?'

'Then treat them. Don't abuse them,' she said icily. 'It's OK.' She held up a hand to stop him. 'I resign.'

Half an hour later, Serena hoisted her bag firmly onto her shoulder and began to walk slowly towards the station.

The panic would rise later. Later when she had slept and could think clearly, when she had called Alex and got that out of the way. At the end of the street she paused to let a black GTi convertible turn the corner before crossing. But instead of driving on it pulled up next to her. 'Serena,' a voice called from the driver's seat. 'Get in.' Cindy pushed back her dark glasses.

Serena's eyes widened. 'Get in? You have to be kidding.'

'Please,' Cindy called. 'I'm sorry. You got fired, didn't you?'

'Thanks a lot,' Serena called back. 'Now the whole street knows.'

Cindy clapped a hand over her mouth. 'Oh God. Oh please. Just get in. I want to say sorry. I want to help.'

An interested little group of pedestrians had now halted, watching this exchange. Oh, what the hell, thought Serena, and got in.

'Where are we going?' she shouted above the noise of the traffic.

'Friend of mine. I rang him just now. I guessed Robert would throw you out . . .'

'For what it's worth, I resigned. And I still think you're in trouble.'

'Oh, fuck off,' Cindy shrieked. 'Do you want a job or not? I know who you are, Robert told me.'

'Great,' Serena sighed. 'What else did he tell you?'

'Oh, that you were being all cool and stuff and wouldn't let anyone help. I meant what I said. I do feel bad about you losing your job. Frankly, my problems are my own. But I don't want anyone to lose a job over me. And I want you off my case.'

'OK,' Serena agreed. 'But I don't need any help getting a job. I'll get by. Now if you could just drop me by the next tube.'

'Don't you want to meet this guy? He's called Ed Stein. He owns Frobisher's. He's been very good to me and I know he'll help.'

'Frobisher's, the club? Businessmen?'

'That's the one.'

'And this Ed Stein, owns it?'

'Well, he's chief executive—same thing.'

'Stop. I can get a tube from here,' Serena interrupted. 'Thanks, Cindy, but no thanks. Listen, good luck. I won't ring your agency, but you should think about what I said. Take care now.'

When she reached home there was a message from Ed Stein. Or rather from his secretary. He wanted Serena to call. She stared, perplexed, at the machine. And then rang the number and asked for him.

He came on the line almost immediately. It was a deep voice, classless, direct. 'Just wanted to thank you for looking out for Cindy.'

'Oh please, don't mention it. I wish she'd get help. Perhaps as you seem to know her you could do something?'

'Good God, not me. I run clubs not clinics.'

'I see,' Serena replied coldly. 'For a moment there I thought you sounded concerned.'

She heard him laugh. 'I am. Her father's an old friend of mine. He's in the USA. I told Cindy if she agreed to go over there and stay with him, I wouldn't get heavy.'

'And is she going?'

'God knows. I've arranged the ticket. I expect she will.'

'Well, thanks for calling, Mr Stein. I'm relieved to know Cindy's in such careful hands.'

'Hold on. What about you? Cindy said you got fired.'

'I resigned.'

'OK, resigned over it. Stop being so touchy. You need a job, I have one on offer. Think about it. Great salary.'

She tried to remain unmoved when he mentioned how much. 'I'll do that, Mr Stein. Goodbye.'

The phone was already dead. Rude sod, she decided, replacing the receiver and making her way upstairs. She stripped off her crumpled clothes and stood under the shower. Later she pulled on a pair of cotton trousers and a white cotton shirt and wandered aimlessly around the kitchen. The doorbell went just as she finished eating an apple.

Alex stood on the doorstep, or rather leaned against the frame. Serena swallowed and instinctively pushed her wet hair out of her face.

'I think we should get this out of the way, don't you?' he said gently.

Serena stepped back and Alex walked past her into the hall. 'Kitchen?' he asked, turning back to look at her. She nodded.

'Drink?' she offered.

He smiled. 'Coffee.'

While she pulled cups and coffee from the cupboard and made a fuss of being busy, Alex pulled out a chair and sat at the table, not taking his eyes from her.

'Alex. I'm feeling pretty ashamed of myself . . .'

'No.' He reached out a hand and placed it over hers. 'I'm the idiot. Rushing you like that, not thinking it through. No, please, just listen to me.' He paused, 'We can't pretend it didn't happen, any more than we can pretend I'm not quite, quite smitten with you.' He gave a shaky laugh. 'But we can do something about what happens next.'

'We can?' She asked doubtfully, sliding her hand from under his.

He moved his own hand to cradle the coffee in front of him. 'Of course. We only have to accept what's happened and not pretend it didn't. I can't disappear out of your life any more than you can disappear out of mine. Because it isn't just you and me.'

She felt so tired she just let him speak. He was making it easy. Just the mere fact they were talking so calmly was having the effect she had been craving all day, the need for someone to lift the weight from her.

'It's about Harry and Alice and Stephen as well,' he told her.

She dropped her head and nodded miserably.

'What is it?' he asked gently, bending his head to try and see her face.

'Stephen.' She lifted her eyes to look at him. 'Stephen's unresolved. Alex, the truth is, if he walked in now I would fall at his feet.'

A flicker of surprise, rather than pain, crossed his face. 'You would?'

'Is that so surprising? We hadn't quarrelled. Our marriage was fine. He just had some kind of breakdown. If you love someone you love them full stop. Stephen is still part of me. Oh God, Alex, I'm sorry. If I didn't feel all this'—she groped for the right word—'this anguish about him, believe me last night I would have been a pushover.'

'Well,' he spoke lightly. 'That's something I suppose. But I have a suggestion. I don't think we should let last night spoil a relationship I value and—and one I hope you do too. You see, I'm sure I can put how I feel in perspective. But not if I only have our last meeting to go on. You see, Serena, I'm now asking you to help me. Could you do that?'

He didn't sound at all resentful. She thought he was remarkable and yes, she did value him. She agreed she could at least try.

Relief flooded his face. 'Look,' he went on eagerly, moving round the table to where she was standing. 'I know you're tired, but let's have a quick dinner together. I'll have you back by ten. Scout's honour.'

And he did. During dinner Alex did most of the talking and she was content to listen. He was, he had told Serena, going to try and to reinvent his relationship with Alice. Too fond of her to cease seeing her altogether, he said with an honesty she thought admirable, but knowing his feelings for Serena must temper that. Perhaps because she was tired she didn't want to tell him she no longer had a job. It was only later after he had dropped her home, kissed her gently on the cheek and watched her go in alone, that she remembered that the chief executive of Frobisher's had phoned and there was a job of sorts on offer.

At the end of the week she phoned Frobisher's. Her call was put through to a man called Mike Griffith. Patiently she repeated her name and explained why she was calling.

'Mr Stein rang me about it on Tuesday,' she finished.

'Tuesday? But it's Friday.'

'I know,' she agreed. 'I wasn't sure I was in a position to discuss it until now. But of course if you've already filled it—'

'Hold on. I just want to check something.'

In front of her on the kitchen table were the application forms for three employment agencies, none of which, given her restricted availability, held out much hope.

Mike Griffith came back on the line. 'Can you come in today? I've got a window at four.'

Frobisher's was tucked away between a restaurant and a firm of solicitors in the middle of a terrace of Queen Anne houses on the edge of Soho. At four on a Friday afternoon, the club was almost deserted. The porter, a grey-haired man wearing a navy jacket with thin gold braid on the sleeves and pocket, took his time about letting Mike Griffith know she was there.

She was wearing a cream sleeveless dress with a matching short-sleeved jacket, which was what she hoped was appropriate for a gentleman's club that she vaguely knew from its reputation was remarkably discreet about members bringing companions with them.

'Mr Griffith will be with you in a moment,' intoned the porter. 'He's with someone. Perhaps you'd like to take a seat.'

He indicated one of two velvet armchairs filling an alcove by the stairs. Through open double doors she could make out groups of armchairs and tables, small red lamps on each, weighty red velvet curtains locking out the sunshine that could have flooded through the floor-to-ceiling windows. While she waited she considered just what the job must entail to justify such a generous salary. A thought struck her. Good God, she panicked. Not that, surely?

There was no time to further consider the thorny question of her virtue. A surprisingly brisk-looking woman in her middle years, dressed in a tailored linen dress, appeared from the door marked PRIVATE. 'Come with me. Mr Griffith will see you now.'

Mike Griffith was, she judged, in his forties. He was very tanned with bags under his eyes, the sleeves of his pink shirt rolled up. As she came in he rose from behind a leather-topped desk and extended a hand.

'Thanks for coming in at such short notice. We have another candidate for the job, but when you phoned we held off telling her. Now, have you done anything like this before?'

Serena blinked. 'I'm dreadfully sorry,' she said. 'I'm not quite sure what the job is. It was a . . . um . . . a friend of Mr Stein's who told him about me. I'd just left my job and she was keen for me to see him.'

'Can't keep up with the man,' muttered Mike. 'I thought the way he spoke about you, he knew you. Must have misunderstood. Let's start again. The job is broadly speaking a club executive. The hours are the tricky bit. Six until two each night, no weekends. But the salary reflects the unsociable hours. We have what Ed calls High Maintenance members. No rock stars but a few film producers. Industry, medicine, politics. That's our bag. We need someone to know who they are, keep them happy and discreetly make sure they behave themselves.'

'Frobisher's is perhaps a little more enlightened than some other clubs but we still don't want them misbehaving, drawing attention to the place. Press being nosy, that kind of thing.'

She took a deep breath. 'Then I don't think you'll want me.'

'And that would be, why?'

'If Mr Stein said he knew me, I suspect it's because he knew my husband, or at least *of* him. Stephen Carmichael. He's missing. Every now and then a tabloid contacts me to see if I want to talk. I never do, of course, but the point is you would have no way of knowing that, would you?'

He gave a soft whistle. 'Banker chap? Good God. Funnily enough I wasn't thinking of that kind of attention. More the fall out from irate wives discovering who their husbands are dining with. Well, it's up to you.'

'Perhaps you should ask Mr Stein,' she suggested, gathering up her bag. 'I'm afraid I don't come with a clean track record in that sense.'

He gave her a sympathetic smile. 'No, I understand. Tough for you.'

He agreed to phone her later that evening and she made her way back home, suddenly wanting the job very much. In fact, if she had someone to stay overnight with the children, the hours were perfect. During the holidays she could be with them during the day, and for most of the time she was working they would be doing homework and going to bed. Well, at least Harry would. Louise was less predictable. Far less.

Ed Stein called her at ten that evening. Serena had been gazing at a moving little note from Edith, in which she let her know she was as well as could be expected and, if ever Serena was passing, to please drop in. Serena glanced at the address. A nursing home in Hove. The letter had been written by a care worker who Edith had said was called Carol. There was no explanation about how she came to be there. Still, better than Maud Frierley, she supposed.

For a moment, when Ed Stein announced himself, she couldn't register what he wanted.

'What's the matter with you?' he asked mildly. 'I hear you were a bit of a tragedy queen with poor Mike.'

'Tragedy queen?' she asked blankly. 'Bilge. I was being honest. I thought that was the right thing to do. Tragedy queen indeed.'

'That's better,' he said approvingly. 'Can't get along with weeping willows. Might as well start as we mean to go on.'

'Go on with what?' she said. 'And I'm not a weeping willow either.'

'No, I can hear that. Mike must have had a touch of the sun. He said you were cut glass and roses.'

'For goodness' sake,' she said impatiently. 'What on earth are you talking about? I'm nothing of the sort.'

'No. I've just said that. What's the matter with you? I'm agreeing with you. Now, do you want this job or not? You can't go on letting that old man of yours rule your life. Frankly, I couldn't give a sod about him. No offence, but I've got other things to concern me.'

In the time since Stephen had disappeared, no one had spoken to her like that about him or intruded so clumsily into her private life. 'Mr Stein.' Her voice was dangerously polite and icy. 'Do you have a pen handy? Good. Now pick it up and draw a line through my name. That way,' she continued, 'you will have no difficulty in recalling that I do not want to hear from you again.'

She pushed her finger on the cut-off button and then slammed the phone down. Afterwards she wasn't at all sure that the noise she heard as she cut him off wasn't the sound of someone laughing.

With no children to worry about, Serena slept late on Saturday morning. They were going to be staying with Minnie until the following Saturday. Serena was relieved because it gave her another week to find a job before they came back. Since there was nothing she could do about it until Monday, she decided to take a train to Hove and see Edith.

At Hove Station she asked directions to the Holewood Nursing Home. It was on the other side of the town, inland from the coast. The bus dropped her at the bottom of Holewood Hill. Opposite there was a small row of shops. Serena scanned them for the one she was looking for and emerged a few minutes later with a tub of ice cream.

Holewood was at the top of the hill, reached by a long curving drive bordered by well-tended flowerbeds. Used to seeing Edith in bleak surroundings, Serena was not prepared for a modest but cared-for home.

Edith, she was told by a surprised Matron, was in the loggia at the back, dozing. Serena promised she wouldn't stay long.

'Relative?' asked Matron, showing her the way.

'No. Friend. I helped nurse her in hospital. I was just concerned about her. I've brought her some ice cream. Would you mind if she had some while I was here? I can help her.'

'No, of course not. Look, there she is.'

She pushed open a door into a long narrow loggia. 'Hello, Edith.' Matron bent over the sleeping figure. 'You've got a visitor. I'll send someone along with a spoon and a napkin,' she murmured to Serena, who crouched down by the hunched figure in the wing chair. Edith slowly opened her eyes and gazed at Serena for a long while.

'It's me. Serena.'

The weak eyes fixed on Serena's face. Then with a tiny flutter she tried to raise a hand. 'Hello, dear,' she said in a whispery thin voice. 'I was expecting you.'

Serena pulled a chair up to Edith's. Thank heavens she'd made the effort. 'Of course I'm here. And with some ice cream. I thought you'd like some,' Serena tucked the napkin one of the helpers had delivered into Edith's collar and began to feed her.

'How are you, dear?' Edith asked faintly, having satisfied her need for the ice cream Serena had remembered she loved. 'Still at Willie's?'

'No,' Serena grinned, replacing the lid on the tub. 'I'll just pop this back to Matron to put in the fridge.'

When she came back, Edith was looking sleepy again. 'Matter of fact, I'm looking for a job. Nearly got one in Frobisher's, but the owner and I didn't hit it off.'

'Oh?' Edith cackled softly. 'That Eddie Stein did well, didn't he?'

Serena sat back. 'Sorry, Edith, do you know him?'

'No, dear, knew his grandma. They all went off to Australia and then . . . I forget, dear. Came back, I think. Lily showed me a newspaper cutting about him. Doing ever so well, he was. Good to Lily.'

All this way to hear about Ed Stein. Serena glanced at Edith who, having finished the longest conversation she'd probably had in weeks, was dozing off again. Serena leaned over and kissed her on the cheek.

'I'll come again, Edith,' she promised. But Edith was already asleep.

On the way out, she stopped by Matron's office. 'Look, will you let me know how she is? I'll try to get down again. Here,' Serena scribbled her name and address on a scrap of paper. 'Keep it in her file.'

On Monday morning, she knew she would never have even entertained Mike Griffith's rather exasperated call if Edith hadn't mentioned how good Ed Stein had been to his grandmother.

'Thanks, Mr Griffith,' she said. 'When would you like me to start?'

There are, she decided, better reasons for taking a job than hearing the boss had been good to his granny. But it's a start, she decided a week later, once again pushing open the heavy oak door to Frobisher's.

Chapter Eight

ED STEIN WAS RESPONSIBLE for the success of several clubs in New York and was on the board of as many companies again. Frobisher's, all red plush and low lights, with a membership fee that made a Fabergé egg look cheap, was the flagship of his business empire in England. Mike Griffith was the only one who had access to him at all times, and Serena was relieved that she was not required to report to Ed. The club executives—as Mike seriously called the half-dozen young women who were employed throughout the club—were not, as Serena had assumed, out-of-work actresses or models. One was a medical student, two were teachers and a fourth had been an advertising executive who had been made redundant.

Between them, the hand-picked, immaculately groomed team made an evening in the casino on the third floor or the library across the hall from the casino a pleasant interlude for the members and their guests. Particularly if the member had no guest.

Serena's role was settled between her and Mike Griffith, who told her that Ed's insistence that she got the job was because he preferred to remain on equal terms with the world. 'A favour is a favour, and I gather you did that stupid goddaughter of his . . .'

'Goddaughter? Explains a lot,' she said, her eyes widening.

It was not the job or the place that Serena would have chosen. But it was, she reflected, a great deal more honest than Robert Merrow's. It was also a chance to get out of Foster Street and into something halfway decent before Stephen came back. The hope of this happening never left her. She also wanted him to be proud of her.

She paused in this reverie. Proud of her? Of course. But even as she said it she knew it was more important to her that she was proud of herself. She gave herself a shake.

Even Cheryl was fine when she heard she would no longer be needed during the day. 'I'll have to get someone who is free to stay overnight,' Serena explained. 'I'm so sorry, Cheryl.'

'Well, that's no problem,' Cheryl beamed. 'I'll do it. I'll just slip over as you leave and I'll be back in time for his nibs's breakfast. Meals—that's what Kev lives for. That and bloody Sky sport. Leave him to me. That spare room of yours will do me fine.'

Serena gave in. Louise and Harry, back a day or two later from Lucca, took the news philosophically. Minnie, she decided, had an amazingly calming effect on them. They could even speak some Italian and Harry's paintings had been really extremely good.

'So,' she said, as the children sat in the kitchen, tanned and full of their weekend at Minnie's friends who had a pool, 'it won't be for ever.' Harry listened intently and Louise, one eye on the television and the other on a copy of *Loaded,* just yawned.

'Just until Daddy is better enough to come back, then all this will stop.'

Louise turned round slowly, pity etched in her face. 'Daddy would never have let us live in a street like this—' She got no further.

'You ghastly, revolting child,' Serena half sobbed. 'Do you think I've done this to you deliberately? Do you think I'm enjoying working in these scrubby jobs, worried sick about what's going to happen to us? And what have you done while I've been doing it? I'll tell you. You have wallowed in self-pity. You have been disloyal and treacherous.'

Louise's eyes were dark and horrified. She seemed to shrink into the wall. But Serena couldn't stop. 'Don't think I don't know what you say about me to your so-called friends. But you have a roof over your head which I put there, not your father. Instead of being ashamed of me you should be ashamed of yourself. Sorry, Harry, sorry, darling. Come here.'

Harry rushed over to her and grabbed her round the waist. Louise stood petrified against the wall, the silence that fell broken only by Serena's attempts to soothe Harry.

She took a deep breath, rationality returning. 'I'm sorry, Louise,' she finally said. 'I shouldn't have shouted. I'm tired. Forgive me.'

A sob broke from Louise, who suddenly flung her arms round

Serena's neck. 'I'm sorry, Mum,' she cried. 'I didn't mean it. I just say these things and I don't know why because I just feel worse after and I say them because they're all gathered here'—she pushed her fist into her chest—'and I want them to stop.'

'Oh, darling, don't . . .' Serena was crying and Harry joined in. 'Don't. It'll be all right. I promise you. You've been through so much. Don't think I don't understand. Harry,' she gulped over Louise's head, 'be a darling. Get LouLou a drink, will you?'

She sat down again, drawing Louise onto her knee, stroking her hair, rocking her until she was able to speak without the awful convulsive sobs that racked her thin body.

'C'mon,' she finally said, as Louise rested her head against Serena's shoulder. 'I think we all need a treat. Let's go out to supper.'

Louise lifted her head. 'I can't.' She blew her nose. 'I've promised Daphy she could come over and copy my Nirvana tapes.'

Serena swallowed hard. 'Of course. We'll do it another time. Harry,' she smiled at his disappointed little face, 'why don't we walk down and bring some hamburgers back for all of us?'

'Cool, Mum,' Louise said. 'Will you get one for Daphy too?'

Serena had been at Frobisher's for nearly a month before she actually met Ed Stein. Once or twice she had seen him stride through the lobby, but he was usually with a group of people *en route* to an appointment. He had also, she learned on the grapevine, been in the States.

Each night Serena changed in the staff room into a short black dress, swept her hair into a coil, slipped on some simple gold-hoop earrings and black suede high heels. With a quick glance in the mirror she emerged to start checking which guests would be in that evening. Thankfully, she was spared the indignity of being stationed in the front entrance, and saw no one until they appeared in the first-floor lobby where there was a bar to one side and a dining room to the other.

She glanced in as she passed, and waved to Tipper who was on duty. She had struck up an instant friendship with him, seeing in the sad eyes and flippant manner a rather lost soul. She had taken to sharing a cab home with him and had grown fond of this thirty-something Irishman with close-cropped hair and a skeletal appearance. His partner, he told Serena, had abandoned him after five years to live with someone else in Italy.

'Gay, of course,' she told Melanie, who had been hard put not to appear shocked when she heard what Serena was now doing. 'But sad. He left Dublin to get over it.'

A KEPT WOMAN

Tipper beckoned her over. 'You look fab.' He admired her dress. 'Just as well, I've heard himself's in this evening.'

'Himself?'

'Ed Stein, you eejit. Back from the States. The girlfriend's playing him up so he's going to be in a right old dander.'

Serena giggled. 'Tipper. How do you know these things? And why don't I ever hear this gossip? Whoops. Here goes.'

She moved away to greet the arrival. 'Mr But—Buttermere,' she remembered quickly. 'We've been expecting you. We have two messages for you. Your wife called and asked if you could call her. She's on her way to Edinburgh. And your secretary will bring the papers over that you wanted.'

'Perhaps you could arrange for her to have dinner,' Mr Buttermere murmured. 'So conscientious. It will be a treat for her.'

'Lucky girl.' Serena smiled at him. Creep, she muttered in her head as he turned to go into the bar.

Halfway through the evening, Serena was able to relax for a few minutes before the rush of guests who, having dined elsewhere, would start to arrive. She slipped downstairs to phone Cheryl, and fought a pang of longing to be home with the children. She turned to go back upstairs and automatically stood aside to let a guest go ahead of her.

'You decided to stay then?' a voice said chattily beside her.

She looked up into Ed Stein's face.

'Heavens!' She was taken aback. 'How do you do? Yes, indeed I've decided to stay. I always do what I say I will.'

'Glad someone round here does.' He paused on the steps and looked her over appreciatively. When they reached the first floor, Serena expected him to walk ahead and take the lift to his own suite. Instead he strolled over to the bar, greeted two or three people sitting there and seemed content to be entertained for a while.

Mr Buttermere's secretary arrived and, with a smile she hoped was charming, Serena led her through to his table. As she left them to greet each other in a way that suggested they had more than dinner planned, she turned round to see Ed Stein watching her and laughing.

'Come and talk to me,' he suggested. 'At least I won't try to pass you off as my secretary.'

'Well, I can't really leave here,' she began.

'No,' he agreed, picking up the phone. 'Mike, send someone up to cover for Serena for half an hour. No, nothing's wrong.'

Tipper brought Ed a whisky and Serena some iced water.

Ed Stein was a big man, but it was his shoulders rather than his girth that gave this impression. What she found jarring was the glimpse of a gold watch-strap when the cuff of his clearly expensive and beautifully cut suit slipped back. She tried hard not to notice or wince at the cuff links that were as big as they were obvious. Solid gold, she guessed. Stephen would have been appalled at such taste. Ed's age was more difficult. Early forties, she guessed.

'This isn't your sort of thing, is it?' he asked abruptly when they were alone at a table.

Serena smoothed her skirt and sipped her drink. 'No,' she agreed, slightly taken aback at such a direct approach. 'It isn't. However I'm perfectly capable of doing it. And besides I couldn't turn down a man who was kind to his granny.'

'My granny?'

'Yes,' she continued, impassively. 'I went to see an . . . old friend of mine, Edith Ambleton. She knew your grandmother. Lily? Is that right? She said you were good to her. A man who is good to his grandmother can't be all—'

'All right, all right,' he interrupted. 'I know who you're talking about. But how do you know Edith?'

She explained about the hospital and how it had led to Robert Merrow and then the sudden departure when she told him what was so wrong with the way he ran his business.

'You told him that, did you?' he asked when she'd finished. For a long moment he just looked thoughtfully at her. 'I'm surprised he didn't strangle you.'

'I have no intention of telling you how to run your club,' she told him, 'if that's what you think. Anyway, I wouldn't have said it was their health that was in danger here,' she added.

'What would you say then?'

'Oh, that's easy,' she said with a charming smile. 'Their integrity.'

His eyes narrowed. 'Mmm. Interesting. Just tell me, none of my business of course, but if it comes to that, what happened to yours?'

She stood up. 'Thank you for the drink.' And then without looking back she walked down the stairs and out of the club.

It wasn't until she was nearly at the corner of the street, furiously pushing her way through the late-night crowds, that Serena realised she had no jacket and her bag was still at the club.

Dear heaven. She glanced uneasily back in the direction of Frobisher's and bit her lip. Now what? She was already regretting a scene she would have found absurd enacted by anyone else. She sank against the wall and dropped her head, chafing her bare arms. Another job gone, she thought morosely. Maybe she could telephone Tipper from a call box, get him to bring her things out to her. Maybe she could . . .

'Looking for business, sweetheart?' A voice leered over her shoulder. She gave a stifled scream and sprang away from the wall.

'Oh my God,' she yelped, backing away from a swarthy-looking man who had minutes earlier been guarding the doorway to a strip club. 'Go away you revolting man. Go away, *away*. Do you hear me?'

'Bugger off, sunshine.' Ed said to the man who had accosted her. He took Serena's arm and drew her away. 'Oh, stop looking so outraged,' he said. 'C'mon back. I shouldn't have said that, but you shouldn't be so fucking rude.'

'Me? Rude?'

'Yes. Rude. You wouldn't have said that to one of those sleazeballs who run the banks in this country, would you? Bit short on integrity there, if you don't mind me mentioning it. But it doesn't matter that you insult my business integrity, does it?'

She had, as it happened, begun to feel ashamed of how she had behaved, but the truth in what he was saying now had the opposite effect on her. She lowered her voice and glared into his face.

'Mr Stein. Believe me, I'm sorry if you don't like the truth, but what do you expect me to say? That I think it's the ultimate thrill to leave my children each evening just to flatter airheads with "For Rent" written across their forehead? You wanted honesty and you got it.'

'So what's the difference between smiling at Brian Buttermere and shits like Malcolm Brisley Jones? Saw you one night at the opera.' He blew a cloud of smoke from his cigar. 'Some fund-raising thing,' he went on. 'You were sitting next to him, charming the pants off him.'

'If you mean I was being pleasant, what's wrong with that?'

'Well, if you want my opinion, you look a great deal more honest standing in the reception at Frobisher's than you did that night. At least everyone knows why you're being nice to them. That stupid twat, Brisley Jones, thought you meant it.'

'You know it's not the same thing,' she said uncomfortably.

'Isn't it? What's the difference, then? Go on, enlighten me.'

'One is a courteous social exchange and the other is . . .' she trailed off. 'This is ridiculous. What does it matter? You shouldn't have said I had no integrity. That was insulting.'

'I never said that. I simply asked what had happened to yours to allow yourself to be in the company of people you despise. I don't despise them. They're clients. That's all. Business. Stop prancing around on the moral high ground, Mrs Carmichael. Morality is only possible if everyone is moral,' adding helpfully as she stared blankly back at him, 'Jean-Paul Sartre.'

'I know that,' she snapped, pretty sure that she didn't. She glanced sideways at him. 'What was I supposed to say, then?'

He shrugged. 'You might have said, "I certainly don't think being paid an honest wage to do an honest job is sacrificing my integrity." Instead of which you stormed off.'

Serena silently berated herself for creating such a scene. They had reached the club entrance. She wasn't sure what to do next.

'I don't come after all my staff,' he told her in a cheerful voice. 'On the other hand, I can't remember that anyone's ever stalked off before, so that might be why.'

She smiled weakly. 'Thank you, I can see you're trying to make it easy for me to return to work, but we both know that's not possible.'

He looked skywards. 'Bloody women,' he breathed. 'We don't know that at all. We both know that we need each other. I can't be without a receptionist—and I don't want another one. I like seeing you when I come in—and you don't really want to go, do you?'

She threw him a startled look.

'Now, buck up. I'm late. Mike thinks you were sick—I told him you'd gone to get some fresh air. Just go back and say you're feeling better.'

He was already walking towards his waiting Bentley, where the driver was holding open the door. She watched as he slid into the back seat and his driver hurried round to take his place behind the wheel.

Alex didn't enjoy the idea of Serena working at Frobisher's. He frowned, listening carefully as she told him what it entailed. His good opinion was necessary because he had been there for her and Harry was, in her view, so much better. And of course because he had made her feel needed. 'I'm just afraid you'll exhaust yourself,' he explained, gently. 'I just want you to be careful.'

She smiled and reached across the table to squeeze his hand. 'I will, of course I will. But I love your concern, it means a lot to me.'

His face glowed with quiet pleasure. The small restaurant in Pimlico was nearly full and they couldn't be heard above the pleasant buzz of conversation. But still Alex lowered his voice to an intimate whisper. 'Some time,' he took both of her hands in his, 'we'll resolve everything,' he said, 'without hurting anyone.'

A small flicker of dismay crossed her face. Too late she remembered her resolve to avoid activating Alex's interest in her. Alice was still in his life, albeit removed from the central position she had once occupied.

But still there. Alex couldn't find it in himself to hurt her by ending it. 'All of us need time to adjust,' he explained to Serena.

Cheryl, on the other hand was enthusiastic about Frobisher's and took to grilling Serena about what happened there and what was worn. She seemed disappointed that understated cocktail dresses were the order of the day.

'I mean, what about when you have to entertain the customers, don't you have to, well, dress up a bit?' she asked, waggling her eyebrows.

'Well, they have their own guests.' Serena piled laundry into the washing machine, trying to envisage Frobisher's awash with full evening dress. 'I'm not required to entertain them. Except if their guest is late or fails to turn up for whatever reason. You step in for a moment or two.'

'You could be talking about my Kev,' she shrieked, as she departed to get her Kevin's lunch.

'What's she on about, Mum?' Louise asked, sitting at the table painting her nails.

Serena shrugged. 'Who knows with Cheryl?'

When Mike phoned to ask if she would come into the club to have dinner that evening as a favour, she groaned with exhaustion.

'Dinner? You mean work?'

'No, I mean dinner. Ed's got some investors coming in from Paris. You speak French, don't you? Well, he's the only one who speaks it and he can't manage them all. I don't speak a word of the lingo. He said he'd make it worth your while.'

Tipper came over to baby-sit. This was greeted with a cheer by Harry who had found a soul mate with whom to indulge his passion for his latest video craze, Fantasy Football. Nor was any serious objection raised by Louise who, Serena suspected, approved of Tipper once she discovered he preferred Nirvana to Damon's unremitting passion for rap. She was to come home from the party she was going to by cab, called for by Tipper at midnight.

Serena had never been to the club at the weekend. Most members disappeared to their wives in the country and it was usually relatively quiet, which is why she was never needed. She made her way up the broad stairs to reception, where she removed her wrap and handed it to a girl called Trish, who was on duty that night. 'He wants you upstairs for a powwow before they all turn up,' Trish said.

Serena pressed the button on the elevator. Inside she tried to see her reflection in the dark oak-panelled lining and gave one last ineffectual tug at her skirt, suddenly wishing it was longer than knee-length and that she'd worn lower heels than the three-inch satin ones that had been bought to match the dress. Suddenly, in a dress chosen to please Stephen, who wanted his wife to look feminine and sexy, she wasn't so sure.

The doors slid noiselessly apart and she stepped out into a large, square, carpeted lobby. The double doors in front of her were flanked on one side by what appeared to be a Turner. On the other a Stubbs, by the look of it. From behind the closed doors she heard the sound of male laughter. Her hand was already raised to knock when the door was opened by Mike, wearing a dark silk suit.

'Serena.' He greeted her warmly, drawing her in. There must have been a security camera watching her. 'Good of you to come at such short notice,' he said, as a white-coated man appeared at his side. 'What'll you have?'

'Oh, just orange for the moment.' She smiled at the manservant. 'Incidentally, why am I needed, I can't quite figure it out?'

'The Frogs suddenly announced they've got their fancy bits with them. Mistresses,' he added, when she said nothing. 'He wants someone to deflect the women if they get in the way of business, or maybe just even things up a bit.' He led her over to where Ed was standing.

She had been expecting something more functional than this elegant drawing room. She gave a quick glance around as they made their way across the cream-and-blue patterned Aubusson carpet. The walls were lined with pictures, among them, she was sure, a Goya. The rest of the room was filled with eighteenth-century sofas and console tables.

Ed was talking to Matthew Turner, the club's finance director. They both turned as she came up to them. Ed smiled.

'Bit rushed? Sorry about that.' He was holding a fat cigar in one hand and the other was pushed into the pocket of his trousers, crumpling the line of his beautifully cut charcoal double-breasted jacket.

'It was no trouble,' she replied. 'Only I should warn you, my French is not absolutely accurate.'

'Doesn't matter,' he said, appraising her. 'Mike says you translated for him the other night. Seemed to do the trick.'

Briefly, and mostly for Serena's sake, he gave an abbreviated account of why it was so important to look after the French. They were courting Ed to transform their club, Les Cages, in Montmartre, in the same way he had turned round Frobisher's some years before.

'Which is only interesting if in return Frobisher's get a slice of the action in France and the benefit of their members coming over here at weekends—special deals, that kind of thing.'

'And where do I come in?' Serena asked.

A KEPT WOMAN

'I wasn't expecting Zizi and Jeanne-Marie or whatever their names are to pitch up. Too many for me to handle since none of them speaks English. And these two can't say good morning between them.'

Mike and Matthew looked sheepish. Serena smiled sympathetically. 'I think you might do worse than let them charm Zizi and Jeanne-Marie,' she responded loyally. 'I'm sure they'd prefer the men to me.'

Mike and Matthew laughed. 'I know what I'm doing,' Ed growled, exhaling a blue cloud of smoke, his eyes narrowing. Serena put a hand to her neck. She wished he wouldn't do that. It made her feel uncomfortable rather than attractive. 'With you speaking French you'll be perfect for what I have in mind. You look terrific. Now, shall we go?'

He stood aside to let Serena go first.

Serena's fractured French became a source of delight to the representatives of the holding company that owned Les Cages. Ed, who spoke the language fluently, placed Serena between Gilbert, the president of the French company, and the finance director, Olivier, at a round table in the corner of the dining room. Their companions sat either side of him. Expensively dressed, immaculately made up, jewellery from the exclusive shops that lined the Rue St Honoré. She recognised every item they wore and at a pinch could have priced each one too.

She looked up and caught Ed's eye. To her they looked exactly what they were. Kept women. Dear God, had she ever looked that obvious?

By the time the French had left it was after one. Serena felt exhausted and hoarse. Slowly stifling a yawn, she turned back to collect her wrap from Trish while Ed and Mike went to see their guests to their cars. She felt tired, but pleased with how things had gone.

As the evening progressed, so too had her French and her wit. She was still smiling about a particularly funny remark Ed had made to Gilbert when she heard a gasp next to her. It took her a minute or two to register the identity of the man in front of her.

'Good God!' She gave a small step back.

'Serena!' exclaimed George Kincaid. 'What are you doing here?'

'Well, George.' She battled for composure. 'I could ask the same of you.' Behind him a woman with red hair and a tight dress hovered. George turned and whispered something to her and she moved away with another couple. Serena did not recognise any of them.

'Well, some friends dragged me along,' he blustered.

She could bluff, say she was dining with friends. And then she stopped, partly because George was looking so flustered himself but mostly because she had nothing to be ashamed about. 'I work here, George,' she told him calmly. 'Tonight was a business dinner.'

His face went pale. 'You *work* here?'

She nodded. 'Why else would I be here at this time of night?'

'But why here?' He registered more horror than was necessary.

A flash of irritation went through her. 'Why not? I have two children to raise. That's why I'm here, George. What about you?'

George looked round. Hastily he grabbed Serena's arm and led her to a quiet corner. Out of the corner of her eye she saw Ed returning with Mike, but seeing her with George they walked on into the bar. 'Serena,' George was saying, 'I'm sure you're aware of my membership.'

'Your membership, George? No, I haven't seen you here before.'

'No, well I only pop in at weekends. To unwind, you know.' He laughed a choking, jovial laugh. 'To enjoy some good conversation.'

Gone was the urbane and chic gynaecologist whom all the mothers loved. In his place was a panic-stricken man with his reputation in her hands.

'Look, Serena, I would appreciate it if you forgot you ever saw me here. What do you say?'

She could see the group of people he had been with waiting for him. 'George, I'm here during the week, so it's unlikely I'll see you again. Now, I think your friends are waiting. Bye, George.'

She turned and walked away, almost colliding with Ed, who was watching her from the doorway.

'Old friend?' he asked quietly.

She looked wearily up at him. 'Sort of. Not any more. Ed, I think I'd like to go home now. Would that be all right?'

'Of course. I was just waiting for you. I'll drive you.'

'No, please,' she protested. 'If Mike could just arrange a car—'

'Oh, stuff it, Serena. You've done me a real favour. I'll drive you.'

'OK,' she smiled back, tiredness triumphing over independence. 'That would be most kind.'

'Most kind,' he mimicked. 'C'mon, Mrs Carmichael. Home.'

Cheryl saw Serena alight from the passenger seat of Ed's Bentley well after two in the morning. The sight filled her with such envy she gripped the net that stood between her and detection from the street.

From where she was on the other side of the road, Serena could see the eerie blue glow from the television in the front room of Cheryl's house, where the hapless Kevin sat transfixed. A slight movement of the curtain in the room above made her eye travel up and quickly look away. For a moment she considered waving. But then pity more than irritation stopped her. Serena knew Cheryl's chief preoccupation was the comings and goings of the residents of Foster Street.

Of late Cheryl had been quizzing Serena quite closely about Frobisher's. It must, Serena thought, be obvious by now that she was not going to get names out of her, but it was also clear Cheryl's interest in the clientele was increasing rather than diminishing. That she was now monitoring her arrival home was not surprising, just rather sad.

On the drive home, Ed neither needed nor wanted instructions on how to find his way to where Serena lived.

'Used to know this area like the back of my hand,' he remarked, as they crossed the river and turned towards Kennington. 'By the time I got back from New York it was nearly razed to the ground, new housing estates, one-way systems. Knocked the life out of it.'

'What made you come back?' she asked. 'New York sounds like it suited you.'

He shrugged. 'Nowhere is for ever. My family—what's left of them— are in Melbourne. America is where I really started, nothing spectacu-lar. At sixteen I was given the choice between joining my old man, running the dry-cleaner's he set up, or jumping ship. What would you have done?'

'So what did you do. In New York, I mean?'

'Really want to know?'

'Of course.' Serena leaned her head back against the headrest. It was a long, long time since she had been so luxuriously chauffeured.

'Well, I didn't go straight there,' Ed was saying. 'Bummed around Europe for a few years, worked in Monte Carlo where I learned to speak French, how to serve drinks and get big tips. Then I got involved with someone that I shouldn't have and when it got heavy I went to New York. I got a job in a bar, then managed it. Then I moved to a club and then managed that and then the guys who owned it asked me to get the "Eighty-One" up and running. And then this mob arrived from here and said come and get Frobisher's on its feet. And it was the right moment.

'Marriage broke up, I wanted to be home for a while. You know that feeling? You just need to get back to the point where it all started and see if you can do it all again without fucking it up.'

Serena glanced at him. 'Did it work?'

'Not sure. Maybe. Still working at it. Here we are, Foster Street. This it?' Ed asked, peering through the windscreen.

She nodded, watching his face to see his reaction to such a faded house. He said nothing, just grunted.

'I'll see you in,' he said, walking round to hold the door as she stepped onto the pavement.

She didn't need an escort on such a short journey, but she was beginning to realise that Ed always did what he wanted. Easier not to argue.

'Would you like a drink? Coffee?' she asked, as she put her key in the door, praying that Ed would decline.

'Why not?' he replied, dashing her hopes and stepping into the hall after her. They both paused. The sound of heated voices was coming from the sitting room. Serena moved quickly forward and opened the door. 'What on earth's going on?'

'Oh, just Tip thinking he's the world's expert on indie groups,' Louise answered, casting a scathing look in Tipper's direction. 'Anyone with half a brain knows Nirvana are brilliant.'

'*Louise*,' Serena rebuked her.

Ed, standing just behind Serena whispered, 'Friends of yours?'

'Friends you choose,' she pointed out, moving aside so that Ed was now visible to them both. 'You don't think I'd choose either of these two, do you?'

'Jesus,' Tipper muttered, catching sight of his boss, scrambling to his feet. Louise stared curiously at him.

'You know Tipper, of course,' Serena said, trying not to laugh as Tipper put an armchair between himself and his employer.

'Evening, sir,' he acknowledged, gripping the back of the chair.

'Tip.' Ed nodded at him.

'Louise, this is Mr Stein who owns Frobisher's. He kindly drove me home. Ed, this is my daughter Louise, who should be in bed.'

'But has kindly waited up to make sure you're safely home'—Ed extended a hand to a suspicious Louise—'and I don't blame you,' he added, as she briefly shook it. 'A night out might have gone right to her head.' He nodded towards Serena. 'My mother was just the same. Went berserk whenever we let her out.'

Tip stared and Louise giggled. Serena let out her breath.

'Louise, as you're up would you start some coffee?' she asked. 'I'll just check Harry. Tip, you've been an angel. Have you ordered a cab?'

'Right away,' he said.

'Don't bother with that,' Ed chimed in. 'A quick cup of coffee and then I'll drop you. Somewhere near here, isn't it?'

Tip looked surprised. 'Oval, sir.' He grinned. 'And that would be grand. Now I'll just give this misguided child a hand with the coffee.'

Serena returned in a few moments to find Ed studying the backs of some of the CDs Louise had left lying around.

'Doesn't look like you, does she?' he remarked, with a nod towards the kitchen where Louise could be heard clattering cups onto a tray.

'No. She's totally Stephen. In every way. Harry looks more like me, I'm told. Do sit down.'

'Come to the opera with me,' he said abruptly, sitting in a corner of the sofa. 'Next week. *Rigoletto*. New production.'

For an awful moment she thought her jaw had gone slack. She began to stammer. 'Opera? With you? I'm not sure.'

'Is that a yes?'

She sat back and surveyed him. 'Look. Ed. I know you might find this odd, but I would be delighted to come with you to the opera, if you weren't my employer.'

'So that's settled then. I'm told the production is trendy.'

'Ed,' she protested. 'Didn't you hear me? I said—'

'Yes, I heard. You sounded like some middle-aged spinster. Don't panic,' he relented. 'Got some guys in from New York. Thought you might perform the same miracle on them that you did on Gilbert.'

'I would have thought,' she replied icily, furious that she had been made to look absurd, 'that as English is their native tongue, trying to grasp the general drift of what they're saying shouldn't be too taxing.'

'Obviously. But I don't say, "Tell me all about yourself",' he mimicked, 'like you do. It's sexy. Makes the hairs on the back of my neck stand up.'

Serena folded her arms round her waist and leaned against the fireplace. 'I don't ever use such a toe-curlingly embarrassing cliché,' she said.

'You see,' he spread his hands. 'I've got so much to learn. So that's all right then? Good. Anyway, it's work. That my coffee, Louise? Good girl. Now, Tip, my man, who do you fancy in the Cup?'

Chapter Nine

~

'I'LL CHECK IN WHEN WE GET to the restaurant, but you can get me here.' Serena scribbled the number of the theatre, adding Ed's name. 'He's got a box so he's easy to find. And we're having supper afterwards here.' She added the number and stood up, handing the piece of paper to Cheryl.

'Night out?' Cheryl asked, reading the itinerary.

'No, work,' Serena replied, checking her bag. 'Nice work for once.'

'Ooh, sounds promising,' Cheryl giggled.

'Well, I like opera.' Serena glanced briefly in the mirror in the hallway. 'I'll just tell the children I'm off,' she said.

She found Louise sprawled on her bed with earphones on and just kissed the top of her head.

'Homework,' she mouthed.

'Done it,' Louise called back above a din only she could hear.

Harry, controller in hand, was sitting on the floor in the living room flicking through Fantasy Football. 'Bye, darling.' She stooped down to kiss him. 'See you in the morning.'

'Tell Tip I'm trying to buy Robbie Fowler so we won't need Alan Shearer.' He barely looked at her as the mouse clicked across the screen.

'I might not see him tonight, sweetheart.' She gazed fondly at him and the mention of his favourite footballers.

'Ye-es!' Harry howled in delight as the screen flashed the successful purchase of the Liverpool striker.

Serena looked thoughtfully at her small son punching the air. She put down her bag and coat and sat on the arm of the sofa.

'Harry,' she said, ruffling his hair. 'Would you like to go to a football match, a proper one?'

'You mean like Chelsea or Arsenal? A proper, proper match? Who would I go with?' he asked nervously.

Serena remained expressionless. 'Well, I'll take—' she stopped and amended. 'I'll go with you. In fact we'll go on Saturday. I'll find out who's playing and at what ground and we'll go. It'll be good fun.'

'Spurs are playing a home game,' he volunteered, hesitantly. 'We could go to that.'

Serena looked blankly at him. 'How do you know?'

'It's here.' He grabbed the paper and showed her the fixtures on the sports page. 'See? White Hart Lane. I read it all the time.'

'Then that's dead easy,' she said, a rush of remorse rising at herself for not seeing how much he had always wanted to go. Louise would have sulked and pleaded until she got what she wanted. Harry just waited to be noticed. 'Spurs it is. Now I must fly. I'll be late.'

Ed had arranged a car to collect Serena to take her to his house in Knightsbridge. It was easy to spot the conflict of cultures in the tall, redbrick house at the back of Harrods. There was the poor-kid-made-good love of gadgets—doors opened, lights were generated by an unseeing hand—and the self-educated man's passion for fine books and works of art.

When the door was opened before she knocked, she saw this conflict at work. The butler, who wore a sober black suit, majestically inclined his head and led her to the library where Ed was waiting. He also had a broken nose and a nasal twang that suggested a former career as something less refined than a gentleman's gentleman in Knightsbridge.

'Mrs Carmichael,' he intoned, stepping aside to let her pass. The library, like the house, was a handsome business. Brass lamps stood on impressive claw-footed tables; leather chesterfields and a velvet wing chair lent a pleasing cultured air to a room she decided looked noble.

He had been in the act of pouring himself a drink when she came in, and saw no reason to stop as he greeted her. 'Terrific,' he approved, taking in her jacket, just shaped at the waist and flaring gently over her hips, and the suede shoes with heels she felt safer in.

'I'm sorry I have to share you,' he grinned. 'Now, let me get you a drink. Wally likes doing it, but he takes it all so seriously you'd expire with thirst waiting for him to do it just right.'

'You mean, the butler?' she asked. 'Thank you. Just orange will do.'

'Wally's great. Used to be in the ring.'

'You surprise me,' she murmured, taking her drink and sitting in one of the wing chairs next to the fire. 'How did he become a butler?'

Ed perched himself on the edge of the fire surround. 'He lived in the next street to me. His dad used to be a fairground pugilist, you know. "Win a pound, if you go a round", and Wally was brought up to do the same. Trouble was he was useless and spent more time flat on his back than a Curzon Street hooker.

'Then Lenny—Lenny Horniman, he's a big noise in Savile Row now, I grew up with him—well, he called me one day and said he'd seen Wally coming out of a dosser's hostel, right mess he was. Anyway, he bundled him into his car, took him home, got him straightened out and discovered that all Wal had ever wanted to do was train to become a butler like his granddad—his mother's lot were in service.'

'So you sent him to be trained?' Serena asked.

'No such thing,' he said, reaching for one of his habitual cigars. 'I wouldn't be that magnanimous. Not like Lenny. He paid for that, but once Wal was trained he had to have a job and poor old Wal couldn't get the accent right, which meant no one would employ him. So I said Wal could work for me. He's been here more or less ever since.'

Ed's guests were surprisingly nice. Equally surprising to Serena was that they didn't appear to be on anything but the closest terms with him, and if business was in the air, it was, she thought, remarkably well hidden. Her recollection of similar outings with Stephen was that Americans did nothing but talk business. There were two couples: Will and Ceri and

Barclay and Bernice. Both from New York and eager to make Serena feel one of them. It was a disorientating experience, since she had been expecting to help them relax, only to find they thought it was their responsibility to do that for her.

It was a memorable evening. Ed was a good host, attentive to everyone's needs including hers. The performance left her near to tears and, when the philandering Duke of Mantua finally sang 'La donna è mobile', she turned impulsively to Ed as they stood to cheer the performance. 'Oh, that was stunning. Thank you for including me. I'm overwhelmed.'

It wasn't until she was making her way through the lobby that it occurred to her that she had been included because she worked for him. Then she froze. Immediately in front were Paula and Richard Van Stuckley, with Miranda Hooper and a man who wasn't her husband, and another couple who looked familiar. She couldn't avoid colliding with them.

'Heavens, Serena,' Paula croaked, clearly horrified. Hemmed in on all sides, there was no escape for any of them. 'Richard, it's Serena. How marvellous.' She turned wildly round. 'Miranda, it's Serena.'

Somewhere behind her she heard Will exclaim, 'Rye. Hey, you old dog. What are you doing here? Where's Meryl? Ceri, look who's here.'

In the commotion of greetings and squeals of recognition, Serena dragged her gaze from the stupefied Van Stuckleys to the American couple they were with. Oh God, Meryl and Ryland Holt.

Miranda was looking dazed. Her companion puzzled. Richard Van Stuckley looked aghast. Only Serena looked composed.

Ed had now joined them and was looking at Serena. Her heart hit her ribs. She had no choice. 'Ed, this is Paula and Richard Van Stuckley and Miranda Hooper. Ed Stein,' she indicated his presence. Paula nodded politely, Richard shook his hand briefly and then turned away, whispering something in Paula's ear. Paula in turn threw a startled look at Ed and then, with a smile that turned Serena's stomach, she moved away. Miranda made no attempt to hang around.

Humiliation swept over Serena. She tried to move away but Ed stopped her, gripping her arm and murmuring, 'Stuckley's an appalling little shit. Tried to be a member. Wouldn't have him. Now, chin up. Smile. Here comes Meryl Holt. Lovely woman. Meryl,' he caught her in a bear hug, 'why haven't you left that no-hoper and run off with me?'

Instinctively, Serena did as she was bid. The second reason she had to stay put was Meryl.

'And you have hidden yourself too well.' Meryl released herself from Ed's arms and kissed Serena. 'Here is not the best moment to catch up. Let's do lunch. Serena and I are old friends,' she explained to

Ed. 'She and . . . and,' Meryl gave an uncertain look at Serena.

'Stephen.' Serena threw a defiant look around.

'Yes, she and Stephen spent time with us out in the States a few summers ago. Don't forget to call.' She looked pointedly at Serena.

Ryland and Ed greeted each other with what appeared to be genuine warmth. Following his wife's lead, he kissed a shaken Serena on the cheek. 'Listen, you guys, must dash. Business. You know how it is.'

It was only then that Serena knew she was shaking. She wanted to sit down before she fell down, just go home. And she would have done if Ed hadn't stopped her. 'C'mon. Take it easy,' he murmured, glancing at her. 'It's over. That the first time you've seen them?'

She nodded, beginning to recover. She gave him a weak smile. 'I'm sorry. Forgive me. Now,' she took a deep breath, 'would you like me to go with Ceri and Will in their car?'

He swore softly under his breath. 'I would like Ceri and Will to take Bernice and Barclay out of my way. You don't need them but you might need me for the next couple of hours.'

She looked up, startled. 'Please,' she said quietly, 'it won't be necessary. But you're awfully kind.'

'Awfully kind,' he mimicked. This time she just smiled at him. 'All right,' he said. 'You know best. Let's move it.'

Throughout dinner Serena struggled to contain the misery she felt rising up in her throat. Seeing the look of disdain on Paula's face when she established Ed's identity, Serena wanted the earth to open and absorb her. The fact that she was working for Frobisher's may not have travelled back to her former world except as a rumour, but it would now be embellished as only Paula knew how.

When Ed brought the evening to a close, Serena felt almost giddy with relief. Outside they all parted company with kisses and hugs and invitations to lunch, which swirled around her. And then they were gone. She was still smiling when she turned to Ed. It was the nearest she'd seen him come to scowling.

'Heavens!' she exclaimed. 'Didn't it go well? I thought it was terrific.'

'Don't lie, Serena,' he snapped, 'you're transparent.'

She stiffened. 'Well, I'm sorry for what happened earlier, but truly—'

'Oh, shut up,' he interrupted. 'Let me tell you something, my girl. They're trash. And you still care what they think. Still care that you're seen with the right people. Yours is the tragedy, sweetheart. Not, as you seem to think, being seen with me.'

'Don't be absurd,' she replied calmly. 'How could you think such a thing? My shame was Paula. That I was forced to introduce my boss to such a vulgar person will not be up there with my happiest memories.' His driver was on the pavement holding the door. 'Come on, get in.'

He grabbed her arm and swung her round, searching her face. His voice held a note of suspicion. 'No messing, Mrs Carmichael?'

She gave an exaggerated sigh and grinned at him. 'No messing, Mr Stein,' she mimicked. 'Now, buck up. In you get.'

'After you,' he argued.

'No. I'm getting a cab. I'm sure you won't mind me charging it. Stop arguing. Bob'—she ignored Ed and turned to the driver—'Mr Stein's had a tough evening. Ask Wally to give him a brandy and put him to bed and, if that doesn't work, tell him I suggest a sock in the jaw. Taxi!'

She ran to the black cab as it pulled up and clambered in. 'Foster Street, Kennington,' she ordered the driver, pulling the window down. 'I'll check if I've still got a job in the morning,' she called out, almost laughing. 'You know something, Ed,' she added thoughtfully, as her driver waited for her to tell him to move. Ed came over to the cab. 'You'd get a gold medal at the Olympics if they had such an event.'

'What event?' he asked, resting one arm on the window ledge, the other on the roof.

'Jumping to conclusions. No contest.'

He began to laugh. 'Only from you.'

'Me?'

'Uh huh. Who said you were working tonight? The guys thought you were my new date.' He leaned in and kissed her swiftly on the mouth, then he stepped back, banged the roof and the cab took off.

Serena let herself into a dark and silent house. Carefully she eased her key from the lock, paused to listen for sounds from above and then walked down the hall to the kitchen. A note from Harry lay on the table saying he'd double-checked and it was definitely OK for the Spurs match on Saturday. Underneath it in Louise's bold script was a note to say a Mrs Harding had called. Mrs Harding? Serena frowned and then remembered. The matron at Edith's nursing home.

Yawning, she glanced round the kitchen and paused, seeing a jacket thrown across a chair that she didn't recognise. A man's leather jacket. She reached out and picked it up. A strong smell of tobacco clung to it. Puzzled, she held it gingerly out in front of her, looking for clues. Probably one of Louise's friends left it behind. That was it.

She doused the lights and as quietly as she could mounted the stairs. Louise's room was next to hers, the door shut. Silently she pushed it open. A lozenge of light from the hallway fell on her sleeping daughter, one arm flung over her head, her earphones still clamped to her ears.

Serena tiptoed over to Louise and gently removed the headphone. Louise stirred in her sleep.

'Only me, darling,' Serena whispered. 'Back to sleep.'

After that she crept up the next flight to check Harry, whose room was next to the tiny room where Cheryl slept when she stayed over. Satisfied all was as it should be, she retraced her steps to her own room. A comparatively early night for once. Not quite one o'clock.

At first she couldn't register what was going on. Light from the lamp just inside the door cut through the darkness of her bedroom as she reached out to switch it on. There was a gasp from the bed. Serena screamed and jumped back.

For one frozen moment no one moved. Serena groped for the switch behind her and blinked as the overhead light flooded the room. 'What the hell are you doing?' Serena demanded furiously, recovering first. 'Get out of my bed. Both of you.'

'What you doing here?' Cheryl bleated breathlessly, trying to clamber off the prone figure of a total stranger.

'I live here,' Serena reminded her. 'Get dressed, Cheryl, and come downstairs. And you,' she snapped at the bemused man now propped on one elbow, 'get dressed and get out before I call the police.'

Serena stood stonily by the front door as the ill-shaven and greasy-haired man came downstairs first, pulling a T-shirt over his head. Serena motioned to him that his jacket was hanging over the end of the stairs. Without a word he shrugged it on and looked Serena up and down.

'Can't get any yourself? That it?' he jeered.

'Get out,' Serena breathed, pulling open the door. 'If I see you even near my house, let alone in it, ever again, you'll be arrested.'

Behind her she heard Louise stumble downstairs.

'What is it, Mum?' she asked, rubbing her eyes. 'What's going on?'

The man shrugged and walked away down the path.

'Nothing, darling,' Serena assured her, trying to control her shaking voice. 'Go back to bed. I'll come up when I've got rid of Cheryl.'

'Rid of her?' Louise's eyes widened. 'You're sacking her?'

'For which she should be grateful. My other option is to murder her.'

They both looked up as Cheryl began to make her way downstairs, wearing the shell suit she had arrived in. She was clutching a carrier bag.

'Bed, Lou,' Serena instructed, pressing her gently in the back.

Louise looked nervously from her mother to Cheryl. 'I'd rather stay,' she answered. 'I don't want to leave you.'

Serena squeezed her shoulder. 'I'll be fine. Promise.'

Reluctantly Louise pushed past the self-possessed Cheryl and disappeared. 'I'm so shocked, Cheryl,' Serena began. 'You of all people. I trusted you. What the hell do you think you were doing? If you're having an affair, that's your concern, but not in my house.'

'Affair? Who's having an affair?' Cheryl gawped at her. 'Gawd, you don't need me to spell it out, do you? A client. Bit of business. OK, I wasn't expecting you home and another half-hour and he'd have been gone. No harm done.'

Serena thought she was passing through a nightmare. A shiver of fear went through her.

'No harm? My children in bed and you think there was no harm? A client? What do you mean, a *client?*'

Cheryl separated the strands of her fringe. 'Well, what else would he be? Maybe not as rich as yours, but they pay about the same I 'spect.'

'What do you mean, "*as rich as yours*"? Are you talking about me?'

'Course. Who else?' Cheryl looked surprised. 'Look, I know this is jumping the gun a bit—and I am sorry about tonight, but everyone's got to start somewhere—but I thought with your contacts I might get in on it. Those guys at Frobisher's, they must want extras, don't they? We could split the money. I mean I might not have your accent but in the sack what does it matter?'

Serena sat down heavily on the stairs, the back of her hand pressed against her mouth. On the game. That's what Cheryl thought she was. A tart. Dear God, dear God.

'Cheryl,' she began slowly, her voice shaking. 'You've made a terrible mistake. I'm not on the game. I would starve in the gutter first.'

Cheryl gazed at her in total disbelief. She gave a nervous laugh. 'Not on the game? Get out of it. Listen, I won't put it about, you haven't got to worry about me. Not on the game?' She began to laugh until she noticed Serena's ghostly pallor and stopped. 'I mean that's what Frobisher's is about, isn't it?' she faltered.

'Believe me, Cheryl, not where I'm concerned. Please leave. I'll drop your money over tomorrow. You can't stay here any more. We . . . we just have crossed wires. Now, please go.'

'Go?' Cheryl whispered. 'Why? You mean you think I'm not up to it. That right?'

Serena looked helplessly at the over-made-up face, the streaked mascara. Finally she said, 'Cheryl, I don't want to continue this conversation. You just don't understand.'

'Oh yes, I do, you jealous hag,' Cheryl screamed. 'You're a taker, that's what you are. What was it they called you? Kept Woman? Bloody whore, more like.' She gazed venomously at Serena. 'I thought you would help me like I helped you. Know what I think? I think you deserve everything that's happened to you. I hope you rot. You vicious bitch with your big cars and flash blokes.'

Serena's face was white with shock. She opened the door and said quietly, 'Leave now, Cheryl. Now. Don't come back.'

At midday she called Mike and told him she was having problems on the home front.

'I'll try to get some cover, but it isn't very likely. You may have to do without me tonight.'

He grunted and told her to ring when she knew for sure. Serena replaced the phone on the wall and leaned against the sink. Who on earth could she get?

It wasn't until well into the afternoon that she remembered the call from Mrs Harding at the nursing home. What she had to say when Serena returned the call did not come as a great surprise. Edith would have to be moved.

'What's happened?' Serena asked.

There was a pause. 'Her daughter-in-law says they've run out of money. Seems rather soon to me,' Mrs Harding said pointedly.

'How long?'

'End of the month. Certainly by the new year.'

'I'll try to get down,' Serena told her.

Ed phoned at seven. 'Thought you were going to do a bunk,' he said when she explained. 'And she just walked out, no explanation?'

'Yes.' Serena winced at her lie. 'But I have to find someone else, Ed. I might need a day or two off. But I could take it as holiday. Rather sudden, but would you mind?'

'I mind that you think I'd be that small-minded. Take your time.'

'I've also got to dash down to see Edith. Her daughter-in-law is having her chucked out of the nursing home by Christmas.'

'Oh? Why?'

'Says there's no money left from the sale of the house.'

Ed grunted. 'Let Mike know what you're doing.'

He hadn't, she noticed, asked her to let *him* know.

It was Stacey who came to the rescue. 'Temporary,' she explained, 'just until you get someone permanent. My cousin needs somewhere to stay for the next three months. Give her dinner and breakfast and she'll baby-sit in return.'

Serena squealed with relief. 'Stace, you're a pal. When can I meet her?'

'She'll be down at the weekend, but I don't think she'll be able to start for a week.'

Saturday dawned cold and windy with a steady drizzle that didn't ease up all day. When she had first suggested a football match to Harry she had immediately regretted it. A mental vision of Harry being attacked by yobs sent her heart to her mouth.

She was relieved to have something to do. The violence of Cheryl's reaction had shaken her and haunted her all week. She found herself hovering over the children, checking where they were.

Tipper, to whom she confided her plans of a football match, insisted on going with them, to her relief and Harry's delight. The idea of Tipper being with them transformed it in Harry's head to real lads' stuff. They caught the tube to Tottenham and then followed the crowd to the home end, which Harry had told her was important so that they wouldn't get into any fights with the away supporters from Leeds.

'Fights?' she asked, staring down at him. 'Harry, don't let go of my hand,' she squealed, catching sight of a sea of supporters, their faces daubed in blue and white stripes, chanting aggressively as they pushed their way through the turnstiles to the stand.

Harry was mesmerised by it all. It was for him a dream. Even if each time a goal was scored or nearly scored his view was obliterated by the roaring wave of bodies in front of him, hurling themselves into the air, he didn't care.

On the way home Serena discovered she was hoarse from shouting. Harry was rapturously clutching the programme and a home strip that she had bought in the team shop. They reached Foster Street in exceptionally high spirits, and when Alex phoned to see if she was free for dinner she said she was but only if they could be back in time to see *Match of the Day*.

In the end, it was nearly five days before she could get down to Hove. She decided to go straight from seeing Harry into school. Serena rang Mike and said she would be back at the club by Wednesday. Bella, Stacey's cousin, would be starting on Tuesday and, to everyone's relief, she seemed to fit in.

In two weeks it would be Christmas and this year Serena was confident it would be a better one for Harry and Louise than the last two. The bottom of her wardrobe was now hiding a stack of presents waiting to be wrapped. Louise raised obstacles about going to her grandmother's for Christmas, but Serena refused to budge.

They would be leaving after lunch on Christmas Eve and would not be back until the new year, when the club reopened.

Serena was aware that she was sinking into Ed's debt. To take time off this close to Christmas couldn't have been welcomed by anyone. In her bag she had a gift for Edith, a pair of slippers shaped like little boots. As she closed the door, she looked across and saw Cheryl coming out of her house. There was an awkward pause.

In the days since she had asked Cheryl to leave, Serena had come to bitterly regret her own actions. The luxury of choice had not been hers, but the danger she had exposed her children to left her shaking and sitting bolt upright in bed at two in the morning. She blamed herself for not listening to Betty Plaxton, who had, in her own way, tried to warn her. Nor could she now trust Cheryl not to ring a newspaper and tell them—albeit a selective version—of what happened.

It was partly in the spirit of protecting herself and the children that she had decided a truce of some sort should be reached. Serena bit her lip and took the initiative. 'Cheryl?' she called over and began to walk across the street. 'Have you got a moment?'

Cheryl paused and turned. Her face seemed older.

'I'm sorry we had such a misunderstanding,' Serena began.

'A what?' Cheryl snapped. 'A misunderstanding? Don't think so, ducky. What's to mistake in you? Slut.'

Serena shut her eyes in disbelief and then turned sharply away.

'Slag,' Cheryl screamed. 'I'll get you for what you did to me. You just see if I don't.'

At Hove Station Serena took the same bus to the bottom of Holewood Hill that she had in the summer. The journey to this point was beyond recollection. Cheryl's rage and the embarrassing public abuse that she had hurled at her had left Serena stunned. Miles away and an hour or so between them, she felt safer but no less distraught.

Alighting from the bus and keeping her head down against a squalling rain, she ran across the street to the row of shops opposite. She bought two egg-custard tarts and then made her way to the nursing home.

'Edith will be so pleased to see you,' said Matron as she greeted Serena in the reception area.

Serena clutched the small box containing the custard tarts. 'I wanted to see you first. Just to see if there's any way I can help.'

'With Edith? Oh, that's all settled.' Matron beamed. 'Some mistake with the accounting on her daughter-in-law's part. I was a bit unsure about giving Mr . . . ' She paused, frowning. 'Mr Turner, that's it. About giving him the details, but frankly if there was a chance that Edith didn't have to be moved, I'm not above bending the odd rule.'

'Who's Mr Turner?' Serena asked, as they walked to the day room.

'Finance director for some company. Someone there knows the family, I believe.'

Serena halted. Turner? Matthew Turner. Ed's finance director. She began to smile. Well, fancy that. Strange to think he had done just what Stephen would have done if she'd asked. What was a sum like that to Stephen? Or indeed Ed. She smiled to herself. Ed's affection for his dead grandmother was clearly the reason for his generosity. As she approached Edith's wing chair, Serena was pleased that she had mentioned it to Ed. How awful if he had heard too late to help.

The visit was brief. Edith had trouble recalling her name. She did however eat half of one of the custard tarts before she fell back to sleep. Serena gazed affectionately down at the crumpled figure, her mouth half open, eyes closed. Gently she wiped the crumbs from around her mouth, adjusting her rug and then left, kissing her lined cheek.

'Come and see her again,' Matron said, opening the door. The wind gusted in. 'She'll love her Christmas present. I'll make sure she gets it.'

Serena decided to phone Ed rather than wait until she next saw him. Walking up Foster Street, the shoulders of her raincoat sopping from the driving rain, she kept a wary eye open for Cheryl, but was determined not to be intimidated about leaving and entering her own home.

Once she had shed her coat she called Ed's house. 'I've just been to see Edith,' she said warmly when he came on the line. 'You are a good person, Mr Stein. You've made an old lady very happy.'

'Well, I hope it helped Edith as well,' he joked. 'Nothing to thank me for. Her daughter-in-law coughed up the money.'

There was a pause. 'But surely Matthew . . . I mean why did he . . . ?'

'Tsk, tsk, Serena,' Ed chided her. 'Practise what you preach. Don't jump to conclusions. I haven't paid a penny. Why should I? Edith has the money herself; it was just a question of unravelling her accounts. Thank me for that. Nothing else, I promise you.'

A ripple of unease ran through her. A vision of a couple of heavies threatening the daughter-in-law flashed before her. 'What did you do?'

'Nothing. I got Matthew to hire a solicitor down in Hove for Edith, got him to explain to her daughter-in-law about fraud. Now Edith's savings are in a bank account set up in Edith's name administered by a solicitor, with a direct debit to the nursing home in place.'

'You mean, you haven't paid the fees?' She was struggling between disappointment that he had not made such a generous gesture when he could afford it and embarrassment that she had clearly expected him to. Not like Stephen at all. 'Well, it was still good of you.'

'Serena? Listen to me. Just think how Edith would feel. A proud old lady like that having to rely on a handout when she knew she had the money somewhere and no home to go back to. Edith might be a bit gaga, but from what I can gather she's a stout old bird at heart and she would have been mortified to hear a near-stranger had to support her. I'm not into that, either.'

'No, of course not,' Serena agreed hastily, feeling deflated.

'When are you coming back?' Ed changed the subject abruptly. It was a habit of his she'd noticed.

'Day after tomorrow,' she told him. 'I've got some temporary cover— breathing space really.'

'Well, now you've got your breath back, come to the dogs with me. You'll enjoy it.'

'The dogs? How brilliant . . . I mean no. I work for you. It wouldn't be sensible. I'm really sorry, Ed.'

'Is this to do with your old man?'

She stiffened. 'Yes, of course, how could it not be. But it's just as much to do with not going out with the boss.'

There was a pause. 'Don't get too trapped in the past, Mrs Carmichael. It's a safe place, but bloody boring.'

'Who said I was?' she tried to keep the anger out of her voice. 'I have friends who I see, go out with.'

'But no one who's interested in you for you?' He sounded sceptical.

She should have been flattered. Instead she was stung. 'Of course. I have . . . a kind of relationship with someone who understands . . .listens.'

'Sounds like a shrink,' he laughed.

'He is,' she replied stonily.

'Oh Christ,' he muttered. 'Spare me. You don't need a shrink, Mrs Carmichael, you need . . . '

There was a long pause.

'What?' she demanded.

'A night at the dogs,' he said flatly. She found herself blushing at what she guessed he'd really meant. 'Let Mike know you're back Wednesday.'

She replaced the phone and leaned her head against the wall. Today was not a good day. She rang Alex. 'Alex,' she said miserably, 'I'm in need of a friend.'

At Alex's suggestion they had supper at his house. She had hesitated. 'It's all right,' he read her thoughts. 'Alice and I have agreed not to see each other for a while. It seemed sensible. God, I sound boring, don't I?'

'You could never sound boring,' she told Alex fondly. 'Not to me. I'm sorry about Alice.'

It would have been folly to have pretended she was entirely divorced from influencing their decision, for which she felt a pang of guilt. However, what he had in common with Alice had always puzzled her.

'Sounds like we both need a shoulder,' she said.

'How about I blow a whistle and we swap over at half time,' he joked, 'now that you're a soccer fan?'

He was, she decided, replacing the phone, awfully sweet.

On reflection, she was not surprised that she had ended the evening in bed with him. A glass or three of a very good Chablis had told her getting sex out of the way with Alex was an exceptionally good idea.

'I absolutely hadn't planned this,' Alex murmured into her hair, as the dinner he had so carefully prepared cooled in the dining room below.

'Nor me,' she murmured. 'It wouldn't have happened if we had.'

'Nothing ever does,' he laughed, softly kissing her. 'I am so happy. So amazingly happy. We must,' he added, 'take this slowly. At this moment I just want to rush off and marry you, but life isn't that simple.'

Serena's eyes flew open. 'Especially as I'm still married,' she said, alarmed at the speed he was progressing their relationship.

Alex rolled off her and gazed at the ceiling. 'Of course,' he said, 'for a moment I forgot. How do you feel about—Stephen?'

Stephen. In four weeks it would be exactly two years since she had seen him, spoken to him, slept with him. Not a word, a sign. It was hard to assemble her feelings about Stephen, now that Alex had asked her.

She shook her head. 'I don't know,' she finally answered, truthfully. 'I know I should be feeling something, but I don't. It's like I'm two people. The Serena that loved him, adored him really, and this other person of whom he knows nothing.'

'Oh, my darling,' Alex whispered, 'it's a start. That's so good.'

'Is it?' she asked doubtfully. She turned and looked at his face smiling contentedly. 'Alex,' she asked quickly, 'would you mind if I didn't talk about Stephen? I'm still not sure how I feel about it.' She smiled a little anxiously. 'You do understand, don't you?'

At once his face filled with concern. 'My precious, of course. Take all the time you want.'

For some reason his understanding response didn't help. A small knot of apprehension tugged away in her head.

Christmas at Margot's was as happy as they could make it for the children. They stayed until New Year's Day and then travelled back to London for Serena to resume work the next day. It was quite amazing, she decided as she drove along, how the children just accepted the fact that they now had a car again. Not the plushest car in the world, but a sturdy estate car that she had bought the Saturday before, secondhand from a garage in Stockwell, with Tipper acting as her adviser.

Life was improving. She was getting there.

She had sent a Christmas card to Ed with a pleasant message and in return she had received a basket of plump winter roses, entwined with tartan ribbon and foliage. The note merely thanked her for all her help during the year and was signed with a scrawled signature.

January gave way to a mild February and a stormy March. Ed had spent the greater part of that time in New York. From time to time he strode through the club and nodded a greeting to her. Once or twice she thought of waylaying him to try to engage him in friendly conversation, but the opportunity didn't present itself. One evening she watched him in deep conversation with Mike in the library.

'Goodness,' she said lightly as he emerged. 'We hardly see you here. You seem so busy.'

He paused and then came over to where she was checking messages for the evening. 'Les Cages reopens in the summer, so I expect I'll be seeing a lot of Paris in the next few weeks. The "Eighty-One" needed a kick in the butt, which is why I had to be in New York these last few weeks. Frobisher's is the one place I don't have to concern myself with. Mike knows what he's doing.'

'Well, that must be a relief,' replied Serena, oddly pleased that it was work and not his mistress who had kept him so long in New York.

'How's your kind-of relationship going?'

Since the kind-of relationship had turned into a sexual one and one in which she felt torn between suffocating at Alex's attentions and enjoying being so wanted, she gave an evasive answer.

'Going, I think is the answer to that.'

'And that would mean what?' he asked. 'Going as in grinding to a halt or going as in getting up to speed?'

'Going well.' She held his gaze defiantly, although she couldn't think why it was suddenly necessary for him to know she was having a sex life.

'Hmm,' was all he said. She was the first to drop her gaze. He glanced at his watch. 'OK, Mike,' he called over to where the general manager was clearly impatient to be off, 'I'm out of here.'

Chapter Ten

~

LIFE IN FOSTER STREET had settled into a routine that worked after a fashion. Bella had decided to stay in London until the end of the summer, which suited all of them, especially since it meant they saw more of Stacey, who Serena could see was trying to loosen the grip the dreadful Barry had on her.

Serena continued to work at Frobisher's, continued to save and continued to hope that within a year or two she would be out of Foster Street and not working at night. The job was not to be knocked, but it lacked the edge she had noticed in her first few weeks, when Ed had nearly always been around. Now she hardly saw him. Since the beginning of March he had been mostly in Paris and New York.

She couldn't say why, because he did not add to her comfort, but Serena missed not having Ed around. All she knew was that when he was present, teasing her or being blunt, she felt the club worked. A buzz lifted the whole evening. Tipper agreed and then gave her a sly look.

'Now, if I were a betting man, I'd say you weren't so cool about him as you make out.' He ducked as she threw a napkin across the bar at him, and strolled out with a toss of his hair to greet some late arrivals.

Every Sunday Tipper would turn up for lunch at Serena's and afterwards, if the weather was reasonable, they would all troop off to Battersea Park where Harry would practise roller-blading. On these occasions they would often be joined by Alex, if he wasn't seeing his own children. At first, it had caused Serena some disquiet that, whereas his children had been encouraged to enjoy a relationship with Alice while they were together, Lorrayne, Alex's ex-wife, had made it clear that she was not prepared to extend the same goodwill to Serena until she understood what her relationship with Alex was.

Curiously Alex had bowed to her demands. 'She has a point,' he explained. 'I don't want them confused.'

Serena said nothing, just squeezed his arm. Since her own feelings had remained unresolved, she conceded that Lorrayne might just have a point. If it had been Stephen, she would not have wanted Harry and

Louise exposed to a series of lady friends, each of whom they would be pressured to like. If she wished for anything, however, it was that Louise would be more polite to Alex. Harry treated him like an old friend, which of course to Harry he was, but Louise found him tame and boring. Just like Stephen, demanding and needing excitement.

It was odd, she thought, how her life had settled into this pattern. Shrewder about how to handle her daughter's almost daily attempts to challenge the rules she laid down, she no longer felt so uneasy about Damon. Not that she approved of his strutting around the streets with his loud mates, but she could see that with Louise he was calmer, perhaps in awe of her. Better to have him under her eye than try to stop it—she was aware that it was not beyond Louise to see him secretly.

Cheryl had waited a long time, but her revenge when it came was vicious. The shock for Serena came more from having believed the danger had passed. And then Cheryl struck.

'Boss wants to see you,' Mike told her as she arrived one evening, giving her an odd look. 'Upstairs.'

Ed was waiting in the drawing room, looking serious. He seemed fit and tanned and Serena thought he had lost a little weight.

'Nice to see you.' She greeted him with genuine warmth.

For a moment she thought he looked surprised. 'And you,' he said. 'Although what I want to see you about isn't entirely pleasant.'

The smile on her mouth faded. 'Not pleasant?' she faltered.

'Have a seat. Drink?'

She shook her head.

'Here, look at this. It came a few days ago. I wasn't here, I only saw it this afternoon.'

He handed her a letter. It was marked personal and private, typed and postmarked in Whitehall. She read it through and then glanced up at Ed. Her face was pale, her hands shaking. She felt sick. In her entire life she had never felt so mortified or dirty.

'I see,' was all she said, handing the letter back to him.

'No address, of course.' He glanced at the envelope and then threw it behind him on the desk against which he was leaning. 'I got a call this afternoon from a couple of guys from the Serious Fraud Office.'

'Serious Fraud Office?' she whispered. 'Why?'

While he talked he poured her a drink. 'Brandy.' He handed it to her. 'Go on, take it. You look done in.'

'Wouldn't you be?' she cried. 'I'm sorry it mentioned you. Truly. Oh God, all I ever do is bring trouble with me.' Her voice began to crack.

'No hysterics,' he commanded, squeezing her hand. 'Promise?'

She nodded. 'Just tell me.'

'Good girl.' He leaned back. 'The letter is from a nutter, but the same nutter wrote to someone at the fraud office, or at least it was passed on to them.'

'It says I'm living on immoral earnings.' Serena clasped her hands tightly in her lap, her mind already back to the letter. 'That I leave the children all night on their own. It's wicked,' she gulped painfully, 'truly, truly wicked. It's Cheryl.' She glanced up at him. 'And it's not true.'

'I know that,' Ed replied, calmly. 'Now, who the hell is Cheryl?'

Serena explained. 'Jeezus,' he whistled softly. 'You mean the sight of my car put all this crap into her head? Why didn't you tell me?' he asked shortly. 'You just said the help had left. You never mentioned the rest.'

She shook her head. 'Not something you tell your boss.'

He stood up abruptly, running a hand through his hair. 'Oh, stop that shit, will you? You know bloody well it's not like that. What do you take me for? Oh, forget it,' he growled, as she protested. 'Let's sort this out first. Fraud office came because of who you're married to and . . .'

'I don't care about the fraud office,' she said. 'They watch me all the time. I'm used to it. They know it's not true.' She took a sip of brandy. She was beginning to recover from the shock. 'My phone is tapped and I'm under surveillance most of the time. After all, what reason could Stephen have for surfacing, other than me and the children?'

'No reason at all,' Ed agreed, tossing back his drink.

'I'm truly sorry you were involved,' she said quietly, 'and I will resign. You don't need the kind of trouble I bring with me.'

'Leave?' he cut across her. 'Why? Because some vicious old hag tells a pack of lies? Give me strength. I thought you were above all that.'

'Don't, Ed,' she said. 'Don't make me feel worse than I do now.'

'Oh, for Christ's sake,' he muttered, sitting down heavily on the edge of the desk. 'Why would I do that? There's no helping you, is there?'

'But there is,' she pointed out. 'Help me by making it easy for me. I don't want to leave. But I know what will happen next and I've got to think of the children. I know, just *know*, she'll go to a tabloid. It's on the cards. I'm surprised she hasn't already. On a slow day, I could fill a column. And then there's the big picture still to be got.'

He looked steadily at her. 'Stephen?' He ground out his cigar. 'You don't believe that will happen, do you?'

She turned away and placed the glass on a small table next to her. 'One day,' she spoke softly, more to herself, 'one day I will see him again, but it will be because I've found him, not the other way round. That's what I think. Odd, isn't it, I've never told anyone that, not even . . . '

'Not even the shrink,' he guessed.

She shook her head as she turned back. 'No. Not even Alex.'

'Don't leave,' he said quietly. 'You're safe here. We'll just tell the bloody hacks to sod off if they try and get to you.' He came back to sit next to her. 'You're safer here with me. I mean working here,' he corrected himself, 'than out there on your own. I can protect you.'

She shook her head. A brief vision of Stephen rose before her, telling her how to do things. Alex trying to shield her from pain, and now Ed. Ed thinking she only had to hide behind him and she would be safe.

'Thank you. You're being kind beyond belief. But I have to do this on my own. Believe me.'

'You mean it, don't you?' He looked her over slowly as if seeing her for the first time.

She nodded. 'I'll fix when to leave with Mike. I'll just slip away so there'll be no big deal. I'll say goodbye before I go.'

He walked with her to the door. 'Thanks, Ed.' She turned and smiled at him as the lift appeared. 'It's been great.'

'Bloody women,' he growled, as the lift doors closed.

'Tough about Serena,' Mike said to Ed as he watched the club emptying out at the end of the evening. 'She'll be hard to replace. There's quite a few faces who have ambitions in her direction.'

Ed just grunted and lit a cigar. Mike looked slyly at him out of the corner of his eye. 'And of course,' he went on, 'I'll put money on it that now she's free from club rules, quite a few of them will be after her. Now she doesn't work for you any more, I mean.'

'That's right,' Ed blew a cloud of smoke. 'I was just thinking that myself. Now that I'm not her boss, anything could happen.'

Alex looked pleased. 'I hated you being there,' he confessed. 'But you needed to prove something and you have.'

'Like I could earn a living?' Serena began to gather up the plates from dinner. 'Not sure I had the luxury of proving anything. Still haven't.'

Almost a month later she still found it odd to be at home in the evening. Each morning she fought down the panic while confronting another day searching for a job, and each night she went to bed comforting herself that this couldn't go on for ever.

Paying the rent was eating into her savings. At the end of the week she knew she should go and sign on. The thought depressed her. All those questions, justifying her life. But what else was there?'

All of that she expected. but it was missing the bustle of the club that was leaving an unexpected hollow. To be fair to Alex, she had kept all this from him. She looked over to where he was sipping his wine, elbows on the table, watching her lovingly over his glass.

'Well, you need another job, of course,' he agreed as she started the washing-up. 'But I think you needed the chance to regain a sense of self-worth.' He raised his glass. 'And you've done that magnificently.'

The dishes slid into the sink. Slowly she turned to look at him. 'Is that what you think?' She wiped her hands on a cloth. 'That I did all this'—she paused, emphasising the words—'for me?'

He got hastily to his feet and hugged her. 'No, of course not. I don't think you ever think of yourself.'

She turned away from him and began soaking the dishes. 'Of course. Ignore me. I'm having an identity crisis in a big way.'

It was a rule Serena had established that Alex would not stay over with her. She had insisted it was because of the children, but she knew it was as much to do with her own need for independence.

'See you tomorrow.' He gazed meaningfully at her as he left close to midnight.

Her hand flew to her mouth. 'Alex, I'm sorry. I forgot. I've promised to take Bella and the children out to dinner. It's Bella's last night with us. I know, come with us. Oh, do. It'll be fun.'

He put his hands in the air to deflect her. 'Whoa. Not for me. This is for you and the children. Wish her luck from me, won't you?'

He strode off, throwing her a kiss. He was gone so quickly she didn't have time to say that Tipper and Stacey were coming too. Louise would be relieved if he wasn't there, because she knew, absolutely knew, she told Serena, that he didn't like Damon, who was also going with them.

Stacey called at seven to say she wouldn't be joining them. When she saw Bella's stormy face as she replaced the phone, Serena guessed.

'Not coming? Barry?'

'Jackpot. He's such a sod,' Bella fumed. 'He doesn't love her, Serena. He's just a control freak and she earns good money, so she's useful.'

Serena slipped an arm round her shoulders. They were close, Bella and Stacey, and Serena knew from Bella that her cousin's parents were frantic with worry about their daughter. 'There's nothing you or I can do until she wakes up,' Serena said. 'Now, come on, it's your last night.'

The phone rang as they were leaving the house. Louise answered it.

'It's for you, Mum,' she shrieked. 'It's Ed.'

'Ed? Ed Stein?'

'And how many Eds do you know?' Tipper teased.

'I'm told you're all going on the razzle,' Ed said when she came on the line. 'Don't let me hold you up. The shrink treating you all?'

Glad though she was to hear from him, surprised too—well, perhaps not totally surprised, she admitted to herself—she did not want Alex disparaged. 'Don't call him the shrink. And no. Family outing.'

'Sounds healthy. I'll call you tomorrow to see what time you want me to pick you up.'

'Pick me up?'

'Sure. Wednesday. Dinner and the dogs.'

She tried not to laugh or to feel quite so pleased. 'Ed. I think you know my feelings about—'

'Yeah, yeah, yeah,' he interrupted, 'but that was last month's excuse. You don't work for me now.' There was a brief pause. 'Do you? Look, Mrs Carmichael, you wouldn't want me to be totally humiliated in front of all my friends, now would you? Naturally I can see perhaps I should have cleared it with you first, but I thought, now who's the person I would like to see most go to the dogs . . . ?'

She tried not to laugh. And she couldn't refuse.

'What did he say?' Tipper asked as she joined them in the car.

'He says I'm finally going to the dogs.'

Several hours later, the whole house was roused by the sound of someone leaning frantically on the doorbell. Dazed with sleep, Serena stumbled from her bed and ran down the stairs. Before she reached the door she could hear Stacey. 'Serena,' she was sobbing, 'please help me.'

She stifled an oath, pulling back the bolts. Stacey was leaning against the door frame, blood trickling down her face. She stumbled into the hall.

Behind her Serena heard Bella scream as Stacey fainted at her feet.

After the doctor had left and the children had been persuaded to go back to sleep, Serena and Bella sat either side of Stacey, who was now tucked up in Serena's bed. A livid bruise was showing on her temple, one eye was closed, her mouth swollen. Stacey had become almost hysterical when Serena wanted to call the police. It was all Bella could do to stop crying at the sight of Stacey's beaten face. On the other side of the bed Serena was trying to decide the next course of action.

Stacey was, by her own calculation, three months' pregnant—the reason Barry had so savagely beaten her. Going home to her parents in Birmingham was not an option. Her God-fearing family would be traumatised at having an unmarried mother in their midst. 'Can't do it to them,' Stacey whispered, 'can I, Bel?'

The younger girl shook her head. 'But you won't go back to him, will you, Stace?' she asked fearfully.

Stacey shook her head on the pillow, large tears rolling down her battered face. 'Never. Never.'

All three jumped as the phone next to the bed jangled. Mesmerised, they gazed at it insistently ringing. 'It's him. Don't let him come here.' Stacey gripped Serena's arm.

'Of course not.' Serena reached for the phone.

A stream of abuse identified the enraged Barry demanding Stacey's return.

'Oh, stop it,' Serena yawned down the phone. 'You're frightening me to death. But you should know, Barry, that every call to my house is monitored by the police. They'll have traced your number in seconds. Don't call again unless it's to apologise.'

She replaced the phone.

'Is that true?' Stacey asked, awed by what she'd just heard.

Serena shrugged. 'Afraid so. He won't call again. He's such a scumbag.'

Stacey looked crushed. 'What'll I do?' she asked. 'I can't go to work like this. My stuff's at Barry's.'

'You stay here, of course,' Serena broke in briskly. 'I'll ask Tip if he knows a heavy who can go round and get your stuff. But the main concern is the baby. Who's your doctor?'

Stacey stared numbly back at her. 'Haven't got one. I didn't know who to go to. I was so scared.'

In the course of the next ten minutes Serena discovered that getting pregnant had not been planned, nor had Stacey any idea if she wanted the child. Until last week, when she gave up hope that her symptoms might be due to stress, she had never thought of having a baby.

'What'll she do?' Bella asked nervously.

Serena swallowed hard. 'OK.' She kept her voice brisk. 'Bella, hop in with Stacey. I'll sleep in your bed for the night. Don't worry,' she patted Stacey's hand, 'first thing Monday morning we'll get the whole thing sorted out. Honestly. Trust me.'

It was soon evident that Stacey's pregnancy was not going to be straightforward. For a start, pronounced the doctor whom Serena had taken her to see, Stacey was nearer five months than three, which ruled out one decision, and a scan at the maternity unit at St Wilhemina's showed the baby was not as developed as they would have liked.

Too absorbed in what was being explained, neither the doctor imparting the news nor Stacey herself noticed Serena stiffen. While they talked, she planned. It was a long shot, but he owed her a favour.

George Kincaid came hurriedly to the phone. She guessed from the affable way he greeted her that someone was listening. She waited while he got rid of them.

'What do you want?' he hissed down the phone.

'Not a lot, George. Stop panicking. Just a favour from you.'

At seven on Wednesday Ed collected her. Stacey was baby-sitting, her face still showing the legacy of her run-in with Barry. Harry was introduced, shyly nodding at him; Louise greeted him like an old friend.

'Nice kids,' Ed observed, as his driver pulled away. 'Nice mother too,' he added. 'Great legs.'

She stopped herself from tugging at her skirt. 'Thank you,' she replied politely, but at the first opportunity she surreptitiously wriggled her skirt down as far as it would go.

They had dinner high above the race track with a group of Ed's clearly regular cronies who included his tailor Lenny Horniman. She recognised the name of the man who headed a major film-production company and another who had recently been in the news, having sold the worldwide television rights to the next heavyweight boxing championships for a million-dollar figure.

It was, she knew, the kind of evening designed to make her forget the bills, the neighbours and Foster Street. Ed showed her how to place bets, laughing at her when she shrieked as her choice shot past the post, and even harder at her dismay when she lost.

Halfway through the evening, she was vaguely aware that her hair had tumbled out of its moorings and she was suffused in a forgotten feeling of well-being. Ed had switched seats so that he was no longer sitting safely opposite her, but beside her, his arm resting lightly along the back of her chair. Every now and then they were interrupted by people who knew him and occasionally he turned away from her to talk quietly to one or two of them. On these occasions she did not want to have to acknowledge that Ed Stein was extraordinary company in spite of the diamond and ruby tie-pin that glinted when the light caught it.

The lift doors opened onto the familiar corridor that led to George Kincaid's suite of consulting rooms.

'Mrs Carmichael,' the sister greeted her, astonishment in her face. 'It's been a long time.'

Serena returned the greeting and asked her to let George know that she and Miss Barclay were waiting.

George rose to his feet as they were shown in by his secretary a few minutes later. With more heartiness than he clearly felt, he greeted

Serena with a handshake. It was not lost on her that in the past a double kiss had been George's preferred mode of greeting. He knew why they were there, and, after the introductions, Serena withdrew to the waiting room, giving Stacey's shoulder a reassuring pat on the way out.

To his credit George was giving Stacey as much time as he would any of his more well-heeled patients. Idly Serena flicked through some recent glossy magazines until a small news item caught her attention. It was about the Stella Bonner Centre, where they actively campaigned for improving the lot of single working mothers. It said they were now in a position to employ a fund-raising manager responsible for raising their profile. Serena read it through twice and then looked thoughtfully into the middle distance. Finally, she tucked the magazine into her handbag and waited for George to finish with Stacey. As she had expected, George agreed to take Stacey without a fee and to deliver the baby himself in the Wendover Wing. 'Thank you, George.' She was genuinely grateful.

He looked at her over his glasses. 'We both know why I'm doing this, Serena.'

'Because I was instrumental in getting the prem unit in place,' she replied evenly. 'That's all, George. Of that you can be quite sure. There is however, one last thing you can do for me.'

She saw him stiffen. 'Here,' she quickly handed him the magazine. 'I need a job and this is one I could do.'

'Well, of course,' he handed it back. 'But how does that concern me?'

'I need a reference, George. Not just any old reference, but one from someone who counts.' She smiled.

The new fund-raising manager of the Stella Bonner Centre sat in a black leather chair behind a teak desk and surveyed her office with pleasure. Her name was on the door. The walls were lined with shelves stacked high with reports on the progress and potential funding for a company committed to improving support systems for single working mothers.

Sitting beside the computer terminal was a basket of flowers from Ed, sent from New York, clearly impressing the secretary she had inherited and whom she would share with the head of counselling.

Ed, on hearing about her new job, had suggested Paris for the weekend and jeered lightly at her when she refused. Alex had taken her to dinner to celebrate, genuinely thrilled for her, but also relieved that now he didn't have to skirt around describing what she did to his friends.

The phone buzzed on her desk. 'Mrs Carmichael? Miss Martindale says would you lunch with her today? You don't appear to have anything in your diary.'

Serena grinned to herself. Windows every day, she acknowledged. But not for long. This was only her second day.

'Tell her that would be most kind,' she told the secretary. 'And Trish? I think "Serena" will be fine.'

Gilly Martindale had been the inspiration behind the centre, the campaigning zeal to change laws, fund crèches and pester local councils until they agreed to fund after-school and holiday care for the children of single working mothers.

Before they left the restaurant, Serena raised the small matter of the diary item in that morning's paper, which had brought her new job to the attention of their readers. It had a picture of Serena taken with her consent as she arrived for her first day at her new offices in Victoria Street. A small story accompanied it, pointing out that, almost three years on, not one word of censure had ever left her lips on the subject of her disgraced husband. It was kind enough, but Serena was wary.

'I spotted him first,' Serena explained to Gilly about the photograph. 'I didn't want a furtively snatched picture so I told the photographer if he wanted a picture he only had to ask. Was that OK?'

Gilly dismissed it with a wave of her fork. 'George Kincaid said you were ace at raising money. That's all I care about.'

'He probably didn't mention I'm also an expert now in sifting the genuine from the curious. So I'll know those who agree to see me who just want to gawp at me. I've had plenty of practice.'

Gilly grinned. 'I bet you have. Anyway, I've made sure everyone at the office understands no one talks to the press. And Serena? I can't say I know what you've been through, but as far as I'm concerned it's history.'

Within weeks the initial interest in her had faded and Serena had become an expert on figures. Each night after supper, while Harry watched television and Louise sat with the telephone clamped to her ear, she mugged up statistics and facts. Alex joked about his rival, and he wasn't referring to another man, when evening after evening he was turned down in favour of preparation for a meeting or a presentation.

Her weekends were filled with the children's needs, but in order to stop Alex fretting she invited Gilly, along with Charles and Melanie, to have supper. And she began cautiously to think about looking for another house. A mortgage was no longer out of the question. A small one of course. But a move in the right direction in every sense.

Minnie phoned to say she was proud of Serena. 'Well done, my dear,' she said. 'You've been amazing. The children are a credit to you. I'm sorry not to have seen you with them, but it was more important for you to get this job under way. Anyway'—she dropped her voice to a conspiratorial whisper—'LouLou is so different when she's here. I get a few days of city-slicker mode and then she's too impatient to keep it up. Really, Serena, she's going to be a stunning girl.' Stephen's name had not been mentioned.

Serena felt quite moved at such a display of solidarity from a woman who had once found it hard to disguise her impatience with her. But mostly it was relief that there was hope for Louise.

Stacey's baby was due in two months, just before Christmas, and they all agreed they couldn't remember what it was like not having her live with them. Slowly, through Bella, Stacey was building bridges with her estranged family. Tipper had collected her belongings from Barry, who had quickly moved someone else in.

Twice Serena had had dinner with Ed and on both occasions had calmly rejected his suggestions for the more exotic end to the evening he had in mind. When he then disappeared for weeks on end and didn't contact her at all, she felt uneasy and couldn't think why she felt better knowing he was around, even if he disturbed her peace of mind. Eventually he would just turn up on the doorstep and she would find herself greeting him as though she was unaware he had been out of her life for up to a month. He flattered Louise and was capable of spending two hours playing Fantasy Football with Harry.

'He'll be in his element when he comes to the Arsenal–Spurs match next Saturday,' Ed chuckled.

Serena's eyes flew open. 'Saturday? Oh heavens, he must think I'm taking him. I'll never get tickets. I'd better ask Tip.'

Ed leaned back, his hands linked behind his head and a smug grin on his face. 'You're not going anywhere. He's coming with me, bringing three of his friends from school, and they're going to sit in the directors' box and give Harry a bit of kudos on Monday morning.'

She stiffened. 'Ed. It's kind of you. But I don't think it's wise to let Harry think he can buy people off.'

'He's not. He's a great kid and he's beginning to make friends at that school of his. Besides, he needs a bit of fun instead of exploring his feelings through whatever it is he does on Saturday mornings.'

'Alex says—' she began.

'Fuck Alex,' Ed snapped. 'Oh, I forgot. You do.'

'Please go.' She rose to her feet. 'You're intolerable.'

'Possibly. But he's worse. He's a bloody bore. OK, I'm out of here.'

If it hadn't been for the fact that Harry would have been devastated, Serena would have refused to let him go on Saturday. There was another reason she felt annoyed. It was the first time she had heard that Harry was making any friends at his new school. It would, she thought furiously, be Ed who discovered the fact.

'They're all right,' Harry mumbled when she enquired who they were. 'I didn't think they'd let me play football with them, but Ed said they would, but not unless I asked. I just said can I play and it was OK. You always said you should wait to be asked, but Ed said that only applied to meal times and being invited to parties but not when you're getting nowhere with something you really want to do.'

'He said that, did he?' she replied acidly. 'I bet he did.'

It was true she never invited him round. He just turned up. Alex respected her need to work. Ed claimed he did too, but never quite convinced her he understood her need for independence.

Tipper thought she was mad to feel worried about Ed's invitation to Harry, especially as he'd been included in the Saturday outing. 'Says he needs a bit of help with the lads. You know you should throw your lot in with him,' he advised, and not for the first time. 'Just think what you'd have. Money, security, never having to work again? Surely, now, it's what every woman wants?'

'Not this one. I've had that. It doesn't follow that you're secure or'—she paused—'or loved. I'm not going to be anyone's mistress. No, I think I'm safer looking after myself. Besides I'm getting good at it.'

And she was. Gone was the charming flirtatious woman knowing what to say to massage the egos of vain bankers and MPs. In her place was a woman who had emerged wiser, sharper, less trusting, but much smarter than the one who had been plunged into poverty.

It was part of her nature to be charming on public occasions; now it was allied to a professionalism and a genuine commitment to the cause she was pleading. Gilly rubbed her hands with pleasure when she could see the effect Serena was having on her audience.

Melanie met her for lunch in a small trattoria in Victoria Street. 'I'm so proud of you,' she told her fiercely. 'It must be wonderful having something fulfilling to do. Everyone says they'll buy tickets for this fund-raiser you're doing.'

Serena's days were filled with meetings, lunches and presentations, and each night she laid the foundations for her first big fund-raising event. Metro Radio had agreed to a tie-in with the Stella Bonner Centre for a fund-raising concert and Gilly was ecstatic. Serena was terrified. Before, she could have relied on her social standing to call in household names to lend their support, but now she was starting from scratch. It was all very well having a hard-hitting young radio station encouraging their listeners to buy tickets, but she had to find an act for them to see.

It was Louise who nagged her to have a rock concert, but Serena who saw how it could be done with a difference. It had not escaped Serena's notice that a lot of Harry's heroes, when interviewed, said they would love to be a rock star. With the station's help she rounded up five young footballers who were game to appear as rock singers. An ad in the music press brought her the offer of a couple of backing groups, who said they would do it in return for tickets to the next Cup Final.

The hard part was getting a big star name to pull the whole thing together, and at least three walk-on surprise guests. Glumly she leafed through her address book, feeling the gap between a smart address in Kensington and a rich husband and the less exalted environs of the Stella Bonner Centre and no husband at all. Well, not one in evidence.

Harry raced through the door. 'Mum,' he yelled. 'Mum, it was brill! We won! You should have been there.'

Serena whooped with delight and hugged him. Tipper, coming in behind, was almost as ecstatic. 'It was ace. And what's more'—he stepped aside as Harry tore past to find Louise to tell her about his after-noon—'himself says if I want to work in Paris or New York he'll fix it.'

She gave him a look of dismay. 'Oh, Tip. I couldn't bear it. How would I manage without you?'

'Ah, now you're worse than the Big Man himself. Full of blarney. You'd all manage a treat. The thing is there's nothing really keeping me here. I don't know what I'd have done without you and the kids. I feel you're my own, you know that?'

She gave him a quick hug. 'Now who's full of blarney? By the way, big news. Breakthrough at last. Stacey's mother phoned. Good old Bella.'

Tipper marched off to find Stacey to share her good news. Serena picked up the phone in the kitchen and dialled Ed's number.

'Just wanted to thank you,' she said when Wally switched her through to him. 'I've never, ever, seen Harry so ecstatic.'

'Nice kid,' he replied briefly. There was a long pause.

She broke the silence. 'Well, that was it really. Just a grateful mother.'

'How grateful?'

In front of her the notice board had a note from Alex saying he would call later about dinner.

'If you think,' she said carefully, 'that I would agree to dinner just because you entertained my son—'

'I haven't invited you,' he pointed out.

'I know that,' she snapped.

'So?'

'*I'm* inviting *you*. But if you're going to be all heavy about it, conditions and that stuff, you can forget it.'

'OK. I'll be there at eight. Black tie?'

She banged the phone down. The note from Alex was staring at her.

'Alex? Can I take a rain check on tonight? Ed's coming to supper. Yes, I invited him. Harry had such a brilliant time.'

'You know, Serena, I understand, I'm just a bit concerned that this rather superficial level of securing Harry's place in his peer group is fraught with dangers. It looks so privileged.'

'Alex,' she cut across him, 'Harry is not privileged and I don't think a boost to his morale will damage him for life. After all, it's a one-off. Ed isn't a fixture in his life.'

There was a small pause. 'I hope not,' he said frostily.

Gilly called almost immediately to ask if Serena and Alex would like her two tickets to the National to see the Brecht, the guest she was taking had cried off and she knew Alex adored Brecht.

Serena paused. 'Gilly,' she said, 'I can't, but why don't you ask Alex?'

Chapter Eleven

❧

HARRY JOINED THEM FOR DINNER. To her surprise, Ed appeared to expect nothing else. Louise, who was off to a party in a pair of skin-tight black trousers and a cropped T-shirt, greeted him with a high five and a giggle when he said she made him feel old.

'No, you're not,' she rushed to assure him, 'you're cool.'

'Tell your mother,' he urged. 'She says I can't go to her concert. I'm not'—he leaned forward looking mournful and mouthed the rest of the sentence—'trendy enough.'

Louise gaped. 'Mum said that?'

Ed nodded forlornly.

'I've only told him he can't come unless he gives Tip the night off. Off you go, Lou. I'll send a cab at midnight.'

As usual Ed confused her. Against her better judgment she allowed herself to be charmed by his wit and beguiled by his stories. He could make her laugh with the same ease with which he could mobilise fury, and it wasn't until he had despatched his driver to fetch Louise that Serena realised that not once had he treated her as anything more than an interesting companion.

In turn she made him chuckle with a wicked impersonation of the agents vying with each other to get their footballers top of her bill and found herself confiding in him more than she had intended.

'Thing is, I've got to find a proper star by the middle of next week, otherwise we've got to keep the ticket price down. A major name and we could double it. I've learned just how tough fund-raising really is,' she grimaced. 'I didn't know the half of it before.'

He looked at her with a careful expression. 'Big miss, eh?'

'Miss?' She looked up, surprised. 'Oddly enough, no. I wouldn't want to go back to that kind of fund-raising. I did it—' She stopped. 'I did it,' she took a deep breath, 'because I lost a child and she might not have died if there had been a prem baby unit there waiting. When I lost my daughter I didn't meet any women who could say, "I know what you're going through." I just contained my grief.'

Ed was sitting very still; his eyes never left her face.

'And now?'

Serena tried to smile and failed. 'I meet single mothers all the time.'

'I meant about your child.'

Ed did this to her. She told him things she never meant to tell anyone. He took her hand. 'Tell me about her. What was her name?'

For a long, long moment she felt his gaze. 'Anna,' she said finally. 'Just Anna. I had her for two days and a part of me has never recovered. When I dream, she's often there. Which is why I truly believe Stephen is alive. If he wasn't he would be in my dreams too. And he never is.'

She realised he was still holding her hand. 'Sorry,' she gave him a bleak smile. 'You don't want to hear this.'

'I wouldn't have asked if I didn't. Tell me about Stephen. Would you have him back?'

'Back?' She swallowed hard. 'Of course. Why not? I mean where else would he go? He would need me.'

'So we'll take that as not sure?'

'We'll take it that I am sure,' she contradicted him. 'He's my husband.'

'That's not a reason. Still in love with him? That's got to be the only reason. Are you?'

Silence lay between them.

Ed finally broke it. 'You've got to confront it some time. How would he feel about, say, the shrink?'

'I'll deal with that.' Her defiance clearly didn't impress him.

'Thought as much. Mr OK for Now, as Louise would say.'

'Ed, if you're going to mock Alex, please stop,' she said impatiently.

'I'm not interested in him. Not any more. If he was important you wouldn't be sitting here entertaining me. He'd be here too.'

'As a matter of fact he would have been, but Gilly Martindale had a spare ticket for the National tonight and she knows Alex adores Brecht, so he's gone with her and it was my suggestion. Satisfied?'

'Don't avoid the issue. Would Stephen be happy for you to entertain another bloke while he was sidelined for the night?'

'Stop it, Ed,' she warned. 'I would never be disloyal to Stephen. Whatever he's done, for whatever reason he's remained in hiding, he knows I will never turn away from him.'

He listened dispassionately. 'He doesn't deserve your loyalty. Don't you ever want a life of your own?' He was beginning to get angry. A familiar surge of panic started to eat away in her chest. She wanted him to stop, but the energy she needed to stop him eluded her.

'You live for a day you have no idea will ever come,' he persisted, 'and if it does, you're expecting the same man to come back. If I cared less about you I would say less. But I do care what happens to you. Oh, for Christ's sake,' he cut across her as she looked up startled, 'it's obvious I do. So what are you going to do? Three years, Serena, that's what it's been, and you're still planning your future with him in it. And you know why? Because you can't face the truth.'

'I don't want to hear.' She pushed her chair back and walked away from him. 'Stop it. You don't know the truth,' she cried.

'Tell me.' He swung her round and gave her a slight shake. 'Go on, tell me what the truth is? I'm interested.'

She could hear the car bringing Louise home drawing up.

'The truth,' she said dully, 'is that until I've seen him, spoken to him, there is no future for me.'

Louise could be heard in the hall. 'Wonderful,' Ed muttered, dropping his hands from her shoulders. 'Hi, beautiful, how did it go?'

Halfway through the following Wednesday morning, a man announcing himself as the agent for the American movie star Brett Bruce asked to be put through to her. Twenty minutes later Serena raced along the corridor and burst in on Gilly whooping. 'I've got a star! You won't believe it. Brett Bruce.'

'Get her a chair,' Gilly murmured to her secretary, 'she's hallucinating. You've got Brett Bruce?' she asked in the manner of one humouring a lunatic. 'In what way, exactly?'

'The concert. He's agreed to be host. We've cracked it. I can't believe it. He's here for the premiere of his film, and Ed—that's Ed Stein, a friend of mine—asked him if he would stay on for a couple of days and do it and he's said he would. I didn't even know he knew him. And I'm going to faint with happiness.'

'Are you a fan?' Gilly asked, watching Serena stride around her office.

'A fan? Not until this moment. Do you know what this means? It means double the price of the ticket.'

'Good grief,' Gilly was as excited as Serena. 'Then I'm a fan, too.'

The only difficulty she faced was to call Ed to thank him. Mercifully he was in Paris so she wrote him a note instead.

The radio-station team screamed with relief and braced themselves to deal with enquiries for tickets. Ed's secretary called Serena and said Ed had bought up two boxes and needed tickets for such an array of dazzling names Serena felt weak. Rock stars, boxers, a string of models who graced the pages of the glossies, a dozen soap stars. Ed's secretary said he hoped Serena would join him in his box because he might need help entertaining Brett's companion.

'Of course,' she agreed instantly. 'Tell him I'd love to. Only I might have to duck in and out if there are any problems.'

It was, Gilly breathed, their finest hour. Long before the show started, the road was packed with fans waiting for a glimpse of Brett Bruce and the tickets could have been sold twice over. A parade of exotically dressed stars drew cheers and screams from the crowd as they alighted from overstretched limos, surrounded by burly minders in the flashiest and most vulgar display of celebrity Serena had ever witnessed. Serena loved every last, glittering, spellbinding moment of it. Louise and Harry arrived with their friends half an hour before the curtain went up, with a heavily pregnant Stacey in tow and all the hostesses from Frobisher's. Two of the hostesses were arm in arm with Harry and his friend, while Daphy and Louise forgot they were cool dudes as their eyes flew from one famous face to another. She wanted to take them to their seats, but Harry wouldn't permit it.

'I know where to go,' he insisted. 'They're all going to follow me.'

She thought she would cry. 'Good for you, my angel,' she whispered. 'See you afterwards.'

The tricky question of Alex and Ed being present together had been solved by her suggesting that Alex escort Gilly, with whom he was now on good terms. They both hugged her and said they would see her after the show.

George Kincaid greeted Serena as though they had never had an estrangement. And she didn't mind. He was being wonderful with Stacey, and his knighthood was virtually assured now that he had swung his weight behind penniless mothers and the Stella Bonner Centre.

Brett Bruce arrived with Mike Griffith and a contingent of bodyguards. Brett was an absolute sweetheart. His companion, a real babe whose fame almost matched his, moulded her perfectly honed body to his side, clutched his hand and replied coyly to shouted enquiries that they hadn't discussed marriage. Yet.

When they were introduced, Brett pulled Serena to him, kissed her full on the mouth and told her Ed was a shit keeping her in London.

'Really?' she gasped, staggering back. 'How kind.'

And then they were on. From the wings she watched nervously, praying she would remember her short speech when summoned on stage. Brett strolled out, unshaven, jeans and a Versace jacket swinging open to reveal a tight black T-shirt, the audience erupting as he stood, arms outstretched, revelling in the attention. For a few minutes he warmed them up, cracking jokes and proving why he was a star.

And then over the speakers she heard her name. A blur of lights, she walked forward, no longer worried that she might trip over in her heels, that the dark blue satin trousers might split, or about the amount of cleavage her jacket revealed.

With a cheery wave to the audience, who were clapping her arrival, she was kissed by Brett, who stood with his arm draped round her as she spoke. Somehow she got through her five minutes about the charity and how grateful they all were for everybody's support. She paid a fulsome tribute to Gilly, whose vision and commitment had been the inspiration for the centre, along with special thanks to Metro Radio, the football clubs who had so generously released their stars, and most of all to Ed Stein for his help. She finished with the fervent wish that the night would be a success and that she would wake up on Christmas morning and find Brett Bruce in her stocking.

To an appreciative gale of laughter she walked off and found she was trembling from head to foot. She was immediately wrapped in a bear hug by Ed, who was waiting for her in the wings.

'C'mon star,' he teased, kissing her gently on the mouth. 'There's a box full of people waiting to meet you. You were stunning.'

Next morning the papers carried pictures of Brett and his babe and some even got the name of the centre right. The amount of money raised looked staggering.

Louise and Harry, who had been allowed to attend the after-show party for an hour and been driven home by Ed's driver, were still in their rooms. Stacey, who had gone straight home after the show, left a note for Serena saying she had gone to spend the day with a friend and would be back by supper. Her answering machine, when Serena finally felt equal to handling the messages, contained a stream of calls congratulating her. Serena sat in the kitchen and gingerly felt her head.

Black coffee, she decided. It was no use pretending any more. Nor could she, since she had fallen asleep with no other thought and woken shortly after nine knowing one thing. Ed was important. How important was something else. She wanted the dazzle, the euphoria of the occasion to wear off, normality to resume.

It was not as though Ed had hovered over her all night. All she knew was that she would find herself searching the room till she found him and when she did he would smile, maybe raise his glass and go on talking to whoever was claiming his attention. She watched him work the room, lowering his head to catch what someone was saying, throwing a joking remark over his shoulder to someone passing behind him.

When she was finally persuaded to sit down to eat by Melanie and Charles she agreed, but could touch nothing until Ed slipped into the chair next to her telling her simply to eat. This she obediently did, while he entertained Charles and Ryland Holt to what Brett's shopping list had included in the deal.

At this point Ed's arm was resting lightly round Serena's shoulders. She was so conscious of it she just wanted to lean back and never get up again. Instead, he gave her shoulders a squeeze, whispered into her hair that he'd be back and strolled off to talk to a captain of industry.

When the room started to empty out around three in the morning, Charles found Ed to say they were leaving, taking Serena with them if that was OK. Ed excused himself to the group he was talking to and came over to where Serena was leaning, exhausted, against the doorway.

'Poor baby,' he smiled down at her, stroking her cheek. 'Of course you must go. Charles, I can always get Bob to drop Serena.'

'No trouble,' Charles shook his head. 'Wonderful night. We must see more of you. Melanie'—he turned to his wife—'arrange for Ed and Serena to come over. Can't think why you haven't.'

Serena wanted the ground to open. Ed grinned. 'Neither can I,' he said, giving Melanie a hug. 'And as for you'—he turned to Serena, still standing leaning weakly against the wall, and laughed down at her— 'Oh God, just look at her, nearly asleep. Charles, take the star home. Call you tomorrow,' he said, pulling her to him and kissing the side of her head. She then found herself being taken away by her oldest and best friends and in the whole of her life she had never wanted anything less.

Hopeless. What was she thinking of? She was still sitting there when the doorbell rang. Yawning, she opened the door.

For a moment she couldn't make sense of her visitor.

'Why, Don,' she managed at last. 'Come in.'

She was vaguely aware of a police car outside and that another man was with him.

A cold stab of fear went through her. Her eyes flew to his. She could feel her heart beating painfully against her chest. He took the door from her hand and gently closed it. 'I'm sorry, Serena.' Inspector Don Trewless placed a hand on her shoulder. 'It's over.'

He had chosen Marseilles because it was big enough to hide in and not, he had decided, an obvious place to search for a runaway banker. Hair dyed grey, his nose reshaped, it was a disguise that had made instant recognition almost impossible. That and his new occupation as a writer.

A bank account established several years before under the name he had assumed, John Mallory, had been pumped up periodically with cash injections from a bank in Bucharest. His work, allegedly as a specialist in East European history, the only cover he needed.

Don told her not to expect much from him. 'He'll be brought back tonight. Held on remand in custody at the nick and then on Monday morning he'll appear before magistrates at Bow Street and be sent on remand to Wandsworth, until a trial can be fixed.'

Prison. Stephen, so meticulous, so energetic, so flawed, in prison. She pressed her hand against her mouth to stop the scream rising up from the pit of her stomach. 'How?' she asked.

'Speeding.'

Of course, she thought dully. Always in a hurry.

'When they checked his licence, the name John Mallory didn't match with anyone granted residential status. Someone over there became suspicious about his source of income. Ran a check on the books he said he was writing. None existed. After that it was easy. They called us about a month ago—'

'A month ago?' Her mind raced, what had she been doing? And last night when he was arrested she was . . . she stopped. It didn't bear thinking about. 'You've known for a month?'

He nodded. She looked away. There was no need to ask why she hadn't been told.

'They'll let you see him tomorrow,' he went on.

'Has he,' she stopped and took a deep breath, 'has he asked for me?'

'Yes. He said for you to get Andrew Beresford to act for him.'

Her face wore a dazed look. 'Is that all?'

Don's face remained impassive. 'All that I've been told. I expect he has said more,' he comforted her. 'They just haven't passed it on. And of course getting him a lawyer is important.'

'Yes, of course. What shall I do? I'm sorry, I can't seem to think.'

'Call the lawyer and get the children out of here,' he advised. 'The press will know in an hour or so. No way we can stop them.'

A bewildered Harry and Louise were roused from their beds, the excitement of the night before forgotten in the haste to get them away. Margot was phoned and calmly agreed to be there in the early evening. Melanie responded by screeching to a halt outside Foster Street less than an hour later. Stacey was urgently contacted by phone at her friend's and ordered to stay there.

By four, when the house was besieged, Harry and Louise were already at Melanie's weekend cottage in the Cotswolds and a policeman had been posted outside the door to deal with the clamour. Andrew Beresford was due back from New York on Sunday night. He would call her then. Alex and Gilly had arrived together and pleaded to be allowed to stay, but Serena refused. It was only later that it occurred to her that no one had phoned them. They must have been coming to see her anyway.

'My mother's coming.' Serena tried to concentrate, just wishing they would go. 'She's the best person. Besides, I don't want you involved in this. You have your own lives.'

Alex hesitated, consternation written all over his face.

At this point Don Trewless stepped in. 'It might be better, sir, if you go. Serena and I know each other well. We'll take care of her.'

A further interruption was caused by Betty and Les Plaxton pitching up in the kitchen. This led to a mini security alert when they were briefly mistaken for the press. Seeing the front was impenetrable, they had simply scaled the back wall and offered the services of a couple of Les's friends to get her to a safe house. Serena told them it would be unnecessary.

'Chin up, love,' Betty whispered, casting a scathing look at the assembled police officers. 'You know where we are,' she added, giving her a significant look. 'Just yell.' And then, in a moment of uncustomary solidarity, they both hugged her.

Serena drew the blinds. The nightmare had resumed. Flashbulbs exploded as anyone left her house, the whole road turned out to watch the amazing sight of the quiet and generally liked Mrs Carmichael being interviewed by the police. 'Arrested, is she?' asked the woman who lived on the other side of Betty Plaxton.

'Gawd almighty, you kidding?' retorted Betty, who had found it impossible to remain indoors. 'Hadn't a clue, poor cow. Always a bit'— she waggled her hands indicating a certain fragility—'you know, bit innocent about the world.'

'Innocent?' screamed Cheryl from the back of the crowd, hungrily devouring the scene in front of her. 'I told you,' Cheryl's piercing voice penetrated the crowd of newsmen. 'I said she was a tart. None of you would listen. "Ere,' she protested, as Don Trewless's assistant pushed his way through the crowd and took her arm, drawing her clear of the mob. Whatever he said made her flush and look defiant. He waited while she returned to her own home without saying another word.

'Stupid bitch,' he murmured, rejoining Don Trewless. Don nodded. He'd grown fond of Serena, even if he felt exasperated by her loyalty to a man who was being escorted to England after three years on the run.

His assistant jerked his head towards the closed door. 'Who's the big fella, just gone in?'

Don squinted at the darkening December sky. 'Ed Stein. She used to work for him.'

'Boyfriend?'

Don shook his head. 'Don't think so. Chalk and cheese.'

Inside the house, Serena faced Ed.

'You shouldn't have come.' Her voice was as stiff as her body. Her hair was pulled back from her face. At some point she must have got dressed, but her efforts had stopped when it came to applying make-up. Her face was pale, her lips colourless. Nervously she pulled at the neck of her black roll-top sweater.

'And done what instead?' Ed demanded. He leaned against the sink, his hands dug deep into his pockets. 'Read about it in the papers? Why didn't you call me? I had to read it on Ceefax.'

'Please,' she whispered, 'not now. Why would I involve you . . . I mean anyone . . . in this mess?'

'Off the top of my head,' he replied furiously, 'because maybe your fucking independence is a pain in the arse and this might just be the moment when you let someone else into your life to help.'

'I can't.' She sagged down into a chair. 'And I have to do this on my own. This . . . ' A lead weight was resting on her eyes. 'This is between me and Stephen. It always was, you see. He needs me.'

'Is that what you think, what you really want?' he asked. His face was drawn and he looked defeated.

'Yes,' she whispered. 'I've always known it would come to this.'

After a long silence she heard him say, 'I see. Well, you know where to find me. Take care.' And he was gone.

The shock was Stephen's hair. Almost silver. And his nose. It was straighter, weakening his face, robbing it of the strength she was so used to seeing there. Maybe she would have had to look closely to make sure it was him, but she would have known the eyes, the mouth, the way he frowned and the way he ran his hand impatiently through his hair. All of it would have betrayed him. But only to her.

Two prison officers stood at the back of the interview room. Stephen was sitting at a plain, square table. He rose unsteadily to his feet when she was ushered in. He was wearing jeans and a leather jacket and Serena had never known him to wear such clothes. Don Trewless, who had accompanied her, walked to the window and turned his back. She went forward, the tears already flowing down her cheeks.

'Stephen.' Her voice was hoarse. Her arms reached out for him. 'Oh my God, Stephen. Are you all right?'

They clung together, Serena weeping uncontrollably, incoherent half-questions tumbling from her, until Stephen untangled her arms from his neck and urged her to sit down.

'Don't,' he said urgently. 'Don't cry. It won't help me.'

She blew her nose and began to apologise. 'No, of course not, but oh, Stephen, why? Tell me, oh God help me, I can't think straight. Say something, tell me.'

'I will, I will,' he promised, taking her hands and pushing her into the seat opposite. 'Listen,' he threw a watchful glance at Don and lowered his voice, 'Andrew Beresford. Where is he? Is he coming?'

'Andrew?' she repeated blankly. 'Yes. He's back from the States tonight. He'll be in court in the morning.'

'Serena. Darling.' He gripped her hands. 'We'll talk and you can tell me everything, but first I have to have Andrew on my case. I must see him the minute he gets back. You'll arrange that, won't you?'

She blinked. 'I already have.' She struggled to focus on what he was saying. It was a litany of instructions on what she should do. Exhausted and drained by lack of sleep, she could not stop the tears flowing. 'Please,' he urged her, 'please try to be calm. Have you any idea what it's been like for me?'

'No. I mean yes. We were the same, the children. Oh God, Stephen, the children—'

'But you were here,' he broke in. 'With them. Not like me. Living in a different country. You didn't have to hide, change your identity.'

'Why didn't you get in touch?'

'In touch?' He glanced behind him. He looked uneasily at her. 'How? Without revealing where I was?'

The tissue she was holding was damp and shredded. 'Why?' She tried to control her voice. 'Why did you do it? We were happy, weren't we? I've been nearly demented trying to think why.'

'Why?' He let go of her hands and threw his head back in such a gesture of despair that her heart was wrung for him.

'I was sick of working,' he told her bitterly. 'Sick of being denied what should have been mine. No one ever thought I was quite good enough on my own. My father saw to that. Gambling everything away, not making a future for me.'

Serena glanced nervously over at Don Trewless.

'Stephen,' she interrupted. 'I'll hear this another time.'

'Another time.' He gave a derisive laugh. 'That's all Malcolm ever said when I tried to talk to him. "Another time, Stephen", "Later old boy". Me? The star negotiator, the trouble-shooter. Anything I took they owed me. Compensation if you like. Yes, that's all it was. And I deserved every penny. And then I discovered that Rupert was lined up for New York, not me. Rupert was going to get my reward.'

It was the first she'd heard about New York.

'I was going to surprise you,' he muttered, 'when I'd got it.'

'Just drop everything and go?' Her voice was almost inaudible. He wasn't listening.

'And it would have been OK if Rupert hadn't fucked up one of the accounts and let them check it without asking me. I knew then it was time to go.'

'And you never told me? Not even a note.' The sobs rose to her throat. 'Why didn't you involve me? Didn't you think about my terror?' She pressed her fist into her chest. 'My shock? Not knowing whether you were alive or dead.'

'Involve you?' He replied with such vehemence that Don Trewless looked round. He lowered his voice. 'Try and understand,' he urged. 'There wasn't time. I had at most three days to clear out before they closed in. I thought once I was safe I might find a way.'

Serena listened in shocked silence. *Three days.*

The door behind him opened. Don indicated it was time to go.

She reached over and held him. As she did so he tipped her face up to his. 'There's my girl. As beautiful as ever. I knew you'd be all right. I knew you'd be there for me.'

She said nothing, just nodded. 'I won't be in court tomorrow,' she said. 'But that doesn't mean I don't want to be. It's just that we, that is, Don, has said it will simply turn into a bunfight.'

A look of alarm leapt to his face. 'Don't listen to him.' He bent his head to whisper. 'Andrew will want you there. Publicly supporting me.'

She released him and walked to the door.

'Andrew,' he reminded her eagerly. 'He'll get me out of here. Don't worry about money. Call Richard—or better still Bill Hooper. They'll stand bail. They owe me.'

It was unbearable. She turned and silently searched his face. Don was holding the door. She signalled to him to give her just a few moments and went back to where Stephen was standing.

'You left me penniless and virtually friendless.' She spoke as calmly as she could. 'No one would touch me. I have lived in virtual poverty for three years. You must have known if you read English newspapers.'

The colour in his face whitened under the tan. 'Penniless? I thought that was all bluff to make me turn myself in. No one? Surely Richard—'

'After I refused to go to bed with him I never saw Richard again.' Her voice was blunt. 'You may have led a lonely but comfortable existence, Stephen, but I led one in near destitution and terror. You haven't even asked where I'm living—'

'Richard did what?' His voice was incredulous. 'But you're OK now.' It was a statement. 'What about Charles? He must have helped. There you are,' he went on eagerly when she nodded, 'Charles will help.'

It was hopeless. He was not even on nodding terms with reality. Shock, of course. From somewhere she mustered a smile. 'I'll do my best.' Don stood aside as she left.

The line of women and children ahead of her was no comfort to Serena as she waited with Harry and Louise for admittance to the visiting room. A dank, sickly smell assailed them as they finally entered the prison remand wing where Stephen was awaiting his trial.

Serena had tried to prepare Harry and Louise for how Stephen had changed. On Alex's advice she had sat them down and described the rituals of prison life, the searches, the rules, and the noise, but she knew that nothing could prepare them for what lay ahead.

'Let them do the talking,' Alex urged. 'They need answers to questions, they need to know he still loves them.'

Before they reached the door leading into the inner courtyard of the prison she could see Harry was struggling not to cry. Louise was more stoic. Catching Serena's anxious eye she grinned bravely. 'Daphy and

A KEPT WOMAN

Damon will think this is really cool. Won't they, Harry?'

For once Serena made no attempt to stop her. Whatever was going to get Louise through the next half-hour was to be welcomed. Harry's face was ashen as Louise leaned across to whisper in his ear. It brought a watery smile to his face. Louise slipped round to his other side and held his hand. 'OK, bruv,' she said in a cockney accent, 'let's do it.' In that moment Serena had never loved her more.

The crowd surged forward across the yard to a small door set in the wall on the far side. Then along a wide corridor to double doors at the end, guarded on both sides by prison officers, their arms folded across navy blue jerseys. It opened out onto a vast room dotted with tables and chairs. She saw Stephen at the back of the room. 'There.' She touched Louise's shoulder, guiding her to look in the right direction.

She led the way, holding Harry's hand. She greeted Stephen with a kiss and then stood aside.

'Hey,' Stephen's voice cracked. 'Look who's here.'

Awkwardly they allowed themselves to be hugged, but it was, she could see, one-way. To his credit, Stephen did his best, but his questions were contrived and they didn't know what to say to him. Anxiously they glanced from one parent to the other for guidance, and in the end Serena, against all Alex's advice, stepped in and filled what was the longest half-hour she had ever spent, in talking and sometimes answering for them to take the weight from her poor children.

And then it was over. Once again they were hugged. Serena told them to wait for her by the door, which they did, trying not to show their relief. When they were out of earshot, she turned to Stephen. 'I can't do that to them again. They've got used to life without you; they must have time to get used to having you back. You do understand?'

'Are you going to stop them coming here?' he asked. His hands were on his hips. He was making no attempt to hold her.

'No, of course not. I will just let them come when they want. Is that OK with you?'

Without speaking he nodded. 'It's been tough on you,' he said. 'Tough on them. Harry's grown, hasn't he? I'm not sure I would have recognised Louise, she looks so grown-up.'

'No,' she said quietly. 'Three years is a long time in their lives, Stephen. Andrew said he's doing what you asked. Ring if you need to talk. Here.' She shovelled a handful of phone cards into his hands. 'He said you wanted these.'

He looked down at them and slowly raised his eyes to hers. 'You're not going to abandon me?' he asked. 'You wouldn't do that, would you?'

'No,' she answered. 'I won't abandon you. You looked after me for so long. Now it's my turn to care for you.'

Relief flooded his face. They kissed. It was not passionate, nor was it the kiss of a man who had been celibate for three years. But then, she acknowledged, neither had she.

Chapter Twelve

~

STEPHEN ADMITTED his adultery first. 'It was nothing,' he insisted. 'Just sheer human comfort. Nothing special. Anyway,' he said, gazing earnestly into her eyes, 'no one could take your place.'

She couldn't look at him. It was her own fault she had made him tell her. And now she'd heard what she wanted to hear and it had solved nothing. 'I understand.' She reached across the table and covered his hand with her own. He looked up and smiled eagerly at her.

'You do, don't you? I knew once the shock had worn off you would be more understanding. You always were. And you?' He levelled his gaze at her. 'Have you met anyone?'

'If you mean'—she had rehearsed what she would say—'have I slept with anyone? Yes. One person. Only in this last year. A dear man, he was good to me and Harry. Harry needed a lot of help.'

She waited, expecting pain to show in his eyes. In the brief moment before he dropped his head it was hard to tell.

'Stephen?' she whispered urgently. 'Please, look at me. I don't want to hurt you. Never did. I was just lonely.'

He lifted his head and looked at her. Finally he reached over and took her hand. 'I don't want to imagine you with anyone else. Is it still going on?' He was watching her carefully.

It was unbearable. 'No. Oh no,' she assured him. 'Not for ages.'

It was almost true. Alex had told her about Gilly and his feelings for her. 'I didn't want you to think my feelings for Gilly had been going on for longer than you imagined,' he said, 'because that would have meant my time with you was a lie. I wanted you to know quickly.'

'So, no one else? And now it's over?' Stephen was asking.

She nodded. 'Don't let's talk about this any more,' she begged. 'No

one in either of our lives. Let's start again. It would never have happened,' she talked rapidly, 'if you hadn't done all this. I never looked at
anyone else in the whole of our marriage and then not for two years.
Please? Stephen?'

'I can't pretend it doesn't hurt,' he said, passing a hand across his eyes,
'but I do understand. Or at least'—he gave her a half-smile—'I'll try.'

It was like talking to someone she'd just met. Unreal because it was
Stephen who knew her so intimately, and here they were confessing
adultery to each other when they had scorned such behaviour in other
couples. 'I understand so easily how it happens,' she insisted, 'so please
try to do the same for me. I'm only human after all.' The clock showed
she had ten minutes left. 'Stephen. Listen. This is so much more important. I want to talk to you about the trial.'

Briefly she outlined how she was going to afford to pay for his
defence, describing the strategy she had agreed with Andrew.

'I think that's it.' She frowned over the file she was reading from.
'Now, is there anything you want? Anything I can do?'

He looked at her with narrowed eyes. 'You've changed,' he said.

'Of course I have.' She returned the papers to her bag. She would not
add to his misery with recriminations. 'Just as well,' she added in a
softer, more rallying voice. 'Someone's got to get you out of here.'

Stacey's baby daughter—to be called Clementine after her grandmother—was delivered safely and on time in the Wendover Wing one
week before Christmas. On the same day, Serena heard that Edith had
died. She was to be buried, at her own wish, alongside her husband
who had died in the war.

The funeral was attended by eight people. Serena sat with Matron
and the care worker, Carol, who had befriended Edith. Of the dreaded
daughter-in-law there was no sign, but Edith's solicitor, Bernard Atkins,
a jolly young man in his thirties, had made the journey from Hove and
was going to give Mrs Harding and Carol a lift back. There was also an
elderly couple, who had lived next door to Edith for years.

The service over, they sang 'Jerusalem' as the pallbearers carried the
coffin outside. They waited while the elderly couple left the pew and
walked, heads bowed, after the coffin.

At the back of the chapel she saw Ed. Wally was with him. They came
forward almost instantly and greeted the old couple, who appeared to
know them both well, and talked quietly together as they walked out
into the cold winter sunshine. The rest of them followed and stood at a
little distance while the priest shook hands with Ed and Wally. At last

aware that he was being watched with curiosity by three of the onlookers and consternation by the fourth, Ed walked to the rest of the group.

He was bareheaded and without a coat. His only concession to the biting wind was a cashmere scarf wound round his neck. 'Hi,' he nodded to her. 'Bill and Poppy,' he indicated the elderly couple, 'knew Lily as well. Wally grew up with their son.'

'Of course.' Serena nodded to Wally, who had raised his hand in a half wave. She found it difficult to speak and hastily took refuge in introductions. 'Mrs Harding,' she managed at last, 'have you met Ed Stein? And this is Carol who was so kind to Edith. And Bernard Atkins you know.'

At that moment the priest asked them to follow him for the burial, so Serena was spared the necessity for further talk. She shivered as Edith's coffin was lowered into the ground. She felt a slight movement beside her and then a warm scarf was wrapped round her neck. A fleeting look passed between them and then she followed Ed's lead and joined in the Lord's Prayer.

When it was over, Bill and Poppy insisted they all come back to their house for a drink to cheer Edith on her way. It was the last thing Serena wanted, but she went as a mark of respect, driving her car behind Ed's, who had ushered the couple into the back with him and Wally.

There was barely space for them all in the living room. Poppy handed round plates of sausage rolls and looked anxiously after her guests. Ed looked perfectly at home, laughing and reminiscing with Bill and Wally, pouring beer from a can into a tall glass. Poppy gazed fondly at him.

'He's always been a one,' she confided to Serena. 'If he hadn't been carted off to Australia, Gawd knows where he'd have ended up.' She dropped her voice. 'Now don't you worry, dear, you being here with him won't get out. Not the kind of thing you want to get back to the old man in chokey, is it? Oh dear. Something gone down the wrong way, has it?'

After the second drink, and feeling her stomach beginning to revolt against a lack of food, she took her leave and the other guests took their cue from her.

'OK to drive?' Ed asked when they were standing outside.

'I'm going to walk,' she explained. 'I think the sherry's having an effect. It's not far. But thank you. How . . . how are you?' She had studiously avoided him in Poppy's tiny sitting room, but with the benefit of time to recover her wits and a couple of drinks, she was feeling braver.

'I've known better times,' he replied, squinting up at the sky. 'You?'

'Oh, you know. Surviving.'

For a moment he looked along the narrow road with its flat-fronted houses and small gardens and then turned away and called to his driver.

'Bob? Take Serena's keys. Drive her car to Foster Street. Wally, go with him and get a cab back. I'll drive myself.'

They drove in near silence to Hans Crescent. Once there, he rang through to his housekeeper and told her he had a guest for lunch, ignoring Serena's insistence that she wasn't hungry. A drink would be fine. He looked a bit doubtful and then shrugged when she insisted.

'When's the trial?' he asked, handing her a vodka with a generous measure of tonic and splashing whisky into a tumbler for himself.

'Beginning of March.' She sat down, still with her coat on. 'He's got no option but to plead guilty. Temporary mental instability is his best chance.'

'And then what?'

'Then? Oh God, I don't know,' she said wearily. 'I can't bear to think of him in that place.'

Ed remained unmoved. 'I was talking about you.'

'Me? It depends on where Stephen is sent. I don't see how I can continue with Gilly if he's stuck miles away from London. When I know, I'll work out how to move nearer to him and get a job somehow.'

'What about the children?'

'Yes. That's a problem. But they'll have to come with me.'

'Perhaps my memory is playing up, but wasn't there something you told me the night of the concert, that Gilly had recommended to the trustees that you go on the board? It seemed to grab you at the time.'

She nodded sadly, holding out her glass for him to refill. 'Yes.' She gave herself a shake and sat more upright. 'But I don't see that being possible. I'm just grateful Gilly didn't tell me to sling my hook when all this erupted.'

'Not when she's nabbed the boyfriend?'

'That's unfair,' she flashed back. 'These things happen. Besides, Alex and I always knew we had no future together.'

'Or with anyone until that fucking crook tells you that you can. Once again, you're all going to dance to the tune of Stephen, bloody bent Stephen. Give me strength.'

It occurred to her that she should just walk out, but the effects of the drink and lack of food prevented her. No one understood. It was suddenly vital that she made him. Without asking, she pushed herself out of her chair and poured another shot of vodka into her glass.

'I don't think that's a good idea,' Ed warned, indicating the bottle she was holding.

'Well, I think it's a brilliant one,' she snapped back, tossing half the drink down her throat and leaning on the back of the chair. 'What none of you understand is that'—she groped for the right words—'is that Stephen looked after me for fifteen years.' She took another gulp of her drink. 'I wanted for nothing and I gave nothing in return. Didn't,' she waved him aside, thinking he was disagreeing. 'Took everything and now'—she took a deep breath, wondering why the curtains were weaving around like that—'and now I'm going to look after him.'

While she was talking he had quietly pressed a bell behind him. 'Black coffee,' he mouthed, as Wally took in the scene. 'In the guest room.' Wally tapped the side of his nose.

Serena woke lying in the centre of a large bed in a room that was unfamiliar if extremely comfortable. The roof of her mouth appeared to be filled with sawdust, small red-hot daggers pricked at the back of her eyes and she had a raging thirst.

At first she couldn't move her legs until she realised there was a light rug over them. Cautiously she felt her feet. Her shoes were gone and a careful investigation showed that so too was her jacket.

Carefully she eased herself onto her side, giving a slight groan as the movement sent shock waves through her head. In front of the windows she could see the outline of a figure, feet up on a chaise longue and reading a newspaper.

The movement attracted Ed's attention. He swung his legs to the floor and strolled over to the bed. 'I hope you've got a hangover,' he said, to the welcome sound of water being poured into a glass. 'You deserve it.'

She waved feebly in his direction, taking the glass he was holding out. 'Don't,' she said. 'I feel like death. What's the time?'

'Nearly five.'

'I've got to get home.' She inched her way to the side of the bed and swung her legs over the side. 'Stacey's coming home with the baby. My mother will be frantic.'

'No, she won't. I told her you were with me.'

'Sorry, Ed,' she croaked. 'What a mess I am. Jesus, my head. I don't think I can drive. Could you possibly get a car?'

He sat down beside her, supporting her with his arm. 'All arranged. Can you concentrate just for a minute?'

She nodded. 'No longer,' she warned. 'I think someone's wrapped my brain in wet cotton wool.'

'You got drunk because you're unhappy.'

'Excuse me,' she contradicted, making an attempt to open one eye, 'I got drunk because I had too much to drink.'

'And what about the night of the concert? You drank then. Quite a lot of champagne as I recall. You didn't get drunk then. And you know why? Because you were happy.'

'How do you know? You hardly came near me. You treated me like . . . anyone else,' she accused him.

He looked thoughtfully at her. 'And you don't know why?'

'How should I know?' she said crossly.

'I'll tell you why.' He pulled her round to face him. 'I could have had you that night.'

'How delicately you put it,' she said, through gritted teeth.

'Oh, knock it off. You'd have been up for it. What I didn't want was you to do it out of gratitude. The same as you are now with him. What kind of man wants you there because you're grateful? Help him, but get on with your life. He hadn't planned to include you in his.'

Slowly she stood up, holding on to his shoulder to steady herself. 'It's not a matter of gratitude. This is a debt.'

He reached out and picked up the phone. 'OK. When you've paid it, let me know. Until then you're on your own. Wally? Tell Bob to bring the car round. Serena's leaving, even though she hasn't quite woken up.'

Clementine's presence in the house was felt by everyone, but most of all by Margot, who departed the day after Boxing Day, taking Serena and the children with her until New Year. Stacey's grandmother had finally persuaded her parents to visit. Serena insisted that they stay with them in Foster Street and remained to greet them before following Margot down the motorway to the tranquillity of her cottage in the country.

Serena tried not to be relieved that there was no visiting allowed for Stephen on Christmas Day. The weekend before she had taken the children, and felt helpless because they were not permitted to take any presents at all.

The visit went slowly but not painfully. Halfway through, as she encouraged them to tell him about their lives, it came to her that it wasn't shyness but boredom that was preventing an easy flow of exchange between the children and their father. He knew nothing of their friends—Tipper and Stacey had to be explained, Alex glided over and Ed spoken of with enthusiasm.

As they were leaving, Stephen pulled Serena back. 'I didn't realise,' he said in a low voice, 'you knew Ed Stein so well.'

She stiffened. 'I worked for him. I told you. He became a good friend.'

'Keen on you, is he?'

'Not that I know of,' she perjured herself, 'why?'

'He's got the right contacts. Money. He could help me. Oh look, I know it goes against the grain with you to consort with someone like him, but give it a go, eh? There's my girl.'

Stephen went down for five years. It would have been longer except the psychologist's report was able to reveal quite truthfully that his separation from reality had been instrumental in his behaviour, caused by stress and unreasonably long hours at the bank. The fact that he had lived so well in his exile was not in his favour. There was little evidence of financial or physical suffering or indeed any record of a doctor being consulted to deal with stress.

It was dreadful to see him being led away. She couldn't cry. The time for tears had long gone. The tan had faded, the dyed hair no longer necessary for a disguise made a sharp contrast between his dark, almost black roots and the skin now tinged with the prison pallor.

Andrew, who knew that the value of the Lowry painting Serena had given him three years before well outstripped his fee, represented him. It was impossible to get anyone to speak up for him.

Minnie made a flying visit from Lucca and only Serena, who had come to understand her, knew the toll it took to remain impassive when the verdict was announced. Both women were allowed to see him briefly in the cells before he was taken away to start his sentence.

It was clear he was shocked. To his mother he was almost a stranger. To Serena he spoke urgently and almost frantically.

'I'll make everything up to you. You must start an appeal. You, Serena, you must fight for me.'

'You know I will.' She could hardly speak. 'Take care.'

The sentence, thanks to the persuasive power of his lawyer, was reduced to three years. Stephen had been in jail for a month when Serena was finally allowed to see him. He had asked that she didn't come until he felt like seeing her. Of Ed there was no news. Tipper said after the trial he had disappeared and told Mike he was not to be disturbed.

'I've got some news,' Tipper told her, sitting in the kitchen. 'I'm going to take up Ed's offer of New York.'

Serena looked at him affectionately. 'I'm going to miss you, Tip,' she said. 'You've been so good to me.'

'Ah, get away with you,' he protested. But she could see he was pleased. 'And you?' he asked gently. 'What about you?'

She sighed. 'I'll move to Manchester when the kids break up from school in the summer. I can't ask Gilly to let me have two days off each

month like this, just to go and see him. If I'm nearer it won't be so difficult. Harry isn't so settled at school that a change will affect him, and
Louise—well, she'll get used to it.'

Tip scanned her face. 'Are you sure that's what you want?'

'No, it's not what I want. It's what I have to do. Stephen needs me.
Who else will visit or write to him? Look at him. He does deals on
phone cards like there's no tomorrow. That's all he ever asks for.'

'Who does he phone?'

'Me, Andrew, maybe Minnie—although I doubt that—he just needs
to keep in touch. And,' she went on, enumerating the reasons that she
counted like a mantra each night, 'Stacey says she doesn't mind coming
with me, which would be nice, and my mother is free to see us any time.
And besides, apart from my job there's nothing to keep me here any
more, not now that you're going. Is there?'

'No one?' he asked, bending his head to see into her face.

'No,' she said firmly. 'No one, Tip. Believe me. Absolutely no one.'

Alex pointed out, rather unnecessarily in her view, that three years was
a long time. 'You've all developed in such different directions,' he
explained. 'You've swapped roles. Stephen is now dependent on you.'

'The trouble is,' she frowned, 'he still seems so distant. Maybe he feels
hurt because I was unfaithful.'

'So was he,' Alex pointed out.

'I know, but not, not in the same way. No real relationship.'

'Maybe he couldn't risk it,' Alex went on. 'I mean, not get close to
anyone in case they told the police.'

She shook her head. 'No. Stephen was never a womaniser. I can't be
sure of many things but he was never *emotionally* unfaithful to me.'

Alex summoned the waiter for the bill. 'You look exhausted,' he said.
'I'll take you home. Gilly says you need a holiday. And she's right.'

'Well,' she drew a pattern on the cloth with her spoon, 'I could go to
Lucca with the children, but I also need to get Manchester sorted out.'

'How does Stephen feel about you moving to Manchester?' asked
Alex, as they walked towards his car.

'I don't know. Haven't told him.'

Alex raised his brows in surprise. 'How's Mr Stein these days?'

'Ed?' she asked carelessly. 'No idea. Don't see him.'

Stephen's reaction was not what she expected. 'Move?' he shouted.
Other visitors paused in their own conversations to look their way. 'I
mean,' he said, lowering his voice, 'what happens if I get moved?'

'That won't happen for at least two years,' she reminded him, stung by his lack of enthusiasm. She was feeling tired and depressed after a long journey in the sweltering heat of an August afternoon and did not, she told herself angrily, need to be greeted by such opposition.

In her sitting room there was a pile of work she would have to tackle when she got home, not to mention the presentation she had to prepare for a big fund-raising push in the autumn. She wanted to leave everything in place for her successor. All this way for half an hour with him in a room full of half-functioning people and misery at every table.

'And besides,' she went on, dragging her dwindling reserves of energy to the surface, 'it means the children will be able to see you more often. I can easily get a job. Remember, we're in this together.' She tried to sound robust, instead she sounded resentful.

Stephen glanced around and then leaned forward. 'Look. Darling. I live for your visits, you know that. But it isn't necessary for you to move. Why don't you apply for a longer visit once a month?'

'Not see you for a month?'

'Sweetheart, it's not for ever. I'm doing this for you. And besides, when I get out what on earth would I do in Manchester?'

She broke the news to Minnie over the phone that she was moving to Manchester to be nearer Stephen.

'And this is his idea or yours?' his mother asked.

'Mine. He was really very noble about it,' she told her. 'He was even prepared to sacrifice a visit so that I didn't have to travel up and down so much. But honestly, I couldn't do that to him. There isn't anyone else. It's so awful for him.'

'It isn't exactly paradise for you, my dear, either.'

A week after her conversation with Minnie she was sitting in her bathrobe, her hair washed and wrapped in a towel, when she heard an excited squeal from downstairs.

'Mum,' shrieked Louise, 'come quickly. Look who's here.'

In the living room, she blinked. Minnie stood hugging her grandchildren, beside a rather ancient suitcase. 'Minnie!' Serena exclaimed, joining in the embraces. 'What on earth brings you here?'

'Tea. Good strong English tea, and then I'll tell you all about it.'

'Why didn't you say? I could have met you at the airport.'

Minnie folded her long skirt neatly over her knees and sank gratefully into an armchair, Harry straddling one arm, Louise the other. They were truly now very fond of her.

'Because,' Minnie said, looking up at her daughter-in-law, 'I flew in early this morning. I've been to Manchester. To see Stephen.'

Long after the children had gone to bed, Minnie and Serena were still talking. As she watched her, Serena was struck by her physical resemblance to Stephen. Minnie was an extraordinary woman, but she had always seen her through Stephen's eyes and as a result had missed the value of her advice and the strength of her support.

'Don't go to Manchester,' Minnie told her. 'Get on with your life here. There was a time when Stephen would have taken precedence over you and the children, but not now. I've always cared about them, but I've now grown to love them. Many times I wanted to say to you, love him less, help him more. Now for your own sake, do it. He's his father all over again with more brains.

'This is so hard for me.' Minnie pressed her fingers against the bridge of her nose. 'And I'm tired so perhaps I'm not making any great sense. I do love him. How could I not? But I'm not blind to what's happening here. He doesn't see that you owe him very little. When he gets out, do you really believe you can live together and be happy?'

'Well, it will take some adjusting,' Serena began, feeling flustered, 'but if we both work at it . . .'

Minnie studied the contents of her cup, swirling it around in an absent little gesture. 'If you were still the same person I might agree with you. But you're not. What he saw in you was perfect breeding and he failed to see your strength. It was there all the time. Look around you. Look at the children. Who else but a woman with strength could have found the resources to have survived so well with everything against you? Could you really love him enough to let him take over once again?'

In the kitchen Serena could hear Stacey moving around preparing Clementine's late-night bottle. Harry's videos were splayed out across the floor and her own workload, stacked on two shelves, cleaved out of the bookcase. The idea of Stephen living in such a place, coping with a teenage son and a daughter who had learned to live without his approval, had learned to live without him at all, was difficult to imagine.

'Love isn't the answer. Not after a while,' Minnie said. 'Once, a long time ago, I loved too much as well. It wore me out. That's why when Wilfred was buried I went to Lucca and found myself. You can start again. Do it, my dearest girl. Do it.'

'I can't,' Serena whispered miserably. 'It would be the final betrayal.'

Minnie left three days later, not entirely optimistic that her visit had achieved much in the way of boosting a calmer future for them all.

Ed's phone call came as Serena arrived home the next evening.

After months of silence he simply said, 'I'm coming over.'

'No. Wait. Ed, please. It won't do any good. I'm moving.'

'Where?'

'To Manchester. To be near Stephen.'

'All the more reason to see you. Before you go.' There was a long pause. 'I've got to talk to you. Just once and then I'll stay out of your life. You owe me nothing. This is a request.'

Barely an hour later, she saw his car pull up. A near riot greeted him from Harry and Louise who berated him for his absence.

'Hi,' he greeted her over their heads. 'Listen, you guys, I've got some serious stuff to discuss with your mother. Let me just take a look at Clementine. Stacey? What are you feeding this child on? She's a cracker.'

Stacey beamed with pleasure. She cast a quick glance to where Serena was standing by the door, remaining mostly silent, and then back at Ed. 'I'm sure you want a drink and you two'—she turned to the children—'supper. Kitchen. Now.'

'But I want to talk to Ed,' Louise protested. 'Oh, OK,' she caved in, meeting a very pointed stare from Stacey. 'Yeah, sure. Harry? You heard what Stacey said.'

Alone they just nodded at each other.

'We could sit,' he suggested after a moment.

So they did. She poured him a drink. 'What is it, Ed? I know that look. What was it you wanted to ask me?'

'You can't imagine the pleasure of knowing you've studied me so closely. Sorry. This is serious. I want you to tell me straight. No messing about. No honourable stuff. Are you seriously planning to stick by this bloke?'

She nodded.

'What would it take to stop you?'

For one awful moment she thought he was going to suggest money, and then felt ashamed, knowing it would never occur to him.

'More than anyone can suggest,' she replied quietly. 'Oh, I don't know,' she shrugged when he persisted. 'That he no longer loved me in any way. Ed, this is a pointless conversation. Because he does.'

He shook his head. 'Maybe. What if there was someone else?'

She rose quickly to her feet. 'For heaven's sake, Ed. He told me about it. Now there isn't'—he couldn't look at him—'anyone in either of our lives. So that's that.'

She was staring out of the window. Behind her she heard the snap as his glass was put down. He came over to her and turned her round.

'I don't play games,' he reminded her, 'and I'm not playing one now.

Look at me, Serena. Tell me what you really feel. Tell me that you feel nothing for me and I'll go away. Tell me.'

'Don't, Ed,' she pleaded. 'Please don't.' She looked at him and there was something in his face that made her halt, made her want to unburden herself. 'All right, all right, all right,' she cried. 'I'm not in love with him any more. I haven't been for a long time.

'There,' she looked up defiantly. 'And it changes nothing. I could no more abandon him now than Harry or Louise. Call it what you like, duty, honour, affection—yes, now I come to think of it, affection for what we had. So,' she finished brightly, 'nothing's changed.'

He reached out and tipped her face towards him. 'Thank you,' he said softly. He leaned forward and very gently kissed her. An odd thing happened to her legs and she had to clutch his lapels. Her eyes were still closed when he pushed her carefully away from him.

'That was much harder to do than what I have to tell you,' he said, moving her hair away from her face. The base of his thumb was by the corner of her mouth. She felt absurdly weak.

'Tell me?' Her voice sounded like a croak. 'Of course,' she tried to recall why he was here, 'you wanted to tell me something.'

And he did. Gently and without preamble and without taking his eyes from her face he told her about Chantal and Stephen's two-year-old son, living in Marseilles. Through Wally he had heard that in prison Stephen was phoning France on a regular basis. When the trial was over and Serena was so determined to stand by Stephen, he thought he might as well take some time and find out about the man standing between him and, he smiled, a good time.

A son. Aged two. Ed watched her face, knowing what she was working out. 'It doesn't take a rocket scientist, my petal,' he interrupted. Her face was a mask.

'Three months after he left,' she faltered. 'He must have met her . . . did he know her,' she asked, the pain not quite kicking in. She knew it would. Later. 'I mean, know her before?'

'Seems not. I found her with the help of a couple of guys who do the odd private job for me. Most people, including the police, bought the story that she was a widow caring for her son by working for him. They didn't socialise much, her family are from Grasse, she had come down to the coast to work as a waitress and met Stephen. When he was arrested, she knew, I gather, that was the moment to pack up and go until he could send for her.'

Serena only half listened to the rest. Her mind had gone back to the day she had pleaded with Stephen to forgive her for her brief affair with

Alex and the guilt that had assailed her all the way home. There was no one, he'd said, no one but her.

'To be honest, for the first few months after he was arrested she did as she was told. Kept up the pretence to the police that she was his house-keeper and now that Stephen had been arrested she was going back to her parents. Only she didn't. She went into hiding.'

'But why?' Serena took the brandy he gave her. 'Why?'

'Because she loves him and did what he told her to do. Oh yes, she knew exactly who he was.'

'Why did he tell her to lie? What was the point?'

Ed gave a dry laugh. 'My flower. He knew if he was arrested, his best chance of being treated lightly was to present a tragic figure, separated from his wife and children. He assumed his friends would stick by him if he was still linked with you. They didn't. That was the shock. Hardly the moment to confess a second family was waiting for the word to join him. Would Andrew have acted for him without you? Of course not. What could a penniless French girl, no more than about twenty-five, do to help him? You held his future. And there's no doubt that with Andrew's resources behind him he got off bloody lightly.'

Her eyes were filled with horror. Nausea rose to the back of her throat. Hastily she gulped the brandy. 'His son? What will happen?'

'God knows. Chantal now wants to come to England but she says Stephen keeps saying not yet. She wants to be near him. And not out of duty, like you.' He leaned forward. 'She loves him. Actually'—He paused and looked down at his glass—'he said in time he would divorce you and marry her. Frankly she thinks that time has come.'

'Ed,' she touched his arm. 'Would you mind leaving me now? I need to think.'

'Sure?'

'Sure.' She swallowed hard. 'Ed . . .' she added. 'I'll call you.'

He hadn't heard. He was already out of the door.

He waited until she finished, his face expressionless.

'It was the only disguise I could think of,' he said when she finally came to a halt. 'They were looking for a single man, living alone. A man with a partner and a child was not so obvious.'

Disbelief gripped her. 'You *planned* this? Planned a family?'

'No. No. Not until I was on the boat going to France.'

Serena stifled a gasp.

'Chantal knew almost from the first something was wrong. And then when—well, when she became pregnant with Jean Patric, I told her.'

'Told her what?'

'You, the children. Why I had to hide. She was frightened for me. But I trusted her because I knew she was in love with me. As long as she stayed that way I was secure.'

If he noticed her wincing he made no sign of it. All she saw in front of her now was a man who needed help. But not—any more—hers.

'Could you—eventually—be happy with her?' She was more curious now than caring. 'Stephen,' she leaned forward making him look at her. 'Think. Do you love her?'

'In a way,' he conceded, without hesitation or apparent surprise at the question. 'I don't see why I have to make that decision. I can make money. It's the one thing I do know about. Chantal will be OK. She has always understood.'

Serena looked at her hands, twisting her wedding ring. 'Understands what exactly?' she asked, steadily meeting his eyes.

He shrugged. 'That I'll see Jean Patric as much as I can, but I'm married to you,'

Speaking slowly, carefully considering each word, she said, 'I will always love you for the happy years—and I was happy, believe me I was. And loved you. So much. But I can't any more. My head says you can't stop loving someone you care about. But I have. I do care. I can't stop that. But we're not the same people we were. I'm not the girl you married, and'—she paused, knowing tears were not far away—'you're not,' she finished brokenly, 'my Stephen any more.'

He didn't move. She thought he would reach out and touch her. But he didn't. It had been too long. She leaned over, half rising out of her chair, and kissed him lightly on the cheek. Her chair scraped noisily as she pushed it back and then she turned and walked to the door. As she was ushered through by the warden, fighting back tears, she turned to look back. But Stephen's seat was already empty.

'It's like this, you see.' She was standing in Ed's library in Hans Crescent. 'I'm free now. But I need time to get used to that freedom. I need to move out of Foster Street, get Lou and Harry back on course, and—of course—make sure they see Stephen whenever they want.'

'And how often will that be?' Ed asked. At almost nine in the evening he had been unprepared for Serena's visit. In the dining room, several guests were assembled, about to start dinner.

She knew she was looking dishevelled, but if she hadn't come straight from the train, she would never have come at all. 'I don't know,' she confessed. 'I suspect not a lot.'

'Why are you telling me all this?'

'Because.' It was the first time she had ever seen insecurity in his eyes. 'Because you're important to me. And I need time to find out just how important. Ed,' she asked nervously, 'what are you doing? You've got guests. Ed, please,' she protested weakly as he pulled her onto the sofa next to him. 'I'll wait,' she offered.

'But I can't,' was the last thing either of them said for some time.

The removal van was blocking Foster Street. Their new home, a small house in Valery Road, Parson's Green, was really nice. Well, it would be once she'd finished with it. The rush to close the deal had suited Serena. Three weeks from the day she had heard about Chantal and Jean Patric she was ready to move on. Harry was already at the new house with Stacey, Clemmie and Tipper, waiting to see in the first of their belongings.

She smiled. In fact she smiled a lot these days. The anguish was over. The past dealt with. There was only the future to tackle. No more decisions to make about Stephen. Her mother had said it was a chance to start again. 'It's not,' Serena told her. 'I did that a long time ago. It's more getting there.'

The phone rang.

'How's it going?' Ed asked.

'Going. I wouldn't put it any higher. See you later?'

'Absolutely,' he said. 'I need some advice.'

'You?'

'Mmm. With your decision-making skills so finely honed I thought you might be just the person to consult.'

'Consult me about what?'

'I've sold out of Frobisher's.'

Serena gasped. 'When did this happen? Why didn't you tell me?'

Ed gave a small cough. 'Well, you've been a bit preoccupied. Actually I was on the point of pulling out of it when you turned up and I had to have an excuse to go on meeting you, so it's no big deal. I mean I don't need a whole club now just to see you, do I?'

He was impossible. 'But, Ed. What now?'

'I thought I might find out your plans first.'

'Well,' she began, slowly tracing a pattern on the floor with the toe of her canvas sneaker, 'I'm going to move house, work hard to pay the mortgage. Bring my kids up, hope they'll be decent about their father, and won't blame me too much. And in between find time to be happy with this man I've met. Only he's not good at telling me important things like giving up a major part of his business life.'

'I would, if you ever stopped still long enough,' he retorted. 'I come quite low down on that list,' he pointed out.

'No you don't,' she contradicted him. 'You come very high on a quite separate one. You know you do. I just need time to merge them. The kids need time. And, Ed? You need time. I don't exactly come uncluttered. Love isn't enough, I learned that the hard way.'

He sighed. 'Doesn't sound like a bad start to me. Oh bugger. I have to go. I'm late. I'll call later.'

When she left Foster Street she didn't look back. The removal van was already at the bottom of the street, turning left into the main road. Parked further down the road, her car was crammed to the roof. Just enough room left for her and Louise, who was sitting on the wall with Damon and Daphy.

As Louise caught sight of her mother she began to sob. Oh God, thought Serena, slipping a comforting arm round her daughter and leading her to the car. Not this all the way to Parson's Green? She slid behind the wheel, reaching over to hand her swollen-eyed daughter a box of tissues and her heart melted. 'Don't cry, darling,' she said, stroking her hair, hugging her. 'Daphy will take care of Damon.'

'Daphy?' shrieked Louise, tearing a handful of tissues out of the box. 'That cow's been trying to snog him for weeks. And I bet he'll let her. Oh God, I hate them all. Where's the Pulp tape? Can I have it on?'

Serena reached over, recognising with relief the imminent signs of recovery, and slotted the tape into the deck. She smiled, giving a swift sideways look at her daughter, whose eyes were closed as she automatically began to mouth the words.

At the end of the road Serena waited for a gap in the traffic. No one noticed she'd gone. Foster Street vanished as she turned into the main road, freezing into an image already shaping into a memory. She drove on, blindly following the stream of traffic taking her to the empty house.

They drove in silence. Louise, forgetting she was heartbroken, changed the tape and rummaged in the glove compartment for a toffee. Decision time, Serena told herself. Her decision, like all the others these last three years. Twice she went to pull the car over and twice she changed her mind. Panic flickered. She could hear her own voice justifying her place in Stephen's life echoing through her head. *Not lower down the list, just on a different one.* Oh God. Had she really said that? There was a knot in her stomach.

'Mum,' Louise said impatiently, 'what are you looking for?'

Up ahead on the other side of the road, Serena spotted a phone box. 'I'll tell you later.' She swung the car into an empty space and got out.

'Hang on,' she called through the window, 'I'll only be a minute.'

She dived between the traffic to reach the centre of the road, then raced through a gap between a bus lumbering heavily along near the kerb and a delivery van, whose driver swore robustly after her as she reached the safety of the pavement.

Inside the phone box she fed money into the slot, tapped out a number and waited. Wally's voice greeted her like an old friend. 'Sorry, he's not here,' he apologised. 'Won't be back until much later. What shall I say?'

She bit her lip. 'Tell him, I've made a new list. Tell him—' she stopped. She was going to say she'd changed her mind, that love *was* enough. Instead she said, 'That's it, Wally. I'll tell him the rest myself.'

Then she hung up and leaned her head against the door, briefly closing her eyes, a small smile on her face, blotting out the snarling tide thundering past outside, shaking the glass pane. It was enough. More than enough. Across the street she could see Louise craning her head out of the car, looking for her. She took a deep breath, opened the door and ran back through the traffic.

FRANKIE McGOWAN

FRANKIE McGOWAN likes nothing better than to write about subjects close to her heart. *A Kept Woman* has provided her with an opportunity to do just this with one of her life's great interests: her committed involvement with charity work.

When her sister-in-law died of ovarian cancer, Frankie McGowan resolved to become involved in fund-raising for ROC (Research into Ovarian Cancer), in order to increase early awareness of the disease among women. In *A Kept Woman,* the heroine, Serena Carmichael, is passionately involved with charity work and is an enthusiastic fund-raiser. 'I wanted to use Serena's character in a way that shows how charities are truly run—the ones that are having an impact and need to raise serious money.'

Drawing from her own experience of learning how to make difficult corporate presentations when working as a magazine editor, Frankie McGowan says that in *A Kept Woman* she 'made sure Serena knew it all in the end: she was mugging up on statistics, she was addressing companies, she was going out there and getting people to listen to her. She was a fine businesswoman and was talking sense.'

However, the charity organiser in Serena is not the only aspect of her character that reflects Frankie McGowan's experiences. At the end of *A Kept Woman*, it isn't a foregone conclusion that Serena will make her future with Ed, but it is certain that she has discovered that she can make her own way through life without relying on the support of a man. It is one of the author's firm principles that a woman should do things for herself, that she should 'not allow a man to be the solution to any woman's problems—the man should just be a wonderful bonus'.

Without doubt, Frankie McGowan's life and career is a shining example of her beliefs. She started writing for teenage magazines and then joined Fleet Street as one of the youngest-ever feature writers for the *Evening News*. In the course of her career, she has contributed to practically every national newspaper, launched four magazines—including *Top Santé* and *New Woman*—has written three novels and two works of nonfiction, and currently has a regular column in *Good Housekeeping* magazine.

Married to Peter Glossop, a feature-film sound mixer, whom she visits on his exotic film locations when work permits, she has two children: Tom, aged twenty-four, and Amy aged twenty-one. Frankie McGowan is proud and delighted that her children, as she says, 'have survived living with such an erratic mother and are so nice they even still speak to me!'

Angela Huth

WIVES OF THE FISHERMEN

❧

Annie Macleoud and Myrtle Duns

cannot remember a time when they were

not friends in the remote Scottish village

which is their home. Their friendship

has survived many testing times, but

suddenly a horrifying accident opens up

a deep rift between them and exposes

the jealousy and betrayals each has

carefully hidden over the years.

❧

PART ONE

It is the habit of fishermen's wives to glance at the horizon many times a day, but only one of their own kind will recognise the furtive looks, the tightening of anxiety behind eyes grown prematurely old from checking distant sea.

A moment too late Myrtle Duns flicks her eyes back from the window. Annie Mcleoud, looking up from her cards, has seen.

'Ach, stop worrying,' she says.

She watches Myrtle lift the black kettle from the range, pour boiling water into a brown pot. Annie knows that Myrtle will now take two mugs from hooks, two tin spoons from a drawer, pour milk into a souvenir jug from Dundee. She will lift the pot with both hands, judging the amount of water before transporting it to the table. The rhythm of tea-making is familiar from hundreds of such afternoons spent together.

All the time Annie watches her friend the cards flicker in her hands. Sometimes they rise in fans. Then quick fingers snap them back into a neat pack. Myrtle stands by the range, waiting for the tea to brew.

She is a large woman, hands rough as salt cod, tall. She moves with practised skill among the narrow spaces, managing her wide hips with dignity. Archie says she sometimes put him in mind of an opera singer, the way she glides. It's as if there are wheels under her skirts. 'Stop scoffing, Archie,' she answers, pleased by his observation, for she recognises the admiration beneath the teasing.

'Archie,' says Annie, slapping down the cards, 'is the best skipper any boat could have. You know that.'

'Aye.' Myrtle sits. She arranges the tea things in front of her.

'How's Janice?' Myrtle asks after a while.

'She's bonny. High marks at school again.'

Annie finds it hard to resist informing Myrtle of her daughter's high marks several times a week.

'That's grand.'

Annie shuffles the cards. 'Mrs Singer said to me, "Mrs Mcleoud, your Janice is on her way to being a great beauty as well as a scholar."' Modesty, or the nearest she can get to it, webs her eyes. 'I couldn't say that to anyone but you, Myrtle. But I believe there's some truth in it.'

'Oh there is, that's for sure,' says Myrtle warmly. She accepts a pile of cards. It's not yet time to pour the tea. Her look slides from Annie's hands to her face: the tiny nose with its nostrils the shape of horizontal petals, the opal eyes, the mouth whose dividing line in repose is the subtlest of shallow curves—a mouth that can jump from solemnity to laughter with astounding speed. In the rubble of dark curls, Myrtle observes that Annie has a few grey hairs. But her friend has changed little over the years. She was the prettiest child in the school, the village, for miles along the coast. Her looks had tempted admirers from Fife to Dundee. It is no wonder her only child, Janice, is set to follow her mother's reputation. Myrtle wonders if Janice has inherited the same powers of persuasion of her innocence, so that she will always be forgiven. Everyone has always forgiven Annie, Myrtle most of all.

As children, Myrtle and Annie walked to school together holding hands. On cold mornings, Myrtle wore mittens of scratchy wool. Annie wore gloves. The bare ends of Myrtle's cold fingers would burrow into the warmth of Annie's angora hand. She longed for gloves. But in her mother's cautious mind they were an extravagance. Locked into the disciplines of a hard life, Dot Stewart's beliefs in everything—from the rewards of the afterlife to the number of blankets a person should be allowed on the bed—were unchangeable.

In the classroom Myrtle and Annie shared a desk. Myrtle's half was sparsely furnished: pen, textbook, exercise books. Annie's was chaotic: school books overstrewn. There were skeins of wool, electric colours, which Annie liked to weave into a long tube that grew into a hideous worm from nails punched into a cotton reel. There were plastic hairslides, boiled sweets and cuttings from magazines—at the age of ten, Annie was a compulsive cutter-outer.

Often the clutter on Annie's side of the desk would drift over its boundaries. Myrtle would gently push the stuff back. She was unreprimanding when it came to Annie's untidiness. And when Mrs Williams began pacing between the desks, eyes straining to detect any hint of something Not in the Rules, in loyalty to her friend Myrtle would hide things under her own books. There was a day when Mrs Williams was particularly disinclined to believe Annie's excuses for the mess, and Myrtle found herself declaring that most of the offending objects were hers. Punishment was just avoided.

When the bell went, Annie turned to Myrtle and hugged her.

'You're my friend, Myrtle,' she whispered. 'I can always count on you.'

In the heat of gratitude and pride Myrtle did not ponder the truth of this. When Annie was at her best, irresistibly endearing, it was easy to forget the other times. The bell rang out the joy of Myrtle's secret feelings. Her loyalty to Annie was often rewarded by a suggestion of doing something together in the playground: she hoped this would happen today. Myrtle waited. Watched Annie's eyes flick round the others. When Ross Wyatt passed he handed Annie an emerald rubber.

'Yours,' he said.

'Thanks,' said Annie. She gave him one of her half-smiles that, despite the braces on her teeth, boys found irresistible.

'Coming outside?' Ross sniffed and wiped his nose on his hand.

'Right.' She turned to the boy standing behind Ross. 'You coming too, Archie Duns?'

He nodded, not looking at her. Flanked by the two best-looking boys in the school, Annie moved to the door. She had forgotten to invite Myrtle.

When all the children had left, Myrtle sat down again. It was during that lunch break, alone in the classroom, voices outside rising and falling like small garments hung out to dry in a wind, that an uneasy thought struck the ten-year-old Myrtle: Annie, her best friend, sometimes preferred to be with boys than to be with her.

Several games of rummy have been played, several cups of tea have been drunk. Myrtle wants Annie to go. She wants to get on with the evening—peel the carrots, take the folded clothes from the airing cupboard and put them in Archie's drawers. But Annie shows no keenness to leave. For all that her own kitchen is a smarter place than Myrtle's—white tiles, the occasional one stamped with a seahorse, formica tops—she seems to prefer the Duns's. Sometimes she does suggest that Myrtle should come over to her place. But then, just as Myrtle is setting out, by chance Annie is passing by. She has come to 'fetch' Myrtle, she says. But as Myrtle has not yet put on her shawl, and

Annie is already taking off her coat, it seems pointless to walk up the hill to the council estate. So they stay. Friendship, as Myrtle points out when guilt spurs Annie to bring the occasional gift of a bannock or oat biscuits, is not about whose house is the meeting place.

'Won't Janice be back?' asks Myrtle. 'Are we forgetting the time?'

Annie smiles. 'She's going over to Joey Brick for her tea. I'll pick her up later. She likes a boy with freckles, Janice does.'

Myrtle waits, weighing caution. She has learned it's all too easy for Annie to detect criticism in anything she might say about Janice.

'Starting young,' she says at last.

'They're grown up at twelve these days. There's no stopping them.'

They hear footsteps outside. The door opens. A smell of sea comes in on the wind. Archie's dark jersey twinkles with raindrops. His face is haggard, exhausted. He smells of cod, rope, pipe smoke. His eyes go straight to Myrtle. Annie stands up.

'Ken's home,' he says to her, sharpness in his voice. The defiance in Annie's eyes that had flared when Archie came in, quavers.

'His supper'll not take a moment in the microwave,' she says. She and her husband, Ken, bought the microwave a couple of months ago. Myrtle and Archie are familiar with the magical way it changed their lives. 'But I'll be going.'

When Archie has shut the door behind her he moves to the range, where Myrtle is standing, and leans his hands against its side. Then he raises his warmed hands to hold his wife's face. He looks at her silently. He will kiss her later. For the moment he lets the sensation of being home flow through him. The warmth of his own kitchen is what he remembers, if there's a moment to think, at sea. When the boat rocks crazily in giant waves and rain hard as sheet glass crashes into his eyes, there's a lightning flash in his mind: the old stove, his wife beside it, ready to pour the tea.

The kitchen was always the warmest room in the house. Until 1953, just before Myrtle was born, it was the place where Dot Stewart baited the lines. She used to throw a tarpaulin over the flagstones and Sandy, who delivered the lines, would drag in a load so huge that sometimes, Dot said, just the sight of it brought tears of despair to her eyes. The lines, with their lethal hooks, were alive with pernicious intent—snagging, pricking, drawing blood. Dot's hands had bled so many times that the scar tissue criss-crossed the ruddy skin in abstract, knitters'

patterns. Once the lines were stacked, Sandy would haul in sacks of mussels. They made a crunching, screeching noise as they scraped the flagstones. On occasions, Veronica gave a hand—one-eyed Veronica who had lost an eye in a fish-hook accident. Veronica baited with a recklessness that unnerved every woman in the village, lacerating herself without complaint, bloodying the mussels as she attached them to the hooks. Veronica made Dot laugh with her scurrilous tales about the fishermen. Her slanderous tongue lightened the long mornings.

The women sat on low chairs to do their baiting, thick-stockinged legs slung wide apart to make a copious lap for a clump of line which, once mussel-loaded, would slip onto the floor. They were skilful with their knives. A flick of the wrist and the shell was jarred open. Then the silvery glistening meat would be gouged out, slipped over the next hook. The women's fingers worked automatically, their rhythm only broken by the quick suck of a damaged finger. They rarely spoke: the small thuds of shell on tarpaulin, and the scrape of line as it was tugged along to the next hook, were the only interruptions in the fish-stinking silence. The smell was always there: in hair, clothes, skin. They did not think of listening to the wireless. With its elaborate façade sculpted like a miniature Odeon, in place of honour on the dresser in the front room, the wireless was for weather forecasts and news, an evening thing. But when the window was open and there was a strong breeze, they could hear the water break against the harbour wall. That was music enough.

Myrtle had listened to her mother's descriptions of all this many times. And now that she was grown up, alone in her kitchen, Archie away at sea, Myrtle often felt that time had intertwined itself and she had actually been with Dot and Veronica, baiting the lines. Sometimes, sweeping the floor, she would come across a glint of mussel shell, a speck of diamond between the flagstones, and she felt awed at knowing how it had been in those hard days. Present life was much less physically exhausting, though never without worry. There was the same fear—no fish, no money. Many was the time—weather too bad to go out—Myrtle and Archie had been down to their last few pounds. And the shadow that could never be erased was the anxiety. Inherited from generation to generation of women whose men make a living at sea, anxiety was a moth trapped in their insides, which flutters, batters, can never escape. When the fishermen come home for a few days, these wings of fear are stilled for so short a time that the places they have damaged cannot hope to heal. As clean clothes are stuffed into a bag ready for another week at sea, the whole inner turmoil begins again.

Archie, at the table, is asleep. His head is couched in his arms. Myrtle touches his salt-crusted hair. She touches his cheek. He hasn't much time for shaving on the boat. The stubble is thick on his jaws. Archie has been away for five days and four nights.

When he wakes, what shall she tell him? Myrtle wonders. There has been no news, apart from the day the washing machine went mad. It was clogged up with fish scales from sea-soaked clothes. Water had gushed out onto the floor. Myrtle, in her panic, had seen it as a surreal cascade, full of living eyes horribly twinkling at her among the bubbles. She had run to find Alan, one-eyed Veronica's son, and the nearest thing to a plumber in the village. He had swiftly dealt with the crisis. There was no reason to trouble Archie with a disaster that was over. With so little time together, important things should consume the hours—re-acknowledgment of love and well-being.

Myrtle loves these moments. Many of the fishermen go straight to the pub, arrive home drunk with no apologies. Not Archie. His priority is his wife. Soon as he's ashore, he hurries home. He's best pleased when he finds Myrtle alone. Annie's constant presence annoys him. He dislikes her, but does his best to contain that dislike. He understands Myrtle needs a friend when he's away. All he asks is that Annie should not hang around when he is home.

Every time Archie returns Myrtle thanks God. But the thought is never far off that one day there will be reason to curse God, just as her mother did when Jock Stewart died. The day that Archie does not come back has festered in her mind for so long that the picture is sharp. She has tried to extinguish such thoughts, but has not succeeded.

When she was eleven years old, her father died at sea, though not on the fishing boat. He was only half a mile from the shore, in his rowing boat. The afternoon he died there was a strong April sun, sea flat as tin, scarcely a breeze. When he didn't appear for tea and darkness gathered, Dot reluctantly put out the alert. His boat was found quickly, empty. No body, no drifting clothes—nothing. Two weeks later Jock Stewart's body was washed up a mile along the coast. Ben Duns told his son, Archie, that it was a swollen mass of blubber, horrible. The eyes were still open. But it was the sight of Jock's feet that made him cry: toes the colour of shale, skin blown up taut. The indignity of seeing a fisherman stripped of his boots was the thing, Archie confessed to Myrtle, that broke his father, and he had seen many a drowned man.

WIVES OF THE FISHERMEN

Archie is awake, eating. He crams butter into a baked potato, splits his sausages and fills them with mustard. Between mouthfuls he leans his forearms heavily on the wooden table. Myrtle can tell by the hunch of his shoulders that he is beginning to relax.

'How was it?' Myrtle can expect only the barest information.

'Not too bad. We had to go a long way for a fair catch. Mighty small fish again. Always the small fish, now. I don't know.'

Archie is weary of the politics of fishing. There are old fishermen in the village who talk about the time when there were limitless fish to catch. It was a hard life, but you could make a decent living. The third cod war, in the seventies, was the end of the good times. And now it is scientists advising about quotas, pontificating politicians who don't know a haddock from a herring, and all the time over-fishing. Early into the next century there could well be no industry left. What then? There is an unspoken rule among the men on Archie's boat that no one should speculate. Archie needs men to function with all the fire they can muster to go further, fish longer, and bring home a decent catch.

Archie smiles. 'Have you been hearing much of the microwave, then?'

'Aye. You can have no idea of the brilliance of that machine.'

Archie studies his wife's face.

'You can always have one if you're wanting one.'

'Not on your life. What would I be doing with it?'

'Just wanted to make sure I'm not depriving you.'

'Never.' Myrtle rises to take a bread pudding from the oven, and two warmed bowls. 'I'm sorry about Annie. God, how she stays.'

'She's not strong, Annie, on knowing when she's not wanted.'

'No, but she's a good heart.'

'I was never interested, you remember, in her heart, nor any of the rest of her.' They both laugh. 'Poor Ken. Does he have any idea what she gets up to? Does she say anything to you?'

'No, but it's not hard to guess,' says Myrtle after a while.

Annie has learned that when the men are home she and Myrtle should see less of each other. She is careful not to drop in on Myrtle if there's a chance Archie might be in the house. What she has not yet done is caution her daughter, Janice. The child, she feels, should remain ignorant of past events that have led to the present situation.

It's the morning after Archie's return. He's in the bathroom, shaving. The first shave, after days at sea, always takes a long time—half an hour, perhaps, among carbolic soap and sweet clean towels. Archie also takes a shower, shampoos his hair, washing out the salt, and brushes his teeth more vigorously than he does at sea. All this is a ritual of the first morning back, before breakfast of porridge and bacon and the thick grainy bread that Myrtle has put in the oven to bake at dawn.

Myrtle stands by the stove stirring the porridge. She listens for Archie's step. She waits, aware of an internal warmth that is never there on mornings when he is away.

The door, rarely locked, opens. Myrtle shifts her position, at once alert, protective of her husband's time.

Janice stands there. She has her mother's enquiring eyes, slanting under heavy brows. She holds a biscuit tin filled with hay.

'Mrs Duns? My mother said . . .'

She moves towards the table. Puts down the tin. Lifts from it a brown hamster that she keeps in her hands.

'There's something the matter with him. My mum said—'

'I don't know what makes your mother think I'm any better than she is with animals.' Myrtle moves from stove to table. 'Let me have a look.'

Myrtle raises Janice's hands so that the animal is on a level with her eyes. It does not move, its nostrils twitch slowly. Its eyes are dull.

'The poor wee thing,' says Myrtle. 'He looks quite poorly.' She sees Janice is close to tears. 'I'm afraid I can't say what's the matter. Go to the vet, would be my advice.'

'Mum says she's not spending money on the vet just for a hamster.'

'Then do your best for him. Keep him warm. Try a little tepid milk.' Myrtle is sorry for the child, but she wants her to go.

Janice returns the animal to the tin. 'Can't *you* do anything, Mrs Duns?'

'I'm sorry, but I really can't, Janice. Now if you don't mind, I must be—' She returns to the stove, picks up a wooden spoon, begins to stir, aware the earlier calm has gone. Bother the child. Her own father home, why isn't she calling on *him* for help if Annie is no use?

'Surely you can do *something*?' Janice is cross now, as well as upset.

'No. Nothing. I'm not an expert on hamsters.'

Archie's tread in the passage is heavy with anticipation. Myrtle's voice rises. 'Now please, Janice—Archie's wanting his breakfast. Go back to your house. Your mother'll be wondering—'

'She won't! She knows where I am.' Janice turns to see Archie standing in the doorway. His look unnerves her. She picks up the tin, smiles straight at him. 'I'm sorry, Mr Duns, if it was too early to call, but my hamster is very ill and—'

'Bugger your hamster when I'm just home,' says Archie, very quietly, and the child, pressing the tin to her chest, runs from the room.

Myrtle spins round. 'What d'you want to say that for? She's upset enough.'

'Little minx. Thick-skinned as her mother.'

'There's nothing wrong with Janice except that she doesn't know when she's not wanted.' Archie sits at the table. Myrtle brings him his bowl of porridge. 'I couldn't be too hard on the child. The creature will be dead before the day's out, and if I know Annie there'll not be too much sympathy.'

In all the years of Myrtle and Annie's friendship there have been many rows, but only a few they can remember. The first was when they were five or six years old. That occasion, never forgotten, they laugh about now, but neither speaks of the crystallising of the differences between them that became apparent that day.

Dot had taken the girls for a picnic on the beach. Annie's mother Mag had agreed to come too, but at the last moment she had changed her mind. She sent a message saying she wasn't well. Of a nervous disposition, Mag was rarely well enough to do anything that did not suit her. She lived on tranquillisers and the practical help of kind neighbours. It was always Dot who dropped Annie home from school. Annie's father, an Irishman, had returned to his native country just weeks after Annie's birth. Life at home for Annie was bleak and boring. It was no wonder that much of her childhood was spent in the Stewart household.

For some reason, that particular day, Annie believed her mother really would come on the picnic. So when Mag changed her mind, Annie felt the familiar pebble of disappointment shift round her insides, a physical pain that made her cry. But it was a fine day on the beach, which they had to themselves, for the breeze was stinging cold, and once Annie had eaten Dot's banana sandwiches, she found herself more cheerful. She and Myrtle wandered down to the shore to look for shells. Dot perched herself against a rock, took her knitting from a cavernous patchwork bag. Lulled by the movements of fingers that needed no eyes to guide them, her glance went back and forth between the empty grey sea and the two small girls, bending and shouting, some twenty yards away. She had no idea how much time had passed before she heard the screams—but their urgency made Dot leap up and fling her knitting down. The children were hitting each other—kicking, scratching, pulling each other's hair. Dot ran.

'I want this one! You've got more than me.'

'*No!* Can't have it! It's mine—'

Myrtle snatched at the shell in Annie's hand. Annie flung a small claw at Myrtle's cheek. Her nails, sharper than shells, tore down the skin. Myrtle grabbed a clump of Annie's curly hair and pushed her to the ground. Annie scratched, kicked—bit her arm. Seared by the pain, Myrtle pushed a thumb into a wet red eye. Annie screamed louder. Then two large firm hands were pulling the bodies apart, Dot's angry voice telling them to stop.

The girls sat one on either side of a panting Dot. She wiped faces, eyes, hands, with an inadequate paper handkerchief. Then she lifted the hem of her long skirt and applied it vigorously to the sniffling children.

'It was her fault,' Annie was the first to say.

'I'm not interested in whose fault it was, just remember you've both spoilt a good day.'

'She's prettier than me,' said Myrtle. 'It's not fair.'

'Life isn't fair and I'm not listening to this stupid talk,' said Dot.

Fight over, they were cold. They huddled next to Dot. They might have remained where they were for some time while Dot gathered the energy to take two unhappy children home. But then the knitting! All three saw it at once—powered by the wind, the long scarf was racing towards the sea. The needles made funny stiff-legged walking movements that made them laugh. With one accord they all leapt up and ran towards the water. By now the scarf was curling about on the white spume several yards out. Ignoring Dot's cries, the children high-stepped towards it, lifting their skirts. They each grabbed an end, and tugged it back to the shore with an air of triumphant partnership.

The days the fishermen spend at home are always edged with the knowledge that time is short: and yet, because these breaks are so regular, they cannot be thought of as holidays, times for treats or unnecessary extravagance.

Myrtle tries to give no hint of her feelings. It would be no help to Archie to know her anguish every time he was away, and she has no wish to hinder him with desire of his constant presence when he is home. The luxurious times are when he is working in the house. As she goes about her own jobs, the tap of his hammer or the sawing of wood, signifying his presence, is the kind of joy that gives lightness to her step.

Between chores, Archie takes trouble with his wife. They go for long walks. They have a drink in a pub. Sometimes, on a fine day, Archie spontaneously suggests a real excursion: the bus to Edinburgh for a day, where Myrtle filters slowly round the bookshops. Sometimes, summer, they get out the old bikes, pedal out to fields of long grass starry with buttercups, where they eat their sandwiches, drink their cider.

There is a particular place they love, where the flat lands behind the village give way to a gentle rise. At the summit is a church from which life has fallen away. Archie and Myrtle love this place best in May, when the cow parsley is breast high and the dense shade of the dark trees is scattered by a warm breeze. From the graveyard they can look down onto fields merged into the darker flank of the sea. Bass Rock, from here, is no larger than a human tooth sticking up from the water.

Once pushing their bikes back to the main road, Myrtle and Archie passed an old grey stone manse. It was simple in its architecture as a child's drawing: four large windows and a handsome front door dividing its façade. Myrtle was excited by the glimpses of lustrous curtains at the windows. She imagined herself looking out of these windows, waking to see the herd of enormous white cows that graze in the field beyond the garden. She wondered who lived in such a place: and did they love it as much as she would, given the chance?

'Imagine living here,' was all she said to Archie.

'I canna,' he said, mounting his bike with a suddenness that disturbed Myrtle's reverie. His mind was on other things.

She stands outside the front door, pot of paint in hand. Archie has gone again. Five more days.

The paint is the Christmas green of holly leaves. Myrtle has been by bus to St Andrews and found the right colour there—a whole afternoon the expedition has taken her. She likes it when whole mornings or afternoons are taken up by a project: such demolitions of time hurry the days to Archie's return. Myrtle's perfectionism sometimes unnerves Archie, though it also makes him proud. It is a wonder, the way she pays such acute attention to detail that others would regard of no importance. But then, with no bairns to keep her busy, time has to be skilfully marshalled.

The days with Archie here, as always, have gone so fast. When time is precious, pottering about, getting on with chores does nothing to slow the hours. Archie spent the best part of one day preparing the front door for the new paint: sanding, filling in, smoothing. Myrtle, in her kitchen, had listened to the scraping and the sanding and had felt the familiar churn of security which alighted when Archie was home.

One afternoon she went with him down to the boat—a thing she did not much like doing, for it was all too easy to imagine such a small vessel at the mercy of tumultuous waves. Archie always assured her it would take a storm the like of which he had never seen to capsize *Skyline II*, but Myrtle could not be convinced. Not long ago, Archie had confessed that his father's boat, *Skyline* (which Ben Duns had bought from Dot after Jock's death), had once rolled right over, but righted itself. If it came to it, he said, *Skyline II* would do the same.

Myrtle, standing on the harbour wall, did not share Archie's faith in the boat, or his affection for her. *Skyline II* was snub-nosed, wide-girthed, her black paint worn away and scratched, yet somehow before returning to sea, Archie and the crew always managed to have her ship-shape. To Myrtle the boat had the look of an old carcass awaiting the vulture gulls, shrieking low overhead, to rip her to pieces. Her decks were an incomprehensible clutter of wires and winches and nets.

When Archie disappeared into the cabin, she could feel her eyes lock with concern. Archie, all smiles as he ran up the ladder carrying a box, caught her stricken face. He put an arm about her and they walked back along the harbour wall, Archie deflecting her thoughts with some story about his mate Ken's eagerness always to be first to help with the worst jobs. In a moment he had recharged his wife's spirits, and they both silently anticipated the long, quiet evening ahead. And on the last night of this leave Archie put his hand round the back of Myrtle's neck, even before they had gone upstairs. He gathered her to him with all the constant love that he found difficult to declare, but which Myrtle had come to recognise in the maze of his natural diffidence.

By noon, the undercoat is finished. Myrtle stands back, contemplates her work. With any luck the paint will have dried hard enough for her to begin the top coat this afternoon.

Until two years ago, when Dot died, the days when Archie was away were charged with duties that did much to speed their length. Dot, who eventually required more expert nursing care than Myrtle could give, went without protest to the Evergreen Home just outside the village. Myrtle and Archie felt guilt at organising this move, but as far as they could judge it caused Dot no traumas.

'I shall no longer be a bother to you,' she said with one of her toothless smiles. 'I'll be able to sit and sit and sit, no trouble to anyone.'

On their first visit, Myrtle and Archie arrived to find Dot had persuaded the nurses to move her armchair to the bay window overlooking the sea, as far as possible from the circle of other fishermen's wives who dozed round a television set. Dot's head, lowered onto her chest, strained upwards so that her eyes could meet the horizon. She was watching, she said, for Jock's boat, the old *Skyline* to return for her: that was occupation enough till she died.

In the two years that Dot was in the home, Myrtle visited her every day. They would not talk much, mother and daughter. Myrtle knew the only news to interest Dot was of tides and winds, so that she could calculate the progress of her dead husband. When Dot died, Archie was at sea. Myrtle, who arrived at her usual time in the morning, was told her mother had had a restless night. Dot was in her usual position, staring out over the white-chipped sea to the horizon.

'He's here,' she said. 'Look: there's *Skyline*! On the horizon.'

Myrtle looked out to sea. There was indeed a ship on the horizon, though it looked a hundred times the size of her father's fishing boat.

'That's good,' she said.

'He'll no' be long now.' Dot did not speak again.

Myrtle had not been back home an hour when the telephone rang. Dot had died moments after she left. Myrtle wished that she could weep away the diffuse sensations that gather when a much-loved mother dies. But for the moment no tears came, and eventually she telephoned the minister of the kirk. Dot's wish was to be buried beside her husband, in a corner of the graveyard that overlooked the sea.

Number five Arbroath Street, East Neuk, had been the McGregor family house for many generations. It was a traditional village house for this part of the Fife coast, comprised of thick stone walls, crow-stepped gables, slate roof and well-spaced windows of more aristocratic proportions than are usually found in small village houses. Two flights of stone steps, joined at the top by a stone landing place, led to the first-floor front door. At the beginning of this century the ground floor, a single large room the length of the building, was a general store, full of ancient nets, rusting machinery and all manner of useless objects. When Dot and Jock were married they lived, at first, with Dot's parents upstairs, until Jock put the old storeroom downstairs to rights. It was cold, sunless, damp, in no way luxurious, but it was private. Myrtle was born in that room. When her grandparents moved to a small modern flat, for the last decade of their lives, Dot and Jock and their daughter moved upstairs. It was warmer, cosier, lighter, and they could see the sea from the kitchen window. Mould grappled the walls of the downstairs room and evil-looking fungi sprouted up through the floorboards. By the time Archie and Myrtle married it was in a state of sad neglect.

Since Dot died, Myrtle and Archie have gradually been putting the house to rights. They sleep upstairs in order to wake up to the view: the two small bedrooms are knocked into one, the old fireplace has been unblocked. In the tradition of Myrtle's forebears, she and Archie spend most of their time in the kitchen. Archie's old armchair is by the stove, Myrtle's books are thrust between china and jars on shelves. It is the place they feel most at ease.

On the landing between the kitchen and bedroom they have put a spiral staircase to the downstairs room. They have painted the walls of the room white, bought a huge old sofa and a desk for Archie. Thus it has become the living room, referred to by the jealous Annie as a 'bloody great ballroom'. But rarely do they use it, for all they can see, from down here, are a few yards of sky, no sea.

Arbroath Street, once only known for the poverty within its thick-stoned houses, is now a generally smarter place. Neighbours preceded the Duns with their improvements: roofs are patched, window frames gloss-painted, old front doors turned yellow and red and blue.

One evening Myrtle sets about polishing the brass lion's head door knocker. The sky is feathered with purple and grey clouds and she is impatient to finish.

'Myrtle? I say, your door looks grand.' Myrtle has no wish to be interrupted, but when she sees Annie, she smiles. Her friend has reached the top of the steps. She stands beside Myrtle on the stone landing, peering at the door. 'I want to talk to you.'

Myrtle sighs. 'We'll go in,' she says.

In the kitchen Myrtle automatically puts on the kettle. Annie remains standing. Myrtle sees a tightness in her face that spells trouble. She knows at once when there is something up with Annie. She wonders if she can deflect whatever it is her friend has come to expound.

'Did you and Ken get to Edinburgh?' she asks.

'We didn't. Ken had to be away a lot with the van. Business.'

'I don't want to talk about that.' Archie has been aware of Ken's 'business' for some time. As skipper he cannot approve, for it means that days ashore are far from a rest for Ken, who returns to the boat exhausted, unable to pull his weight. Archie has warned Ken several times he cannot put up with Ken's double life. There have been rows. At some point, both wives know, there will have to be a showdown. Archie is suspicious as to the nature of Ken's 'deliveries'. He does not think they are all furniture removals. He has reason to believe that crates of black fish—fish surplus to the legal quota that should be returned to the sea—are stowed among the furniture and delivered to someone in a chain of traders flouting the law.

'You asked,' says Annie. 'But I want to know what you meant by Saturday. You upset Janice. She came back in tears.'

Annie pulls back a chair with an angry scrape. Sits down.

'There was nothing I could suggest to cure the hamster,' Myrtle says.

'It wasn't that. It was the feeling you gave Janice of not being welcome.'

'Well, she was right there. She wasn't.' Myrtle slams down two mugs. 'Archie just home, wanting a bit of peace and quiet. Not what I'd call good timing.' She pours tea. Annie, silent, has deep pink cheeks, the same marks that used to appear when she was an angry child.

'The hamster died,' she says at last.

'I'm sorry.'

'I thought you loved Janice as if she was your own daughter.'

Myrtle sits down. 'It's true I'm very fond of Janice.'

'Sometimes, you wouldn't know it. You're often sharp with her.'

'There are moments when a child must know the truth. It's not up to me to tell her how to behave in general. But I've every right to tell her how to behave here. She should learn when she's not wanted. When Archie has just come home—that's one of the times. Doesn't seem unreasonable to me. You should tell her, Annie, not to—'

'So that's it.' Annie pushes away her mug. 'You know what your problem is, don't you? You're just jealous of any couple with a child.' She takes in the scorn that travels across Myrtle's face. 'That accounts for your behaviour—everyone says so. Of course, it's not that you don't have our sympathy. You know that. There can't be anything much worse than wanting a bairn and not being able to have one. But how do you think I felt, having a bonny wee daughter when you were unable—'

'Stop it!' Myrtle is pale. Her hands grasp her mug of hot tea. After a while she says, 'I've told you before: if we're not going to quarrel then we should avoid this subject. You've no idea how I feel about not having—'

'You can't tell me you like the fact I have a daughter and you don't.'

'I don't like it, no—not the fact that you have something I don't, but the fact that I can't, ever, for Archie. I can't have Archie's child. That doesn't make for jealousy. It makes for something far more deadly: the persistent sense of failure. Nothing can compensate. Failing to have a child smoulders away . . . you accuse yourself, all your life. There, I've said my bit. That's it, please. End of subject.'

Annie folds her arms, looks up at Myrtle. 'I'm sorry,' she says. 'I don't often fly off the handle like that, do I? We've been having a time, Ken and me. Up and down, all over the place. What do I do once he's gone? Take it all out on you.'

Myrtle gives her a distracted smile. 'That's no matter,' she says. There's a long silence between the women. While both want to regain the old equilibrium, both are still too encumbered with their own preoccupations to come up with a declaration of good intent. 'If I was jealous of you, Annie, there'd be all sorts of good reasons, nothing to do with a bairn. You were always the pretty one, the one the boys fought for. But I didn't mind because you were always such a loyal friend, sticking up for me, insisting I share everything except for the boys—well, they didn't want me, so that wasn't your fault.' She gives a small laugh. 'You did everything to make sure I couldn't feel jealous and I was very proud that you, the most popular girl in the school, were my friend.'

The anger in Annie's cheeks, long since vanished pink, now returns, diffused, in the guise of a blush.

'Well,' she says. 'You were my rock. Still are. Besides, you're remembering wrong. I'd make you cross as anything. Still do.' Both women laugh. Annie moves towards the door. 'Will I come for cards tomorrow?'

'Aye.'

'I must be gone. Janice'll wonder where I am.'

Myrtle takes a bar of chocolate from a shelf. 'Give her that from me.'

When Annie has left Myrtle feels such desolation that to remain sitting is all she can do. After a time, the emptiness of the room is so acute she knows she must leave it for a while. She will go to her mother's grave.

Annie's acts of kindness to Myrtle, as a child, sometimes caused her trouble. There was the day when Ross Wyatt, who had been pestering Annie for months, made a final stand for her, and was rejected in favour of Myrtle.

'Come in the playground, Annie. I've something to show you.'

'I'd rather not, thanks, Ross.'

The boy, Myrtle remembers, was desperate to appeal to the snooty girl before him.

'I didn't mean the playground. I meant, let's go down to the harbour. Get us some chips.' His voice was breathless, odd. Myrtle was alarmed.

'No, thank you,' Annie shouted. She was used to boys weak with love. 'I don't want to go anywhere with you, ever. So don't bother to keep asking. Do I, Myrtle?'

There was confusion in Myrtle's mind. Three weeks ago Annie had told her how much she fancied Ross. So this change of mind took Myrtle by surprise. What should she do? Annie nudged Myrtle.

'No, she doesn't,' said Myrtle, quietly.

'There! What did I tell you, Ross?' Annie was thrilled by her friend's quick thinking, her loyalty. 'Myrtle knows. Myrtle's my friend.'

Ross spun round and fixed Myrtle with a look of total scorn.

'You! Friend? You're an ugly great parcel, guarding Annie, for you know *you'll* no' ever get a man wanting to get into your pants—'

'You foul-mouthed bugger! Don't you dare speak to my friend like that,' screamed Annie, and threw herself towards him. Annie kicked Ross hard in the balls. He went white, moaned, bent double.

Myrtle dragged Annie back. 'Leave him, Annie,' she shouted above Ross's moaning.

'You'll pay for this, bitch.' Ross unfurled himself painfully, one hand clutching his groin. 'You stick around with your friend Myrtle, and I'll tell my friend Hamish if he wants you then he'll have to have your ugly friend too!' He laughed.

'Don't you dare!' There was a quiver in Annie's voice. Myrtle knew at once that Ross's threat meant something to Annie. Hamish?

'Get out,' Annie screamed again, 'before I fetch Mrs Williams.'

Ross turned and left the classroom with the air of one who had no intention of wasting any further insults on such despicable girls.

Myrtle put an arm round Annie. 'You shouldn't have stuck up for me so hard like that,' she said.

'Course I should. I won't have anyone saying such beastly untrue things about you. It's wicked.' She sniffed. 'I'll kill him if he goes and messes up everything with Hamish.'

'I don't know what's up, you and Hamish, do I?' asked Myrtle.

Annie suddenly giggled. 'I liked Ross for a bit. Then when he started up with all his pestering and soppy notes I thought he was revolting. Then this morning in assembly Hamish winked at me and I thought he was nice. I mean, I like curly hair.'

Myrtle smiled, conspiratorial. She always enjoyed the turbulent progress of Annie's love life. 'But how,' asked Myrtle, 'could Ross know already that you—?'

'Och, he just guessed. And next time he insults you I'll kick him so hard he'll never get up again.' She was punching the air with a clenched fist, pretty eyes flashing. 'No one's rude to my friend.'

It was one of Myrtle's proud moments. She knew she had no chance with boys, anyhow. They either ignored her or were rude to her. But none of that mattered so long as Annie loved her and stuck up for her.

Myrtle stands beside her mother's grave. The flaked clouds of early evening have given way to a smooth darkness that becomes faded rags round the moon. Its light makes a highway across the sea. There are no ships, no waves. The meeting of sky and sea is lost in velutinous black.

She finds it hard to picture her mother as a whole figure. The images in her mind are scattered miniatures. There are the scarred hands, the deep-lidded eyes, the wary smile, some small gesture of head. The scent of her comes back frequently: fish—the powerful whippy smell of brine—and the lavender water Dot would dab on her neck to disguise the fish. Dot's sweet, melodious voice was the part that lived most clearly, the Scots accent brittle as glass, the intonations choppy as small waves on a windblown sea. 'Myrtle: will ye come here?' 'Myrtle look: there's *Skyline*. He'll no' be long now.'

Dot's voice chimes ceaselessly through Myrtle, all times of night and day. Perhaps the voices of those we love will never die, she thinks, and that is of some comfort.

'Myrtle, is that you?'

This is not a voice from the grave, but a man's voice. Canadian. Myrtle turns.

Martin Ford stands nearby, one hand at rest on a granite cross. His hair blonded by the moon, his face is in deep shadow.

'Och, Martin.'

'Hope I've not given you a fright.'

'Never.'

'I was caught up on a job, back late. Just wanted to see where I have to start digging in the morning.'

Martin is a stonemason. He came over from Canada with his parents when he was seventeen—now they share a divided house just beyond the village. Lack of work has always been his problem. He has established a reputation for being the most skilled stonemason on the east coast. He is kept fairly busy with headstones, the odd monument, but each job is long and painstaking and his profits do not reflect the value of his craftsmanship. To supplement his paltry income he digs graves. His reliability is renowned—always ready to help others, he has never been known to let anyone down. He is generally liked in the village, but no one, so far as Myrtle knows, is close to him.

Martin shifts his position. 'Your mother was a rare woman.'

'Aye, she was.'

'And you? Archie away so much. Must be hard for you wives.'

'You get used to it.' The lie reverberates down Myrtle's spine. She pulls at her shawl.

'I must be on my way. Would you like me to walk you home?'

Myrtle shakes her head. 'Thanks all the same,' she says. The fingers of one hand alight on the headstone of her mother's grave. Dot's name and dates were beautifully carved by Martin. There is no epitaph. Myrtle has still not been able to think of one that she considers perfect.

'You've not come up with something for me to add?' Martin asks.

'Not yet. But I'm thinking.'

Somehow they are walking down the path, their feet making a shushing noise in the stone chippings. Martin shuts the cemetery gate behind them. Myrtle stops while he does this. It is the smallest indication that she does not mind his company. She has said she does not want him to walk her home, but when he continues by her side down the road she does not think of objecting.

No one is about in the village. The houses, so friendly looking by day, have shuttered themselves behind a haughty, defensive look, which is their custom by night. Myrtle and Martin walk in silence. Number five Arbroath Street is soon reached. Myrtle, who has been wondering whether to spend the rest of the evening with the radio or her book, stumbles on the bottom step.

'Careful.' Martin whips a torch from his coat pocket. A bright beam carves the stone staircase into wodges of light and shadow.

'Whatever am I doing?' she asks. She can feel Martin's hand under her elbow as she remounts the step, easily this time. She pauses there, turns to him.

'Cup of tea? Something to eat?'

Martin thinks for a moment. Releases her elbow from his hand. 'Better be getting back,' he says. 'Thanks all the same. But I'll have to be up at four.'

'Very well,' she says. 'It was good of you to walk me home.'

She flies up the steps now, keen to be inside. Martin keeps his torch shining for her. He waits till she has turned the key in the newly painted door before he puts it out. Then he waves, but it's too late. Myrtle has shut the door. Martin is as alone outside as she is within.

It is almost midnight. Myrtle shifts about, unable to sleep. As always, she envisages Archie far out to sea—an image she hates, but which recurs every night. Then the endless black water in her mind turns to sea dancing with sunlight, a calm day in the harbour. Martin, newly arrived in the village, strolling along the harbour wall. He was well over six foot tall and wore his blond hair in a wild mess. Already he had become the object of desire of all the local girls. Annie, who at the time was going out with one Roddy Fairburn, found that her affection for a good but dull Scots boy did nothing to impede exciting possibilities provided by the Canadian.

'He's a smasher,' she whispered to Myrtle. 'I could do with a bit of him.' Myrtle could not deny the desirability of Martin, but kept this to herself.

'Why don't we just go over and be friendly?' said Annie.

'Not me.' Myrtle learned long ago the disadvantages of acting as chaperone to Annie. 'You can go alone. But he's too old for you, seventeen.'

'I'm nigh on sixteen,' said Annie, whose fifteenth birthday was not a week past. 'And anyhow everybody takes me for seventeen.' She fluttered her eyelashes, stiff with mascara.

'I thought you were going out with Roddy,' said Myrtle.

Annie laughs with a scorn too sophisticated for her years. 'Roddy? What good's he?'

Myrtle guessed Roddy's days were numbered. She had heard that laugh before. Martin had moved to the far end of the harbour wall, back to them. His concentration was now on the horizon.

'Thoughtful type, Martin, if you ask me,' Annie said. She shrugged, then laughed more agreeably. 'Course, the one he'd be really good for is you. He's about the only boy around taller than you, isn't he?'

'Don't be daft.' Now that Annie seemed to have forgotten about approaching Martin, none of her silly suggestions could alarm Myrtle.

'I'm not so daft, you'll see. All I ask is a chance to have first go.'

'You do what you like,' said Myrtle. 'I don't *want* Martin.'

The unexpected meeting with the Canadian has brought back this long-past scene to the sleepless Myrtle. She goes on to remember Annie's next move, and smiles to herself. Then at last she sleeps.

Annie, shuffling cards at Myrtle's kitchen table, is unusually quiet. She has brought a small pot of crocus bulbs which, she says, will be out for Christmas. This, too, is unusual. She does not describe the bulbs as a peace offering, but Myrtle knows they are and makes much of her pleasure and thanks.

Although the women play in silence for a while, Myrtle is aware that something is on Annie's mind. She knows her friend so thoroughly. She knows the fingers that jump faster through the cards when she is harbouring some thought she finds hard to contain. Myrtle watches her patiently, amused. Her inability to conceal, her candour, are among the things Myrtle loves her for.

Annie enjoys keeping Myrtle waiting. She pretends to concentrate very hard on her hand of cards. But eventually she says, 'So you caused a scandal last night.'

Myrtle meets Annie's mischievous eyes, gives a deprecating smile. 'I don't know what you mean.'

Annie flings out a look that says, Of course you know what I mean.

'Arm in arm with Martin, all through the village.' Myrtle is already laughing. 'He sees you in, right in. What happens then Myrtle?' In Annie's playfulness there is an edge of suspicion. Myrtle's laughter increases, the warm, bubbling noise that Archie calls audible hot chocolate.

Myrtle cuts off the laughter, takes a deep breath. 'This village! I've never heard anything so ridiculous in all my life.'

'The truth, then. Tell me the truth.'

'I went to the graveyard. Martin was there, looking at some plot. Aye, we walked home together—not arm in arm. I asked him in for a cup of tea. He said no. I shut the door. Big scandal, that, I suppose.'

'Big scandal. I believe you. He's a mystery, that Martin. There's not one of us knows about his life.'

'You got the closest.' It's Myrtle's turn to tease though she thinks, too late, that the subject of Martin is probably no joking matter.

'Didn't get very close, as far as I can remember.'

'I do believe you were really taken by Martin, all that time ago.'

'I was. Well, you know me. Not being able to *get* spurs the attraction. If my carefree days were still here, I could still fancy him. There! Now I've said it. It's brought on your disapproving look.'

Myrtle laughs. 'You'll be fancying people till the day you die,' she says. 'I can just see it, when you have to go into the home. You'll be chasing the old boys down the passages on your Zimmer.'

'Now you're being daft. Besides, Ken'll be in there with me.'

'How is Ken?' asks Myrtle. They don't normally enquire much about each other's husbands. Annie shuffles her cards, eyes down.

'It's not a good time,' is all she says.

Ken, at school, was for some years proud to be the joker in the class. He was always the one to come up with the cheeky answer, to make the others laugh; the one to be punished most often. The standard punishment was to be made to stay in after school and learn a hundred lines by heart, either from the Bible or Robert Burns. Thanks to this, Ken discovered he had an astonishing memory. Not ten minutes after he had been shut into the classroom with a passage from Corinthians, he would hail the teacher with the news that he had 'got it'. To the teacher's amazement, he would gabble the whole thing off, word perfect. With glee he would recount this to his classmates who, already admiring of his cheekiness, doubled their respect. In order to be given more passages to learn, Ken had to continue in his irreverent ways to gain punishment. Soon he began to ask if he could branch out from both Burns and the Bible. He was given the *Oxford Book of Verse* and told to learn whatever he liked. Thus he was introduced to the poets, and came to love them. For two happy years he kept to the routine of punishment and learning. He was kept so busy that he had no time for thoughts of girls.

The summer term that Ken turned sixteen there was a post-exam expedition to St Andrews. There was to be a picnic by the beach, swimming, games. Ken arrived late to find there were just two seats left at the front of the bus. He sat by himself, took out his copy of *Hamlet*. The coach was about to go when there was a cry from Myrtle: Where was Annie?

Five minutes later, delayed not wholly by chance, Annie made her entrance. It was clear she had made a stupendous effort. She wore tight black jeans and a scarlet elastic top, so thin and tight it might have been skin. The nipples of her breasts played hide-and-seek between the chunks of stone, beads and leather thongs of her ethnic necklaces. It must have taken her an hour, Myrtle thought, to perfect her face: lips a creamy gloss, cheeks burnished a coppery pink. The sight caused a general intake of breath, followed by a whooping that spurred Annie to smile benevolently up and down the bus. The only free seat was next to Ken. She smiled. Ken moved as close as he could to the window, and opened his book.

Annie swivelled round and started chattering to those in the seats behind her. The journey passed in a cacophony of voices that Ken tried to shut out. The thing he could not ignore was the smell of Annie: some kind of warm, honeyed flowers. It gave him a strange new feeling. He looked up to see the bus was entering the town. At that moment Annie gave one of her flashing turns—towards him. For an infinitesimal second she dropped a hand on his knee. The second was also an eternity, for in it Ken had time to observe in the minutest detail the shape, weight and contours of that small hand. It carried some strange venom which punctured his own skin with a thrilling sensation that sped up his thigh and reverberated through his body. As he climbed down the steps of the bus a few moments later, Ken felt curiously weak and tired, as if he had just accomplished some mammoth physical feat.

That day was not perfect for a picnic. There was an unbroken grey sky and a cool wind that whipped the sea into petulant waves. But the pupils made the most of it. They set up a ball game to keep themselves warm, and ran random races, pulling each other onto the ground for a skirmish in the sand. Myrtle detached herself from the crowd and went to sit next to the solitary spectator, Ken. His melancholy air enclosed him like a shadow. He sat hugging his bare, goosepimpled knees. As Annie raced about, followed by some dozen boys, his eyes never left her. There was a moment when Sandy Strachan flung her to the ground. He rolled quickly over her, mashing her breast with his hand and plunging his mouth into her hair. Ken winced.

'You all right?' Myrtle asked.

'Fine, thanks.'

Annie fled down the beach, classmates stringing out behind her. Suddenly she swerved towards the sea. Myrtle and Ken could see the splashing and chasing of the faraway crowd. Spume freckled the sky, and the squeals of laughter came to them, tiny as the sounds of distant seabirds. Ken kept his agonised silence. Oh Lord, Myrtle thought: another one.

When the others returned for the picnic lunch, Annie invited Myrtle to sit next to her, thus dashing the hopes of at least four boys hoping to be granted this privilege. Ken got up and wandered down the beach.

'What's the matter with him?' asked Annie, uninterested. Myrtle shook her head, didn't answer.

On the way home, Myrtle took the place next to Ken. He looked terrible, she thought. As soon as the engine started up she enquired if anything was the matter.

'I feel as if I've been in an *accident*,' he said.

'Anything to do with Annie, could it be?'

Ken nodded miserably. 'Your friend,' he said. 'Is she a witch, or what?'

'She's a beguiler,' said Myrtle. 'But she's good, too. She wouldn't want to hurt anyone intentionally.'

'I never really looked at her until today. Then she sits next to me and next thing I know . . .' Ken sighed. Myrtle suspected his discovered tragedy was not altogether disagreeable. 'There's a Keats ode,' he said. '"But when a melancholy fit shall fall, sudden from heaven like a weeping cloud . . . then glut thy sorrow on a morning rose . . ." Bloody stupid suggestion.'

'Quite,' said Myrtle. 'You need more than a morning rose.' She looked at his miserable face. 'I'll tell you something. The thing that really intrigues Annie is a boy who doesn't notice her. So maybe if you give no indication she's made you feel so . . . sick, it might come into her head that Ken Mcleoud is the one to interest her.'

Ken gave a pessimistic shrug, but half a smile. 'Thanks for the tip,' he said. And then, later, he asked: 'Do you know that melancholy ode?'

'Yes, I do. It was after I first read it I thought to myself I'd like to be a teacher.' Ken seemed to be listening. His interest encouraged Myrtle to confide. 'I thought, if I can get so much out of it there must be others who can too, if only they had the chance. That's why it came to me maybe I should be a teacher, help children to love poetry.' By now Myrtle's cheeks were crimson. She knew she had gone too far and would regret this silly outburst.

'You'n me've got quite a lot in common,' he said.

Myrtle felt the heat of relief. He wasn't scoffing. But quite a lot in common was of little worth if you were the plainest girl in the class. The pity of it would remain one more secret in her heart, for she warmed to his sympathy and liked the good nature in his brown eyes.

After this exchange Ken did not mention Annie again. But the day at the sea marked some profound turning point in his life. The cheekiness, the spirit went out of him. He no longer entertained the class, he no longer committed deeds fit for punishment. Myrtle watched his confusion and pain with concern. But his aloofness was not easy to broach. She liked to think, though, that he trusted her, and one day they would talk to each other again.

For once, Myrtle is in Annie's house. They stand edgily in the kitchen. The microwave has been placed in a position that catches the eye as soon as you're through the door. A bright sun polishes the lime green of the formica tops, and reflects on Annie's face. She boils the kettle with the air of one who is reluctantly using an inferior machine. Had Myrtle wanted a cup of coffee, Annie would have boiled the milk in the microwave. Myrtle smiles to herself. Their various pleasures have always been so different, she thinks. Annie regards nature, landscape, walks, as boring. For her the pleasure of an afternoon alone is to lie on her sofa studying a high-class mail-order catalogue.

This morning the lime-tinged Annie has something on her mind.

'I'm the one to be causing a scandal now,' she says.

Myrtle assumes a look of interest. Nothing puts Annie out so much as a blank face in response to an important fact or opinion.

'Martin,' she says, and hands Myrtle pale tea that sways in a cup stamped with an orange flower of no known variety. 'Ran into him not an hour ago. We walked a good hundred yards down the street together, seen by everybody.' She smiles.

'Big scandal,' says Myrtle, smiling back. In joining in the joke she knows that Annie will be assured that their recent squabble is forgotten.

Annie gives a beguiling toss of her pretty head so that the green light scatters into a translucent mosaic over her skin. 'So, anyway, to make conversation I tell him the news.'

'The news?'

'Let's go next door and sit down.' Annie is amusing herself tantalising Myrtle by drawing out the suspense.

She leads the way. Each of them has one hand beneath their saucer, the other controlling the cup that is in danger of skittering on its bone-china base. Myrtle finds all this cup-and-saucer business tiresome. Status symbols of a household kind Annie finds irresistible. It is her persistent desire to spend that drives Ken to his nefarious ways.

In the living room, the carpet is a frozen sea of blue and green whirls. A sofa and armchair, covered in imitation leather the colour of cement, are at an angle to the complicated fireplace, a patchwork of overdefined brick and filigree wrought iron that surrounds and overwhelms the small gas fire. The wall above is hung with horse brasses, though neither Annie nor Ken has ever had any interest in horses.

Myrtle sits down. The armchair squeaks. Annie is twitching her spiky little ankle on the sofa. Northern sky full of slow, drugged clouds is bright through the panoramic window, illuminating her uncontainable smile. She can hold out no longer.

'I've taken a job,' she says. She shifts excitedly.

'Oh Lord, Annie girl,' Myrtle replies, 'Whatever is it this time?'

Annie has tried so many jobs. Up and down the coast she has

worked, for grocers, hairdressers, butchers, bakers and newsagents. The last job was in Ladies' Fashions, an elderly establishment in a staunch old building close to the harbour. Annie enjoyed selling clothes, but she could not reconcile herself to the fashions themselves. Her boss Mrs Helen Grundy's vision of what high fashion on the east coast of Scotland should constitute was not a little out of keeping with current fashion in the wider world. Annie took the liberty of pointing this out, one customerless morning. Mrs Grundy was so affronted that tension between boss and employee became high. The end came when Mrs Grundy asked Annie to cover the windows with transparent yellow paper that would, she said, prevent the merchandise from fading. Annie pointed out that behind the yellow glare the slumped dresses and lifeless cardigans would look even less alluring. Mrs Grundy asked Annie to leave within the hour.

Dismissal meant nothing to Annie, was certainly not a sign of failure, but the evidence of how unreasonable employers are. She could always get another job, she said, when she felt like it. And despite the lack of work locally, and her reputation for unreliability, she always did.

'Come on,' says Myrtle. 'I've waited long enough.'

'The new café up at the museum,' Annie says. 'I'm to be a waitress.'

'Waitress?' Myrtle is surprised. Annie serving others is a role hard to imagine. 'Surely that's not the sort of thing you enjoy?'

'It's so nice up there,' Annie says, 'The place always full. You feel life is *going on* up there.' She gives Myrtle a look. 'You're not being too hasty with your congratulations.'

'Congratulations,' says Myrtle. 'I'm pleased for you. I really am. Though I don't understand. You don't need the money.'

'That we certainly do. Besides, I want to see the wider world.'

Myrtle laughs. 'It's just tourists you'll get up there. Not much time to chat, I don't suppose. You could be disappointed.'

'Think what you like, I'm looking forward to it.' Annie's faint huffiness shows in her risen shoulders. 'It's not often we get the chance to see new faces.' She gazes longingly out of the window at some convivial imagined scene. Suddenly, she gets up. 'Come on, let's go out. I start Monday. No more free afternoons after that.'

'Where?' asks Myrtle.

Annie shrugs. 'The harbour, why not? We might run into Martin.'

In the harbour lies the brown silk water of a low tide, matching the mud beneath. They can see the bones of the harbour wall, steel girders fixed into the stone. On the wet stone steps they can see the sparkle of barnacle and the slimy curl of seaweed. They walk closely side by side, alert to the possibility of something to laugh at. A man in a municipal plastic overall of livid orange, a few yards ahead of them, switches on his machine. He begins to power-hose the empty fish boxes. The jet of water makes a savage hiss. Steam rises, chasing low-flying gulls. They scream in protest. Annie clutches Myrtle's arm.

'Do you see who I see?' she asks.

Myrtle, following Annie's glance, sees Mrs Grundy slink out of Ladies' Fashions. She hurries off towards the newsagent.

'Stupid bitch,' says Annie. 'You go and hide yourself round the corner, make sure she doesn't see you on the way back. I'm going to fix her.'

There's no time to question Annie's demand: Myrtle simply obeys. She finds herself running. What has Annie in mind? Myrtle takes her position, panting, in a doorway.

Annie is whispering to the man with the hose. Myrtle can tell from the way her friend tilts her head she's using her coquettish act to persuade him of something. Then she sees them both laugh. Annie then darts away to a hiding place of her own.

Mrs Grundy comes out of the newsagent. A magazine is under one arm of her emerald jacket. She totters uncomfortably across the uneven ground, eyes down. Daft shoes for such a place, Myrtle thinks.

The hosing man has his back to Mrs Grundy, apparently concentrating his water jet on boxes. How he hears her step Myrtle will never know. But without turning, his hosing arm swerves to the left—an involuntary movement, it seems—then speeds back to its old position. An arc of sparkling water catches Mrs Grundy's high-fashion jacket with its full force, at once darkening the terrible emerald stuff and disarranging the neat package of her hair. Her mouth opens, but her scream is killed by the noise of the jet. She hobbles to her shop.

Annie and Myrtle run from their hiding places, meet in a laughing embrace. Tears are falling from Annie's eyes, mascara zigzags down her cheeks. Myrtle sways in her mirth, joy at the silly prank scattering inside her, making her weak, keeping her closely locked to the small Annie in her arms. For several hours the anxiety, the longing for Archie, have been curtained off, unable to disturb.

'It's good to know we can still be so daft, sometimes,' says Myrtle.

When Archie is away Myrtle wakes every morning at four thirty. This is the time that his first shift begins and she likes to feel he is in her thoughts as he wakes. She lies imagining him disentangling himself from his duvet—that does little to disguise the discomfort of the bunk—and taking a single step to the vile little sink whose tap provides a thread of water to splash on his face. She thinks of him pulling on his trousers and salt-stiffened jersey before pushing an egg round the frying pan that none of them ever considers cleaning. She sees him eating fast, efficiently, stomach lurching in time with the rise and fall of the boat. Myrtle imagines it all so hard that sometimes she feels she is transported out to sea, she's an invisible passenger. It's only when she slides a foot to Archie's side of the bed and finds the sheet, smooth and chill, that she knows she is not there, but here, alone. Myrtle shuts her eyes but she will not sleep again. With a great effort of will she puts Archie from her mind, and thinks of Annie.

For years she has tried to analyse Annie's powers, for years she has failed. What is it about Annie that draws people to her, wanting to please her, wanting to be in her presence? The pretty face is far from the whole solution. The solution—and after years of trying, Myrtle is beginning to understand—is to do with the feeling Annie conveys that she is the centre of an important part of the universe, and whoever is with her shares that place. Myrtle remembers well that feeling as a child. In Annie's company, she felt important, courageous. Without her, time was flatter, duller. Annie brought a gladness to bear wherever she was, and it brushed off on others like gold dust. The fact that she was petulant, spoilt, sometimes ill-mannered, frequently thoughtless and constantly selfish made no difference. Boys, snubbed by her, never gave up hope that at some future time they would be forgiven. While grown-ups declared they could 'see right through her', they were no less enchanted than Annie's contemporaries when Annie chose to concentrate upon them. Nowadays, whatever disagreements they had, Myrtle found she could never go for more than a few days before returning to Annie— who bore no grudges when Myrtle berated her, and was always pleased to see her back. Even when Annie's trivial chatter most annoyed Myrtle she felt the warmth of her presence, which had been essential to her since childhood, and she could not imagine life without such nourishment. Myrtle liked to think that Annie would feel equally deprived were she to lose her own devotion.

In the last couple of years at school, still too lacking in attraction for any girl to think of her as competition, Myrtle found herself in the role of confidante. Her peers were grateful for her careful listening, her considered opinion. Of all the vicissitudes of young love that Myrtle listened to, there was none half so interesting as Annie's. Since the age of seven Annie had been receiving notes from boys. She used to gather them together, a day's takings, crumpled bits of paper torn from exercise books inscribed with passionate and ill-spelt declarations. After school, she and Myrtle would go behind a bush in the Stewarts' garden and read through them. At first, Annie enjoyed the notes, but over the years, as there was no decrease in their delivery, they began to bore her. 'Same old thing,' she told Myrtle. 'There's no real romance to be found in this place.'

It was real romance, she confessed to Myrtle a thousand times, that she was after. Her suitors were not of like mind. All they wanted was sex. Annie, who had made flirting into her highest art, let them have a little of their way. (By the time she was sixteen, she once confessed, she had kissed twenty-three boys.) Their impatience was their undoing. No sooner had they made their carefully plotted pass, clutched her with sweaty hands and whimpered oh, so soppily, Annie's interest died. She would push them away, regard their silly look of frustrated desire with undisguised scorn, then run to tell Myrtle all the details.

Two boys in the class never attempted to kiss Annie: Archie Duns and Ken Mcleoud. Archie, alone of all the boys in the school, did not fancy Annie. When asked why, he declared her too small, too spoilt and too flirtatious. Looks were not what interested him as much as kindness and calm. Annie, lured by Archie's resistance, did once offer her mouth behind the coal shed. But it was her turn to be rejected. Archie told her firmly to go away. It was three days before Annie, more amused than humiliated, was able to bring herself to pass on this information to Myrtle. She'd never really *fancied* Archie, she said—too dour. She was just annoyed he ignored her so blatantly.

As for Ken, since the day out at St Andrews, he had been so tortured by love for Annie it was impossible for him to speak to her. If by chance he found himself close to her, he would move quickly away. When she noticed Ken's avoiding tactics she found herself faintly intrigued. His lack of response to her most coquettish appeals became a challenge. Eventually she gave up, puzzled. Myrtle advised her there was no point in fretting over one shy boy when she could have her choice among so many who were eager. Even as she produced that homily, Myrtle suspected her own motives.

Myrtle is in the kitchen alone at the table. Archie will have been at work for three hours. It's funny to think that the only two men in her life, Archie and Ken, end up on the same boat. Not that Ken was ever exactly *in* her life. Her hopeless love for him was a secret she had kept from everyone. She was sometimes amazed that Annie did not guess, but then it would never occur to Annie that Myrtle, so plainly unappreciated by boys, might fancy anyone. 'You'll find yourself a good solid husband one day,' Annie once told her. 'Older men aren't so worried about looks. They want a faithful wife who'll cook their dinners and be happy with a quiet life.' Myrtle knew this was Annie's idea of consolation.

Myrtle goes to the window, waits for the kettle to boil. Outside, the sky is that naïve grey peculiar to early mornings in October. Myrtle can smell the sea, but not hear it. The calm, usually some comfort, is disturbed by her thoughts of Ken. The truth is that of late she has come to despise him, his betrayal of Archie. When Ken first became mate on *Skyline II*, his loyalty was total. Now, since he has taken up his second job of 'removals and deliveries', that loyalty has become divided. He returns to the boat a weak link in a strong and devoted crew. Myrtle senses the rows between the two men are increasing and dreads the moment control is lost. She also finds it hard to accept that Ken has turned into a weak and dishonest man. He is taking law-breaking risks merely to pay for the silly status symbols his wife demands. He is a fool. He should condemn Annie for her greed, not pander to it. Then Myrtle remembers that, in his early teens, Ken was daring in his lack of respect for authority. When Myrtle had loved him it had been during his quiet phase. Withdrawn, melancholic, his sad dark eyes had wrenched her heart, though shortly after the day at St Andrews she had given up the idea that he might confide in her again, and her foolish spurt of hope had subsided into calm compassion.

But she had always remained on the alert, lest one day there should be a hint of things changing. *Had* Annie won him over—well, that was a situation, in those days when Ken was Myrtle's only hope, she could never let herself contemplate. And when Annie declared herself not interested in pursuing Ken further, at least there was consolation in knowing that Annie would leave him alone. This comfortable, if unfulfilling, state of affairs lasted three years. Then came the day of the gala.

Even as she remembers it, Myrtle pulls her shawl tighter. There is still the echo of the pain that she buried long ago, for the sake of her friendship with Annie. Myrtle thinks there is reason never quite to trust even the closest of friends.

There were galas, then, every year. As children Myrtle and Annie would go down to the harbour, watch as the boats, dressed up for the day in flags and flowers, sailed out of the harbour in their fancy dress. They made such a pretty flotilla, their hulls hidden under skirts of looped flowers, greenery and ribbons that fluttered with every bounce of the waves. Each boat had its chosen Fisher Lass, a beautiful young girl in some extravagant dress that was the result of weeks of excitement in its creation (and happily paid for by the skipper and crew). The Fisher Lass would sit at the head of the boat, unmoving as a masthead. Behind her, family and friends would drink and sing. Myrtle and Annie longed for that time someone would invite them onto their boat.

It came the summer they were both seventeen. Archie Duns's father, Ben, had been an old friend of Jock Stewart. Ben's wife, Sarah, suggested Dot help with the food. She was invited to bring the two girls, whose intense excitement was increased to breaking point when they learned that Annie had been chosen to be the Fisher Lass. There followed weeks of flurried plans concerning her dress, hair, make-up, shoes, which, seeming to occupy every moment of Annie's thoughts, Myrtle found a little tiring. Her greatest contribution was in persuading Dot, a natural seamstress, to make the dress. Annie explained she would recognise the material she was looking for when she saw it, which meant visits to drapers up and down the coast, Myrtle her weary companion. Eventually she settled on a bale of pale mint lace.

As the dress progressed, Annie came more and more often to try it on, querying every seam, every tuck, requesting that the neck should be a pinch higher, an inch lower. While Myrtle slouched in a chair, Annie jiggled in front of a mirror. Dot, tried to the limit by Annie's ungracious striving for perfection, let fly. 'Och, stop your complaining, girl, or I'll no' put in another stitch.'

Annie's quick smile of contrition, her apology for her nervous state, quelled Dot's fury. She stopped jiggling her hips; the skirts—pink imitation silk beneath the mint lace—froze round her knees. Myrtle realised with awe that Annie's prettiness had given way to looks of wondrous and extraordinary beauty. She thought how lucky she was, being Annie's friend, to be part of all this excitement.

On the morning of the gala, Annie came round to the Stewarts' house soon after seven. While Dot cut sandwiches, Annie jittered about, touching the dress. She'd never seen anything so beautiful, she said. Every few minutes she hugged Dot, which interfered with the sandwich-making, and thanked her a dozen times. By eight o'clock she could wait no longer. She slithered into the dress and spun about. Everybody laughed at her happiness.

Suddenly, facing Myrtle, she stopped. 'What about you, Myrtle? What are you going to wear?'

In all the flurry of organising the Fisher Lass's clothes, Myrtle had given no thought to her own appearance.

'I'll think of something,' she said. 'It's early yet.'

There was too much on Annie's mind to concentrate further on anyone else: silver shoes to be taken from their tissue paper, earrings to be secured, hair brushed to a shine that would defy the wind—so much trouble all for so few hours of glory, Myrtle thought. But perhaps that was the whole point of glory—the anticipation.

As they walked to the harbour, Myrtle looked at her friend with silent awe. She marvelled at the incandescence of Annie's skin, and the black-lashed eyes whose every restless movement sparked a chip of diamond in the blue irises. From today, Myrtle realised, things might happen to Annie that had never happened before. And she, Myrtle, would be left far behind. Perhaps now their close ways would diverge.

When they reached the harbour wall, they stood looking down at the waiting boat. At the bows a chair had been transformed into a magnificent throne of greenery dotted with flowers. Myrtle was suddenly afraid, though she could not define the fear. She moved closer to Annie, in attendance, before the Fisher Lass was urged towards her seat. Myrtle's forebodings were further strengthened by the sight of so many passengers: a crowd of Archie's friends—Ross, Sandy, Roddy, Ken, Hamish. Annie was waving to them, acknowledging their catcalls of praise with small bows. A gust of wind flattened her lace skirts against her legs and scrambled her hair into a thousand curls. Then Ben Duns lifted Annie up in both arms and carried her down into the boat. There was more laughter and cheering.

Myrtle and her mother, clutching boxes and baskets, made their way down the slippery steps. Archie, the only boy who seemed to have no interest in Annie's enthronement, received them, putting a firm elbow under Myrtle's arm as she stepped onto the deck. She knew that Annie, despite all the clamour around her, would not be too preoccupied to notice that Archie was paying her no attention. Only recently Annie had observed that the god Archie had *never* paid her any attention since the 'silly incident' when they were children. At some point his stand-offish behaviour would have to be challenged.

Myrtle made her way to the back of the boat where Dot was sorting food. Beside her sat Ken, pale face well back into the hood of his waterproof. He nodded to Myrtle. She sat next to him in the only empty seat. This proximity to Ken stirred Myrtle in some vaguely pleasurable way. She would enjoy sitting beside him, would not mind his silence.

The boats set off at last, a line of seven of them, their loops of flags all twittering in the breeze, their Fisher Lasses upright in the bows, heads high, stiffly smiling.

Skyline rose and dipped with a rhythm that sometimes broke. Then the boat would tip at an unexpected angle, jostling the passengers. On several occasions Myrtle found herself pushed into Ken's side. She apologised each time. He did not seem to mind. But he kept his silence, so Myrtle concentrated on the distant Lammermuir Hills, and the way Bass Rock was becoming gigantic as they approached it. By midmorning there was a high sun, though the breeze was still cold. The light on the sea had a strange thinness, as if it had been dragged over by a feather to enliven the dense navy. This light made a wide path across the waves which the boats seemed to be following.

Myrtle had not thought of sharing her observations, but suddenly she was aware of herself murmuring to Ken, 'Don't suppose the fishermen are surprised by all this sort of thing.' She nodded in the direction of the path of light. 'Probably don't even notice.'

Ken gave a reluctant movement of his closely packed lips, which Myrtle took as a comprehending smile. Before he could reply, Dot pointed out that they were turning for home now. And indeed Myrtle saw that all seven boats were curving round, their backs now to the Rock, and were facing the home coast.

Myrtle helped Dot unpack sandwiches and pour out lemonade. 'Take something up to Annie,' said Dot. 'She'll be famished, behaving all this time like a regular masthead.'

Myrtle made her way along the deck, the wind keener now she was upright. The boys, still crowded round Annie, made way for her.

'She's gone all silent, silent as a bloody statue,' said Hamish.

'We canna get a word out of her,' said Ross, 'and it's very boring.'

Myrtle saw at once what Hamish meant. Annie sat upright, rigid, her head thrown back, staring at the horizon, apparently unconscious of her surroundings, impervious to the boys' gibes which had replaced the compliments. For a moment Myrtle was alarmed. Annie's eyes seemed to be fixed on some invisible place. Her cheeks shimmered with a thousand tears of spray and the front of her green lace dress was darkened with water. Myrtle touched Annie's arm. It was icy cold.

'Here, Annie, I've brought you something to eat,' she said. Annie did not respond. Myrtle touched her again. 'Come on, Annie. What's the matter? You're so cold. Shall I get you a jacket?' After a long moment Annie very slightly shook her head. The boys cheered. Annie murmured that she would like Myrtle to leave her. Myrtle, defeated, moved away. The boys jeered at her for having no effect on the sleeping beauty. Fed up, now, they began to move towards the boat's stern and help themselves to food and drink. Myrtle stood watching Ben at the wheel.

ANGELA HUTH

Archie stood behind his father, some two inches taller: broad and strong and stern, his blond hair jagged about his forehead. He smiled briefly at Myrtle, shrugged: a message that Annie was a hopeless case, the least entertaining Fisher Lass he had ever seen. The thought flashed through Myrtle's mind that Archie was the most desirable boy along the coast, and had she been a different sort of girl then she might have allowed herself to fancy him. As it was, there was not the slightest possibility that Archie would ever have reason to be interested in her. Ken, on the other hand—with his sullen ways—if she waited patiently, perhaps one day Ken would turn to her.

As a large wave, which had sneaked up on them from nowhere, tipped the boat, Myrtle was flung to one side and fell. In the next instant she saw one of Annie's thin white arms, pearled with water, shoot into the sky as the boat righted itself. Then she felt a strong hand under her own arm, and the blue of Ken's waterproof filled her vision as clumsily he dragged her to her feet. She turned to thank him, but he was gone. And Annie's arm had returned to her side. Still rigid as before, her head was tipped further back.

Months later, Annie explained she had wanted the journey just for herself, holding the brief hours to her so that they would be imprinted in her mind for ever: sun, sea spray, cloud; the movement of the boat, the noise of gulls and boys. She went into a kind of trance, she said, which she could not allow anyone to break.

Early afternoon the boats reached a harbour some miles up the coast, a prettier place than Dot and Myrtle's village. Behind the harbour, white-painted houses clustered on a small hill. Some had scarlet geraniums at their windows, and front doors of yellow and green. A makeshift dais had been put up a few yards from where the passengers alighted from the boats. It stood in a tangle of torn nets, lobster pots and coils of tarred rope: a precarious-looking structure to which a skirt of salmon-pink crepe paper had been inadequately pinned. Quite a crowd had gathered to watch the proceedings.

Myrtle could see that Annie, tripping up the wobbly steps with the other six Lasses, was showing some sign of nerves. She clutched at the damp skirts of her dress and looked vaguely about with an unnatural smile. In bright sun, close at hand, the other girls' dresses were painfully clear—bundles of spangled netting, glossy red satin cobbled together with clumsy seams, wilted muslin fit for milkmaids. All the girls' cheeks were buffed to a deep red-brown by the wind, and their carefully organised hair blew free from various combs and ribbons. They were happy, bonny faces, as Dot observed, but only one was beautiful.

382

They stood for what seemed an age, shifting from uncomfortable foot to foot—stilettoes of pearly leather seemed to be the order of the day—casting expectant smiles and giving shudders of exaggerated fear. Annie's statue-pose a thing of the past, she now allowed herself the odd anticipatory jiggle of the hips to encourage the compliments of her admirers, proud of her now, which flew up from the crowd.

'This part always takes too long,' said Dot. 'It's terrible, the waiting.'

'Do you reckon Annie's going to win?' Myrtle's heart was beating fast. She could imagine just how it was for Annie, up there on the dais, so many calculating eyes on her.

'You can never account for the judges' taste. They might think Annie too wee for a good Lass. I've seen certain winners disappointed.'

There was a movement in the crowd. The harbour master, another man and two women, with undisguised looks of self-importance, moved towards the dais. The harbour master alone mounted the steps—the added weight of his fellow judges would have meant disaster. Revelling in the attention, he took his time, milking his moment of eminence. Myrtle, her ears pounding with impatience for the climax of his speech, missed the sonorous words that led up to the announcement of the winner. But she saw the harbour master bend to take a sash from someone in the crowd and then approach Annie with a lascivious smile on his face. There was a roar of approbation. Dot jumped up, shouting Annie's name like a wild thing. Myrtle, clapping, saw the harbour master fumbling to put the sash over Annie's head. Then he handed her a silver shield. For a second Annie held this away from her, smiling at her own reflection, then she moved to the edge of the dais, shut her eyes and stretched both arms above her in a gesture of ecstasy.

She leapt, impossibly high, into the sky, eyes still shut. A dozen arms shot up to catch her. But somehow, midair, her body twisted, avoiding them all. Annie fell onto a bare patch of cobbles. Myrtle caught sight of her shocked face and a badly grazed arm, but her own help was unnecessary, because instantly a group of Annie's admirers was there to retrieve her. She moved her eyes from the crowd and saw that Archie was walking towards the harbour's edge. And that Ken was talking to a fisherman, plainly not interested in Annie's triumph or her fall.

By the evening, having rested on the Stewarts' sofa, Annie's energies were restored. Her object tonight, she told Myrtle, was to win over the elusive Archie. When she entered the supper room for the traditional gala dance at the Seafarers' Hotel, everyone else was seated. As she made her way to the place of honour at the top of the table, there was a general gasp of admiration. Myrtle had no doubt of Annie's power tonight.

After supper the reels began. By now Annie's stand-offish demeanour had disappeared. She was revelling in the race among her admirers to be her partner. With good humour she tried to distribute her favours fairly. As she twirled up and down the lines, she bestowed smiles on whoever was the current partner, making each feel he was in with a serious chance again, no matter how many times he had been spurned in the past. But Myrtle saw that Annie's eyes were also conducting secret hunts. At safe moments they darted towards Archie. Whenever a reel came to an end, Annie led her partner towards the place where Archie stood or sat. Her proximity signalled many times her desire to dance with him, but Archie refused to recognise her invitations.

Myrtle watched from a chair at the side of the room. She was deeply curious. How would the evening end? She did not want Annie to be hurt by Archie's obvious rejection. She had faith in her friend's powers, but by eleven thirty it was plain she was far from achieving her goal.

Dot came to sit next to Myrtle. 'You should take to your feet, dear,' she said. 'When I was your age you couldn't keep me off the floor.'

'I don't like dancing,' said Myrtle, sullen.

'Nonsense! All girls like a reel. Why don't you go over to the bar? There's a crowd of your friends. One of them's sure to ask you for a dance.'

Myrtle blushed, furious. She resented her mother's well-meaning help. She longed to go home. But she knew she could not leave until Annie's predicament was resolved.

Ben, Archie's father, came up.

'I can't get Myrtle here onto the floor,' Dot said, feet tapping.

'Perhaps she doesn't care for reeling,' Ben said. He turned to Myrtle, smiling, sympathetic. 'Is that it?' Myrtle nodded, aware of the hot red of her face. 'But how about you and me have a go at this eightsome?'

Ben was a kind man. Myrtle could not refuse him. She stood, realising she was taller than him. He made her feel like an awkward giant, dingy in her beige skirt and white blouse. She wished she had made more effort, but had reckoned that not to be desired when you have made no effort is less humiliating than not to be desired when you have done your best to look alluring.

Myrtle and Ben joined three couples. One was Annie and Sandy. Before a friendly smile could disguise it, Myrtle saw Annie's look of pity. Myrtle, forced to dance with Archie's father . . .

While Annie's delicate little feet twinkled skilfully through the steps, and her lean back and arms bent like saplings as the boys twirled her keenly round, Myrtle's huge clay feet tried to keep in time and place. She felt the boys struggling to get their arms round her waist. She felt them pushing her as if she was some piece of large and awkward furniture. Only Ben gave her an encouraging smile. Myrtle felt the tears burn her eyes and thought the misery would never end.

When it did, she thanked Ben and made her way to the crowd by the bar. If she helped herself to a glass of wine, she thought, and just stood there, perhaps no one would notice her. She drank fast, took up a position. A moment later Archie passed by.

'Saw you give my old man an enjoyable time,' he said. As far as Myrtle could tell he was not laughing at her. 'That was kind of you.'

'It was kind of *him*,' said Myrtle. They both laughed.

'I've had enough of all this,' Archie said. 'Not my scene. I'm off. Like me to walk you home?'

For an immeasurable time Myrtle was unable to answer this question. The surprise was too great to be digested instantaneously. Archie, the most elusive and desirable boy for miles along the coast, asking her, Myrtle . . . While her cheeks burned outrageously, two very obvious things came to her: Archie was only asking her out of kindness. Escorting her home—he had to pass her house on the way to his— would be no trouble. And were she to accept, Annie would never speak to her again. Even as these things were balancing in her mind, Myrtle turned and caught the full blast of Annie's look. Annie was at the other side of the room, furious, puzzled eyes perched on the rim of a glass of lemonade. The knowledge of her misery was like a physical blow to Myrtle. She would sacrifice anything to avoid Annie's unhappiness. She looked straight at Archie. A terse voice disguised her real feelings.

'I think I'll stay on a while, thanks.' She forced a smile. 'My first Fisher Lass dance—better make the best of it.'

Archie shrugged. He did not care one way or the other whether Myrtle came with him. He just wanted to leave as soon as possible.

'Very well, then. I'll be off.'

Myrtle saw Annie's eyes follow his exit. She saw the tears. But in her own misery she had not the heart to go over to her friend to try to comfort her. Suddenly she was exhausted by the day. As soon as she knew Archie would be well on his way, she slipped unnoticed from the room.

Myrtle hurried through the passages, the patterned carpet moving like shoals of red and blue fish beneath her feet. Although she had drunk nothing but a single glass of wine, she felt unsteady. Sharp lines trembled; wall lamps had the hazy, perilous look of jellies. In the reception area she ran towards the revolving door. Captured within two spread glass wings, she found herself going round so dizzily that she missed the moment of escape. She was forced to go round again, and suddenly, trapped in two opposite wings, was a figure, the face cut into jagged reflections. In irrational panic, this time Myrtle managed to slip out onto the pavement as the doors spun by. Then the other figure escaped too.

It was Ken. He was smiling. 'More fun than the reels, going round and round,' he said. 'Not my sort of evening.'

Myrtle smiled back. Gradually, the spinning of her head was slowing down. 'I've had enough, myself,' she said.

They began to walk. In silence, at first.

'It was certainly Annie's day,' said Ken at last. Shyly, he took Myrtle's arm, but she could tell it was not her he was thinking about.

'It was.' Myrtle sighed. She slid Ken a sideways look. 'Do you still love her?' The unplanned question came out with a harshness that Myrtle instantly regretted. 'I'm sorry, I shouldn't have asked. It's none of my business.' But Ken was not perturbed.

'You don't stop loving someone just because there's no visible hope, do you? You keep thinking something might be possible, one day.'

By now they had reached the house in Arbroath Street. They stopped at the foot of the steps. In the light from the bright moon Myrtle could see the fatigue of long, hopeless love in Ken's eyes.

'As I told you, that day. Annie's intrigued by what she can't easily capture. If you're patient enough . . .'

'But she's so many after her. Do you think she's ever actually . . . ?'

Loyalty to Annie rose at once in Myrtle. She could not discuss such private matters. On the other hand—the devious serpent that thrives on the convolutions of all friendship stirred uncomfortably within Myrtle—if she could be the one to put his mind at rest, then his gratitude to her might even flower into some closer friendship.

'If you're asking what I think you're asking,' she said, 'the answer is no. No.'

Ken's relief was visible. He straightened himself, grew taller.

'Thanks,' he said. 'You've a good heart, Myrtle. Annie's lucky to have such a friend.' He put a hand over Myrtle's. She could feel it was strong with resolve, and felt pleased. This was some compensation for the yearnings of the day. Then suddenly Ken moved his head towards her and kissed both cheeks. She believed the edges of their mouths just touched. Emboldened, Myrtle ran a cautious finger up his bare arm, under the rolled-back sleeve: warm muscle under hard skin. Ken pulled swiftly back. Her prying hand was left at a loss.

The speed and unexpectedness of Ken's kiss left Myrtle with a feeling of ecstatic disbelief. His kiss may have been merely out of kindness, but the secret warmth for him, contained so long, rushed back.

Wholly preoccupied with the sensations of her body, and panting audibly as she turned the key in the door, Myrtle did not see in which direction Ken had gone.

Neither did she see, or guess at, the ending of that gala day. She observed that Annie was unwilling to talk about it, which was puzzling. Myrtle had expected her to relive each moment. All Annie said about Archie's exit was that she was briefly put out. She had enjoyed the dance, she said. But that was all. Perhaps Myrtle had misjudged the significance of the event in her friend's mind, she thought, and questioned her no more.

Three months went by in which nothing more about the gala was said. Myrtle was working hard for her exams. She spent less time with Annie. When they did meet, Myrtle observed Annie to be curiously withdrawn, edgy. At school she almost gave up her flirting. All at once she was grown up. Sometimes, when Myrtle caught a sly look between Annie and one of the boys, she wondered if something was going on that Annie had decided, in a new phase of life, to keep to herself.

But Annie's habit of telling all to Myrtle, demanding her opinion, was strong. At the beginning of the summer holidays they took a picnic lunch up into the fields and Annie confessed.

'I've done it,' she said.

'Done what?'

'You know.' She was plaiting grass. Concentrating hard.

'Who with? Sandy? Ross? Harry?'

'Ken.'

'*Ken?*' Myrtle held a sandwich halfway to her mouth. She dropped it. Annie shrugged, careless. 'It seemed like a good idea at the time. After the gala dance.'

'*After—?*' Myrtle could not repeat the words.

'I was getting fed up, Archie behaving so rottenly and everything. I saw Ken leave—just after you, I think it was. But then he came back.'

'He came back.' It wasn't a question, but a dumbfounded echo. Annie had no idea what she was doing to her friend.

'All the others were arguing about who'd take me home, so I put an end to it all by saying I was going home with Ken as he was the only one who hadn't asked. He looked pretty surprised, I have to say. Blushed deeply.' Annie laughed. 'It was quite awkward, actually, Ken being so silent. I began to think I would have done better to have taken up one of the other offers, though of course the only one I really wanted to be with was Archie. And he'd buggered off, the bastard. Anyhow, Ken was rather sweet. He put his jacket round me. Then somehow we were walking towards St Monan's Church. Ken said, "Let's go down onto the beach." From him, it didn't sound at all like a filthy suggestion. I really believed he just wanted to walk on the sand. So we climbed down. My feet were hurting like hell by now, so I kicked my shoes off and we walked by the water's edge. It was lovely, the cold sand under my squished toes. I couldn't be bothered carrying the shoes. I threw them into the waves. Don't know why. It was a spontaneous thing. Anyhow, it made Ken laugh. He laughed and laughed.'

While Annie smiled at the remembrance, Myrtle said a small prayer for strength. *Please God, don't let me break down until I'm alone.*

'We went back up to the stones—you know, those big flat stones— and sat down. The moon was so bright it was almost like daylight. If it'd been with someone I'd really fancied, it would have been pretty good. So there I am, end of the best day of my life, thinking, Here's the moon and the sea and all that stuff—what a waste. Next thing I know I'm asking Ken to kiss me.'

Annie paused, scrutinised Myrtle's face. Myrtle prayed she would think the watering of her eyes was caused by the hurting sun.

'And we do it.'

Myrtle could think of no response. She could not speak.

'It wasn't up to much, really. Ken hadn't a clue. Not at all what I'd imagined.' She paused again. 'Then, well, it was over. No big deal. Then an awful thing happened.' Annie bit her lip. 'He began to cry. Really sob. I said, "Come on, Ken—what's the matter?" Took him ages to calm down. He said something about not wanting me to think it was just any old occasion—it meant more to him than he would ever be able to tell me. I reckon he 'was overcome—his first time, too. I said, "Brace up, Ken, you don't have to say anything. I'm glad the first time was with you," lying through my teeth. "But don't let it give you any ideas. It was just the end of my Fisher Lass day. We're not going out, or anything." He said that was fine, he was sorry about the crying, and we walked home. Sun coming up.'

Annie lay back and shut her eyes. Myrtle, convinced God had answered her prayer, gathered herself. Caution tightened her words.

'Why didn't you tell me before?'

'I tried, but I just couldn't bring myself. I had to work out how you'd take it. You always used to warn me, so sternly, when we were younger.'

'We're seventeen, now.' Myrtle's light tone was edged with laughter.

'Exactly. So you're not shocked?'

'Of course not.'

Annie sat up, brushing grass from her hair. Their eyes met.

'And since then?' Myrtle could not resist. The agony of not knowing would be unbearable. 'You and Ken?'

Annie shrugged. 'I wouldn't go with Ken again. He was just the end of the Fisher Lass thing, like I said. He doesn't pester me, I'll say that for him.'

'He's someone you can trust,' Myrtle said.

'More than you can say for the others. Most of them can't keep their bloody mouths shut, can they?'

'What about?'

Annie lowered her eyes to concentrate on plaiting more grass. Her demeanour suggested a closeness to shame Myrtle had never seen before and she answered quietly. 'After Ken, I found myself saying I don't mind. Ross . . . poor old Ross, he'd waited so long. Harry, Sandy . . . don't know why really. They were all so impatient.'

'Archie?' Myrtle asked at last.

'Not yet. I've been too occupied to have a go at him. One day.'

'They must have been rather surprised, the other boys.'

'I think they were, rather. Maybe they just thought the right time had come. Sandy said I was showing a green light. You're not shocked?'

'A bit concerned. I wouldn't want you to be thought of as an—'

'Easy lay,' interrupted Annie, who knew Myrtle was uneasy with such jargon. 'That's a risk you have to take if you want a bit of fun. Just hope they're not laughing too much behind my back, comparing notes. As for the other—don't worry. I make sure they all take precautions.'

'Good.' A feeling of great weariness had begun to overwhelm Myrtle. She was eager to be by herself. Reflect on the things Annie had confessed. She wanted to be free to cry without restraint, as Ken had.

'Sandy's top of my list at the moment,' Annie broke in. 'He's a sweet lad. And a quick learner.' She giggled. 'We came up here one evening—'

Myrtle did not want to know. Quickly she stood up. Unable to bear any more, she hurried off, leaving Annie to pack up the picnic bag. When she had gone some way she heard a shout.

'Have I said something?' Annie cried.

Myrtle did not answer, but ran faster into the lacerating sun.

The impact of Annie's confession and the thought of Ken's innocent betrayal consumed Myrtle for the first few weeks of that summer holiday. She and Annie continued their normal life together, when Annie wasn't off with one of the boys, and Myrtle managed to conceal her own disturbed feelings. The last thing she wanted Annie to know was that she had ever entertained hope of serious friendship with Ken. It was the first time in their lives Myrtle had kept anything concerning her own most private feelings from her friend. The friendliness Ken had shown Myrtle after the dance had briefly fanned her hopes. It had not occurred to her a boy would kiss (albeit chastely) one girl and make love to another within a matter of hours. Then Annie's news, that Ken plainly still loved her, added to the shock. She felt deeply for Ken, she felt for herself. So much suffering, and it had to be kept secret. She could only sob at night when Dot was asleep.

Then, perhaps because she was determined to be rid of the discomfort, her own feelings for Ken slid invisibly away. She awoke one morning to find they had evaporated. Her affection for him, and her sympathy, were still there. But the idea of having some deeper relationship with him made her laugh. She laughed out loud at breakfast, surprising Dot. Ken! However could she have maintained the slightly excited feeling since she was fourteen? She laughed again. Dot observed she hadn't seen her so happy for weeks.

In the void left by thoughts of Ken, Myrtle tried to sort out the sensations Annie's promiscuous life caused: alarm, worry, some diffuse thing that could be jealousy. Not that Myrtle would want or approve such behaviour herself, but she would like occasionally to experience the chance to say no. Not one of the boys had ever given the smallest indication he fancied her. As for her friendship with Annie—it was a difficult time. In her daily exuberance, charged with hormones, part of the excitement was to relate every detail to Myrtle. But Myrtle had no wish to hear the sexual skills or failings of the boys she had known most of her life. She begged Annie to keep them to herself.

'Very well,' Annie eventually agreed. 'I won't tell you a thing except the really dreadful bits, or the really funny bits . . .'

They laughed over this arrangement. But it was the beginning of the parting of their old ways. There was now careful choice in the exchange of secrets, conscious restraint. Myrtle began to wonder, too, whether there was an element of treachery somewhere in her friend.

Myrtle walks through the village weakened by her day spent dwelling on the past. She sees Annie come out of the museum café. Myrtle curses herself. Had she been less preoccupied with her own thoughts, she would have remembered it was Annie's first day at her job and dropped in to see how she was getting on. She shouts. Annie turns. They run to each other.

'It was marvellous!' Annie is all smiles. 'I'm going to be happy there. Like I told you, the whole world is drawn to the café.'

'Really?' Myrtle knows Annie's world probably has a single name.

'There was this chappie, Bruce, from the north. Gave me a huge tip, all for one cup of unspilt tea.' She laughs. 'We get talking. He asks me would I like a drink after work. He's on his way tomorrow.'

'What about Janice?'

'She'll think something's held me up, first day.'

'I'll go round, tell her. Stay with her till you get home.'

'That would be kind.' Annie's mouth puckers. So often Myrtle has seen her like this, torn between right and wrong. To urge in the right direction is always counterproductive. 'Only a drink,' Annie repeats, suddenly impatient. 'There's no need for that face.'

Myrtle finds Janice in Annie's kitchen. She sits at the table, exercise books unopened before her, watching television. Janice's eyes flick from the screen to Myrtle and back without interest. Since the death of the hamster her usual warmth to Myrtle has been noticeably absent.

'Mum's late,' she says.

'I caught sight of her. She said to tell you she'll not be long. Will I get you something to eat?'

Janice shakes her head. 'Not hungry,' she says. 'I'll wait till Mum's back.'

At eleven, Janice is nothing like as pretty as Annie was at the same age, but she has the same wide-apart eyes with thick lashes, and a languid smile that could lead to success when she is older. What she lacks is Annie's spirit, animation. She suffers from lethargy, or boredom. No childish ambition seems to goad her. She tolerates the attentions of boys but her natural disinterest means they keep their distance. But, of late, there have been signs of her mother's character. Janice strikes provocative poses. Even alone in the kitchen, there is an elegance in the slouch across the table. This fills Myrtle with misgiving.

'Very well, I'll go next door. Don't want to disturb your homework.'

Her lack of admonition is greeted with a cheeky grin. 'OK. I'll start soon as this is over.'

In the front room Myrtle lowers herself onto the sofa. The imitation leather gives its usual squeak. She wonders if she would have been a good mother—better than Annie, most probably, though at moments, at times convenient to herself, Annie takes great trouble with Janice. Through the panoramic window she can see the sky is darkening—a gathering storm rather than nightfall.

The distant scrape of voices stops. Janice must have kept her word, turned off the television. Myrtle continues to sit, unmoving, in the ever-huskier brown light of the room. Then there is a tap at the window. Myrtle turns: it's a small clutch of pebble-hard raindrops. They begin to tadpole down the glass. They are jolted into sudden speed by a loud crack of thunder. The terrifying noise is sharp, clean as gunshot. It is followed by a second of absolute silence. This is broken by a livid crashing and growling and rain squalls across the glass so hard Myrtle fears it will break. She jumps up to run to the kitchen: Janice is clearly alarmed. At that moment lightning flares through the room. Janice's cries chime like small disjointed bells in the clamour of more thunder.

Myrtle takes the child in her arms. Almost hysterical, she clings to Myrtle, hot-limbed. Her tears darken the wool of Myrtle's jersey. With each new bark of thunder Janice tightens her grip.

Myrtle concentrates on soothing Janice, stroking her head, murmuring it will be over soon. Janice is curled into a babyish position, cheeks blotched with tears. Myrtle thanks God she came. What if Janice, so afraid of storms, had been alone here?

Half an hour goes by. Anger with Annie, and pity for her child, clash within Myrtle. She rocks back and forth, willing Annie to return. Gradually outrage drains from the thunder. Its fury almost spent, the growling after each clap gives way to quieter murmurings.

'I hate thunder,' says Janice, for the third or fourth time. 'I think it's coming to get me.'

'It was a nasty old storm but it's on its way out now.'

'Do you think they'll be all right in the boat?'

'They'll be fine. They've been out in weather much worse than this.' Myrtle tries to sound convincing.

'I hope so.' Janice sniffs. 'I'm hungry now.'

'I'll get you something.'

'You're very kind, Myrtle. Were you sad to hear my hamster died?'

'I was. Of course I was.'

'I cried a lot. Mum said, "Stop blubbing, Janice, it's only a hamster, we'll get another one." She couldn't understand it wouldn't be the same.' Janice puts her arms round Myrtle's neck. Myrtle is touched. Janice is a child who makes little show of her affection. To disguise her feelings, Myrtle knows she must be brusque.

'Now run upstairs and wash your face. I'll butter you a scone.'

Janice obediently slithers off Myrtle's knee.

'We've no butter,' she says. 'We're always out of butter.'

'We'll manage with jam, then.'

'Don't suppose there's any jam either. Mum's not so good at remembering things like that when Dad's away.'

Ten minutes later Janice is eating a hot butterless scone, when Annie returns, clothes dripping, sodden curls flat against her cheeks. Her eyes skitter with guilt—well they might, thinks Myrtle. Were Janice not there she might have risked telling Annie what she thought of her as a mother.

'I'm sorry,' Annie shakes her head. Water patters onto the floor.

'Where were you?' Janice gets down from the table.

'First day in a new job—I was kept, didn't like to hurry away—'

Janice is out of the room. They hear her running upstairs. A door bangs. Annie picks up a dishcloth and rubs her hair.

'She wasn't alone. You were with her,' she says.

'I might not have been.'

'You said you would be. I would have come straight away, otherwise. Always ready to jump down my throat about Janice, you are, Myrtle Duns. Always accusing. What do you know about children?'

'I know that if you're lucky enough to have them, then they should be your priority. How was he, this important Bruce?'

Annie picks up a bunch of spoons and forks from the draining board, throws them into the sink to make an infuriating clatter.

'If you must know, he didn't turn up. Stupid bastard. I waited. Gave him half an hour then ran back here fast as I could.'

Myrtle stands up. 'If I hadn't been here,' she says, 'God knows what Janice would have gone through on her own.'

'I've had enough of your preaching, Myrtle,' Annie shouts. 'Your *goodness*, your *thought* for others, your *priorities*—they make me sick. You may be more saintly than me, but there's one thing you know nothing about: that's *motherhood*.' She is scarlet-cheeked, furious.

Response flares up within Myrtle, but she fights against it. She hates such quarrels. She curses herself for her lack of restraint. This row will mean days of unhappy tension, each waiting for the other to apologise.

'I'll go now, leave you to Janice,' Myrtle says.

Home, the telephone is ringing. Archie, on his ship-to-shore telephone, says the storm has hardly touched them: all is well. Myrtle sits heavily. The news is clouded by the scene with Annie. Fury with those you love best, she thinks, is unlike any other fury in its destruction. She sits listening to the rain, gentler now. The telephone rings again, startling. It will be Annie—to apologise. Charged with unexpected relief, she hurries to answer it. For a moment she does not recognise the voice, a man's. Martin. 'Yes, Martin,' he says. Happens he's been given a lobster. Would she like it if he brought it round to share?

'That would be grand,' says Myrtle. She is still confused, heavy. Stupid to have supposed Annie would make amends so soon. She fills a pan with water, puts it on the stove. It will be good not to spend the evening alone, but she doesn't relish the thought of having to make conversation with Martin. Through the window, as she waits for him, she can see a scattering of stars in a sky suddenly cleared. Moments later there is a knock on the door.

Martin is embarrassed to find Archie not at home. Had he been down to the harbour, seen no boats, he would not have come, he says. Myrtle smiles to see him clutching at his parcel, not sure that sharing his supper with a married woman is in order.

'Perhaps I'd better go,' he says. 'I'll come when Archie's back.'

'Put your lobster down,' says Myrtle. 'Archie'd never forgive me if I turned you both away. Besides, I'm in need of company tonight. Shall I beat up some batter for pancakes while the lobster's boiling? I seem to think you like a pancake with treacle.' How did she remember that? He must have mentioned it, the Lord only knows how long ago.

'Can't think of anything better, if it's not too much trouble.' Martin sits at the table, avoiding what he knows to be Archie's chair. As Myrtle prepares the food they talk about the shortage of fish, problems with the delivery of marble.

When they have finished eating, Martin congratulates Myrtle on her cooking. 'I could do with a wife like you,' he says, laughing. 'I dream of coming home and finding a supper like this on the table.'

Myrtle likes the Canadian drawl of his voice. She grins, trying to imagine him as a husband. Signs were he'd be a good one: faithful, sensitive to his wife's desires. Had Archie not existed, Martin was the sort of man Myrtle would have aspired to, though not with much hope.

'But you've not got one for the lack of offers, have you?' she says. 'Every girl along the coast was after you.'

Martin looks down, reddens. Myrtle sees him as he was: blond hair, bronze skin—diffident among all the sea-going young men of his age. She remembers the excitement he caused among the girls, very clearly.

'I had a picture in my mind of just what a wife should be. None of them came anywhere near it,' says Martin. 'I could never bring myself to go for second best. And now I've given up looking, I suppose.'

'That's ridiculous,' says Myrtle. 'There are good women about. One of them'll cross your path one day when you're least expecting it.'

'Perhaps,' says Martin, not meeting her look.

Later, when the dishes are cleared and the lamps are lit, they move to the wooden chairs either side of the stove. Martin declines Myrtle's offer of a dram of Archie's whisky, but accepts a bottle of lager. Myrtle herself makes do with a mug of tea. The conversation turns to Annie.

'I see your friend, Annie, darting about,' Martin says. 'A real will-o'-the-wisp. Marriage hasn't changed her, I'd say. How is she?'

'She's fine.'

There's a long, easy silence between them. Martin wipes his mouth with the back of his hand. 'I suppose I could have married her,' he says.

'Married Annie?'

'Well, don't think me boasting if I say this, but there was a time when—if I read the signals right—she seemed keen.' Martin meets her eye now. 'I imagine you know . . . about Archie. I mean, it was when she was all out for Archie, trying to add him to her list.'

'Lord, I did. Was she a pest, forever telling me about her pursuit of the elusive Archie?' Myrtle laughs so Martin will see all that—events so long ago—means nothing to her, now.

'Then she seemed to give up on Archie. Turned her attention to me, instead. Heaven knows why. I didn't do a thing to encourage her. Rather, I kept my distance.'

'That's always been the challenge, in Annie's case,' says Myrtle.

'The impression I got was that she was a little . . . afraid of me. There was none of that come-hither stuff I'd see her exercising on others. Then the letters began to come. Strange, wild, beautiful letters. It seemed she thought she'd fallen in, eh, love with me. For all the boys she had accommodated—I remember thinking what an unlikely word for her to use—she'd felt nothing. But she was eating her wretched little heart out for me. She said nothing of this to you?'

Myrtle shakes her head. Her heart begins to beat as wildly as it did some hours ago, when Annie shouted at her. Somehow, she must keep her astonishment to herself. Her mind spins back to that time: Annie daft and laughing as ever, looking vaguely for a new job. Annie drinking with all her short-time lovers in the pub, a bit too much sometimes, perhaps. But not unhappy. As for writing good letters—the idea is beyond comprehension. Myrtle scours her memory for any incident which would in retrospect indicate the truth. But she can remember nothing. Not a hint of hidden, unrequited love.

'So what did you do?' Myrtle, desperately curious to hear the rest of Martin's story, feels this question is permissible.

'I have to say I was touched by those letters. Anyone would have been. Beautiful writing, poetic sort of stuff straight from the heart.'

Annie who never put pen to paper if she could help it: Annie consistently bottom in English, scoffing at Myrtle's love of Keats.

'Does that surprise you?' Martin asks.

'It does, a little.' Myrtle's incredulity is so overwhelming she wonders that Martin cannot see it.

'She became what I can only call obsessive. Following me, jumping out at me at unexpected moments to declare this great love. I never gave her one iota of encouragement. Quite the opposite. I tried to explain she was caught up in some fantasy. Wanting affection, I said, she'd fixed upon me to provide it. She wouldn't listen to a word of that.' Martin pauses, smiles. 'I'm no analyst, but I think I had a point. Father gone long ago, little love or attention from her mother. Then this great flurry of boys—quick fancies, disillusioning sex. She was after something more solid. So happened she picked on me, almost the only one she hadn't known all her life. She wanted love. But I couldn't give it to her.'

'You didn't feel anything for her at all?'

'Only pity. Of course I saw she was an exceptionally attractive girl. But not for me.' Myrtle fetches him another lager. Presses him a little.

'So how did you resolve it?'

Martin sighs. He opens the bottle, fills the glass then puts it on the floor without drinking. 'It had to stop. I was worried about her. Inevitably the end was untidy. She taxed my patience once too often. She came round in the middle of the night. She was sobbing, desolate. She'd come to tell me of her resolution to wait for me, no matter how long. I said, "Annie, don't you understand? I don't love you, I never will love you, and all this nonsense must stop." I rather lost my cool I guess. I wasn't as gentle as I might have been. All I wanted was to stop her preying on me. As usual, my words had no effect. So I told her I loved a different sort of woman—a quiet, gentle soul who'd never flirted in her life. Unattainable, sadly, but so entrenched in my heart I've no hope of ridding myself . . .' He petered out, embarrassed to have gone so far.

'I didn't know that,' says Myrtle.

Martin reaches for his glass. 'No, well, I keep things to myself.'

'And how did she take the news?'

'She said I was making it up to try to put her off. She said it wouldn't make a jot of difference to what she felt—ever. Poor Annie. Then—well, I regret this. She said, "I'll strike a bargain with you. Give me one kiss on the cheek, and I'll not bother you any more. I can see it's useless, now. But one day you'll see how foolish you were—and I'll still be there." She sounded so pathetic. I said I was sorry I had shouted at her, but I didn't know how to get the truth through to her. Then I did what she wanted. I kissed her gently on the cheek. But as soon as my mouth touched her skin, she fell away from me as if I'd struck her—fainted. I gave her some whisky, brought her round. She apologised for being a nuisance. I couldn't help seeing how real her fantasy had become—girls don't faint when they're kissed on the cheek, these days. Anyway, true to her word, she stopped her pursuing after that. Avoided me for a while, then just acted normally as if nothing had ever happened. But that was all a long time ago,' he pauses. 'I can't say we're close friends, but she's not unfriendly. She seems to be happily married to Ken, doesn't she?'

'Aye. Ken's a good husband to her.'

Martin looks at his watch, stands up. 'My, how I've been going on,' he says. 'I'm sorry. It's late.'

Myrtle goes with him to the door. 'And your own . . . unrequited?' she says, not meaning to say anything. 'I'm sorry about—'

'Yes, well, you get used to the insurmountable. Even if the shade—is that the right word?—never quite goes. Anyway, thank you for listening. I've never told that story before.' He puts a hand on Myrtle's arm for a moment. His touch ignites a flare of sympathy—is it sympathy, exactly?—through her body. The sensation is unnerving.

'Thank you for coming round,' says Myrtle. 'Thanks for the lobster.'

'My pleasure.' He inclines his head.

Myrtle smiles at his old-fashioned courtesy. She sees that once more his face is blazing. Funny how she has never noticed his easy blushing before. But then in all the years they have known one another they have never had anything like tonight's conversation. It is past midnight when Myrtle closes the door.

Sleep is not possible. Myrtle returns to her chair. In her confusion the words *betrayal, disillusion, disaster* swarm through her head. It has never occurred to her that Annie, the person she has loved so much for so long, has carried on keeping important parts of her life to herself. The fact that Annie, obviously so unhappy at the time, did not require Myrtle's help, or sympathetic ear, is a blow of such magnitude that she is consumed by a physical wrenching. How many other events, loves, losses, has Annie not told her about? How was it that she failed Annie so badly? How could she have been so unobservant, not even suspecting her secret traumas? They had sworn, at a young age, to be best friends and tell each other everything, always. A childish pact, perhaps. But one they had believed in. Annie confided so many thoughts that it had never occurred to Myrtle there could possibly be much she was keeping to herself. For Myrtle's own part, with the single exception of her feelings for Ken, she tried to supply Annie with private information. Most private of all her secrets was to do with the shame of her large hands and feet. She had told Annie that while she knew she would never be the kind of woman who would attract men, she wondered if physically she might improve? Annie had said yes, of course; everyone gets better once they've lost their puppy fat. In truth, Myrtle was aware Annie was not much interested in Myrtle's confessions. But she had no intention of breaking her promise, so continued to supply some secrets, no matter how dull Annie found them.

Myrtle remains in her shocked state for a long while. She hears a gentler rain than earlier, shimmying down the window panes. And she remembers a day of light rain. Annie had red, puffy eyes. She said she had some infection: they had been to the chemist for ointment. Myrtle asked what was the matter? Nothing, said Annie. Nothing now. *Now* meant *Now that something important is over. Now that I've given up all hope of Martin's love.* How *could* Myrtle have had no inkling of what her friend was going through?

And one further memory returns. It is in the street, possibly later that day. Annie told Myrtle, with a pathetic attempt at light-heartedness, her plan to have one more attempt at seducing Archie. Myrtle thought nothing of this declaration at the time. Now, Myrtle sees the bravado of it, and the fury against Annie, that has been uncoiling itself since Martin's story, begins to ebb. She remembers instead all Annie has been to her: the exuberant leader, the encourager, the one so generous in her small acts of kindness—the joker. Their friendship has often astonished others. But they understand it—Myrtle the rock, Annie the spark, it suits them both. And perhaps, Myrtle thinks, deceit of a certain kind among friends is a form of self-preservation. Small betrayals must be forgiven. She is calmed by the thought.

When Archie returns the following evening, Myrtle can tell at once that he is in good spirits. A slow, ponderous tread is his normal gait. But happiness, or relief, spur him a little faster. This evening he slaps down two hunks of fish on the table rather than bothering to find the usual tin plate that raw fish is kept upon. He throws his damp jersey at Myrtle rather than hanging it over the back of his chair.

'What's all this, Archie?'

Archie smiles. The taut solemnity of his face is broken up into unaccustomed lines and dips and puckerings round eyes and mouth.

'Here, wifey,' he says. She goes to him.

'I thought of you through your storm yesterday evening. Wish to God I'd been here.' Myrtle privately rejoices: she never likes to ask Archie whether he thinks of her at sea. She can taste salt on his lips. His hands are on her breasts, covering them.

'Let's not eat for a while,' Archie says.

They go to the bedroom. Archie smells powerfully of sweat and fish and cold salt water. Myrtle smiles to herself: storms have always been an aphrodisiac to Archie. Archie puts out her smile by clamping his mouth to hers. She guides one of his hands to her neck. His salt-stiff fingers pull at the small buttons. Clumsy in his impatience, it takes a long time to undo them. Myrtle, engaged in other overtures, does not help him. She likes his urgency. She likes the way he begins tunelessly to hum, or moan. The noise reminds her of wind in sails, the calls of dolphins and the depths of the sea.

After supper Archie says he is going down to the boat to fetch his torch. He wants to inspect the roof. Myrtle says she will go with him. She feels that curious combination of melting weakness and newly lighted strength that comes from perfect lovemaking.

'Annie's not going to be so pleased with Ken.' Archie says. 'He made me a promise. We thrashed it all out—finished up shaking hands on it. No more of his bloody stupid "deliveries". He's going to sell his van.'

'That's all good,' says Myrtle.

'I've told him. If he's off again, that's it. He's out of the boat. None of that'll please Annie, I reckon.'

'She's got a new job,' says Myrtle. 'That should make up a little—'

'That won't last long if the others are anything to go by.' Archie cannot resist a trace of scorn in his laugh.

'Who knows? Maybe she's found the right thing this time.'

A feeble moon struggles for recognition among passing clouds. Myrtle and Archie stand looking down at the scarcely visible deck of *Skyline II*. Archie lowers himself down the iron ladder cut into the harbour wall, jumps onto the deck.

It is cold now. Myrtle draws her mother's shawl more tightly round her. Patiently she waits. At last the skipper's face appears over the wall, and she takes his arm again.

'How about going for a drink?' Archie says. 'Would you like that?'

The invitation is so unusual that Myrtle has to pause before answering that she would love a small whisky. The thought of the noise and warmth of the pub is appealing.

'Very well, then. A wee drink it shall be. Tomorrow we must up to the cemetery, you remember.'

'Och, aye.' The anniversary of Archie's father's death. How many years is it? Myrtle cannot remember. A long time. Gone so fast.

Ben Duns died of cancer, a slow and appalling process observed by Archie, aged twenty-three, with increasing horror and desolation. Only to a very few did Archie reveal his profound sense of loss and despair. At first, he occupied himself with reorganising the boat, replacing old members of the crew who wished to retire, now Ben was gone, with younger ones. He arranged longer trips than usual to sea—the new young crew, all unmarried, did not seem to mind. On his return home he would find flowers and kindly notes from girls he had briefly fancied at school. 'How can I help?' 'Let me do your washing.' 'I'll send you over a pie, just needs warming up.'

Archie was touched by such kindness, but never requested help. And after some months, instead of passing most of his shore leave in his house, where Ben's things lay untouched, he began to pass the days in the Stewarts' house. Dot and Ben, after the deaths of their respective spouses, had become great friends. Dot had mothered Archie after Sarah Duns had died. So it was in Dot's kitchen he felt most comfortable, eating her copious meals, listening to her familiar stories. He was used to Myrtle's silent ways, her diffident smile, her care not to intrude. Myrtle regarded Archie with the affection of a sister, and she was able to act towards him with an openness, a lack of awkwardness, that eluded her in the company of other young men.

One day, some three months after Ben's death, Dot gave the command that Archie should go through his father's things—take the clothes to a charity shop, generally reorganise the house. 'Go on with you,' she said, 'it's got to be done some time. Myrtle here will help you.'

The house, untouched by a woman's hand for the last decade, was a sad shambles. In the stuffy air there was a smell of dust and salt, and Archie's efforts at domesticity were not impressive.

'It's not usually this bad,' he apologised. 'Just lately it's all got rather out of hand, being at sea so much. Let's get the worst over first.'

He led her up to Ben's bedroom. This had plainly not been visited since the day Ben was taken to hospital. A smell of impending death had been horribly preserved in the airless room.

'Oh, God,' said Archie, hand to his nose.

'Open the window,' said Myrtle.

He struggled with the small casement. Fresh sea air gushed in, cutting through the stench within, but not extinguishing it. Myrtle made her way to the cupboard and pulled open the little door. There was Ben's

Sunday suit, a brown pinstripe. The stripes were worn and smudged round the back of the collar, where two grey hairs clung and moved like ghostly tendrils. Two pairs of stiff, sea-stained heavy jeans, and a light jacket. Pushed to one side was a dress of drooping crushed velvet.

Archie turned, saw the clothes.

'Oh, God,' he said again. 'Mother's wedding dress. My dad would never throw it away.'

He sat heavily on the bed. Then slowly his head descended into his hands and he began to sob. At first it was silent as his body swayed back and forth. Tears fell over his fingers onto his knees. Then he began to moan, a deep, pitiful noise.

Myrtle had never seen a man cry before, and was alarmed. Bereft of comforting words, she sat on the bed beside Archie. After a while she put a hand on his heaving shoulder. Eventually, the sobbing lost its strength. Finally drained of tears, Archie fiercely scrubbed at his eyes. Myrtle removed her hand. He stood up.

'Sorry,' he said. 'Thanks for being here.' He picked up a plastic rubbish bag. 'I'll hold it. You shove in the clothes.'

'No,' said Myrtle, rising too and taking the bag from him, 'It's a job best done by Ma and me. We'll do the whole house for you next week when you're at sea. We're good at that sort of thing.'

Archie shrugged, attempted a smile. He had no energy to protest.

Myrtle smiled strongly back. 'You'll come back to find everything sparkling,' she said. 'Ma and I will enjoy that. Let's go now. There's a stew for dinner. You must be hungry.'

Downstairs a pink envelope lay on the doormat. Exhausted, Archie opened it without interest. He read the single page quickly to himself, then handed it to Myrtle.

Dear Archie, she read, *Just to say how sorry I am about your dad. He was a good man with not an enemy in the world, wasn't he? I will never forget when he chose me to be Fisher Lass on his boat and told me that as skipper it was his duty to pay for my dress. He said you go ahead lass and spend whatever is necessary. I thought that was very nice of him, very generous. Do hope by now you are not still too much down in the dumps. Love for now, Annie.*

'Good of your friend,' said Archie.

What was Annie up to? wondered Myrtle. What was her idea? Her threatened one last assault on Archie had had to be postponed because of Ben's death. Myrtle chided herself for such uncharitable thoughts: Annie was merely showing her sympathy, like everyone else.

Archie threw away the letter. He and Myrtle returned to the Stewart house for Dot's long-simmered stew. As they sat at the table, Myrtle was aware of the warmth of the thought of rescuing Archie's house from its present depressing state. To have Archie's house all ready for him when he next got back from fishing . . . a curious excitement was simmering, a new feeling she could not name.

She and Dot worked hard on Archie's house. He returned to find it transformed into a welcoming place, clean and shining and full of fresh air. Archie's delight, though apparent, did not inspire him to unusual rhetoric. He merely said the place hadn't looked so good since his mother was alive, and he thanked them. His pleasure was evident in his absence, after that, from the Stewart house. He still paid visits, did small jobs for Dot, but he spent far more time at home.

Myrtle found herself carefully observing Annie. Annie's moods fluctuated, as they always had, but she seemed restless, more prone to melancholy. She was irritated by Myrtle's job (coaching children to read for several hours a week) while she herself was unemployed. She did mention one afternoon that she thought her best plan would be to marry soon. 'Though God knows where I'll find a good man in our neighbourhood, Myrtle.' Myrtle replied that Annie would do better to put her mind to employment. It had effect: Annie made no further reference to her matrimonial hopes, but took a job in the post office, and bided her time. For a while she went out with a fisherman from Aberdeen. But he was given his marching orders after six weeks and then she was manless and restless again. Her past boyfriends were marrying girls from their old class. Archie, on the few occasions she saw him, looked more cheerful. Time, Annie told Myrtle, to have one last light-hearted attempt. 'Nothing serious,' she assured her. 'I'd never think of marrying a man like Archie. Archie will end up marrying some serious woman just like him, and they'll be happy ever after.' She laughed her scoffing laugh, and Myrtle felt so sick she turned away.

A week or so after Annie's announcement Myrtle went to the post office early one morning for stamps. Annie was behind the counter.

'Didn't work,' she said. 'Silly bugger. Doesn't know what he's missed.'

'It was a bit soon after Ben's death,' ventured Myrtle. There was such a leaping of relief within her that she had to control her words carefully.

'You can't mourn for ever. Life's got to go on. I'll tell you all about it one day. It was quite funny, quite amusing, I'll say that.'

Later that day Archie came round for tea before returning to the boat for a long trip. He hung a picture for Dot, asked if Myrtle would keep an eye on the flowers on his parents' grave. No mention of Annie. From his behaviour, it would have been impossible to guess anything untoward had taken place. The only unusual thing was that he asked Myrtle if she would walk to the boat with him: she could carry Dot's cake while he managed other supplies. He was to sleep on board; departure was at dawn next morning. He took the stuff on board, then told Myrtle to hurry home, patting her arm. Myrtle obeyed him, much though she wanted to linger. She wondered if her imagination was playing cruel tricks, but did not allow herself to think too far in that direction.

It was not till some years after she and Archie were married that she learned the full story. Archie had had a feeling, he said, that for some time after the pink letter, Annie had been following him. Several times she turned up at the same place as him, too often to be coincidence. Then came the winter evening Archie had gone for a walk in the woods.

He had not gone far along the path when he heard someone calling his name. Archie turned. Annie stood some yards behind him, an innocent-looking Red Riding Hood figure in a knitted cape with a hood. She carried a bundle of twigs under one arm. Having observed that it was funny to run into Archie here, of all places, she explained that she was gathering firewood for their elderly neighbour. The story was very unlikely. Annie was not a known walker. From harbour to pub to home was as far as she ever went. Annie chattered on, impervious to his silence. When her bright little remarks ran out, she suddenly pushed past Archie on the path, and made her way ahead of him, calling out that she was going back to the road and it had been nice seeing him.

Archie remained where he was, wondering what to do. The enjoyment of the evening had been spoilt by Annie's unexpected presence. He had the uneasy thought that the meeting had been arranged by devious means. But he also felt that it was not safe for a young woman to be alone in these woods on a dark evening. He had better make sure she was all right. Archie walked quickly down the path expecting to see Annie after a hundred yards or so. But no sign. Then from behind a tangle of bushes, he heard laughter. His name was called. Annie urged him to join her in a little clearing she had found.

Annoyed, Archie made his way through the bushes. Annie was sitting on the trunk of a fallen tree. She was swinging her legs against it, banging the bark with her heels, childlike. She grinned up at Archie, laughed at what she called his solemn face.

At this moment in his story Archie paused to try to impress upon Myrtle the strangeness of light in the small clearing. On the path it had been a normal winter gloaming, but here the density was a surprising blue-white, like sea mist. Annie had thrown off her cape. Beneath it she wore a cardigan the blue of her eyes, made of soft, fuzzy wool, done up to the neck with a line of small pearl buttons.

They stood looking at each other. The flutter of wood pigeons in high branches was the only sound. Eventually, Archie asked Annie if she wasn't cold. She replied the only thing she felt was romantic. Even as she said this, head tilted, eyes fluttering, one hand ran up the line of buttons, pulling them apart. The two sides of the garment were thrown open and it was flung to the ground. Archie's eyes followed the progress of its silent wings till it landed, then looked slowly, reluctantly, up to Annie's bare breasts. 'There,' said Annie.

At twenty-three, this was Archie's first view of naked breasts. To date his knowledge of girls' bodies had been confined to their curious, soft rises and slopes explored under cover of darkness. In the strange light, the outlines of her breasts were hazy, but clear enough to make Archie feel a shortness of breath. He sensed his hands stirring—desperate, for an appalling second, to cover the skin which must surely be icy cold. He clenched his fists and kept them firmly at his side. Annie wriggled her shoulders. The milky, ethereal shape of her moved gently in invitation. 'I'm here for you, Archie,' she cooed.

It was her voice, the pathetic little phrase attached to her offering, that broke the spell. Archie's turmoil of feelings was replaced by embarrassment, anger. He shouted at her to put on her clothes. He didn't want her—he never had wanted her and never would want her. She was nothing more than the village slag—used by everybody, loved by no one, and serve her right for her years of revolting behaviour. If she had any plans for future happiness she had better change her ways. Yes, he went too far—spurred by guilt, perhaps, for having briefly contemplated an ignoble act.

By now it was completely dark. Archie could hear Annie sobbing and was unmoved. He knew that the smallest word or gesture of compassion would be misconstrued. He left her to her misery in the cold night. After that, Annie avoided Archie. They did not speak again for many months.

It's the last afternoon of this shore leave. Both Archie and Myrtle have had a particularly good time. Some shore leaves are too cluttered with jobs for any real peace or pleasure. This time there has been little to do but enjoy themselves. The four days have flown.

Archie is down at the boat. Myrtle is not expecting him back for a couple of hours. She is aware that the pleasure of the last few days has softened her edges. She feels sleepy, although she is not tired. She drifts about the kitchen, while she waits for the bread in the oven she has baked for Archie's tea, enjoying her dreamlike state.

There is a knock on the door. A visitor will break the spell Myrtle wants to last till Archie leaves. Her shout to come in is reluctant.

Ken enters the room. He is agitated, she can see. He keeps rubbing a hand over his mouth as if with an invisible towel. Myrtle tells him to sit.

'Annie wants a car,' he says.

'What?'

'A *car*—can you believe? How can we afford a car?'

'She's not mentioned it to me.'

'It just came to her last night, late, all of a sudden. Says she's stuck here, a prisoner. Can't get out. She's at the mercy of public transport, she says. What she wants is to get in a car and drive about when she feels like it.' Ken sighs, pushes his thin fingers through his hair.

'Perhaps the novelty's worn off the microwave and she has to have something new to aim for. You know our Annie.'

'I do,' says Ken. He sounds rueful. 'I expect Archie's told you,' he goes on, 'of our agreement. It's a relief, I can tell you. Apart from anything else, working nights when I come home is taking its toll. But I only did it for Annie. She wanted so many things I couldn't afford to buy otherwise. I like to keep her happy.'

'But Annie must be pleased you and Archie have sorted things out. She must have seen you couldn't keep it up much longer.'

Ken shrugs. 'To be honest, I'm not sure she was all that bothered.'

'Oh, I'm sure she was.'

'You're a good friend to Annie, Myrtle. Don't know what she'd do without you. But I sometimes wonder what the hell you get from her in return. I used to wonder that even when we were at school.'

'I get a lot,' says Myrtle, a defensive look hardening her eyes. 'I've loved her ever since I was a small child, no matter what. Beneath all the nonsense there's a good heart, and a special way with her that's hard to describe. When she's concentrating on you she makes you feel on top of the world. There's nothing I'd not do for Annie.'

'I know what you mean,' says Ken. 'It's that mostly unseen bit I fell in love with when she was a girl.' He pauses.

'How can I help you?' Myrtle asks.

'I thought you might persuade her that it's a bloody silly thing to want, a car. Make her see sense. She knows we can't afford it.' He stands up: a thin figure with arm muscles lean as leather straps. Myrtle looks at him with complete dispassion, wondering how she could ever have been so drawn, even for a short time, to the difficult, clever but bloodless, Ken.

'I'll do what I can if she mentions any car nonsense to me,' says Myrtle. 'Try to avert her mind to something cheaper.'

They smile: recognition of their mutual love for Annie, and understanding of her singular ways. Then Ken makes his way to the door.

'Have you seen anything of Janice, of late?' he asks. His back is to her, so Myrtle cannot see his face.

'I was with her during the storm. She's growing up fast—'

'Where was Annie?'

'Her first day at the museum café. She was held up.'

Ken nods. 'Well, thanks.'

Myrtle, standing by him at the open door, sees a quick, grateful smile, but the anxiety still there.

When he has gone, Myrtle takes the bread out of the oven. It is a little burnt on top. She curses herself for leaving it too long. She continues to think of Ken. It's evident all is not well between him and Annie. For Ken to come to Myrtle signifies a seriousness Myrtle has not guessed at. She catches her breath, saddened. Her mind takes refuge in the past. She remembers a cold afternoon, here in the kitchen, a week or so after Annie had announced that her assault on Archie had gone wrong. They were eating Dot's scones. Annie piled hers high with raspberry jam.

'You'll never guess what I'm doing tonight, Myrt,' she said.

'No,' agreed Myrtle. Her friend was wriggling about, good-humoured, licking up jam from the plate with her finger.

'I'm going for a drink with Ken.'

'*Ken?*'

'Well, he asked me, didn't he? Why not? I thought. Ken's an old friend, isn't he? He's kept his word, not bothered me since the Fisher Lass dance. So, anyway, I said, "All right, Ken. But no funny business, mind." He didn't seem to mind. Understood. Can I have the last scone?'

'Go ahead,' Myrtle said. The warmth of her own feelings for Archie guarded her against any retrospective jealousy. But she was not unshaken by an irrational irritation: here was Annie messing with a kind and innocent man.

'Don't you go causing him harm,' said Myrtle, lightly. 'Not that you would on purpose. It's just that Ken's held a candle for you for so long. Suddenly taking his hospitality might make him think there's hope.'

Annie sighed, impatient. 'Trust you to take it all so seriously. One drink is all that's on the cards. We may never go out again. So you don't need to worry.'

The next day Annie reported Ken had borrowed his father's old car and they'd driven to a pub several miles inland. Had a good time, Ken the perfect gentleman. Top marks, he got, first evening, Annie said. As a reward, she accepted another invitation. From then on, although she still went out with one or two others, her chaste relationship with Ken continued. There was no hope of that ever changing, she said.

The men have returned to sea. It's late afternoon, almost dark. Myrtle plans to sit down with a cup of tea and ring Annie. It's been six days, now, since the storm, since they last spoke. Too long.

The door opens. Myrtle spins round from the stove, kettle in hand. Annie, who never knocks, stands there smiling.

'Janice is over with a friend for the night,' she says. 'Thought I'd come round. It's a long time since we had a game.'

She takes a box from a paper bag she is holding, puts it down on the table. A new pack of cards.

'That's great,' says Myrtle. 'We needed some new ones.'

They sit at their usual places at the table, pot of tea between them. Annie pushes the cards over to Myrtle. Their stiffness will take some getting used to. Myrtle prefers the soft slappiness of the old cards. But she shifts them about, shuffles them.

'Do you know what happened?' asks Annie. 'I asked Ken for a car.'

'Why ever do you need a car?'

'Freedom. Not to have to be forever at the mercy of the awful buses.'

'Like a lot of us.' Myrtle pushes the cards towards Annie.

'I dare say. That doesn't stop me wanting . . .' She pauses. 'Did Archie tell you he and Ken have come to an agreement?'

'He did. I'm glad. The whole business is over, now. Let's not talk about it again.'

'Aye, you're right.' Annie begins to deal the cards.

There is nothing to lose, Myrtle decides, in just one attempt to make Annie see reason. 'Isn't it pushing Ken a bit far? He gives up the source of income that's paid for all the gadgets, and you immediately ask for something beyond his means. Is that fair?'

Annie sighs. 'Perhaps not. He went away worried, I'll say. Perhaps I'll shut up about the car for the moment. Suggest a better telly.'

They begin their game. Both rub their fingers round the edges of the cards, unconsciously to speed familiarity with their strange feel.

'You were very good to Janice the other night,' Annie says after a while.

'That's all right. You know I love the child.'

'I don't think I said thank you. I felt badly when you'd gone.'

'I would have rung you tonight to say—'

'We always get over these silly skirmishes, though, don't we? You can't expect even the oldest friends not to drive each other potty now and then. It was my fault the other night, Myrt. I know that. You're very forgiving. I've not been myself lately and you still put up with me.'

They smile at one another, lay down their cards in fans on the table. 'Shall we have a glass of whisky?'

Annie nods. Myrtle fetches bottle and glasses. They chink their glasses together. 'Archie'd never believe this, would he?' Annie laughs again, more easily. Her cheeks are pink after the first sip of her drink. 'I've a favour to ask you . . . concerning Janice. Recently, she's not been doing too brilliantly at school. She says she's bored out of her mind. She doesn't try, she's getting rotten marks. I was wondering, might you have time to fit her in with a little coaching? I'd pay you.'

'I'd love to help.' The idea instantly appeals. 'But I'll not take a penny.'

'What would I do without you? You're a brick.' Annie giggles. 'You've been a brick, the best brick ever, all my life, though I could only say that after three sips of this. Come on, your turn to deal.'

Warm and flushed on their unaccustomed whisky, the women return to their game. The hours, secure, pass magically fast as always. Annie does not pull on her coat till past midnight. Myrtle puts on her shawl so that she can see Annie down the steps. At the bottom, they hug.

'Will you be all right, walking back alone?'

'What do you think I am? A helpless woman?' They both laugh, happy. 'You know what? Ken says there'll be snow before Christmas.' Annie moves away. In a moment she is consumed by darkness.

With a small shiver, Myrtle returns up the steps. There's a hard, dark scent in the black air that often comes before snow—a smell Myrtle will associate with a particular Christmas for the rest of her life.

That Christmas, almost twenty years ago, Archie was coming for lunch. The kitchen was fugged up with steam. Dot was preparing mince pies and chopping up chestnuts—enough food for half-a-dozen hungry eaters, though Archie was to be the only guest. Myrtle opened the window to clear the air, clear her head. It was then she sniffed the bright crispness of impending snow, and Dot said the clouds would break tomorrow, Christmas Day.

She was right. Archie turned up at one thirty, flakes on his shoulders. It was so dark outside that they lit candles as well as the lamps, and afternoon felt like evening. After they had eaten they exchanged small presents and drank Archie's gift of a bottle of red wine. Intrigued by the snow, no one wanted to draw the curtains. They watched it slam silently against the window and pile high on the ledge outside. The tree, with its tiny coloured lights, stood on the window ledge inside, speckling in the high ridge of white with dots of red and blue and green. In the warm room Dot and Myrtle and Archie played three-handed whist until it was time for the Christmas cake bound in scarlet ribbon, and Myrtle wanted the day never to end.

But Archie would not stay for supper. Myrtle stood watching him hunch his way up the street in the falling flakes, white figure soon invisible in the greater white that swirled through the darkness. He had not said when he would be round again, Myrtle thought, with a heaviness of heart. That evening she could not hide her sudden melancholy, and was aware of Dot's enquiring looks.

Next day she wondered how she would pass the time, and how she would keep from Dot the agitated feelings that made her so restless she could not concentrate on any task for more than a few moments. After breakfast she looked out of the window.

'Snow's melting.'

It was, too. Melting fast under a bright sun. Myrtle longed to go out, walk. Walk anywhere, very fast. But she could not leave for fear of questions, surmises. Dot gave her some chore at the table—carrots: scraping, chopping. The morning loomed up like the side of a vast mountain Myrtle had no energy to climb. Then there was a bang on the door.

Archie. Such a fine morning, he said. Pity to waste it. Would Myrtle like to stretch her legs? He planned to walk a few miles.

'I'll do the carrots,' said Dot, with the voice of one who had had every intention of doing them all along. 'Don't you bother, child.'

Myrtle, exasperated by her mother's approving eyes, could not stop herself blushing. She and Archie hurried down the steps. The village was deserted, silent except for the wail of a lone gull. They made their way up the wynd that led to the main road. The thaw had destroyed the untrammelled whiteness of yesterday. Roofs were slatted with thinning snow, gutters ran with melting water.

'How many days do you have off?' Myrtle asked. She hoped Archie would not observe the new unease within her.

'A week or more, depending on the weather.' He took her arm to cross the road, something he had never done before.

They walked along a path beside a ploughed field. Dark earth showed through its chipped icing of snow. Sometimes one was ahead of the other, sometimes they were abreast. A thorn hedge protected them from a southeasterly wind and the sky, flax blue, was stripped of cloud.

'The postcards never get the blue right,' said Myrtle. She instantly regretted so foolish a remark, but was relieved when Archie laughed.

'You do say the oddest things. You're a very precise woman.'

Myrtle smiled. 'I would have thought fishermen were acutely aware of every shift in the sky,' she said.

'No. It's just fair weather or foul. We're not poets.' Archie turned to look at her. 'What are we doing, talking about the sky? Wouldn't it be better if we talked about getting married?' he said.

Myrtle stumbled backwards off the path. She could feel thorns snarling into her coat, tearing at her hands as she stretched them to support herself.

'Am I to drag you out of the hedge before I get an answer?'

Archie took both her hands, impatiently pulled her back onto the path. Myrtle's immediate thoughts were for the snagged wool at the back of her coat. Archie was dragging her towards him, smudging the stupid thought as he put his arms round her shoulders. He kissed her on both cheeks with an ironic formality that seemed to please him, for there was a smile on his lips. So this is a proposal, she thought.

'So is it to be aye?'

'Of course, Archie. Aye a thousand times. Yes, yes, yes.'

'I've not proposed before. It's not worked out too delicately.'

'Oh, I don't know. I'm not experienced in proposals, either. But I'd say you've managed it beautifully.' Both laughed, newly shy.

'I'd been working up to it. Christmas Day, I'd planned. But somehow there was never a chance. So it's late, but at least spontaneous. It suddenly came to me. Ploughed field, I thought; good as anywhere.'

A long silence then quivered between them.

'Why do you want to marry me?' Myrtle asked at last.

'Always known you'd be the best wife in East Neuk. Always loved you.'

'*Always loved me?* You never gave the slightest clue.'

'Course not. Had to be sure. Takes a long time to be sure, when a man is choosing a wife.'

'But . . . all those other girls after you. I always knew you were quite out of my range—just a distant hero. Then you became a friend, and I couldn't believe my luck.'

'And then?'

'And then, quite lately, friendship turned into something else. I didn't dare admit it, even to myself.'

'Thank God it's turned out like this,' he said.

'I love you,' said Myrtle.

'That's all I wanted to hear. I'm a lucky man, but I'll have to warn you: I'm not a man of many fine words.' He patted Myrtle's hand. 'But you'll know it's there, my love for you, for ever, God willing.' Archie was a little brusque, looking at his watch. 'Maybe we should be getting back to Dot, tell her.'

'She won't be surprised,' said Myrtle.

'That she won't,' said Archie. 'There's nothing your mother misses.'

Dot, in her total delight, offered them the ground floor of her house so that they could sell Archie's house and have money to invest. Archie put the house on the market and returned to sea early in the New Year. Not until he had been gone for some days did Myrtle tell Annie: harbouring the secret had provided a peculiar pleasure. Until now she had had so little excitement to share with Annie. When she did break the news, Annie went so pale that Myrtle thought she was close to fainting. Then Annie took hold of herself and managed suitable congratulations.

'Oh, Myrtle, it's wonderful! I never thought you'd make it up the aisle before me.'

'You probably never thought I'd make it up the aisle at all.'

Annie laughed. Then they hugged, glittery-eyed.

'Nonsense. I'll never make as good a wife as you.'

'Course you will. To be honest, I never imagined I could end up so lucky. I still can't believe it. Archie Duns! . . . *Me!*'

'I hope you won't think too badly of that silly business when we were at school,' Annie said. 'Me threatening to go after Archie. Dreadful mistake. But you know me: always spurred on by a challenge. I always knew I'd never get anywhere. I'm sorry.'

'I'll never give it a thought. It's forgotten for ever.'

'Do you think Archie forgives me?'

'I doubt it ever enters his mind. Besides, he knows you're my friend and nothing will ever alter that.'

'Marriage will, a bit.' For a moment Annie was downcast. 'I'll have to find myself a husband too. God forbid—where to start? So what will the wedding dress be? Big and white?'

Myrtle laughed. 'My size, I'd look like a fridge.'

They laughed and hugged again. In their twenties, they were on the brink of a new era in their friendship.

'So what do you have in mind? Oh, I'm so excited for you! So jealous.'

'Ma's got out the yards of velvet she's had stored away for years. She bought it in a sale for curtains, then never had time to make them.'

'Old curtains won't make you a very fashionable bride.' Annie sighed at her friend's lack of romantic vision. 'But I expect you'll get away with it. Long as you expect me over first thing, morning of the wedding day, Carmen rollers to the ready. By the time I've finished with you, you won't know yourself.'

'Well, I wouldn't want to surprise Archie too much,' said Myrtle doubtfully. 'He seems to love me as I am, amazing though that is.'

Dot spent a week cutting out and sewing yards of velvet the colour of loganberries. The fittings were silent, serious occasions: Dot pinning and tweaking with slow and loving care, Myrtle impatient and uninterested. She was agitated by Archie's absence—the beginning of feelings that were to grow and torment for many years to come. There had been storms. There was scarcely a moment of the day she did not imagine the man she loved exposed to a wild sea.

One afternoon a fitting was interrupted by a knock on the door. Martin came in. He carried a small box. He was silenced by the sight of the bride swathed in the gloomy velvet. They stared at each other: Myrtle in friendliness, Martin too surprised to speak.

'I'm sorry,' he said at last. 'It seems to be an inconvenient time.'

'No, it's not,' said Dot, through the pins in her mouth which kept their balance on her lips. 'Sit down and tell us what's going on.'

'You're the ones with the news,' said Martin. 'You and Archie. That's good.' He held out the box. 'Small wedding present.'

'Martin! There was no need. Thank you. Our first wedding present.'

'I was wondering if I might appoint myself . . . official photographer?'

'I'm sure Archie wouldn't mind,' said Myrtle. 'Though there'll be nothing much to—I mean, it'll be a very small affair.'

'All the same, it should be recorded.' Though his voice was light, Myrtle found herself touched by his clouded look of joy and regret.

Myrtle did not open the box until Martin had left. It was a lump of rock crystal, its tiny milky peaks glittering with a faint voltage. But Myrtle could imagine how it would be on a bright day.

The very small affair took place on a bitter February afternoon in St Monan's Church. It was so cold Myrtle was forced to wear her grandmother's old cape, thick as a horse rug, over the velvet dress. She and Dot and Annie were driven to the church by a taxi that heaved over the lumpen roads like an old boat. Annie, her dress more appropriate wedding material than Myrtle's, carried a small bunch of snowdrops, which she remembered to give to Myrtle just as they were alighting into heavy rain. They found Archie and Ken waiting in the porch, shifting uneasily in their unaccustomed suits.

The small group went into the church, where the priest was lighting the altar candles. Bride and wedding guests stood beneath a fine model of a sailing ship that hung from the ceiling, unsure how to proceed. The priest invited them, being so few, to walk down the aisle together. Ken and Archie flanked the bride. Dot and Annie followed them. Myrtle wished her father were here, escorting her up the aisle.

After the simple ceremony was over, they were all standing at the church door looking out at the rain that bulleted down on the sea, when a sodden figure suddenly appeared—Martin, camera in hand. First he photographed them huddled in the porch, then he persuaded them out onto the squelchy slopes of the graveyard, backs to the sea, for more pictures. One of these, blown up and framed, caught the spirit of the moment: Bass Rock, thrashing waves, granite crosses above gravestones and the startled, disbelieving faces of the wedding group.

Later, after food and drink in a pub, Myrtle and Archie made their way to the Isle of Mull. There they spent a week in a guesthouse. The honeymoon was a time of relentless bad weather. They ventured out only briefly each day. Mostly they kept to their room. Archie confessed that, desirable though he may have been to local girls, he had never slept with anyone. Myrtle laughed at his solemnity, deeply relieved. She liked to think of their starting out to discover this unknown territory of physical passion together. On the first night she walked naked across the room to the bed, where Archie awaited her, huge shoulders looming above the sheet. He murmured about the wonder of her.

It was on Mull that Archie fell in love with his wife, and she with him. The exhilaration of those early days of lovemaking never seemed to flag. But Myrtle grew to understand that it was the chronic anxiety when Archie was at sea, the threat to life itself, that heightened the value of the times they had together. Each homecoming was a celebration, a reason to be thankful. For their entire married life Myrtle and Archie remained alert to the shadow of mortality, which endows all love and pleasure with its cutting edge.

In the eighteenth century, Myrtle explains to Janice, fishing boats were still remarkably similar in design to their Viking forebears. She shows her a picture of a *sixern*, or six-oar boat, found rotting in the Shetland Isles quite recently. Janice, close to her, is intrigued.

They are at the kitchen table. Janice is at work on a project on the local fishing industry. Myrtle has agreed to coach her in several subjects. This project, it turns out, is Janice's favourite. Originally, she had hated the whole idea of such a boring old fishing project.

But somehow, with Myrtle, fishing has become fascinating. Myrtle puts things quite differently from her boring new teacher, Miss Simmons, who drones on in a voice that sounds as if she's talking through a mouthful of scones. Myrtle tells stories, asks Janice the sort of questions it's actually fun to answer. Myrtle *listens*, as if she is really interested, which makes Janice want to go on with her ideas to please her. Her school marks are rapidly improving. She loves the poetry Myrtle is introducing her to. In just a few weeks, as Annie observes to Myrtle, the child has blossomed.

'You ought to be an all-the-time teacher,' Janice says, 'so that lots of children can have all this fun, not just me.'

'Maybe, one day. I've often thought of it. But I've no training.'

Myrtle is gathering up photocopies of pictures of ancient fishing boats. In preparation for these lessons she has spent hours in the museum. Mornings, thus engaged, have flown by. Sometimes she has broken off to go down to the café to see Annie. Annie brings coffee, 'on the house'. 'You the tutor, me the waitress,' she says, laughing. There is both admiration and jealousy in her comment. She would like to inspire her daughter herself, ignite her enthusiasm for learning, but she knows that is beyond her. And she is pleased that at least her childless friend is able to play an important part in Janice's life.

'On to the herring industry, tomorrow,' says Myrtle. 'It's time to go now.'

Janice does not move. She concentrates on writing HERRINGS in elaborate capital letters. Eyes down, her lashes, thick and curly as Annie's, make spiked shadows on her cheeks. Her hair, of late, has become curlier, more abundant. It falls over her eyes. She makes no attempt to push it back. Annie was just the same at that age: stubborn about her rebellious hair. For a moment Janice is the child Annie. She looks up, smiles the same smile. Dimples press into her cheeks, plumper than Annie's ever were, and she's herself again. Her father's heavy jaw means her own looks will never quite equal her mother's. But there is an unruly appeal, a wicked eye, that will be both invaluable and dangerous when it comes to grown-up life.

'I'd better be off, then,' says Janice. 'Though I don't want to go.' She stands, gathers up her things. 'There's a boy at school called Arthur Dilk. He writes me such silly notes.' Myrtle smiles. Again, history repeating. 'I haven't told Mum—don't say anything.'

'Of course not.'

Janice kisses Myrtle quickly on the cheek. This is something she has not done since she was a very small child. Myrtle goes with Janice to the door, big hand lightly on small shoulder. 'See you tomorrow at five.' She fears for the girl. She loves her.

The time when Archie and Myrtle were trying for a child is a time that both have closed away. They never reflect on the disappointments of those days, there is too much else to be glad of in their lives. But to deny that regret did not assail them—Myrtle in particular—from time to time, would be an untruth. News of friends giving birth, the sight of babies in prams, could not but remind of their own 'failure', as Myrtle saw it. Long ago both she and Archie had come to accept this 'failure'. But growing used to the idea of impossibility savagely eluded them.

Myrtle's attempts to conceive went on for almost five years. She was subjected to tests, questions of a loathsomely intimate nature, examinations. She would spend many hours waiting in hospital corridors, hope writhing like some wretched, dying bird within her. Sometimes the pregnant Annie would come with her.

'Well, if nothing happens, you can share this bairn. How it kicks! Feel it kicking, Myrtle.' Innocent of Myrtle's reaction to this offer, she would tap her stomach with long silver fingernails. 'Oh, it's not fair. Though you mustn't give up for a long while yet. Then just when you're least expecting . . .' Annie did her best to raise her friend's hopes and spirits, always innocent of her own blundering.

When months of examinations came to an end, the answer was that nothing seemed amiss. Perhaps Archie was the 'culprit', as the gynaecologist put it. But there was nothing amiss with him, either. 'All a great mystery,' the consultant said in their last interview. How about trying the fertility drug? With one accord Myrtle and Archie dismissed the idea. Then it was in God's hands, the man said, attempting to be helpful. He closed the Duns's file before him. Yes, God was the best hope, he went on, standing up. Indeed, his own father was a minister of the kirk and had taught him the power of faith. He looked down on his patients with an encouraging little turn of his mouth. Archie and Myrtle stood up. The consultant's final advice was not to give up hope—and, who knows, the good Lord might provide them with a surprise in his own time. Remember, His ways were mysterious, He could not be hurried.

But God's mysterious ways did not include, for them, the provision of a baby. Meantime Annie gave birth to Janice. Myrtle, for the first two years of the child's life, helped greatly with her upbringing. She grew to love the child—not like her own, no use pretending that—but without reserve. Archie understood how she felt, and was grateful that there was a baby upon whom Myrtle could bestow her naturally maternal feelings. But he himself harboured an amorphous kind of antipathy that he could not fathom. Something to do with resentment? Why should the unde-serving Annie be blessed with a child, while his own, far superior wife was denied this gift? Janice was a beguiling and pretty child, but by three years old she was showing the dangerous precocity and petulant ways of her mother; Archie could never feel much affection for her.

The day after Myrtle and Archie came back from their honeymoon, Archie went to sea. Within moments of his departure, Annie dashed round to the house. Her state of excitement was unconnected with Myrtle's return. She hurried through some questions about whether Myrtle had had a good time, then her own news burst forth.

'I'm engaged!' she shrieked.

'*Engaged?* Who to?'

Annie fluttered her eyelashes, blushed, put on her most mischievous look. She liked to surprise.

'Ken,' she said at last.

'Ken?' Myrtle sat down, heavy with astonishment. 'How on earth did that come about?'

'Well, he's loved me for ages, hasn't he? I made up my mind following you down the aisle. I thought to myself—why not marry Ken? He's a good man. I'm fond enough of him. Not everyone has to be passionately in love, you know, to have a happy marriage.' There was a faint sneer in her voice. 'Are you so surprised?'

'Yes, in truth.'

'I thought you'd be *pleased.*' Myrtle's less-than-enthusiastic response was not at all what Annie had envisaged. She pouted, petulant. 'It may not be the love match of the century like you and Archie, but he loves me all right, and I'll try to be a good wife.' She gave a wisp of a smile. 'We'll get on, see if we don't.'

Myrtle sighed. She made a quick decision to ask just one question, and then to brace herself for loyal support.

'But you scoffed at Ken for so long,' she said. 'You've never loved him. As far as I know you don't even fancy him. Is it fair to marry him?'

Myrtle's tone was less harsh than her words. Annie shrugged.

'You have to be a bit practical when it comes to marriage,' she said. 'There's not much choice left, locally, is there? I've never had anything positive against Ken. I think I could grow to love him. I respect him, and that's important. So, if one half loves and the other half respects, well, that's more than can be said for a lot of marriages. We'll be fine.'

'I hope so.'

'Don't look so worried. There's lots going for us, I promise.' She giggled. 'I'll tell you something: he's a grand lover, Ken. I can hardly walk.' Annie moved round in a small circle, legs bowed, limping like a wounded bird. She laughed.

But Myrtle looked away, a confusion of feelings contorting her face. She controlled them, rose and kissed her friend on the forehead.

'I'm pleased for you, Annie,' she said. 'I hope you'll be very happy.'

'We will be.' Annie laughed again. 'It gave him quite a shock, I can tell you, when I proposed. You should have seen his face!'

'When *you* proposed?' The calm now erupted again into shock.

'Not an hour after you and Archie left for Mull, Ken was walking me home. I said, "How about you and me getting married, too, Ken?" He said I'd had too much to drink. I said, "No, I'm serious." He said, "If you're serious, of course I'll marry you. I've loved you for years."'

Myrtle's determination to disguise her horror failed her at this point. Annie was quick to try to quell her friend's misgivings.

'The wise thing Ken said was—and he's a wise man, believe me—he said all marriages involve risks, and we've got a lot more going for us than some. Provided, he said, I make it my business to be a faithful wife.' She fluttered her eyelashes, suddenly red-cheeked.

'Then there's cause for celebration,' Myrtle said primly, for there was no point in speculating on the likelihood of Annie's future fidelity. 'I'll make us a cup of tea.'

An hour or so after Janice has gone, Myrtle notices a darkening in the room. She goes over to the window. Outside, a fog, thick as custard, obliterates everything in its greyness. There are no gulls' cries to splinter the silence. Myrtle wonders whether the fog has spread over the sea, where Archie should be casting his nets.

Then the dense quietness is split by a shriek—the shriek everyone dreads: the rockets. The alarm scorches through the walls of the house. Myrtle trembles. Some boat is in trouble. She grabs the big torch, runs without her cloak from the house. There's confused shouting in the street. The rockets continue to savage the air.

Down at the harbour, other blobs of light are gathered at different heights, like lanterns held by a group of carol singers. There's not a woman in the crowd unshaken. 'A boat's on the rocks,' someone says. 'The *Swallow*,' says another. Myrtle's heart contracts with relief. The fear still grips, but is different.

Myrtle feels a cold hand in hers: Annie. She is trembling too.

Then the screech of the rockets stops. A man's voice shouts the good news: boat located, crew all safely on their way back in the lifeboat.

Now the lamps bob about faster, almost gaily. The wives of the *Swallow's* crew hug each other. Annie takes Myrtle's arm and the two women push their way out of the crowd. Relief, almost tangible, runs like a lighted fuse through the figures.

'Thank God,' says Annie. 'It could have been . . .'

'This has happened so often, hasn't it?' says Myrtle. 'There's good weather, the worry has faded a bit, then something like this comes to shock you. I suppose we can only ever have limited moments of peace, when our men come ashore.'

It is with grateful joy that fishermen's wives welcome their husbands home after there has been a drama at sea. When Archie returns, Myrtle leaps from her chair when she hears his footsteps outside, and runs out to greet him. He looks surprised. He takes her in his arms, kisses her briefly on the cheek, but without attention. His mind is elsewhere.

'They got the *Swallow* off the rocks,' she says. 'She's not badly damaged.'

'So I hear.' He conveys no interest. Normally, if one of the harbour boats has been in trouble, Archie is the first to go down and offer help. Myrtle is puzzled. Anxiety, which usually fades when he comes through the door, spirals through her. What has happened? She waits.

Archie takes his place at the table, eats hungrily, preoccupied. Myrtle keeps her silence. She knows he will not welcome questions. It's the belief of fishermen that wives should be spared from incidents at sea. When the men come home, they want to forget the savagery of storms tossing the boats without mercy from one cliff of waves to another, drenching decks and men, leaving them frozen, exhausted, numb. They have no wish to recollect the flaring of tempers, the sickening disappointment of a poor catch.

So Myrtle allows this heavy silence. She thinks an explanation must come soon. She polishes the stove, going over bits that have no need of polishing. Her back is to Archie.

At last she hears him put down his glass, push back his chair.

'It's Ken,' he says. 'He'll no' be on the boat if he carries on.'

Myrtle turns. Archie must have run his hands roughly through his hair. It stands up in stiff, clownish points. He looks a little crazed. Saddened.

'I thought it was all agreed. What's Ken done now?'

'Same old thing. For a week or so he was back to his old self. But this trip he wasn't pulling his weight, hell he wasn't. Driving us mad with his complaints of chronic tiredness. He's not been keeping his word. I'm afraid a lot of it is Annie's fault. He says she's given up asking for a car, but now it's other stuff she's demanding—shoes for the bairn, a tumble drier, whatever. But he's going to have to make up his mind finally. Is he a fisherman or a removal man? I tell you, my patience is running out.'

Archie gets up, moves over to the window. He is flushed. He stands, looking out, back to Myrtle. Unnerved by the strange atmosphere, Myrtle keeps her place by the stove.

'Annie told me Ken was planning to sell the van,' she says carefully.

'Well, he's obviously made some effort, but has changed his mind. I warned him before we came off the boat. I said, "Ken, you sell that bloody van or get off the boat." God, how I hate all this. Until Ken went to pieces we were as good a crew as you could find. Now there's an atmosphere. I want it cleared. I only mention it because a crisis is looming. I'm surprised Annie hasn't been on at you about it all.'

'Sometimes,' says Myrtle, 'even after all these years, I get the impression I don't know anything that's going on in Annie's head. She likes to make me think she's telling me everything, but I doubt that's the truth.'

'If Annie betrayed you one day, I wouldn't be surprised.'

'She'd never do anything calculated to hurt. She has a good heart. You've never liked her,' Myrtle hears her voice rising. 'You've never tried hard enough to understand her.'

'Oh, I have. But seeing her through different eyes from you, it didn't seem worth the effort.'

Myrtle wishes Archie would turn to face her. But he remains mesmerised by the view beyond their window.

'Well, anyway,' she says, attempting a lighter voice, 'whatever you think about Annie will make no difference to my feelings for her. You know that. She's my friend.'

Archie gives an almost inaudible laugh. Myrtle can just hear the note of scorn within it. 'Aye, she is, too,' he says. 'More's the pity, sometimes.'

Silence flops between them again. Myrtle wants this exchange to come to a quick end. Then the quiet is blasted by an angry banging on the door. Before Myrtle can urge the caller to come in, it's flung open.

Annie runs in, scarlet-faced. She does not look at Myrtle, but pummels the table and screams.

'Archie Duns! What the hell have you been saying to Ken?'

Archie turns round slowly. He looks down on the woman battering his table.

'What seems to be the matter?' The languid voice of Archie's question infuriates Annie further.

'What d'you think's the matter? I'm here because Ken comes home a broken man. You've been getting at him again and he can't take it any more, nor can I. I don't want a broken husband. You're nothing but a sodding great bully, Archie Duns, and I hate you for it.'

'Calm down, Annie—'

'Shut up, Myrtle. This is between Archie and me.' Annie moves to the window. With small fists still whitely clenched, she punches Archie on the chest. 'I want an explanation!' she shrieks.

'Stop it, Annie!' Myrtle cries. 'Stop it, please. For heaven's sake . . .'

She sees Archie looking down on Annie with a disparaging smile. Her pathetic gesture seems to amuse him.

'You shouldn't go hitting people,' he says, 'especially those a lot larger than yourself.'

'I'd willingly kill you for what you've done to Ken.' Annie no longer shouts. Her rabid fury is abating.

'I've been warning him for months,' says Archie. 'We made what I took to be a final agreement. He broke it. I said to him this morning he could have one last chance—sell the van and give up his deliveries, as we agreed, and get back to being his old self. We can't afford to carry a man like him on the crew. He's useless.'

'Ken's done nothing wrong.' Annie is sullen now.

'I'm sorry to say, Annie, he has. Last week he couldn't even cope with the nets. When Ross came to help him, he got nothing but abuse. Ross flung him on a bunk where he slept for three hours. Woke up saying he wasn't used to brandy and he'd had a slug or two to give himself energy. Meantime, two hands short, we were up against it. This can't go on. You must see. Can't have a man on board who could be a risk—'

Annie cuts him off with a laugh. 'Don't be so dramatic, Archie! How could Ken be a risk? If you'd stop nagging him, he'd be all right. I'm telling you, if you ever put Ken off the boat, there's no accounting for how the score will be repaid.'

'Please, both of you . . .' Myrtle feels an outcast, kneads her skirt.

'I'll not put Ken off the boat if I can help it,' says Archie. 'Last thing I want. But you better stop pestering him for things he can't afford. *You're* a lot to blame for all this, as you must know.' His eyes are hard on her.

'*Me?* I do nothing but support him.'

'You goad him. You make him feel a wimp, not being able to afford the things you want. Because he loves you, Ken spends his shore leave trying to earn a few quid just to buy the junk you want.'

'I don't want to hear any more such rubbish!' Annie cups her hands over her ears. Anger flares in her eyes again. 'I ask Ken for a few mod cons, yes, all right. What wife doesn't?' Her eyes lash from Myrtle to Archie. 'But to say I goad him . . . That's just the vicious side of you, Archie Duns.' She looks at Myrtle.

'Vicious?' says Myrtle, appalled. 'There's not a kinder man in the world. Archie says nothing without good reason.'

Annie gives a small laugh. 'The supportive wife! The perfect couple, so brave about no children—'

'Shut up.' Archie goes white.

Annie tosses her head at him, defiant. 'But here's one thing you know-alls don't know—Ken *likes* his moonlighting, earning a bit to get me things. That's why he broke the agreement. And anyway, what we do with our time is bloody well nothing to do with *you*, Skipper Duns—'

'It is if it affects Ken's job as one of my crew.'

'Ken would be better off without you. There's plenty who'd like him.'

'Then he can go.'

A trace of alarm flickers over Annie. 'I'm not saying he wants to go.'

'What's that?' Ken's voice startles them all. He stands in the doorway. None of them has heard him coming up the steps.

'I told you not to come here, Annie,' says Ken. He is pale, but there is no evidence of the broken man Annie declared had returned to her.

'If you won't stick up for yourself,' Annie says, 'I'll have to do it for you.'

'I can stick up for myself, thanks. Sorry about this, Myrtle. Archie and I can work it out between us. It's nothing to do with the wives.'

Myrtle sighs, misery coming at her from all directions. 'Tea, every-one?' she asks, and registers a general nodding.

Annie slumps, all energy spent, into a chair. Now Ken has arrived, the fight is leaving her. Ken remains standing, eyes warily on Archie.

Then Archie moves towards Ken, hand outstretched. 'Look here, Ken,' he says, 'this has all gone too far. Things shouldn't have got to this.' Ken looks at the hand with suspicion. 'Can't we call it a day? You know what I'm asking. I don't want to lose you from the boat.'

The men shake hands. Ken turns his head so that he does not meet Archie's eye. Myrtle, in a warm rush of pride at her husband's magna-nimity, puts mugs on the table. Ken gives a wan smile, sits beside Annie, who sniffs. Archie takes the pot from Myrtle and sits beside Ken. Myrtle sees beneath the charitable front he has fought for, Archie remains determined to carry out his threat should Ken fail him again.

It's a long time since the two couples have sat down together round a table, and this is not the easiest of occasions. But united in their disturbed feelings they make an effort to cover the awkwardness. The simplest way is to resort to talk of the shared past. Archie tells a story of some childish escapade and they manage to laugh. But a void remains beneath the paper-thin politeness. Not one of them is free of concern that the smallest mistake could cause a further explosion. They drink their tea swiftly.

Then Archie gets up and says he is taking Ken to the pub: they deserve a drink. The gesture is so out of character that Myrtle is unable to suppress a look of astonishment. It is for the sake of Ken, she realises. So the final agreement about Ken's future can be decided.

As they scrape back the chairs, in Myrtle's eyes Archie shines with benevolence. Ken has caused Archie serious trouble for the last few months, and Archie has put aside his anger about Annie's insults and accusations. He has offered forgiveness. Never has Myrtle been so moved by his goodness. Through a blurring of vision she sees that Ken, following Archie out of the door, wears a feeble, guilty smile.

The two women are left alone. Now is Myrtle's chance to berate Annie for all the loathsome things she said about Archie. She takes a deep breath, for control. Then, as she knew they would, sympathy and forgiveness surge over her. Annie, in a rage, had surely been saying things she did not mean.

'Glad that's over,' Annie says, airily, as if the whole incident had been nothing to do with her.

'Aye.' Myrtle sighs. 'No one can have enjoyed it. Perhaps it was best it's all come to the boil. God willing, everything'll be back to normal.'

Annie gives Myrtle a look in which defiance is still just visible. 'Maybe. Hope so. Bad things were said.' This, Myrtle realises, is the nearest Annie will ever come to an apology. Annie pulls an old packet of cards from her pocket. 'Shall we?' she says.

Myrtle nods. For a while, they play in silence. Then Myrtle looks at the clock.

'Gone two hours,' she says. 'They must have a lot to talk about.'

'Ken's got to be off at nine. A delivery first thing in the morning.'

Myrtle puts down her cards. 'But I thought . . .?'

'Just one final job, worth a bomb,' Annie says quickly.

'For God's sake, Annie! We have all this discussion here not an hour ago, and Ken fails to mention he's another job lined up for tonight. Archie'll . . . I don't like to think what Archie'll do.'

Annie looks impatient. 'None of you understands. It gives Ken a real buzz to hand me over a wodge of notes and tell me to spend them.'

'Well I don't know . . .' Myrtle is determined to say nothing that will resurrect the row. But fear for a troubled future returns.

Annie shrugs. 'Don't worry, Myrt,' she says. 'It'll all work out all right.'

Myrtle has little faith in this declaration. Unsettled, she concentrates hard on the cards again until they hear the sound of footsteps. The women's eyes meet in relief. But the man who enters is Martin.

He carries, as he often does when he drops in on the Duns, a newspaper parcel. There's usually a lobster or crab inside. Tonight, Martin has miscalculated. He thought he would find the Duns on their own. Seeing Annie at the table, he is confused, put out.

His feelings are transparently clear to Myrtle, who makes a quiet show of welcoming him. While she fetches beer, he hesitates over which chair to take. Eventually he seats himself beside Annie.

His choice delights her. In a trice her moods of the past hours are gone and a rosy blush spreads over her face and neck. She taps Martin's forearm with mock severity.

'So! You bringing a lobster to my friend! You never bring a lobster to me.' Annie pouts, childlike. Martin smiles, lifts his arm to take a bottle from Myrtle so that Annie has to remove her hand.

'I wanted Archie's advice,' he says to Myrtle. 'I've been offered a job part-time filleting. I've got the time. I could do with the money.'

'There!' Annie bangs her hand on the table, triumphant. 'How about that? Another one who isn't afraid of two jobs! If you're offered the work, Martin, you'd be a bloody fool not to take it.'

Martin and Myrtle exchange a look.

'Part-time grave digger, part-time filleter, part-time stonemason—and I'd still be far from a wholly employed man,' Martin says.

'Well,' says Annie, deflated. 'I dare say.' She tries another tack. 'So what have you been up to? Why haven't I seen you for so long?' The questions are accompanied by her most flirtatious look, a beguiling widening of the eyes. Perhaps Annie imagines she still loves him, Myrtle thinks. Perhaps, in the blindness of this love, she will fail to see how pathetic are her small efforts still to attract him. For all her appeal, Annie has had nothing but empty disasters with men. Ken is a compromise husband, not the man she loves. Martin has little respect for Annie—no interest. It's unlikely his feelings for her will change.

Annie is now talking in a more ordinary way, and Martin is paying more attention. She is talking about how Janice is enjoying her private lessons. Myrtle busies herself unwrapping the lobster. She sees that Annie has pulled up her skirt over her crossed knees. The top leg swings gently while she spins her tiny ankle. Martin's eyes trail the foot for a moment. Then, with surprising suddenness, he rises and leaves with a perfunctory excuse.

'Well, that was a nice surprise,' says Annie, when he has gone.

Myrtle is saved from answering by Archie's and Ken's return. Archie is sober, while Ken sags by his side, with a stupid grin on his face.

Archie turns to Annie. 'As you can see, Ken will have to postpone his job. But he'll be off in the morning, and that'll be his last job.' He says this with good humour, but casts a forbidding look at Annie. 'That's our agreement and I have every reason to suppose Ken will keep to it.'

Various reactions cross Annie's face. But what Myrtle sees most powerfully is the hopelessness of a woman married to a weak husband. Annie opens her mouth to say something, but thinks better of it.

'That's our agreement,' Ken says, slurrily, and puts out a hand in Annie's direction. 'Home.'

He needs support. But Annie sweeps out through the door without a word. Archie takes pity on Ken and guides him to the door.

Archie and Myrtle, with the place to themselves at last, silently acknowledge the need to extinguish the traumas of the evening.

'Let's hope that's final,' Archie says.

'Yes,' says Myrtle.

They move to the window. Myrtle opens it. Frosty air gushes past them. It's a clear night, full of stars. Myrtle never ceases to wonder at Archie's knowledge of the stars, how he uses them to chart his path on the sea and warn him of the weather. To her they are a confusion of twinkling specks.

'See if you can find me the Great Bear,' Archie says. This is an old tease. For years he has been trying to teach his wife the way round the night sky.

Myrtle's eyes are frantic, searching. She wants to please him. But tonight the sky is smeared too densely with scintillating light and the air is cold on her bare arms. 'I'm trying, Archie, but I can't. It's cold.'

Archie puts an arm round his wife's shoulders, and laughs. 'One day you will,' he says. 'You'll suddenly see it clear as anything, and you'll wonder however you couldn't see it before.'

Myrtle bends her head against him. She wonders how it's possible to be so close, and yet so far apart in knowledge. Archie knows about winds and currents. He remembers where hidden rocks lie, across hundreds of miles at sea, without having to consult his radar screen. He knows where the fish are gathered; some instinct draws him to them like a magnet. Archie's knowledge has always filled her with excitement, awe, respect. She loves learning from him.

After a while, too cold to remain standing against the night air, Myrtle shuts the window. 'You *are* cold, too,' Archie is saying. He is rubbing her arms, her shoulders, her cheeks—gently, with his thumbs. He is urging her to leave things till the morning. Relieved, but longing for further comfort, Myrtle follows her husband to bed.

'Is Ken happier, do you think, now everything's resolved?' Myrtle asks Annie. It is three weeks since the row.

Annie looks up from her cards. 'I'm not sure it's all been resolved in his mind.' She suddenly giggles. 'You know what? He never made that last job. He didn't get out of bed till three in the afternoon. I said, "There goes our last chance of a few savings." He didn't seem to care—his head was throbbing that badly. "Savings!" he said. "You'd have spent it in an afternoon." I don't know what he thinks I am.'

In her anxiety not to be trapped into a conversation about Annie's material desires, which could lead back into dangerous territory, Myrtle finds herself taking an unwise path to deflection.

'Archie's been contemplating buying a bit of land,' she says. 'There's a small field going. It's nothing much, just over an acre, but protected.'

Annie eyes her with contempt. 'You're to be *landowners*? What would you want that old field for?'

Myrtle regrets her mistake. Annie is bound to be unreceptive to the idea that she and Archie have so enjoyed for the past few weeks.

'Archie has it in mind to plant this coppice, this small wood.'

'What on earth for?' In her amazement, Annie puts down her cards.

'He's always liked trees. He thinks it would be a challenge, finding trees to withstand the weather up here . . . besides,' she says, quietly, 'Archie and I have nothing to leave behind. You've got Janice. We've nothing. We just have this feeling we'd like to plant something.'

'Well.' Annie's astonishment is enfeebling. 'I don't know what to make of that. Seems to me to be a funny way to spend money.'

Myrtle, desperately wanting Annie to understand, tries further to convince. 'Just imagine: in twenty years or so there'd be this wood—for birds, wildlife, people to walk in, bluebells . . . Don't you see?'

'Not really.' In silence she wrestles for a long time with thoughts that

Myrtle cannot guess at. 'It must be nice to be rich,' she says at last. 'Able just to go and buy a field if you want one.'

'We're not rich,' says Myrtle, quickly. This is another conversation she would prefer to avoid.

'You got a fair price for your father-in-law's house, didn't you? You got this place for nothing from your ma. You don't know what it's like paying rent.' Annie's mouth is twisted, resentful. 'The funny thing about you and me,' she says, 'is that you're rich and don't care about money. We're poor and I mind very much.'

'We're not rich, I tell you. I'm not denying we've a bit more than you, but if we buy this field there'll not be much left.'

'We're up to the limit of our overdraft, you know. You in your cushy position can't understand the worry of that.'

'Of course I can, Annie—'

'You've no idea what it's like, the feeling of having nothing to fall back on. Don't try to pretend you can understand.'

'What can I say? Except that money's not the most important—'

'It's bloody important if it's not there.'

Both women are flushed. Myrtle feels provoked; Annie, unreasonably angry, would like Myrtle, for once, to respond in equal anger. But Myrtle's way is to hand out patient advice.

'Perhaps,' she says, 'if you could sometimes resist the extravagant things you always seem to crave, that might ease the strain.'

'I'll take no such criticism from you,' Annie explodes. 'You're always criticising, Myrtle. When you keep back the words I can see them in your eyes. I get fed up with your disapproval.'

Suddenly she is sobbing. Myrtle is unnerved, shocked.

'Whatever's the matter, Annie? You can't expect us to agree on everything. We've never done that, have we? And ever since we were children we've spoken our minds to each other, haven't we?'

Annie looks up, her stricken face streaked with mascara. 'Hell, it's nothing to do with you and me.' She sniffs, dabs at her eyes with her sleeve. 'Ever since the new agreement Ken's been . . . well, he's become *obsessed* with earning more money, with providing me with things he thinks will make our marriage better.'

'Oh, Annie. I thought everything was well. Archie's not said a thing.'

'Archie wouldn't know. Ken's keeping his word. But he just keeps on and on . . . how's he going to afford this and that for me? Now he thinks he'll never keep me unless there's a constant stream of stuff. I keep saying he's got it all wrong. I've got everything I want—except the kind of husband I once imagined. But it's become a sort of madness. He starts up as soon as he's through the door, goes on and on. I find myself long-ing for him to go back to sea. I don't know what to do.'

'I'm so sorry. I'd no idea.' Myrtle's sympathy rises automatically: she also feels helpless and tired. A picture of Ken, all those years ago comes to mind: Ken eaten with an obsession. 'Tell him to come and see me,' she says. 'Perhaps I could—'

'He never would,' says Annie. 'He keeps things to himself—always has. Still, thanks.' She looks at her watch. 'I must be going.' She stands, her face calmer. 'Sorry I flared up, said stupid things.'

'That's all right.'

The two women briefly hug, a signal that differences have been wiped from the slate again.

The few weeks since the row have been particularly happy for Myrtle and Archie. Each time he has been home they have been involved in negotiations for their field. The contract is ready for signing. This will be done tomorrow, when Archie gets home. Myrtle has been engaging her-self in the study of trees. Catalogues arrive. She goes through them slowly, marking the possibilities she can point out to Archie. She selects reference books in the library, makes notes. For the first time since her mother died, what with Janice's lessons and the planning of the copse, her days are fully occupied. She revels in the feeling of busyness, and the joy of working towards something with Archie. Not since the reno-vation of the house, after Dot died, have they shared anything so closely and with such anticipation.

On the morning of Archie's return, Myrtle is sitting at her table drink-ing a mug of tea. She does not put on the lamp, but watches light slowly unfurl across the small bit of sky framed by the window. In ten minutes she will put on her cloak and go down to the harbour. She enjoys the moment when *Skyline II* pushes its way through the harbour's entrance. She likes to watch the way Archie skilfully manoeuvres the vessel into its place beside the wall. She knows that if she witnessed the homecomings regularly, they would become commonplace events. As it is, Myrtle goes to greet Archie's arrival so rarely that her pride and pleasure never fade.

She picks up her mug, puts it by the sink. As she goes to take her cloak from the peg behind the door, the telephone rings. She curses it. She does not want to be held up. The crackling, as she picks up the receiver, tells her at once it's a ship-to-shore phone. The voice she can't immediately distinguish. Ross, perhaps. Shouting.

'Get an ambulance down to the harbour. At once! Quickly.'

'What?'

'There's been an accident.'

'Who?' The line is indistinct. Her immediate thought is Ken. One of his mistakes . . .

'Myrtle—?'

But she has slammed down the receiver and fled down the outside steps. She runs so fast that when she arrives at the harbour icy knives of pain are shooting up through her chest. Several boats are already in, unloading their catch. No sign of *Skyline II*. A group of fishermen some yards away are talking. One of them turns to Myrtle, shakes his head. What do they know? What should she ask? Oh God! In her panic she has forgotten to ring the ambulance. Myrtle turns to run to the telephone box outside the chandler's. At that moment she sees the ambulance slowly coming down the hill. Ross, or whoever, must have rung someone else as well. Thank the Lord. And the ambulance's siren isn't screaming. It must know this mission is no great emergency.

Others have gathered. Word has flown round. It always does, when something out of the ordinary happens. There they are, the villagers, a mixture of loyal support and curiosity.

Myrtle moves along the harbour wall. She does not want to catch anyone's eye. She looks out to sea. There is a low, light mist. She sees that there's no horizon. It's one of those moments when the sky—a deep storm blue—is an arc that curves right into the water, no demarcation line, making one vast bowl of the elements.

Jutting through the mist, which lazes round its bows, comes *Skyline II* at last. She moves very slowly across the flat grey water, like something filmed in slow motion. Myrtle runs back to the place where she will berth. Others are there before her, gathered round the ambulance. A stretcher is waiting on the ground.

Skyline II is nosing close to the harbour wall. Two ambulancemen, in livid orange coats, move to the edge of the wall and the iron ladder that Archie and his mates hurry up and down as if it is no more difficult to negotiate than a domestic staircase.

'Are you going down first, Jock, then? Or am I?'

'You go. You're nippier on your feet.' The two men laugh.

Skyline II is now in place. The engine stutters, then cuts out. The crowd is quiet. Ross is running up the ladder, rope in hand, to tie up. As his face appears, Myrtle enquires with her eyes. But he doesn't see anyone.

'Hurry,' he whispers to the ambulancemen. One of them lowers himself, dithers a foot among the top rungs of the ladder. The other picks up the stretcher. Myrtle forces herself to look down.

Among the clutter of the deck a body lies covered in blood-soaked rugs. Only a sprout of hair is visible, and a hand. The fingers are splayed: it could be a bleached starfish. Dozens of dead fish lie beside the body, tipped from a box meant for the hold. Their silver scales are streaked with blood. Chains and nets are splattered with blood. The man must have erupted like a volcano of blood. It's everywhere.

Myrtle hears an echoing moan within her, like the call of dolphins in the sea's depths. She thinks she may faint. Someone has an arm round her and is saying things that make no sense.

Both ambulancemen are on board now. As the body is lifted gently onto the stretcher, a rug falls from one arm. Myrtle sees Archie's jersey, but for a moment the fact means nothing to her. Once the fisherman is in place, the ambulancemen stand rigid with concern. How will the stretcher come up the wall?

She does not see how it is done. She turns away, unable to watch, for by now the connection between Archie's jersey and the injured man has made insane sense. When she next looks, the bloody parcel of her husband is rising up the harbour wall. It swings perilously for a moment, then is secured firmly by Ross, sweat pouring down his face. Myrtle finds herself pushed towards the open doors of the ambulance.

She sits opposite the bunk where Archie is lying. His hand hangs down under the sodden rug. She leans over and touches it. It's icy cold. She's pushed gently back into her place by one of the ambulancemen, who is doing something to Archie she does not want to see.

The doors are slammed shut, cutting off the faces of the crowd. Myrtle is aware that Ross is by her side. She wonders vaguely, where is Ken? Surely Ken ought to be here? And why isn't Annie here?

The ambulance moves forward, its siren shrieking. Myrtle looks through the clouded window. In the watery view beyond it, Myrtle sees Ken vomiting over the harbour wall. Annie stands beside him. As the ambulance gathers speed, Annie's shocked white face is a thin frame round the great black hole of her open mouth. The image dances in the blackened window all the way to the hospital: ugly, ugly.

Myrtle sits on a plastic chair in the hospital waiting room. There are shiny tiles halfway up the wall, the colour of beetroot. The detached part of her mind asks who on earth could have chosen such a colour for a room where people await bad news. She shuts her eyes. The beetroot makes her feel sick. Cold sweat is guttering down her back. Ross, beside her, keeps patting her knee. She has no energy to ask him to stop.

A long time has passed since the bloody mound of Archie was rushed past her. She managed to ask a doctor what hope there was.

'Your husband's suffered a terrible injury, Mrs Duns,' was all he said, and ran from her.

A nurse had shown Ross and Myrtle into this beetroot cell. Tea was offered. Myrtle shook her head. Her throat was closed, so she was unable to ask Ross a single question, or utter a word. They sit in silence.

Suddenly the door opens. The nurse ushers in Annie, and Ross's wife, Jean. Annie is red in the face, making a lot of noise, sobbing. She dashes over to Myrtle, flings her arms round her neck. Myrtle, rock hard in her upright position on the plastic chair, doesn't yield. She seems scarcely to notice Annie is there.

'Stop that noise, Annie,' says Ross. 'Doesn't help any of us.'

Annie, jarred by the note in his voice, stops crying at once and sits on the empty chair beside Myrtle. 'Is there any news?' she asks.

Myrtle shakes her head. 'We're waiting,' she says. Then she asks, 'Where's Ken?'

'Ken?' It is as if Annie has never heard of Ken. 'I don't know.'

The door opens again. A doctor Myrtle hasn't seen before comes in. He looks towards her.

'Jean and I will wait outside,' Ross says, and they leave the room.

Annie puts a shaking hand over Myrtle's. The doctor swallows.

'I'm afraid I have to tell you, Mrs Duns, that your husband has passed away. We did everything we could.'

Passed away? For a moment the phrase is confused in Myrtle's mind with *passed by*. 'He's just passed by,' someone once said when she was looking for him. *Passed by* it couldn't be.

'You mean he's dead?' she asks at last.

'I'm afraid so. He stood no chance, really.'

Annie's fingers are cold spiders all over the clump of Myrtle's hands. She tries to shake them off. Annie is whimpering.

'I'm so sorry,' the doctor adds. 'Now, if there's any way in which we can help . . . When you feel ready, we can make arrangements.'

'Thank you. I can manage. Annie here will come home with me.'

The doctor coughs. 'I don't know if you'd like to see your husband.'

'No, thank you.'

'Go on,' says Annie. 'You must say goodbye to Archie.'

'I want to remember him alive, not dead,' snaps Myrtle. Her eyes are hard and dry as glass, not a tear in them.

'Very well,' says the doctor. 'Whatever you wish. But if you change your mind, just let us know. Mr Duns will be tidied up within the hour.'

The doctor looks as if he's aware of his own clumsiness. He backs out of the room, muttering further words of regret.

When he has gone, Annie says, 'Oh, Myrtle, how could this happen?'

'*How did it happen?* That's the question.' Myrtle stands up very fast. Her hands hang at her sides, heavy as buckets.

Annie shakes her head. 'I don't believe any of this,' she says.

'It's happening,' says Myrtle, 'and I want to go home now.'

Annie goes to fetch Ross and Jean. The three of them walk with Myrtle back to the house. As they pass, people lower their eyes and murmur words of sympathy. Myrtle keeps herself very upright, silent.

At the house Myrtle runs up the steps. She goes in and the comfortable sight that has met her on a million ordinary entrances is there as always. The only difference is that the contract for the field lies on the table awaiting their signature—hers and Archie's.

For the rest of the day, Myrtle is surrounded by kindness, sympathy, friends, offers of help, offerings of flowers. She is brought soup and pies and shortbread biscuits, in the pathetic belief that at some point she will feel hungry. People come and go. They try to find words, try to hide their tears, marvel at Myrtle's apparent calm. 'When she takes it in,' she hears one of them whisper as soon as she is outside the door, 'she'll crack.' Annie is a constant presence, making endless mugs of tea. She offers to stay the night, but Myrtle insists all she wants is to be left alone. Annie hugs her friend.

'Where's Ken?' Myrtle asks.

'I don't know. When he comes home shall I send him over?'

'Aye. Tell him I want to know, from him, how it was.'

'I will. Ring if you want me in the night. And I'll be round in the morning first thing. Oh God, Myrtle. What did Archie ever do—?'

Myrtle cannot contain her impatience, though she tries to be gentle. 'There's no accounting for the Lord's decisions, I've always known that. Now, thank you for being here . . .'

When Annie has gone Myrtle moves brusquely about in the emptiness, drying mugs left to drain by the sink. She watches her actions from some distant place outside herself. She watches herself move towards Archie's old jacket hanging on the door, bury her head in its coarse wool stuff that is alive with the smell of him. Then she goes to the table and sits down. She picks up Archie's pen. On the back of the contract she begins to make a list of arrangements that must be made. She stays up till midnight, but Ken does not appear.

Five days later, an hour before the hearse is due, Annie comes round. She carries a bunch of bright flowers wrapped in cellophane.

'Didn't think he'd want anything gloomy, knowing Archie,' she says, putting the flowers on the table.

Annie didn't know Archie at all. Her claim is annoying, but Myrtle manages a faint smile.

'Thanks,' she says. 'Lovely. Do you want to come in the hearse with me? There's room.'

Annie nods, pleased by the offer. She sits, undoes her coat.

'Ken came home last night,' she says.

'Did he say where he'd been?'

'No. But then I didn't really ask. It's not as if I cared.'

'It was worrying,' says Myrtle.

'Aye, on top of everything else. I'm sorry for the extra—'

'I'm just glad he's back. It must have hit him badly, his old friend . . . for all their differences. Is he coming to the funeral?'

'He didn't say. But I imagine so. He wouldn't miss Archie's funeral.' She glances at the clock. 'Nearly an hour. Shall we have a game?'

Annie takes a pack of cards from her pocket and begins to shuffle them. Myrtle pulls the flowers towards her so that she can read the message. *Dear dear, Archie,* it says, *missing you already and always will. Much much love, Annie.*

Again Myrtle has to quell a stab of annoyance.

'All right, is it? Took me ages to think what to put.'

'Fine, fine,' says Myrtle.

They concentrate on the cards till the hearse arrives. Annie sits one side of the coffin, Myrtle the other. Tears pour down Annie's cheeks. Myrtle's eyes remain hard and cold. On the journey to the church she sees nothing but the transparent salmon skin of the driver's ears that stand to attention under his black hat.

Late that night, when it's all over—the ceremony, time, reality, all an incomprehensible flotsam in her mind—Myrtle goes automatically to the kitchen window to close it. She feels a weariness unlike any she has ever known. But she takes a moment to look up at the clear night sky, full of stars as it was that last time she and Archie contemplated it. In a single glance Myrtle sees the Great Bear. It shines out at her more clearly than any other star gathering. The sadness of not being able to please Archie by her discovery is what causes her finally to weep.

PART TWO

IT'S EARLY MORNING, two years after Archie's death, at the fish market. In the large shed, where neon bulbs fizzle sourly against sunlight, the floor is covered with plastic crates of fish. Through the covering of crushed ice, their heads all face the same way. Myrtle, shawl over her head, wanders about looking at them. Within hours each one of these thousands of creatures will be reduced to separate flesh and bone by a few lethal flicks of a knife.

Men in grubby white coats and yellow rubber boots stomp about among the crates making notes, shouting prices. There is a sense of urgency. Many of the fishermen, having dumped their fish, want to go straight back to sea. Political problems in the fishing industry are taking their toll. They must go much further, these days, to find their fish, come back with a much reduced catch. The fight for survival, now, by those who have not abandoned it all and gone off to the rigs, is harder by the week.

Myrtle leaves the shed for the harbour's edge and looks down at the fat, grubby boats. The decks are a favourite lookout place for gulls: enormous birds standing on stilt legs, of voracious eye and savage beak. As a load of boxes swings on the crane, a single flat-fish falls to the ground. The gull whose anxious watch happens to be in the right direction swoops and catches it. The gulls who missed their chance keep up their moaning. There is no sharing among birds who must fight for survival.

'They're starving,' says a voice. Myrtle turns to see Alastair Brown, the harbour master. He, too, is watching the desperate little scene. 'The Lord knows what'll happen to them.'

Alastair Brown is a newcomer to the village, a Cornishman by birth, who likes to give the impression that he has inherited Mediterranean blood. Perhaps it is to underline this fiction he wears dark glasses, no matter how overcast the sky, perched on a nose shaped like a parrot's beak. No one has ever seen his eyes. His excessive black hair is disciplined by quantities of Brylcreem, a trick he has learned from forties films, the passion in his life. He always wears the kind of sunset-streaked tie that is laughed at for being poncy. In all, he is a singular character, standing out in a community of unflamboyant men, but efficient at his job and generally liked.

Alastair Brown is a bachelor. On his arrival in the village he was treated to the scrutiny of every unmarried woman of approximate age. Some fancied his harbour-side house, some saw themselves as the first to rip off the dark glasses. Polite though he was to all these ladies, no definite relationship seemed forthcoming. Sometimes he is seen leaving his house with a suitcase on a Friday night. There is a rumour that there must be a woman who has something the locals lack.

Annie, unsurprisingly, was one of the many who cast eyes on the harbour master. Bolder than most of the others, she wooed him first with free cups of coffee in the café, which he accepted with pleasure. But he made no suggestions of returning her hospitality. Annie grew impatient. She saw him as a challenge that could not go untried. She laid her plans and was rewarded in part.

The reward was to be granted entry into Alastair's house, something none of his other pursuers had achieved. Annie's way was to knock on his door one night, and his politeness prevailed. He invited her in to join him watching the end of one of his favourite films. He ushered her to a chair, gave her a glass of milk and whisky, and returned to his own armchair for the rest of the film.

As the credits of the film came up at last, Annie handed him a small paper bag, explaining she hoped he would not think her . . . Annie could not find the right word, but Alastair Brown did not notice as he pulled a multicoloured tie from the bag. As he looked at it in surprise, Annie explained she had come across it at a car-boot sale and thought it just the thing for his collection; since it had only cost ten pence she felt it could not be considered as a gift with a message. To this Alastair Brown was bound to agree. He thanked her and put the tie back in the bag.

But Annie, encouraged, felt she should go one step further in her mission. She asked him if he ever took off his glasses. Alastair Brown answered by rearranging his spectacles across his beak nose. Finally, he said *no* was the answer to that question. Except, of course, in bed.

When it came to tactics, Annie told Myrtle, never had she been so stretched. She decided to take the bait she was convinced he had offered her. She wondered if he would allow her to be the first one to see his eyes. Alastair Brown remained unmoving, in astounded silence. Annie quickly explained that, of course, it had never entered her mind that bed was the only place in which he could be seen with naked eyes. How about snatching off his glasses just for a moment, and in return she would give him a kiss?

Suddenly Alastair Brown stood up very fast. The dark glasses were turned hard on her. 'That would be most improper,' he said. 'And now if you don't mind, Mrs Mcleoud, I'll show you to the door.' He shook hands, and bade her a polite good night. Myrtle has managed to make Annie promise not to repeat the story to anyone else, both for her own sake and Alastair Brown's.

While subtle competition for his favours continue, the story begins to go round that the woman he is actually waiting for is Myrtle Duns. She is one of the few who has never shown the slightest interest in Alastair Brown. They are mere acquaintances. Annie is not slow to pass on the rumour to Myrtle. The absurdity of the whole idea makes Myrtle smile. She hopes Alastair Brown has not heard the gossip too. It would be embarrassing, make their brief encounters awkward.

The morning at the fish market, when the harbour master observes the seagulls' plight, Myrtle is ready to go along with his friendliness.

'You're right,' she says. 'Archie was always concerned about the gulls.'

Alastair is standing beside her now. He rests a bare hand on a stack of full fish boxes. He picks up a handful of crushed ice, watches it melt and run down his thumb. 'Going to be another fine day,' he says at last.

'I think it is, aye.'

Alastair Brown moves towards the ice house. Myrtle follows for a few paces. Ice is being pumped from the machine into the hold of one of the boats. The process makes a loud scrunching noise, like hundreds of feet on gravel. Ken must be at work, she thinks, and stops. She does not want to run into Ken. After Archie's death he never went to sea again. Two months later the job came up at the ice house and he took it. His life is now duller. But Annie likes the regularity of the wages. And Ken, Annie says, likes the fact he has more time for reading. But none of this is any concern to Myrtle. Her wish is simply to see him as little as possible.

She turns her eyes to the harbour mouth, half expecting to see *Skyline II*. But the boat has been sold. She works from Aberdeen. Ross and two other members of Archie's crew have a small red boat now. They fish up on the west coast, near Inverness, away for several weeks at a time. Myrtle looks at her watch. A quarter of an hour before she must be at school. Time to fill in. She has managed to structure her life well—part-time job at the school now, the planting of the coppice, one day a week at the Evergreen Home, Janice's lessons: yes, she is busy. But unexpected feelings come upon her still, jagged and cutting as broken glass, reminding her that she must always return to an empty house, an empty bed, an emptiness that reaches far beyond the horizon.

Myrtle turns quickly to walk up the hill to the shed where Martin does his filleting in the mornings. Martin is hard at work. He stands behind the slab, intent on the fish. The thin blade of his knife makes the barest sound of splitting silk as it runs through the raw flesh. Myrtle wonders at Martin's constant cheerfulness. She looks down at his hands, so skilful, trained to chip stone, not to slice fish.

'Myrtle! What are you doing here at this hour?'

'I don't seem to be able to stay in bed much after five thirty. I wake up so alert. I went down to the harbour.'

'What's going on down there?'

'Nothing much. I ran into Alastair Brown.'

They smile at each other. Martin is aware of the rumour. He throws the carcass of a small haddock into a crate on the floor. He lays the fillets beside a row of others, iridescent silvery strips of matching neatness.

'Any progress in his courting?'

'Don't be silly! We've scarcely exchanged a word.'

'Maybe he's a slow mover. Though I have to say I don't see him as quite the ideal man for you, should you ever want to marry again.'

'I'll never want to do that.'

'No. Well. That's understandable.' Swish, swish goes his knife. 'Have you thought any more about the headstone? I'm keeping aside that fine bit of marble I showed you. You only have to give me the word.'

'I'm still trying to choose something. I'm being slow, I know. I want to get it absolutely right.' Martin nods. 'I must be on my way.'

'Shall I bring you a piece of haddock on my way home?'

'Well, that would be nice.'

'See you later, then.'

The second evening after Archie died, Martin went round to see Myrtle. He found her alone. She seemed calm, and glad to see him.

'I'll be the one to dig Archie's grave,' he said. 'It's all arranged.'

'Thank you. That would be best.'

'And as for the headstone, when it comes to the time to think about it, you can rely on me to find the finest bit of marble.'

Myrtle, grateful for a visitor who did not offer well-meaning platitudes, made an attempt to smile. 'You're a good man, Martin,' she said, and turned her eyes to the window.

'Is there anything I can do?'

'I think it's all done. I've been making arrangements all day.'

'If there's anything at all . . . you know you only have to call on me.'

'I know.' Myrtle nodded. 'Thanks.'

They fell into silence for a while. Eventually she said: 'I don't know why it happened. Nobody has told me. I don't want to ask. I expect one of them will come and explain when they can find the words. Ken was meant to come. I was expecting him.'

'I'm sure he will.' Martin moved uneasily in his chair. He had heard bloody rumours.

'Also, I don't know when he died. No one told me. I didn't ask. I couldn't ask. I held his hand, but did he know I held it? How will I live without knowing? How can it have happened, Martin? Archie was the most conscientious man you could ever find when it came to safety.'

'There's no use asking yourself all these questions when the answers aren't ready. You must try not to let them torment you in the next few days. You must keep your strength.' Martin stood up, aware of his clumsy sympathy, sharing her grief. 'I'm sure Ken knows he has to be the one to tell you. Imagine how he must feel. He'll need to gather his strength to come to you.'

'Aye, you're right. I'll wait.' Myrtle shrugged, and stood too. 'It's not *how* I really want to know. All I want to know is *why*? Why did Archie die?'

Martin shook his head, unable to speak. He wanted to stretch out a hand to her, touch her—make some gesture to show he understood the magnitude of her sorrow. But he felt that to do so would be inappropriate.

Myrtle and Annie sit playing cards. The aged wall clock ticks—relentless, hollow, nagging the concentration. One of Archie's old navy jerseys still hangs on the back of the door. The wool on a sleeve is snagged in a couple of places.

Annie arrived a little late, and flustered. In the museum café, she is now in charge of three waitresses. She works longer hours than she needs, lingers long after the last customer has gone. Anything, as Myrtle observes, to put off the moment of going home.

Myrtle is used to reading Annie's hands. Today she sees that they are a little shaky. Indication of some sort of confrontation: a thin blade of dread stabs at Myrtle's innards. There have been too many since Archie's death. Too many arguments, apologies . . . Peace, then, for a week or so before Annie provokes some new unease between them.

Today Myrtle knows she is not going to get away with a peaceful game. Some accusation that she cannot guess at is boiling within Annie, whose eyes glitter dangerously. Annie slams down her cards.

'Myrt: I can't not say this any longer. You should see someone.'

'See someone?' Myrtle says lightly. 'What sort of person?'

. 'You know: one of those people who help. A counsellor.'

'Why should I want to see one of them? Why do you suppose I need help?' Despite herself, she knows there is scorn in her voice.

Annie sighs. 'The fact is, it's almost two years since Archie died, and as far as I know, you've never broken down, never given in to hysteria, never acted like any normal woman whose husband has been killed. You didn't even cry at the funeral. Just watched all the rest of us snivelling, a superior expression on your face.'

'Is that how you saw it?' Myrtle tries for patience. 'I appreciate your concern,' she says, aware of her own formality, 'but I've no intention of seeing anyone. I don't want that sort of help, I don't need it, it's just how I am. We all react differently.'

'You're impossible sometimes,' says Annie. 'The fact is, you've been shutting yourself away. I know you love your pupils, and Janice. And I know a lot of your time is taken up planting your wood—none of us ever invited to see it, mind. And you're not the same to me, in a way. Here I am: cards as usual. Chit-chat, cups of tea. But you've left me, your friends, for somewhere of your own where no human company seems to be needed.'

'I'm sorry,' says Myrtle, 'if it feels like that.'

'All I'm trying to say is, it's time for you to try to return to a less solitary life. Archie'd want you to carry on as normally as possible.'

'I do,' says Myrtle. 'At least, I'm trying.'

'And quite apart from that, you don't tell me much now, about how you're feeling—it's as if you don't want me to know what's going on in your—well, your soul.'

'I don't,' says Myrtle, firmly. 'I'm sorry if this distresses you. In the first place I could never describe it. And if I could, I wouldn't want to. Not even to you.'

'I see.' Annie's wounded look now meets Myrtle's. 'It didn't used to be like that.'

'Perhaps you don't remember. You were the one who confessed—well, not everything, but a good deal. I was the one who said less.'

Annie's head snaps back. 'What didn't I tell you? I told you everything.'

Confronted by this untruth, Myrtle feels reckless. She answers before she can stop herself. 'You never said a thing about the seriousness of your love for Martin.'

'For Martin?' The blood blows across Annie's face, reddening it from forehead to chin. 'Who told you about Martin? The bastard. It must have been him. No one else knew.' There's a long silence. Then, 'Well, since you know, I don't mind telling you it's true. I loved Martin. I mean I really loved him. But he didn't love me. Funny, really. I suppose I didn't want to admit to you my *failure*. I'd always been so good at getting every man I wanted. Although all *they* ever wanted was the same thing—except Ken.' She gives a small laugh. 'Whereas you, big plain Myrtle—you've only ever looked at one man, and that man loved you completely. He may have died too soon, but you don't know how lucky you've been.'

'Aye, I do,' says Myrtle. 'There's not a day I don't remember that. But you shouldn't underrate Ken's love for you.'

'Ah! Ken. The loving husband. We scarcely speak these days.'

'There you are! That's another thing you haven't told me.'

'Not something I want to speak about, think about.' Annie sounds weary now. 'I'll find it hard ever to forgive that man.'

'But you should,' says Myrtle. 'I mean, I have. And if it wasn't for Ken, Archie would be here today.'

'You're a saint, then.' The words are forlorn. 'How can I forgive, Myrt? I haven't let him lay a finger on me since . . .'

'I'm sorry,' says Myrtle. 'Perhaps, time—'

'Time? Time makes no difference, does it? You must know that.'

'Not to . . . no,' agrees Myrtle.

Annie pulls on her coat. 'I came here to try tactfully to suggest you need help, and you snap my head off . . . and then I go and tell you about not letting Ken come near me. Oh, I don't know. I'm not sure I care.' Tears begin to run down her cheeks. 'Maybe I'm the one who needs the help. Well, you've always been the strong one, really. I've always relied on you. I hate your new distance.' She stretches out her arms. 'Please come back.'

Myrtle holds out her arms, with some reluctance, and allows Annie to shift her head on her shoulder. She murmurs comforting words, assures Annie she'll always be there, but since Archie died there are great tracts of life she wants to deal with on her own. Annie nods, wipes away her tears. Myrtle has no idea whether her friend understands. And in a strange, hard way that puzzles her, she doesn't care very much. A selfish longing to be alone consumes her. She disentangles Annie from her arms, stands up and goes to open the door. But Annie does not move.

'Shall I tell you something, Myrt?' she asks. Her red eyes are mischievous now. 'Seeing as you know . . . I have to confess I wrote Martin smashing letters. Know how? I went up to the library, studied love letters between famous people. I took a bit from one, a bit from another, joined them up with a word or two of my own. I was proud of them, I can tell you.' She is laughing now; so is Myrtle. 'But if he ever says anything about those letters, you won't let on, will you?'

'Of course not. Never.' The laughter, which has lifted them, dies. 'But please, Annie, don't suggest any more counsellors.' Myrtle manages to say this lightly. 'If I've inherited anything from my mother, it's how to deal with things on my own.' She manages a smile as Annie leaves.

'I'll remember that,' says Annie. But she can't return the smile.

When Annie has gone the memory of Ken's confession returns to Myrtle, as it has done many times since Archie's death.

Ken came to the funeral, silent, pale, unweeping. He made no attempt to speak to Myrtle. As she stood throwing a handful of earth into the grave, she was aware of his slipping away down the path. His mysterious exit merely added another puzzle to the dreadful mystery of the day: why had Archie died?

Two weeks later Ken paid his visit to Myrtle. He confessed he could find no adequate words to express his sympathy and sorrow. All he could do, he said, was to explain what happened.

'This is difficult for me to say, Myrtle,' he began, 'but if I don't tell you the truth I'll never be able to live with myself.'

'I dare say it will be just as difficult for me to hear the truth as it is for you to explain it. But I'd be obliged if you'd just get on with it.' Myrtle had never heard herself speak like that, so roughly.

Ken kneaded his hands, lowered his eyes, further unnerved. 'There was this argument. Archie and me.'

'Argument? I thought you'd sorted out all your differences.'

'We had. I was about to sell the van. No more deliveries. But I just couldn't get it out of my mind that we on the *Skyline II* were being a bit foolish . . . the only honest ones. I was just selling a few fish that the bloody stupid law says should be thrown back. I was just helping a friend, delivering a crate or two for him. All I said to Archie was that if others were doing it, why not us?'

'You were stuffing crates between the furniture?' Ken nodded. 'You're a fool, Ken.' Myrtle's voice was a knife-slash. 'Besides, you knew nothing would persuade Archie to contemplate anything dishonest.'

'Of course I knew that. But this wasn't exactly dishonesty on a large scale. Just the occasional crate or two. Didn't think there was much harm in that. Once again there was a shortage of money. Annie always wanting more than we had. This was to have been my last try at persuading him. Then I would have given up—hell, I'm not a crook, just worn down by disappointing my wife. Anyhow, that day I made my suggestion . . . and Archie lost his temper. I've never seen a man so angry, bawling me out. Just for that moment he lost his concentration. Then the chance in the million happens: winch snaps. Cable snaps back at the speed of light, gets him in the throat . . .' Ken's voice was thickened by a rising sob. But Myrtle, hearing the facts at last, felt no mercy. Now she desired to know the full horror.

'And then?'

'One minute he was screeching blue murder at me. The next—Archie was slewed over on the deck. Blood gushed out. Jugular sliced. He didn't make a sound. No cry, nothing. It happened so quickly, and it was all so terrible, the most terrible thing I've ever seen, that it's still confused in my mind. In the daytime, that is. Asleep—nightmares—clear as anything . . .' He broke off to blow his nose, tried to stop the sobbing.

Myrtle sat very upright, eyes on something out of the window.

'Archie always believed that a fisherman should keep his concentration. Let it lapse for a moment, he used to say, and disaster can strike.' She spoke in the high, thin voice of her younger self. 'If you hadn't been having a row, Archie would be here now.'

'Possibly,' said Ken. His sobs were ebbing. 'He could still have had his back to the winch, might not have got out of the way in time . . .'

Myrtle turned on him, rigid in her contempt. 'You know that's not true, Ken Mcleod, so don't go trying to soothe your conscience with any such delusions. Archie could sense disaster a mile off. There's no possible chance he would have been caught by that wire if he had been concentrating—' Her normal voice had returned now, deep and scarred.

Ken stood up. 'Myrtle, please. I know how it is for you—it's bad for me, too. How am I going to live with myself?'

'I don't know.'

'You'll never forgive me—how can I cope with that?'

'Oh, no need to worry there.' Myrtle gave a small laugh. 'If that's what you want. I forgive you. You didn't set out to murder Archie. Your foolishness—was beyond belief. But the thing you should worry about is keeping out of my way. I don't want our paths to cross any more, Ken. Not easy in a place this size, but possible. Nothing's changed between me and Annie, of course. Not her fault, your—'

'Annie's not all innocent in this. Her pushing me—'

'I'll not hear a word against Annie, and I'd like you to go now.'

'Very well.' Ken left the room in silence.

Myrtle remained in her chair. Visions of the accident crowded her mind, worse than anything she had imagined. Archie's bloody head, almost severed from his body, rose before her. She heard herself moaning. Archie's voice was in her head, his presence so strong she was convinced he would soon be back to comfort. In her stillness she realised she was waiting for him: she also knew the uselessness of that wait. The absurdity of her position struck her with a feeling of utter helplessness. It was to strike again and again in the months to come.

Ken, for his part, kept to his word. He avoided Myrtle. Until the afternoon of Annie's outburst, the two friends never mentioned Ken's name. He became a ghost between them.

In the five minutes before Martin arrives, Myrtle wonders if she has been too hard on Annie. Annie meant well. Others, concerned for her, mean well too. But she wants to be left to deal with her aloneness in her own way. These things will pass, she believes. The chasm that surrounds her will never be filled, but the footholds will become stronger. She vows to try to be less distant, less defensive.

Myrtle gets up and moves round the room. Under her long skirts her feet shuffle in shy dance steps. Her body sways. Her big hands sprawl on her hips, clutching at her waist. She moves cautiously as a ship coming into berth: from table, to stove, to chair. As she passes the door she slows down. The smell of Archie's jersey is still there. Like his voice in her head, it has not faded a jot. Perhaps this is madness, she thinks. But she has found this criss-crossing the room, weaving in and out like the wool of a darn, is comforting.

When Martin arrives with his parcel of fish, she looks at him gladly. She suggests they should walk out and see how the trees are doing.

This is the first time Myrtle has invited anyone to the coppice. As they walk up the road she feels an irrational guilt. The wood was Archie's idea: he should be the first one to check its progress. But Martin is talking about other things. He is trying to describe how hands deal so differently with different materials. There could hardly be a greater contrast between the rubbery flesh of fish and the unyielding hardness of marble, he says. Martin's voice is soothing. The guilt disappears.

And when it comes to showing Martin round the wood, she begins to enjoy herself. The enjoyment runs up the veins of her arms, tingling. They walk up and down the paths between the trees—young saplings, each one strapped into a protective covering, just a few thin branches and tiny leaves sprouting out at the top.

Martin is impressed. He nods his head. 'You organised all this your-self? Choosing the trees, planning the planting? It's quite something.'

'We'd decided on a good many things together, it wasn't all me. At one moment, I thought I should abandon the whole project. But then I thought, no: Archie was so looking forward to getting it under way. The least I could do was to go ahead. And I have to say it's taken up a lot of time, which has been a good thing.'

They reach the centre of the wood, where all the paths end.

'This,' says Myrtle, 'I'm going to keep as a clearing. I might put a bench here. Somewhere to ruminate in my old age.'

'I could make you a bench,' says Martin. 'I enjoy a bit of carpentry.'

He's not sure Myrtle has heard his suggestion, for she does not answer, but moves to the centre of the clearing.

'Here,' she says, 'I want a rock. Do you think that would be possible? I want a rock to be a memorial stone to Archie.'

'I think that would be possible.'

'Could you find me one? It would need some sort of . . .'

'Simple carving? Name and dates? I'd like to do that for Archie.'

'I'd be so pleased—though you've already done a lot for Archie. Do you like it here? Can you see how it will all be eventually?'

Martin nods again. He is touched by her excitement. She moves, pointing to the only path they have not tried. Then she trips over a stone and falls. It's not a bad fall, though she clutches an ankle. In a moment Martin is by her side.

'It's nothing but a slight twist,' says Myrtle. 'Give me a hand.'

Martin grips her hand, puts his other one beneath her elbow, pulls her to her feet. For a moment they stand close while Myrtle tries putting weight on her foot. There is a stab of pain, but nothing unbearable.

'It's fine,' she says. 'Thanks.' She moves awkwardly away from Martin, turning her head so that he shall not see the scarlet flush that has spread over her. This is the first time since Archie died she has had any physical contact with a man. An enjoyable sensation. This is betrayal indeed.

'Let's go back this way,' she says, and hobbles down the new path.

Archie, she tells herself, would have thought it the natural and right thing to do, to help Myrtle up when she stumbled. So why had such an innocent event caused her such anguish? Could it be because leaning on Martin, she had felt hopeful—hopeful of something to do with the kindness of a good man still having the power to touch her?

She and Martin walk slowly back along the road to the village. When they reach the house, Myrtle, her calm restored now, invites Martin in for a glass of beer. But he declines.

'I promised Annie I'd deliver a bit of fish for her supper. Thank you for taking me to your wood,' he says. 'It's a grand place. Archie would have been proud of what you've done.'

As Myrtle fries the haddock Martin has given her, she wonders whether Annie has invited him to join her and Janice for supper. The thought ruffles her very slightly. To deflect it she takes out her old copy of Matthew Arnold's *Sohrab and Rustum* to prepare herself for Janice's tuition tomorrow.

Morning comes and Janice arrives early. She is pink-cheeked and bright-eyed as she empties her satchel of books onto the table. Myrtle knows this restless mood so well: Janice is Annie at thirteen, inflamed with anticipation, almost visible sparks flying off her.

They sit. Myrtle eyes Janice fiercely. The girl is here to study Matthew Arnold. She must put aside whatever has caused this excited state. Myrtle picks up her book. She begins to read the poem.

'Oh, Myrtle, I'm sorry. I can't concentrate today. I'm all of a dither.'

'So I can see.' Myrtle fixes Janice with a look in which interest is underlined with impatience. 'What's clogging your mind?'

Janice laughs. Her hands fidget about. 'I'm in love,' she says.

'In love?' Myrtle feels her face being scanned: Janice is eager for a reaction.

'Don't ask me who,' says Janice.

'I won't. It's nothing to do with me.'

'Shit: it gets you in the guts, doesn't it?'

'That's horrible language,' says Myrtle.

'Sorry. Slipped out.' Janice is taken aback by Myrtle's admonition—a rare thing. But still she is unable to drag herself back to the poem. 'Spend all my time looking out for him. Anything to catch a glimpse.'

Myrtle's glance, despite herself, is sympathetic. 'Is this love requited?'

'Does he fancy me, you mean? Don't suppose he even knows I exist.'

'Then you shouldn't waste too much time on him.'

'How can I help it? I only have to see him and my legs turn to jelly and my heart batters like I'm going to die.'

Myrtle smiles. 'Does your mother know?'

'No, she doesn't. Please don't tell her. Promise not to tell her.'

'Promise.'

'What shall I do?'

'Such feelings wear off. It can't last at fever pitch for long.'

'Hope not.' Janice is petulant. 'But I still can't do anything about it. It's, like, *gripped* me.'

'Janice, if I were you I should try to concentrate on the other bits of your life that give you enjoyment. Our lessons, for instance.'

'Sorry. I'm trying.'

'Like something to eat?'

'Please. I'm starving, though I feel sick when I eat.' She looks very young.

Myrtle goes to a cake tin. When her back is to Janice she asks. 'Didn't you manage the nice piece of haddock last night?'

'What haddock?'

'I thought Martin brought round a bit—'

'Oh, he did, aye.'

Myrtle has a quick struggle with herself, and loses. 'And did your mother ask him to stay and share it?' she asks, despising herself.

'She did,' says Janice, 'but he said he had to be on his way.' There is a sadness about her now, thoughts far from Martin and his fish.

'Try this,' Myrtle says, and hands Janice a slice of recently made ginger-bread. At the news about Martin a sensation she would not like to scrutinise flows through her. She watches Janice hungrily eat the ginger-bread, her eyes confused, grateful.

'Oh, Myrtle, thanks,' she says.

'It's something most people go through,' Myrtle says. 'When it's over—and you might be surprised how soon that is—you'll look back at yourself and laugh.'

'No, I won't,' says Janice, very serious, licking crumbs from her fingers. 'I'll never laugh about this.'

'Well, whatever. There's not much time left and we've hardly read a thing.' She picks up the book and Janice sighs.

Later, when Janice leaves, Myrtle feels she has failed to divert the girl's thoughts. It was impossible to regain her interest, concentration, enthusiasm. She hopes this is but a temporary phase.

It's a Saturday morning. The exercise books Myrtle was intending to mark she finished late last night. They sit in a neat pile on the table. There is nothing to do. With no one to cook for, no plans to meet Annie, the hours stretch emptily ahead.

A long silence is interrupted by a knock on the door. It is Alastair Brown. The shaky smile on his face indicates he has been practising its uneasy stretch. He holds a bunch of yellow roses.

'Mrs Duns, might I step over your threshold for just a moment?'

'Of course. Please do.'

Myrtle shuts the door behind him. She sees his hands are shaking and offers him coffee.

'That would be a kindness,' says Alastair. He puts the roses on the table. While the kettle boils he filters back and forth round the kitchen. Why has he come? Plainly he's ill at ease. His whole being suggests he has misjudged the wisdom of calling on Myrtle. He is cowed by regret, but it's too late to escape without some explanation.

Myrtle hands him a mug of coffee. He thanks her too profusely. She sits in her usual place at the table, indicating he should sit opposite— she doesn't want him to take Archie's seat. Sitting, he stares at his coffee. Silence hangs between them.

'Not having been here at the time of your husband's death,' he begins at last, 'I offered no condolences. But I imagine that when a spouse dies the need for sympathy does not run out. I've taken my time in coming here to offer my . . . but I could not be sure it would be appropriate.'

'It's very kind of you to . . . thank you,' says Myrtle.

Alastair allows another silence while he forms his next words.

'I hear that you are very brave, crying on nobody's shoulder, as happy as can be expected in yourself. I hope that is the case.' Myrtle senses that behind the dark glasses Alastair's eyes shut with relief now the worst part of his little speech is over.

Myrtle nods. She sees her visitor's confidence rising.

'I also hear,' he says, 'as I dare say you do, that there is a rumour that the woman I am in fact awaiting is you, Mrs Duns.'

Myrtle senses she is blushing, can think of no reply.

'But worry not. My reason for coming here is to assure you that there's not a jot of truth in the rumour. The thought had never crossed my mind. I mean, we've scarcely met. But I didn't want you to suffer any embarrassment.'

Myrtle allows herself a moment in which to think how best to answer. 'That's very thoughtful,' she says. 'It's good to hear from you that the idea seems as absurd to you as it does to me.'

The muscles round Alastair's mouth relax. Myrtle warms towards this awkward man: she would like to put him completely at his ease, and wonders how to guide a conversation into a new direction.

But before she can come to any decision Alastair braves his next difficult point. 'There is something I should like to put to you, Mrs Duns, now we have cleared the air. I hope you won't take this as speaking out of turn. There is something I am after, something precious, very innocent, but proving elusive to a bachelor of middle years.' Myrtle, is amused by his formal use of language.

Alastair pauses only to register a blurred query in her eyes, then hurries to enlighten. 'As you must know, to be a single figure in a society crowded with couples has its drawbacks. It's assumed one is looking for a partner, and to that end people offer up enthusiastic suggestions. You must have experienced this.'

'You flatter me,' says Myrtle, feeling herself redden again, 'but that really isn't the case.'

'Whatever. For my own part, and forgive me if this sounds like vanity, many ladies have pressed their suits upon me'—the visual image forces Myrtle to control a smile—'and I've had to discourage them because their aims have not exactly coincided with mine. I've no wish to be married, though I have every wish to be companionable. I can offer plain food by my fireside, a drop of double malt, old films on the video, excursions in my little boat—but nothing more, really. My old mother lives in a home in Dundee. I visit her regularly. What a dull life, you must be thinking. But it's all I have to offer. In return I would enjoy an occasional agreeable female presence.'

'I'm not thinking it's a dull life,' Myrtle interrupts.

'Then you're a woman in a million.'

'Just one of simple tastes. I've little ambition beyond getting through each day to the best of my ability.'

'Funny, I'm of that school, too.' Alastair now smiles. 'It's also funny that any woman should ever consider pursuing me. Dark glasses that never come off are a mystery, a challenge, I suppose. Well, mine don't come off for a very good reason.'

With no warning, the harbour master snatches off his glasses.

'This, Mrs Duns. Take a good look and you'll see the reason I can never hope to offer any woman—'

He stops. Myrtle is too surprised to contain a gasp. One eye has a permanently lowered lid. The rim of white that shows beneath it is a cloudy brown, the iris invisible. The eyeball of the other eye is surrounded by a mess of scarred and puckered skin. Ashamed of her initial reaction, she attempts an impassive face.

'Accident,' says Alastair. 'I can see all right. Sight's not impaired, but, you have to admit, I look pretty monstrous.'

'I'm sorry,' says Myrtle. 'But I don't think you should be so sure that a scarred face will put people off.'

'I do think that. I'm quite sure of it.'

Myrtle shakes her head. To her the scarred face remains curiously fine, with its strong parrot nose and engaging smile. Reflecting on this, she fails to come up with quick words of comfort.

'You've seen enough,' Alastair says. He puts the dark glasses back on. 'I didn't mean to . . . I'd be grateful if you would keep this to yourself.'

'Of course.'

'But just to return for a moment to my request for a companion. I came to you with the thought that perhaps, as a widow, you might be looking for something of that nature yourself. Nothing more.'

'I haven't consciously thought in those terms,' says Myrtle, anxious in her delicacy, 'but I like to see friends. I'm no hermit.'

'Then from time to time we could get together?'

'Why not?' Myrtle smiles. 'I do enjoy a game of cards.'

'Why, so do I!' Alastair smiles back. His eagerness is almost pathetic.

Myrtle plans a small lie to ensure the visit will have a definite cut-off time, for she feels that given the slightest encouragement Alastair could still be sitting at her table at noon.

'I have an engagement at twelve,' she says, 'but we could play a game now, if you like.'

The effect of this offer is out of all proportion to the invitation: Alastair beams at the prospect.

'I would not want to prevail upon your kindness,' he says.

'You're not prevailing on anything.' Myrtle slaps down the cards.

'Now you're making a mockery of my language.'

'Well, it is quite distinctive,' Myrtle answers in a teasing voice. 'I can tell you watch a lot of old films. You're not a man of your time.'

'Nor do I want to be,' says Alastair, cutting the pack with an elegant flick of his wrist. He's beginning to enjoy himself.

Two hours pass. Myrtle and the harbour master are still silently at their cards. Myrtle seems to have forgotten her engagement. Alastair is taxing Myrtle. He is a much better card player than Annie.

The door opens, and Annie hurries in. Myrtle looks up to her friend's incredulous face.

'Oh, Annie,' she says, 'Mr Brown, here, has just dropped by—'

'I'm so sorry.' Alastair, rigid with confusion, leaps up. His cards fall from his hands to splatter over the table. 'I just dropped in—'

'Well, don't mind me,' says Annie. Her eyes are on the roses, which Myrtle has thrust into a jug. 'I was just dropping in, too, to see if Myrtle fancied a game of cards. But I see I've been beaten to it.' The words are quiet and furious.

'I am on my way.' offers Alastair. 'Thank you for your hospitality. Mrs Duns. I enjoyed our game. Perhaps we can have a return match, one day.' This is said with a small defiant toss of his head in Annie's direction. 'Mrs Mcleoud, good to see you again, too—'

He is gone. Annie sits in her usual place.

'So? What was all that about?' she asks.

'Annie!' Myrtle laughs. Her friend's entrance has done nothing to affect her good humour. 'Mr Brown dropped by unexpectedly. He had a cup of coffee and played several games of two-handed rummy.'

She smiles. Annie sniffs. 'So they're true, then, the rumours? Harbour master pants after the widow Duns.'

'Don't be ridiculous. He strikes me as short of friends up here.'

'Not for the lack of opportunity.' Annie is mellowing. 'Well, he's all yours. Not my type.' She begins to shuffle the cards. 'Actually, I came over to tell you something funny. Janice is in love.'

Myrtle dislikes the triumphant way Annie produces the news Myrtle already knows. She barely raises her eyebrows. 'Who's the boy?'

Annie shrugs. 'She won't tell me. She'll only say I'd be surprised. A lot of boys walk her home after school. She comes back very pink in the cheeks, sometimes.'

'What's been your advice to her?'

'Advice?' Again Annie laughs. 'What advice can a mother give a daughter that she's going to listen to these days? I said don't do anything I wouldn't do, but have fun.'

'Hope the whole business won't detract from her work,' says Myrtle, shoulders rising prissily. 'She's doing so well.'

'Heavens above, Myrtle, you're too nervous, overcautious. Of course a crush on some spotty boy isn't going to put Janice off her work. Feel like a quick game?' Annie is dealing out the cards. 'You'll find me pretty boring to play with after Mr Romantic Hero Harbour Master, I dare say. But at least you're familiar with my game.'

'Don't be silly, Annie.'

Half an hour later a white envelope is slipped through the door. Myrtle does not hear it drop onto the mat. Annie, vicariously expectant, puts down her cards and hurries to pick it up.

'From Martin,' she says.

'How do you know?'

'He left me a note once.' She looks at Myrtle with such powerful curiosity that Myrtle, despite herself, slits open the envelope and takes out a sheet of paper. She reads quickly to herself: *Bench settled. All in place. Hope you won't take this as a liberty. I'll be up at the coppice at 5.30 for your approval if that is convenient. If it isn't, ring me and I'll remove it at once and apologise for acting with such haste. I was spurred by what I thought was a good idea. Yours, Martin.*

Myrtle feels herself blushing and is annoyed with herself. 'Martin's arranging some sort of memorial thing for Archie. He says he's found the very thing.'

'He's a kind man, Martin,' says Annie. 'I mean, he showed no resentment over my silly behaviour. Real gentleman!' She pauses. 'He's bringing me a dressed crab tonight. If I'm patient enough, who knows? One day he might have more to offer than fish.'

'He might, too,' agrees Myrtle, keeping her eyes firmly on the note.

When she arrives at the coppice, 5.30 precisely, Martin is already there. He sits at one end of the bench, eyes on a wheeling swallow.

The bench is a firm and ancient thing of dark wood: not at all what Myrtle had in mind. But quickly she sees it is better than her imagining.

Martin jumps up. He seems nervous. 'What do you think?'

'I like it. It's good, solid.'

'Funny thing is, it's been outside my workshop for as long as I can remember. I suddenly thought—why, it's just the thing. Here, try it.'

Myrtle sits. She puts an arm on its wide wooden arm. She shuffles herself, feeling the safety of the thick planks beneath her skirts.

'Oh, Martin,' she says, 'it's lovely. Thank you very much.' She smiles up at him. 'Would you mind if I sit here alone for a while?'

'You do that.' Martin turns at once and walks down a path edged with waist-high saplings. Myrtle is grateful for his instant understanding.

But once she is alone she does not think of Archie. She looks up at the broad evening sky, lavender blue unbroken by cloud, and is aware that there has been some change of the tides within her.

Myrtle's eyes follow the tiny arrow of the swallow. What strange rites people go through, she thinks. What subtle junctions they make for themselves between one era of their lives and another . . .She stands, stretches, yawns, looks round at the healthy young trees, then sets off for home knowing that Archie would be glad.

On the road Myrtle see Janice running towards her. The girl is wearing a light-coloured dress with a hem that rises and falls in small waves as she moves. She reaches Myrtle: pink cheeks, high spirits.

'What's up with you, Janice?'

'I'm just so *happy*.'

'That's good. Done your homework?'

'Oh, Myrtle . . . I'm going to. You know what? I told my mum I was in love. She said, "Don't do anything I wouldn't do. Have fun." That gives me a pretty free rein, doesn't it?'

'You shouldn't speak of your mother like that,' says Myrtle.

'But it's the truth. I know my mum was up to all sorts. I've heard things.' Janice scans Myrtle's face, but finds no response.

Myrtle is glad they have reached the village. 'Run along now, no more skiving,' she says, ruffling the girl's hair.

As Myrtle watches Annie's daughter skipping into the dusk, bent on some foolish action, she feels a profound sense of misgiving—a feeling horribly familiar from her childhood, when she had helplessly watched Annie's compulsive behaviour.

'Janice,' she calls. She wants to say something, warn her, stop her, but Janice does not hear. Myrtle sighs. She knows she must do something before it is too late. But what?

Life, Myrtle senses, is beginning to speed up. People seem to come and go more frequently; Annie comes again to play cards several afternoons a week, other fishermen's wives invite her to drop by, Martin arrives regularly with a piece of fish, and the harbour master comes round once a week for a game and something to eat.

One Tuesday evening there is a particular feeling of bustle. Myrtle is marking books when Martin comes in—these days, although he knocks, he also takes the liberty of pushing open the door at the same time. The confidence of this action indicates a deepening of their friendship, thinks Myrtle.

This evening, Martin is pacing about. 'Look,' he says, 'I have to collect a consignment of marble next week. Somewhere up near Perth. I was just wondering if you might like to come with me. It would only be a very minor outing, but I was thinking it's about time you went somewhere. You haven't left the village since Archie died, have you?'

Myrtle puts her hand onto the kettle. She leans against the stove, needing support. The implications of this innocent invitation have ungrounded her. Martin watches her carefully. He sees her hesitation.

'It wouldn't be *much* of an invitation,' he says. 'But the van's comfortable and it's fine country up there in the hills. I have to pick up the stuff by five. Then we could find ourselves somewhere for an early supper— be back here soon after nine.' Myrtle has turned very pale. The internal argument with herself, the weighing up of her various feelings, is almost visible. 'Or we could skip supper altogether,' says Martin, gently.

The growl of the kettle is the only sound in the room for a while.

'That's a very kind thought,' Myrtle says at last. 'A lovely invitation, and I'm tempted.' She pauses. 'But I think I'm not quite ready yet . . .'

'Ready for what?'

'Ready for sitting beside a man, being driven by someone who isn't Archie.' She gives a small laugh. 'It sounds silly, I know.'

'I'm sorry,' says Martin. He suppresses a sigh. 'I was trying to find the right moment. I misjudged.'

'I find it hard to judge, myself. At the moment, anything beyond the village, the wood, would seem like infidelity.'

Martin smiles. Wry, disappointed. 'It's been two years, Myrtle.'

'I know. And things are beginning to change. I'm beginning to feel a little less unsafe. But there's still a way to go.'

Martin moves closer to her. She can see he considers putting an arm round her shoulder, but resists, and she is grateful for that.

'I understand,' he says. 'I'll try to be patient. Then one fine day I'll suggest we go off for a drink to some far-off place—at least two miles away—and you'll say yes. You might even enjoy yourself and think it was just what Archie would have wanted.'

Shortly after that, having refused a cup of tea, he leaves.

For all his cheerful countenance, Myrtle knows he is disappointed. She reruns the short scene in her mind. Her refusal, she knows, was irrational, foolish. It would have been an enjoyable day. She trusted him absolutely: he had become the best male friend she had. She had no fears that he would take the liberty of making some untoward physical gesture. So why had she been overwhelmed by reluctance to accept his offer? Myrtle could not answer. She could only be sure of an amorphous apprehension. And now she was faced with the worrying question: had her decision endangered their friendship? Would Martin, once rejected, wait patiently for a more opportune time? Myrtle had it in mind to run after him, say she'd love to come to Perthshire with him after all. But so quick a change of mind was not in Myrtle's nature. It would be undignified; an almost-middle-aged woman should know her own mind, stick to the firmness of her purpose.

There is another knock at the door. Myrtle hopes it might be Martin returning. Yes, she would say, I would love to come.

It is Ken. They stand looking at each other.

'What are you doing here?' Myrtle asks at last.

'Please, let me in for a moment. It's important.'

Myrtle stands aside to let him enter. She doesn't know why. Touched by Ken's look of desperation, perhaps.

'Thanks,' he says. He hurries to the window. 'I need your help. Annie says she's going. Leaving. Has she said anything to you?'

'Not a thing.'

'That's curious. I mean, with your being such friends.'

'Even the best of friends cordon off certain areas,' says Myrtle. 'What's the problem?'

'Hard to say. I've done my best. Earned the money, tried to keep out of her way. She's on about Archie all the time. Won't listen to a word I say. There seems to be no such thing in her nature as forgiveness. I don't know how to persuade her there's nothing I can do about something in the past—no way I can bring Archie back, God that there were.'

'I'm sorry,' says Myrtle. Despite herself, she has pity for the man.

'She says she can't stand being under the same roof as me any longer. There's probably someone else. Leopards don't change their spots, do they? And I haven't been allowed to lay hands on her since the day Archie died. She must be getting it from somewhere—'

'Ken—'

'Well, you know Annie. If there is someone, though, beats me who it is. Martin's the only one who comes round, bringing his do-gooding pieces of fish—it couldn't be St Martin she fancies, boring man. No, I think there's someone visits her at the café. I've seen her talking to some fellow in a big car. Annie wouldn't last a minute without a man. As for me, I wouldn't last long without her. She may be a right bitch, Annie, but I love her.'

'What do you want me to do?' Myrtle asks.

'I don't know. Find out what's going on. You'd best not tell her I've said anything. She'd go mad.'

'We'll have to risk that,' says Myrtle. 'I'll do what I can, but she'll have to know you've been here. Otherwise what reason would I have for suddenly enquiring about her private life?'

'Very well. You know what's best. I leave it to you. Thanks, Myrtle. You can imagine how grateful . . . letting me in like this.' Ken moves towards the door, a trace of relief on his face. 'It's taken me weeks, making up my mind whether or not to come. It was only her outburst last night finally decided me. You're a good . . . well, I suppose not a friend any more.'

'It'd be difficult ever to forget the part you played. But in my heart I can't bear you any hatred. Anger runs its course. All the avoiding, I'd say there's no point any more. It might help with Annie, if she sees my forgiveness as well as knowing it exists. Come round whenever you want.'

Ken rubs his eyes, incredulous. He opens the door.

'You're a woman in a million, Myrtle,' he says.

When Ken has gone, Archie—whose presence has been less vivid of late—comes roaring back, so close to flesh and blood it is only the rational part of Myrtle's mind that stops her from putting out a hand to touch him. Archie's jersey still hangs on the back of the door. Myrtle takes it down, slaps at it. Sprays of dust fly out. She rolls it up and stuffs it into the bin. Should have done this long ago, she thinks. But her eyes are filled with tears.

She must employ her old standby, deflection. This evening she is lucky enough to have some positive action to hand. Annie must be confronted as soon as possible. She pulls on her coat, averting her eyes from the bareness of the door.

As she hurries up the path to Annie's house, she sees through the window that Annie is lying on the sofa watching television. Myrtle lets herself in. There is dread in her heart, but her blood is up.

Annie furrily turns on the cushions, a lazy-cat movement, as Myrtle comes in. Her bare feet nuzzle each other, twirling in a sensuous way that Myrtle finds repellent. The toenails are painted dots of scarlet. The sight of them enrages her. Annie smiles up at her friend's censorious face, enjoying the disapproval.

'Here's a surprise,' she says. 'So what brings you here—?'

'Ken's just been round,' says Myrtle. She sits, back to the window.

'He's obviously said something to put you in a rare old mood. I told him not to go round to your place, ever.'

'I'm glad he did.'

Annie sniffs indelicately. 'What was he on about, then?'

'He's says you're threatening to leave. I felt we ought to talk about it.'

Annie begins her usual beguiling laugh, but Myrtle detects scorn.

'Could this be called poking your nose into matters that have nothing to do with you?'

'You could call it that, I suppose,' Myrtle says. 'But when it's something this important, surely—'

'You know me,' butts in Annie, 'always threatening to leave Ken. We had a particularly noisy row last night. I suppose that alarmed him.'

'You mean you're not about to go?'

'Course not. It might come to that one day. But not yet. What would I do? What about Janice? There's her to think of.'

Myrtle feels herself falling more deeply into the chair. Relief makes her heavy, calm. 'I'm glad to hear it,' she says.

'He shouldn't have come running to you.'

'Don't be stupid, Annie. Ken's in a bad way. All I said was I'd try to talk to you, make you see sense.'

'No need for your good advice, thanks very much. We've always had different ideas about right and wrong, haven't we? Well I'm quite able to make my own judgments. I'll stick around with Ken till I can't bear it a moment longer. But it's a high price to pay for a roof over my head. I can barely stand the sight of him, those eyes begging for forgiveness.'

'I told him I'd be glad if he comes round when he wants to,' says Myrtle. 'No point in carrying on with all this avoidance. It was an accident. I forgave him right from the start. It's time to show I mean it. Ken's had punishment enough.'

'That's up to you.' Their eyes meet. 'At least he's got *your* forgiveness.'

'It's not enough.'

'That's all he's getting.'

'I wish you weren't so adamant.'

'You've always wished me to be things or do things that wild horses wouldn't make me . . .' She swings one leg onto the floor. 'And I suppose Ken mentioned a certain gentleman with a large car?'

'He did say something.'

Annie laughs. 'Jealousy's his problem, always has been. The chap he's referring to gave me a lift home one night from the café. Ken went berserk. Banged on the windscreen, shouted bloody murder, hauled me up the path by the scruff of my neck. The man hasn't been back since, as you can imagine.' She smiles, casts a wan look out of the window. 'There's no one I've met recently I fancy in the slightest, so you needn't worry. I'm beginning to think there may never be anyone else again. The sterile life from here to the grave.'

When Annie subsides into self-pity it's time to change tack.

'Do you remember,' Myrtle asks, 'how when we were first married we so hated it when the men went off?'

'I'd do anything, now, for Ken to be off for a week,' says Annie. 'Fishermen's wives don't know how lucky they are having time to themselves . . .' She glances at Myrtle, sees the tight mouth and big clenched fists. Remorse comes too late. 'Oh, God, Myrtle,' she cries. 'How could I be saying that to you of all people. You with no choice but being alone . . .?' She leaps up, rushes to put an arm round Myrtle. 'What was I saying?'

'Just carrying on in your usual blundering way,' says Myrtle. She stands up, pushing Annie from her. 'With no thought for others.'

'I'm sorry. I really am. Don't go. Stay a bit. Have a cup of tea.'

But Myrtle is sweeping out of the door. 'I'm away,' she says.

In her brisk walk home Myrtle allows herself to wonder what it would be like were she and Annie no longer friends. Such a situation is unimaginable. But in the safety of her own kitchen her friend's voice rings out. *You with no choice but being alone . . .* It's odd that Annie, in her cruel moments of truth, can be so accurate. Drained by her day, Myrtle sits and listens for Archie's voice. But at moments when she most needs it, it fails her.

Five days have passed since Myrtle turned down Martin's invitation. She has not seen him since. But they have been busy days and she has not thought much of his absence. Now, on the sixth day of no sign of him, she fears she may have caused him offence. She wonders what she should do, hesitates to be the one to get in touch.

On the afternoon of the sixth day, a strong wind from the sea attacks the coast. Myrtle walks home from school. It occurs to her she has good reason to get in touch with Martin: at last she has chosen an epitaph for Archie's headstone. The wind scrapes across her eyes causing streams of tears. She has no free hand to wipe them away. Her vision is blurred. But in the distance she thinks she sees Martin. She blinks rapidly. It *is* him. A woman walks beside him. They are arm in arm.

She is aware of the battering of her heart, and is puzzled. Why should she be so shocked at the sight of Martin with a woman? It has never occurred to her that he might have a girlfriend. Simply, she does not think of Martin in those terms. For the most part they skirt one another's private feelings by mutual, though unspoken, consent.

She sees Martin wave, smile, begin to cross the street. At once she summons a generous smile in return. She is determined to welcome whoever this woman may be: how very good that Martin has found someone, perhaps, with whom to share his life. Martin greets Myrtle, shouting through the wind. He puts his arm round the woman's shoulders. She's smiling. She has a friendly face, no denying.

'My sister, Myrtle,' Martin is shouting. 'Gwen. Suddenly over from Canada—no warning. Sorry I haven't been in touch. We took a small trip up to Perth.' Gwen is nodding. She and Myrtle are smiling at each other, trying to concentrate against the elements.

'Why don't you both come and have a cup of tea?' Myrtle shouts.

Martin moves nearer. 'We're on the way up to the cemetery. Want to show my sister some of my work. Could we drop by later?'

'Supper?' shouts Myrtle. Then she remembers something. 'Alastair Brown is coming round, but . . .'

'We'd like that.' More smiling. Then they go their separate ways.

Myrtle turns into the wind. She sails home as if carried by a buoyant sea, dipping and tossing like a small boat. There, her mind whips through the almost empty fridge. She will have to add vegetables to the venison stew. She will make a quick treacle tart (the harbour master's favourite). It has been so long since Myrtle has entertained that she finds herself in a dither. Her hands shake as she rolls pastry. Time goes so fast there is no moment for Myrtle to change her old skirt. She knows, as she opens the door, she is all awry, far from the picture of a calm hostess.

But the evening works. Alastair is plainly surprised but gratified to find himself one of a *party*, as he calls the evening. He and Martin know each other slightly and seem keen to refurbish the acquaintance. There is an enjoyable moment when each takes it upon himself to open the wine—a slight race, indeed, to the corkscrew. This Martin wins, knowing its place in the drawer. But Martin is adamant the harbour master should be the one to open the bottle. All this is amid laughter. Myrtle is conscious that a sense of competition has been established as to whose proprietorial rights are strongest in this kitchen.

Myrtle's cooking is much appreciated. Over supper she reflects she has never seen the harbour master in better spirits. He tells anecdotes, encouraging laughter in stories against himself. Myrtle feels a warm rush of surprise at her ability to have organised this spontaneous evening, and pleasure at seeing it work so well.

It's past midnight when Gwen and Martin leave. Martin says he will come round when Gwen has gone. It is plain, in the out-of-character profusion of his thanks, he has much enjoyed the evening.

The harbour master, still sitting at the table, does not look inclined to depart. He has poured himself one of his strange drinks—whisky with a touch of milk. Myrtle has lost count of how many of these he has consumed since he arrived. He stands up, begins to unbutton his blazer.

'Let me help with the washing-up,' he says.

'No, please. I can do it in the morning.' There is urgency in her voice. Myrtle is anxious that the blazer should remain buttoned.

'Very well.' His quick agreement fills Myrtle with relief. 'But the night is young. Should we have a game of cards?'

'It's not that young,' says Myrtle, lightly. 'Getting on for one o'clock. So I think it's too late for me.'

Alastair leaps to his feet as if a bomb has gone off beneath him, rebuttoning the blazer. He is mortified by his own impropriety. He should have seen how late it was. These musings are clearly visible to Myrtle who, shocked by his leap from the chair, tries to contain a smile. He stands looking at her, a little unsteady.

'Oh, forgive such an inconsiderate thought. I'm on my way . . .'

Myrtle follows him to the door. He is having trouble with the handle.

'Calm down, Alastair.' She does not often use his Christian name. It has effect. It also gives the harbour master courage to make a final gesture. He takes both Myrtle's hands in his and rubs them gently.

'This was a wonderful evening,' he says. Her hands are still in his.

'Good.'

'You're a fine-looking woman, Myrtle,' he says.

To humour him, Myrtle thinks quickly, is the best way. She does not want a tussle. Perhaps the mention of Archie will caution him.

'Archie used to say he loved my smile,' she says, 'and my height and my weight. But in all his love for me he never tried to pretend he saw me as any kind of beauty. Luckily for me, looks weren't a priority in Archie's mind.' She laughs lightly. Her plan has worked. Alastair releases her hands. But his train of thought is not deflected.

'God knows, Myrtle,' he says, 'you underrate yourself. You do something to a man. I asked only for companionship, but I find myself wanting more: your love.'

Myrtle is unnerved but also, despite herself, intrigued.

'You're like a distant mountain in my life,' Alastair goes on, 'which more than anything in the world I want to—'

'Climb?' suggests Myrtle. She is still trying to make a joke of it all.

Alastair smiles reluctantly. Then his mouth is on hers. There is no taste of salt on his nibbling lips. Nothing like Archie. Instead, intimations of tea, whisky, milk. As the harbour master's tongue worms gently round her teeth she is both scandalised by her own behaviour, and excited. She shifts her position. Alastair moves back at once.

'Have I offended you?'

'No.' No, he hadn't offended, exactly.

'Not for the world would I do anything to lose our friendship.'

'That's all right.' By now, curiously, it is all right.

'Then farewell, dear Myrtle. I'm on my way.'

He goes. Myrtle reruns the evening in her mind. The success of it, and the unexpected ending, have filled her with spinning energy. Her admiration for the dignified way in which Alastair comported himself, when his feelings overcame him, has added to the warmth of Myrtle's affection. Archie would have wanted her to make new friends. One day, perhaps, she can imagine the sympathy she feels for Alastair could change into a kind of love. The kiss, now, does not seem like a betrayal. Rather, it was a relief to know physical pleasure could still flare. This realisation adds to the sense that her life is in some curious way speeding up, and she is glad.

The next afternoon Alastair is waiting for her when she arrives home from school. His unexpected presence is not altogether welcome. There is a load of books to be marked, then she wants to write down the epitaph for Archie. Myrtle can see the harbour master is in an agitated state. Her previous feelings of warmth are suddenly overcast with annoyance. But she invites him in. They will once more share a pot of tea.

Alastair's cheeks are pale. His behaviour of the night before has obviously caused him remorse. He paces the room, in a warm-up to his apology. He does not take off his waterproof jacket, indicating his stay will not be a long one. By the time they are sitting at the table with their mugs of tea, her irritation is replaced by sympathy.

'I do hope my inappropriate behaviour last night has not caused you the anguish it has caused me, dear Myrtle,' he begins. 'My only excuse is that I got carried away by the enjoyment of the evening. I do apologise.'

'There's no need,' says Myrtle, smiling. 'So stop tormenting yourself. As far as I was concerned, you were the perfect gentleman.'

'Oh, Mrs Duns, Myrtle . . . you've no idea how good it is to hear you say that,' he murmurs. 'Your understanding means more to me than—'

'Yes, well, let's put the whole incident aside now, shall we?' Myrtle is brusque in order to deflect his course. 'And for heaven's sake don't brood any more on something of so little importance.'

Alastair struggles with his mouth and produces a tepid smile. It's this grappling with himself, and winning, that inspires Myrtle's admiration.

'Of so little importance?' he says, sadly. Then quickly continues, 'I wonder if I could persuade you for a little jaunt in my boat? We could take a picnic—just go for an afternoon.'

Myrtle remembers her foolishness in refusing Martin's invitation.

'Of course: I'd love to come one afternoon,' she says. 'When it's warmer. In a few weeks . . .'

The harbour master, like a man who has snatched what he wants and feels he must escape before it's taken back from him, makes a sudden leap towards the door.

'Then *there's* a plan to look forward to,' he says, and runs from the room. Myrtle goes to shut the door, to find Annie on the doorstep.

'Just collided with your fancy man again,' she says.

'Och, Annie. Come on in. I'll make a fresh pot.'

Since the confrontation concerning Ken, their mutual avoiding of the subject of him has caused only the faintest shadow between them: Annie has been in high spirits, full of stories about customers at the café. Today she is in no less good humour, though her face is serious.

'Come on, what's going on?' she says. 'He's always here.'

'Nothing,' Myrtle says. 'He's just a friend. He knows that's all I want.'

Annie laughs. 'Seems pretty keen to me,' she says. 'Are you sure you're not being naïve? I've been trying to imagine it: my friend married to the harbour master. Has the thought never crossed your mind?'

'Never. Archie's only been dead two years.'

'How long must a widow wait?'

'Depends what she wants.'

'How long must it be to feel something for a new man when the man she's always loved has died?'

'God knows. It's not something I think about.' Here, Myrtle questions herself silently. Is this quite true?'

Annie sighs. 'You know what? I've been trying to imagine what it's like being you.'

Myrtle laughs. 'You've been overtaxing your imagination then. You're not usually by way of thinking how things are for other people.'

'Right as usual,' concedes Annie with a smile. 'But I find myself curious. I imagine widowhood must be so empty.'

Myrtle dislikes the way this conversation is going, for the impossibility of conveying the feelings of loss will make it worthless. But Annie is in a rare mood of sympathy and concern. Myrtle tries to be patient.

'I don't feel empty,' she says. 'It may be true for others, not for me.' She pauses, taking in Annie's incredulous eyes—she feels renewed love for her at this moment.

'That sounds to me like boasting,' says Annie.

'Then I've put it badly,' Myrtle says. 'It's not meant to sound self-satisfied. I'm trying to explain that I feel overfull of new things. The wreckage within has to be sorted out—a long process, I dare say. But I think there's a lot that can be rescued. So I wait, quite patiently.'

'Not at all as I imagined,' says Annie after a silent reflection. 'You make me feel there's hope for you. I'm glad about that.' She sips her tea, then looks directly at her friend. 'I let Ken have it last night. First time for so long.'

Myrtle's answer is the merest lift of an eyebrow. She has never been able to respond to Annie's naturally crude language.

'It was nice,' Annie goes on, entertained by Myrtle's blush. 'I don't suppose it'll mean anything amazing like me suddenly falling in love with him, but perhaps it'll make things easier. This morning, Janice says to me: "Mum, do you realise it's the first morning for months you haven't shouted at Dad? What's got into you?" Trouble is,' Annie goes on, 'if you can't stop thinking about another man, it's difficult to concentrate on a husband you've never really loved.'

WIVES OF THE FISHERMEN

Myrtle can bear no more. She takes a pack of cards from the drawer. 'How about a quick game? Just one, before I get down to work.'

Annie responds silently to the look of familiar severity that locks her friend's features. With distracted fingers she picks up the pack and begins to shuffle.

When Annie has gone, Myrtle tries out the epitaph, finds it satisfactory. She writes a brief note to Martin, which she will post—no energy to walk up to his cottage this evening. Then she begins to go through the exercise books, marvelling as always at the singularity of each of her pupils. But her concentration is interrupted by the telephone. It is the matron of the Evergreen Home, desperate for help: two members of staff are sick. Myrtle agrees to go as soon as she has finished her books.

It is almost dark by the time she arrives. As soon as she is through the door, she is greeted by the grateful, harassed matron, and hurries to the parlour. There, every chair in the semicircle round the television is occupied. Heads are slumped low on chests and hands droop from the arms of floral chairs, lifeless as old gloves.

'All this lot—bed,' says the matron. 'It's way past time. If you could start moving them, I'll get the Horlicks.'

For the next few hours Myrtle does her best. She tries to understand confused murmurings—mostly grumbles. She peels off warm wrinkled stockings. She wishes each old person a good night.

On the walk home, Myrtle decides never to go to the home again. She is angry and depressed; not so much by the sadness of the home's function, as by being the widow who can always be counted on to help out. She wants passionately to rebel against that role.

She is by now very tired and longs for bed. There is no moon, but a mass of small, hard, dense jet clouds, as if the contents of a coal scuttle have been scattered in the sky. She turns a corner and sees the figure of a man just ahead of her—he has obviously just come out of the pub. It's Ken. She calls him. He turns, and is at once by her side. She can smell whisky, smoke.

'Myrtle! I'll walk you home.' He takes her arm. He's in good humour.

'You been out enjoying yourself?' he asks.

'I've been up at the home, helping out.'

'You're a good woman, Myrtle. A woman to be relied on.' His own high spirits preclude further interest.

'I'm not, you know. I've all sorts of uncharitable thoughts.'

'Well,' says Ken, not up to finding a pertinent response to this surprising fact, 'I'll tell you something: I'm a happier man, Myrtle.'

'Good. I'm glad.' They have reached Myrtle's house.

'I'm not swearing on this, mind,' says Ken, 'but God knows why, I think maybe Annie's coming round . . .'

'I hope so,' says Myrtle. She is halfway up the steps. 'Good night.'

Ken hurries off with a bounding step, a lightness of heart, knowing what awaits him at home. Myrtle is caught unawares by a thrust of something very painful. She loathes herself for her base feelings. How, just two years since Archie's death, can she possibly be jealous of Ken and Annie's renewed physical joy. A picture of the harbour master presses into her mind. It would be so easy . . . It takes Myrtle a long time to find her keys and let herself into the dark emptiness of the house.

The day Martin gets Myrtle's note about her decision for Archie's epitaph, he hurries round.

'This is cause for celebration,' he says. 'I'll get working.'

Behind his smile Myrtle sees a look of unusual weariness. The smile faded, his mouth is grim in repose. He sits in his usual place. Myrtle fetches a bottle of beer, and sits too. She decides to ignore the signs of trouble. She asks if his sister enjoyed her stay.

'I think she did. She needed a break—running a smallholding on her own, it's a lot for a single woman.' Martin pauses. 'The real reason for her visit was to tell me that there's a man who wants her to move in with him in Vancouver. She's thinking about it.' He swigs at his beer, tosses back his head, closes his eyes for a moment. 'I've decided to give up the filleting job, end of the month,' he says. It's not a way to spend the mornings. Besides, the pay—' He opens his eyes. 'I went round to Annie last night. Ken there for once. Quite a surprise.' He flicks another smile, conveying nothing. 'Janice was there, in a foul mood. When I arrived she dashed straight up to her room and stayed there.'

'Teenagers,' says Myrtle. 'She tells me she's in love with some boy.'

'Annie said that was the explanation, too. She's pretty enough to cause trouble,' says Martin. 'She should be warned.'

'I try,' says Myrtle, 'but I doubt I make much impression.'

When Martin makes to leave, his expression has mellowed. She assumes he has been worrying over the decision about the filleting.

'You're a wonder, Myrtle,' he says, as he goes. 'So many of us wouldn't know what to do without you.'

WIVES OF THE FISHERMEN

When she is alone, Myrtle crosses the room with her dipping gait, half dancing, enjoying her imitation of a small boat on a buoyant sea, her silly secret. Outside there is blue sky. It's very warm. Then she remembers: now this good weather has settled in there's no excuse to delay the excursion on the harbour master's boat. Her strongest desire is to get the whole thing over. She is convinced the picnic will straighten things in her mind, though the precise nature of her thoughts is not easy to define. I'm floating, she thinks, on a sea of unknown depths: no idea which way I'll drift. But at least I'm not drowning any more: I'm stronger, though the missing will never change.

With the delicacy and tact that he considers his speciality, Alastair Brown proposes a date for their excursion and makes arrangements. On the morning of the appointed day Myrtle prepares herself—head-scarf, and a jacket in case the weather should change. She thinks with amusement how very differently Annie would prepare to go out on a date. Myrtle wears her oldest summer skirt, nothing on her face, and ties back her hair.

She enjoys the bus journey five miles along the coast to a neighbour-ing fishing village where she is to meet Alastair at the harbour. There is a hot sun, the sea a tightly stretched blue a shade deeper than the cloud-less sky. She has not been out of the village, except to the copse, for a long time. The short journey feels like an adventure.

At the harbour, Alastair sits at a wooden table provided for customers at the stall where lobsters and crabs are sold. Myrtle taps him on the shoulder. He jumps to his feet like a man surprised: perhaps this is to disguise the fact that he has been waiting, anticipating, for a long time. He pulls his shoulders back, stands very upright. Myrtle reads his mind. He is nervous. She smiles to convey her understanding of this fact. They move towards the steps in the harbour wall that lead down to the water.

The *Swift*, unsurprisingly, is an immaculate little boat. Everything is swept and polished. There is a cushion on one of the wooden seats. A wicker picnic basket is lodged under another.

Myrtle takes her place on the cushion. Alastair wedges himself into the tiny cabin that houses a steering wheel. Slowly the *Swift* putters out to the open sea. The water's tautness, seen from the bus, Myrtle realises, was an illusion. Here, it dips and sways in a lively way. Sometimes a small wave is driven to break, its peak flurrying like a white bird before its feathers are dashed back into the darker water.

The sun is hot by now, despite a breeze. Myrtle is lulled by the rocking and the heat. She sits looking at the waves, trying to read the signals in her stomach. She recognises a feeling of pale anticipation—nothing specific, nothing either certain or troubling. Just the comfortable sensation of good companionship. No sooner has she made these calculations than Archie appears. How he would laugh, the very idea of her off on a sea picnic with the harbour master! His voice is so loud she jerks her head round, expecting to find him beside her. But boat and sea, empty of him, tighten the void within her. She knows that the rest of her life will be a double life: on the one hand there will be reality—on the other, always haunting that real life, will be the spirit of Archie.

Myrtle is jolted from her cogitations by a slowing-down of the boat. The harbour master shouts that he thinks it's time to eat. Myrtle agrees. They go to within a few yards of the shore. There is no one on the small grey beach, just rocks scarved with blowing seaweed.

'Shall we wade ashore? Make ourselves comfortable.'

Myrtle pictures a picnic as perhaps he sees it: an opportunity . . . a second kiss. Her pity and affection for the harbour master, her new desire for arms round her, could wing beyond set boundaries here under the sun. Is this what she wants?

'I'd rather stay here,' she says.

'Very well. Whatever you wish.' If the harbour master is disappointed, he conceals it nobly. He drops the anchor, moves to sit opposite Myrtle. He pulls the basket between them and begins to sort out carefully wrapped packages. There are crab sandwiches, lemon biscuits from the bakery, peaches and grapes. Myrtle is touched by the trouble he has taken. She accepts a glass of dry cider, chilled in a special box. For himself, the harbour master has brought a carton of milk.

As Myrtle's guest, playing cards, Alastair Brown is not a keen talker. But now, on this sea picnic—a time he has perhaps been waiting for with impatience—he takes his opportunity to tell Myrtle of his life.

Myrtle shuts her eyes but keeps up a small smile to show she is listening. In truth his story becomes a little hazy—the many jobs, his inability to find a wife; his love of milk stemming from some week on a farm of Jersey cows . . . through the mists of her sleepiness it is all very endearing but confusing. Soporific. Almost asleep, she suddenly feels a hand on one of hers. She snaps open her eyes.

'I've been looking forward to today,' the harbour master says.

Myrtle broadens her smile, shifts on her cushion. She hopes that this will show she has felt the same. She leaves her hand beneath his, lest moving it away in under a minute would seem impolite.

'Hope I haven't bored you, babbling on.'

'Not at all. What a life you've had. I've hardly been anywhere. Archie and I had plans for a holiday in Italy one day. But now . . .'

'Ah! *La bella Italia!*' The harbour master is suddenly vivacious. 'I once had to transport a crate of mallard out to Rome. Some rich Florentine prince had this sudden desire for English ducks on his lake. Four hours of driving through the Italian countryside in a hired car, ducks quacking beside me, is my only experience of Italy, I'm afraid.' Myrtle laughs. Her response triggers a squeeze of her hand, which she now gently removes. The harbour master begins to gather up the picnic things. 'You could take off your scarf, here,' he says, subdued again.

Myrtle unties it. Her hair blows about. The wind on her neck is wonderfully cooling. A gust snatches the scarf, drops it in the sea. At once Alastair leaps to Myrtle's side of the boat, leans perilously over. The boat tips alarmingly. Myrtle, convinced they are about to capsize, pulls at the harbour master's jacket. He falls back into her arms. He quickly moves back to his seat, put out by his failure.

'Sorry, sorry, sorry, so very sorry,' he says. The incident has unnerved him. 'I'll get an oar, I'll easily reach it with an oar.'

'Please don't bother.' Myrtle cannot bear another attempt at rescue. 'It's not at all important. I've plenty more scarves.'

'Oh, my dear Myrtle, as you can see, I'm not a man nimble in his ways.' His melancholy sense of failure touches Myrtle. She puts a hand on his arm.

'It's a lovely day,' she says. 'I'm enjoying myself so much.' Behind the glasses, she is convinced, his eyes are incredulous.

'Dear, dear Myrtle,' he says, 'I was so anxious to make it a happy day for you.' Myrtle retrieves her hand. 'I'm bound to admit that a not inconsiderable amount of hours a day are spent wondering . . . how best to please you. I find that my desire merely to be a companion has changed immeasurably. I know that any alternative to your husband is beyond contemplation. But if ever you so had it in mind to require anything beyond our happy companionship then you must know that I would be far from averse to changing the solitary nature of my life.'

Even as the harbour master labours with his convoluted declaration, Myrtle finds herself editing it down to simple English. She takes some time to answer.

'What you say is a great comfort,' she begins at last. 'I'm lucky to have you as a friend and hope that any visions you may have of a change in the future won't disturb our present friendship.' Even as she speaks she can see her reply brings disappointment, dashed hopes. But there has been no time to prepare a more delicate response. She can only try to reassure her companion-turned-suitor she will take his words seriously. 'I'll think about what you said.'

'I'd be grateful for that. Well, I'll not bother you with the matter again.' The harbour master stands. 'I rather think it's time we were getting back.'

The boat tips rapidly from side to side as he returns to start up the engine. They move off, heading back the way they've come. Myrtle studies Alastair's parrot profile as he lifts his carton of milk to his mouth, drinks. There is no reasoning, here, Myrtle tells herself: but the heart can be a wayward thing. She suddenly now knows, beyond any doubt, that the idea of life with the milk-drinking harbour master is not, and never will be, something she would want. She is grateful to have come to her senses.

Back in the harbour Alastair seems withdrawn. There is the pretence of a smile, courteous thanks for having given up her day. Myrtle's own thanks seem not to touch him. On the bus home Myrtle is convinced he was aware of the swift turn her thoughts took on the homeward journey.

She is so preoccupied that it takes a moment when she reaches home to register a girl sitting at the bottom of the stone steps. Janice. A furious and sulky Janice, by the look on her face.

'Where've you been? I've been waiting half an hour,' she says.

'But I thought . . . ?' Myrtle is confused, put out by the child's hostility. 'You said you didn't want any more lessons this term.'

'Changed my mind.'

'Well, I'm sorry, but you didn't let me know. Come on in.'

The kitchen is cool. Myrtle opens the window, makes tea. She's glad to be home. Janice slams her books down on the table, sits in her usual gawky position, knees together, calves widely spread. Her grumpiness fills the room.

'I've written something about *Michael*,' Janice says, 'though I have to tell you, I think Wordsworth is bloody gloomy.'

'Janice, your language,' says Myrtle. She scans the paragraph, a crude attack on the poet unlike anything Janice has ever written before.

Janice watches her face. 'You know what? The other day at school I mentioned Wordsworth, and course none of the others had ever heard of him. They'd never heard of any of the stuff I do with you. They thought I was bananas, wanting to know poetry. If they thought I was having extra lessons they'd think like I was a bloody swot, do me over. You'll never, ever tell anyone, will you?' Her eyes are hard, but hold a suggestion of tears.

'Janice, what's happened? Of course I won't tell anyone.'

'What's happened is, I don't want any more lessons, thanks very much. I've gone off of poetry. That's what I've come round to tell you.'

Myrtle thinks quickly. Janice is in no mood to be persuaded. 'Well, I'm sorry to hear that. I've enjoyed our lessons. I thought you had, too.'

'Oh, I have.' Janice shrugs. 'It's just I don't want any more.'

'I would be very sorry,' says Myrtle slowly, 'to see you go the same way as your father. He was a clever boy, very keen on literature. But he went to sea and his interest seemed to dry up.'

'First I've heard of it. Anyways, I don't want to go to university. I want to be an air hostess. Get out of this dump.' A single tear glitters down Janice's cheek. She wipes it away with the back of her hand, suddenly childlike. 'Have you ever been mocked by a whole class? Jeered?'

Myrtle passes Janice a handkerchief from her pocket.

'I know it's hard,' falters Myrtle, 'to be brave enough to do something different from the crowd. But it's always worth trying to stick to what *you* really believe in, no matter how much ridicule that may earn you. Sometimes you get recognised in the end . . . one other person thinks it worth following you, and then others all do the same.'

Myrtle knows she is not doing well. Further tears are running from Janice's eyes now. She gives a choking laugh.

'Very funny,' she says. 'I can just see my class all suddenly thinking Janice Mcleoud and her swotty love of old poets is the hip thing. And I don't want to be lectured. One thing I liked here, you never lectured.'

Myrtle forces a smile, attempts lightness. 'I can see I'm getting nowhere. I'll not try further. How's the boyfriend?'

For a second Janice's face crashes, then she sticks up her chin, controlling herself. 'I don't know if you've ever fancied someone so rotten it gets you everywhere like all the time, but it's a bloody nightmare.'

She gives a leap towards Myrtle—childlike, again—flings her arms round her. Myrtle wipes away the tears, strokes the frenzied head.

'Anyways, thanks, Myrtle,' Janice says, pulling herself away. She runs out, dragging her satchel, and bangs the door purposefully behind her. Myrtle feels the pleasures of the day seeping from her.

A few days later Alastair returns at his usual time. They settle down to a game of cards.

It's very warm in the kitchen, despite a thread of air that hangs between open window and open door. After several days of sun the thick stone walls have relinquished their cooling influence. The harbour master asks permission to take off his jacket. Beneath it he wears a shirt no other man in the village would contemplate—a fancy garment of blue, yellow and green stripes, expensive cotton, sharp collar.

Myrtle smiles. 'That's very smart,' she says. 'Did you get it abroad?'

'Hong Kong airport. Over there to deliver a panda.' His answer is deadpan. Myrtle sees that his spirits are still withdrawn. He is behaving in his usual companionable way, but something has gone from him. Myrtle pours glasses of homemade lemonade. They play in silence for a while. Then the harbour master frowns.

'I suppose,' he says, eyes on his fan of cards, 'that for the wife of a fisherman, widowhood is in some respects easier. You must be so used to being on your own.' The difficulty he has saying this indicates to Myrtle it's something that has been occupying his mind.

She cannot believe that a man of such keen sensitivity, in some ways, is so lacking in imagination. But she is careful not to seem to snub him.

'I can quite understand that's how it could appear,' she says, nicely. 'But it's not so. This is an absence that will never end, that you never get used to. It's always there. And the hardest thing is that you know that sometimes it'll leap out, take you in a stranglehold, causing havoc again with all the things you believed you'd managed to get into some form of order. Fishermen's wives never quite get used to the constant absences, but at least there's hope, a very good chance, the men will be back. Archie's death is the end of that hope for me.'

Alastair lays down his hand of cards.

'I'm sorry, Myrtle,' he says, 'I seem to have presumed something very thoughtless. I've said the wrong thing again.'

'Oh, no. No you haven't.' Myrtle is quick to reassure.

The harbour master now shuffles sadly. 'I'm honoured—that you should have explained so well things which you have no reason to explain to another living soul.'

'You're a good friend to me,' Myrtle says. 'You asked. It would have been cowardly not to have tried to answer.' Once again she finds herself drawn to this awkward man, and yet detached. The pathos of the man moves her deeply. Alastair has dared to hope, been rebuffed, and now must return to the emptiness that had been his life before.

The air of mutual anguish is scattered when Annie comes running in, laughing, restless. She wears a muslin summer dress that mists her limbs, clings to the points of her knee bones, breasts. In the low shadows of the kitchen she could be eighteen again, running in to urge Myrtle out. Myrtle loves her again now: it suddenly comes upon her, a vibrant, smothering warmth, a gladness at her presence. Also, she is grateful for this visit. Now Myrtle will be spared any further explanations when Alastair decides to leave.

Which he does at once. The presence of Annie always causes him unease. 'Here, take over my hand,' he suggests, getting up.

'Willingly.' She looks at him with an enchanting smile that makes him hurry on with his jacket. Myrtle follows him out.

'Come again soon,' she says. Then she kisses him on the cheek. The gesture causes them equal astonishment—Alastair cannot know this, but Myrtle has never kissed a man on the cheek in her life: meaningless social habits are not her way. She watches the harbour master skim down the steps. At the bottom he turns to give a small wave—the wave of a man grateful for kindness shown, but fully aware of the limitations between them that will always exist. Myrtle turns back into the kitchen.

'So!' Annie is laughing. 'Caught you and the harbour master at it again. I think it's bloody marvellous. When's the happy day?'

'Don't be so daft, Annie. He's a good friend, but that's all. You're in high spirits.' Myrtle pours more lemonade.

Annie gives her a triumphant grin. 'Ken took the afternoon off. Have to take our chance when Janice is at school.'

'You're happier, then? Things still going better?'

'They're far from perfect, but a few per cent better. We don't row so much, but we have our time cut out dealing with Janice and her moods. Don't know what's got into her. Bloody nightmare to live with, I can tell you. All due to hormones, I suppose. Still, in some ways she's brought us closer. That and . . .' Annie looks away from Myrtle. 'I don't know. I suppose you can't go on blaming someone for ever. I've come to see Archie's dying was enough punishment for Ken. Then, he's been so patient. I respect that. It's made me feel much fonder of him. Not the love I feel for Martin—but a nice comfortable sort of old fondness. And now the sex is back, that's terrific.'

'Oh, Annie, I can't tell you how pleased I am,' says Myrtle. 'It's what I kept hoping for.' She makes no mention of the piece of information that troubles her: Annie's admission of her continuing love for Martin. Myrtle must never confess to Annie that her friendship with Martin provides a growing warmth in her life.

'I think you should seriously consider Alastair,' Annie says. 'Of course you couldn't love him like you loved Archie, but he could widen your life. You've never been anywhere, you don't show any signs of wanting to explore other places. If you never set foot outside this place you'll never meet anyone. The harbour master is a golden opportunity.'

'I've no particular wish to meet anyone else, I'm one of those who finds more than enough in a small world.'

'Wish I could feel the same way. I keep wanting to be off, though God knows where to. You're stumped, really, without some rich bloke behind you. Ken's doing his best, I'll say that, but we'll never be rich. He says one day we might go to Australia. Don't suppose we'll go. It's only an idea.' Annie's exuberance has mellowed. She picks up the cards. 'Here: cut.' They play until late. Annie says Ken is getting a takeaway for Janice this evening, so she can have a night off. Myrtle says there's cold meat and tomatoes in the fridge. They smile at each other, enjoy the thought of a late supper. This evening all the love and admiration Myrtle has ever felt for Annie are reassembled. In the void left by Archie, this peace with Annie, sometimes so elusive, must not be allowed to escape.

Their evening is a merry one. They talk about the old days, laugh at old jokes. She knows there will never be a time she does not worry about Annie's firecracker ways, her thoughtlessness, her dubious morality. But a kind of maturity seems to be reaching Annie. On an evening like this it is impossible to imagine ever falling out with her again.

When at last Annie leaves it is almost midnight. Myrtle goes out of the door with her. The women hug each other for longer than usual.

'Bugger Australia,' says Annie, as she runs down the steps.

A week later, another warm summer's evening, Martin has sent word that he has finished work on the headstone and would like her opinion on a few last details in the carving.

Myrtle walks with lightness of step towards the cemetery. Martin is to come back with her for the fish he brought her that morning, which she will grill with a little butter. They will sit talking in their easy way. She sees the quiet pattern of her life stretching for years ahead. It will be cards with Annie, suppers sometimes with Martin, visits with the harbour master: the pleasure of teaching and the time to read all the books she has always wanted to read. What else could a widow, bound for ever to her husband's spirit, ask?

Myrtle lets herself through the gate, shuts it behind her. She turns towards the sea: the grave is close to the wall that divides graveyard from shore. She can just see the kneeling figure of Martin. He is backlit by the sun: the illusion is of a halo surrounding him. The halo also frames a second figure, a slight young girl, it seems to be, leaning against the headstone.

Myrtle approaches warily. She wants to see more before she herself is seen. Ten yards from Archie's grave she stops, conceals herself behind a mausoleum. She can now see the figures clearly. The girl is Janice.

Janice leans against the headstone, one skinny arm along its top. She wears a very short dress. It clings to hips and small breasts, only knickers underneath it. Her free hand swoops to the buttons at the neck: languorously, like some caricature film star, she undoes two. She flutters her eyelashes, as she must have seen her mother do a thousand times.

'For shite's sake look at me, Martin,' she suddenly screams. 'Please!'

From the speed with which Martin rises to his feet Myrtle can measure his anger. For a second she registers the two figures—the man with a hand on the girl's shoulder, shaking her, shouting at her, and the girl's open, screaming mouth. She runs towards them.

'Janice! Whatever can you be thinking—? You little trollop, you—'

Myrtle is too horrified, too angry to fashion useful words. She pushes past Martin and slaps the defiant, upturned face.

The screaming stops. Silence. Myrtle is aware of Martin's arm on hers.

'How dare you?' Janice's face is defiant. 'You'll be sacked for this.' There are red slashes on her cheek.

Myrtle is conscious of little beyond her thundering heartbeat. Martin is pulling her away.

'Leave her alone,' he says.

'*Do up your buttons*,' says Myrtle. Her voice is a long way off, nothing to do with her. 'What do you think you were doing?'

Janice smiles, the nastiest smile Myrtle has ever seen on a child.

'What would you know about anything? About passion, desire, months seeing Martin being nice to my mum, kind to you, and not even *noticing* me? I wasn't doing anything wrong. Only trying to make Martin *notice* me. Say something to me. Realise I exist.'

'Go on,' says Martin. 'Home. I think we should forget all this as quickly as possible.'

'Forget?' Janice laughs. She picks up a jersey, slings it round her shoulders. 'I'm off. Leave you two to it. Hey! Perhaps that's what got you, Myrtle. Perhaps you fancy Martin yourself! Well, you're old and plain and no man in his right mind would give you a second—'

'Get away!' Martin now shouts, all gentleness gone. 'Now. Go on.'

Janice, barefoot, runs through the tombstones towards the gate.

Myrtle sits down on Archie's grave. Martin lowers himself to sit beside her. Myrtle longs to weep, but she cannot.

'Whatever did I do?' she asks at last. 'Hitting a child . . . Hitting Janice, who I've loved since she was a baby. What happened to me?'

Martin raises his head. He puts an arm round Myrtle. 'She deserved it. She's out of control, that child. Disturbed.' He sighs. 'For months now, she's been tracking me down, making suggestive remarks, doing all she can to provoke me. As for the letters . . . page after page of how she loves, will wait for ever—pathetic, childish stuff. I stopped opening them. I told her I would read no more. Then she started phoning. I was going to go to Annie and Ken: I didn't want to get the child into trouble. But she needs help . . . And now this.'

'Oh, God,' says Myrtle. 'What do we do now? I've hit a child. She may have deserved it—that's no excuse. That's goodbye to my job, she's right.'

'It won't come to that,' says Martin. 'We'll work it out with Annie and Ken. They know how Janice has been of late. They'll understand.'

'I can only hope so,' says Myrtle. 'Just when I thought Annie and I were on an even keel again . . .'

They remain sitting for a long time, listening to the occasional gull. The sun is hovering on the horizon, the sea is grazed with gold light. Myrtle stares at the fine-grained marble of Archie's headstone where Martin has done his careful work. But she has no heart to discuss it.

'Would you mind, another evening?' she says, and struggles to rise. 'I can't concentrate on the headstone just now. But it's beautiful.'

'Of course.' Martin helps her up.

'And would you mind if . . . I cooked the fish tomorrow? I've no doubt Annie will be round. I'd rather face her on my own.'

'Fine. Shall I walk with you to the house?'

'I'll be all right, thanks.'

'You look as if you're in a state of shock . . .'

'You look pretty shocked yourself.' Myrtle is aware of the strained lines under his eyes, and the sadness of the eyes themselves. They hold each other's hands for a moment, then Myrtle turns to go.

Home, Myrtle has scarcely settled to a few moments reflection when Annie comes bursting in, cheeks scarlet, furious-eyed.

'You hit Janice,' she shouts. 'How dare you?'

'She deserved it,' says Myrtle.

'It's not up to you to decide what anyone else's child deserves. You know nothing of Janice, what's been going on. The last thing in the world the child needs is to be attacked by you. I could have you up for assault. But I'm not going to. I'm going to give you a piece of my mind in a way that'll give me far more satisfaction—'

She rushes at Myrtle, swings at her cheek with a hard open hand. She slaps with every ounce of strength in her furious body. The blow sends

Myrtle tottering backwards to the stove. Her cheek stings, flames. Her heart is beating wildly, but she feels no desire to shout back. A heavy calm seems to have drugged her.

Annie steps back, shocked. But her fury is not spent.

'That's what you deserve, Myrtle Duns. Maybe it'll make a chink in your bloody superiority, your high-mindedness, your arrogant ways, your *smugness*. And don't you go thinking, St Myrtle, that in a few days' time we'll make up as usual. Because we won't. You've gone too far this time. There'll be no more of this . . .' She snatches up the cards from the table, raises her hand above her head and throws them. They drop like heavy leaves all round the room. When they have landed, there is a moment of quiet again. Then Annie thrusts her head into her hands and begins to sob. Myrtle fingers her cheek.

After a while she says, 'I shouldn't have struck Janice. I'm sorry.'

'You bloody shouldn't.' Annie's shoulders are heaving.

'Spontaneous fury. I couldn't believe what I was seeing. It was mad, I know. I've no explanation, beyond the shock. You can imagine how I feel, letting fly like that. You know I love Janice as if she—'

'I don't give a toss how you feel. Serve you right if you're up to your neck in remorse for ever.' Suddenly Annie locks eyes with Myrtle. 'Are you sure your fury wasn't to do with the fact that the man Janice was being stupid with was *Martin*?'

Myrtle's mouth opens. Her hand drops heavily to her side. 'Of course not,' she says. 'I don't know what you mean.'

'Don't tell me Martin doesn't mean something to you—you're always asking Janice if he's been bringing us fish. I've got ears.'

Myrtle sighs. 'Martin's a good friend, he's been wonderful since Archie died. So has Alastair Brown, in a way. I don't know what I'd have done without them,' Myrtle falters on, 'without you.' She lifts the kettle, puts it on the stove.

'I don't want any of your tea.' Annie stands, tears over. 'I'm going.'

'Shouldn't we talk about Janice? I've been worried for some time.'

'Janice is none of your business. Spare yourself the worry.'

'For the Lord's sake, I've known her all her life, I love the child. I don't know what's got into her lately, but it's something very disturbing.'

'You don't know the half of it,' says Annie. Her hostility is waning. Myrtle pours two mugs of tea. Annie takes one.

'She's been mentioning this boy she's fallen for. Did you know it was Martin?'

Annie shrugs. There's a long pause. 'Not till Janice comes screaming in,' she says. 'I must admit. And that's not the all of it.' She goes to the window. 'I told you I've never stopped loving Martin. So you can see what it was like when Janice comes running home in tears to tell me you hit her because she was having a bit of fun with the man she's been doing her nut for these last months, and that man is the man I love most in the world.'

In this icy revelation Myrtle senses a core of toughness. Annie, she has no doubt, will sort out Janice in her own way. The chances are Annie will win Martin in the end, though God knows what that will do to Janice.

'The pity of it,' are the only words she can find.

'Anyhow, she wasn't doing anything wrong. Only having a bit of fun. Flirting—just trying to make him look at her, say something nice.'

'That may be what she intended. It didn't look like that. She was acting provocatively. Reminded me of a child prostitute—'

'You prissy woman!' Annie flares up again. 'How dare you call—'

'Let's not shout at one another any more,' says Myrtle. 'The point is, whatever she was up to, something's got to be done about her.'

'Yes, well, I'd be grateful if you'd not interfere. I'll deal with it. Martin never gives her a glance. She'll soon learn how hopeless it is. I'm buggered if I'm going to stop him coming round. She'll soon find some boy of her own age.'

Annie has finished her tea, bangs down the mug on the table. Her face is a mess of mascara, her hair a stormy tangle of curls. Myrtle tries to picture their last, happy meeting. But she can't.

'I hope we can get over all this,' she hears herself saying.

'I'm not as good as you at forgiveness, remember? Pity, but there it is. There's too much against us now to carry on. So best not to have anything more to do with each other, isn't it? And don't look at me like that. If you don't like what's happening, blame yourself. Janice is an innocent child, head over heels about some man, acts stupidly one day. She's never given him so much as a sign before . . .' Annie is near Myrtle now, looking closely at her still reddened face. 'That's what she told me, that's what I believe. If she'd been causing Martin any aggravation he'd have told me, wouldn't he?'

'I dare say.' Myrtle turns her head from her friend's glare. She is in no doubt that she must keep her knowledge to herself. To reveal what she knows would not help, now.

'So I'm going,' says Annie. 'I'm off.'

She hurries to the door. Everything within Myrtle cries out to her to say stop, this is ridiculous, let's not leave it like this. But no voice emerges from the chaos within her.

WIVES OF THE FISHERMEN

It has been the bleakest week since Archie died. Myrtle has spent many hours in reflection, cursing her own untoward behaviour that has brought about this crisis—condemning herself for not having tried to help Janice. She also blames Annie: a self-obsessed, irresponsible mother, always wanting to win her child's approbation by giving in to her wishes. But Annie has always been deaf to all constructive suggestion concerning Janice. Long ago, Myrtle gave up, kept her silence as she watched Janice yearning for the barriers of discipline that are every child's right.

Myrtle goes over the last quarrel, the lacerating words. Despite the wounds they have left, she misses Annie. She misses Janice. She fears for them both. She plays patience, waiting for one of them to come round. But Martin tells her Ken has hired a caravan and the whole family has gone off somewhere. This is so unusual that she is further alarmed. The days are long. She has noticed that when she goes out to shop she causes a disagreeable stir. People give her looks: she feels the tension, the disapproval. She ignores them, with as much dignity as she can manage. Never has she missed Archie so much. The ache, which she had thought was beginning to dull, has returned more piercingly than before. And the feeling of the new bustle in her life has disappeared. Now there is nothing but the maturing of the trees to look forward to.

The harbour master remains loyal. The day after Annie ran out he appeared with a bunch of poppies and daisies and long grasses. Myrtle was touched by the thought of him pottering along the hedgerows, choosing the flowers. He told her he had heard the silly rumours, but she could rest assured he would always stand by her, always be there if needed. Indeed, in the week since Annie's departure he has been round three times: gentle, his sympathy alive in his quietness. He asks no questions and Myrtle makes no effort to explain. They merely play their card games. There is that ease between them which comes to people who recognise their friendship will never converge, but never fade. The small element of tension fired by their different desires does nothing to trouble their pleasure in each other's company.

Martin, too, comes round most days. He tells her he saw Annie only for a moment before she went away. She slammed the door in his face. He could hear Janice crying upstairs, and Ken shouting. The whole household was in an unhappy state, he said. He left quickly, had no intention of returning. 'They'll have to sort it out themselves,' he said.

He and Myrtle did not speak of Annie after that. Instead, Martin—a little wanting in spirits, Myrtle thought—reported progress on the finishing of Archie's epitaph. He hoped it would be completed in days.

In the long hours between visits from her two loyal friends, Myrtle sits thinking that, if you look around, everywhere you see people frightened of beginnings, frightened of endings. She is not unusual in that, and this present time is both some kind of ending, and some kind of beginning that she cannot envisage. She is a little afraid, but Archie's voice comes to her, strong, firm, wise—encouraging her in some way she cannot exactly comprehend, but comforting.

Martin comes round to say he has finished the engraving. He would like her to come to see it. They walk together through the warm air of a late summer evening. They stand by the headstone. Martin has done a wonderful job, but Myrtle does not want to stay long. The ghost of Janice is still too raw. So when Myrtle has given her thanks, they decide to walk on up to the copse.

The saplings are strong, bright with young leaves—noticeably taller since the last visit. The sight of them provides Myrtle with the first dart of real pleasure since Annie left. She cries out loud in delight, tripping fast up and down the paths. They reach the clearing and sit on the fine old bench which is Myrtle's memorial to Archie. In silence she and Martin look about them: at the trees, the brightness of the grass, the unclouded blue sky, where swallows swoop in lazy whiplash circles.

'I'd still like to put a rock here,' says Myrtle. 'Did you manage to find one?'

'I've been looking,' says Martin. 'And I think I've found the perfect thing—I was going to tell you. I found it on a small beach, a couple of miles up the coast. Only trouble will be transporting it. There's no access to the beach for a van. But I'll work that out somehow soon. It'll have to be soon.'

'That's wonderful news,' says Myrtle. 'I look forward to it.' She pauses. 'It's the thing I most look forward to, now.'

Martin sighs. He allows a few moments to pass before speaking. 'I've news for you, Myrtle,' he says at last. 'I fear it's not a good moment, but time is running out. I'm going back to Canada.'

Myrtle turns her head and looks at him.

'I'm off at the end of the month if everything's tied up by then. It was my sister who made up my mind. As you know, she came over to tell me she couldn't really cope any more with the smallholding where we lived with our parents. Then there's her man, who wants her to move in with him. It will be good for her. I'm pleased. She didn't like the idea of selling the old place, wondered if I might consider . . .'

As he speaks, Myrtle sees the years ahead. No Martin with his fish and his devoted friendship. She sees the harbour master, his hair turning to grey, beating her at cards for years to come. She sees her own funeral: the widow Duns laid to rest beside the good fisherman Archie, who died many years before her.

'So I've been considering,' Martin goes on. 'The decision was very difficult. I scrape around for work here, earn very little. Besides that, I don't really fit in—never will. I'm a friend to a lot of the fishermen, but I'm not one of them. I shall miss my parents, though they might join me in a few years' time. But I'm tired of the sense of my own uselessness here. In Canada, I could be working to some real purpose.'

Myrtle sees herself in the kitchen, through the seasons, listening for Archie's voice, living with the spirit of him but denied the flesh, and wonders if that is the proper plan of things. She thinks of Annie's return: surely they will forgive each other. But she sees years of watching the friendship become more threadbare as ever more wearying quarrels outweigh the love.

'Besides,' says Martin, 'there's one other thing.' He speaks quietly. 'I once confessed to you there was just one woman I loved. I never told my love because she married another. She was widowed. She became my greatest friend and I never stopped loving her. I waited for a very long time, wondering how long it takes for widowhood to heal. I tested the water very gently. I asked her to come for a small trip to Perth with me.' Here, he allowed himself a small, grim smile. 'But no, she said: she wasn't ready to come even as far as Perth. I took that as a final no, for she must have seen where I was leading, and wanted to stop me in my tracks before I did anything that might upset our friendship.'

'Oh, Martin,' says Myrtle, turning to face him, cheeks blazing. She sees his eyes are dull with resignation.

'And so I gave up, I suppose,' he says. 'I have never left off loving her. But when my sister made her suggestion . . . I thought, there's nothing to keep me here. The sensible thing to do is to return home, work hard to make it the thriving farm it once was. And who knows, I may meet someone who'd like to join me there, even become my wife.'

Myrtle thinks of some Canadian wife, without a face, greeting Martin as he comes into his childhood house.

'So, I'm off. It breaks my heart, but it would be foolish not to go.'

Myrtle remembers the times she's been jealous of Martin taking fish to Annie. Her regret over refusing his invitation to Perth. The flash of lightning between them the day Martin helped her to her feet. She remembers how constantly she has relied on him since Archie died. But because of her fidelity to a dead man, she has not allowed herself to accept what her feelings have become for one who is alive.

We could write, she thinks. *I'd write more than Annie, of course, but still. Maybe she'd come for a visit one day—always wanted to see the world.* Myrtle sees a single swallow, spinning so fast it's hard to imagine how the bird will right itself as it tumbles towards the ground. But it does, and the next moment it's soaring very high again in unpremeditated pleasure. She keeps her eyes on its flight.

'I could always come with you,' she says.

Then for a long time she and Martin remain sitting on the memorial bench, looking at each other in astonishment and wonder.

ANGELA HUTH

'I AM A GREAT BELIEVER in writing about what I don't know much about,' says Angela Huth. 'If you can't imagine things, you can't be a novelist.'

Wives of the Fishermen is a triumphant testament to this belief. It creates such an authentic atmosphere of a small Scottish fishing community that it is almost impossible to believe that the author has not spent her whole life in one. In fact, she took only four days to do her research among the fishing villages on the country's east coast. The village in which her story is set is an amalgam of all of them and none of the characters bears any resemblance to anyone she encountered. Again she insists, 'I write purely from my imagination, never about people I have met.'

Apart from imagination, she attributes her success to another important talent: 'a painterly eye that absorbs landscape'. Her father, Harold Huth, was a renowned film producer and a star of the silent screen who, she claims, was a huge inspiration to her. It was he and her mother who encouraged her to paint, which she did at the Beaux Arts in Paris, Annigoni's Art School in Florence and the Byam Shaw School of Art in London. At heart, however, she had always wanted to be a writer and, indeed, she had written her first collection of short stories when she was only five years old. She started out in journalism at *Harper's Bazaar* in 1959 and then moved to *Queen* magazine, where she met and subsequently married Quentin Crewe, her first husband, with whom she had a daughter, Candida. At the age of twenty-two Angela Huth had her own page in the *Sunday Express* and soon afterwards became a freelance writer for all the major newspapers and magazines. She has also written for film, television, radio and the stage. In 1987 she wrote and presented *The Englishwoman's Wardrobe*, a documentary for the BBC featuring Margaret Thatcher.

When asked how the idea for *Wives of the Fishermen* came about, the author says it just 'came out of the blue, as all the ideas for my novels do. I wanted to write about Scotland—I love Scotland—but I also wanted to write about what it must be like to love someone who is not only away a lot of the time but is also in possible danger. However, the book quickly developed into a story about the perversity of friendship. After all, many friendships have a darker side—most of the time we don't confront it, but if you've just one friend in this kind of remote place you probably have to.'

Angela Huth is currently at work on her next novel. Now married to Oxford historian, James Howard-Johnston, her writing is punctuated by 'thinking about baby matters', as Candida, her elder daughter, is about to be a mother. She has also been advising on the film script for one of her recent novels, *Land Girls*, to be released in August 1998 as a film starring Anna Friel (from television's *Brookside*). She and her younger daughter, Eugenie, are both thrilled to have been given minor parts in the film. Our photograph shows the author as she will appear on screen.

601-001-4